Going Home

Danielle Steel

To the endless list of people who have meant so very much to me, and this book. I address you alphabetically, because there is no order to how I needed you. I loved and needed you all.

Kate Reed Cains
John Mack Carter
Sidney M. Ehrman
Charles Flowers
Franklin K. Gray
Edward Kessler Jr.
Timmie Scott Mason
Inez Nutzman
Mary Evans Richie
John Schulein-Steel
Kuniko Schulein-Steel
Fred R. Smith
Norma Stone
Phyllis Westberg

and especially to Clo and Beatie, for putting up with it all.

Now by the path I climbed, I journey back.
The oaks have grown; I have been long away,
Taking with me your memory and your lack,
I now descend into a milder day.

Edna St Vincent Millay

I

It was a gloriously sunny day and the call from Carson Advertising came at nine-fifteen. The stylist was sick and they needed someone to assist with a shooting up the coast. Was I free? Would I do it? And how much? I was, I would, and the price was right. One hundred and twenty dollars for the day, plus expenses. After working as a stylist in New York, I had been lucky in California. They were impressed, and they paid well. And it was easy work. All I needed was a job or two a week and, added to my alimony, Samantha and I could live well. Sometimes there was no work for a few weeks, but we made out anyway, and we were happy.

We had left New York one grizzly, rainy day, like pioneers off to another world. I was twenty-eight, she was almost five, and I think we were both scared. Brave New World. And off we went. To San Francisco, where we knew no one, but it was pretty and it was worth a try. So we were trying.

We'd been there for a little less than three months the day that Carson called me for the job on the coast. We lived in a tiny flat in the Marina, with a peaceful view of the bay and Sausalito in the distance. We could look out the window and see the sailboat masts just out front, as the boats bobbed around tied up at the Yacht Club dock. And on sunny afternoons when I wasn't working, I could take Sam down to the tiny strip of beach, and I'd lie there while she raced up and down the sand and then up the steps on to the grass. It was still snowing in New

9

York while we were lying on the beach. We had done the right thing, and we'd come to a lovely place. We were happy there. We were alone and still very green at being pioneers, but everything was going to be okay. I'd look at my daughter, all brown and healthy, and I'd look at myself in the mirror in the mornings, and I'd know we had been right. I looked ten years younger, and at last I was alive. Gillian Forrester had been reborn at twenty-eight, in a city that spread itself over a series of beautiful hills, next to the mountains, and within breathing distance of the sea. San Francisco.

I looked out the window at Mount Tamalpais in the distance that morning, and then at my watch. It was nine-thirty, and the truck from Carson was due at ten. The crew was driving out together, except for the people from the film company who were shooting the commercial. They had their own truck. And probably their own ideas. I wondered briefly what they were going to think of having me to 'help' them. Probably not much. The advertising agencies always liked to have an extra hand, but cameramen and the like never thought much of the idea. Thus far, it had been kind of 'Who's she? . . . What? . . . A stylist? . . . Man, you've gotta be kidding . . . From New York? . . . Oh, Christ . . .' Yeah, but what the hell. I was getting paid for the job, and they didn't have to like me. As long as the agencies liked my work and kept calling.

The school bus had already picked up Sam, and I had just enough time to shower and climb into a pair of ancient jeans, a denim shirt, and my safari jacket. It was always hard to tell about the weather. It was early April, and it might be cold if the shooting got late. And sooner or later the fog would roll in. I dug my feet into an old pair of riding boots, put my hair in a knot on top of my head. And I was all set. A quick call to a neighbour who would wait for Sam to pile off the school bus at noon and keep her till I got home, and I was all ready for Carson Advertising.

We were to shoot a cigarette commercial on some cliffs overlooking the sea, north of Bolinas. And they were using four models, some horses, and a fair amount of props. It was going to be one of those healthy looking ads with the deceptive air of nonchalance and fresh air. Fresh air there would be, but nonchalance relatively little. Hence the need for me. I would spend the day making sure the models looked right, setting out the picnic, making sure the two female models didn't sit on the horses the wrong way round, and no one fell off the cliffs. Fairly easy work for a hundred and twenty dollars, and it might be fun.

A horn honked outside at exactly ten o'clock, and I sped out the door with my 'magic bag' over my arm. Band-aids, aspirin, tranquillisers, hair spray, a variety of make-ups, a note book, a collection of pens and pencils, safety pins, clothes pins, and a book. The book was an anthology of short stories I never got to read at shootings. But it gave me a nice illusion of 'one of these days'.

As I hopped down the three steps outside our flat I saw a dark green pickup truck and a military-looking jeep out front. The truck was filled to the gills with equipment and props; there were two sleepy-looking girls in the back with sweaters pulled up to their chins and scarves over their heads. They looked like the Bobbsey Twins. Our female models. Sitting in front were two frighteningly virile-looking guys, also in turtle neck sweaters, with carefully kept ear-length hair and strong jaw lines. Their whole look told me that they were gay, and I knew that they were the male half of our modelling team for the day. All set. At least they'd shown up for the shooting. But I had stopped worrying about things like that. In San Francisco, people show. It's not like New York. They don't get as much work, so when they get a call, they show. The male beauty queen seated nearest the window waved, and the man in the driver's seat slid out and came towards me with a smile. He was small and sturdy-looking with jet black hair and bushy eyebrows, and I had met him at other shootings with Carson Advertising. He was their chief art director, and a hell of a nice guy. His name was Joe Tramino.

'Hi, Gillian. How've you been? I'm glad you could make it.'

'So am I. Looks like a nice day for the shooting. Are the guys in the jeep with you too?' We stood on the sidewalk and he rolled his eyes in semi-Neapolitan style.

'You bet your ass. Those are the account guys. Three of them. This commercial is for our biggest account. I'll introduce you.' He strode over on his short legs and one of the men in the jeep rolled down the window. 'This is our stylist, Gillian Forrester. Gill . . . John Ackley, Hank Todd, Mike Willis.' They all nodded, smiled, and shook hands with me, without looking particularly interested. They had a fifty-thousand-dollar commercial to get out for an important client. And that was all they cared about. Making charm with the stylist wasn't what they had in mind.

'You wanna ride with them or with us? It's gonna be crowded either way.' Joe shrugged his shoulders and watched me for a minute, wondering what I would decide. I could tell that he liked me and thought I was a 'good looking broad'. I was a little taller than he, and my complexion was as fair as his was dark. That was probably what fascinated him. My brown hair and blue eyes had never seemed like such a big deal to me, but he seemed to like the combination, and I could tell he liked my ass.

'I'll ride with the crew, Joe. No sweat . . . Nice to meet you, gentlemen. We'll see you there.' I looked at Joe as we walked away from the jeep, and broke into a laugh. 'Surprised? What do you think I am? A snob?' I gave him a friendly shove and then hopped in the back seat of the truck with the girls. One of them was asleep and the other was reading a magazine; the boys up front were talking 'shop'. According to them, men's fashion was going all to hell. I saw Joe roll his eyes and give me a wry grin in the rearview mirror and then we were off. He slid the gear into drive, let out the brake, and stomped on the accelerator, and we sped around the jeep and off towards Lombard Street, which would get us on to the Golden Gate Bridge.

'Jesus Christ, Joe, you drive like a goddam Italian.' I was hanging on to the front seat so as not to squash the girl sleeping next to me.

'I make love like an Italian too.'

'I'll bet.'

'What's the point of betting? Try me some time . . . Try it . . . you'll like it.'

'Yeah, sure.' I smiled back, and then sank into my own thoughts as we approached the Golden Gate Bridge which never failed to have an effect on me. A feeling of overwhelming power and beauty would sweep over me, and I'd raise my eyes to dizzying heights, like a child, feeling pleased with the effect. The deep orange colour of its spires stood out in the blue sky, and its sweeping lines reminded me of kite strings.

'Whatcha looking at, New York?' Joe had seen the slow smile spread over my face, and I leaned against the window and looked upward.

'I'm looking at your bridge, Joe, just like a hick.'

'Come on, I'll give you a better view than that.' He leaned backward in the seat, turned a handle in the ceiling of the car, and slid a panel back. It was a sun roof, and by opening it the view had improved still further. The Golden Gate Bridge stood over our heads in the sunlight, and the fresh Northern California air whipped our faces.

'Wow . . . this is neat. Can I stand up?' The opening looked just big enough.

'Sure. Don't step on the girls though. And look out for the cops. They'll give me a ticket.' I saw him watching my behind again as I gently placed my feet between the two sleeping girls and disappeared through the roof. He was some Italian. And that was some bridge! It was hard to breathe, standing unprotected in the wind, and my hair started to whip around my head. And up above was . . . it. My bridge. And my mountains and my sea. And off in the distance behind us, the city. My California. It was stupendous.

I felt Joe tug at my jacket as we approached the end of it, and I came back in and sat down.

'Happy now?'

'Yeah.'

'All you Easterners are nuts.' But he looked pleased with what I'd done. There was a nice atmosphere in the car, everyone was minding his own business, we were all going to work, and no one was feeling hassled. It was a far cry from what I'd experienced working in New York, first at an ad agency and later at a decorating magazine. Everything was different in California.

'Who's shooting the commercial? Shazzam or Barclay?' I had learned that Shazzam was the 'in' new group that did most of the really with-it movie production in town and Barclay was the most established production house around.

'Neither one. That's why all the account guys came along. They're tearing their hair out. I'm using a new house. They're young, but they're good. They're not even a house, really, just a team. A crazy young guy and his crew. They look like lazy, good for nothing freaks, but they've really got it. And their bid was terrific. I think you'll like them, they're easy to work with.' I nodded, wondering if they'd like me. 'Freaks' don't usually like stylists from New York, even if I didn't look like one any more.

We were past Sausalito and Mill Valley by then and already on the winding mountain road towards Stinson Beach. It was lined with immense trees, and the smell of eucalyptus was everywhere. And it was beginning to feel more like a day in the country than a job.

The models were all awake by then and everyone was in a good mood. We started down the other side of the mountain and the view was breathtaking. Great splashes of panorama would appear, the mountains would drop down to cliffs at unexpected moments and the sea roared up to meet them with a great gush of spray. Everything was lush green and soft brown and bright blue. God's country.

We came down the mountain singing songs and then drove on past Bolinas up the coast to a place I didn't know. But it was more of the same. More mountains, more sea, more cliffs, and more splendour. And I was glad I'd come.

'You look like a kid at a birthday party, Gill.'

'Oh shut up, you blasé dago. That's the way I feel about this place.'

'It sure as hell ain't New York.'

15

'Thank God.'

'Is that so?' He grinned at me again and pulled the car off the road on to a dirt track which led across some hills, high above the coastline.

'Where the hell is this place?' The models were craning their necks but there was nothing to see. We were miles from civilisation. There was still no sign of a waiting film crew.

'You'll see in a minute. It took the camera boys three weeks to scout this place. It's fantastic. Belongs to some old lady who lives in Hawaii and hasn't been here in years. She rented it to us for the day.'

We came to a bend in the road then and swooped down towards a plateau lodged between the hills and the cliffs. The sea was hurling itself at the shore with greater force than I'd seen at Big Sur, and there were trees sticking out along the cliffs like giant flags. Huge boulders stood in the water below and the spray sprang up from them so high that is seemed as though it could have watered the trees. Maybe it did.

I saw the jeep then and wondered how they got there before we did, especially the way Joe drove, but there they were, parked alongside a horse trailer, an old car, and a dilapidated truck with a lot of hippies crawling all over it. We hopped out of the pickup truck and the various groups merged into one as everyone prepared to do their bit and get the show on the road.

The account men from the Carson agency stood slightly aside in a nervous little clique and began to look over their notes. The models jumped back into the pickup and started doing their faces and hair. They left me with Joe and a bunch of rag-tag-looking boys who looked like they had run away from home the day before.

I watched them unload their heavy equipment as though it were weightless and saw Joe standing near the cab of the truck with a tall, blond boy. He had a strong, muscular body, a full head of shaggy hair, strangely wide-set eyes, and an incredible smile that exploded two deeply entrenched dimples. And I saw that he was watching me.

'Gill, come here a minute,' Joe called out to me with a wave and I wandered towards them wondering which of the crew this boy was. He looked younger than the others and seemed to have less to do. 'Gillian Forrester, Chris Matthews. He runs this madhouse.'

'Hi.' The smile widened and I saw that he had beautiful teeth. His eyes were of a soft green colour. He didn't hold out a hand to shake, or seem particularly interested in who I was. He just stood there, nodded at me, seemed to keep an eye on his troops, and went on talking to Joe. It made me feel a little out of place.

'Hey . . . where you going?' Chris asked. I had decided to go back and check up on my models.

'I thought you two were busy. I'll be back.'

'Wait a sec, I'll come with you. I want to see what I'm shooting.' He left Joe and strode along the hillside with me, kicking through the weeds in his boots and looking up at the sky. He had all the mannerisms of a young boy.

The models introduced themselves and I was pleased to see them looking about right. They were pros and it was nice not to have to start from scratch with them. I had been on a shooting the week before with a bunch of kids who hardly knew how to comb their hair.

Chris stood aside from the group after a moment and then shook his head. 'Joe!' His shout rang down the hill and caught Joe's attention instantly. The kid had a hell of a voice. He beckoned to Joe and I could see there was a problem but I didn't want to intrude. It was obviously between him and Joe.

'Okay. What's up?' The little Italian huffed and puffed

as he got there and he didn't look happy. He sensed that there was trouble and that was all he needed, with the account boys sitting on his neck.

'We've got a problem. And it's going to throw the budget out of shape. You've got five models. We only needed four.' Chris looked unhappy about the excess and Joe looked baffled.

'We do?' He cast a glance into the truck and shook his head. 'No, we don't, you jerk. What'sa matter? You can't count? One, two, three, four.' He pointed to them one by one, and he was right. Four.

'Five.' Chris shook his head and pointed again. And Joe and I both burst into laughter as he did. He was pointing at me.

'Four. Relax. I'm the stylist. I thought you knew.' Joe gave him a friendly shove. Chris burst into a laugh himself and the dimples came to life. Then he shook his head.

'Christ, you should've told me. What the hell do I know? All I do is take pretty pictures. I wouldn't mind taking some of you some time either.' He faced me with a long appraising look.

'Flattery will get you nowhere, Mr Matthews.'

'No. But it'll get me a friendly stylist. Get your ass in gear, lady. I start shooting in five minutes. And if your models aren't ready, you know what happens?' He was looking at me in a fierce, unfriendly way, and I suddenly decided that I wasn't so far from New York after all. They're all the same. I shook my head in answer to his question and waited for him to threaten to fire me. 'If they're not ready, it's simple. We all quit and get stoned. You think I want to bust my ass working all day? No way.' He shook his head and threw up his hands with a gentle look as Joe and I started to laugh again, and then Joe tried to put on a serious face. He could see that the men in the jeep were watching us.

'Listen, you lazy bastard. Stop threatening my fancy stylist. And get off your ass. Move it out.' He gave a military sounding yell, and Chris ran back down the hill. We were finally about to start.

The horses were led towards us, the models were in full uniform, and the camera equipment was all set. Some of Chris's men lit a blazing campfire and I went to check out the food to make sure it looked right for the 'picnic' we were shooting. The food was all cemented into place and heavily lacquered so as to look right, and it seemed fine to me. I spread it on the ground, loosened a scarf around the neck of one of the boys, calmed down the female models' hair, put a little more rouge on the second man, and moved back. I'd be busier later in the shooting when things started to look rumpled.

I watched Chris with amusement as we got under way. He joked with everyone, shot from a variety of strange positions, and heckled the models. He had everyone in hysterics at the end of half an hour and the account men looked alternately thunderous and panic-stricken. At one point he disappeared down the side of the cliff, and with a clutch of fear in the pit of my stomach I assumed we had lost our photographer. Joe and I raced to the edge to see what had hapepned, fear in our eyes. As we leaned over, Joe bellowed Chris's name towards the water, but there was no answer and there was nothing to see. He had vanished . . . Oh my God . . .

'Chris . . .' Joe tried again, and the echoes seemed endless, but then I saw him.

'Shhhh . . . what'd you want to do? Scare the shit out of me? I'm having a smoke. Come on down.' He was sitting on an indented and well hidden ledge, not six feet down from the top, straddling a sturdy looking bush and smoking a joint.

'You crazy sonofabitch, what the hell . . .' Joe was incensed, but visibly relieved. And I burst into nervous laughter. The guy was obviously nuts but he was so natural about everything he did that he was easily forgiven the outrages he perpetrated on the world.

'Is this our break?' I tried to seem as though I were not impressed, but I was. For a moment, I had been so sure that he was gone.

'Yeah. Sure. You smoke?' I nodded and then shook my head.

'Yes. But not on a job.'

'And neither should you, you crazy bastard. Get the hell up here and come back to work. What am I going to tell the account guys?' Joe looked genuinely nervous.

'You really want to know what to tell them?' Chris looked pleased at the idea. 'Tell them that they can . . .' Joe cut him off and looked apologetically at me.

'Come on, Chris . . . please . . .' By then I was in stitches again. The whole scene was so absurd. Joe and I were leaning down talking to an invisible bush off the side of a cliff, and our chief film genius for the day was enjoying a leisurely smoke of dope. We had already waved to the rest of the crew to let them know that everything was okay, but it must have looked ridiculous anyway.

'Okay, little Joe. I'm a-comin'. Up, up, and away.' And with that, the long, lean, muscular body of Christopher Matthews sailed past us and landed back on the plateau. He took something out of his pocket and the next thing I knew there was a shrill whistling sound in the air. He had blown a little toy whistle and pulled a water pistol out of his pocket. 'Come on, you guys, let's get this show on the road.' He then proceeded to squirt everyone within range, including the account men from Carson, and he looked immensely pleased with himself. He was having a good time. 'Places . . . action . . .' A pair of sunglasses emerged from another pocket and he was busily playing director when I went back to set up the picnic again. One of the horses had walked across the set. It took me ten minutes to get everything back in place, and after that I sat back on the running board of Chris's truck to watch them shoot, feeling useless, but amused. It was the best shooting I'd been to in years.

'What do you think, Gill?' Joe collapsed next to me and lit a cigar.

'It's hard to tell. Either he's brilliant or he's a disaster. I'll reserve judgement till I see the film. He's nice to work with anyway. How old is he?' I figured he was about twenty-two and maybe fresh out of some new-wave film school.

'I'm not sure. Somewhere in his thirties, but nobody's told him yet. He acts like he's twelve. And man, I hope he does some good stuff for me today, or else I can forget my job, starting now.' We both glanced over towards his colleagues and Joe shook his head. He was right, with the show Chris was putting on his work was going to have to be fantastic to justify the fooling around.

I watched in mild amazement as everyone went through their paces though, and there didn't seem to be any problems. His men did precisely what he wanted, the models were marvellously loose and unselfconscious, and things were moving along. It was hard to tell exactly where things were at, but it looked as though the shooting was almost over. And then suddenly I knew that, whether or not the work was done, it was. Chris stopped dead for a brief moment, looked around blindly at the crew, and then began to reel to one side, clutching his heart. This time I was sure he wasn't faking, he was sick. I wondered briefly if it were an overdose of something as he slid to the ground and lay there unconscious.

Joe and I arrived at his side within the same instant and Joe gently turned him over. He had been lying face down on the ground. And as we rolled him on to his back and I reached for his pulse, his face broke into a vast, boyish grin, and he giggled.

'Fooled ya, huh?' He was delighted. But not for long. Joe pinned him to the ground and pointed towards something behind him while looking straight at me. And I knew what he meant. The water bucket for the horses. I ran to get it, emptied it a bit so I could carry it, and rushed back to dump it on Chris. All of it. But he only laughed harder, and then I was pinned to the ground and he was pulling my hair, which had come undone.

With that, the agency men ran up to see what was going on and Chris's men and the models joined in the fray. It was a free-for-all. I heard Joe shout over the din that we were all through shooting so not to worry, and I went right on wrestling with Chris Matthews until I felt Chris put something strange and pointed between my ribs. I tried to see what it was.

'Don't move, Forrestal. Just get up and start walking.' His face and dialogue were straight out of a grade B Western.

'In the first place, the name's Forrester, and in the second place, just what exactly do you think you're doing?' I tried to sound unruffled and at the same time awesome, but didn't succeed.

'We're gonna ride, little lady. Just step lively . . . nice'n easy . . .' I knew the guy was nuts as I suddenly realised that he had a gun in my ribs. What the hell had Joe gotten me into for a hundred and twenty bucks? I wasn't working for him to get shot in the back for chrissake . . . what about Samantha? 'Keep moving . . .

that's it . . .' He was walking gingerly at my side, and my eyes searched wildly for Joe in the tangle of arms and legs and water on the ground. They were still going at it. I saw that Chris was walking me towards the horses, and watched him deftly untie one from the back of their trailer with one hand while still keeping the gun on me, which I couldn't see.

'Come on, damn you. Cut it out. The fun's over.' At least it was for me.

'Nope. It's just beginning.' He spotted a megaphone lying near the trailer, dragged it closer with his foot, and then kicked it into the air so he could catch it, never loosening his hold on either the horse's reins or the gun. He seemed to know exactly what he was doing and punctuated most of his actions with his dazzling smile. To hell with his smile. I had had enough. 'Bruno!' The sound of his voice boomed through the megaphone. 'Pick me up at the Watson in Bolinas at eight.' I saw an arm wave in the crowd and then felt the gun push harder into my flesh. What was the Watson? And why eight? It was only a little after one, and what the hell was he going to do to me? 'Get up. You do know how to ride, don't you?' A momentary worried look crossed his face, like a little boy who's been given a cap gun with no caps in it.

'Yes, I can ride. But I don't think this is funny at all. I have a little girl and if you shoot me you're going to wreck a whole lot of lives.' It was a dumb melodramatic thing to say, but it was all I could think of under the circumstances.

'I'll keep that in mind.' He looked singularly unmoved by my speech and I swung into the saddle, glad I'd worn my boots, and wondering what was next. He hopped up behind me, I felt the gun still in the same place, and burst into a fresh wave of worry as he nudged the horse into a fast trot and then a slow gallop. What if the gun went off by mistake? What would happen then? The mountains were rough terrain to ride over and the horse might stumble, and then .. . . .

In less than a minute, we were out of sight of the plateau where we'd been shooting and we were faced with the splendid range I'd admired on the drive over. But it was a whole other thing to ride over the mountains and I didn't give a damn if they were beautiful, I'd had it. Suddenly a wave of fury swept over me at this insane boy-man who was playing with my life. He was a snotty, pompous, careless, stupid hippie who thought he could do anything he damn well pleased, from getting stoned on a job, to pretending he had died or fainted, to shooting me . . . Well, he was wrong. He couldn't shoot me at least. My body had tensed into a steel beam and I swung around with every intention of knocking him off the horse. But when I turned around my attack was temporarily delayed by a squirt of cold water in my face. The water pistol . . . that's what he had been holding in my back all along.

'You lousy, rotten . . .' I spluttered within two inches of his face, trying to wipe the water out of my eyes, and wanting to kill him. 'You big shit . . . you . . . I thought . . .'

'Shut up.' He squirted the pistol in my mouth this time, and I choked on a burst of laughter. Christopher Matthews was something else.

The horse had come to a stop at some point during Chris's watery attack on me, but I didn't notice until I had wiped the water from my eyes and saw that we were standing near another cliff again, with the Pacific stretching as far as we could see.

'Pretty, isn't it?' His face was peaceful and he looked like a cowboy in repose. The mischievous child was momentarily gone. I nodded and looked out to sea, again with that immense feeling of having found my way to where I had been meant to be all my life. The hysterical feeling of riding over the mountains at gunpoint was gone, and I was watching a bird swoop slowly down towards the water and wondering what it would feel like to do that when Chris slowly turned my face towards his and kissed me. It was a long, tender, gentle kiss. Not the kiss of a lunatic juvenile. The kiss of a man.

When we pulled away from each other and I opened my eyes, I saw him smiling at me and looking pleased. 'I like you, lady. What did you say your name was?'

'Oh, go to hell.' I pulled the reins from his hands, exhorted him to hang on, and I took over the horse. That was one thing I could do well. I had been riding since I was five and it was a marvellous, heady feeling to be pounding over the mountains, not a house or a human being in sight, just a lovely, leggy horse under us and a beautiful man in the saddle behind me, however crazy he was.

'Okay, smartass. So you can ride. But do you know where you're going?' I had to giggle to myself as I realised that I didn't, and I shook my head in the wind, my hair whipping his face, but I didn't think he'd mind. His hair was almost as long as mine anyway.

'Where do you want to go?' As if I'd know how to get there. We were in his world and I was just a tourist. But a happy one.

'Bolinas. Head back towards that road down there, take the first right, without falling into the water, please. I can't swim.'

'Bullshit.' But I followed his instructions, walking the horse down the mountainside and then cantering along near the road in silence until I saw another road off to the right.

'That's it.' He kicked the horse for me and I tried to slap him playfully but the water pistol was suddenly aimed at my ear again.

'You know what you are, Mr Matthews?' I shouted into the wind. 'You're a pain in the ass. And a bully.'

'So I've been told. Hey, take this next right too, and then a left.' There were only one or two cars on the road, and I moved the horse on to it and took the appropriate turns. It was fun riding again, and I was beginning to like the nut with the shaggy hair and the water pistol. He had a nice grip on my waist and I could feel his thighs pressed into mine.

'Is this it?' We were in a nondescript-looking place, down on shore level, but there was nothing much to see but trees.

'Ride through those trees over there . . . you'll see.' And I did. A long sandy strip of beach, the sea, and an inlet. And on the other side a still more beautiful beach which stretched for a couple of miles and then was stopped by the mountains again, dropping down to meet the sea. It was a splendid sight.

'Wow!'

'This is Bolinas and that's Stinson Beach. Can you swim?' He looked pleased at the expression on my face and he dismounted and held out his hands to catch me. I realised again how tall he was as I slipped to the ground next to him. I'm five feet seven inches and he must have been at least six feet three inches.

'Sure I can swim, but you can't. Remember?'

'Well, I'll learn.' I watched what he was doing with sudden surprise and wondered just what he had in mind. He had pulled off his jacket and boots and was proceeding to remove his T-shirt. What next? His jeans? I wasn't quite sure what this was all about. 'Whatcha looking at?'

'Let me ask first. What are you doing?' He stopped

and looked at me for a long moment.

'I thought we'd swim the horse from here to the end of the land spit over there – it's an easy distance – and then we can ride on the beach. And swim, and stuff. Take off your clothes, I'll tie them to the saddle.' Yeah . . . sure . . . and swim and stuff. Stuff, huh? . . . Oh well.

I tied up my hair again and then pulled off my own jacket and boots . . . and then my T-shirt, my jeans, and my pants. There was no one else on the beach. It was warm that April, yet on that side of the bay and on that Tuesday afternoon there was no one on the Bolinas Beach but us. Christopher Matthews and I stood facing each other beneath the mountains, stark naked and smiling peacefully, while the horse seemed to wonder what was next. And so did I. I wondered if Chris were going to leap at me and rape me, or squirt me with the water pistol again, or what. He was hard to predict. But he seemed matter-of-fact as he strapped my clothes to the saddle and led the horse towards the water. The three of us walked in, Chris showing nothing of the shock of the cold water, only slowly leading the horse into it and checking back over his shoulder to make sure I was okay. I was, but I was freezing my ass off and hated to show it. I dived under the water to see if that would feel better, and swam past him towards the opposite shore. It felt fabulous, and I smiled to myself as I surfaced and looked over my shoulder at Chris. Here I was in California, swimming from one beach to another with a horse and a crazy young film-maker. Not bad, Mrs Forrester, not bad at all.

We walked slowly up on the beach on the other side and Chris tied the horse to a long piece of drift wood. Again, there was no one on the beach but us. It looked like a movie and felt like a dream. He stretched out in the sun and closed his eyes, making no move towards me. He was doing what he wanted to do and I was free to do the same.

'Do you always run your shootings like this, Chris?' I was stretched out on the sand, with a respectable distance between us, my head was propped up and I was looking out to sea.

'Not always. Just most of the time. There's no point working if it's going to be a drag.' Apparently he really believed that.

'Joe says you're good.'

'Joe's got his head up his ass, but he's a nice guy. He's been giving me a lot of work.'

'Me too. And I need it. He's nice to work for.' We were roaming around comfortable subjects and it seemed a little funny to me to be making small talk about work as we lay naked in the sun.

'Where are you from, Gill? Back East?'

'Yes. New York, but I hate to admit it.'

'That's a bad place. Bad for the head. I wouldn't go near it flying forty thousand feet above the ground.'

'You're probably right. I've been here three months and I'm beginning to feel that way myself.'

'Married?' It seemed a little late to ask, but maybe that was his style.

'No. Divorced. You?'

'Nope. Free as that bird over the water.' He pointed to a gull drifting slowly downward in a lazily swooping arc. 'It's a nice way to be.'

'Lonely sometimes though. Isn't it for you?' He didn't look as though he'd suffered from much loneliness. He didn't have that sharp look about the eyes that one gets from trying to survive.

'I guess it's lonely sometimes, but . . . well, I work a lot. And I guess I don't think about being lonely.' I envied him and wondered briefly if he was living with a

28

girl, but I didn't want to ask. I didn't want to know. He was the first man I'd met in a long time who had guts and style and a sense of humour. 'You look like a thinker. Are you?' He had rolled over on his stomach and was watching me with an amused grin.

'A thinker?' He nodded. I was stalling . . . yes . . . I was a thinker . . . what was wrong with that? 'Yeah, I'm a thinker.'

'And you read a lot.' I nodded. 'And you're lonely as hell.' I nodded again, but what he was saying was beginning to bother me. It was as though he lived on the top of Mount Olympus and was looking down.

'And you talk too much.' I stood up and looked at him for a second before walking towards the water and slipping into the waves. I liked him but I wanted to be alone for a bit. He seemed to stand very close and see a lot. And I suspected I could care about him. A lot. About what he thought, and what he was. I even liked how he looked . . . Chris Matthews was what I'd been waiting for, but now that he'd arrived I was afraid.

A sudden splash in the water next to me caught me by surprise and I turned quickly to see if I was being attacked by a local sea monster. But it was only Chris swimming by, and then turning back to swim at me again. He was really just a giant kid. I waited for him to dive at me from underwater, or try to dunk me, but he didn't, he just swam towards me and then kissed me as the waves swept by.

'Let's go back.' He had a quiet look on his face as he said it and I was glad. I was getting tired of the games.

We swam towards the shore side by side and I started to walk towards where we had lain before, but he took me by the hand for a moment and looked at me.

'There's a nice cove back there. I'll show you.' He kept my hand in his and walked me slowly around the

29

point to a tiny cove nestled in the tall dune grass, like a secret garden. And suddenly I felt stronger and more desirable than I'd felt in years. I wanted him and he knew it and I knew he wanted me . . . But it was too soon, I hardly knew him . . . it couldn't be right . . . it . . . I was scared.

'Chris . . . I . . .'

'Shhh . . . everything's going to be okay.' He wrapped his arms around me as we stood in the tall grass with our feet dug into the sand, and then I felt my body swaying with his, until we lay in the sand, and I was his.

2

'Do you do this a lot, Chris?' The sun was still bright in the sky and we were still lying in his secret cove.

'What? Screw? . . . Yeah . . . I do this a lot.'

'No, you smartass bastard. I mean like this. Here, in this cove. With someone you don't even know.' I was serious. It had all seemed a little bit set up, the way he knew about the hidden cove and all.

'What do you mean? Hell, I know you. Your name is . . . uh . . . hang on just a sec and I'll get it . . . your name is . . .' He scratched his head with a feeble-minded look on his face and I felt like hitting him, but instead I laughed.

'Okay. I get the message. Mind my own business, right?'

'Maybe. I'll let you know when you bug me. New Yorkers just like to ask a lot of questions.'

'Oh . . . is that so?' I looked mock pompous as I said it

but I knew he was right. New Yorkers are nosier than Californians for some reason, probably because they're used to living in closer quarters with more people underfoot in a world of terrifying anonymity, so when they sink their teeth into someone for questioning they go all the way to the bone.

'Wanna go for a ride, Gill?'

'On the beach?' He nodded as he scrounged in the sand looking for shells. 'I'd love it. But I'll ride behind you this time.'

'Bareback okay with you?'

'Terrific.'

'So are you, New York.' His words were the barest whisper, and he leaned over and kissed me as he pulled me slowly to my feet. Everything he did had a sensual quality about it, as though he enjoyed life to the fullest, but as though what he liked best was making love. 'Here . . . I found a present for you.' He pressed something into my hand as we walked towards the horse, and I looked down to see what it was. With his sense of humour, I figured I'd be lucky if it wasn't a jelly fish he'd found on the beach. But it wasn't. It was a sand dollar. A strange fossil-like shell with imprints of a flower on either side. It was so delicate you could almost see through it, and it was lovely.

'Hey . . . it's beautiful, Chris, thanks.' I reached up and kissed him on the neck and felt another stirring deep within me. I hadn't had a man since I'd come to California, for a while before even, and Chris was quite a man.

'Quit kissing me or I'll make love to you right here on the open beach.'

'Don't make promises you don't intend to keep.' I was teasing and he knew it, but he grabbed me by the arm, spun me around, and the next thing I knew we were lying on the beach making love again. And when we stopped we both broke into delighted chuckles.

'You're crazy. Do you know that, Mr Matthews?'

'You forced me into it, so don't blame me.'

'Bullshit. And if you're trying to make me feel guilty, forget it. I'm glad.'

'So am I. Now . . . as I was saying, let's go for a ride.' He unbuckled the saddle and put it down on the sand, stroking the horse's head and flanks with a knowing hand, and then he jumped gracefully on to the mare's back and held out a hand to me.

'Whatcha waiting for, Gill? Chicken?'

'No, something else. Happy. You're nice to look at.' And so he was, sitting tall and proud astride the sandy-coloured horse, his bronzed flesh standing out against her pale hide, and the grace of their two bodies making me think of poetry I'd read as a girl. Chris looked so beautiful.

'You're nice to look at too, now hop up.' He gave me a hand and I slid up behind him, put my hands around his waist, and leaned into him as we sailed into the wind. It was the most marvellous feeling I could ever remember. Racing down the beach on a pale golden mare with a man I loved . . . loved? . . . Chris? . . . I hardly knew him. But it didn't matter, I was already in love with him. From that first day on.

We galloped up and down the beach until sunset and then took a last swim before reluctantly taking our leave.

'Do you want to swim the mare back to the other side?' I asked. I was a little worried, the tide was coming in, but he had seen it too.

'No, we'd better go by the road this time. It's less fun but it makes more sense.'

'It does, huh? You're beginning to make me wonder if

you just swam her over so you could make me take my clothes off.' I hadn't even thought of that at the time.

'Is that what you think?' He looked hurt and I was sorry I'd said it. 'Well, you happen to be right.' He let out a delighted laugh, and I stood watching him again. The giant boy who'd taken my heart at water-pistol point. Not bad.

'What's next on your agenda, Conceito Bandito? You leave me tied naked to a telephone pole till morning?' He would be capable of it.

'No. I feed you. How does that sound?'

'Intravenous or regular?'

'You're disgusting, Gillian, Regular, of course. The Watson House, the best Bolinas has to offer. Have you ever been there?'

'Nope.'

'Wait and see.' We got back on the horse and trotted slowly down the beach to the part that belonged to the state, then walked the horse slowly past the empty parking lot to the road. It was a fifteen-minute ride into Bolinas and we got there just as the sun was setting; it seemed as though the entire world were lit in red and gold.

We stopped in front of a small dilapidated Victorian house and tied up the horse as I looked around. There were a number of hippies wandering in and out of the house and a discreet sign said 'The Watson House', but it offered no further information as to what it was.

'What is this place?'

'A restaurant, dopey. What did you think?'

'How do I know? Hey . . . by the way, I have to call my neighbour and tell her I'll be late. She's taking care of my little girl.'

'That's okay. They have a phone inside.' He swung slowly up the steps to the house and opened the screen

33

door without knocking. It had the look of a private house belonging to a large family and certainly no suggestion of a restaurant about it. Vast quantities of laundry hung on a clothesline, and a strange assortment of bicycles and motorcycles stood outside, while two cats and a dog played in the grass. It had a friendly, homely look to it which appealed to me and seemed well-suited to Chris Matthews.

'Hi, gang. What's doing?' Chris walked straight into the kitchen and sniffed into a pot on a brilliantly clean, museum-piece stove. There were three girls in the kitchen and a man. The man wore his hair to his waist, tied neatly back with a leather thong. He was wearing what looked like a pyjama top over his jeans, and it probably was, but what struck me most were the bright, kindly eyes that stood out above his beard. Without moving a single muscle in his face, his eyes seemed to smile and say a dozen welcoming things. The girls were all pretty, young, and simply dressed.

'Gillian, this is Bruce . . . Anna, Penny, and Beth. They live here.' Bruce and the girls all said hi, and Chris shepherded me back to a little room decorated in cheerful Victoriana and Tiffany lamps.

'What is this place, Chris? It's neat.'

'Isn't it? It's actually a hippie commune, but to support themselves they run a restaurant, and it's the best goddam food this side of the bay. You should try the escargots, they're terrific.'

'I will.' And I did, and they were. And so was the coq au vin, and the home-made bread, and the salad, and the mousse au chocolat and the tarte aux fraises. It was a royal repast. Chris had been right, the food was superb. But there was more to it than that. The friendliness of the place was endearing too. I had been right on the way in – it had the feeling of a home with many children in it.

34

There were twenty-seven people living there at the time, and each one contributed his or her efforts to the restaurant. They drifted in and out as we sat there in the candle-light at one of the eight small tables. Everyone seemed to know Chris, and a few stopped and sat at our table for a few minutes before going into the kitchen, or back upstairs.

'Do you come here a lot?'

'Yes. Especially in the summer. I rent a small shack in Bolinas and sometimes I just come by to bullshit with the gang. Sometimes I come here to eat. But only on special occasions.' He was teasing me gently, but he had a nice way of doing it His smile lit up his face as he did, and his eyes said that he meant no harm. He was a gentle man.

'How old is your little girl?' He seemed only vaguely interested, but it was nice of him to ask.

'She'll be five next month. And she's something of a terror. Her main ambition in life is to become a cowboy. If she'd known we'd spent the day with a horse, and without her, she wouldn't speak to me for a week. I think she was under the impression that we came out here to be cowboys.'

'Maybe we could take her riding some time. Is she a brave kid?'

'Brave enough. She'd love it. I was her age when I started.'

'I figured, but you don't know your ass from a hole in the ground when it comes to Western Saddle. I could see that too.' I blushed faintly and wound myself up to say something insulting, but then broke into a laugh and threw up my hands in defeat.

'You're right.'

We talked on for another hour or so, of nothing in particular, California mostly, and work, and why the simple life was better for both of us, when a group came in that looked vaguely familiar.

'Whatcha looking at?' Chris had noticed me looking at them.

'Nothing. I thought I knew those people, but I don't think I do.' They were three hippies much like Chris and the ones in the house, and I think it was just the familiar type that had struck me.

'You know them?' He looked surprised.

'No. I just thought I did.'

'Well let's find out. That's really funny.' He signalled to them to come over to us and I began to wish I were dead.

'Chris . . . no . . . really . . . look, I . . .' But then I knew where I had seen them before. They were Chris's crew. He saw the recognition in my eyes and he and his boys started to laugh. They had heard the brief exchange and knew Chris was up to one of his tricks again.

'Oh you big, lousy bastard, Chris Matthews . . . Hi, boys. Nice to see you again. How did the fight wind up? Did anyone drown the account guys from Carson?'

'No, they went back in the jeep almost as soon as you two left. And we spent the afternoon drinking wine with Joe and the models. They were paid for the day so we all figured what the hell. How was it with you?' They seemed to be addressing Chris more than me, and I let him carry the ball. He also wanted to know how they felt about the shooting and what they hoped they had gotten on film. Everyone seemed to feel it had gone well, and I was relieved for Joe Tramino from Carson. I would have hated to have him suffer for our craziness. Our? . . . Well, I had ridden off with Chris, and that was bad enough. They hadn't been expecting that from their 'stylist from New York', but then again neither had I.

We paid the check at the Watson House then and the

36

five of us ambled outside where Chris's truck, the car, and the horse trailer stood near our mare. It was nice to see her again. She reminded me of what had happened on the beach.

'I'll take the car. Thanks for dropping it off.' They said good night and took charge of the horse as we hopped into Chris's somewhat dubious chariot. As Chris fought with the choke, I wasn't sure I was going to enjoy driving back over the winding mountain road in that, but maybe with Chris I would.

As it turned out, it was an easy drive. There was no fog that night, and the moon lit up the road with a lovely silver glow.

I sang old ballads that I had known as a child, and once in a while Chris joined in. We looked at each other in the moonlight, and kissed from time to time, and very little was said. We didn't need to. It was just nice to be there.

I saw the entrance to the freeway with regret and wished that there were a longer way home. I hated to see all the people and cars again. I had liked our lonely mountain road . . . and our deserted beach.

'Where do you live, Gill?' We were already crossing the bridge, and it was pretty to see the lights of Sausalito, Tiburon, and Belvedere on one side of the bay and San Francisco on the other. Usually the fog was in by sundown, so it was a rare sight.

'I live in the Marina. On Bay.'

'Fine.' He took the first turn off, I gave him the address, and we were home in a few minutes.

'This'll be fine, Chris. I have to pick up Sam next door.'

'Sam?' He raised an eyebrow and looked surprised.

'My little girl.' He nodded, and I was pleased to think he might have been jealous.

'Shall I wait, or will that screw up your scene?'

'No, that would be nice. I'll be right out.' I rang my neighbour's bell and went inside to scoop my half-sleeping child off their couch. She was groggy but not in a deep sleep yet. And I was surprised to realise that it was only nine o'clock. I thanked the neighbours and went out to find Chris sitting on our stoop. I put a finger to my lips and handed him the key, so as not to wake Sam. She had already drifted back to sleep in my arms.

He looked at her for a moment and then nodded his head in approval as he turned to open the door, and then Sam's croaky four-and-a-half-year-old voice rang out in the night.

'Who's he, Mommy?' I grinned and Chris laughed. He had the door open and I set her down inside.

'This is Chris Matthews, Sam. And this is Samantha . . . now, time for bed, young lady. I'll get your pyjamas and then you can have a glass of milk if you want.'

'Okay.' She sat in a chair and eyed Chris sleepily as he sprawled on the couch, his long legs straight out in front of him, his hair looking shaggier than ever after our day on the beach. I got Sam's pyjamas and was walking back towards the kitchen when I heard her ask Chris in a hoarse whisper, 'Are you a real cowboy?' There was hope in her voice, and I wondered what he would say.

'Yes, I am. Do you mind much?'

'Mind? No . . . no . . . I wanna be a cowboy too!' The tone was conspiratorial.

'You do? That's great. Maybe we could ride together some time. But first do you know what you have to do?' I couldn't see her face but I could imagine her eyes opened wide, waiting to hear what he was going to say. 'You have to drink a lot of milk, and go to sleep when your mom tells you. Then you get to be big and strong, and you'll be a really extra terrific cowboy.'

38

'I have to do all that yucky stuff?' Sam sounded disgusted.

'Of course not. Only if you want to be a cowboy, silly.'

'Oh . . . well . . . okay . . .' I walked into the room with her glass of milk and was grateful for Chris's speech. For the first time she drank it in what looked like one gulp and headed for bed like a flash, with a last wave towards Chris and a mumbled, 'Goodnight, Mister . . . Mister Crits . . . see you at a rodeo someday.' I tucked her into bed, kissed her goodnight, and went back to find Chris looking pleased with himself.

'Thanks. That made things a lot easier for me.'

'She's cute. I like her. She seems like a nice kid.'

'Wait, you haven't seen her in her full glory. She was half-asleep. Next time she might try a new lasso trick on you and give you rope burn. She's something else.' But I was pleased that he liked her.

'You're something else, too. And I'm not sure I'd trust you with a new rope trick either. You might try to strangle me. I really think you were trying to knock me off that horse today when you thought I had a gun on you. But I was waiting for you.' He looked amused at the memory of it.

'Good thing for you that you were. I was planning to knock the bejesus out of you.'

'Wanna try again?' He held out his arms to me as I stood across the room and I walked towards him with that feeling of having been reborn again. It had been so long since anyone had given a damn about me, or wanted me as a woman. And now I had someone who wanted me as a woman. Whether or not he gave a damn about me was something I'd find out in time.

3

The phone rang at nine-fifteen again on Wednesday morning, and I was torn between hoping it was Chris and wishing it would be another job. I needed the money.

'Hello?'

'Gillian? Joe.'

'Oh. Hi. That was quite a shooting yesterday.'

'Yeah. I just thought I'd call and check that you weren't pissed off at me for getting you into that madhouse scene. And I wanted to be sure he hadn't dropped you off a cliff or something.' Pissed off?? Wow!

'Nothing of the sort. I had a great time. That was the easiest hundred and twenty bucks I've ever made. He had me a little worried with the water pistol though.'

'He did? I thought you knew.'

'No, I didn't. And he almost got himself knocked off the horse as a result, but it all turned out okay.' Yes . . . it did . . .

'I'm glad. Say, listen, I called to ask you something. Are you free on Friday night?' Huh? Friday night? Shit, no job. A date. And I wanted to go out with Chris, not Joe. 'It's the annual Art Directors' Ball, and it's a bit of a free-for-all, but I thought you might like it.' Oh hell, why not?

'Sure, Joe. I'd love to.' But what if Chris should call? What if . . .

'Great. Wear anything you want. Sort of far-out type stuff, nothing formal. We're having it in a warehouse downtown. Sounds a little crazy but it might be fun.'

'It sounds terrific, Joe. And thanks for asking me.'

'Prego, prego, Signorina. I'm delighted you can make it. I'll pick you up at eight. See you then. Bye, Gill.'

'Bye.' We hung up and I wondered if I'd done the right thing. Joe had never asked me out before and I didn't want to get into a heavy scene with someone who could give me work. It was bad policy. And Joe wasn't really my type . . . and what if Chris wanted to . . . oh shit. I figured he'd understand, and anyway I'd accepted, so why stew about it. I could talk it over with Chris . . . I could have that is, if he had called.

As it turned out, the week ambled by without a call from Chris. Sam and I went to the beach, I painted the kitchen floor with red, white, and blue stripes and painted stars on the ceiling, I got a job from Freeman & Barton Advertising that took me all of two hours to do on Friday afternoon, and still no sign of Chris. I could have called him, but I didn't want to. He had left me early Wednesday morning with the first light of day and he had said he'd call. But he hadn't said when . . . next year maybe? Or maybe he was just playing it cool, but that didn't seem quite his style. Maybe he was just busy . . . making movies . . . but all work and no play wasn't Chris's style either, and I was getting very down about it by Friday evening when I fixed Sam's dinner.

'Why are you going out tonight, Mommy?'

'Because I thought it might be fun, and you'll be asleep, so you won't miss me at all.' I tried to sound light-hearted for Sam's sake, but I was feeling lousy.

'Yes, I will. Am I having a sitter?' I nodded and pointed to her dinner she wasn't eating. 'Maybe I'll tie the sitter to a chair and set the rope on fire. That's what Indians do. It's called being an Indian giver.'

'No, being an Indian giver is giving something to someone and then taking it back.' I thought of Chris and

41

cringed within myself. 'And you're not going to tie the babysitter to anything or I'll give you the spanking of your life when I come home. Is that clear?'

'Okay, Mommy.' She sank into her milk with a look of boredom and despair and I went to my room to pick out something to wear for the Art Directors' Ball. He had said something far-out, so I dug around and came out with a flowery gypsy skirt I'd forgotten I owned and an orange halter top. I had a new pair of orange suede boots and a pair of gold loop earrings, and I knew that would do it . . . and maybe after a bath I'd feel more like me again.

I could hear Sam rummaging around in her room and at ten to eight I went in to check on her and announce bedtime.

'Okay, Sam. Put your stuff away and get your pyjamas on. The sitter'll be here any minute.'

'You look pretty, Mommy. Are you going out with Mister Crits?' My heart rose and sank almost simultaneously, and I shook my head. No, I wasn't going out with 'Mister Crits,' but I wished I were, and I suddenly began to wonder if Chris might be at the party.

The doorbell rang at eight and Joe Tramino and my babysitter walked in together.

'Hi, Sam's in her room. It's time for bed and I'm all ready to go. Hi, Joe. Goodnight, Barbara. Bye Sam.' I blew a kiss towards her room and walked outside with Joe. I didn't want to get into any of Sam's editorials on the situation and I wanted to get the hell out. I was feeling restless.

'Christ, Gill, you look fantastic!' I could see in his eyes that he meant it and felt briefly guilty for being unenthused about the evening. Hell, maybe it would be fun.

42

'You look pretty good yourself, Mr Tramino. Very snazzy.' He was wearing tobacco-coloured suede levis and a dark red turtleneck and it struck me that, side by side, we clashed terribly. But maybe that was just how I felt inside. We walked to his car parked at the kerb and he helped me in. It seemed a little funny to be a girl to someone you had played 'one of the boys' with, but that's all part of going out with someone you've worked with. It always seems a little funny to me.

'I thought we might stop for dinner somewhere on the way. Do you know Nicole's?'

'No, I'm a new girl in town, remember?'

'You'll like it. French food. It's terrific.' He was trying so hard to please that it was painful. Poor Joe. I knew he was considered a prize catch at the agency. He wasn't beautiful, but he was thirty-six years old, had a good job with an impressive salary, a nice personality, and a good sense of humour. And he didn't turn me on. He hadn't before, but now it was worse. He wasn't Chris.

We joked with each other through dinner and I tried to keep a spirit of camaraderie in the conversation. But Joe was trying to turn the tables on me. He was plying me with a heavy red wine and we had one of the best tables in the house. He had chosen a really pretty little restaurant. It was decorated like a large summery tent at a garden party, the tables were covered in red and white checked cloths, and the room was ablaze with candles.

'Who's going to be at this party, Joe? Anyone I know?' I tried to make it sound like idle conversation, but it wasn't.

'Just the usual troops. The art directors from most of the agencies in town, a lot of models, some film guys, nothing special.' But he was on to me. He knew I had meant Chris and he was waiting to see what I would say next.

'It sounds like a good group. There's a thing like that in New York every year, but it's so big you never really see anyone you know. Just a great thundering horde, like the rest of New York.'

'It's different out here. Everything's smaller. San Francisco is a very small town. And everyone knows everyone else's business.' What was this all about? 'Like I know that if you fall for some people you could get hurt. I mean Chris, Gill.' There, he'd said it.

'Oh?'

'Look, I wasn't matchmaking the other day. I was setting up a job. I even had another stylist lined up but she got sick. Gill, he's a terrific guy and I'm crazy about him, but he has no morals, he collects women, and he doesn't give a damn about anyone but himself. He's a lot of fun. But don't go falling in love with him. Maybe I'm way out of line, but I thought I'd say it. And just so you don't get your hopes up, he won't be there tonight. He hates these kinds of parties. Look, the guy's a hippie. You're a nice girl from New York, probably from a good family. And you've had your troubles, you're divorced . . . don't mess around with him.' Wow . . . quite a speech.

'You haven't left me much to say, Joe. Of course I'm not in love with him. I just met him last Tuesday, and I haven't seen him since' – goddam it – 'and I agree with you, he's fun to work with but probably lousy to get involved with. But I'm a big girl and I can take care of myself. And I'm not involved . . . okay?' . . . Who says?

'I'll take your word for it. But I'll be sorry if I hear that you two get into something serious with each other. I'd feel guilty as all hell . . . and I'd probably crawl

44

the walls of my office in a frenzy of jealousy! Here's to you.' He toasted me with the last of the bottle of wine, and, as I drained my glass, I silently wished that he would be having that jealous fit before too long.

We left Nicole's then and drove downtown on Broadway, past the neon hysteria of the topless dance parlours, and then turned on to Battery Street, near the entrance to the Bay Bridge. It was a district that had once been a port, and the shipping lines were still within a block or two. They had put in landfill in the early 1900s and the area had only recently become one of the more interesting parts of town. A lot of the ad agencies were moving in there, and the decorating business had taken over years ago. The result was a series of dismal-looking warehouses interspersed with well-designed new buildings with brick sides and glass fronts.

Joe parked outside one of the warehouses and we went inside. It was a hell of a scene. Miles and miles of shiny mirror-like Mylar had been hung from ceiling to floor and flashing strobe and neon lights made the room look as though it were about to explode. There was cellophane confetti all over the floor and an acid rock band dressed in silver lamé jeans and shirts was blasting their message through the building at an ear-shattering, heart-pounding pace. There was an ingeniously designed bar in one corner of the room. It looked like an iceberg, and the girl doling out the drinks was wearing a skirt made of plastic icicles, and no top. And in the centre of the room and along the walls were the guests. And they were wearing just what Joe had suggested . . . really far-out stuff. Fuchsia satins, and green suedes, dresses that were frontless, or backless, or seemingly both, hair of all shapes, colours, and varieties. Boots by the truck-load and blue jeans by the ton. It was a crazy scene and one that only the artistic community of any city could produce. No one else would dare. I almost felt like Little Bo Peep in my gypsy outfit, but I was glad I'd worn it. It gave me a chance to stare at everyone else in reasonable anonymity while still looking fairly with-it.

I noticed a group off to one side of the room staring up at the ceiling then, and Joe tugged at my arm.

'Take a look.' And when I did, what I saw made me laugh. Suspended from the ceiling, about twelve feet off the floor, was a small but perfectly normal ice-skating rink, with a girl in an ice follies outfit quietly doing her number. She moved to her own slow, graceful beat, totally apart from the crazed sounds of the acid rock band. She was marvellous.

'Where the hell did they get her?'

'I don't know, but you haven't seen anything yet. Take a look over there.' He pointed again and this time I saw a ballerina doing quiet spins in the corner, and every few minutes or so she went into a dead faint on the floor. Then she'd revive, pick herself up again, and do her pirouettes for a while before seeming to die on the floor again. She was even better to watch than the skater. And I began to look around the room myself for more oddities. As it turned out, there was only one, a gentleman who looked like a well-dressed, well-stuffed bank president, and who walked sedately around the room, speaking to no one, and blowing huge bubbles with what must have been a wad of bubble gum the size of my fist. They were terrific. And eventually, enquiries disclosed that they and the room's ingenious decor had come from an enterprising service organisation called 'Rent-a-Freak' run by a young San Francisco artist who thought it was a good idea. He was right, it was. And it made the party.

Joe and I lost and found each other several dozen times in the course of the evening. I met a few people

I knew from other agencies, and danced with what seemed like an endless series of similar faces. They all looked the same, none of them looked like Chris, none of them was Chris. And Chris wasn't there. But I was, and in the end I had a good time.

We left a little after 3 a.m. The party was still in full swing, but we'd had enough. Joe took me to the Buena Vista for an Irish coffee and a pleasant view of the bay and Sausalito sparkling on the other side, and then we called it a night.

He pulled up in front of my house and I noticed with some dismay that all the lights were out. Which meant the babysitter had passed out. Nuts.

'Thanks, Joe, it was a really super evening. That was one of the best parties I've been to in years.'

'And you're one of the best dates I've had in years. Could we make it again sometime?'

'Sure, Joe. And thanks.' I pecked him lightly on the cheek, pointed my key in the lock and turned it quickly, and was relieved to see that Joe was on his way back to his car. No sweat. No hassle at the door. Peace.

I woke the babysitter and offered to call her a cab, but she said she had her own car, so she vanished only moments after Joe, and Sam and I were alone again in the quiet house.

Too quiet. The sitter had said the phone hadn't rung all night. No messages. Damn.

4

On Saturday morning the sun was up before we were, and Sam and I headed for the Marina Beach next to the Yacht Club for a little sun before lunch. We had a lengthy discussion on the sand about the merits of the life of a cowboy, and I described the party to her. She was impressed. A ballerina and a skater and a man who chewed bubble gum? Wow! That had to be some party! And I noticed with amusement that the newspaper said it was, in roughly the same terms as Sam.

At noon, we munched hot dogs and potato chips on the stone steps near the boats and threw bits of the rolls to the seagulls who waited to be fed.

'Mommy, what are we going to do today?'

'Nothing much. Why?' I didn't have any plans, and I was a little tired from having only managed three hours' sleep before Sam arrived to order her corn flakes. Sleeping Beauty I was not privileged to be.

'Let's go see some horses.' . . . Christ . . . how about a game of football? . . . You're a girl, Sam . . .

'Maybe we can go see the horses in Golden Gate Park.' But I wasn't particularly enthused.

'That sounds like a nice idea to me.' But the voice that spoke behind me wasn't Sam's. It was a man's voice. I turned to see, but I already knew. It was Chris.

'Hi, Gill. Hi, podner. Don't you girls ever stay home? I dropped by twice this week. No one home.' I was feeling unglued.

'You did? Why didn't you leave a note?'

'I never thought of that. Anyway, I figured I'd catch up with you sooner or later.' Yeah, but it turned out to be later than sooner dammit. But who cared? He was back.

'It's nice to see you. How did our film turn out?'

'Great. Tramino's going to love us.' Us? That was a nice touch. And I could see that he was genuinely pleased with the film. 'But let's not talk about work. I take it you're going to see the horses in the park. Can I come?' Are you kidding? Of course you can come! After three days of not seeing him he could have come to the dentist with me if he'd wanted to. The three days felt like years.

'Will you come with us, Mister Crits, please?' She stretched out the please and my heart with it, and I nodded happily.

'Why don't you, Chris?'

'Thank you, ladies, I'd be delighted. But don't call me Mister Chris please, young lady. Or I'll call you Samantha. How would you like that?'

'Yerggghh.' She made a face that illustrated the point and Chris and I laughed.

'That's what I thought. So you call me Chris. Just Chris. Okay?' She was about to burble into ecstatic speech but I shook my head and Chris raised an eyebrow. 'No go, Gill? Come on, don't be so stuffy. Okay, how about Uncle Chris?' He seemed amused at the idea and I felt better. Sometimes my stiff childhood training stuck out in funny places.

'That's better.' I gave my dowager's approval and all was well.

'Okay, Sam. Call me Uncle Chris. Sound okay to you?'

'I like that better. Uncle Crits. That's good.' She nodded thoughtfully and then smiled and offered him the last of her potato chips.

'Thanks, Sam. How about a piggyback ride back to my truck?'

'Yes! Yes!' She hopped on his back and grabbed him around the neck and off we went. I carried the beach towels and a happy heart and we were on our way to a merry day.

We stopped at the house to feed Chris a tuna fish sandwich, send Samantha to the john, comb my hair, and collect a few odds and ends of gear, like Sam's teddy bear and a bottle of wine to take to the park. And then we loaded ourselves into the cab of Chris's truck and headed for the park. We found the horse paddock there and took rides on two rather tired brown horses. Sam rode with Chris and he told her a modified version of our riding on the beach the day of the shooting and swimming from one beach to the other with the horse. Sam thought it sounded wonderful. And on hearing it again so did I.

Then we went to the Japanese tea garden and munched strange little cookies and drank tea. And after that we lay on the grass in the botanical garden till five. Sam played with her teddy bear, Chris and I drank the bottle of wine, we played tag and hide and seek, and it was a glorious day. We hated to go home but it was gettng cold.

'How would you like a home-cooked meal, Mr Matthews? Pot luck.'

'Can you cook?' He seemed to be weighing the invitation and I was momentarily reminded of Joe's warning. Maybe he had something else to do.

'I can sort of cook. But if you're going to be picky you can go to hell.'

'Thanks a lot. I'd rather eat at your house than do that. If that's the choice, I'll come to dinner.' He nodded

50

his head sagely and Sam let out a delighted whoop which said everything I felt.

We picked up some groceries at the supermarket, and Chris gave Sam her bath when we got gome while I made spaghetti and meat sauce and a giant salad.

Chris and Sam came out of the bathroom hand in hand. She looked terribly pleased about something and I figured maybe they'd faked the bath. But what the hell? No one ever died of a little dirt.

'Hey, Gill . . . you've got a problem with the dinner.' He was speaking to me in an undertone and I wondered what was wrong.

'What is it?'

'There are worms in the meat sauce . . . but don't tell Sam.'

'Worms? Where?' I practically screamed the words. Worms? Never mind upsetting Sam, the very idea made me feel sick.

He nodded his head again, reached into the bowl with a fork, and came up with a long slithering piece of spaghetti. 'Take a look at that. That's the biggest worm I've ever seen.'

'Oh you ass. That's a spaghetti.' As if he didn't know.

'It is? No kidding?' The boyish smile happened all over his face as he said it, and I could have hit him with my frying pan.

'Worms my ass. Now, everybody, let's eat dinner.'

'Gillian!' His face froze into a look that reminded me of my father and cracked me up. The three of us sat down at the table. And chaos reigned for the duration of the meal, until Sam went to bed and the dishes were done.

It was a far cry from the evening I'd spent at the crazy Art Directors' Ball the night before with Joe. It was a happy time for all three of us. And Joe Tramino's warning be damned. There was nothing wrong with Chris

51

Matthews. He had his own style, he liked to play jokes and indulge in pranks, he had an enchanting childish side that made me think he was more Sam's friend than mine, but he was a good man, and I could only see happy days ahead.

'Can I take you two to the beach tomorrow?' He was sprawled out on the couch, drinking wine and waiting for me to finish in the kitchen.

'Sure. That sounds like fun. Stinson?' Our eyes met for a long moment as we both remembered what had happened there.

'Yes, Stinson . . . and Gill, maybe there's something you want to know. There's this girl I live with . . . is that okay?'

5

The revelation that Chris was living with someone had come as something of a shock. The possibility that he was had crossed my mind the first day, but I had shoved the thought away. I didn't want to know. I didn't want him to have anyone else. He said she wasn't terribly important to him. Not to worry. He would work it out. And he had said it all with such ease that I knew he would. I trusted him.

He spent the night at my place and was a good sport about moving from my bed to the couch before Sam got up. I didn't think she ought to know. Not yet. It was too soon.

We left for Stinson Beach at ten after an enormous breakfast of French toast and scrambled eggs and bacon. And we packed a picnic lunch for the beach. It was another glorious day, and this time when we got to the beach I was a little sorry to see that there were people on it. It wasn't just ours. Sam sped off to play with some children down by the water and Chris and I were left alone.

'Does it make a difference to you, Gill?' I knew what he meant the minute he asked.

'About your room-mate?' He nodded. 'Yes and no. It's sort of a pain in the ass, and I'm jealous. But I'll leave it to you. If she's not all that important to you, I guess it won't make much difference. What are you going to do about her?' That was the key.

'Oh, she'll go. She's just a hippie chick I took in last winter. She was out of money, and she's very young, and I thought I'd give her a hand.'

'More than that, I suspect.' I was beginning to feel sour about it. She was taking on flesh. She was a real live girl. And she lived with Chris.

'Hey . . . you really are jealous. Cool it, baby. She'll go. And I'm not in love with her, if that's what you want to know.'

'Does she have a nice body?' . . . Oh shit . . .

'Yes, but so do you, so come off it. There's only one girl who's ever really meant anything to me, and she doesn't any more, so you're home free.'

'Who's she?' I wanted to know everything.

'A Eurasian girl I lived with a long time ago. Marilyn Lee. But she's in Honolulu now. Far, far from here.'

'Do you think she'll come back?' I was feeling paranoid.

'Do you think you'll shut up? Besides, I'm in love with your daughter. So get off my back. As a mother-in-law you're tremendous. Type-cast for the role.' I slammed him with a fistful of sand aimed at his chest and he pinned

53

me to the sand and kissed me.

'Whatcha doing, Mommy? Is Uncle Crits playing a game with you? I wanna play too.' She lay down on the sand and nuzzled her head in with ours.

'It's called artificial respiration and only grownups can play. Go make me a sand horse.' Sam thought that was a terrific idea and our game didn't look like much fun to her anyway, so she went back down the beach to her friends while we laughed and watched her go.

'You're good with kids, Chris. It makes me wonder if you have any of your own.'

'That's a hell of a left-handed question, Gill. No, I don't. My own would freak me out.'

'Why?' It seemed funny. He was so good with Sam.

'Responsibility. I'm allergic to it. Come on, I'll race you to the water.' He did, and I beat him by half an inch, which won me an earnest dunking in the chilly surf . . . allergic to responsibility, eh? Okay. Sorry I asked.

'Is anybody interested in Chinese dinner?' We were rounding the hair-raising bends in the road home from Stinson Beach and everyone was in a good mood. Sam had played all afternoon and Chris and I had talked film. He was crazy about his work, his eyes lit up with passion when he spoke of it. And I envied him that. Being a stylist just doesn't work up the same kind of emotion. All you do is add your own touches to someone else's work. Like his work. He was doing all the creating.

The invitation to Chinese dinner was well-received, and Sam was thrilled at the sights of Chinatown when we got there. Many of the buildings were made to look like pagodas and the streets were lined with shops filled with fascinating junk. The smell of incense was heavy in the air, and there were tiny, tinkling bells over every doorway.

'Do you like Chinese food, Gill?'

'I love it.' It seemed funny that he didn't know. I expected him to know everything. It felt as though we had been together for years.

The three of us wrestled over chicken foo yong, sweet and sour pork, shrimp fried in batter, sharks' fin sauté, fried rice, fortune cookies, and tea. And at the end of the meal I felt as though I were going to explode. Chris looked as though he felt about the same, and Sam went to sleep at the table.

'We're some group,' he said. I giggled as he looked around and threw up his hands. 'I was expecting the last fortune cookie to tell me I'd turn into an egg roll by morning. I feel like one.'

'Me too. Let's go home.' I saw a funny look in his eyes as I said it, but he didn't say anything, so I didn't speak. The moment passed.

'I want to show you something pretty before we go back. Sam can sleep in the truck. I'll carry her.'

We walked slowly to the parking lot where Chris had left the truck and I was sorry Sam couldn't get one last view of the wonders of Chinatown, but there'd be other times.

'Where are we going?' He was driving west up Broadway, and we had just crossed Van Ness Avenue and were entering one of the better residential districts.

'You'll see.'

We drove all the way up Broadway to the intersection of Divisadero and then he stopped and made a right turn. We stood on the crest of the hill and looked at the bay and the mountains on the other side, and it was splendid. Everything was terribly quiet and heartbreakingly beautiful. The glory of San Francisco was ours.

He put the truck in low gear and we rolled quietly down the hill towards the bay, past the rows of important-looking, well-kept houses in Pacific Heights, until we reached the cheesy flamboyance of Lombard Street and I was sorry it was over.

We drove into the Marina district and I knew he was taking us home.

'Don't look so sad. It's not over yet.'

'It's not?' I was pleased.

He drove along the docks and then parked next to the Yacht Club.

'Let's get out. Sam's sound asleep. We can sit out there for a bit.' We walked out into the cool night air and looked across the bay at the view. The water was lapping at the narrow rim of beach and it made a pleasant sound. It was the most peaceful moment of the day and it was lovely. We sat on the low retaining wall, dangling our feet and looking outward, and there was nothing left to say. It was all right there. And I didn't feel alone any more.

'Gill . . .' He seemed to hesitate as he looked out across the bay.

'Yes?'

'I think I'm in love with you. That's a hell of a way to say it, but I think I am.'

'I think I am too. And don't worry how you say it, it's nice to hear.'

'You may be sorry that you love me one day.' He looked at me earnestly in the dark as he said it.

'I doubt that. I know what I'm doing. And I think I know what you are. I love you, Chris.' He leaned over gently and took me in his arms and kissed me, and then

56

we smiled at each other in the dark. All was well with the world.

We drove the few blocks to my house in silence and he lifted Sam gently out of the truck, took her inside, and put her down on her bed. And then he looked at me for a long moment and left the room.

'What's bugging you, Chris?' We were standing in the living-room and I could tell he had something on his mind.

'I'm going back to my place tonight. And don't try to make me feel guilty about it. Ever. Do you understand that? Never, Gill, never . . . and besides, you couldn't anyway.' I started to answer him, but he was gone. There had been a strange fire in his eyes as he said those words to me . . . and then he was gone.

6

Monday was a horrifically busy day. I got a super job from an advertising agency that had never used me before and I spent the entire day getting accessories for the shooting of some textile ads the following day. It was fun work and I kept busy bouncing in and out of boutiques and department stores looking for jewellery, shoes in the right sizes, handbags, hats, and great odds and ends. All a stylist really needs is taste, imagination, and good, strong legs. You have to run around a lot.

The art director of the agency took me to lunch at Ernie's and it was fun to see the chic people come and go. He was a man of about forty-five, was recently divorced, and had the worst case of the hots I'd seen on anybody yet. He kept trying to talk me into coffee and brandy at his apartment after lunch, on Telegraph Hill where he had a terrific view . . . Come on, baby, are you kidding? I had work to do. And I had Chris.

My last stop of the day was at I. Magnin's fur shop, and I had a ball picking out sable capes, ermine throws, mink this, and leopard that. They would work well with the textiles, and it was a lovely, luxurious feeling to be picking out furs, practically by the gross.

Sam had been parked with the neighbours again for the afternoon and she was visibly annoyed at me when I swept in in good spirits and a new black wool dress that I'd bought at Magnin's on the way out. I was feeling chic and successful, like the people I'd seen at Ernie's at lunch.

'Is that a new dress, Mommy?'

'Yes, do you like it?'

'No. It's black.' Tough, Sam, I like it. But I knew she was mad that I'd been busy all day and hadn't been able to take her to the beach. But this was a big job. Two days for four hundred dollars.

'Come on, Sam. I'll cook dinner and you can tell me about your day.'

'Well, it was miberatzil.'

'Miserable? As bad as all that?' But suddenly she had taken off towards the house like a shot. And then I saw why. Chris was in front of the house, all cleaned up, the shaggy blond hair immaculately clean, and a fresh pair of jeans, and he was carrying an armful of flowers.

'Wow! How pretty.'

'So are you, Gill. Listen . . . I was lousy to you last night and I'm sorry. Really, really sorry. We'll have a nice night tonight, and . . .'

'Relax. I had a nice night last night and the night

58

before. Everything's okay, Chris. I understand. It's okay.'

'What are you talking about? I don't understand.' I had forgotten that Sam was in our midst and she was looking confused.

'Nothing, Sam. Go wash your hands. I'll cook dinner.'

'No, you won't, Gill. I'm taking you out. Get a sitter.'

'Now?'

'Now. I'll make the peace with Sam.' He pointed at the phone and then left the room to talk to Sam.

He had come through . . . flowers and all. And he was right, he had been kind of lousy. But not very. He had only told me that he was living with someone, which was honest, and he had gone home to sleep, which hurt, but he had to go home some time. The funny thing was that I really did understand, and I knew he didn't mean to hurt me.

I called the sitter and she agreed to come by in half an hour. But there was still Sam to contend with. I wasn't so sure Chris could snow her. Maybe me, but not her. I put his flowers in a vase and waited for her to emerge. It didn't take long.

'Uncle Crits says you're going out. But I guess it's okay. He said you worked hard all day, and something like that. You can go out, Mommy.'

'Thanks, Sam.' I wasn't so sure I was pleased with getting permission from a child three feet tall, but it was best that she wasn't mad about it, whatever he'd told her. Then, Chris took charge of me, and it struck me again how nice it was to have a man in the house.

'Now, you go get dressed. Put on something beautiful and sexy and I'm going to show you off. And wear your hair down. And by the way, Mrs Forrester,' he lowered his voice and whispered in my ear as I walked by, 'I'm so goddam in love with you I can hardly think straight.

59

You're wrecking me.'

'I'm glad to hear it.' I planted a kiss on his mouth and practically floated into my room, where I dressed to the sounds of Chris neighing like a horse and Sam playing an ardent cowboy scene. It was nice to hear them, and I felt great.

'Where are we going?'

'Dinner on Clay Street. The competition is giving a party. But I've got something I want to say to you first.' What now? He stopped the truck, pulled over to the side of the street, and turned to me with a funny look, then he took me in his arms and kissed me so hard it hurt. 'You look fantastic. I said dress sexy, I didn't say make me drool for crissake.'

'Flatterer.' But I was pleased. I had worn a green and gold Indian shirt à la hippie, and tight black velvet pants with black suede boots. My hair was down, as per his orders, and I had nothing on under the shirt. And it seemed to be effective. Chris looked absolutely lecherous as we drove along.

The party was given by a San Francisco film-maker who had made a recent hit with a film about drugs, and he was giving a party to celebrate in his brand new house. When we arrived, there were easily two hundred people roaming in the empty house to the sound of a wailing blues singer that was coming at us seemingly from all over the house. That seemed to be the only thing the new tenants had set up. The stereo. There was no furniture, nothing on the walls. The only decorations were the people, and they were exceedingly ornamental, all young, and nice to look at, in the style of Chris. There were girls in hippie shirts and skin-tight jeans with electric-looking hair and Bambi eyes, and long-haired boys in the same kind of clothes. Almost everyone was

60

stoned and the smell of grass hung heavy in the air.

The house itself was a large bastardised Victorian, with a huge, sweeping staircase that seemed to soar towards a skylight miles above. There were people draped all over the banisters in earnest conversation, or necking heavily. It looked just like the parties I'd heard were typical of San Francisco but had never seen.

'Too heavy for you, Gill?' I felt a little bit square in that ambience and Chris's question made me wonder if I looked it.

'No. It's neat. I think I like it.'

'And I think I like you. Come on, I'll take you around to meet some of the troops.' He took me by the hand and we drifted through the crowd, occasionally accepting a hit of hash or a puff on a joint as we went, and stopping for refills of red wine from one of the gallon jugs sitting on the floor. There must have been at least fifty of them in key points.

It seemed like a particularly low-key party. And much quieter than the scene at the Art Directors' bash on Friday. I was expecting exciting things to happen at any minute; it looked like the sort of group that would take off its clothes and begin to writhe on the floor in orgiastic glee. But instead, the crowd seemed to be thinning. We had been watching the scene for almost two hours, and then I looked up at Chris, wondering.

'It looks like more ought to be happening. Or am I missing the point?' He looked amused at my question, and seemed to hesitate.

'Like what?'

'I don't know.' I felt silly having asked. Maybe this was it.

'Well, little Gillian, you're not too far wrong, but I thought we'd stick with the gang downstairs.' We were still on the ground floor of the house. If you can call it that in San Francisco. Ground floor in this case had been two dizzying flights up the side of a hill as we approached the house from the street.

'Is something else happening upstairs?' I was curious.

'Maybe.' Chris looked vague. He could have been dodging me, or it could have been the grass and hash.

'I want to see, Chris. Show me.'

'We'll see.' He introduced me to a few more people, necked with me in a corner for a while, and then we sat down on the floor to talk. But I noticed after a while that the crowds on the main floor seemed to walk up the stairs never to return. The party had moved on, and we were left like pebbles on the shore after the tide goes out. There were only a dozen people left sitting on the floor around us.

'Is the party over, or has the action moved on?'

'Gillian Forrester, you're a pest, but you asked, so . . . here goes . . . get up. We're going upstairs.' He made it sound like a major event. 'But I'm not sure you're going to like this.'

'What lurking evils are you protecting me from, Mr Matthews? Or should I wait and see?' We were weaving our way through the remaining bodies on the stairs; they were either drugged or drunk, but there seemed to be little life in them. The blues music on the stereo had turned to hard-core jazz, and the sounds wailed through the gut as they did through the house, with a kind of strange pull and tug.

At the top of the first flight of stairs, Chris turned and looked at me for a long moment before kissing me longingly with his hand on my breast. The shirt I was wearing was so thin that I felt naked to his touch, and I suddenly longed to go home and make love to him.

'Gill, there are two scenes here . . . in there a bunch of people are dropping acid. It's not much to see, and I don't recommend it, and upstairs they're doing other stuff.'

'What other stuff? Heroin?' My eyes were wide and I wasn't happy. I didn't like the idea of that scene at all.

'No, dopey. Not heroin. Other stuff . . . come on, at least I know you can handle that.' He grinned to himself as he tucked my hand under his arm and raced up the stairs with me in tow. We were just under the skylight then, and that and two huge candles provided the room with its only light. It took a minute for my eyes to adjust. I knew that there were a lot of people where we were, but I couldn't tell how many, or what they were doing, or what kind of room we were in. It struck me only that there was relatively little noise. And then I saw where we were.

We were in a room the width and length of the house, a kind of loft that lay just beneath the skylight and had few windows, and like the rest of the house no furniture. But it had more action. Lots. In the sea around us were most of the two hundred bodies we'd seen downstairs, their jeans and shirts off, their bodies pretzeled into odd positions, locked into each other in groups of four and five and six, and they were all making love. It was an orgy.

'Gill . . . is this okay?' I saw him watching me in the candlelight.

'I . . . uh . . . yeah . . . sure, Chris . . . but . . .'

'But what, love? We don't have to get into this.' A scene behind him had just caught my eye. There were two girls making love to each other while two men stroked their bodies with hungry pleasure and yet another girl wove her tongue between one of the observers' thighs.

'I . . . uh . . . Chris . . . I don't think I want to.' I knew I didn't want to, but I was still a little too stunned

63

to speak coherently. I was twenty-eight years old and had been hearing about stuff like this for years. But it was different seeing it . . . and I didn't want to do it.

Chris took my hand and led me slowly back down the stairs, smiling over his shoulder at me, and stopping to kiss me on the way. The kiss was a gentle one and his smile was warm. He didn't seem sorry we had left.

'I'll take you home.' . . . And come back here alone? . . . My heart sank and my face must have showed it. 'Not like that, dopey. No sweat. I can do without that. Group sex is a bore.' I wondered how often he'd tried it until it became a bore, but I didn't say anything. I was grateful for his reaction. And I was glad we were going home, I'd seen enough. My education was complete, without joining in a gang-bang. I'd seen it. Basta cosí.

'Thanks, Chris. Am I a horrible stuffed-shirt?'

'Nope. Kind of a nice one.' He grinned happily at my transparent shirt, leaned down to kiss one breast, and led me out the door. We were going home.

The ride back to my place was brief and comfortably silent, and I felt even closer to him than I had before. He parked the truck in front of the house and helped me out, and I wondered if he was going to stay.

I paid the sitter and she left. And before she did, she diligently told me there were no messages, which made me smile. I was with the only one I would have wanted anyway.

'Some wine, Chris?' He shook his head and looked at me for a long moment as we stood there. 'Are you angry we left?'

'No. I like your style. Come on, Gill, it's late. Let's go to bed. I've got a lot of work to do tomorrow.'

'So do I.' There was a nice homey feeling as we turned off the lights in the living-room and crept past Sam's room to mine. I was glad he was staying and thought it funny that we had so easily slipped into the kind of relationship we had – 'let's go to bed, it's late, I've got a lot of work tomorrow.' I expected him to peel off his jeans, sit lazily on the edge of the bed as he set the alarm, and then kiss me goodnight before going to sleep. I didn't even mind not being made love to, it was comfortable the way it was.

I was smiling to myself as I brushed my hair and Chris looked surprised.

'What are you doing, Gill?'

'What's it look like? Brushing my hair, you dopey.'

'The hell you are. I don't give a shit about gang-bangs, but I brought my orgy home . . . Come here, you, let me do that.' He stood up and met me halfway across the room, his hands already stretched towards me to peel off my clothes. I unbuttoned his shirt as he did mine, and then we stood there chest to chest, the smoothness of our skin met and melted into one, as my slacks came off in unison with his, and his whole body seemed to enter mine.

7

'Hey . . . Chris . . . it's getting light outside. And you didn't get any sleep.' I felt faintly guilty about that, but not very.

'I'm not complaining. Are you? But I've got to get to work soon. We start at six.' It was already five. 'Let's get dressed and go outside. I want to see the sun come up.'

'So do I.' But inside me, it already had. We climbed back into our clothes which still lay in a jumble on the floor and walked outside to sit on the tiny patch of lawn in front of where I lived. It was chilly and the ground was damp, but it felt good as we sat there and watched the sun come up over the East Bay.

'No fog today. That'll be good for my shooting. Want to come watch?'

'I'd love it, but I don't think I can. I've got to get Sam to school, and I've got a shooting at ten. Textile stuff. They're shooting just the fabrics somewhere outside first, and then we do the models at ten. At the Opera House yet. It sounds like fun.'

'Of course it does . . . who do you think's doing the camera work?' He looked amused as he grabbed my hair and pulled it back so he could kiss me.

'Hey . . . are you on that job?'

'Who do you think recommended you?' He tried to look pompous.

'Bullshit you did. They told me Joe Tramino gave them my name, you big phoney.'

'Well, okay . . . but I told them you were a great stylist.'

'After I had the job.'

'After you had the job. Boy, the ego of some women.'

'Not to mention some men . . . I'm glad we'll be working together. Think we can ride a horse across the orchestra pit and down Van Ness?'

'We can try . . . baby, we can always try.' He rolled his body on to mine on the wet grass and we lay there smiling for a moment in the early morning sun. 'I gotta go, Gill. I'll see you at work.'

'That's the most unusual morning good-bye this neighbourhood has ever seen, Chris Matthews. But I like it.'

'Good, because it isn't the last. And this neighbour-

66

hood can't do a goddam thing about it if they don't like it.'

'They could evict me.' I was feeling playful and I walked him to the truck.

'We'll talk about that sometime . . . but not just yet.' He slammed the door to the truck, put it into gear, and I wondered what he had meant as he drove away. Whatever he had meant, it would be fun to work with him that day, and it was nice to know that the head of the film crew would be at as great a disadvantage as I. I knew exactly what he'd been doing the night before. And neither of us had had a moment's sleep. To hell with the Clay Street orgy. Chris and I had had our own.

I arrived at the Opera House at exactly ten o'clock, stood back to look at its splendour for a moment before going in, and then smiled. It looked like a funny place for Chris.

I went in the stage door, and was told where to go, and arrived somewhere behind the stage to look at the clothes and props I'd picked out the day before, and check in with the agency people who seemed pleased with what I'd dug up. It was going to be a pretty shooting.

They had seven of San Francisco's top models and three they'd imported from Los Angeles for the day. They were beautiful girls and the clothes they were going to wear in the commercial we were filming were superb. Everything from evening clothes to beach wear to show off some new man-made fibre.

I assigned the appropriate clothes and accessories to each girl and then went off to find Chris. It didn't take long. He and his crew were lying in the string section of the orchestra pit, eating tacos and salami sandwiches and drinking cherry soda.

'Breakfast or lunch? Hi, boys.'

'Neither. This is just between the two. Come on down and have a bite.' Chris looked wicked for the briefest second, and then looked pleased with his double entendre. It made me wonder how little or how much he wanted his crew to know. I suspected less than more. And I was glad . . . I didn't want Joe Tramino to offer his condolences quite yet. Not till we were sure.

I hopped into the pit, landed on my feet near Chris, and then sat down to guzzle cherry soda and munch on tacos.

'You know what, boys? This stuff is disgusting. Blyergh.'

'You know what? She's right.' Everyone looked pleased to agree, and we went on eating happily until they told us the models and the scenery were ready to go. We had been allowed the use of some of the opera's stage props for the day, and it was fun to see it all from backstage. As I stood in the wings, checking each girl as she went out, and watching for lack of continuity as girls went out for a second or third time in the same clothes, I looked towards the Boxes, and the Grand Tier, and wondered what it would be like to sing to them . . . or to be in the audience again on the snobby, social nights when everyone would wear white tie and tails. Those days were so far behind me, it was funny to think of them.

'Whatcha thinking about, Gill?'

'Nothing much. What are you doing back here?'

'We're all through.'

'Already? It's only . . .' I looked at my watch and gasped. It was four-fifteen.

'That's right. We've been working six hours straight. Let's go pick up Sam and put in some beach time at the Marina.'

'Yes, boss.' I saluted sharply, and we left hand in hand.

The day of working with him had flown. This time there had been no crazy escapades, just a lot of hard work. And stolen kisses in the pit.

We picked up Sam and wandered over to the beach where she chased sea gulls and we played word games in the sand until the sun began to fade.

'Sam, time to go home!' She was far down the beach and had other things in mind. But Chris changed it for her quickly.

'Come on, podner, I'll give you a ride.'

'Okay, Uncle Crits.' She galloped down the beach to meet us, hopped on Chris's back, and I watched them hobble home. The child and the man I loved . . . Samantha Forrester and her 'horse'. My man.

'What are you doing today, Gill? Any work come up?' He had been staying with us every night for a week, and breakfast à trois had become an ordinary thing. It looked routine, but it felt like Christmas to me every day.

'Nope. How about going out to Stinson, Chris? We could take Sam after school.'

'Can't. I've got a job today at three. Another cigarette job.'

'That's nice. I'll do stuff here. Will you be home for dinner?' That was the first time I had asked him that, and I held my breath.

'Maybe not. We'll see.'

I did. He wasn't. He was gone for two days, and when he reappeared on Thursday there was nothing to show that he'd been gone. He looked and sounded the same, but he had left a tiny dent in my heart. Not to mention Sam. I had finally decided that if he didn't show up by the end of the week I was going to use her much dreamt of trick and tie her to a chair and gag her. I couldn't stand the questions any more.

I wanted to ask him where he'd been but I didn't dare. I made hamburgers and French fries and we all went to Swensen's on Hyde Street after dinner. They had the best ice cream in town.

'Want to take a ride on the cable car, Sam?' She was dripping strawberry, and we were dripping rocky road. We had made the appropriate choice.

'A cable car ride? Wow!' And so it was. We hopped on when it came by and reeled down towards Fisherman's Wharf where Chris bought her a painted turtle. How can you stay mad at a man like that? He ran around us playfully like a big dog, kissed me back into a feeling of almost-security, and further seduced Sam. By the time we got home we were a solid trio again and all was well. Almost.

'Want to go to Bolinas tomorrow, Gill?' We were lying in bed and the lights were out.

'Let's see what the weather's doing.' I wasn't sure.

'Don't be a grump, Miss Gillian. I meant for the weekend. I got someone to lend me their shack till Monday.'

'You did?' I was pleased. 'That would be nice.'

'That's what I thought. And now, stop being grumpy. I'm back, and I love you.' He kissed my neck and put a hand gently across my lips to silence them, and we lost another night of sleep. But we won each other back.

The weekend in Bolinas was lovely. The shack which someone had lent him was almost that, but not quite. It was a small two-bedroom house buried in the woods. We went to the beach every day, had dinner at the Watson House one night, and the rest of the time spent quiet evenings at home. There was a marvellous aura of peace

70

about the few days we spent there. San Francisco seemed quiet to me after New York, but the time in Bolinas even managed to make San Francisco seem too busy. There was a golden stillness to those days. And I was sorry to leave on Monday.

The week following the Bolinas weekend was busy. I got another job from Carson, but Chris wasn't on it this time; he had other things to do. He came to dinner with us in the evenings though, and most of the time he spent the night. He vanished again that weekend but reappeared Sunday night and never left us for a week after that. It was a bit strange the way he came and went, but I got used to it, and everything was rolling smoothly.

We were unbelievably happy together, and I got to the point where I didn't even mind his disappearances – they gave me some time to myslef and I needed that too.

The weeks rolled by and I realised at the end of May that we had spent two months together, which seemed more like two years. I had become a combination wife-mother-girl-friend-pal to Chris Matthews and I could no longer imagine a time when I hadn't known him. He was my best friend, and the man I loved. And he was always fun to be with. There was a selfishness about him too – he never did anything he didn't want to do, he couldn't be pressed into anything – but I didn't try. I understood his ways, and I accepted them. In many ways I felt older than he, but I had led a different life. And I had Sam to make me feel grown-up. He'd never had anything like that. He only had Chris Matthews to think of and, when he felt like it, me.

We were lying under a tree in the park one Thursday morning, with nothing much to do except enjoy the world and love each other, and I remembered that Memorial Day weekend was that week. Not that it changed things for us a great deal – almost every weekend we had was a long one, unless one of us had a job on Monday, which was never sure for either of us.

'What are you doing this weekend, Chris? It's a holiday.'

'Yeah. I guess it is. I'm moving out of town as a matter of fact.'

'Very funny. But I get the message. I was just asking.' I picked a blade of grass next to where we lay and tickled the side of his face with it, wondering when he'd get rid of the girl he lived with. He hadn't yet.

'I wasn't kidding, Gill. I am moving. Out to Bolinas for the summer. Want to come?'

'Are you kidding or are you for real?' This was the first I'd heard of it, other than vague mention two months back that he usually spent his summers in Bolinas. But with Chris very little was 'usual' and nothing ever seemed to be planned.

'I'm for real. I thought I'd move out tomorrow or Saturday. I meant to tell you. Why don't you and Sam come and stay?'

'And after that? She's already so attached to you, Chris, if she gets used to having you around all the time it's going to really hurt when we come back to this. She's already had that once, with her father . . . I don't know . . .'

'Don't be so stuffy. She'll be happy with us, and you said you were going to send her East to see him anyway, so that'll wean her off me.' . . . But what about me? . . . 'When's she going to see him?'

'Middle of July till the end of August. Roughly six weeks.'

'Okay. So what's the sweat? She'll spend six weeks with us and six weeks with him. And we can be alone for a while . . . Gill, please . . . I'd really like you to.' He turned

72

to me with the expression of a starving, lonely child, and my heart melted. I didn't know whether to laugh or jump at the chance. It would be so nice to live with Chris . . . but what then?

'We'll see . . . anyway, what would I do about work?' That was a lame reason not to do it, and we both knew it.

'Don't be a jerk. I work out of Bolinas, so can you. There's a phone over there. You'll get your calls . . . oh hell, if you don't want to, screw it.' Suddenly I was the bad guy, and he was hurt. But he hadn't even told me he was moving. That was so like Chris.

'I want to, I want to, for chrissake . . . okay, I'll come. I'm just afraid I'll get used to you that's all. Can't you try and understand that? I love you, Chris, and I want to live with you, but when we come back to San Francisco at the end of the summer I go back to my place and you go back to your room-mate.' I hadn't mentioned it in a long time.

'As a matter of fact, Gill, you're wrong. She's moving out next week or something. I gave her notice.'

'You did? She is? . . . Hey . . . wow!'

'That's right, little lady. Wow. And I thought that if it works out this summer you and Sam could move in with me in September. The house is big enough for all of us.' . . . But what about your heart, Chris? . . . It was a dumb thing to think. I knew he loved us. And I was thrilled the girl was leaving . . . at last.

'Chris Matthews, do you know what? . . . I love you. And Bolinas is going to be super. Take me home, I want to pack.'

'Yes ma'am. At your service.'

It dawned on me as we drove back to the Marina that I had never seen his house in the city. I knew it was on Sacramento Street, but that was all. I had a sudden urge to see it, to take a long drunken look at the place where we would live in the fall, but that could wait. He had said 'if it works out this summer'. But why shouldn't it? I couldn't see any reason why it shouldn't. No reason at all.

8

'Chris! . . . Sam! . . . Lunch is ready!' A large red enamel plate was buried under a dozen peanut butter and jelly sandwiches and a pitcher of milk stood next to it. We were going to eat under the big tree behind the tiny house Chris rented every summer, which had become our summer home. It was a gem. He had painted it the year before, and everything was a bright, sunny yellow, and there were splashes of colour everywhere. It was simple and rustic, but comfortable, and it was close to the beach, which was all we needed.

'I'm coming, Mommy. Uncle Crits said he'd take me riding this afternoon.' Samantha staggered to the lunch table under the weight of the cowboy holster Chris had given her and shoved a sandwich into her mouth with a look of satisfaction.

'You want to come too, Gill?'

'Sure.' I looked over Sam's head at Chris for a long moment, and we shared a secret smile. Things were working out. Beautifully. We had been in Bolinas for a month, and it was like something out of a fairy tale. We went riding and swimming, we sat outside at night, and we were so in love with each other we could hardly see straight.

74

Sam was supposed to leave in two weeks to spend the rest of her vacation with Richard, and for once I felt less badly about Samantha leaving. I was looking forward to being alone with Chris. Even though I couldn't see how things could get any better than they were.

'Hey, Gill . . . what's the matter?' I suddenly felt ill and it must have showed. My stomach rolled slowly towards my throat and then down again, in a kind of slow-motion roller coaster feeling.

'I don't know . . . must be something I ate.'

'Peanut butter? Can't be. Maybe too much sun. Go lie down. I'll keep an eye on Sam.' I followed his suggestion, and half an hour later I felt better.

'You still want to ride with us, love?'

'Maybe I'll skip it. I'll go tomorrow.'

'Oh shit . . . I forgot to tell you. I'm going into town tonight. I have a job tomorrow.'

'Lucky you.' I hadn't had a job in almost three weeks. Summer was slowing things down. But it didn't matter much. We were living cheaply in Bolinas. 'When will you be back?' It didn't make much difference, we never had any plans, and we were leading a lazy life.

'Tomorrow night, or the day after. It depends how long we take to shoot. This is a documentary for the state.' He smiled at me for a moment. 'Don't worry, I'll be back.'

'I'm glad to hear it.'

But he wasn't back the next night, or the night after that. He came back three days later, and I had been worried. I had called the house on Sacramento Street and had gotten no answer.

'Where the hell were you, Chris?'

'I was busy for chrissake. What were you worried about? You knew I'd come back. So what's the big deal?'

'The big deal is that something could have happened to you, that's all.'

'You worry about you, and I'll worry about me.' And that's the way it was. End of discussion.

'Fine. I'm going into town tomorrow myself. Joe Tramino called me for a job at Carson.'

'Great.' Yeah . . . great . . . but you were still gone three days and what the hell were you doing? You didn't even call . . . But I didn't want to ask.

That evening, he acted as though nothing had happened, and I left him in charge of Sam the next morning as I set out to drive across the mountains in his car. I was due in town at nine. And Joe had invited me to lunch if the shooting was over in time. It was. He took me to a late lunch at Enrico's, on lower Broadway, looking down Montgomery Street towards the newly built up financial district. We sat outside, and it was warm and sunny, with a nice cool breeze that rustled through the trees out front.

'You did a nice job today, Gill. How's life been treating you?' He looked concerned. He knew.

'Fine. Everything is really fine.'

'You look like you've lost some weight.'

'And you sound like my mother.' But he was right, I hadn't felt really well since the day the peanut butter sandwich had gone sour on me at lunch. That had been almost a week, but it was probably just worry over Chris's absence.

'Okay. I'll lay off. But I was right. I'm still kicking my ass in for introducing you to that guy . . . and I am crawling my office walls in a jealous frenzy. Haven't you heard?' We both broke into a laugh, and I shook my head.

'You're full of shit, Joe. But you're good for my ego. And just for the record, Chris and I are really happy. You did a nice thing for both of us. All is well.' I felt silly having to reassure him, but his concern seemed genuine

76

and I meant what I said. He had done a nice thing for all of us, including Sam.

The lunch was pleasant, we talked about the shooting and a variety of other things, and when we rose to leave I was sorry. He was good company, and it was pleasant to just sit there, watching people come and go, and talking about nothing in particular.

I stopped at my apartment on the way back, picked up my mail, a few odds and ends, like a new kite for Sam, and then I went back. I was a little earlier than planned, but it would be nice to get back into sloppy clothes and go for a swim. The day had gotten hot.

'Hi troops, I'm home.' But it appeared that no one else was. It was after five, but they were probably at the beach; they might even have gone to Stinson. 'Hello! Anybody here?' But it was obvious that there wasn't or Sam would have come screeching out to meet me.

I kicked off my shoes in the living-room, headed towards the kitchen for a glass of something cold, and then noticed that the bedroom door was closed. Closed doors were unusual in our house in Bolinas, and for some reason it suddenly made me wonder if everything were okay. Some maternal instinct spoke up deep within me . . . Sam? . . .

I walked to the bedroom door with three deliberate steps, stopped, took a deep breath, and turned the handle. But what I found was not Sam. It was Chris. Making love to someone else in the bed we shared.

'Ohhh . . . I . . .' I stood rooted to the spot, my mouth frozen into what felt like an iron 'O', and my eyes began instantly to blur with tears. Chris turned his head to look at me as I opened the door, and the only thing that struck me was that his face was as expressionless as his buttocks which stared at me from the bed. No dismay, no horror. Nothing. The girl had leapt beneath him as I entered, murmuring a horrified gasp, and looking around the room with terrified eyes, as though she might have wished to escape through the window. I couldn't blame her, I felt precisely the same way. Perhaps that's what we should have done, both left together via the window, leaving Chris alone. But we didn't. She lay there, pinned down by Chris's firm grasp on her arms, and I slammed the door. What could I say? But then it occurred to me that there was something I had to say, and anger welled in me as never before. I spun around on one heel and flung the door open again, addressing Chris.

'I don't give a shit what you're doing or who she is, but where's my daughter?' Another gasp emanated from the bed, and Chris turned to me with a look of fury on his face, but it was no match for my own.

'What the fuck do you think, Gill? That I tied her up and put her under the bed? The Gillmours picked her up for a picnic hours ago. I said I'd pick her up at six.'

'Don't bother.' The girl was squirming under Chris's vicelike grip, and the ignominy and horror of the entire scene struck me like another blow. 'I'll be back to pick up my things in an hour.' I slammed the door again, picked up my shoes in the living-room, grabbed my handbag, and ran barefoot towards the car. To hell with Christopher Matthews. If this was what it was going to be like, he could take his lousy life and do anything he damn well pleased with it. I didn't want any part of it . . . no, thanks . . . the rotten . . . lousy . . . cheating . . . miserable . . . Tears streamed down my face and sobs choked me as I drove towards the Gillmours' place. All I wanted to do was get Sam and then get the hell out of Chris's house. For good. I was suddenly relieved that I

78

hadn't given up my apartment in the city. Sam and I could go back that night and make believe nothing had ever happened. Chris had never existed . . . Chris was gone . . .

The tyres squealed as I drove into the Gillmours' driveway. I pulled up behind their station wagon, put on the brake, turned off the ignition, and wiped my face. I felt as though the world had just come to an end, and how was I going to face Sam?

Elinor Gillmour came out as I got out of the car and waved as she stood barefoot in the doorway.

'Hi, Gillian. How was your day?' . . . How was my day? Are you kidding?

'Fine. Thanks for taking Sam on the picnic. I bet she loved it.' The Gillmours had five children, two of whom were close enough in age to Sam to make an outing with them really fun for her. Visiting them was like going to a playgroup.

'Hi, Mommy, can I stay for dinner?' Sam had come thundering out at the sound of my voice.

'No, sweetheart, we have to go home.' You bet . . . home . . . San Francisco, to our place in the Marina.

'Awww . . . Mommy ' She wound up for a good long whine and I shook my head.

'I'm not kidding tonight, Sam. We're going home. Thanks, Elinor. Now, let's go.' I took her firmly by the hand and led her to the car, as we waved a last wave to the Gillmour brood trickling out of the house. 'Did you have a nice time?'

'Yes. Can we do something special for dinner? Like have a picnic with Uncle Crits?'

'No, you just had a picnic, and I have a surprise for you. We have to go back to the city for a few days, so Mommy can do some things.' A few days seemed like enough explanation, I had decided. She was going off

79

with her father in a week anyway.

'Why? I don't want to go back to the city. Is Uncle Crits coming too?' She seemed cheerier at the thought.

'No, sweetheart. He has to stay here.' You're damned right he does. I was absolutely livid by the time we got back to Chris's house. I didn't even feel hurt any more. I just wanted to kill him. But I didn't want Sam to know that there was trouble underfoot.

'Gill . . .' He was waiting for us outside the house when we got there.

'Hi, Uncle Crits. It was a nice picnic.'

'Hi, Sam. Would you do me a big favour and go water my plants for me again. They look thirsty as a cowboy in the desert. Thanks.'

'Sure, Uncle Crits.' She looked delighted with the errand, and ran off behind the house to comply.

'Gill . . .' He followed me into the house as I headed for the bedroom.

'Forget it, Chris. Don't bother saying anything. I'm not interested. I saw what was going on and I don't dig that scene. I'm going back to the city tonight with Sam. I'll see that you get the car back somehow tomorrow.'

'Fuck the car.'

'That too? My, my . . .' I was yanking drawers open in our room by then, and most of my things were already lying in a heap in my suitcase on the unmade bed. The bed. Where he screwed that girl. The bastard. 'You could have at least made the goddam bed.'

'Look, Gill, please . . .'

'No. No "please". Just nothing. I'm getting the hell out. Now.'

'Look, it was no big deal. I don't give a damn about her. It doesn't change anything between us. She's just a girl I picked up in town.' He sounded desperate.

'Oh? Is she? I'm thrilled. Just thrilled, to know that she

doesn't mean anything to you. But it seems to me that neither do I. The whole time I've known you you've been living with some girl. You come, you go, you arrive for dinner, spend the night, and then disappear for three days. And now you fuck some girl, just for the hell of it. In our bed, and hell . . . it's your goddam bed, but I don't give a shit. We're supposed to be living together. And I don't do stuff like that. That's probably my big mistake.'

'No, Gill, it's not your mistake. I love you the way you are. But I'm a man for chrissake, and I need to have some fun.'

'Then what am I?' My voice seemed to shake the rafters.

'You're not just fun, Gill. You're for real. I love you.' His voice had dropped to an almost whisper, and he looked at me earnestly from across the room. 'Please don't go, Gill. I need you. I'm sorry this happened.'

'Well so am I. But I'm going anyway.' But my resolve had been shaken . . . I was for real? But what did that mean? 'Chris, it's going to happen again and again, I can smell it. And I just can't take it. I'm sorry.' . . . Sorry? . . . Why the hell should I be sorry? . . . But I was.

'Why do you have to turn it into such a goddam major happening? Because it just isn't. It really isn't.'

'Maybe not to you. But it is to me. Do you have any idea what it felt like to walk in and see you pumping your prick into her, your ass staring me in the face, and her legs spread fifteen yards apart.' The mental image made me sick.

'You make it sound terrific.' He had calmed down and he wasn't letting me get to him any more.

'Well, maybe it was terrific. What the hell do I know? It sure looked like it from where I stood. Do you know what I feel? I feel stupid and inadequate, and like I'm not enough woman for you. If you're not happy with us, then tell me. But all I know is we ball our asses off, and the minute I turn my back you go off and screw somebody else. Joe Tramino was right.' I regretted that the instant it was out of my mouth. I should have left Joe out of it.

'And what did that little dago fart have to say about me?' Chris was suddenly livid.

'Nothing. Forget it. He just said you'd make me unhappy, and it looks like he was right.'

'Bullshit. We've been plenty happy. And the fact is if you'd come home when you said you were going to you'd have found me and Sam eating dinner in the kitchen, and nothing would have changed. You wouldn't have known. And if you really cared about me, you'd understand, and nothing would be changed now that you do know.' . . . Huh?

'Are you kidding?'

'No, I'm not. It could happen to you too, Gill. And I wouldn't walk out on you. You're right, we live together. And I love you, and I understand how people work, which is something you don't.' I was beginning to wonder if he was right, and it shook me. There was something so cool and knowledgeable in his voice. Maybe those things did happen all the time. But why to me? . . . And why did I have to see it? 'Gill, will you spend the night, and see how you feel in the morning? This is silly, and you'll get Sam all shook up going back into town now. I have a job in town tomorrow; if you still want to call it quits, I'll drive you in.' I didn't want to sleep on it, but he had a point about Sam. I was wavering, and he knew it.

'Well . . . all right. For Sam. But stay out of my way. I'll sleep on the couch. You can have your bedroom back,

82

as of right now.' I swung my badly packed suitcase down on the floor and walked out of the room.

'I'll cook dinner, Gill. You take it easy. You look rough.'

'I feel rough, thank you. But I'll do the cooking for Sam. I'm not hungry, and you can take care of yourself.' I walked outside to check on Sam before making dinner. She was still devotedly watering Chris's plants and showed no sign that she had heard the fracas. But I was afraid she had.

'Sam, whatcha want to eat, love? How about some cold chicken?'

'That's fine, Mommy.' I knew then that she had heard, at least some of it, because she was being inordinately good-natured. But I was grateful.

'You're a good girl.'

'Thanks, Mommy. Is Uncle Crits gonna eat with us?'

'No, he's not.' My mouth tightened uncontrollably over the words.

'Okay.'

She ate the chicken almost soundlessly and then put her pyjamas on by herself and told me she was ready for bed. My heart went out to her as I tucked her in. I hated to have her think, yet again, that men wandered through our lives only to go away again. Or have me walk out on them. It didn't seem fair. And I hated Chris for making it all happen again, and myself for letting it. I should never have moved in with him in Bolinas, and I felt nothing but regret as I kissed Sam good-night and turned off the light.

'See you in the morning, sweetheart. Sweet dreams.' A tear crept down my cheek as I walked back to the kitchen for a cup of coffee, and I felt as though all of me were sagging. It had been such a rotten afternoon. And I couldn't see how tomorrow would be much better.

'How are you feeling, Gill?' I hadn't heard him come into the kitchen.

'Fine, thank you. Would you mind listening for Sam? I'd like to go for a walk.'

'Yeah, sure. Okay.' I felt his eyes on me as I quietly closed the door and walked down the road towards the beach. It was a quiet night and the air was still warm. The fog mustn't have come in. But I had been too busy earlier to notice. I looked up and saw the stars brightly etched in the sky above, but even that didn't make me feel better.

The sea was lapping gently at the beach when I got there, and I lay down on the cool sand, to think. Or not to think. I didn't really care what I did. I just wanted to be alone, and away from Chris. And as far away from the house as I could.

I watched a stray dog amble slowly past and sniff at the water, and then, without thinking, I began to take off my clothes. I slipped into the water, naked, and swam slowly towards the land spit at the end of Stinson Beach, remembering the day Chris and I had crossed that stretch of water with the horse from the Carson shooting. The day we'd met. The first day . . . that had been three months before, and this was such a different day.

Once on the other side, I lay on the sand in the bright moonlight and wondered what would come next, and if I'd ever trust anyone again. It seemed as though I lay there for hours, and then I heard footsteps in the sand behind me and turned in sudden fear.

'Gill?' It was Chris.

'What are you doing here? You said you'd stay with Sam.' He could have at least done that much.

'She's fine. She's sound asleep, and I wanted to talk to you.'

'There's nothing to say. How did you know I'd be here?'

'I just knew. I would have come to the same place too.'

'I didn't think you'd have cared that much.' The tears started out of the corners of my eyes again as I said the words.

'I only wish you knew how much I do care, Gill.' He sat down on the sand beside me, and I could see his wet flesh glisten in the dark.

'I'd better get back to Sam.' I didn't want to wait and be told anything.

'Sit with me for just a minute . . . please.' Thére was something in his voice that caught at my heart, almost the way Sam's quiet good behaviour had when she went to bed.

'Why, Chris? What's the point? We've said it all.'

'No, we haven't. Or if we have, then let me just be with you here, quietly, for a few minutes. I can't stand the thought of your leaving me.' I shut my eyes hard and squelched a sob before it rose in my throat. 'Want to take a walk?' I nodded silently, and we set off down the beach, side by side, but far apart. I still felt terribly alone.

'We'd better go back, Chris. Sam.' We had walked halfway to the point at the other end, and we still had to walk back to the inlet, swim back to the Bolinas Beach, and then get back to the house. It would take at least a half-hour to accomplish, and I had really begun to worry about Sam being alone in the house. She'd be frightened if she woke up and there was no one there. It wasn't dangerous, but it still wasn't nice.

'Okay, Gill. I wanted to stop at our cove.' His voice sounded like that of a small boy who has just suffered an immense disappointment, but his words were like a slap in the face.

'Chris, how could you? You really don't understand a goddam thing.' The peace of the silent walk on the

85

moonlit beach was totally interrupted, and I began to run towards the inlet. When I got there, I dived into the water and swam as hard as I could towards the other side. But he reached the beach even before I did and he swung me into his arms and held me tight when I got out of the water.

'You just shut up, goddam you, Gillian Forrester. I did a lousy thing today. But I love you, and if you don't know that by now you aren't worth a damn.' He crushed his mouth down hard on to mine and his kiss touched my very soul.

'Chris . . .'

'Shut up. We have to go back to Sam.' He took my hand firmly in his, walked me over to my pile of clothes, and watched me dress as he slid into his jeans. They were all he'd worn.

When I was dressed, he took me by the hand again, and we walked back to the house without saying another word. The lights were on, and all was quiet when we got in. I checked and was relieved to see that Sam was still asleep. And as I walked away from her room I saw ours. Chris had tidied up, the bed was made with fresh sheets, and there were flowers from the garden in a vase.

'Are you coming to bed?' He was sitting on the edge of it, and smiled a tiny smile.

'You did a nice job.' There was no sign to remind me of what had happened that afternoon, except what was already lodged in my head, like an aching splinter.

'You didn't answer my question. Are you coming to bed?' He flicked out the light, and I stood there in the darkness, wondering what to do. I didn't want to get into the bed, but I didn't want to leave him either. I wondered if he had been right when he had said earlier that if I had come home as late as I'd planned I wouldn't have known, and nothing would have changed. Except

I hadn't come home as planned.

He turned over on his side in the darkness and I walked slowly into the room and began to take off my clothes. I would sleep with him, but I would not make love. Maybe he didn't want to anyway. He had had his for the day. The memory made me cringe again as I slipped between the sheets, turned my back to him, and fell asleep, exhausted.

I woke up next morning to the smell of bacon frying, and looked at the clock. It was 5 a.m., and it was foggy outside.

'Good morning, sleeping beauty. Breakfast's on the table.' I felt more like sleeping ugly than sleeping beauty, and the smell of the bacon made me feel sick. The nausea I felt reminded me again of the day before. My nerves were obviously falling apart.

'Hi, Mommy. We made you waffers.'

'Waffles. And you're all dressed. Looks like you two have been up all night.' And I felt as though I had, but I had to put a good face on it, for Sam at least.

I got up and brushed my teeth and felt a little better after that, and the waffles were good. I ate two and Sam was thrilled.

'Aren't they delicious, Mommy?'

'Terrific, Sam.' I cast a brief glance at Chris, but he was busy cleaning up the kitchen. 'What's everybody doing up so early?'

'I have to be on location at six, and if you still want to go to the city we've got to get moving. I'm already late.' He looked at me pointedly across the room.

'Fine. Thanks. I'll get Sam's stuff packed up, and I'll be dressed in ten minutes.' Blue jeans and a shirt. I had nothing to do in town anyway. Except congratulate Joe Tramino for his good judgement.

Sam looked downcast as we left, and I tried to get her

87

to sing songs as we wound our way over the mountain road. I was grateful for the fog; I didn't have to see long sweeping views of Stinson and Bolinas stretching behind me as we left. All we could see was a brief patch of road ahead of us, and the fog-crowned hills stretching above us.

The roads were deserted at that hour, and we were in the city in thirty minutes. Chris pulled up in front of my apartment and gave Sam a piggyback ride to the front door.

'I'll be seeing you, podner.' She looked as though she were about to cry, and then he leaned down and whispered something in her ear which sparked a smile on her face like a sunburst.

'Okay, Uncle Crits. Good-bye.' She ran into the house and slammed the screen door as I turned to Chris.

'What did you tell her?' I wanted to know. I didn't want him telling her any lies about his coming back. 'I want to know.'

'None of your business. It's just between the two of us. And I have a message for you too. Only that this isn't the end. And don't waste your time thinking this is it, because it just plain isn't. I won't let it be. Do you hear me?' He stared into my eyes for one long moment and then kissed my forehead before he turned his back, walked away, and drove off.

He had made a big mistake. For me, it was all over.

I dropped Sam off at her old playgroup at nine and was pleased to see that she didn't seem to mind being back. And then I went home to unpack.

I also had to call all the advertising agencies I did freelance work for and tell them I'd moved back to town. And then what? Cry, maybe? Yeah, why the hell not?

But as it turned out, I sat around the house drinking coffee until I picked Sam up at school and we went to the zoo. I couldn't face the suitcases or the calls to the agencies, it was too depressing. We ate dinner at the Hippo on the way home, and Sam and I had a minor fight over the menu.

'But I don't like gorillas, Mommy. They're scary.'

'It's just a hamburger, Sam. They only call it a gorillaburger.'

She was dubious, but she finally decided to try it, threatening me with an instant walkout if it turned out to be scary. Apparently it wasn't, and the hamburger and French fries disappeared in minutes, while I tried hard to hide a smile.

We went home in the fading light of what had turned out to be a very pleasant summer day, and I gave her her bath and put her to bed. But I knew that sooner or later it would catch up with me. Chris was gone.

'May I come in?' My heart soared as I saw the shaggy blond mane poke through the door. 'You should lock your door.'

'And you should listen to what people tell you. I told you to stay away.' But I was so glad to see him there that I felt like throwing my arms around him. His absence had weighed on me like a hundred-pound backpack all day.

'You're full of shit, Gill. And anyway, I had to come back. I promised Sam.' He had already sprawled on the couch and was looking pleased.

'Well, you shouldn't have.'

'I'm taking you both back to Bolinas tomorrow. I figured the day in town would do you good.'

'It did. And we're staying.'

'In that case, so am I. But it's asinine to let the place in Bolinas just sit there empty.'

'So don't let it. Go back. I don't care where you stay.'

'Oh really?' He had gotten off the couch and was walking slowly to the chair where I was sitting, smoking a cigarette, and shaking inside. 'Well, it just so happens that I care plenty where you are, Mrs Gillian Forrester. And I want you to be with me. Have you gotten that message yet?' He was leaning over my chair, with a hand firmly clenched on each arm of the chair. His face was lowering slowly towards mine and I knew that he was going to kiss me.

'Chris, don't!' I shoved at his chest but he kept right on coming at me anyway, and then he kissed me. 'Stop it!'

'No, you stop it. This has gone far enough. I'll eat crow for the next week. But I'm not going to let this thing get out of proportion. So get that into your head.' And with that, he swept me out of the chair, carried me into the bedroom, and dumped me on the bed.

'Chris Matthews, get out of this house!' I stood on the bed and shouted at him, but he swung his arm gently in the air and knocked me down on the bed. And then in one swift movement, his body was on mine, and the end was over. We had begun again.

'Are we going back to Bolinas this morning or not? The weather looks lousy, by the way.' We were in bed, and we could see from the window that the fog was in again.

'I don't see much point, Chris. I have three jobs next week, and Richard is picking up Sam on Friday anyway. Let's stay in.'

'Okay.' He was being very amenable.

'But I want to stay here, not Sacramento Street.' Chris's place.

'Why?'

'For a number of reasons. For one thing, there's no

point feeding Sam stuff that's going to make waves with her father. I'd just as soon she not be able to tell him we've moved out of our place and into yours. It was different in Bolinas. And ... well, the other stuff's not important.' But it was to me. I just didn't want to be someplace where I'd know he had already slept with a hundred different girls. Some of them in the past three months. Even Bolinas still had a faint sour taste. I wanted to stay at my place in the city.

'I think you're silly. But I'll go along with it. I've got a lot of work to do anyway.'

So we spent the next week in the city, living at my place, and putting the pieces of the broken dish back together. I was surprised how easy it was, but that was because of Chris. It was impossible to stay mad at him, he had the charm of an irresistible six-year-old boy, and besides, I loved him.

At the end of the following week, I got Sam's bags packed again, shooed Chris out of the house, and we sat down to wait for Richard, Sam's father. He had called to tell me that he had to go to Los Angeles on business and he would fly up to San Francisco to pick her up at noon on 15 July. Which meant he planned to get to the house by two o'clock on that date. And when Richard said that, he meant it. He was as irritatingly punctual as ever.

It was then 15 July, and he arrived promptly at two-ten, looking painfully neat and well put-together in a dark grey suit, with a navy and white striped tie, white shirt, and highly polished black shoes. It was an odd feeling to watch him come in the door and realise that this had been the man I had been married to and had once gone home to the end of each day. He seemed like someone from another world. And I suppose I did too. I was no longer the Gillian he had known.

'She's all set.' I tried to keep my voice firm and wear a cheerful face for Sam's benefit. But I hated to see her leave for six weeks. The days would seem so quiet and empty without her.

'You look well, Gillian. You've been out in the sun?'

'Yes. Across the bay.' I kept it deliberately vague, and was struck again by the inane conversations we had had since the divorce. What did we used to talk about? I really couldn't remember.

'I have a list of where Samantha and I will be for the next six weeks. And if you move around, please send my secretary your itinerary so we can reach you in case of emergency.' His face looked like a dry bone.

'Don't worry about it. You'll be hearing from me. I'll be calling Sam.' He didn't look overwhelmingly pleased at that, and I stooped to give Sam a giant hug and a big mushy kiss as she stood at the door.

'Good-bye, Mommy. Send me some pretty cards . . . and say good-bye to Uncle Crits!' . . . Whoops . . . I saw Richard's eyes register the name and look towards me.

'Nice to see you, Richard. Have a good trip. Good-bye, sweetheart. Take care.'

I waved as the limousine pulled away from the kerb and Sam's small face shrank at the rear window as she waved back. It was going to be lonely without her.

The phone was ringing as I came back into the house, and I picked it up, grateful for someone to talk to.

'Can I come home yet? Has the big bad wolf gone?'

'Yes, and so has Sam. I feel lousy.'

'I figured you would. I'll be over in ten minutes and we can leave for Bolinas as soon as you want.' Suddenly the memory of the girl Chris had slept with didn't bother me as much, and I wanted to go back. The sour taste had faded in the course of the week in town, and I wanted to get out of my apartment. It would be gloomy as all hell without Sam clattering around.

Chris was as good as his word and was standing in the living-room ten minutes later with a large bottle of wine in each hand.

'I wasn't sure if you'd want red wine or white. So I brought both. Want a drink?'

'You bet. Several. And then let's go.' We each had two glasses of the red wine, and then we were off. Back to Bolinas. Alone this time, and in remarkably good spirits.

9

The next month was once again like something out of a dream. Neither of us got many calls to go into the city and we spent most of our time hanging around the beach, lying in a hammock under the big tree next to the house. And making love.

I had one job in town during the entire month, and Chris had two. Which made finances tight, but we were happy. I pitched in my alimony, and Chris didn't seem to mind the financial assistance.

We had a glorious time. I got into doing some painting, Chris took what seemed like a thousand rolls of film of me in the nude, and the days flew. Brief, frozen letters from Richard told me that Sam was well, and she seemed happy when I spoke to her.

The episode of the girl in Chris's bed never repeated itself, and he was more devoted than I'd ever dreamed. Joe Tramino had been wrong. And Chris and I didn't have a care in the world. Except one small one. I had had what appeared to be sun poisoning twice and food poisoning four times. And in between I had a fair amount of dizzy spells. It didn't seem like anything serious because the rest of the time I felt fine, but Chris wanted me to see a doctor.

'It might be an ulcer, Gill. Why don't you come into town the next time I go in. That's in two days. You could try for an appointment now.'

'I just think it's nerves. But if it makes you happy . . . okay, I'll go.'

I made the appointment the day before we went in and tried to forget about it. I didn't want anything to be wrong. Life was so good just then.

'Rise and shine.'

'What time is it?' I felt like hell again, but I didn't want to admit it to Chris.

'It's seven-thirty. That's plenty late enough. Get up. I made you some coffee.' He was painfully matter-of-fact about the morning, and I tried not to show how I felt as I closed my eyes and attempted not to gag on the coffee fumes.

We left the house at nine. He had been delayed looking for stuff for his shooting, and I was glad. I felt better by the time we left, but I knew the drive over the hairpin turns on the mountain road wouldn't help. They didn't.

'You look lousy, Gill. Do you feel okay?'

'Sure. I feel fine.' But I must have looked green. I felt it.

'Well, I'm glad you're going to the doctor anyway. My sister had something like you and she ignored it for a year. The next thing I heard she was in the hospital with a perforated ulcer. And that's no joke.'

'I bet it isn't. Is she okay now?'

'Sure. She's fine. So don't worry. But at least you'll

know.' . . . Yeah . . . at least I'll know. 'I want to take you by the house sometime before we go back to the beach. You can see if there's anything you want me to do before you move in. I have Sam's room all picked out too. I hope you like it.' He gave me a shy, nervous look that made me smile from deep in my heart. I felt like we were about to be married. There was that funny almost-newly-wed feeling about the way he talked about the house.

'I told my landlord I was giving up my place on first September. He said it's no problem to rent furnished places, so he'll have a new tenant in no time. I'm glad. I felt shitty giving him such short notice.' We had waited till the last minute to discuss it, but things had in fact 'worked out', as Chris had put it earlier. 'I can't wait.'

Chris leaned across the seat and kissed me, and we drove into town making small talk and telling bad jokes. I was feeling fine again and we were having a lovely time.

He dropped me in front of the Fitzhugh Building in Union Square a half an hour early, and I decided to go to I. Magnin's across the square to pass the time.

I noticed a mime on the corner and laughed out loud as I saw him imitate my walk, and then I disappeared into the fairyland delights of the elegant store. I was briefly tempted by the men's department to the right of the entrance, but decided against it. Chris wouldn't wear anything I'd find there anyway. Somehow they didn't look like they'd carry denim shirts. I smiled to myself and walked on until a row of ladies' sweaters caught my eye, and I started to sift through them.

Twenty minutes later, I emerged wearing a new red turtleneck in a thin silk knit, and reeking of a new perfume. I needed something to give me courage. I had

95

the feeling that what I was going to hear wasn't going to be easy to take.

I checked the directory on the ground floor of the Fitzhugh and found the doctor I was looking for. Howard Haas, MD, Room 312. The Fitzhugh was a medical building, and as I rode up in the elevator I had the funny feeling that I could walk into any door in the building and come out all right. But my appointment was with Dr Haas. My doctor in New York had recommended him when we came out.

I gave the receptionist my name and took a seat with six or seven other people. The magazines were dull, the air was stuffy, I was starting to get nervous, and the new perfume was beginning to make me feel sick.

'Mrs Forrester, this way please.' It hadn't taken long.

I followed the nurse to a heavy oak door at the rear of the office and followed her as she stepped inside. There was something laboriously old-fashioned about the entire scene, and I expected Dr Haas to wear horn-rimmed glasses and be bald. He wasn't though. Instead he looked as though he were about forty-five and played a lot of tennis. He had only slightly greying hair and a warm blue-eyed smile as he shook my hand.

'Mrs Forrester, won't you sit down?' In spite of the winning smile, I was thinking of saying no, but I didn't have much choice.

'Thank you.' I felt like a child called in front of the principal in a new school. I didn't know what to say next.

'Let's take down a little of your history first, and then you can tell me your problem. If there is a problem.' He smiled at me again, and I reeled off my vital statistics, which seemed hardly worth putting down. A tonsillectomy when I was seven, a lot of earaches as a child, and Sam. That was about it. 'That all sounds very healthy. Now, why did you come to see me?'

I told him about the dizziness, the nausea, and the vomiting, and he nodded, without making notes. He didn't seem impressed.

'And when was your last menstrual period?'

'My period?' I had wondered about that, but I think I hadn't wanted to know. 'It was a few weeks ago, at least I think it was.' I was feeling faint as we sat there.

'You think it was? You're not sure?' He looked at me as though I were very stupid.

'No, I'm sure of when it was, but it only lasted a few hours.'

'Is that unusual for you?'

'Yes.' I would have been amused by his tone, but I couldn't be. He was speaking to me as though I were a very young, slightly retarded child, and his words came across the desk in slow, painfully deliberated tones like slow-motion tennis balls.

'What about the period before this one?'

'The same thing. But I thought it was from the change in coming out here. Or worry, or whatever.' It was a very lame excuse.

'But you have not actually missed a period?'

'No.' I wanted to add 'sir', but restrained myself. He had me feeling very humble though. And scared.

'Any change in your breasts? Fullness?' I hadn't noticed and told him so. 'Well, let's take a look.' He flashed the dazzling smile at me again, and I started to pray, but it was a little late for that. The entire exercise of coming to see him had been like checking the list of who passed and flunked an exam, when you knew you hadn't studied anyway. But you always hope. At least I do.

So Dr Haas took a look. And he saw. I was two months pregnant. Maybe two and a half. Sonofabitch.

'Congratulations, Mrs Forrester. I think the baby is

97

due in March.' Congratulations? 'We'll do the A-Z test just to be formal about it, but there's really no doubt about it. You're pregnant.' He smiled.

'But I'm not . . . that is . . . uh . . . thank you, Doctor.' I had told him about my tonsillectomy, but I had forgotten to tell him I wasn't married any more. Congratulations, my ass.

He told me to make another appointment in a month and I rode down in the elevator, like a stone going down a mine shaft. At least that's how I felt. And what would I tell Chris? He was going to pick me up downstairs, and I saw by my watch that he had already been waiting ten minutes. Maybe he wouldn't be there. My spirits lifted at the thought . . . maybe he had forgotten . . . maybe . . . I decided to wait and tell him when we got back to Bolinas, when we'd be sitting under the tree next to the house and things would be peaceful.

As I stepped outside I saw him waiting for me and my heart sank again. I wanted to cry.

I opened the door and slid in next to him and tried to smile. 'Hi.'

'How was the doctor?'

'I'm pregnant.'

'You're what?' The entire exchange was like something out of a Laurel and Hardy movie as we dodged through the downtown traffic. It was not at all what I had planned, but it had just slipped out. I guess I wanted it to. 'Wait a minute, Gill. What do you mean, you're pregnant? You use a thing.'

'Yeah, okay, so I use a thing. But I'm pregnant anyway. Congratulations!'

'Are you out of your mind?'

'No. That's what the doctor told me.'

'Did you tell him you weren't married?' Chris was looking pale.

'No. I forgot.'

'Oh for chrissake.' I giggled hysterically and looked up at him and then regretted my mirth. He looked like he was going to explode. 'How pregnant are you?'

'Two or two and a half months. Look, Chris . . . I'm sorry . . . I didn't do it on purpose, and I'm wearing it for chrissake.'

'Okay, I know. But this comes as a hell of a shock to me. Didn't you know when you didn't get your period? And why the hell didn't you tell me?'

'I did get my period . . . sort of . . .'

'Sort of? I can't believe this thing.'

'Where the hell are you driving me to, by the way?' We had been roaming aimlessly on Market Street for a quarter of an hour.

'What do I know?' He glared in the rearview mirror and then back at me. And then his face lit up. 'Come to think of it, I do know. We're going to San Jose.'

'San Jose? What for?' Maybe he was going to murder me and dump my body somewhere on the peninsula.

'Because there's a dynamite Planned Parenthood in San Jose and they set up abortions. I have a friend there.'

'Bully for you.' The drive to San Jose was accomplished in total silence. We stole occasional glances at each other, but neither of us spoke. I guess he didn't want to, and I was afraid to. I felt as though I had committed the most heinous crime of all time.

In San Jose, Chris's friend was very nice, took down all the information, and said he'd call us, and I walked out to the car feeling lonely and nauseous. The drive out had taken an hour and a half, and it would take us longer to get back in rush-hour traffic, and we still had the drive back to Bolinas to contend with. I was exhausted thinking about it, and I didn't want to think of the abortion. Anything but that.

99

Chris tried to make lighthearted conversation on the way back to San Francisco, but I couldn't stand hearing it. I could tell he was feeling better. The fact that he'd done something to set up getting rid of it gave him a sense of relief. And me a feeling of desperation.

'Chris, pull over.' We were just outside South San Francisco when I said it, but I didn't give a damn, I couldn't wait.

'Here? Are you sick?'

'Yes. I mean no, not like that. Look, just pull over.' He did, with a worried look, and I faced him as we sat in the car. 'Chris, I'm going to have the baby.'

'Now?' The word was a squeak, and he looked like his already frayed nerves were going to give out.

'No, not now. In March. I don't want the abortion.'

'You what?'

'You heard me. I'll have the baby. I'm not asking you to marry me, but don't ask me to give it up. I won't.'

'Why? For chrissake, Gill, why? It'll totally fuck us up, not to mention what it'll do to your life. You've already got a kid, what do you want two for?'

'Because I love you, and I want to have our child. And deep in my heart, I don't believe in doing that if you don't have to. When two people love each other enough to live the way we've been living, then it's a crime not to have the child that results from it. I can't help it, Chris, I have to.' My eyes were brimming with tears as I looked at him.

'Are you serious?'

'Yes.'

'Jesus. Well, you've got to do it the best way for you. We'll talk about it. But you're taking on a hell of a lot to handle, Gill.'

'I know that. But it would do worse things to my mind if I got rid of it. I'm going to have it, whether you stand by me or not.' The last words had been sheer bravado, but he didn't respond.

'Okay, little lady. The decision's yours.' He slammed the car back into drive and sped off towards the city without another word.

IO

We drove back to Bolinas that night, without stopping to see his house on Sacramento Street, without dinner, and without wasting many words. But I was too tired to care. It had been a heavy day and I collapsed into bed and passed out.

I rolled over in bed the next morning and saw Chris staring at the ceiling with an unhappy expression on his face which matched the way I felt.

'Chris . . . I'm really sorry.' . . . But in a way, I wasn't. I was too chicken to tell him that though.

'Don't be. And maybe you're right for you. To have the baby, I mean.'

'What about for you?' I had to know. And he rolled over on his side and propped himself on one elbow, looking at me, before he spoke.

'No, Gill. Not for me. But you said yesterday that that doesn't matter. Do you still feel that way?'

'Yes.' But my voice had shrunk to the barest whisper. He was leaving me. 'We split?'

'No. You go back to New York.' Which meant the same thing. My heart sank and I wanted to scream, or cry, or die. And I didn't want to go back to New York.

'I won't go back, Chris. You can leave me, but I won't go back.'

'You have to go, Gill. If you love me at all. You're doing one thing you want to do. So you owe it to me to do one thing I want.' He made it sound so reasonable, but it wasn't. Not to me at least.

'What does my going back to New York have to do with anything? And then what? I never see you again?' . . . Oh Jesus . . .

'No. I'll come visit. I still love you, Gill. But I just couldn't handle the pressure of your being here. You'll be pregnant, and everyone'll know about it. Hell, Gill, we work in the same business, and don't you think everyone will know? Joe Tramino will see to it. And there would be others.' He sounded bitter and sad.

'But who gives a damn? So, okay, we're having a baby. Lots of people do. And we love each other. So what's the big deal? Are you suddenly so establishment that you feel we have to be married? That's pure, total, one hundred per cent crap. And you know it.'

'No, I don't know it. Besides, it'll make me feel guilty. You see what happens, I come, I go, I disappear sometimes. I won't always do that, but right now I need to. Or at least I need to know I can. And if you're sitting around with a long face and a big stomach, I'll go crazy.'

'So I won't wear a long face.'

'Yes, you will. And I wouldn't blame you. I think you're nuts. In your shoes, I'd get rid of it. Today.'

'Well, we're different, that's all.'

'You said it. Look, I told you in the beginning, responsibility blows my mind. What do you think this is? It's like a giant commitment.'

'What the hell do you want me to say, Chris?'

'I don't want you to say anything. I want one thing. For you to go home. And you're going to, if I have to carry you there. You've already given notice on your apartment, so you're free and clear. All you have to do is call Bekins, pack up your stuff, and get your ass on a plane. And that's just what you're going to do, if I have to gag you and tie you up. And if you're planning to argue with me, don't bother. You haven't got a chance. You've got two weeks. You can stretch it a couple of days, and stay at my place while you do, but that's it. Go back to New York and we've got a chance, but if you stay in San Francisco we're through. I'll never forgive you for it. I'd always think you'd stayed to get at me. So do me a favour . . . go.'

He left the room as I rolled into my pillow, choked with sobs, and in a few moments I heard him drive away.

He came back that night, but he had made up his mind. I was leaving. And by the end of the week, I knew I was. There was no other way. He had finally made me see that. And his forced cheerfulness during the days before I left was crueller than anything else he could have done to me. He was kinder and more loving than I had ever seen him. And I was more in love with him than ever before. He did some brutal things to my heart in those last weeks, but somehow I loved him anyway. He was Chris. And he was made that way, and you could never blame him for anything. In the end, I felt as though I had first done him wrong making the decision I had, and by getting pregnant in the first place. But I had no choice. Morally, I had to have the child.

He helped me tell Sam we were leaving when her father brought her back, and he packed all my things. He wasn't taking any chances. Chris Matthews may have loved me then, but he made one other thing a great deal clearer. He wanted me to go. And I was going.

After what seemed like a thousand days, we got to that

all-time horror, the last day. The last this, and the last that. I couldn't stand it any more, and the last night was the worst of all.

'Good night, Chris.'

'. . . 'night.' And then, 'Gill, do you understand at all? I . . . I hate doing this to you, but I can't . . . I just can't. I think maybe I want you to have the baby too, but I don't know. Maybe I'll get it all together. Soon, I mean . . . I feel like such a sonofabitch.'

'You're not. I know, everything got kind of screwed up.'

'Yeah. It did. And I'm sorry you got pregnant. God, I wish . . .'

'Don't, Chris. I'm not sorry. I'm kind of glad, even if . . .'

'Why do you want to have it, Gill?'

'I told you. I want to have you near me always. It's sort of a corny thing to say but I . . . I just want to. That's all. I have to.' We lay there in the dark, holding hands, and I kept thinking, 'This is the last time. The last night. The last time I'll lie here in his bed. Ever. The last . . .' I knew he'd never come to New York, he hated the place, and he had no real interest in seeing his child.

'Gill? Are you crying?'

'N-no.' But I choked as I said it.

'Don't cry, oh please don't cry. Gill, I love you. Please.' We lay in each other's arms, crying. The last time. The last . . . 'Gill, I'm so sorry.'

'It's okay, Chris. Everything's going to be okay.' He fell asleep in my arms after a while, the boy I loved, the man who loved me and was sorry, hurt me and failed me, and filled me at other times with a kind of joy I'd never known before. Christopher. The giant child. The beautiful man with the soul of a boy. The man who had

104

ridden bareback on the beach with me the day we met. How could I burden him with the weight of my existence? I know I should have. But I didn't quite dare.

I lay awake until the room started to grow light and then curled into his back and fell asleep, too tired to cry any more. The last night was over. The end had begun.

II

'Look, dammit! Don't look at me like that. It'll do you good to get back to New York. You have lots of friends there and I'll come East in the next couple of months. You'll . . . goddamit, Gill, I'm not going to explain this thing to you again, and I'm not going to stand around here like this, if you're going to wear your crucifixion look.' We were standing in the airport, and he was looking crucified himself, guilt was nibbling at him. My fault again?

'Okay, okay, I'm sorry. I can't help it, it's . . .' Oh shit. What's the use? 'Did I give you back the key to the house in Bolinas?'

'Yes. Do you have your ski boots? I saw them out in the garden yesterday, and they looked pretty shot to me. You shouldn't leave them out there.' Good boy, Chris, keep it to the practical.

'I didn't . . . Sam . . . yes. I have them.' I looked up and he was giving me one of his encouraging smiles – 'there, there, that's better, now you're doing it.' We were playing a little game. Nice Uncle Chris sees Auntie Gillian off at the airport, and Auntie Gillian does not have hysterics. There we are. Smile for the birdie. I wondered who we were putting on the show for, the people at the airport, each other, or ourselves. We were acting out all the bad endings I'd ever read about in books; we were really blowing it, no longer reaching each other, just filling the minutes before Sam and I would get on the plane. But filling them with ugly things to remember.

Chris's gentle voice and empty words, punctuated by his little smiles, shrieked at me. 'Don't make me feel guilty,' they said, and my martyred face shouted back, 'I hate you!'

'I put your rain slicker in the back of the car.'

'Good.'

'Where's Sam?' The general panic of the morning touched everything within me.

'Relax. She's over there, playing with that kid. Don't be so nervous, Gill. Everything's going to be fine.'

'Sure.' I nodded, looking at my feet, trying not to say something nasty. 'I'll call you when we get in tonight.'

'Why don't you wait till Sunday; the rates are lower and we can't start this calling every day routine.' He was looking at something over my shoulder as he said it.

'Not every day. I just thought you'd want to know we got in okay.' Tinges of irritation blazed in my voice.

'If the plane crashes, I'll hear about it. Get settled, then call in a couple of days.' I nodded again. I was running out of things to say. 'Want a piece of gum?' I shook my head, turning away again, crying towards the lady who stood behind me. She must have thought me very strange, but I couldn't face Chris any more. I couldn't stand it.

'Will all passengers holding green boarding passes for American Airlines Flight Forty-four to New York please board the aircraft through Gateway D, at Gate twelve.

Will all passengers . . .'

'That's you.' I nodded, gulping, looking for Sam again.

'I know. We can wait. Too many people . . . no point . . .'

'No point waiting around, Gill. When it's time to go, it's time to go.' Thank you, Mr Matthews, you sonofabitch . . . but I kept nodding, trying not to cry.

'I . . . uh . . . oh God, Chris! . . .' I clung to his jacket and touched the side of his face with my hand, one last time, and turned away blinded by tears. I wanted to scream, and kneel down on the airport floor, to cling to one of the huge chrome airline desks, to stop all the things that were happening without my consent. I wanted to stay, oh God, how I wanted to stay. And I wanted Chris to put his arms around me, but he didn't. He knew I would fall apart if he did.

'Sam, you carry your teddy, and take your mother's hand.' Our coats were being lumped into my arms, Sam's hand took mine, and the crowd moved us towards the plane. I could feel Chris angry beside me because I had made a spectacle of myself, but I didn't give a damn. I had never felt so lonely or unhappy in my life. I thought I was losing what I loved and wanted most, I even doubted that I'd ever see him again. And I was positively keening for him, even before we left. Loving and hating him all at once.

'Chris . . .'

'Good-bye, Gill, have a good flight. Talk to you Sunday.' I turned away, squeezing Sam's hand, and started moving through the gate with the rest of the crowd. Half a dozen people already stood between us, and I was looking ahead, not wanting to look back again at what I wouldn't see.

'Gill! . . . Gill!' I stopped in the flow of people, and turned to see him, Sam and I being jostled by the people pushing past us, but I had to see. I just had to. 'Gill! . . . I love you!' He said it! He said it! It was always that kind of thing that made me go on loving him, the last-minute contradictions that caught my heart just before it shattered on the bathroom floor.

'Gabye, Uncle Crits! . . . Gabye! . . . Mommy, can I watch the movie on the plane?'

'We'll see.' I was looking back at Chris, our eyes saying to each other what we hadn't been able to say that morning. It was easier this way.

'Mommy . . .'

'Later, Sam. Please.' Please, please, later, anything, but just later. We were herded into the plane, and then San Francisco was shrinking below us. And then gone. Like Chris.

12

Samantha was angelic on the flight, the plane was full, the food was lousy, and I was numb. Shellshock. I sat back in my seat, nodded to the stewardess at the appropriate times, or shook my head, and did my best to smile at Sam to give her the illusion that I was sharing in her conversation. I wasn't. My brain had died in the San Francisco airport, and somewhere in my chest was something called a heart. But it felt more like a marble watermelon, and I wondered what would happen if I stood up. Maybe it would fall out?

We had spent almost eight months in San Francisco, and now we were going back to New York. Why? That was stupid. I knew why, except I didn't really. I was going back to New York because I was pregnant and Chris didn't want me around. But why didn't he? That's what I didn't want to think about. I just couldn't. It was too much to face. As was the thought of what he'd do now that I was gone. Meet someone else? Fall in love? Have another girl move in? . . . Screw his ass off . . .

He said he'd come to New York, but would he? I didn't believe he would. In fact, I knew he wouldn't. Which left me where? Nowhere. Alone. Pregnant. And back in New York.

I spent the first three hours of the five-hour flight back to New York pining within myself, the fourth hour asleep, and the fifth hour getting steamed up. To hell with him. To hell with it all.

I was going back to New York and I was going to make it. I would take that town and grab it by the neck until it gave me what I wanted. Chris Matthews wasn't everything, and then, as the plane circled low over the lights of Long Island, I knew I was excited to be back. San Francisco may have been beautiful and a place of peace and sunshine, but New York had something else to offer. Excitement. It was alive, it breathed and writhed and made you want to spring into action, it almost had a musical beat of its own, heavy, hypnotic, irresistible, and I could already feel its lure as the landing gear touched the runway.

'Mommy, are we here?' I smiled at the question, and nodded, taking Sam's small warm hand in mine and looking out the window, into nothingness, only the blue runway lights, but I knew what lay beyond, across the river. We were back in New York now and we were going to use it well. Hallelujah. Amen.

We got off the plane and headed towards the baggage

claim area. And suddenly, all I wanted to do was to grab our stuff and see that skyline as we came over the bridge. I wanted to see it and hear it and smell it. I wanted to know that New York was standing there like a naked gypsy, waiting for me.

'Where are we going to sleep tonight, Mommy?' There was a faintly worried look in her eyes as she clutched her teddy bear, and I had a sudden idea.

'You'll see. We're going to stay someplace special.' I stopped at a phone booth on the way to the bags, looked up a number in the directory, and dialled. Samantha and Gillian Forrester had just changed their plans.

The apartment we had lived in before had been sublet, furnished, and I had given my tenants a month's notice two weeks before. Which left us with two weeks of living in a hotel, and I had chosen a quiet, inexpensive residential hotel not far from where we'd lived before. But that was bullshit. This was New York. To hell with 'quiet, residential'. I had had an idea. And for two weeks, I could afford it.

'Who did you call, Mommy?'

'The place where we're going to stay. I think you'll like it. And in two weeks we'll be back in our own apartment.' I realised that she needed to hear that. Maybe I needed something grandiose to drag me out of the dumps, but she needed familiarity. It was all right. We were going to have both. First, two weeks for me. And then she'd be home, safe and sound.

Our bags were revolving aimlessly on the turntable when we got there, and I found a porter to carry them to a cab.

'Where to, lady?' The driver had the standard New York cabdriver look, a dead cigar stuck out of his face which was covered with a two-day beard stubble.

'The Hotel Regency, please. Sixty-first Street and

Park Avenue.' I settled back with a gleam in my eye, and Sam on my lap, and we drove into town. Our town, Sam's and mine. This one was ours. And it was going to be mine, all mine, in a way it never had before.

13

In typical New York style, we sped towards the city, darting from one lane to another and threatening lives as we went. It didn't seem to impress Sam much but it gave me that heady, hysterical-giggle feeling you get on a roller coaster, everything moving too fast and the view beyond a blur of lights and indistinct forms. I was only aware of the motion and speed, not of the dangers. In New York, you don't learn to live with danger, you thrive on it, you expect it, you come to need it. It's built in.

We raced across the Queensborough Bridge, down Sixtieth Street, and stopped for the light at Sixtieth and Third. And there it was, it was just beginning. Hordes of shaggy-haired young 'groovies' sat at Yellowfingers restaurant, eyeing each other, and viewing passersby with a critical air, the sweaters on the girls were tight and transparent, the pants on the men bordered on the obscene, and through it all a look of carefully calculated 'laissez aller'. In the quick glance I threw at them, I noticed the baubles, the Afro wigs, the painted faces, all the little details you never see in California because nobody dares, not like they do in New York. Across the street, Bloomingdale's Department Store, and in the canyon between the mammoth store and the restaurant, a flood of frantic traffic, horns bleating, fenders dented,

Con Edison adding an obstacle course for the entertainment of drivers and pedestrians alike. The entire area seemed to be seething with lights from restaurants, shops, street corners, and movie house marquees, and there was a kind of aura that held me in its spell. We turned right on to Third Avenue, and made our way a few blocks uptown among the other cars, crowding us on either side, tailgating and racing to make the lights. Left towards Park Avenue then, where we circled the island of greenery in the centre and came back down the avenue to a screeching halt in front of our hotel. And I was suddenly glad that I had made the call from the airport. That 'quiet' hotel would have killed me. I needed this. The Regency.

A liveried doorman helped us out and smiled at Sam, and two bellboys rushed up to take the bags. I paid the cabdriver and doled out tips like Hershey bars on Halloween, but I didn't give a damn. It was worth it.

We whirled through the revolving door, Sam's hand clutching mine, and then we swooped up to the reception desk. It was an immense baroque-looking marble and gilt affair, with a fleet of men standing at attention behind it.

'Good evening, Madame. May I help you?' He wore a dinner jacket and black tie, and the accent was French. Perfect.

'Good evening. I'm Mrs Forrester. I called for a reservation an hour ago. A double room with twin beds.' Sam's eyes peeked over the counter and he smiled at us.

'Yes. Indeed. But I regret, Madame. There has been a problem. A little misunderstanding.' . . . Oh shit. No rooms. And I suddenly felt like Cinderella, gone from satin frills to ashes in the flick of an eyelash.

'What sort of misunderstanding? Nothing was said

on the phone.' I tried to look commanding and not as disappointed as I was.

'Only that we have no more double rooms tonight, Madame. I was thinking that perhaps you would agree to two adjoining singles until the morning, but I see that that may not be suitable with Mademoiselle.' His eyes pointed at Sam and he smiled. 'You would surely prefer to sleep with your Mama.' I was about to leap at the proffered singles, but he burst into speech again. 'I have a much better idea though. We have one unoccupied suite. It will be a little larger than you wanted,' and a lot more expensive. That much I could very definitely not afford to spoil myself. A suite? No way. 'But I will make the appropriate adjustments on your bill, if you will allow. As you were promised a double on the phone, we will charge you that rate. I hope Madame will be pleased with the suite. It's one of our nicer ones.'

'How very kind of you. Thank you.' I smiled warmly at him and noticed with pleasure that he looked quite overwhelmed. At least I hadn't lost my touch completely. And I was briefly very glad I'd worn the good black dress I'd bought at Magnin's that summer. At least I looked the part. And I felt just right as the elevator rose sedately to the twenty-seventh floor.

'This way, please.' We followed the bellboy and our bags, turned left twice, and I'm sure I felt quite as lost as Sam. We walked down what seemed like endless pale beige halls with rich red carpeting and small Louis XV marble-topped tables at appropriate distances from each other. The doors were quietly marked with small gold numerals and had big brass handles.

The boy unlocked a door at the end of the hall, and it swung open wide. 2709. That was us. Wow! It was a corner room, with a real New York view. Skyscrapers twinkled impressively at us, the Empire State stood far in the distance, and at closer range we had the Pan Am Building and General Motors. Far below us, we could see the elegance of Park Avenue stretched out like a long grey-green ribbon, dotted here and there with stoplights. And at right angles to the panoramic cityscape of sky-scrapers was the East River, with all the lovely little town houses of the East Sixties between the water's edge and where we stood. I couldn't have asked for more.

The bellboy retired discreetly from the room after I thanked him and gave out yet another tip, and I looked around the room. It was decorated in yellow and off-white, in thick carpets and rich upholstery fabrics, there were heavy cream satin damask curtains, and an air of opulence throughout. Near the door where we had come in there was a bar and tiny kitchenette, a small dining alcove, and, across from it, a large marble-topped desk. I felt as though I were expected to do something impressive here, like write a $400,000 cheque.

The bedroom beyond was bright and cheerful; the furniture looked French provincial, the wallpaper and bedspreads were in a tiny floral print, and there was a vast bouquet of fresh flowers. What luxury! And the bathroom! . . . The bathroom! . . . It was a dream. All done in porcelaine de Paris, marble, and bronze. The towels looked seven inches thick, and the tub looked three feet deep. And there was a dressing room which looked like a boudoir in the French court.

'Sam, how do you like it?' I was grinning to myself in self-satisfied greedy glee.

'I don't. I wanna go back to San Francisco.' Two huge tears slid down her face, and I felt time stop. Poor Sam.

'Oh, sweetheart . . . I know . . . so do I. But we're back here for a little while now. We'll go back some time. And this will be nice. You can go to school here, and . . .' My arguments sounded lame and I felt suddenly guilty

114

to be so pleased to be back, and Sam looked as though she felt betrayed.

'Can I sleep in your bed tonight?'

'Sure, sweetheart. Sure. Let's get you to bed. Are you hungry?' She shook her head and plopped herself down on the edge of the bed, still clutching her teddy bear. She was a portrait of despair. 'How about some milk and cookies?' Maybe that would help.

I picked up the streamlined beige phone, consulted the little card beneath it, pushed the right buttons for room service, and ordered milk and cookies for her and a split of champagne for me. I hadn't given up the satin frills yet. Cinderella was still at the ball.

Sam sat on my lap when the enormous pink linen-draped tray arrived from room service, and she sipped milk and munched cookies while I guzzled champagne. It was quite a scene.

'Time for bed, love.' She nodded sleepily, let me take off her clothes, and climbed into bed.

'Will we go back soon?'

'We'll see, sweetheart . . . we'll see.' Her eyelids already drooped heavily over her eyes and they flickered open only once more to cast a piercing look at me.

'I'm gonna write a letter to Uncle Crits tomorrow . . . first thing!'

'That's a nice idea, Sam. Now get some sleep. Sweet dreams.' Her eyes closed for the last time, and I smiled at her as she lay in the bed which dwarfed her small frame. She would 'write' to Chris tomorrow, which meant a great, loose, lovely scribble . . . just for him.

I turned off the lights in the bedroom and wandered back into the living-room of our suite, the champagne glass still in my hand, the vision of Samantha asleep in the bed still in my head . . . and a vision of Chris too . . .

The scene at the San Francisco airport seemed a

thousand years behind us, and the days in California seemed like a distant dream. And as I looked at the dragon city which lay at my feet, I wondered if we'd ever go back. Or if I'd even want to. In one brief hour, New York had already bewitched me. I had conquered other worlds, but now I wanted to conquer my own. I wanted to enter the contest with New York, and emerge victorious, no matter what the price to pay.

14

'Good morning, Mademoiselle. How did you sleep?' For once I had woken up before Sam.

'Okay.' Sam looked at me sleepily; she was a little confused.

'We're in a hotel. Remember?'

'I know. And I'm going to write a letter to Uncle Crits.' She had remembered that too.

'Fine. But we have lots of things to do today. So, up you get. And we'll go out in a little while.'

I had a few calls to make first. I checked with the tenants at my apartment to be sure they'd be out on time, and called schools for Sam. We were just in time for the beginning of the school year, but by New York standards we were a year late with our application. Too bad. I knew that if I called enough schools one of them would take her, and I was right. It was just down the street from the hotel, and I made an appointment to see it with Sam that afternoon.

I also got a babysitter to come and help with Sam. She was to live out for the two weeks we would be at the hotel and live in after that.

And there was something else to set up too. A job. And I wasn't at all sure it was going to be easy to find one. The economy had tightened up during the year I'd been gone and jobs were scarce. My experience was limited to advertising and magazine work, but according to reports I'd heard they were the two tightest fields to get into just then, and I'd been away for a while. My last job had been at a decorating magazine called *Decor*, but I had little hope of getting a spot there again. Freelance styling as I had done in California was a possibility too, but I knew that in New York I could never survive on it. The cost of living was too high. So my only hope was *Decor*. At least it was a start, and maybe Angus Aldridge, the senior editor, would have an idea, or know of a job available on some other magazine. It couldn't hurt to try.

'Angus Aldridge, please. This is Mrs Forrester. Gillian Forrester . . . No . . . F-O-R-R-E-S-T-E-R . . . that's right . . . No. I'll hold.'

He was charming, elegant, and a damned good editor. All Bill Blass suits, and warm smile, and omniscient eyes, showing all those ladies in Wichita 'how to'. He was thirty-nine years old, his vacations were spent skiing, preferably in Europe, he had been born in Philadelphia, spent his summers in Maine with his family, or in the Greek Islands on his own, and had gone to the school of journalism at Yale. Our Editor. Our God. Our Mr Aldridge.

Underneath the warm smile, he could be as cold and heartless as an editor should be, yet I liked him; there was very little pretence about him, he was Philadelphia and Yale, and East Sixty-fourth Street, and he liked being those things. He believed in them. He didn't give a holy damn about Wichita or Bertrand, or the other places like it that he was sending a magazine to once a month. But he put on a good show, and if you played by the rules he was good to work with.

'Yes. I'm still holding.'

'Gillian? What a surprise. How are you, dear?'

'Fine, Angus. Great. It's super to talk to you, it feels like years. How's life? And the magazine, of course?'

'Marvellous, dear. Are you back in the city for good? Or just coming back to the watering hole again to revive after San Francisco?'

'I think I might be back for good. We'll see.' But I had a sudden twinge for San Francisco again as I said the words.

'Gillian, dear, I'm late for a meeting. Why don't you stop by sometime. No. How about lunch tod . . . no, tom . . . Thursday? Lunch Thursday. We'll talk then.'

'Thursday's fine. That would be wonderful. Nice to talk to you, Angus, see you then. And don't work yourself into the ground before Thursday. I'm dying to hear all the news.' Which was a lie, but that's the local dialect.

'Fine, dear. Thursday. At one. Chez Henri? . . . Fine, see you then. Good to have you back.' Bullshit, but more of the same dialect.

Chez Henri. Just like old times, when there was something to 'discuss' . . . good afternoon, Mr Aldridge . . . over here, Mr Aldridge . . . a dry martini, Mr Aldridge? . . . the expense account, Mr Aldridge! . . . balls, Mr Aldridge.

But I wanted a job, and I had always liked Angus for what he was. But why was I sounding so New York all of a sudden? Where was Chris? San Francisco? The new me? Or even the old me . . . where in hell was I? I had become so engrossed in just being back in New York that I felt almost schizophrenic, as though I'd become another person when I stepped off the plane.

I had made up my mind to ask Angus for a job on Thursday, and it was perhaps more easily done over lunch after all. Or maybe harder. We'd see. In any case, it couldn't hurt to ask. All he could do was say no. And it would be a start.

What next? Whom to call? Should I wait till I saw Angus, or call a bunch of people all at once? Well, maybe just one more. John Templeton. Editor of the less elegant, less witty, more earthy *Woman's Life*. The magazine was tougher, straighter, and more diversified. It told you what to feed your child after he had his tonsils out, how to apply Contac paper to bathroom walls, what diet to go on when you were losing your man, and how to sew 'at-home' skirts out of remnants of curtain fabric. John Templeton, like his magazine, was a no-fooling-around species, fish or cut bait, produce or you're out, slightly scary individual. But he and I had liked each other, the few times we'd met, and he might remember me. I had done freelance work for him a few times before I'd gone to *Decor*. So I called.

Once again, the whir of a switchboard, the clicks, staccato, and almost swallowed 'Wmm's . . . Lfff.'

'Mr Templeton, please.'

And then, 'Mr Templeton's office' cooed by a mildly intimidating, highly poised youngish voice. The executive secretary. Who believed, knew in fact, that she was perhaps not better or smarter than Mr Templeton, but surely almost as powerful, in her own way. Secretaries invariably intimidate me; they want you to 'tell it to them', because of course they too can handle your problem just as capably – except if you had wanted to talk to them, and not the boss, you'd have asked for them in the first place.

'Mr Templeton, please. This is Gillian Forrester.'

'I'm sorry, Miss Forrester. Mr Templeton is in a

meeting . . . No, I'm afraid he'll be tied up this after-noon, and tomorrow he's going to Chicago for the day. Is there something I can help you with?' There it was. I knew it!

'No, I'm afraid I wanted to speak to Mr Templeton directly . . . that is . . . I just got in from California, and I used to freelance for *Woman's Life* and . . .' Oh shit, why do secretaries do that to me?

'Perhaps you'd like to speak to our personnel office?' Ice in the voice, and comfortable condescension that says, 'I have a job. Don't you?'

'No, I really wanted an appointment with Mr Templeton.' Now watch her tell me she can't commit him just now because his schedule is very heavy this week, and next week they're closing the book (i.e., finishing the issue, before it goes to print), and the week after that he'll be in Detroit all week . . . just watch!

'Very well. How is Friday at nine-fifteen? I'm afraid that's all he has open . . . Miss Forrester? . . . Miss Forrester?'

'Sorry, I uh . . . nine-fifteen? I . . . uh . . . ahh . . . yes, yes, nine-fifteen is fine, I mean . . . this Friday? . . . No . . . no . . . that's fine . . . the number where I can be reached? Oh, yes, of course. The Hotel Regency, Room 2709 . . . I mean six . . . no. Sorry. Room 2709 . . . That's it . . . That'll be fine. See you on Friday.' Well, I'll be damned.

So I was off to a start. And if nothing worked out with either *Decor* or *Woman's Life*, I could look elsewhere. At least I had a momentum going.

'Sam? How about a trip to the zoo?'

Sam and I walked out to Park Avenue and then west towards Central Park. She had two pony rides while I stared at the skyline, and it was a hell of a sight. Fifth Avenue stretched as far as I could see in either direction, and I could imagine people living in grand style in penthouses to my left, and business tycoons making million-dollar decisions in offices to my right. The General Motors building had sprung up, dwarfing all on its periphery. Everything seemed new to me again, and enormous.

'Hey, Sam, how about a special lunch?'

'I'm not hungry yet.'

'Come on, don't be a drag, love. Do you want to see some more of the zoo?' But she only shook her head, and I stooped to kiss her. She was still desperately hanging on to the world we had just left, the world I was trying so hard not to think about. Chris. 'Let's go, Sam.'

'Where are we going?' She was beginning to look intrigued.

'Just across the street. You'll see. Right over there.' I pointed. 'That's the Plaza.' We stopped to look at the horses and the hansom cabs and then mounted the steps into the fairyland magic of the Plaza Hotel. Once inside, it was like another city in itself, and it had the same independent elegance as an ocean-going liner, totally self-sufficient and reeking of luxury. The carpets felt like mattresses beneath our feet, palm trees hovered above us in great profusion, and crowds of determined-looking people came and went, some staying at the hotel, others just stopping in for lunch. It had a worldliness about it which pleased me. It was New York.

'Who's she?' Sam had stopped beneath an enormous portrait of a chubby little girl, posing next to a pug dog, wearing drooping knee socks, and a heavy pleated skirt. Her expression was one of outrageous devilry, and just by looking at her you could tell that her parents were divorced and that she had a nurse. Miss Park Avenue herself. The painting was somewhat caricatured and I knew who she was meant to be.

'That's Eloise, sweetheart. She's a little girl in a story, and she supposedly lived here, with her nanny and her dog and her turtle.'

'Where was her Mommy?'

'I'm not sure. I think she was on a trip.'

'Was she real?' Sam's eyes were growing larger. She liked the looks of the girl in the painting that loomed above her.

'No, she was make-believe.' And as I mentioned it, a small sign on the table beneath the painting caught my eye. 'See Eloise's room. Just ask the elevator man.' 'Hey, want to see something?'

'What?'

'A surprise. Come on.' We found the elevators easily, I asked the elevator man in veiled terms to deliver us to our destination, and we rose slowly towards the floor in question. The elevator was full of over-dressed women and overstuffed men, and behind me I heard Spanish, French, and what sounded like Swedish.

'Here we are, young lady. The second door to your right.' I thanked him and he winked. And I gently opened the door. Eloise's room was a little girl's dream, and I smiled when I heard Sam gasp.

'This is Eloise's room, Sam.'

'Wow! . . . Oh boy!' It was a veritable showcase of pink chintz and gingham, full of every toy imaginable, and cluttered with the kind of mess and disorder that most children dream of leaving in their rooms but can't get away with. A tall spare woman with an English accent was playing 'Nanny', and she showed Sam the key points of the shrine with utter seriousness. The visit was an enormous success.

'Can we go back and visit again some time?' Sam had torn herself away with difficulty.

'Sure. We'll come back. Now, how about some

lunch?' She nodded, still dazed from the ecstasy of the visit, and she floated alongside me into the Palm Court, where piano and violins combined their sounds beneath the trees as a myriad of ladies indulged themselves at small tables covered with pink linen tablecloths. It still had the Victorian elegance it had had when I was a child and had been occasionally treated to tea there by my grandmother.

Sam had a hamburger and an enormous strawberry soda, while I dabbled with six dollars' worth of spinach salad, and then we started home, satisfied with our morning.

We stopped at the school for Sam on the way and, being pleased with what I saw, I enrolled her starting the next morning. And as we arrived back at our hotel, I was amazed at what we had accomplished. There is so much happening in New York at any given moment, that one seems to do a week's worth of anything in half a day. I had made two appointments to enquire about jobs, had enrolled Sam at school, had had lunch at the Plaza, and had seen to Sam's entertainment as well. Not bad at all.

And now I had a few hours off. The babysitter had arrived and I turned Sam over to her. I wanted to call Peg Richards. I had been itching to all morning and could hardly wait.

Peg Richards and I grew up and went to school together; she is the closest thing I have to a sister. We are totally different, yet we understand each other. Perfectly. And we care about each other. Always. Like some sisters, and some friends.

Peg Richards is rough and tough, uses incredible language, is a no-nonsense sort of girl, stocky and direct, with freckles and immense lively brown eyes. Always the first one to raise hell in school, yet to get things organised too, to tell off the girl who'd done her dirt, and to look out for the girl nobody liked or paid attention to. She'd grown up with a dutchboy haircut, oxfords, and a total lack of interest in clothes and make-up and all the things that most of us were intrigued with. She liked boys less and later than some of us. She was just Peg. Peg. Tomboy. The head of the field hockey team who changed completely while I spent two years in Europe, pretending to study art. When I came back, Peg was at Briarcliff, taking life very seriously. Her language was a little worse, but I thought I could see the glimmer of mascara on her lashes. Three years later, she was a buyer of children's wear at a poshy department store, her language was incredible, and she was definitely wearing mascara, and false eyelashes. She was living with a journalist, playing a lot of tennis, and spending a lot of time knocking the Establishment. She was then twenty-three. And five years later, when I had just come back from California, she was still single, not living with anyone for the moment, and still had the same job.

Peg had done everything for me, mothered me in school, kept me company after I had Samantha and was feeling helpless at home, she'd been around to hold my hand through the divorce, and had seen me through every sort of scrape over the years. Peg is my staunchest friend, strongest ally, and most vehement critic. There is no shame, there are no deceptions, with someone you know that well, and who knows you.

The switchboard answered at the department store where she worked, I asked for her office, and she was on the line in half a minute.

'Peg? It's me.' Just as I had reverted to ultra-New Yorker when speaking to Angus, I felt like a schoolgirl again when talking to Peg.

'Holy shit! Gillian! What the hell are you doing in town? How long are you here for?'

'A while. I got in last night.'

'Where are you staying?'

'Would you believe at the Regency?' She chuckled and I laughed back.

'Well, la-dee-da to you. What happened? Did you get rich out West? I thought the Gold Rush was all over.' Leave it to Peg.

'It is. In more ways than one.' She had made me think of Chris and I sobered quickly.

'Oh? Are you okay, Gill?'

'Yeah. Sure, I'm fine. What about you?'

'I'm still alive. When do I get to see you, and my friend Sam? Is she with you?'

'Of course she is. And you can see us whenever you want. I feel like a stranger in this goddam town, and I don't know where to start first. But I'm having a ball.'

'At the Regency, who wouldn't? But just a sec, let me get this straight. Are you moving back or are you here on a visit?'

'Mentally, the latter, but practically . . . we're back.'

'Your romance busted up?'

'I don't know, Peg. I think so, but I don't really know. It's a long story, and I had to come back.'

'You're confusing the hell out of me. But I wouldn't have been surprised if the love story had ended. That business you told me about the girl in his bed at the beach house didn't sound good.' I had forgotten that I had written that to her in my misery.

'We got over that.'

'Something else happened? Christ! That would have been enough for me. Good old Gill, you never learn, do you? Anyway, you can tell me whatever you want to tell me when I see you. How about tonight?'

'Tonight? Sure . . . why not?'

'Such enthusiasm. To hell with you. I'll come to the hotel for a drink after work. I want to see your monster daughter. I'm so glad you're back, Gill!'

'Thanks, Peg. See you later.'

'Yeah, and by the way, be dressed when I get there. I'm taking you to dinner at Twenty-One.'

'You're what?'

'You heard me. We're celebrating your return.'

'Why don't we celebrate with room service?'

'Nuts to you.' And with that she hung up and I grinned to myself. It was nice to be back. The whole time span with Chris was beginning to seem as though it had never happened. I was in New York where I had begun, hopefully I'd soon be jobbed, and that night I was having dinner at Twenty-One. It was as though New York was putting on its best face and everything was beginning to go my way.

15

Peg had reserved a table downstairs near the bar at the illustrious Twenty-One Club, and we were ushered to our seats by the maitre d' who seemed to know Peg quite well.

'Well, well, at least you've been hanging out in the right places since I left. Not bad.'

'Expense account.' She grinned with her pixie look and ordered a double martini straight up. That was new too.

The reunion between Peg and Samantha at the hotel

had been boisterous and joyful and ours had been scarcely less so. She looked better than ever, and her tongue was even sharper than before. She squeezed Sam in a vast hug, and then called me names while we pushed and shoved and giggled. It was so good to see her again.

I glanced around the restaurant as she sipped her drink, and marvelled at the clientele. The cream of the cream. Moneyed New York was out for dinner. And so was I.

In terms of dress, San Francisco alternates between acute hippiedom and 1950s stock brokerage, with almost no middle ground. The women are conservative and still wear pastel wools, sleeveless and knee-length, hats, gloves, the whole scene. But New York offers a rainbow of looks that overwhelm the eye. Intense funky, quietly elegant, outlandish chic, a myriad of looks and colours and styles. Just as I had noticed as the taxi stopped at Yellowfingers on the way in from the airport, in New York people dare. And how.

The table next to us consisted of heavily bejewelled 'Nyew Yawwwk,' successful garment centre wearing chic Paris, rich silks and creamy satins, hair fresh out of the hairdresser, and manicures that made me want to amputate my arms. At the bar were a slew of fifty-year-old men with astounding-looking models, statuesque-looking young women with elaborate eye make-up and closely cropped hair. It surprised me to see that short hair was 'in' again. In California they were still wearing it long and straight, but in New York the natural look was dead, it had no charm at all, and proved only that you weren't trying.

The room itself was dark, and the tablecloths were so starched they looked as though they could have stood up on their own. Overhead hung a vast array of toy cars and aeroplanes. All you had to do was look at the ceiling and you knew you were at Twenty-One. The discreet sounds of good silver, fine china, and paper-thin crystal mingled with the soft buzzing of conversations, and the entire room seemed to come to life.

'Whatcha looking at, you hick?' Peg looked amused as she watched me.

'That's about the size of it. I'd almost forgotten how New York looks. It's so weird to be back. I feel as though I have to learn the language all over again, and get myself together.'

'You look like you're doing okay to me. You haven't lost your touch yet.' I was wearing a white wool dress, the pearls my ex-mother-in-law had given me, and had pulled my hair into a tight knot at my neck. 'That guy on your right looks as though he's got the worst case of the hots for you I've ever seen. You're looking good.'

'Thanks, but you're full of shit.'

'Mrs Forrester! Such language at Twenty-One. Gawwd! I can't take you anywhere.'

'Oh shut up!' I giggled at her over my Dubonnet.

'Not until I hear what brought you back to New York. I smell a rat.'

'Come on, Peg.' I averted my eyes and looked around the room. I didn't want to talk about Chris. I just wanted to enjoy the evening.

'That confirms it. Okay, close-mouth, you want to tell me now or later?'

'There's nothing to tell.'

'Oh yeah? Didn't your mother ever tell you the story of Pinocchio, Gill? You should see your nose . . . it's growing longer, and longer, and . . .'

'Peg Richards, you're a pain in the ass. I just came back, that's all.'

128

'I'm insulted. I thought we were freinds.'

'We are.' My voice got small, and I started on my second Dubonnet.

'Okay, I'll let it go. What do you want to eat?'

'Something light.'

'You sick?' Peg eyed me seriously then, and I reached quickly into a mental grab bag of possible excuses, and then gave up.

'Nope. Pregnant.'

'What? Holy shit! So you came back for an abortion?'

'No. I moved back.'

'What about Chris? Does he know?'

'Yes.'

'And?'

'I moved back.'

'Did he walk out on you, Gill?' Fire kindled in Peg's eyes; she really was the most loyal friend I had.

'No, we just decided it was best this way.'

'We? Or he? It doesn't sound like your style.'

'It isn't important, Peg. He doesn't want to get tied down just now, and I can see his point. He's not ready. It's really better this way.' But I could see I wasn't convincing Peg. I wasn't even convincing myself.

'You're out of your mind. You're going to have the baby, Gill?'

'Yes.'

'Why?'

'Because I love him. And I want to have the baby.'

'That's a hell of a big decision. I hope you know what you're doing.' Peg looked as though she had just been hit with a bucket of ice water.

'I think I do.'

'How about another drink? I don't know about you, but I think I need one.' She looked up at me with a rueful smile and I shook my head.

'Look, don't let it put a damper on our evening. Everything's okay, I'm fine, and I know what I'm doing. Honest, Peg. So relax.'

'That's easy for you to say. I enjoy worrying. Besides, you're only the mother. I plan to be the godmother, and that's a big responsibility.' I laughed and she raised her drink to me in a toast. 'To you, you goddam nut. Sonofabitch. I never expected this. What happened to your upbringing for chrissake?' We both laughed at that and then we ordered dinner. The subject never came up again, but I knew Peg was rolling it around in her mind and I'd hear more about it at a later date. She'd let it go by too easily, for Peg, and she wasn't going to feel right about it unless she did what she thought was her duty by me at some point and gave me hell. Maybe she thought I couldn't take it just then. Maybe she was right.

We stayed at Twenty-One until after eleven and were just getting ready to ask for the check when a tall, attractive man stopped at our table.

'Hello, Peg, can I offer you two a drink?' He was speaking to Peg, but smiling straight at me.

'Hi, Matt. What you doing here?'

'I could ask you the same question, but I won't.'

'Oh, I'm sorry. This is Gillian Forrester, Matthew Hinton.'

'Good evening.' We shook hands over the table and Peg looked pleased about something.

'How about that drink, ladies?' I was about to refuse but Peg gave me a filthy look and accepted.

We sat and chatted with him for half an hour. He was a lawyer, worked on Wall Street, and belonged to the same tennis club as Peg. He looked as though he were in his early thirties and had an easy-going manner but a little too much charm for my taste. I felt as though he were looking me over, like a large hunk of meat he might or might not want to buy, and I resented it.

'How about if I take you two ladies to Raffles for a drink and a little dancing.' But this time I beat Peg to it.

'No, really I couldn't. I just got back from California last night, and I haven't caught up on my sleep yet, but thanks anyway.'

'She's my best friend, Matt, and the biggest pain in the ass I know. Party pooper.'

'Why don't you go, Peg? I'll take a cab home.'

'No, I'll pass too. Sorry, Matt.' He made a mock tragic face, threw up his hands, and we all paid our various tabs, or rather he and Peg did. I cringed, thinking what she must have paid for the dinner, but it had been a lovely evening.

Matt offered to drop us off at our respective homes in a cab and Peg accepted. And in a few minutes we were at the Regency. And I noticed that Matt seemed to like what he saw. I kissed Peg on the cheek, thanked her for dinner, and tried to stop her from saying anything. Whatever she could have come up with would surely have been mortifying. Matt was patiently waiting on the sidewalk as the doorman stood by.

'You like him?' she whispered in my ear as I disengaged myself from her hug.

'No, goddam you! And don't you dare start any matchmaking! But thanks for dinner.' My response was spoken in a hoarse whisper like her own, and I punctuated it with a stern look. But she didn't answer, which is always a bad sign with Peg. I had visions of her setting up a whole scenario for Matt while he took her home.

'Good night, Matt. Thanks for dropping me off.' I shook his hand coolly as we stood on the sidewalk and started towards the revolving door with a last wave at Peg.

'Gillian!' It was Matt.

'Yes?' He reached my side in two long strides.

'I'll call you tomorrow.'

'Oh.' But he was already gone, the taxi door slammed and the cab pulled away and was instantly lost in the city's eternal traffic.

16

The telephone rang while I was struggling with my second cup of coffee the next morning, and I reached for it absentmindedly, holding the paper in my other hand.

'Hello?'

'How did you like him?'

'Peg! You're a bloody nuisance. Will you cool it, please? I told you how I felt about that last night. And I meant it.'

'What the hell is wrong with you?' She sounded immensely irritated.

'For one thing, I'm still in love with Chris.'

'And that's not going to get you anywhere. He dumped you, remember?'

'Okay, Peg, that's enough. Let's just drop it. Last night was really nice.'

'I thought so too. And . . . oh hell. Okay, Gill. I'll lay off. I'm sorry. Except I wish you'd go out with him. It would give you a good start back here. He's very social.'

'I'm sure he is, but that doesn't turn me on any more.'

'Okay, so I'll find you a hippie, ya nut.' She laughed briefly and I felt better. 'Well, I just thought I'd put in a good word for Matt. Gotta go to a meeting now. I'll call you.'

'Okay, Peg. See you soon.'

I no sooner hung up than the phone rang again, and this time I suspected who it would be. And was right.

'Gillian?'

'Yes.'

'Good morning. This is Matthew Hinton.' So what else is new?

'Good morning.' Now what? I really wasn't in the mood.

'I was going to ask you to dinner, Gillian, but something else has come up.' It seemed an odd way to start, but I waited for him to go on. 'One of the senior partners in the firm just offered me two tickets to the opening of the opera tonight. How does that sound?' I was ashamed of myself for the sudden change of heart, but that sounded too good to miss.

'Wow! That would be lovely, Matthew. I feel very spoiled.'

'Don't be silly. The opera starts at eight and we can have a late dinner afterwards. I'll pick you up at seven-thirty. Sound all right to you?'

'Sounds fine. I'll see you then. And thank you.'

I looked at myself in the mirror and felt briefly guilty for accepting his invitation just because of the opera, but what the hell, it would be a real treat.

Matthew arrived promptly at seven-thirty and gave a long, slow whistle which almost swelled my head. I was wearing a cream satin dress which set off the remainder of my California tan, and I had to admit that I'd been

133

pleased myself when I looked in the mirror before leaving the room.

He was looking very precise and rather handsome in a dinner jacket, with small sapphire studs, and for a moment he reminded me of my ex-husband. I was stepping back into the sedate, establishment world again, even if only for an evening. And it was a million light years from the world I had shared with Chris.

The cab pulled up to Lincoln Center, and the fountain rose in graceful, erratic leaps in the plaza. Little clusters of well-dressed opera-goers headed in the same direction as we, and I ignored Matt in favour of the bright dresses and beautiful people. It was obvious that this was an Event.

Photographers leapt out from oblique angles and invisible corners and flashed lights in the darkness as people went inside. You could tell who would occupy the boxes – they were even more elaborately dressed than the others, and the jewels were blinding.

'Mr Hinton, just a moment please.' Matthew turned his head to the left to see who was calling him, and I followed his gaze, just as a light went off in our faces and a photographer snapped a picture.

'May I ask who the lady is?' a lithe-looking black girl at the photographer's side enquired. She was dressed in brilliant red and was wearing her hair in a natural. She raised a small notebook and took my name with a smile, while I looked on in disbelief. It was quite a scene. Pandemonium seemed to reign everywhere, and people were attempting to filter through the assembly of reporters and photographers.

Matthew shepherded me up the flight of stairs to the boxes, and an elderly usher smiled at him. 'Good evening, Mr Hinton.' My, my.

'Do you come to the opera often, Matt?'

'Once in a while.' But something was beginning to smell fishy.

The opera was *Lucia di Lammermoor* with Joan Sutherland, and the performance was breathtaking. During the intermissions, the champagne flowed like water, and the photographers continued their field day.

'I ordered dinner at Raffles, since you wouldn't do me the honour last night. Is that all right with you?'

'Lovely.'

And at Raffles we were besieged with 'Good evening, Mr Hintons' from every waiter in sight. Peg was right, he was very social.

But the evening was pleasant, the conversation was superficial, and he had a nice sense of humour. He had ordered smoked salmon, roast duck, and a soufflé au grand marnier. We drank more champagne, and danced for a while in the muted gaiety of the club. The decor was done by Cecil Beaton and lacked warmth, but the crowd was obviously New York's elite.

We arrived back at the Regency at one, and I shook his hand in the lobby as the evening came to a close. It had been precisely what I'd expected. The opening of the opera. It meant no more to me than that. Until I saw the papers the next day.

The phone rang once again at nine the next morning, but this time I was asleep.

'I thought you said you didn't want to go out with him.'

'Huh?'

'You heard me.' It was Peg. 'How was the opera?'

'Very nice, thanks.' I struggled to wake up and then a question came to mind. 'How did you know I went to the opera? Did Matt call you?' The possibility irritated me, like a ninth-grade report to the 'gang'.

'No. I read it in the papers.'

'Bullshit. He called you.' I was sitting up in bed by then.

'He did not. I have in hand today's *Women's Wear Daily*, and I quote "Who is Playboy Matthew Hinton's latest love? Mrs Gillian Forrester, of course. They attended the opening of the opera last night, which was ... etc., etc. They occupied his father's box, Q, and were later seen at Raffles' private discotheque where the B. P. congregate. They sipped champagne and danced till dawn."'

'For chrissake. I was home by one!' I was stunned, 'Playboy Matthew Hinton's latest love'? Oh Christ.

'Shut up, I'm not finished. "Mrs Forrester wore a gown of cream-coloured satin, off the shoulders, and it looked like last year's Dior. But she is a most attractive young woman. Right on, Mat."'

'Thanks a lot. As a matter of fact, the dress is six-years-ago's nobody. For God's sake, Peg. That's the worst thing I've ever heard. I'm mortified.'

'Console yourself. *The Times* only ran a picture. You looked pretty good. Now ... do you like him?'

'Of course not. Oh hell, what do I know? I was excited about going to the opening of the opera, and he's about as colourful as papier-mâché. He's stereotyped and terribly proper. And frankly, I don't enjoy being smacked all over the newspapers as some playboy's "latest love". Jesus!'

'Don't be a bore. Enjoy it.'

'Bullshit.'

'Well, at least go out with him for a while.'

'What? And have all the papers analysing what we had for dinner. It's not worth it, Peg. But thanks for the introduction.'

'You're a creep. But maybe you've got a point. He is a

136

little dull. Anyway, I'll put these in my scrapbook. My friend, Gillian Forrester, latest love of playboy.'

'You jerk.' And this time I hung up as I broke into a laugh. It really was pretty funny. It would have almost been worth sending the clippings to Chris.

An immense bouquet of roses arrived as I ordered breakfast. The card read, 'I'm so sorry about the newspapers. Hope you can weather the storm. Next time dinner at Nedick's,' And it was signed 'Matt'. Weather the storm was right. And that wasn't at all what I had in mind for myself. I put the flowers on a table and answered the phone. Probably Peg again.

'Gillian? Have you forgiven me?' It was Matt.

'Nothing to forgive. That's quite a coming-out party for my second day in New York. It would appear, however, that you're rather notorious, Mr Hinton.'

'Not nearly as much as *Women's Wear* seems to think. How about dinner tonight?'

'And confirm the rumour?'

'Why not?'

'I'm sorry, but I can't make it, Matt. But I had a lovely time last night.'

'I'm not sure I believe you, but I'm glad if you did. I'll give you a call at the end of the week and see what else we can think up to tantalise the press. How do you feel about horses?'

'In what sense? As a meal or for transportation?'

'As entertainment. In terms of the horse show. Does that appeal?'

'As a matter of fact, it does, but I'll have to see, Matt. I have a lot of organising to do.' And I had no intention whatsoever of letting myself into a press-inspired romance.

'All right, busy lady. I'll give you a call. Have a nice day.'

'Thanks, and the same to you. And thank you for the roses.'

Wow! Three days in New York, and I had roses on my table, had had two pictures in the social columns and dinner at Twenty-One and Raffles, and had gone to the opening of the opera. Not bad, Mrs Forrester. Not bad at all.

17

Thursday arrived, and with it my lunch with Angus. I was anxious about getting a job from him, but not really nervous. It was a glorious, sunny autumn day. I was feeling well and in good spirits.

I arrived at Chez Henri at three minutes after one, Angus was already waiting at the bar, looking more Bill Blass than ever, and perfectly groomed. His hair was a little thinner on top, but it had been exceedingly well-disguised by a loving barber. His smile fixed into place instantly as I stepped through the door.

'Gillian! You look marvellous! Just divine. You're looking so well, and brown. And wearing your hair differently, aren't you, dear?'

What seemed like 147 'Gillian dears' later, I got up the nerve to ask him about the chance of finding a job in the hallowed halls of *Decor*, and got turned down, graciously, elegantly, charmingly, the smile broadening just a little more to let me know that he really 'cared', and would 'love to but' . . . He said all the right things about 'just feel terrible about it . . . things so slow . . . but you wouldn't be happy at *Decor* any more, would you, dear?'

He was half right, but I wanted a job and had thought of him first. Actually, I might have liked working there again, but once you left *Decor*, you left forever. Like the convent, or the womb. Never to return.

It was a nice lunch anyway, and I still had the meeting with John Templeton to look forward to the next day. But unlike Thursday, Friday happened with pouring rain and an acute case of nerves which told me just how badly I wanted the job at *Woman's Life*.

I bumped along on the bus, on the way to the magazine, wishing that I had had another cup of coffee to give me that wide-awake, bouncy busy look people get when they're all stimulated by what they're doing. I knew I had the whole thing backward and wanted to cover it up. You have to be put together, in need of nothing, sailing along under full steam, and then jobs fall into your lap like ripe apples. Need a job, for financial or emotional reasons, and it shows. You get that desperate look, that pathetic hungry look, and the tree shakes absolutely nothing into your lap. Need scares people off. Nobody loves the poor little hungry guy sitting in the corner of Riker's. You feel for him, but you don't want to get too close, or give him any-thing, because maybe proximity and/or recognition will give you his 'disease'. Maybe his sadness will be contagious, and nobody wants to take that chance.

At nine-ten I arrived at the black marble entrance of *Woman's Life*, with the bronze numerals at the side of the door: 353 Lexington. The slightly tacky chandeliers were being dusted, and as I headed for the second of four banks of elevators I began to get excited. There was Muzak in the elevators. And as we rose slowly I was beginning to hope, to really want to believe that in an hour I'd walk out of there 'jobbed'.

Nine-twelve. The third floor . . . the receptionist . . .

'Mrs Forrester, will you have a seat, please. Mr Templeton's secretary will be right out.' Seven copies of *Life* Magazine, two issues of *Holiday*, and all the current issues of *Woman's Life* lay on the low table next to the Naugahyde couch that tried to look like Mies van der Rohe but didn't quite make it. Seventh cigarette of the day, second wave of nausea, brief reminder of what was happening inside my body, brief realisation that my palms were wet, and then a smiling girl of about my own age, and looking as though she might be from Cleveland, appeared to take me in to see 'Mr' Templeton. I suddenly felt younger, dumber, less competent, and infinitely less useful than she. After all, she had a job, didn't she? . . . Come on, Gillian, pull yourself together . . . down three different corridors whose only apparent purpose was to impress visitors and make them totally lose their sense of direction, which I accommodatingly did as we reached the second corridor. Then, a beige on beige anteroom, with a large orange ashtray on Miss Cleveland's desk, and another almost-Mies-van-der-Rohe chair, and a door. The Door. John was standing in the doorway, smiling at me, looking wiry and nervous, full of energy, and welcoming. He whisked me in, shut the door, offered me coffee, lit up his pipe, smiled a lot, made a lot of small talk, praised all the virtues of San Francisco, and was 'John Templeton: friend' to 'Gillian Forrester: expatriate free-lancer returned'. I could handle that, that was easy. I could be Gillian Forrester. I knew how to do that. And if he would play Friend, then everything would be okay. I relaxed, looking at the view, enquired about his kids, said the usual things about New York, and asked how *Woman's Life* was weathering the publishing crisis. I didn't ask as an interviewee, but as someone who used to be in publishing. I forgot about the job.

A capsule report on the business ensued, along with reports on which of the other 'books' were threatening to fold, and which ones weren't threatening but were in real trouble, 'as we all know'.

Seemingly mid-sentence, during my second cup of coffee, John looked up, watched me for a minute, and said, 'Gillian, why'd you come back?' Whammmmmm. John Templeton was not such a close friend that I could speak truths from the depths of my heart. At least I didn't feel that I could. So? 'I had to,' 'I wanted to,' 'I missed New York,' 'I wanted to come to *Woman's Life* to find a job,' – the only thing that might have rung true would have been the truth and that was so outlandish that I couldn't begin to offer any part of that as an explanation. What seemed like eight years, and was probably three seconds, passed as I stared into my coffee and listened to my ears buzz and pound: then I looked up and said the most articulate thing I could come up with, 'I wanted to leave San Francisco for a while, I thought I should come back here,' which made a little sense, and sounded like nothing much, except that maybe I had been wanted in California on a morals charge or something. But he accepted that and only asked me if I thought I was back for good. Which I didn't know. And I said so. I said I was back for at least six months. maybe a year, maybe forever, it depended on what I found in New York, what happened to my life in the next year.

'Have you been looking for a job?' John asked.

'Yes . . . no. That is I called you because, well, because I like *Woman's Life*. I don't want to go back to advertising, and, as you said, publishing is pretty well closed up. I thought it might be worth a try to give you a call.'

'What about your old job at *Decor*? Did you talk to Angus Aldridge?'

'Yes. No go.' He nodded, and I was pleased with myself for being honest. I had always suspected that there was rivalry between them, but whatever the case, at least I was playing it straight.

'. . . Julie Weintraub . . .' What, Julie Weintraub? How did she get into this? What in hell is he talking about Julie Weintraub for?

'Julie Weintraub?' It seemed the only thing to say to get back into the conversation. Maybe he'd repeat what I'd missed.

'Sure, you remember her. You two worked on a couple of projects together. Christmas, and . . .' Of course I remembered her, but I still didn't know why John had brought her name up.

'Well, as I said, she broke her pelvis last week, and she's going to be flat on her back for a while, at least eight weeks, maybe ten, maybe even twelve. Jean Edwards and two other girls are trying to take over the mainstream of her work, but we're having some problems. So I'm at the point now where I was thinking that I could get someone in on a short-term basis, maybe even part-time, three, four days a week, and see how that works out. And I was thinking you might want to give it some thought. I warn you, Gillian, slave wages and no by-line, but it wouldn't be a full work week either which would give you more time with your daughter. What do you think?' . . . What do I think? What do I think? I think somebody, somewhere, loves me, that's what I think! Hallelujah! Wait till I tell Chris! 'Gillian, stop grinning at me and say something.' John was smiling back. He knew the answer from the look on my face.

'I think, dear Mr Templeton, that the tree shook an apple into my lap after all. I'll take it. I mean, I want it. I mean . . . it sounds great! Like an absolute dream!'

'Can you start Monday?' I nodded, still feeling tongue-tied. 'Fine. And you can plan on having the job for at least eight weeks. I want you to talk to Julie about what she's been doing. And we're working on the March issue right now. I guess that's all you need to know for a start. We'll let you have it with both barrels on Monday.'

I just grinned and grinned, and silently blessed Julie Weintraub's pelvis.

'That's fine, John. That sounds fine.' And still that dumb grin on my face.

John stood up, we shook hands, I picked up my coat, and seemed to float out of his office, as they say. The secretary in the beige anteroom no longer had anything I didn't have, the elevators were playing my song, and the bronze '353' on the front of the building made it look like home. As of the following Monday, I had a job.

When I got back to the hotel, I thought of calling Chris. I hedged about it because I was afraid he'd quell my enthusiasm, be indifferent or nonchalant about it, and I wanted him to be excited too. It's like half the excitement of a new dress you're crazy about is waiting to hear what Prince Charming is going to say about it. You can hardly wait for him to gasp and tell you that you've never looked more beautiful. So, when he tells you it's a great dress but you ought to lose another ten pounds, or that it would be terrific on a girl with bigger bosoms, or it's too bad your legs are too short for that look . . . you die a little, and the glitter falls off your star. I felt that way about the job. I didn't want him to take the glitter off it, but I really wanted to tell him. So I waited . . . But at four o'clock I couldn't stand it any more, and I called, sat holding my breath for a minute while the phone rang and rang at Chris's end, disappointment beginning to back up in my throat as I realised he might not be at home.

'. . . Yeah? . . .' Whew, he's in . . . and me feeling about fourteen years old at the other end.

'Chris? It's me. I've got a job. Stylist at *Woman's Life*. I start Monday for eight or ten weeks, taking over for one of the editors who's in the hospital. I just got the job. Isn't that super?' All of it pouring out in one breath. Why couldn't I make it sound more grownup, or professional, or something? My excitement and something like embarrassment at talking to Chris made it sound so small and kind of foolish. Or maybe that was just me, feeling small, and sounding foolish.

'That's nice, Gill. It'll keep you busy for a while. Why didn't you look for something longer term? You'll just be out looking again in two months this way.' He would think of that . . . i.e., 'too bad the dress has that hemline, with your legs' . . . oh well, nice try.

'Look, Gill, I don't think you ought to call here any more. Now don't get all excited and mad, it's no big deal. Just temporary. I've got a room-mate. She's going to pay half the rent, and it really helps.'

'A room-mate? She? Since when? And who the hell is she that all of a sudden I can't call you any more?? What the hell do you mean?' Oh God, why am I doing this, it's none of my business. Why am I dying and shaking all over? Third cigarette . . . who cares about John Templeton's old job anyway? It's over, everything is finished with me and Chris, the Queen is dead, Long Live the Queen . . .

'Look, it's really not important, Gill, you don't even know her, and it's just for a while.' You rotten bastard, you big son of a bitch . . .

'I do too know her. I can hear it in your voice. Who is it? It's no big deal, you said so yourself, so tell me, just out of curiosity. Who is she?' A slightly hysterical pitch getting into my voice.

'Marilyn Lee.' Sonofabitch, I knew it. She was the one he had told me about at the beach one day. The only girl he had ever really cared about. But it was supposed to be over. And now it wasn't over at all. She was back. 'Hey, Gill, come on, cool it. It's just for a while. She called yesterday and she's in town for a couple of weeks, so she's staying here, maybe for a month, no big thing.'

'Stop telling me it's no big thing, will you please!' That hysterical note again. 'And if it's no big thing, how come I can't call? Afraid you might upset her, Chris? Would it bother her to know that I'm calling? Is she just a little teeny tiny bit jealous? Why should she be, baby? she's been getting you for years, she's not losing anything.'

'Will you take it easy, it's not good for the baby if you get upset.' The baby? The baby? Since when is he so interested in the baby?

'Look, forget it, Chris. It's your life. I just wanted to tell you about the job. Got to get off the phone now anyway. Take it easy. Oh, and Chris . . . I won't call any more. Have a nice life.' Stupid, stupid, sophomoric thing to say. Why can't you be glib and cool? He can hear you crying, you big ass.

'Gillian . . . I love you, baby, you know that.'

'Try telling that to Marilyn. Chris . . .' And there I was, sobbing. Humiliating myself, begging him to love me. Why did I have to be that way? Why? I hated myself, but I couldn't stop.

'Gill, I'll call you next week.'

'Don't bother. Just don't bother. Marilyn might not like it. For once in your life, Chris, just this once, do something all the way, not half-assed. If you want to be with her, be with her. If you want to be with me, come to New York. But don't shit up her life, or mine, or your own, by double-timing everyone you ever spend an hour with. Try being honest with yourself for a change.'

'If you're going to behave like an ass about this, I won't call you.'

'Fine. Tell it all to Marilyn.'

'You're supposed to understand me, Gill. You're the only one who ever knows how I feel. What do you want me to do? Be something I'm not? Well, I can't. This is how I am.' Christ, now he's making me feel sorry for him. The little boy kicking dirt around with his toes, being misunderstood by the world. Poor sweet Chris, and big bad Marilyn, and mean old me. Shit. 'Let's talk about it another time. I love you, Gill.'

So Chris was living with someone else. The excitement of the morning was dispelled and forgotten. The hour I had spent in John Templeton's office felt as though it had been a month before. Who cared about goddam *Woman's Life*?

18

But Monday was a day of bliss. I was busy. I had a job. And I lost myself in it all day long.

I shot out of the hotel at twenty minutes to nine and headed downtown with the crowds. It was a heady feeling. I took the bus to work, and by the time those bronze numerals announcing '353' loomed into view I felt as though I owned them. I exchanged a smile and good morning with the maintenance men who were

146

once again polishing the bronze and dusting the chandelier, and I felt as though I belonged. At that precise moment I belonged to New York and had been born under the sign of those bronze numerals. The Muzak was blaring fuzzily in the elevator, and the coffee wagon was ringing its bell and doing a sizeable business on the third floor when I stepped off. Welcome home.

I looked for John Templeton's office and, after a few wrong turns, found it, with his secretary still sitting in the same place, wearing beige-on-beige to match the anteroom.

'Mr Templeton is in a meeting, Mrs Forrester. He said you were to go in and see Jean, Mrs Edwards, and then he'll see you and the whole decorating group at eleven.' Another exchange of smiles and . . . 'Oh, Mrs Forrester, Mrs Edwards will show you the office you'll be using. And please see Mr Porcelli about your social security number. Payroll is on four.' Magic words. It was real.

Further down the maze lay Jean Edwards's office, tucked in between two larger ones. Hers was tiny, disorderly, littered with fabric samples, needlepoint kits, bright posters, dirty coffee cups, and scraps of paper with eight or nine messages scrawled on them in different directions. Her office was bright and friendly and full of potted plants. An arrow with 'Up' painted on it in red letters pointed down, and a huge poster that said 'Smile' showed a photograph of a little girl in tears, looking at her ice-cream cone lying on the pavement at her feet.

I waited for Jean while people came and went, looked in, rushed by, and had the air of very busy people. I felt like a guest.

I remained alone, nervous, and itching to get to work. Where was Jean? Where was everybody in fact?

147

It seemed like everyone had something to do except me; it was like a giant game, and I wanted to play too. Faces continued to appear in the doorway and then go away again, and the minutes ticked by as I glanced through the three most recent issues of the magazine.

'Waiting for Jean?' I looked up when I heard the voice, and a tall man in his mid-forties met my gaze. He had black hair, bright blue eyes, and was sporting a well-trimmed beard.

'Yes. I am.'

'Friend or foe?' The eyes twinkled as he asked.

'I'm not sure, but I think I work here.'

'Oh, the new secretary. Right.' His face lost interest, and he sped away down the hall before I could respond, with irritation mounting in my throat. Secretary indeed!

I continued to wait, and just after ten o'clock Jean raced in with an arm full of folders, fabric samples, and contact sheets. Her smile brought the morning back into perspective, and the long wait in her office seemed like only a moment.

'Hi. I hear I have a new secretary waiting in my office.' Her dark eyes flashed in amusement as she looked up at me, and then I had to laugh. 'Don't let him get to you, that's just his style. He's a little brusque. When I told him you were the new wife of the French Ambassador, and you had agreed to come here to discuss our photographing your house, he almost died.'

'Good. Who is he. Anyone important?' I suspected he was. There had been an air of officialdom about him when he walked into the room.

'More or less. He's Gordon Harte. Senior Art Director and Assistant Managing Editor.'

'That sounds like "more" rather than "less". Hard to deal with?'

148

'Sometimes, but mostly just standoffish. And we all get bitchy when we're getting ready to close an issue. You'll see.'

'I remember that much.'

'Good. Look, I haven't got time to brief you now. We have a decorating department meeting in Templeton's office in five minutes, and I've got to get this crap off my desk. There's a list on Julie's desk of the stuff you'll be doing for the next week at least. You've got to find me a very unusual dining-room for a shooting, and we're doing children's bedrooms, and . . . what the hell was that other thing? . . . Christ! . . . Oh! Right! You're supposed to talk to the food editor about something tomorrow morning, and John has an interview for you to do next week. It'll get a little saner in a week or two, before that though you'll mostly be shovelling your driveway, so to speak. Okay? Ready? Off to our meeting. I have to stop and look at the slides from last Friday's shooting on the way. Lamps. We'll talk later, and Julie's office, yours, is two doors left of mine.' The entire time she had been speaking to me she had been sorting through papers on her desk, shoving things into files, stacking photographs, and making notes, but the stream of conversation never lagged for a second. She was one of those wiry, dynamic women in her late thirties who lives for her career. She was tough, competent, and nice, which was a rare combination. And I guessed correctly as I watched her that she was also divorced.

The meeting in John Templeton's office was brief and to the point. Mimeoed sheets were handed out listing future features in the magazine, and I listened intently, feeling as though I had somehow missed the first two weeks of school and already needed to catch up.

149

By noon, I was following Jean back down the hall. She zipped into her office, and I proceeded two doors down to mine.

I gingerly opened the door, wondering what I would find, and then stood and looked around for a moment, liking what I saw. Two walls were blue, one was orange, and the fourth was brick, there was thick brown carpeting on the floor, and the walls were covered with photographs, posters, and funny little plaques. 'Too much of a good thing is wonderful' was attributed to Mae West, two others said 'Mierda' and 'Courage', and behind the desk was one that said 'Not Today, Johnny Boy'. There were two plants on the desk, and in the corner an immense array of multicoloured paper flowers. It was a small room, but it looked like a pleasant place to work and I plopped myself down in the chair that said Madame Director and momentarily felt like the winner on 'Queen for a Day'. I felt every bit the part, and the first day at school feeling began to wear off.

'I hear I owe you an apology. And how is the Ambassador, by the way?' It was Gordon Harte, standing in the doorway, with a solemn expression, watching me try my office on for size.

'I trust he's well, Mr Harte. And how are you?'

'Busy, thank you. Why aren't you?' I wondered for an instant if he were serious, and groped for an icy retort, but then I saw his face relax.

'I feel like I've taken a job in a factory all of a sudden.'

'Don't kid yourself, you have. And don't ever let Eloise catch you sitting around with empty hands. Even a spoon will do. You can tell her it's a prop for a photograph you're checking out.'

'That bad, huh? I hear the Art Director's pretty bad too.' I raised an eyebrow and tried not to smile as I gave him back a little of his own. But I knew he was right about Eloise. Eloise Franck, Managing Editor, and resident terror. I still remembered her from the days I had free-lanced at *Woman's Life*. She was an ex-newspaperwoman who was at least sixty, and looked forty, and had a heart of ground glass and cement. But she was a pro. From head to foot, a pro, hated by her underlings, feared by her colleagues, and valued only by John Templeton, who knew her worth. She knew how to run a magazine, never lost control, and had an infallible sense for what was right for *Woman's Life*.

'By the way, Mrs Forrester, there's a general staff meeting at nine sharp tomorrow morning. You're expected to be there.' I had almost forgotten Gordon's presence while I remembered the terrors of Eloise Franck.

'Fine. I'll be there, Mr Harte.'

'You'd better be. Now get to work.' And then he vanished, still something of an enigma. It was hard to tell when he was serious and when he was joking, or if he joked at all. There was an edge of sarcasm to everything he said. Those eyes would look at you, and take hold . . . turn you around . . . squeeze you for a moment, and then drop you when you least expected it. As though life were a game. His height and slimness exaggerated the leanness of his face, which somehow reminded me of an El Greco portrait . . . what was it? I wondered to myself that day. Perhaps that despite the glint of humour in the eyes there was something else there, a quality of hurt, something that made him seem just out of reach.

'Oh well, Mr Harte, you do your thing and I'll do mine, and hopefully we won't get on each other's nerves.' I mumbled to myself as I began to ferret through the stack of notes on my desk. It looked as though I had a lot to do. And a lot to catch up on.

I was so totally engrossed in sorting out what lay ahead that I didn't pick my head up until almost five, having forgotten everything but my work, including Gordon Harte.

I poured myself a cup of coffee from the machine across the hall and returned to my desk as the phone began to ring.

'How's it going?' It was Jean Edwards.

'Okay. But I feel swamped. I've just spent the entire day going through the stuff on Julie's desk. But I think I'm catching up.'

'In one day? Not bad. Have you been notified of the staff meeting tomorrow?'

'Yes, thanks. Gordon Harte came by to tell me.'

'That's quite an honour. As a rule, he speaks only to John Templeton and God. And I'm not even sure he speaks to God.'

'That doesn't surprise me. He looks like he could be a real . . .'

'Don't say it, Gillian. But you're right. Just don't step on his toes and you'll be all right. He's a perfectionist, but you can't quibble with it; he drives himself even harder than he drives the rest of us. He's had some kind of a chip on his shoulder for years.'

'Sounds like someone to stay away from.'

'That, my dear, is up to you. And now I've got to run. I'm having people in tonight.'

'Okay, Jean. See you tomorrow, and thanks for the help.' I hung up slowly and wondered about Jean's last remark about Gordon. One thing was for sure, chip on his shoulder or no, he was a very attractive man.

I looked at my watch then and decided it was time to pack up and go home. I had promised Sam a pizza, and it would be nice to have a few hours together before she went to bed.

As I left my office I took a last look over my shoulder and smiled. It had been a lovely day. I felt useful again, and busy, and pleased with the job I had found.

I walked slowly down the corridor and turned right into the maze. One more right and a left, and I was at the elevator bank. And so was Gordon Harte, looking pre-occupied, and carrying a large manila envelope in one hand and a huge portfolio in the other.

'Homework?' I asked him.

'Yes, in the left hand. No, in the right. I teach a life drawing class on Monday nights. The portfolio has some of my old nude studies in it, to show the class.'

The elevator arrived then, and we moved into the Muzak-infested aura of people from other floors. Gordon saw someone he knew and was busy talking, so I thought I'd walk out quietly without saying anything more. But when I reached the revolving door he was just behind me, and we hit Lexington Avenue one after the other, like gum balls out of a nickel machine.

'Which way are you headed, Mrs Forrester? I'm walking uptown to pick up my bike. Would you care to join me?' I wasn't sure, but I acquiesced, and we walked slowly through the crowds on Lexington.

'Do you ride the bike to work?'

'Sometimes. But it's not the kind I think you mean. It's a motorcycle. I picked it up in Spain last summer.'

'Sounds terrifying in this traffic.'

'Not really. There is very little that terrifies me. I just don't think about it much.' . . . Or maybe you don't care? . . .

'Do you have children?' It was something to talk about as we walked along.

'A son. He's studying architecture at Yale. And you?'

'A daughter, she's five, and she's still at the stage where she enjoys taking houses apart more than putting them together.' He laughed and I noticed as he did that he had a nice smile, and he looked more human when he forgot to look fierce. I had noticed too something odd in his eyes when I asked about his son.

We talked about New York on our way uptown, and I mentioned how strange it seemed to be back, how different it was from California. I liked it but I didn't feel at home any more. It was like watching animals at a zoo.

'How long have you been back?'

'About a week.'

'You'll get used to it again, and you'll probably never leave. You'll just go on talking about how weird it all is. That's what we all do.'

'Maybe I'll go back to California one of these days.' It made me feel better just to say it.

'I used to say that about Spain. But those things never happen. One never goes back.'

'Why not?' I felt naive as I asked the question, but it just slipped out as I looked up at him.

'Because you leave when you have to, or when you're meant to. And part of you dies when you go. You leave it there, it stays there. And what's left of you moves on to someplace else.' It sounded pretty heavy but I knew myself how true it was. Part of me had died when I had left San Francisco, and part of me had stayed with Chris.

'I hate to admit it, Mr Harte, but your analysis sounds apt. What made you go to Spain in the first place?'

'It was a moment of madness, as they say. My marriage had just broken up, I was bored and frustrated with my job, and I was thirty-two years old. I figured that if I didn't get going right then and there I never would, and I think I was right. I've never regretted going there. I spent ten years in a tiny town near Malaga, and in retrospect they were the best years of my life. The people

154

in our business call them "wasted years" but I don't. I cherish them.'

'Have you ever thought of going back?'

'Yes, but at thirty-two, not forty-nine. I'm too old for grandiose gestures like that now. That's behind me. This is it – ' his right hand swept across the skyline – 'for better or worse, until death do us part.' It struck me that he was a little morbid.

'But that's absurd. You could go back any time you want to.' Somehow it bothered me that he should be so loath to run after his dream. It was as if he didn't even care any more.

'Thank you for your concern, my dear, but I assure you I'm far too old to cherish delusions about living on bread crusts in Spain, or being an artist.' He punctuated his words with a dry little laugh and I saw then that we were standing on the corner of Sixtieth. I was almost home. He shook my hand while I noticed that the spark of amusement hadn't died in his eyes. For some reason he had apparently enjoyed our conversation and I had to admit that, despite his penchant for sarcasm, away from the office he was almost an agreeable man.

I turned right towards Park Avenue as he walked away, and reached the Regency thinking of Sam. Gordon Harte had already vanished from my mind.

'Hi, sweetheart. What did you do today?'

'Nothing. I don't like Jane. And I want to go back to Uncle Crits. I don't like it here.' Sam looked unhappy, tear-stained, and rumpled. Jane was the baby-sitter, and neither one looked too smitten with the other. Sam could be tough when she worked at it.

'Hey, wait a minute. This is home, you know. We'll go back to our apartment soon. And it's going to be nice, and Uncle Chris will come and visit us in a while, and you're going to make new friends in school, and . . .'

'I don't want to. And there was a big, bad dog in the park.' God, she looked so cute, those big eyes looking up at me. 'Where were you all day? I needed you.' Whamm. The nightmare of the working mother all rolled up in that 'Where were you all day?' and the clincher, 'I needed you.' . . . Wow! . . . But Sam sweetheart, I have to work . . . we can use the money and I . . . I have to, Sam, I just have to, that's all . . .

'I needed you too. But I was working. I told you all about that. I thought we agreed. Hey, how about our pizza? Mushroom or sausage?'

'Ummmmm . . . mushroom and sausage?' She had brightened at the mention of the pizza.

'Now come on. Pick one.' I was smiling at her, she was so nice to come home to.

'Okay. Mushroom.' And then I saw her look up at me, and I could tell she had something on her mind. 'Mommy . . .'

'What, love?'

'When is Uncle Crits coming?'

'I don't know. We'll see.' And let's not get into that dammit . . . please . . .

The pizza arrived half an hour later, and Sam and I lunged into it, seemingly free of our problems. I didn't know when or even if Chris was coming, and maybe I didn't even care. I didn't want to care. Sam and I had all we needed. We had each other, and a great big, drooling, cheese and mushroom pizza spread all over the Regency's best Louis XV. What more can you ask of life? On some days, not much. Not much more at all. I looked at Sam and wanted to laugh I felt so good, it had been a beautiful day, and she looked up at me and smiled back. She could feel the good vibes too.

'Mommy?'

'Uh huh?' My mouth was full of food.

'Can I ask you for something?'

'Sure. What? . . . but not another pizza.' I felt like I was going to explode.

'No, not a pizza, Mom.' She looked at me with disgust at my simplemindedness.

'Then what?'

'How about a baby sister some time soon?'

19

The second day at work was even better than the first. I felt as though I belonged. The staff meeting was no different than any other, but it gave me a chance to take a look at the other faces I'd be working with, and what was going on.

John Templeton conducted it like a board chairman in an early fifties movie, and Gordon Harte stood at the back of the room watching the show while I sat with Jean. I half expected Gordon to say something when we walked past him on our way out, but he didn't. He was involved with briefing one of the junior editors on some project John had discussed. He didn't even try to catch my eye.

The only thing directly pertaining to me during the two-hour session had been that Milt Howley, the black singer, had agreed to give *Woman's Life* an interview, and John Templeton had assigned me to do the job. It sounded like the proverbial plum.

When I got back to my office, Matthew Hinton called, and I succumbed to the lure of the opening of the horse show the following night. Once again, I couldn't resist.

And before lunch, I called Hilary Price. I had tried her a few days before and had been told by her secretary that she was in Paris for the collections.

I had met Hilary Price during my early years of work. We worked on the same magazine briefly, and she had since risen to rather impressive heights on one of the more important fashion magazines. A far cry from *Woman's Life*, it was one of those super fashion books that paint women's faces green and then paste peacock feathers on them.

We took a liking to each other when we first met. It's not a deliciously noisy, rude, obvious friendship like the one with Peg, but, though more polite, relaxed in its own way. I always feel I have to rise somewhat to Hilary's level though, which in a way is good for me. But the effort is never overwhelming. I can still let my hair down and kick off my shoes. In a way she's kind of mind expanding . . . Hilary. Always calm, always unruffled, discreet, elegant, witty. Obviously strong, but basically kind. Very chic, very 'New York', an intelligent woman whose mind appeals to me immensely. She looks amazingly flamboyant because she has a lot of style and a look that classifies easily as 'sophisticated'. But in spite of the looks, she's actually quiet. About thirty-five, or thereabouts, her age is permanently veiled by an aura of mystery . . . She never tells . . . or gives herself away. Divorced also, she has lived in Milan, Paris, and Tokyo. Her first husband was an ageing Italian Count, whom she refers to once in a while as 'Cecco', short for Francesco, I gather. He had been on the verge of death when she married him, or so she had thought, but he managed to revive long enough to marry a seventeen-year-old girl three weeks after their divorce.

The phone rang in Hilary's office and on the second ring she picked it up herself.

'Hello?'

'Hilary? It's Gillian.'

'Welcome back, my dear. Felicia gave me your message. And what brings the little bird of peace back to the Mecca?' She was laughing in her funny way.

'Who knows? God, it's good to hear your voice. How was Paris?'

'Exquisite. And rainy. The collections were abhorrent. Rome was much better. I ran into my ex-husband Cecco. He has a new mistress. Delightful girl, she looks rather like a palomino colt.'

'How was he?'

'Alive, which is in itself remarkable. I cringe to think of how old he must be . . . It must be costing him a fortune to keep having the dates changed on his passport . . . the paper was wearing thin years ago . . .' and we both giggled, she was so bad sometimes. I had never met Cecco, but I had these terrible visions of him.' And you, Gillian . . . how are you, dear? You didn't answer my last letter. I was a little worried.'

She sounded throaty and sarcastic and the same as ever. There was a warmth beneath the sarcasm, and a tone which suggested that she cared about the person she was speaking to. It was a knack she had, which might have been cultivated, but I thought it was sincere. Hilary sounded great, and asked for a brief résumé of 'all the news, please' – 'in other words, Gillian, the bare essentials: when did you get back? how long are you here for? and what are you doing?' I answered the first two briefly, and then told her about the job at *Woman's Life*, about John Templeton and the miracle of an eight-week job that was made to measure, about Julie Weintraub's broken pelvis, and even about my dining-room search. I thought she might have an idea.

Hilary's laugh came back at me again, and an order to 'slow down, there, what's all this about Julie Weintraub and a dining-room? If I understand you correctly, you are looking for a broken pelvis, and just bought Julie Weintraub's dining-room, or you bought Julie's pelvis, and broke your dining-room . . . and do I have a what? A pelvis or a dining-room? I have both, but you are welcome to neither, my dear, and it is quite clear that New York is too much for you.'

By then I was laughing harder than Hilary, and trying to unsnarl the whole thing which I knew she understood perfectly well anyway.

'Actually, Gillian, I've never met Julie Weintraub, but I'm delighted you have the job; it sounds like just your cup of tea. By the way, I have a very old friend who works on the magazine, fellow by the name of Gordon Harte. Have you met him yet? Though I suppose one could hardly expect you would have in two days.'

'Actually, we did meet. He seems nice enough. Kind of a sarcastic bastard though. I didn't know he was a friend of yours; you've never said anything about him.'

'Oh, not that kind of friend. I knew his wife years ago, when she was a model and I had just arrived in New York. They were getting divorced, and he was on his way to Spain to make like the Ernest Hemingway of the art world, or some such. Then I bumped into him myself in Spain years later, and afterwards we began meeting at official functions for the magazine types. He's one of the few redeeming features of those events. He's a very capable man. And a nice one; the sarcasm is . . . well, something he uses to keep the world at bay . . . There's a wall around him a mile high . . . In any case, Gillian dear, how's your Christopher, the Big

Romance?' Like Peg, I had written to her from California.

Silence at my end, and brief paralysis of the mouth, or was it my heart? 'Hilary, I don't know for the time being. Can't talk about it.'

'Good enough. The less said the better for now. But if you need me, you know where to find me. Why don't you come up for drinks on Thursday night, after work, and we'll have a good long chat about anything you do want to talk about, and I'll see who I can get for dinner. Maybe Gordon, and four or five others. It's awfully short notice though. Anyone special you'd like me to ask?'

'No, I'll leave it to you. It sounds marvellous. But will you think about a dining-room for me too, please, genius lady? Hilary, you really are super. And thanks. What time on Thursday?'

'Six?'

'Fine. I'll be there.'

Now that would be an invitation worth accepting. Hilary gave the best goddam dinner parties in New York. And she was also a marvellous scavenger. She called me back that afternoon to say that she had remembered 'just the dining-room!' It belonged to a couple who were both actors, and in the course of taking a class on scenery design the wife had attacked their dining-room with brush and paint. She called it an environment; Hilary's description was more specific: '. . . looks like the whole goddam jungle looking over your shoulder while you eat.' But she convinced me it was worth a try. So I called and made an appointment to see the place on my way home.

It was a wow. It looked like a movie set for a jungle scene: trees and fruit and flowers were painted every-where, clouds hung overhead, the floor was a lake, and animals peered out from behind the painted shrubbery. The furniture was like the kind you'd use on safari, with the exception of a handsome glass table and an immense network of candles. It was really something else.

After that, I called it a day. At least there was one mission accomplished for the magazine. I headed for the Regency with the intention of having a nice, cold glass of white wine and a nap before Sam came home from the park.

As I unlocked the door to our suite the phone was ringing, and for once I didn't even think about it being Chris. Which was just as well, because it wasn't. It was Gordon Harte.

'Hello. I understand from Hilary that we're to be dinner partners tomorrow night. Can I give you a lift?' His voice sounded mellower than it did at the office, and more like it had during our walk the day before.

'That would be nice, but I'm going over early for a drink. I haven't seen Hilary since I left New York.'

'Then I won't intrude. How are you finding the job?'

'Great fun, and a wee bit hectic. I'm out of practice.'

'I'm sure you're doing fine. I was going to ask you to lunch today, but you vanished. We'll make up for it another time.'

'I'd like to do that.'

'Then consider it done. Have a good evening, Gillian. See you tomorrow.'

'Good-bye.' Strange call, strange man, it was as though there was an enormous gulf between him and the rest of the world. He seemed cold even when his words were friendly, and it was a little bit confusing. But at least there seemed to be more to him than to Matthew Hinton. Gordon Harte had spirit and texture and soul. And you could tell that somehow, somewhere, at some time in his

162

life, he had suffered. But over what? Or whom? I fell asleep on my bed as I mulled it over.

I woke up to the sound of the phone ringing again and reached out groggily, not quite aware of what I was doing, and far from awake. This time it was Chris. And all I could think of were warm thoughts, and kind things, and how much I loved him. I smiled sleepily, blew kisses, listened to the sound of his voice. And then rolled over and looked at the clock to see what time it was . . . four-fifteen . . . that's one-fifteen in San Francisco . . . and then, for some reason, I remembered Marilyn, and before I could stop it I had let loose with a bitchy sounding 'And where's Marilyn? Doesn't she come home for lunch?' . . . Ouch. I blew it. I could feel Chris bounce back as though I had slapped him. After that, we talked about my job, the weather, Chris's projects, his films, and we pointedly stayed off the subject of Marilyn, or anything else of any importance. It was a lousy conversation. We played our little games, and Marilyn was as much with us as though she had been listening on the extension. We were ill at ease, I was angry and hurt, and Christopher felt awkward. He should have. He should have felt much worse than that. But he didn't know how.

20

On Wednesday, the opening of the horse show was similar to the opening of the opera, from a social standpoint. It was something to see, and someplace to be seen. Matt was as charming as ever, but I thought the polish was beginning to wear a bit thin. I was already bored with his scene. Afterwards, we dined at La Caravelle, where again everyone bowed and scraped to 'Monsieur Eeentone'. And the newspapers were kinder this time than they had been the first, though they didn't ignore us entirely. They merely made note of our existence by publishing a photograph of our attendance. But this time Peg didn't call.

On Thursday, I appeared for my interview with Milt Howley. He was living in a penthouse at the United Nations Plaza and for a brief moment, as I braced myself for the interview, I stood on the sidewalk and gazed upward, impressed once again with the towering heights of New York. Everything was up, everything was big. There was a breathless, overwhelming bitchiness to it, and every minute of every day you knew that you were 'there'. It was the Mecca. It was Sodom, it was Hell and the Garden of Eden, and, like any other human being with a thrill for life, I was enthralled. And I knew then that even if I left the city the next day, never to return, for one brief moment I had looked at a building fifty stories high, and New York and I had come to terms. It was just what I had said I would do as our plane had landed in New York. I had the city by the balls. But it had me by the throat.

I was let into Milt Howley's apartment by a tiny, blonde girl who was Howley's current 'old lady', as he put it. His mistress. And from that point on, a whirlwind day began. He ran from Rockefeller Center for a meeting to Doubleday's to autograph records, to his agent's office to sign contracts, to a three o'clock lunch at Mama Leone's, where between the salad and the spumoni I managed to squeeze in some interview time. He was an interesting man. He had started singing blues in Chattanooga, Tennessee, ten years before and had made a minor hit in Hollywood before being lured into the protest scene which landed him in jail thirty-seven times and kept him so busy he let his career slip. But now he was up. Mr Superstar, three albums in one year that had sold over a million copies each, two movie contracts, and appearances in Las Vegas, Hollywood, and New York. The whole bit.

After lunch, I rode to the airport with him in a rented limousine. He was going to the White House for dinner. It was exhausting and exhilarating and I liked him. He was all man, and he had been good to interview. He was direct and human and had a raucous sense of humour which made the pressure of his schedule more bearable.

His valet had put his suitcase in the car during the afternoon, and as we drove to the airport he calmly answered my questions as he checked its contents and took care of a double bourbon, seeming totally unflustered by the fact that he was in a moving car, having a drink, being interviewed, and on his way to have dinner with the President. He had a lot of style.

The last I saw of him was as he went through the gate to his plane and stooped to kiss my cheek while he purred in my ear. 'You're one all right woman, Gillian

. . . for a honky chick.'

I laughed and waved as he got on the plane. I had exactly seventy-one minutes to get to Hilary's.

When Hilary opened the door, she looked wonderful. A mixture of Henri Bendel and Paris and Hilary. Put together to perfection, the kind of woman other women envy but that make men feel a little uncomfortable – they wouldn't want to get her hair messed up. She is the kind of woman who spends a lot of time with homosexuals, other women, and old friends. All her lovers are temporary, some of them indecently young, but very attractive, and most become friends eventually. Hilary must be hard to love. I would have felt sorry for her, except I wouldn't have dared. Pity was something you did not dare to think about in the company of Hilary Price. Respect was more like it. In fact, a feeling akin to what my grandmother had inspired. Tough, ballsy women like that make you stand taller, command their due. These are the women whom friends put on pedestals, the same women who would do anything for those friends with one hand while castrating their men and their sons with the other.

Hilary has an incredible amount of style. Everything she touches is done to perfection: her manicure, her home, the dinners she prepares, her work, and her friendships. There is another side of Hilary which is cold, and could be very cruel, but she reserves that for the people who cross her. I have never had the occasion to incur her wrath, and for that I'm grateful. I have seen her take people apart verbally, and it is formidable and terrifying to watch. Perhaps it is that that men sense, which makes them keep their distance, or move on quickly.

Hilary and I have never had the sloppy ease with

166

each other that I share with Peg or some of my other friends. I wouldn't pick my teeth, use all the curse words I might otherwise, or show up at her house in blue jeans and a ragged sweat shirt. But I share something else with Hilary which I do not share with the others. The others have known me as a child, and there is still much of the school-girl in all of us when we meet – we still look upon our relationships with each other in the same spirit that they began. The friendship with Hilary, however, began when we were both grown up, so perhaps we expect more of each other. Besides, Hilary as a school-girl is unthinkable, unless she went to school in Chanel suits, with perfectly arranged hair. I just can't imagine Hilary playing hockey. In the drawing-room of Mme de Sevigne surely, but not on the hockey field looking the way we had.

We had an hour and a half to talk before the first guest arrived, and we covered most of what we wanted to know and say. Hilary mentioned briefly and without much passion that she had a new beau. A young German boy named Rolfe. He was a poet, younger than she, and a 'beautiful child', according to Hilary. He was expected for dinner. She continued to live alone because it suited her better. And I envied her that. That sort of thing would never suit me better. Hilary's dream princes were all dead and gone, if they had ever existed. Mine was still waiting in the wings of my dreams. For however much I may have loved Chris, he was a far cry from a dream prince, even to me.

I had planned not to talk about Chris, but Hilary brought it up while she was making her second drink. 'Gillian, if it's going to work out, it will. And better yet, if it works out on your terms. And if not, hard as it is for you to think that way, try and believe that you haven't lost a great deal. I'm sure Chris is a charming boy, but I don't think he's for you. Frankly, I think you deserve better. And you need the kind of things Chris will never be able to give you. He's too much like me, he doesn't believe in the kind of things you believe in, and I don't think you're ready to stop believing in them either. But whichever way you go, I want you to know I'm around to help, or to listen. I can't tell you much more than that.'

Hilary's words touched me, but it disturbed me that she should think Chris wasn't good enough for me. He was, he was . . . I wanted him to be, no matter how much I had to swallow, or bend over backwards. I still wanted it to work.

Hilary then walked over to her library, looked for something for a few minutes while I gathered my thoughts, and came back with a book in her hands. Leather bound and very old, it looked like something Hilary, or my grandmother, would have. 'Here, this may sound trite to you, but there's a great deal of truth in that,' and she held it out, open to the fly leaf, where a strong hand had written in brown ink:

> He who bends to himself a joy,
> Doth the winged life destroy;
> But he who kisses the joy as it flies,
> Lives in Eternity's sunrise.

and it was signed with the initial L., and a date.

'That was the first man I ever slept with, Gillian. He was thirty years older than I, I was seventeen at the time. He was the greatest concert violinist in Europe, and I loved him so much I thought I'd die when he told me that I was "a big girl now" and he felt I didn't need him any more. I wanted to die, but I didn't. One never does, and I have learned that there's a great deal of truth in those words. I live by them.'

I was moved, and was still holding the book in my

hands when the doorbell rang. Hilary got up to answer it, and in walked a tall good-looking boy about three years younger than I, with blond hair and big green eyes. He had the grace of a very young boy, with none of the awkwardness. It was a totally sensual pleasure to watch him, and a little embarrassing to watch him stare adoringly at Hilary. This was Rolfe. He kissed my hand, called me 'Madame', and made me feel a thousand years old. Except this was what Hilary expected, what she liked. It put no strain on her. And in a brief flashback, I realised that she had become her concert violinist, the man she had loved twenty years before. She sent all these little boys on their way when she felt they didn't need her any more, like a dancing mistress at a finishing school. It was an odd realisation, and I wondered if she gave them each a bronze plaque inscribed with the lines I had just read as their graduation present. It was a funny thought, and I giggled, which snapped Hilary's attention towards me and made Rolfe look confused, as though he might have said something he shouldn't have. Poor Rolfe.

The rest of the guests arrived shortly thereafter. Another editor from Hilary's office, an extremely elegant Italian girl, Paola di San Fraschino, the daughter of some nobleman or other. She spoke charming English and was obviously very well-bred. After her, a lively girl who looked very horsey, had a rather odd laugh, but a kind face. She had just published her second book and didn't look at all the type. She had a very definite sense of humour and livened up the group considerably. Her husband was a music critic for an English paper, and they had the air of country squires about them. She wore some kind of caftan with Moroccan jewellery, had none of the super chic of either Paola or Hilary, but nevertheless a certain style. And her husband had none of the ethereal qualities of Rolfe, which was refreshing. I was beginning to find the golden poet a little hard to talk to. The doorbell rang twice more after that, once for a terribly pompous but good-looking Frenchman who owned an art gallery on Madison Avenue, and the last time for Gordon Harte, who seemed to know Paola and Rolfe. He and Hilary embraced, and he then proceeded to the bar to make his own drink, looking very much at home. Much more so than Rolfe, who looked as though he was not allowed to touch anything without Hilary's permission. Before doing anything, or opening his mouth to speak, Rolfe seemed to check with Hilary first, and it made me nervous. It reminded me of the way I had been when I got married, and it was embarrassing to watch someone else doing it.

The evening passed delightfully. It was like flying back and forth on a trapeze, being part of an acrobatic act. We rushed from Japanese literature to French tapestries, to the new rages in Paris, to Russell Baker's latest editorials, to the political implications of American literature vs Russian literature at the turn of the century, on to homosexuality in Italy, and speculation as to the demise of the Church and organised religion in our society . . . on to Oriental cults, yoga philosophy, and the *I Ching*. It was exhausting and exhilarating, the kind of evening you can only stand about once every six months. It takes you that long to get all your faculties refurbished afterwards. It was a typical evening chez Hilary, with people from the arts, and publishing, and a smattering of literati.

The lady writer and Gordon impressed me the most. They seemed knowledgeable, and informed, but more down to earth than the others. Infinitely more aware of 'reality', something which had become important to me since my days with Chris. My days of enjoying the purely theoretical were over. And I had come to have a healthy respect for the real.

Gordon took me back to the hotel, and we spoke of nothing in particular, the excessive intellectualism of the evening having been dispelled when the group disbanded to go home. As we reached the hotel I expected him to invite me for a drink. But he didn't. Instead, he looked down at me and said, 'How about dinner tomorrow?' He looked suddenly vulnerable, and kind. And I wanted to have dinner with him.

'I'd love to.'

'Good. I'll give you a call in the morning and let you know what time. I have a meeting with John at five, so I doubt if it will be much before eight.'

'Suits me. Thank you, Gordon. And thanks for the lift home. Good night.'

I could hardly wait till dinner the next evening, and as I rode up in the elevator I made a mental note to buy a new dress.

21

'Where are you going, Mommy?'

'Out to dinner, love.'

'Again?' Ouch. Oh, Sam . . .

'Yes. But I promise to be home this weekend.' Meagre compromise.

'Is that a new dress?'

'What is this? The inquisition?'

'What does that mean?'

'It means you're asking a lot of questions, Sam.'

'Well, is it a new dress?'

'Yes.'

'I like it.'

'Well, that's a relief. Thank you.' She was sprawled on the couch and checking me out with a critical eye.

'You know, you're getting fatter in the middle, Mom. You don't look skinny like you used to.'

'What do you mean fatter?' My heart sank. I didn't think I showed yet.

'Just a little. Don't worry.' The phone rang then and I kissed Sam on the top of her head.

'I won't. Now you go take your bath and I'll answer the phone. Scram.' She took off, and for a sad instant I thought it might be Gordon calling off our plans. He would be held over at the office, or had been poisoned at lunch, or had broken an ankle, something . . . like cold feet maybe, or another date . . . That's okay, Gordon . . . I understand . . . but what about my new dress?

'Hello? . . . Yes, Operator, this is she . . . Hello, Chris . . . Yes . . . What's up? . . . No, I am not uptight . . . no . . . no . . . I'm alone . . . Okay, okay . . . I was just getting ready to go out to dinner . . . What the hell do you mean "it didn't take me long"? . . . Just dinner with a friend of Hilary's (why did I have to put it that way?) . . . No, he is not a greasy Italian count, he works at the magazine. *Woman's Life* . . . You know, I think you could really hold off on those remarks. For someone who's living with a girl, you're awfully touchy, dearest . . . Oh really? . . . And why is that so different? . . . Would you like me to tell you why? . . . Hardly. I'm still pregnant, or have you forgotten that little detail? . . . It's not too late for what? . . . Forget it, that's out of the question . . . How's Marilyn? Okay, I don't want to hear about it . . . Don't explain, Christopher. It's very clear as it is . . . Leaving? . . . When? . . . I'll believe it when I see it . . . Look, Chris, will you please get off my back about tonight . . . I'm here because you wanted me here, it wasn't my idea . . . All right we'll talk about something else . . . Wouldn't want to get Uncle Chris upset, would we? . . . She's fine . . . Yes, she still asks for you . . . Concerned with our little family tonight aren't we? . . . Why? . . . Marilyn giving you a rough time???? . . . Look, Chris, I think it'd be better if you didn't call for a while. I can't take it. It just makes things worse. You've got Marilyn, you don't need me, and I can't handle it. I'll call you . . . Oh, I see, fine . . . Look, go to hell, you've got her, so just get off my back, please . . . Write to me then . . . No, I'm seeing the doctor next week. I guess everything's okay, I don't know . . . A little tired, but okay . . . Chris how are you really? . . . I miss you so goddam much I can't stand it . . . No, that is not why I'm going out with Hilary's friend . . .' The doorbell rang then, and I panicked. 'Look, Chris, I've got to go. I'll call you . . . Okay, okay, fine . . . No, don't call . . . all right then, call . . . Not till Monday? . . . Oh that's right, the weekend . . . I forgot . . . Look, I have to get off the goddam phone. I love you . . . Chris? . . . Yeah, baby, I know . . .' It was quite a phone call, with Gordon waiting at the door.

Gordon and I had a wonderful evening. He took me to a tiny Italian restaurant somewhere in the east twenties and then we went uptown to a penthouse restaurant on Central Park South for a drink. The restaurant was housed in a faceless little office building and the moment we stepped off the elevator it was like entering another world. The decor was East Indian. A girl in a gold sari greeted us and parted richly embroidered curtains to lead us into the rooms beyond. There was a heavy aroma of incense in the air, the tables were long and low, and the room seemed to pulsate with a music I didn't understand but couldn't help but respond to. It made me want to sway and close my eyes, in rhythm to the sensual sounds of the East. There was a single rose on each table, and the waiters were tall and dark, many of them had beards, and some wore turbans.

We drank exotic drinks and I looked at the view in silence. It seemed as though everywhere one went in New York there was a new vista to be seen. This one from yet another angle, facing north, Central Park lying below like a child's toy bedecked with Christmas lights, and framed by the buildings on three sides of the park. I felt a million miles from anywhere I'd ever been, and the scenery beyond the windows was merely a skilfully achieved decor, meant to remind one of New York, and nothing more.

Gordon ordered a delicate white wine and rose cakes, and after the waiter served us and proceeded to disappear Gordon held my eyes for what seemed an interminable time. It was as though he were asking questions without using words, and perhaps finding his own answers.

'Why didn't you stay out West, Gillian?' He looked as though he already knew, but his gaze continued to hold mine as he waited for me to answer.

'I wanted to come back.'

'That is not the truth. All right then, did you run away? I imagine that you'd be capable of that.'

'I'm not sure I know what you mean. But, no, I didn't run away. I just came back.'

'Because of a man?' I hesitated for a long moment and then nodded.

'And you? Why did you leave Spain?' Tit for tat.

'I was hungry.'

'Now you're not telling the truth.' I smiled at him and

pulled the rose from its vase to finger the petals.

'Well, let's just say that the time for me to be there was past.'

'Did you run away? Or did she?' It seemed the right question to ask in view of what he had asked me.

'Neither and both. She committed suicide, and after that I ran away.' His face held a quiet sadness, but none of the shock I felt. He was the most incredibly direct man I'd ever met.

'I'm sorry, Gordon.' I looked away, sorry we had begun the questioning. It was a dangerous game to play. We both had our painful pasts.

He looked away, a sad, serious look on his face. And I couldn't see his eyes. 'That's all right, it was a long time ago. Her name was Juanita. She was the most beautiful girl I've ever known. Good and pure. Like a child. I found out that she had been a prostitute in Malaga. So she killed herself. The funny thing is that I wouldn't have cared. I didn't care, it didn't change anything, and I had suspected something like that anyway. But she never knew that. The man who told me, told her, and before I got home she was dead. And after that I left. I couldn't handle it there any more. I never really belonged in the first place, but I had loved it.' I nodded again, there seemed to be nothing to add to what he had said. 'And your man, Gillian, who was he?'

'Just a man.' I didn't want to talk about Chris because I couldn't give Gordon the kind of honesty he was giving me. Chris was not as far back for me as Juanita was for him, I hadn't come to terms with it yet, and whereas his story was narrative, mine was more likely to sound like true confessions.

'Is it still a going thing?'

'No . . . well, not really. We still talk. But I think it's over.' I knew deep in my heart that I was lying, because

I didn't think it was over. I thought it might be, but I didn't really believe that.

'What was he like?'

'My father.'

'And what was your father like?'

'In a word . . . a bastard.' I looked up with a grin. There was a nice feeling of relief in saying it.

'And what does that tell you, Gillian?'

'Bad things. But I didn't see the similarity until just recently.'

'Were you happy with this man?'

'For a while. Yes, very happy. He has some good points after all, or I wouldn't have stayed around as long as I did. But I think, underneath it all, he's a bastard just like my father. Not a nice man. I don't think so anyway. He's incapable of a lot of things I need. I knew that, but I didn't want to know it.' It felt so strange to be talking about Chris as though he were a thing of the past.

'Why did you stay with him then, since you can't tell me why you left, because the fact that he was a "bastard" doesn't explain anything. You liked him that way.' Ouch. Gordon was right, I think I did.

'All right. I left because he forced me to. I stayed because . . . because I loved him, I needed him, I wanted it to work. As long as I stayed on his terms, it was okay. Oh, and I stayed because there were other things. It's sort of a complicated story.'

'And not over yet, is it, Gillian?'

'Yes, and no. Oh hell, Gordon. There's a lot to this thing.' I looked up and let my eyes take hold of his. 'It's over because I don't believe he loves me, and it's not over because I'm having his child. In that sense, it'll never be over.' And then panic at what I'd just said.

'Does anyone know?' He looked perfectly unruffled.

176

'Only one friend. And he knows, of course. But it doesn't seem to make much difference.'

'Have you thought of having an abortion? I suppose you have.'

'Yes. I've thought of it. But I want to have the child. I'm going to bring an awful lot down on my head, but this is how I want to do it. I'm sure.'

'Then you're doing the right thing. But I wouldn't tell anyone, Gillian. However much I admire your determination, it isn't the accepted lifestyle for someone like you, after all.'

'I know. And I had planned to keep it to myself. I don't know what happened tonight. It just slipped out.' I tried to smile without looking at him, and felt him take my hand in his.

'Don't look so sad, Gillian. You're going to make it through.'

'Thanks for the vote of confidence . . . Once in a while I need it.' I tried to smile at him. And it was strange. It was almost as though we were on a carousel of revelations. In less than an hour we were covering every inch of each other's scars and markings. As though we both felt we had to know what had come before. And then, almost unconsciously, I hurled the ball into his court again.

'What about your marriage?'

'In a sense it never existed, Gillian.'

'But you said . . .' I was puzzled. He seemed too honest to lie about something like that.

'For Heaven's sake, don't look at me like that, child! I was married. What I meant was that it might as well not have existed. It was brief, painful, and devoid of all emotion.'

'How in hell did you ever get married then?' It seemed so unlike him.

'Easy. I had to. Or felt I had to. That was twenty-five years ago, and I had seen a young lady briefly, and . . . well . . .'

'She got pregnant.'

'Right. She refused to have an abortion, so I decided to do the noble thing. I married her. But it was untenable. As soon as Greg was born we got a divorce, and that was it.'

'Well, at least you got Greg out of it. Are you two close?' His eyes hardened at the question and took on a strange kind of bitterness.

'Hardly, my dear. Greg is a charming young man. Intelligent, witty, independent. And a stranger. When I left, I cut him out of my mind and tried to forget he existed. I never saw him as a small child, and you forget, I was in Spain for ten years. When I came back he was fifteen. It's difficult to become a father to a fifteen-year-old boy you don't even know.'

'Perhaps one day you will.'

'Perhaps. But unlikely. He thinks me a dreadful materialist. And he's quite right. I am. To earn his respect, I'd have to do something grandiose. Like become an artist for a cause in Afghanistan, or something of the sort. And that's not in my plans. And now, young lady, we have both talked long enough about our grisly pasts. Let's get you home, it's late.' He signalled to the turbaned waiter, and it was clear that the confidences had come to a close. Gordon Harte had the evening well in control. And then he looked at me and the brief tenseness left his face.

'You must have a strange power over me, my dear. I haven't talked like this in years.' It was a nice compliment, and he reached for my hand as we rose from the cushions we had been sitting on. His hold was gentle but firm, and he kept my hand in his as we rode down in the elevator and stepped outside. It was a lovely night, the air was warm and there was a slight breeze, and the horses tethered to the hansom cabs neighed softly from across the street.

'This city looks like a movie set to me. So unreal.' I looked around again and saw Gordon watching me.

'Come, Gillian. Let's walk back to the hotel.' It was only three blocks to the Regency and his arm around my shoulders felt just right. We said nothing on the brief walk, and at the hotel he stood outside the revolving door and looked down at me with a small smile.

'How about lunch in the country tomorrow? I'm going to see friends in Bedford. The country air would do you good.' Not 'I'd like you to be with me,' but 'the country air will do you good'. I would have liked him to say the words, but I could see that he meant them anyway as he waited for an answer.

'I'd like to, Gordon.'

'Would you like to bring your daughter?'

'She has other plans. But thank you. She's spending the day with a friend from school.'

'Fine, I'll pick you up at eleven then. And don't be sorry about tonight, little one. You needed to talk . . . and so did I.' He made no move to kiss me then, but only touched my shoulder gently before he walked away.

We waved at each other one last time as I went in, and I floated past the desk, wondering what lay in store, and fearing that the magic would be gone by the next day.

'Would you mind getting the map out of the glove compartment for me, Gillian?' We were racing along the East River Drive with the top of his car down, and he

179

had been cool when he picked me up. There was no reference to the confidences of the night before, and very little warmth.

'Sure.' I snapped open the little door on the dashboard, pulled out the map, and handed it to him.

'Open it, please.' I was a little surprised by his tone, but dutifully unfolded the map, and then laughed. There was a cartoon, showing a much caricatured portrait of myself and Mr Gordon Harte, eating hot dogs under a lamp post outside the building that housed *Woman's Life*; a Chihuahua and a St Bernard were dutifully lifting their legs on the lamp post, and what looked like the entire magazine staff was leaning from the windows of the building. The capsion read 'Let's get away from it all,' and when I looked up, Gordon was looking pleased by my obvious delight.

'That means you owe me lunch this week.'

'You've got a deal. This is super, Gordon.'

'So are you.'

The lunch in Bedford was pleasant, I liked his friends, and the afternoon sped by.

By five o'clock I was back at the hotel, in time to meet Samantha.

On Sunday, Sam and I moved back to our old apartment with Peg's help, and the absence of the Regency was sorely felt, by me at least. As for Sam, she was ecstatic to be home. I was less so. Sunday night was spent scrubbing floors and scouring closets, and it seemed as though I hardly had time to go to bed before another work week began.

'Samantha! . . . Breakfast! . . . Hurry up, you'll be late for school!' And I for work. It was quite a major feat of organisation to get the show on the road, Sam ready for school, and myself for work. I had lost the knack, and getting it all together at eight o'clock in the morning was like climbing an iceberg wearing roller skates. It had been easier to be up and dressed at six in San Francisco. Maybe it was the clothes.

'Sam! Come on! . . . Where are you?'

'Here I come, Mommy!' and she arrived in a burst of cowboy gear Chris had given her. 'Here I am!'

'Okay, love, eat the cornflakes. We're in a sort of a hurry.'

'Cowboys don't eat cornflakes.' She looked insulted.

'Oh yes they do. Now come on, Sam. Eat!' I was trying to juggle coffee and the paper, while wondering if my shoes needed a shine.

There were the usual thousand phone calls to make at work, shooting of the children's rooms to be set up, the dining-room assignment to be finalised, and John Templeton had a horde of minor things for me to attend to.

Gordon and I had our promised lunch on Tuesday, and he invited me to a black tie press party at the Museum of Modern Art on Wednesday night.

On Wednesday afternoon, I rushed home from the office, got out a black velvet dress and raspberry satin evening coat, and waited for him to pick me up at seven. I realised as I waited for him to arrive that mixed with the elation of going out with him again was a sagging feeling. Chris hadn't called all week. And as usual, it hurt. I ached for Chris Matthews, for his arms around me, for his quiet voice, even for his indifference, anything.

'Mommy! The doorbell is ringing!' Sam's voice rang through the apartment.

'Okay. I'll get it.' I hadn't even heard it. It was Gordon.

'All set? My! Don't you look smashing! You look just lovely, Gillian.' He studied me appreciatively and gave me a peck on the forehead.

'Thank you, sir. How was your day?'

'As per usual. Gillian, is there anything wrong?'

'No. Why?'

'You look as though you've had a rough day, as though something hurt.' Very perceptive, Mr Harte.

'No. Really. Maybe a little tired, but that's all. Would you like a drink before we go?'

'No, I think we'd better get started.'

'Who are you?' Samantha was suddenly in the doorway, studying the scene.

'Gordon, this is Samantha. This is Mr Harte, Sam.'

'Who's he?'

'Someone I work with and a friend of Aunt Hilary's.' I watched them carefully, afraid she'd set his back up by saying something rude. I knew he wasn't used to children.

'Can I touch your beard? Is it real?' Samantha approached carefully and Gordon stooped down to talk to her.

'Yes, and it is real. Hello, Samantha.' I watched with trepidation to see if she would give it a yank, but instead she just patted it and I stopped holding my breath.

'Feels kinda like a horse. You know?'

'That's a compliment,' I interpreted.

'Do you like horses, Samantha?'

'Yeah! A lot!' A lengthy discussion followed, and I was surprised to hear how much Gordon seemed to know about them, and even more surprised when he reached for a pad on my desk and did a few quick sketches for Sam, which delighted her. Gordon and Samantha were discovering each other.

'Gillian, we'd better go now. Samantha, I hope to see you again sometime.'

'Sure. Come back and visit, Mr Gordon.'

'Mr Harte, Sam. Good night, sweetheart. Be a good girl with Jane.' We exchanged great big hugs and a series of watery kisses, and then Gordon rang for the elevator.

'That was nice of you, Gordon. Thanks.' We were waiting for a cab downstairs and my spirits were restored. It was nice to see Samantha enjoying him.

'I like her. She's bright and very direct.'

'That's for sure!' I laughed and shook my head as a cab pulled up and we sped off towards the museum.

The evening was wonderful, it was delightful to be swept along in his wake, being introduced to everyone and having a fuss made over us. Gordon was on the board of the museum, something he had neglected to tell me when he had invited me. Hilary was there, sans Rolfe, looking smashing in a long skinny black knit dress and an equally long skinny white coat. Gordon asked her to join us for dinner afterwards, which I thought was nice, but she refused.

This time Gordon took me to Lutece for dinner, where he was received as though he owned the place or, at the very least, paid the rent.

We had run into Matthew Hinton at the museum, accompanied by a striking redhead who clung to his arm as though in desperate gratitude. We greeted each other, but coolly, and it was apparent that he had as little interest in what *Women's Wear* had called 'his latest love' a week before as I had in him. He was nice, but there just wasn't much to him.

And I may not have been making the social columns with Gordon Harte, but I was having a beautiful time.

22

Friday was pandemonium. The actors who owned the eccentric dining-room stood amidst a bevy of people, ready to begin the shooting. And four hours later we were still only beginning. They managed to get loaded during the shooting, kept the setting constantly rumpled and disorderly, and drove the photographer crazy. At midnight it was over, and I wondered if we had a single usable shot. And we weren't through yet; we had promised everyone dinner in compensation for their 'patience'. At 2 a.m. I finally crawled home, exhausted and feeling as though I were about to die.

An hour after I went to bed, I got up, vomited, had chills, cramps, and panicked, thinking I was losing the baby. I should have called Peg, or the doctor, or even Gordon. Someone sensible. But I wasn't feeling sensible. I had that wild animal feeling one gets when surprised at feeling suddenly sick. So I operated on reflex and emotion, and dialled Chris.

'Hello?'

'Chris? . . . I think I'm losing the baby, I feel so awful. We worked until one o'clock . . . No, for God's sake, I mean it. No, I'm not drunk . . . I'm sick . . . what am I going to do?'

'For Chrissake, Gillian, stop crying. Why did you call me? I can't do anything about it, and you know what I told you. Call the doctor . . . Look, I can't talk to you now. I'll call you Monday.'

Monday? Monday? What the hell does he mean,

'Monday'? Sonofabitch . . . I put on some clothes and went to the emergency room at Lenox Hill Hospital where I spent the night and was treated for exhaustion and hysteria.

I was sent home at noon, feeling sheepish, and still very tired. Gordon called almost as soon as I got home.

'And where have you been so bright and early this morning? I called you at nine. I hear the shooting was a madhouse last night.'

'Yes, it was.' And then I told him about the night at the hospital, omitting the part about my call to Chris.

Gordon was sympathetic, and said he'd check on me on Sunday, and why didn't I take Monday off?

I slept all day and when I woke up there were flowers from him, a small basket that looked like a nest, filled with tiny blue and orange flowers. The card read, 'Work is the opiate of the masses, but it sounds like you had a bad trip. Have a good rest. Apologies from your Senior Art Director, Gordon Harte.' Funny and thoughtful and nice, because it wasn't pushy and signed 'G.' or something equally irritating.

He called again on Sunday, and I was feeling better, but still pretty tired, so he agreed not to drop by, but instead invited me to dinner on Thursday.

As I lay in bed on Sunday afternoon, pleased with the easiness of the Gordon situation, and maybe feeling a little supercilious about it, as though for once I had 'control', the doorbell rang. Who the hell is that? I got up to answer it. It was Gordon.

'Changed my mind. Besides, Hilary says you love having people drop in on you on Sundays. We just had lunch and she sends her love. May I come in?'

'Of course,' but I was angry, really mad. I looked a mess, he had agreed not to come by, I didn't feel well, and unannounced visits from him constituted an 'act of pressure' in my book.

'You don't look too pleased to see me, Mrs Forrester.'

'Just surprised. Would you like a cup of tea?'

'Yes. But I'll make it, you go back to bed.'

'No, that's all right, I'll stay up. I'm really fine.' . . . I wasn't about to get into one of those 'now tell me, doctor', scenes with him on the edge of my bed . . .

'You look fine to me, but I don't know much about these things. I'll make the tea.'

He returned from the kitchen after much scraping and banging, and he sat there looking unaffected by it all, making easy conversation and looking around pleasantly. Samantha was out and the apartment seemed horribly quiet.

I was in the midst of making stiff, pompous remarks about nothing, and looking into my cup of tea to cover the fact that I was uncomfortable, when Gordon got up, came around the coffee table, sat down, and kissed me. His beard felt scratchy, and his mouth felt soft, and I was too embarrassed not to kiss him back. He kissed me, and then leaned back a little, looked down at me, and hugged me.

He hugged me. A nice hug. The kind I had longed for when I was eight years old, and still longed for twenty years later. And there was Gordon Harte, hugging me, while I sat in the circle of his arms and was suddenly in tears.

I tried to make light of it after that, for fear that he was going to try to take it too many steps further, and I didn't want to get into a scene like that with him yet.

'You want to be wooed, don't you?'

'What?' It sounded so ridiculous, it made me laugh.

'Mrs Forrester, we could spend the next few weeks eating dinner together twice a week and enjoying preambles, I could "woo" you, and we could say agreeable things to each other, and in three weeks you would probably agree to go to bed with me, or we could go to bed now, and enjoy the three weeks more. What do you say?'

'I can't. I'm sorry, but I just can't. I know I'd get upset, and I couldn't handle it. I know myself.' I was almost whispering when I said it, and looking down at my hands clenched in my lap.

'All right.' . . . I was a teensy bit sorry that he agreed so readily, but for the most part I was relieved.

We sat talking in low voices, and listening to the rain, kissing on the couch in my living-room for a while, and each time we kissed I wanted him more, and we held each other for longer, until he kissed my breast, and my whole body surged upwards towards his, and we were suddenly hand in hand, heading for my bedroom, still kissing and touching and holding along the way, almost knocking over a lamp, and in a great hurry to get to bed. He took off his clothes, and I noticed with a shock that he didn't wear any underwear . . . 'Why Gordon Harte, you look so goddam serious all the time, and there you are walking around that magazine all day with no underpants on! What if your zipper breaks?' I was laughing, it really struck me funny.

'It never has.'

'What if you get in an accident? My grandmother always said . . .'

And he roared with laughter, and walked over to help me take off the rest of what I had on . . . 'Gillian, you're beautiful.' He sounded as though he meant it, and for the rest of time our bodies rolled together, merged into each other, touched and fell away, and joined again. We made love, and lay together feeling close, and familiar, easy with each other. We had become friends. We had fallen in like. It was the first time in my life that I didn't feel I had to shout 'I love you' to justify doing something that I had been told all my life was not a nice thing to do. Instead, we hugged and laughed, and I felt right with the world.

It was better with Gordon than it had ever been with Chris, which seemed odd to me because I didn't love Gordon. But that afternoon I stopped being angry with Chris. I didn't make love with Gordon to wreak vengeance on Chris for Marilyn. I made love with Gordon because I wanted to, and I liked him. Nothing more than that.

And I lay in Gordon's arms, smiling, while he drew figure eights around my breasts with his finger, and I thought of the poem on the flyleaf of Hilary's book . . . 'he who kisses the joy as it flies, lives in Eternity's sunrise . . .'

23

In every possible way, October was a good month, a warm month full of people and things to do. Samantha was happy at school and, while I hadn't come to love New York, I had done a little better than just resign myself to it. New York was being good to me, it was looking its best, and was on its best behaviour. There is a time of year in New York, in the fall, which comes suddenly, and doesn't last long, but is enough to make you love it for the rest of the year. If you go away then, you will always think of New York in golden hues, but if you stay you see the filth, the soot, the slush, and, later, live in the stench and torrid heat of a New York summer.

But in the fall, it becomes beautiful, it is red and gold and brown, it's clear and windy and crisp, the streets look cleaner, people step as though walking to a march, the smell of hot chestnuts is everywhere, young people are in the city on weekends, making it look as though there are some nice young people who live there after all, because summer weekends are over and it's too early for skiing. It's the time of year I love best, and if there is a warm spot in my heart for New York it is for that city at precisely that time of year. And the spell it weaves for two, or three, or four weeks in the late autumn.

And as though the city itself had planned it that way, on my last year in New York, those magical weeks happened, and were crisper and livelier and more beautiful than ever before. To me, New York is like a bitch of a woman, she's too much to handle, and I don't admire her lifestyle, but, in deference to what she is and what she stands for, I have to admit it when she moves out in style. And in October she does.

Gordon and I were seeing each other two or three times a week, went some place really 'nice' about once a week, met some place after work sometimes, or one of us cooked dinner at his place or mine. Halfway into the month, we pooled our resources and address books and threw a party. It was crazy and fun, crowded and full of amusing stereotypes, like most parties in New York.

Gordon had a full schedule, and I had enough to do, so that it never became an everyday thing.

There were no assumptions made about each other's time, but everything just seemed to fall into place, like the weather. And life moved on.

Halloween came and went leaving Samantha richer and happier with the loot she had collected from our building and Gordon's. He had taken her over to his place to test his neighbours' mettle, and she was delighted.

By then, she and Gordon were fast friends.

We decided to spend Thanksgiving together, quietly, at my place, and I was just leaving the office to pick up our turkey when the phone rang. It was Julie Weintraub.

'Hi. I just spoke to my doctor, and it looks like you've got the job for another month. How's that for a bitch? Actually, I'm enjoying the rest, and there are a couple of interns worth staying around for. Who needs John Templeton with a setup like this?' Her words sounded funny, but she sounded disappointed. Lying on your back with pins in you, and traction pulling at you, just isn't a whole lot of fun, interns or no. Given a choice, I'd even take Eloise Franck. Poor Julie.

'Have you told John yet, Julie?'

'Yeah, I just called him. He ought to be barrelling down the hall any minute with the good news.'

'Come on, you know everybody here wants you back. All anybody ever says to me around here is "when's Julie coming back?"' which wasn't entirely true, but I thought it might help.

'Bullshit. But that was a nice try. I saw stats of your last issue by the way. Looks good to me. Maybe I won't have a job any more when I get out of this place.' . . . And that was something I knew was worrying her.

'Bullshit to you, lady. I'm just making like a Kelly girl here. Purely temporary. I'll start wearing white gloves if it'll make you feel any better,' and she broke into a more Julie-like laugh . . . 'Listen, seriously, what did the doctor say? How's it mending?'

'I don't know, nobody tells me much of anything. All I know is that they want to reshift something, which means yet another orthopaedic surgeon, and the operating room again, which is not exactly my favourite scene. It also means another four weeks. Kinda depressing,' and that's just how she sounded.

'Well, keep the chin up. Might as well get it all done now rather than have to go back in six months. That's nothing to mess around with. Besides, you don't think I'm going to break my ass for you here every six months, do you?' and I heard Julie chuckle again. 'I'll come up and see you this weekend and give you all the news . . . which reminds me, you remember that little love seat in John's office?'

'Yeah.'

'Well, I hear Lucius Barclay humped Eloise on it yesterday afternoon,' Lucius being the faggy beauty editor. Even women's lib couldn't get upset about our having a male beauty editor. There was absolutely nothing male about Lucius. Nothing.

But the crack had served its purpose, and Julie was in hoots at the other end of the phone.

'Hey, listen, don't do that to me . . . it hurts,' and then more chortles and chuckles . . . 'Anyway, you got it wrong. I heard that story this morning: Eloise humped Lucius,' and we both laughed.

'Okay, Julie, gotta go, but I'll come by this weekend. Anything I can bring you?'

'Yeah. Sex.'

'What about all those interns? Listen, save one for me. Hang in there, Julie, we miss you. I can't wait to give you this job back anyway. I want to start collecting unemployment.'

'Screw you, you don't qualify. Gotta work six months and then get fired. And if you think I'm gonna lie here for six months, you gotta be nuts. So just take damned good care of my job . . . See you soon. Hey, and Gillian? . . . Thanks.'

'Don't be an ass. The thanks go to you, now get off the goddam horn before we get sentimental, or I get fired. See you . . . take care.' Poor Julie, it didn't sound good, and I wondered what the score really was, as the phone rang and I was told that 'Mr Templeton would like to see you in five minutes, Mrs Forrester.'

Half an hour later, when I came out of John's office, I was not feeling like laughing any more.

John had spoken to Julie, as she had said, but he had spoken to her doctor too. Julie was not healing at all, and her haemoglobin was low. They suspected bad news. They weren't sure, but they 'suspected' it, and they were going to operate to find out. They thought she might have bone cancer. Julie didn't know.

When John had finished talking, I felt weak, and rotten, and sick. He told me not to tell anyone. And thank God he had the good taste not to mention the possibilities of extending my job into a permanent one. I would have thrown up at that point, or burst into tears.

As it was, I walked straight back to my office, shut the door, and leaned back against it with tears pouring down my face, wondering how in hell I was going to face Julie on Thanksgiving Day. It was one of those horrible soap opera ironies that happen all the time, sometimes even to people you know.

The following day, Sam, Gordon and I had Thanksgiving dinner. It was lovely and comfortable, and I tried not to think about Julie.

At that point, I was five months pregnant, and hadn't seen Christopher in over ten weeks. I still missed him but I had settled in. I was happy with my job, enjoying Gordon, and rolling along nicely. The baby was more mine than Chris's, and men on the street didn't look quite so much like Chris any more. They were beginning to look a little more like Gordon, and a lot more like themselves.

So when Gordon left my apartment shortly after midnight on Thanksgiving night and the phone rang at two, I almost fainted when I heard Chris on the line.

'Gill, I'm at the airport now. I've got a film to do in New York for the next month. The plane gets there about six hours from now. American Airlines. Meet me.'

24

The plane came to a stop just in front of the window, and rumpled-looking passengers began to disembark. Mostly men, carrying suits on hangers covered by plastic bags, and attaché cases. And a few women. One woman with two small children. People. And more people. And no Chris. Where was he? Had he missed the flight? Had I heard the wrong airline? Would he be on the next flight? ... And then there he was, smiling, looking a little sleepy, and more beautiful than I remembered him. Had he stopped walking, I would have thrown myself into his arms, but he just walked up to me, and we kept right on walking, never breaking stride.

'Hi, Gillie, how's it going?' ... How's it going? ... After almost three months? ... You big shit ...

'Fine.'

'Don't I get a kiss?' and he held out a cheek for a peck as we neared the baggage claim area.

'Wait till we get home.'

'Oh is the young lady playing it cool now?' and he looked amused.

Everything amused him, mostly me, and I felt silly, in my fur hat, looking for something to say that would pass for conversation.

He was totally engrossed in collecting his bags. The flight had been fairly full. I stood watching him, wondering what it really was that held me close to this man. Why did I still feel the way I did, how could I still feel as though the world stood still for him, how could I still believe in dream princes when I looked at Chris? But I did.

I was frowning as I looked over at him. He seemed taller and wider than I had remembered. And he looked so brown and healthy. So different from the pale, city-looking people you see in New York.

He picked up the last of his bags and we headed for the exit to look for a cab. The ride into the city was a little uncomfortable because it seemed odd not to have a phone resting between us. I had grown accustomed to dealing with a disembodied voice, not to looking into the eyes of this big, suntanned man. He noticed my hat and liked it, and commented briefly on the fact that I didn't look pregnant.

'What'd you do, get rid of it?'

'It's the coat, Chris. My clothes still hide it pretty well.'

'Yeah, I'll bet you're not even pregnant.' I knew he didn't mean it, but it was a typical Chris remark, which annoyed the hell out of me, but somehow I managed not to snap back.

When we got home, Chris walked in, dumped his bags in the hall, and headed for the kitchen where we could hear Samantha expounding on the virtues of her teacher.

'UNCLE CRITS!' Screams, and yells, and hugs, and much tossing around, and more yelling. It was so nice to watch them together. The two people I loved most in the whole world crawling all over each other, and hugging, and laughing. It made me laugh too, and brought back all our days in California. It was sunshine and beaches and love.

'Uncle Crits, I'm going to show you my room, and you can't come in, Mommy.'

'Okay, I'll make breakfast.' They disappeared down the hall, hand in hand, with Samantha telling him all about school and Chris asking if she'd been a good girl, and had she been putting honey on her corn flakes like he'd shown her?

Poor Sam, she needed Chris almost as much as I did. He had been the closest thing she'd ever known to a full-time father, and our days in California had been the closest thing she'd had to a normal home life.

'Breakfast! Come and get it!'

'Okayyyy . . .' came back, muffled, from down the hall. And then Chris appeared with a jump-rope tied around his head and Samantha shouting 'Giddyap horsey' as she skipped behind him.

'Horses don't eat at my breakfast table, Mr Matthews.'

'Since when? Things must have changed a lot in the last two months,' and we all laughed and ate eggs and waffles, and toast, and bacon. We ate and talked and joked with each other, and I knew how terribly I had missed Chris. Just as much as I had thought, and then multiplied by twenty.

My mother's helper appeared when breakfast was over, to help clear up and take Samantha to the park . . .

'I don't wanna go, I wanna stay with Uncle Crits.' She looked as though she were going to cry.

'Come on, podner. Your mother and I are going to talk. You go to the park and see if you can't find some hay for the horses. I'll be here when you get back, now giddyap, there . . .'

She looked dubious, but she went, waving back over

195

her shoulder, 'Gabye, Uncle Crits, see you later. Bye, Mommy.'

'Bye, sweetheart.'

'You've still got her spoiled rotten, Gillian. Nothing's changed.'

'Look, she needs a lot of love.'

'She's got a lot of love, she needs a lot of time. And spoiling isn't going to make up for that. If you didn't have your goddam alimony you wouldn't have that girl taking her to the park and you'd both be better off.'

'I have to work for chrissake.'

'That's not the point . . . I'm going to take a bath. Which way's our room?'

'I'll show you,' and as I walked down the hall I was annoyed at Cris. What did he know about children?

'Run my bath, will you, Gill? I'm going to open the bags.'

I turned on the taps full blast, and felt a little baulkish about taking orders again . . . Yessir, Mr Chris, sir. Yo baff is fillin up dere, yo honour, sir . . . Run your own goddam bath . . .

He walked back into the bathroom, stark naked, and I noticed the bathing suit marks which hadn't quite faded since last summer.

'You're peeking.'

'Don't be ridiculous.'

'Come on, take your clothes off, and let's take a bath.'

'I had a bath before I went to the airport. I'll unpack for you.'

'No, I'll unpack for me. Take your clothes off and get into the bath. I want to see that belly of yours.'

'Chris, I don't want to take a bath.'

'You're taking a bath. Now, move your ass, girl . . .'

He was stretched out in the tub, looking up at me, with

196

that look of his . . . 'You can take your hat off now, too. I said I liked it, but I think you could take it off now.'

'Thanks. Yeah, okay,' and I was pulling my clothes off, feeling silly about it, as Chris watched.

I was standing naked next to the tub, and Chris held out a hand to help me in. 'Yep, you're pregnant.'

'Who told you?'

'Wash my back, will you Gill?'

'Sure,' and there I was, lathering his back, with my gardenia soap, smiling at the moles and freckles. I could have drawn a diagram of where every spot was on his body. I knew him, his soul and his body, every inch of him. It was a happy thing to be doing . . . If anyone had told me that week that I would be washing Chris Matthews's back the day after Thanksgiving, I'd have laughed in their face. But there we were, and I was grinning from ear to ear.

'Watcha smiling at, little fat girl?'

'What do you mean, "little fat girl"?'

'I mean little fat girl, now what are you smiling at?'

'Nothing. Us. You. It's so nice to have you back, Chris. It's just not the same on the phone, it's no good. I get hung up on the words, I forget the looks that go with things, and you can't squeeze them into a telephone. I've missed you so terribly.'

'Yeah, I know.' And for some reason, there was Marilyn again. I could see him thinking of her too, and she was there, blowing bubbles up to the surface of our bath water, like a fart.

'Okay, now wash my chest.'

'Come on, Chris, you can do that yourself.'

'No, I can't. I want you to do it. Wash my chest. And listen, will you do me a favour on Monday? Get some decent soap, will you please. Get rid of this orchid crap.'

'It's not orchids, it's gardenias. From Magnin's.'

'Well get rid of it, try something from the grocery store.'

'You plebe.'

'I may be a plebe, but I am not a fag, and I don't want to go around smelling like a goddam gardenia. Now wash my chest.'

So I soaped up his chest and leaned over to kiss him . . . he was smiling again.

'Come here, little fat girl . . . come here, you,' and there we were slathering soap all over each other, like some ridiculous French movie, and trying to make love, slipping around, slapping water all over the floor, and laughing hysterically, like two kids.

'Come on . . .' and Chris pulled me out of the tub, still half-covered with soap, and we lay down on the bathroom floor and made love.

Afterwards, we lay there and grinned at each other . . .

'Chris?'

'Yeah, baby?'

'I love you.'

'I know. I love you too,' and then he squeezed me a little and stood up. 'I'm going to take a shower to get this soap off. Get me a glass of milk, will you?'

'Sure,' and life was back to normal again, Chris was singing his lungs out in the shower, and there I was with soap drying on me, my pregnant belly, standing naked in the kitchen, pouring him a glass of milk. As I stood there I thought of Gordon. This was a far cry from what I had with him. He was my old side, this was my young side. This was the side of me that still had all the dreams left in it, and they just wouldn't quit.

I left the glass of milk on the bathroom sink and walked back into the bedroom while Chris continued to steam up the bathroom, when the phone rang.

'Gillian? How about some lunch?' It was Gordon . . . oh, Jesus . . . what could I say? At least Chris was in the shower, so he couldn't hear.

'I can't. Something has come up, the weekend is kind of screwed up.'

'Anything wrong?'

'No, but I really can't go into it now. Let's have lunch Monday.'

'You're sure nothing's wrong?'

'No, really, I'm sure. Don't worry. And Gordon . . . I'm really sorry.'

'That's all right. I have some work to do anyway. See you Monday. But I'll give you a call later. Good-bye.'

'Who was that?' Chris's voice, between gulps of milk. I hadn't heard the shower stop.

'A friend from the office.'

'Oooohhh . . . does little fat girl have a lover boy?'

'No. And stop calling me little fat girl.'

'Okay,' and he blew me a kiss.

It struck me that he seemed to feel totally at home, which was a quality Chris had. And I headed for the tub to rinse off the soap and wash again. I was thinking of Gordon, and what I had said to him, and to Chris. No, Gordon was not a 'lover boy'. And no, 'nothing was wrong'. Except that I had lied to both of them, and I didn't like doing it. Chris's stay was going to be an interesting month.

Chris slapped my ass as I walked back to the bedroom . . . 'Put on your grubbies, Gill. I want to go for a walk.'

'Okay, love,' . . . and the door slammed and Samantha's shrieks of 'Uncle Crits' reverberated through the apartment. 'Uncle Crits! Uncle Crits! . . . Hi, Mommy. Guess who I saw on the way home? Gorrrdon.' She rolled it around her mouth like a marble. 'I told him Uncle Crits is here, and he said that was very nice. He said to say hello.'

Oh shit. Happy Thanksgiving . . . and at that point in time I felt an overwhelming kinship with the turkey.

25

I stood before the door to Gordon's office, and hesitated for a moment. What in hell was I going to say?

'May I help you with something, Mrs Forrester?' His secretary eyed me curiously as I stood there, and I no longer had any choice. I had to go in. I turned the knob carefully in my right hand, as I knocked with my left, and then stopped with one foot in the room. He was in the middle of a meeting. As he saw me, the look he gave me chilled me to the bone.

'Yes, Gillian?' His eyes were cold and blank, and his face looked taut beneath the beard.

'I'm sorry, I didn't know you were busy. I'll come back later.'

'I'll call you when the meeting is over.' His eyes moved away from me then, and I felt unwelcome in the room. I closed the door softly behind me and walked slowly back towards my office, wondering what lay in store.

Distractedly, I bought a cup of coffee and a Danish from the coffee wagon and sat down at my desk. Whatever was coming, I could tell it wasn't going to be pleasant. And I couldn't blame him. I know how I'd have felt in his shoes. Rotten. And pissed.

The phone rang almost an hour later, when I was

absentmindedly trying to get into my work, without much success.

'Gillian, meet me downstairs in ten minutes.'

'Gordon, I . . .'

'I don't want to talk about it, we'll discuss it downstairs.'

'Fine.' But the word went unheard, he had already hung up. I closed my eyes and tried to clear my head, and then got up to go. It would have been ironic had we met in the elevator on the way down, but we didn't. He was waiting on the street when I got there, and as soon as I reached his side he started walking uptown on Lexington Avenue at a pace I could hardly keep up with.

'Why didn't you tell me he was coming? Did you think I couldn't take it?'

'Of course not. I didn't know he was coming. He called right after you left, and a few hours later he was here.'

'By what right?' That was a tough one to answer. And we were crossing streets against the lights, taunting traffic and moving along at breakneck speed. It was obvious that Gordon was livid.

'It's not a question of rights, Gordon. He's making a film here and he doesn't realise how things stand.'

'And precisely how do they stand? I'm not sure I understand myself. Is he your lover or am I?'

'He's the father of my child. I lived with him. And we left each other under difficult circumstances.'

'How terribly tragic. And if I recall, the difficult circumstances you just mentioned were that he threw you out? Have you forgotten that? Or doesn't it matter? All he has to do is get on a plane and arrive and everything's fine. I imagine he's staying with you.' My 'yes' caught in my throat, and Gordon grabbed my arm and spun me around. 'Isn't he?'

'Yes! He is! So what for chrissake?'

'So plenty. I don't want that sonofabitch near you, Gillian! Not for an instant!' People were beginning to stare at us in the street, and the grip Gordon had on my arm brought tears to my eyes.

'Gordon, I've got to get this thing sorted out. Please.'

'Grow up for God's sake, and be honest with yourself. There is nothing to sort out. The man doesn't want you. Don't you understand that?'

'Maybe he does.' And then I was horrified at what I'd said.

'So that's it, is it? Well at least now I understand. I make a good fill-in when he's not around. You bitch!' He pulled back his arm and for a moment I thought he would hit me, but he restrained himself. 'Well, I'll tell you something. Do you want to know why the men in your life have treated you badly? Because you want them to. You wouldn't know what to do with them if they didn't. You eat it up. I'm the first man who's ever been decent with you, and look at what you're doing. Take a good long look, because it's the last look you'll take.' He stared at me with fire leaping from his eyes and a sense of horror grew within me as I realised what he was saying.

'Gordon, there's nothing I can say. I don't want to be dishonest with you. I loved the man. But you mean so much to me too. I love you. I need you.'

'You want to use me. And I'm not up for that. It's too goddam late for that. I'm too old for that bullshit. I haven't gotten this far to play games with some hippie film-maker and his fucked-up girl friend. Because that's just what you are. Fucked up!' He had a grip on both arms then and was shaking me until my teeth rattled, and with sudden shock I saw a policeman approaching us from across the street.

'Gordon! Let's talk about this someplace else . . . there's . . .'

'There's nothing to talk about.' He gave me one last shake and then pushed me away. 'To hell with you!' And then he walked away and turned the corner, just as the police officer reached me.

'Lady, are you all right?'

'Yes, Officer, I'm fine thank you.'

'Looked like that guy was giving you a bad time. I thought I'd check it out.'

'Just a little misunderstanding.' And feeling shaken, I started back towards the office. The whole scene with Gordon had been awful, I had lost him, it was over. And for what? In a few weeks Chris would be gone again. Maybe this time for good. What in hell was I doing?

The prospect of returning to the office was dismal. I had no desire to face the tasks of the business day any more. I just wanted to go home and hide. But I didn't want to see Chris, so I was better off at work.

The day crawled by, and my heart felt like it was sitting on my feet. And suddenly I couldn't stand it any more. I put my head down on my arms and sobbed. The phone rang and I didn't answer it, I didn't give a damn who it was, it could wait, and the tears just wouldn't stop. Goddam Chris Matthews, all he ever did was screw up my life.

'Gillian?' I heard a voice, but before I could look up to see who had come in his arms were around me. 'Darling . . . I'm sorry.' He pulled me gently to my feet and I went on crying in his arms.

'Oh Gordon . . . I . . . I . . .' I couldn't find the words.

'Sshh . . .'

'I'll tell him to go away, I'll tell him that . . .'

'Quiet. You won't tell him anything. We'll wait till he goes and see how you feel.' I looked up at him, stunned.

'You can't do that!'

'I can do anything I want. And I think you're right,

203

you've got to get it out of your system. So if you can put up with an occasional fit of the glooms on my part, let's just let it ride. How does that sound?' He kissed me tenderly above each eye, and the tears began to flow again. He was so incredibly good to me. Always.

'That sounds beautiful if you're sure.'

'I'm sure.'

He held me tightly in his arms, and half an hour later he walked me home.

And as I turned the key in the lock, I dreaded seeing Chris.

When I walked in, Chris and Samantha were roughhousing, her toys spread all over the living-room floor.

'Hi, Sam. Hi, Chris, how'd it go?'

'Okay. They're a funny bunch though. Very "Nyeww Yawwk". And they're still trying to get their heads straight and figure out what they're making a movie about. It's all fucked up.'

'Watch the "forks and spoons" with the little people around please!'

'Yes, ma'am. How was your day?'

'Okay. Nothing special. Looks like I'll be pretty busy for the next few weeks though. I might have to work late.' Which meant I wanted time with Gordon.

'No sweat. Once this thing gets started I probably won't be home till eleven or twelve most nights.'

'That's okay.'

'Maybe it's okay with you. But it's not my idea of a swell time, but bread is bread, and in this case the money's good.' I noticed that he wasn't offering to pay the grocery bills with it.

'Hey, listen, you didn't unpack the small suitcase, Chris. Want me to do it?' It was cluttering up the room.

'Okay, just dump it all in a drawer.' As though I had twelve empty ones just sitting around, waiting for Chris.

He really was incredible, in New York for three days and I was beginning to feel as though I were visiting him.

I went into my bedroom with the package of soap I'd bought at the drugstore and unwrapped it, waving a mental farewell to my gardenias from Magnin. I stooped down to open Chris's suitcase and fiddled with the catch for a minutes before it opened. When it did, I saw that the bag was full of sweaters, and some extra underwear, and his ski clothes, and little yellow slips of paper – 'i love you, m.' . . . 'who's kissing you now? m.' . . . 'more than yesterday and less than tomorrow, m.' . . . 'come home soon, m.' – I gathered them up and put them in a pile on Chris's bed-table. There she was again. Marilyn in my bedroom, in my bathtub, in my kitchen, ramming herself down my throat incessantly. Chris walked in and said, 'What're those?'

'Take a look. Messages from your lady.' It was almost as if Chris had left that bag for me to find them.

'Hey, you don't think . . .?' His voice trailed off.

'No I don't think . . . but I don't enjoy them anyway. There are about a dozen of them. I only read four or five. Sorry.'

He didn't say anything but read them, tore them up, and threw them in the toilet. He had to read them first though. Each and every goddam one.

The time I spent with Chris that first week was odd. We alternated between heading straight into the subject of Marilyn, and rather delicately trying to stay off it. Either way she was right in the forefront of our consciousness most of the time, or mine at least. I realised too that I had changed, that I had in fact gotten a little more independent. I had depended on the idea of Chris, but had stopped leaning on the reality of him. The flesh and blood reality of him was a little harder to live with than I had remembered. I saw him in a different light, a light which was not always flattering. I also realised that Gordon had spoiled me in a number of ways. He was easy to be with, he was thoughtful, took care of me, spent a good deal of time smoothing over rough spots rather than creating them. But in spite of it all, I still continued to glow and grin and love Chris, and feel foolish, falling all over myself, loving the fact that I was able to reach out and touch him again. In spite of how I felt about Gordon. Chris was Chris.

On Thursday of that week, Julie was operated on again, and the hospital would only say that her condition was satisfactory and that she was in the Intensive Care Unit and could have no visitors. My knowledge of hospital language was meagre but nevertheless adequate enough to make a reasonable translation of what they were saying. Satisfactory didn't mean a whole hell of a lot, but the Intensive Care Unit meant plenty You didn't go there for a broken toe, you went there with a good chance of not coming out again, and you weren't liable to enjoy your stay while you were there, if you even remembered it. It was a highly specialised unit, for very, very sick people, with monitors that told the staff exactly what your body was doing and what the chances were that your body would go on doing it. They didn't relay that kind of information to anyone except each other, so there was no way of knowing how Julie really was, other than 'Satisfactory'.

On Friday, John Templeton called me into his office, with Jean, Gordon, Eloise Franck, and three other people who looked familiar but whom I didn't know. I realised once we were seated and John started to talk about Julie that we were the select elite who knew the truth about

Julie. And we were about to get the next bulletin.

'Julie was operated on yesterday, as you all know. They did a biopsy of the bone tissue. She has . . . (pause; count on John for a little drama) . . . bone cancer. The prognosis is a little vague. It could be a year, or even two years, or it could be a matter of weeks. They just don't know. A lot depends on how she rallies from the shock of the operation. She's very weak, and we're keeping close tabs to see how she's doing. She can't have visitors, but as soon as we know something I'll let you know. In the meantime, all we can do is pray, and once again I'd like to ask you not to share this information with the rest of the staff. There will be time enough for that later. And if she rallies in the next few weeks, then she'll enjoy as many visitors as possible. Until then, I don't think there's much point in talking about it. Thank you, and I'm very sorry. I feel just as rotten about this as you do.'

With that, there were murmurs of 'Thanks, John,' and a shuffling of chairs, there were a lot of cigarettes lit, and we all walked out of the office, without speaking to each other, looking sombre, feeling alone.

Gordon walked me back to my office, and walked in with me, closing the door behind him. He took me in his arms, and we rocked back and forth together. We were both crying. Gordon Harte, the man who had seen everything, who had lost Juanita, the girl that he hadn't minded finding out had been a prostitute, was crying for Julie Weintraub, and we stood in each other's arms, crying also for each other.

26

Surprisingly, the relationship with Gordon suffered little from Chris's sudden appearance. Thanks to Gordon. He was making a tremendous effort not to change the pace. There were no mercurial ascents, or descents, no pressure, despite the fact that we saw each other less. And, inevitably, slept with each other less.

In contrast to things with Gordon, life with Chris was stormy, up and down, subject to hourly changes, as always. There were beautiful moments, followed by anger, and tears, and bitterness on my part about the recurring theme of Marilyn. We spent increasing amounts of time discussing our problems, and it was apparent that the situation needed action, either repair or commitment to one alternative or another. It had stood too long in one place and, whereas Chris was willing to let it stay there, I was not.

As for Julie, she stayed in a coma for two weeks following the operation and then proceeded to rally beyond everyone's hopes and prayers. She looked thin and wan but sounded wonderful. Her sense of humour was the same as ever, her interest in the magazine continued, she gave us some very good suggestions for the next issue, and she ran a sort of Rest & Recreation Club, cum bar, for everyone at the magazine. People were in and out of her room all day long, and at any given time you could find at least five or six editors sitting by her bed. And, to be honest, Eloise Franck was unbelievable. She was there every day, not hanging on like the hospital ghouls who come to sniff the ether-flavoured air and watch the dying, but she was there being herself: tough, cheerful, efficient, and bitchy. She organised a blood donors' committee at the magaizne, and at other magazines where she knew the editors, to minimise the cost of the constant transfusions they were giving Julie. Eloise may have been a tough number, but I respected her, and there was a heart somewhere beneath it all. She surprised me, and so did some others. It's amazing who crawls out of the woodwork when the chips are down. The people you expect to surface first sometimes let you down, and the guys way out in left field come in and knock you off your seat with a whole lot of loving. It was nice to watch. Eloise became human, and so did the rest of us. We all stood around in a magic circle, trying to keep Julie buoyed up, giving blood, and trying to give her something more, that magical life serum which makes you want to keep going.

I had asked Chris to come up and see Julie with me, but he wouldn't.

'What's the point, Gill? It's not going to do anything for either of us, and she doesn't even know me. Besides hospitals and funerals are against my principles. It would be hypocritical, like going to church, which you know I don't believe in either.'

'It's called humanity, Chris. Or don't you believe in that either?' ... And there was one more thing to bitch at each other about.

Nothing is ever cut and dried, however, and neither was the situation with Chris. Had it been all bad, had he really appeared as the Villain from the Far West, it would have been simple. But it wasn't. He was good and bad, loveable and hateful, beautiful and ugly. It was all very grey, and even if it had been black, the fact was that I loved him.

As our month together drew to a close, I hadn't come to any further conclusions about it, and neither had he, but he hadn't come East for me to come to conclusions anyway. It would just have been nice if I had.

The last few days had a kind of tenderness to them, because we didn't know when we'd see each other again and once again I was trying to drink it all in to hold on to it in memory. It was like twilight, like a beautiful summer night when the fireflies begin to come out once again. I loved Chris as much as I had in California, and the bitterness about Marilyn was momentarily forgotten. I was resigned to the fact that he was going back to her; there was nothing I could do.

Gordon seemed to sense what was happening and didn't ask me to see him the last five or six days before Chris was to leave. He steered a wide berth, and I was grateful. I just wanted to be alone with Chris. I took an extra day off from work and we took Samantha to the country after the first snow, had snowball fights and walked in the snow, kissed and laughed and sang Christmas carols.

Christmas was the following Wednesday, and I had hoped to spend it with Chris, but he seemed to want to go back. His job was over and he had no reason to stay on, except for me. That never played much on Chris. Whenever he decided to go, he went.

I expected him to leave that weekend, though he hadn't said it, and I was bracing myself for the impact. I had Christmas shopping to do but was putting it off until after he left. I didn't want to waste a second of our time together.

On Friday, I woke up and Chris was already dressed. He had that 'I've got something to tell you' look on his face, and I braced myself to hear that he was leaving that afternoon.

'I've decided when I'm going.'

'Pray, hit me with it quick.'

'Christ, Gill, will you please not look like that. You make me feel like such a bastard. You almost make me think I should leave now, just to get it over with.'

'I'm sorry. It's just that . . . well, you know how I feel.'

'How could I help it? I was going to tell you, you big worrier, that I'm going to leave the day after Christmas, Thursday, the twenty-sixth. Sound okay? Hope I'm not messing up any plans.'

'What plans? Christopher Matthews, I love you!!! Hurrah!!!! Hallelujah! Let's go Christmas shopping today.'

'Oh Christ . . . I'm leaving . . . in New York? Do you know what the stores look like? And you shouldn't be in crowds like that.'

'Come on, don't be such a drip, we don't have to stay long. Anyway, I want to take Sam to see Santa Claus.'

'Why does she have to see Santa Claus? Don't you know it's not healthy to fill kids' heads with all that bullshit?'

'Come on, Chris, be a sport. Please???'

'Okay, okay, but after that we get to do what I want.'

'Deal . . . Chris? . . . What about Marilyn?'

'What about Marilyn?'

'Well, I mean, with Christmas and all?'

'Look, you seem to forget that I'm not married to her. And it's my problem, and Gillian I'm just not going to discuss it with you any more. I mean it. The subject is closed.'

'Okay, get me a cup of coffee will you. I'll be dressed in half an hour.'

I bought Chris a Patek-Phillippe watch, which was insanity on my part, but I knew he'd love it. He loved fine things, and the watch was beautiful. Like a Salvador Dali painting, it was as flat as they could make it, and had a beautiful simple face, and a black suede watch-band. For my mother I got a dressing-gown, for my father a humidor, which I knew he'd have twelve of, but I couldn't think of anything else. For Hilary and Peg I got small, silly things. For Julie the sexiest bed jacket I could find and three dirty books. And for Gordon, I bought an old leather-bound volume of Don Quixote. I had ordered a rather spectacular doll's house for Samantha a few days before. I knew Chris would disapprove of it and she would love it.

I had decided to send John Templeton some scotch, unimaginative, but it seemed okay and for Jean Edwards and the girls at the magazine I had gotten funny hats in a thrift shop weeks before, thinking we'd have some good laughs out of them.

On the twenty-third, Gordon and I went up to see Julie at the hospital, and she didn't look well at all. She had that bright, glittering look that people get with a fever. We brought her a bottle of champagne, and our presents, and there was something so unbearably sad about the whole scene that I had to turn away once or twice to pull myself together.

Afterwards, I gave Gordon his present and he gave me a lovely hand-wrought leather box, 'a magic box for your treasures, Gillian . . . and old love letters.' In it was a card with a poem, signed 'Love, G.' . . . and I was touched. It was an odd gift, not personal and yet terribly personal . . . very much like Gordon . . . I had always wanted a box like that, something to put eucalyptus nuts in, and dried flowers, and buttons from shirts, and things like that, things which mean nothing to anyone because they're so ordinary, except they mean everything because of what they stand for. Gordon was going to be with his sister in Maryland for Christmas, which made things easier for me.

On Christmas Eve, Chris and I stayed home and made popcorn in the fireplace and chased Samantha back to bed every ten minutes. We decorated the tree and kissed, and he did the top while I did the bottom, because ladders were off limits to me.

'Well, little fat girl, want your present now?' He had a gleam in his eye.

'Yup. How about you?'

'Sure.'

I brought out the Cartier box and began to worry. Maybe it was the wrong gift for him after all, the wrapping looked so pompous next to the little box wrapped in cheap paper that he put in my hand.

'You first,' I said. Chris agreed, and began to tear off the paper, while guessing what might be in the box. He sat there with it in his hand, unwrapped, and the box still closed, while I held my breath and wished I had bought him something for his stereo, or a ski sweater, or new ski boots . . .

He opened the box and his wide little-boy grin appeared and he just chortled. I felt like Santa Claus. He liked it! He liked it! Hip! Hip! Hooray! He had it on his wrist and was winding and checking, polishing, and looking at it, and he almost squeezed me to death he was so pleased.

'Your turn . . .'

'Okay, here goes.' I began tearing the blue foil paper off the little box. Underneath the paper was a silver and red cardboard box, the kind you get at the dime store. I pried open the lid and there was a midnight blue velvet box that snapped open on a stiff hinge to reveal bold letters saying 'Tiffany & Co.,' and an unbelievable flash of blue-white diamond lying on the velvet. It lay there staring at me, attached to a thin gold chain. It was a pendant. I could hardly breathe, I was so stunned, and it made me want to cry.

'You sneak. You big fraud, you phony shit. I love you so much, how could you give me something like this?' and I hugged him and squeezed him and gulped. 'It's so beautiful, darling . . . wow!'

'I don't know, I might take it back and sell it some time.' Typical Chris remark.

'You will not. Put it on for me. My hands are shaking too hard.'

And I headed for the mirror and saw it staring back at me, like a headlight. Wow!

We turned off the lights and looked at the Christmas tree for a while, and then went to bed and made love, and lay there, holding hands, almost asleep.

'Hey, Gill . . .'

'Yes, love?'

'Let's get married some time before the baby's born.'

'You mean marry you?'

'Uh huh. That's what I said, isn't it?'

'I accept!' I didn't ask about Marilyn, but I thought it. I didn't think he meant what he'd said. But I hoped to hell he did. As I hugged him closer, I saw that he was wearing his watch, and I smiled and touched the diamond around my neck before I fell asleep.

27

The next morning was Christmas, and it was chaotic, and full of squeals from Samantha. As predicted, the doll's house got rave reviews from Sam and a disapproving look from Chris.

At the end of the day, we went for another long walk in Central Park. There was more snow on the ground, and the park was empty. Everyone was busy with family and friends. It was nice to have the park to ourselves.

'Chris?'

'Hmmmm . . .?'

'Did you mean what you said last night?'

'Yeah. Why not? You only live once, and it'd be too bad to have the kid be a bastard.'

'Is that why you're doing it?'

'No, you ass. What do you think? I'm not made that way. I just figure maybe I better keep you off the streets before that guy, Gordon, decides to marry you from his wheelchair.'

'Chris! He's not that old, and what makes you think he'd marry me anyway?'

'I may be good-natured, but don't think I'm stupid. Besides, I can read.'

'Oh, the poem.'

'Yeah, that. And some other things. Besides I had a feeling . . . How soon do you think you could come out? I think you ought to give me about two weeks . . . ahhh . . . "to get my house in order."'

'Yes. I'd think you'd need that. I can't leave before

215

that anyway. I can't leave then in the lurch at the magazine. Chris? How're you going to handle that . . . I mean out there?' What I meant was Marilyn.

'You let me worry about that. You just keep your ass in line, and come on out when you get squared away.'

'You know, it'll take me a little time to rent the apartment again and get everything settled here. Besides, the magazine . . .'

'You and that goddam magazine, woman. I need you more than they do.'

'Since when? . . . Do you Chris?'

'What do you think?' We kissed again and walked home hand in hand.

In bed that night, I lay there looking at his stuff all piled in a corner and the impact of his departure began to hit me. And I began to cry, because I was sorry to see him go, but there was more.

'Chris, it's not that simple. There are a lot of problems. Like Marilyn, and the other Marilyns; maybe there'll always be a Marilyn. I couldn't stand it. And we're so different, and I irritate you so much sometimes, and . . . oh hell, I don't know. I really worry about us sometimes.'

'Are you trying to tell me you don't want to marry me? Give me my diamond back.'

'Nuts to you. No, I'm serious. I'm not telling you I won't marry you, but I'm telling you I'm scared.'

'Of me?'

'Well, no . . . yes. In a way.'

'So don't marry me.'

'But I want to marry you . . . oh, you don't understand . . .'

'I understand. Now just shut up and go to sleep. Jesus, if you were in Heaven you'd find something to worry about. Stop bitching and go to sleep.'

'I'm not bitching . . .'

'Yes you are. Now go to sleep. I have to get up early tomorrow.' . . . That was so like Chris. I wanted to talk.

'How soon do you want to get married, darling?'

'Are you still at it? As soon as you're ready. In the delivery room, if it makes you happy. Okay?'

'Okay. Good night. Hey, Chris?'

'Now what?'

'Merry Christmas.'

'G'night.' He was already half-asleep.

The next morning I watched him go with the proverbial heavy heart. Departures always make me sad, and I felt so alone after he was gone.

Strangely, when I got back to the apartment I had a desperate urge to call Gordon and cling to him, but it seemed like a dirty trick, and I hadn't yet decided what to say to him. Basically, it was simple. 'Gordon, I'm leaving. Chris and I are getting married.' But how do you say that to someone? How do you even start?

I gave John Templeton notice on Monday and managed to avoid Gordon for the entire day, berating myself for being a monster and a coward. The rest of the week I spent at home with a bad cold, hovering between bed and the living-room, where the packing cases for our move were rapidly filling up. I was going to leave right after New Year's, come hell or high water.

I hadn't heard from Gordon all week, but I had decided that somehow I'd tell him at Hilary's on New Year's Eve. Maybe the champagne would make it easier for both of us.

She had another of her quiet, but stimulating gatherings. And at midnight, Hilary made a lovely toast, and held her glass up in honour of her guests. We rose and drank to her, and then everyone sat down again in small groups. The conversation was carried on in low voices, the room was bright with candlelight, and the magical sad/tender aura of New Year's Eve surrounded us all.

And then Gordon looked up and saw me watching him, smiled a tiny smile, and spoke softly so the others couldn't hear.

'To you, Gillian. May the new year bring you wisdom and peace. May your child bring you joy, and may Chris be good to you. Vaya con Dios.' Tears sprang to my eyes as he lifted his glass and his eyes reached into mine. He knew.

The next time I saw John Templeton in the hall, he looked at me with a harried air of fatigue.

'Why is it that I always lose the best people I've got?'

'Thanks for the compliment, John, but you'll do fine without me. You did before.' He only shook his head and moved on down the hall, and that was the last I saw of him until the farewell party they gave me on Friday. Gordon and I went together and we said little to each other. He had been kind but remote since the party at Hilary's and he seemed to have a lot on his mind. And then I caught the gist of what was happening as I said good-bye to the staff. Gordon was leaving too. As he took me home, I wondered why he hadn't told me. He must have been thinking about it for a while.

'When did you decide?'

'Oh, I've been thinking of it for some time.' But he avoided my eyes and sounded vague.

'Are you taking another job?'

'No. I'm going back to Europe.'

'Spain?'

'No. Eze. It's a little town in the South of France. It may have gone to hell by now, full of pizza parlours and tourists. But it was beautiful ten years ago and I thought

218

I'd go back and take a look. I want to spend the rest of my life painting somewhere like that, not wasting the years in this bullshit jungle.'

'I'm glad you're going, Gordon. I think it's the right thing.'

He nodded, smiled, and kissed me on the forehead as he left me at the hotel.

'See you tomorrow.'

'Fine, I'll give you a call.' But he didn't look as though his heart was in it. We had agreed to spend my last day in New York together, Saturday. I was leaving on Sunday morning.

That night, I went up to see Julie at the hospital, and it was the hardest thing I did before I left. What do you say? 'Thanks for the job'? 'Good luck'? 'See you soon'? No, you just try not to cry.

We made small talk, but Julie's mind was wandering, and before I left she fell asleep. Her mind was greatly affected by the Demerol and whatever else they were giving her. She had shrunken, and faded, she looked old and grey, so tiny and frail in that bed.

I watched her sleep, and patted her arm, and she opened one eye and smiled. I kissed her cheek, and mumbled something without thinking, probably just 'Thanks, Julie,' and she closed her eyes again and drifted off. As I looked at her one last time, I heard myself murmur, 'Vaya con Dios.' The same thing Gordon had said to me.

28

Sam and I were staying at the Regency again for our last two days in New York. And through some miracle we had ended up with the same suite. We were going to leave as we had arrived. In style. Except that so much had happened in the four months we'd been in New York that it was hard to believe we hadn't been back for years.

The phone rang as we were finishing breakfast. It was Gordon.

'This is your tour leader and social director, Mrs Forrester. We have your schedule all planned for you,' and I giggled, wondering what was coming next. 'First, you will be picked up by the tour leader, and you will proceed to point one on the day's itinerary: Fifty-ninth Street and Fifth Avenue, where you will be drawn by an ancient horse around Central Park. The horse may or may not die *en route*, and in case he does, your tour leader will place you on his shoulders and continue the journey. Please do not wear shoes with spurs, as your tour leader has very sensitive ribs. Thank you for your consideration, Mrs Forrester. Next, you will go to the Hotel Plaza for lunch in the Edwardian Room, and after that you have a choice between (*a*) a quick stop at Parke-Bernet Auction Galleries, (*b*) a tour of the Museum of Modern Art, (*c*) a shopping tour, or (*d*) you may tell your tour guide to fuck off, and you may go home and rest. After that, you will be taken to the Sherry-Netherland Bar for one and one half drinks, please present your coupon to the bartender. And then you will be taken to La Caravelle for dinner, check your camera at the cloak room, and be sure to wear gold shoes, a sweater with a mink collar, or fox will do fine. After dinner at La Caravelle, you will then go to Raffles, where you will dance with your tour leader. Again please do not wear spurs; your tour leader also has sensitive arches. And after that you will go to one of New York's most charming hide-aways, for our mystery surprise. And that, Mrs Forrester, is the day we have planned for you. Welcome to New York.' And it struck me again what a good man he was and what a hell of a good sport.

'Gordon Harte, you are something else. What time do we start?'

'How about eleven?'

'Well . . .'

'Make it eleven-thirty. I'll meet you in the lobby.'

'Oh, listen, Gordon?'

'Yes?'

'I promised Sam I'd take her to the zoo "one last time."'

'No problem. When?'

'I have a sitter for her now. After her nap? Say around four?'

'That's fine. Ask her if I can come too.'

'I think that can be arranged. See you soon, and thanks.'

Gordon appeared in the lobby at eleven-thirty sharp, looking terribly pleased with himself.

'Well, Mr Tour Leader, what's next?'

'The hansom cab, but first your chariot awaits,' and as we pushed through the revolving doors of the hotel I looked for his car, and wondered who belonged to the outlandish fire engine red Rolls Royce parked smack in front of the hotel. It had licence plates with a 'Z' at the end, which meant it was rented, probably for some Texan, or at least someone with a sense of humour.

'Madame,' and there was Gordon holding open the door of the red Rolls, with a sweep of his arm, and a huge grin. The chauffeur stood by in a liveried uniform, looking as though he took the whole scene seriously. It was absolutely absurd, and I stood there and whooped. I laughed so hard I felt like doubling over. I looked at Gordon, and back at the car, and then laughed until tears ran down my face.

'Oh, Gordon, really.'

'Come on, get in. I thought your last day in New York should be memorable,' and so it was. Once inside the Rolls, there was a bar, a television, a stereo, a telephone, and a vase with a red rose. It was definitely something from a Rock Hudson-Doris Day movie.

We did all the things Gordon had planned, except that after lunch we went for a walk instead of choices (a), (b), (c), or (d), and then we went to pick up Sam at the hotel. She was thrilled with the red car, and the first thing she said was, 'Is it a present? Can we keep it?' with wide eyes. Gordon and I started to laugh again.

'No, sweetheart, it's just for today, kind of a joke. It's a present from Gordon, just for today.'

'I don't think it's a joke. I like it.'

'Samantha, you remember that when you're a big girl,' Gordon said with a serious expression and I added the suspicion that she probably would.

When we got to Sixty-fourth Street and Fifth Avenue, the chauffeur stopped the car and whipped around to my side to let us out, and we headed for the zoo. Gordon was carrying a camera I hadn't noticed before.

'I want to take some pictures. Do you mind? I won't if you'd rather not.'

'No, it's okay. I'd like to have some myself. But be sure you take one of the car,' I said grinning over my shoulder, trying to keep track of Sam.

'I don't have any pictures of you, Gillian, and I'd like to have some . . . Who knows, we may not meet again . . .'

'Oh, Gordon, don't be silly. Of course we will,' but I wondered too.

'Eze and San Francisco are not exactly next door to each other, my dear. And when you leave someone, you never know what will happen. When I say good-bye, I always believe that it will be forever.'

'That's funny, when I say good-bye I always tell myself that we'll be seeing each other again.'

'Do you believe it?'

'No, I guess not. Not deep in my heart,' and I felt sad then. I looked up at Gordon, but he looked away.

So for an hour Gordon took photographs of Samantha with balloons, Cracker Jacks, on the pony ride, watching the seals, and of me. They were quick photographs. He kept catching us with our mouths full of Cracker Jacks, and our eyes closed, or a hand up, or laughing. He shot, and he shot, and he ran around the other way and took more pictures . . . click, click, click, click, click, click . . . the last day in the life of Gordon and Gillian . . . 'sing me no songs, tell me no tales, cry me no tears' . . . but remember me kindly.

The last photograph on the roll of film was taken by the chauffeur of all three of us as we stood in front of the open door of the red Rolls, Samantha holding a bright red balloon, and I realised as we stepped into the car that it would be the only photograph that would include Gordon.

The rest of the day went according to the 'tour leader's' plan, and at midnight we were ready to leave Raffles and head for the big 'mystery surprise'. The Rolls was still with us, and we headed uptown and East, towards what I assumed correctly would be Gordon's apartment.

We arrived and went upstairs. He opened the door, stepped in ahead of me, flipped some switches, lit candles, and then came back to help me with my coat. The room looked lovely – it was full of flowers, and there was champagne in an ice bucket on the coffee table, in front of the couch. He lit the fire and turned on some music, and it all looked perfect. Kind of a funny scene for a lady about to go off and get married to someone else three thousand miles away, and expecting that man's child. But it was lovely. I knew that life with Chris would have its own kind of beauty, many tender moments, and many problems too. But life with Chris was of another texture; it would not be of candlelight and champagne. Sadly enough, one rarely marries the candlelight and champagne. One marries instead the blue jeans and rumpled T-shirts, the Coca Cola and burnt toast, and one puts away the candlelight and champagne in a magic box. In the long run, I guess Coca Cola and burnt toast are easier to live with.

As though he had read my thoughts, Gordon handed me the champagne cork and said 'for your magic box.' I took it and smiled back at him, and then he took the cork back for a moment and wrote something on it. When he returned it, it had the date, only that, nothing more.

'I don't want to confuse your children in fifty years with a lot of initials they won't know.' It was kind of a sad thing to say, because I knew he meant it.

'When are you leaving for Europe?'

'Oh, I'd say in about a month.'

'How does Greg feel about it? Have you told him yet?'

'Yes, I called him yesterday, as a matter of fact. You know something, Gillian, I think he's impressed. I think

I've finally gone and done something that my son approves of. I'm "abandoning" all the materialistic things he holds me in contempt for, and doing something he thinks he understands. He said he'd come over and see me next summer. I think he means it.'

'I'm sure he does. I can't blame him. I wouldn't mind a summer in the south of France myself.'

'What, and leave sunny California?'

I tried to smile and then looked at him for an interminable moment. 'Gordon, will you write to me?'

'Maybe. I'm not very good about that though. And I don't think Chris would think it such a great idea. But I'll let you know where I am.' He had already taken his distance, and it showed.

'Chris won't mind.' . . . And I want to hear from you . . . please . . .

'Don't be so sure. He's no fool, and he doesn't like me. That much I know. And I don't blame him. I wouldn't like me either, in his shoes. Gillian, don't leave yourself open to where he has an excuse to hurt you.'

I nodded silently and he poured two more glasses which emptied the bottle. Louis Roederer 1956, the champagne of Charles de Gaulle. And Gordon Harte.

We emptied our glasses and then sat looking silently into the fire, each with our own thoughts. We had been so very civilised, so controlled, and had said so much with the way we looked at each other, and so little with our words. And I knew that leaving Gordon was going to be one of the most difficult moments of my life . . . that last instant . . . that very last look. I had already been through that once, with Chris, and in its own way this would be no easier.

I turned towards his profile next to me on the couch. The splendid head was turned slightly away from me, the beard jutting out, the eyes closed, and then his hand made a brutal gesture, and there was the sound of tinkling glass as his glass crumbled in the fireplace. I knew what he had meant by the gesture. Perhaps by hurling the glass away and watching it smash it was easier to understand that what we had had was over too.

Gordon stood up without speaking, got my coat, and we walked slowly towards the door.

All the way back to the hotel, we sat without speaking, holding hands, and looking out at the city rolling by. Leftovers of the last snow still lay in the gutter, freezing one more time, getting a little greyer.

The car stopped at the hotel, and Gordon moved to get out as the driver held upen the door on my side of the car.

'No, don't get out. Please.' My voice sounded hoarse. Gordon took me tightly in his arms and kissed the top of my head. I moved my face up to his and we kissed, my eyes squeezed tightly shut, tears oozing slowly out of the corners towards my hair. I opened my eyes then and saw that Gordon was crying too . . .

'I love you, Gordon . . .'

'Good-bye, my darling. Know always how much I care.'

I stepped out of the car and ran towards the revolving door, never looking back . . . good-bye . . . good-bye . . . au revoir, not adieu . . .

But there was no point thinking of what I might have had with Gordon. I had chosen Chris. I loved Chris. And I went up in the elevator, with my eyes tightly closed, whispering to myself . . . I love Chris . . . I love Chris . . . I love . . .

29

The flight to California was peaceful and a little strange. I felt as though I were suspended in a cocoon between two worlds, a special place in which to hide and think. I had five hours to totally abandon Gordon's world and re-enter Chris's, and I was grateful for the few hours I had to belong to no one but myself. It was eerie how the metamorphosis took place.

As I soared high over the skyscrapers of New York, my heart tugged painfully as I looked down to the rapidly shrinking places which had meant something in the past few months. And as though I were sliding down to the other side of my rainbow, I began to feel excitement grow within me as we circled low over the peninsula, nearing San Francisco. I was going back to Chris . . . to Chris . . . to Chris!

I looked at Sam and squeezed her hand. I had the feeling that we had finally made it home. Hallelujah, baby!

We arrived exactly on time, and when we emerged into the terminal building, there was Chris. And I lit up inside. He smiled that little boy smile of his just for me. We looked into each other's eyes, and all was right with the world. New York, Gordon, Julie Weintraub, they were all a million miles away, on another planet.

'You look tired. Bad flight?'

'No, good flight. Bad week in New York. It was one hell of a lot of work,' not just work, but easier to put it down to that.

We collected our bags and piled into the Volkswagen bus Chris had borrowed from a friend. I waited for Samantha to tell him about the Rolls the day before, and kind of held my breath. I didn't want to have to get into explanations just then. But she didn't say a thing. I figured it would come out instead one day when it was least expected, maybe two months later. And by then it wouldn't matter any more.

We drove into town and I looked around with this incredible feeling of, 'My God, here it is . . . wow!' San Francisco does that to me, it takes my breath away, and scoops me up, and I feel like I'm going to fly away. I wanted to drive all over the city and see everything I loved, but that was not Chris's style. It would never have occurred to him that that was what I wanted to do. We drove straight home, where we dumped the bags in the living-room, and I went to see what there was in the refrigerator. Nothing. Welcome home. Two half-full bottles of club soda, three cokes, a mouldy lemon, and a jar of peanut butter that had probably been untouched since last July.

'There's nothing to eat in here, Chris.'

'I know. It's still early though. We can go to the store. You drive my car while I take the bus back.'

'What about Sam?'

'We'll take her with us.'

'Okay, but I want to get her to bed early. It'll be late for her with the time difference and she's tired from the trip.'

'She doesn't look tired to me.' She was racing through the place and had taken possession of 'her' room.

Well, I knew I was back. The refrigerator was empty and we were going to the store. No roses or champagne in sight. That had been yesterday. But I had known that. I had chosen mouldy lemons and flat club soda over roses and champagne. I knew I could have had the roses and champagne, but I didn't really want them. I wanted to go to the store with Chris, and ride around in a borrowed Volkswagen bus.

'Whatcha thinking, Gill?'

'That I love you,' and I meant every word of it. I was home, and it felt great. I put on my jeans, with a safety pin to cover where the zipper wouldn't close, and a sweater of Chris's, with my raincoat, and we went out to return the bus and buy food. We looked like a family, and Chris looked beautiful. I was so happy I felt as though I were about to burst.

As we walked out of the house I thought of something, 'Chris? Where are we going to put the baby?'

'Cool it, will you. You've been here one hour and you're already bitching at me. We'll put it somewhere. Don't worry about it now for chrissake.'

'I'm not worrying. I just thought of it.'

'Well, stop thinking. I'll meet you at the Safeway in ten minutes.' He gave me a peck on the cheek and drove off with a wave. Then he shot back in reverse, almost hitting the car, as I got ready to start it.

'Watch the choke!'

'Okay . . . Hey! . . . And stop bitching at me!' I was giving some of his own back.

'Fuck you.' He grinned and drove off.

'Same to you, fella.' . . . God, it was so nice to be back. It wasn't elegant, or anything like a fairy tale, but it was my fairy tale, and at the same time it was real. Beautiful and real. Like Chris.

30

Chris lived in a ramshackle Victorian-style house on Sacramento Street, just near enough to the elegant Pacific Heights district to make the neighbourhood pleasant, but not so close as to be actually in it. We were up at the west end of the city, and the fog would stay up in that section till almost noon on mornings when the sun would be shining downtown. At five o'clock the fog would roll back in, and at night you could hear the fog horns, very faintly in the distance.

To me, San Francisco has always been an enchanted city, something of a dream place. It has all the physical beauty that the postcards suggest, and an easy lifestyle that reminds me of Europe. People are friendly, not in the put-on way of Los Angeles, but in the way of smaller towns in the West. It is a city, and a non-city. Within minutes you can be in the country or at the beach, and the mountains are only a couple of hours away. The air is still fresh, and we had a tiny garden where Samantha used to dig for worms and look for snails.

The house itself was something of a bomb shelter. It could have been really super if Chris had wanted to spend any time fixing it up, but there was always something else he wanted to do, so it got a little shabbier and a little more weather-beaten all the time. Victorian houses are fairly common in San Francisco. The exteriors have a lot of charm, and inside the floors slope, the ceilings are arched, and the windows are often bayed.

The morning after our arrival I turned over in bed and

looked up at the ceiling, and out the window, at the trees that reached up from the garden. It was quiet and I felt as though I were in the country. I looked over at Chris, still asleep, and grinned. I thought that even without Christopher I would have loved San Francisco. After all I had fallen in love with the city before I had fallen in love with the man. I heard Samantha walking around and got up to make her breakfast. No more mother's helper. That had been part of the deal with Chris. Sam and I came out alone.

Chris rolled over as I got out of bed and opened an eye. '. . . time is it? Come on back to bed . . .'

'Got to feed Sam,' and I kissed him. 'Good morning. It's so nice to be back, Chris.'

'Sure, honey. Bring me a glass of orange juice, will you?'

'Better than that. You stay in bed, I'll call you when breakfast is ready.'

'Okay.' And he turned over again and went back to sleep, looking like a boy, his hair all rumpled up and his head tucked under his arms, the covers almost over his head.

Breakfast was long and noisy, and we decided what to do for the day. Chris had some things to do and Sam wanted to 'go see Julius,' i.e., the Julius Kahn playground in the Presidio.

'You can see Julius tomorrow, Sam. We're going to stay home and unpack and clean up the house a little. How about helping Mommy today?'

'I don't want to,' and the whining started.

'Well then, how about looking for worms in the garden.' Yech, me suggesting that?

'That's a good idea, Mommy. I'll see if I can find some for you.' Wonderful.

I wanted to unpack, but what I really wanted to do was

231

get the house in order. Before, it had been Chris's place, but if we were going to get married the house was going to undergo some changes. The mechanical stuff Chris would have to do, but I was going to attack it with a lot of soap and water, and at least put up new curtains, and get a bedspread . . . and the bathrooms! . . .

I dug around for some cleaning equipment as Chris headed out the door shouting, 'See you later, gang!' I was busy thinking that, whatever else Marilyn may have been good at, she had been one hell of a lousy house-keeper. That had probably been part of the charm.

By two o'clock the place looked a lot better, and Sam and I went to buy some flowers. 'How about woses, Mommy?'

'How about daisies, Samantha, and corn flowers, and maybe some nice red flowers?'

'Wed woses.'

'No, wed something else. Roses cost too much money.'

'Are we poor now? Are we gonne staaaarve?' Her big eyes looked up at me, half-filled with fear, and half-seeming to enjoy the prospect.

'No, we are certainly not going to "staaaarve". We just don't want to spend too much money, that's all.'

'Oh.' She seemed disappointed. 'When do we pick up the baby?'

'Not for a.while yet. Almost two whole months. That's still a long way off.'

'Oh . . . why not today?'

'The house isn't ready yet,' which reminded me that I had discovered the right place for the baby that morning and wanted to tell Chris. It was kind of a walk-in closet with a window, just about the right size for a crib and a chair and a little chest. It was right next to our room and had two doors, one leading to the hall, the other to our room. We didn't need the closet and, fixed up, it could

232

be really cute. That way the baby would be right next to us, without actually being in the room. It wouldn't work forever, but for six months or so it would be just right. After that, we could put the baby in Sam's room.

Chris's house was roomy, though small. It had a living-room, a tiny dining-room and kitchen downstairs, two bedrooms on the second floor, and above that a bright studio room which Chris used as his office. That was sacred territory, and there was absolutely no question of putting the baby up there. Besides, it was draughty, and the heating didn't reach up there. It had a great fireplace, though, which Chris had going most of the time.

When Chris came home I told him about my idea for the baby's room and he promised to get some paint and to get to work on it.

'Hey, Gillian, it smells funny in here. What is it?'

'That, my love, is an unfamiliar odour called clean. I scrubbed the place all morning.'

'Should you do that? Don't go around being an ass now. Did you pick anything up?'

'No, I did not pick anything up,' and I kissed him and smiled over his head. He was beginning to sound as though he cared about the baby, or about me. It was new and made me feel kind of tingly.

Chris leaned over and whispered in my ear, 'Get rid of Sam.'

'What do you mean?'

'I mean, get rid of Sam . . . want to make love to you . . .'

'Oh . . . Sam, sweetheart, how were the worms this morning? Find any?'

'Nope, they musta been sleeping.'

'How 'bout taking another look before it gets too cold?'

'Okay. You want some too, Uncle Crits? Mommy loves worms.'

'Sure, you bring me some too,' and she banged out the back door and marched off to the garden with two old spoons, a toothpick, and a paper cup.

Chris grabbed my hand and we started running upstairs. 'Hey, wait a minute, you nut.'

'Wait nothing. I've been horny all day. Come on, woman!' And we ran up the stairs, laughing and giggling, and I almost tripped on the top step, which kind of sobered us a little, but not for long.

'I found 'em. Three of them,' and there was Sam. The door burst open and she had a whole handful of dirt and something that was squirming. 'Hey, you all sick? What's everybody sleeping for?'

'We're just having a nap. Your mother's tired.'

'Oh, well, here they are. I'll give 'em to you,' and she placed the whole revolting mess in Chris's hand and walked out singing to herself.

'Oh Jesus, Gillian, I think I'm going to throw up.'

'Me first,' and we both rushed for the bathroom, laughing.

Chris got there first and threw them into the toilet and flushed. 'Bllyyyyeeeeerrrgggggghhh. Who said all that shit about girls being sugar and spice? Hasn't anyone told Sam yet?'

'Come on, Chris, be a sport.'

'Be a sport? I didn't see you holding out a hand for that little handful of delicious.' And we started laughing again, while I ran the tub.

'Let's go for a drive before dinner. I haven't gotten a good look at the place yet. We worked in the house all day. I want to take a look around.'

'What d'you want to do that for, Gill?'

'Come on, Chris, please. As a special favour to me?'

'Okay, okay, but a short one. There's a game I want to watch on television.'

'Yessir.'

'Say, Mrs Forrester, by the way, when are we getting married? Or haven't you made up your mind yet?' He said it facetiously, but I knew he meant it. I had made up my mind, so it was all right.

'Well, I'll have to check my appointment calendar. How about Saturday?'

'Why not tomorrow?'

'Do you have a licence?'

'No.' He looked crestfallen.

'That's why not tomorrow. Today's Monday, we can go and get the licence tomorrow, which leaves Wednesday, Thursday, Friday . . . we can get married Friday, if you want.'

'No, I've got a job to do Friday. Saturday'll be okay . . . Gill? . . . Are you sure this is what you want? I mean, do you really know? I'm not the best husband material in the world.'

'Sounds like you're changing your mind, Mr Matthews.'

'It's not for me to change my mind. You're the one who's got to be sure.'

'Boy, talk about a switch! I'm sure, now just shut up and get in the tub, or I won't get to go for my drive.'

Chris took us down Broadway past the big old mansions, and then left on Divisadero down the steep hill where Steve McQueen had filmed the chase scene in *Bullitt*, and the house where they filmed *Pal Joey*, and as we came down the hill there was the bay, and Sausalito on

235

the other side, with the mountains behind it. As I came down that hill, I felt the way the pioneers must have as they came across the mountains and saw the Pacific. The roads had changed, but I was willing to bet the feeling hadn't. It took my breath away, and always gave me that same feeling. We drove all the way down to the Marina, and sat in the parked car at the waterfront, looking at the water, and watching the fog roll in slowly, coming through the Golden Gate Bridge, as though it was being held together by the structure of the bridge. It headed towards Alcatraz, and the fog horns started up. After a while, Chris said, 'Had enough?'

'No, but you can take us home now.'

'No, no, I wanna see Onion Square!' Sam squealed from the back seat. 'And the Hare Krishna people with the orange sheets and the bells.'

'They're probably home by now, Samantha, but we can go to Union Square if you want.'

Chris was really being a good sport about it.

'What about your game?' I didn't want to push a point . . .

'We've got time,' and he smiled over at us. I think he was enjoying it too.

We drove down Lombard, and down the part where it gets all crooked just before you get to Leavenworth Street. Sam squealed all the way down and loved every minute of it. We could see the Bay Bridge and Oakland as we were coming down. Up Powell, behind a cable car, waving at the people, mostly tourists, and they waved back. Union Square looked the same as always, and that is one part of the city that doesn't excite me a whole lot, but Sam loved it, even though she was disappointed that the Hare Krishnas had gone home. On the way home, Chris drove through Chinatown, which was another treat for Sam.

236

'Hey, want to have Chinese dinner?'

'No, come on, you want to watch the game. This has been plenty. But you're a love to ask.'

'No, I mean it. Let's stop and have an early dinner.'

'No, Chris, come on, let's go home.'

'Quiet . . . Sam, what do you think?'

'I want to eat dinner here. Can we, Uncle Crits, can we????'

'Yes, ma'am,' and we drove into the St Mary's garage and walked towards the milling people on Grant Avenue.

Dinner was delicious, and as usual I ate too much. Chris and Samantha worked it out with chopsticks or at least Chris did. Sam ate most of it with her fingers, and poked with the chopsticks. I ate with a fork, which got me a lot of scornful comments from both of them. But I was hungry and never could manage chopsticks.

Driving home we went through the Broadway tunnel, and that completed an evening of Heaven for Sam. A tunnel!! And it was an evening of Heaven for me too. Chris and I looked at each other over her head, and I blew him a kiss and mouthed, 'Thanks, I love you.' He mouthed back, 'Me too,' and by God we did. Whatever the last months had been, whatever Chris had done, or Marilyn, or I, or whomever, it was all buried by that look. Bad times may come again, but a prophecy had been fulfilled. 'The good times are coming,' the song said. And they had. They really, really, finally had.

31

On Tuesday, I put Sam back in her old playgroup in the morning, and then Chris and I went downtown to get the marriage licence. The place was crawling with Mexicans, and little kids, and odd-looking people who either looked too old to get married or as though they didn't really want to. I guess most of the young people weren't getting married any more, because we were about the only people our age that I saw. But then again, we didn't look so typical either – I was seven months pregnant and had suddenly blossomed. I stood there in my jeans and Chris's sweater, leading with my belly, and the clerk looked over and shook his head. 'I hope you make it, lady.' And then he shot a nasty glance at Chris, which made him squirm, and cracked me up.

'Did you see that old bastard, I mean did you see him?'

'Yeah, so what? What do you care?' Look who was getting sensitive. Poor Chris.

We picked up Sam and he dropped us off at the house. 'Got some stuff to do, see you later.'

'What stuff?'

'Just stuff, now come on, get out of the car.' He'd been in a bad mood since the marriage licence bureau. Stupid to let something like that bother you, but he was really upset.

'Okay, see you later,' and as Sam and I walked into the house I wondered if Chris were going to see Marilyn. It was just a thought, there was no reason why I should think of it, and the last couple of days had been perfect, but the thought crept up on me and took hold. I wondered if I'd always worry about that, or distrust him. He had learned one thing, and that was that his old openness had cost him something. I doubted if he'd be as honest about it next time he pulled a stunt like that. So I worried all afternoon, and started getting mad, and then worried again, and by the time he came home I was so relieved to have him back I didn't care where he'd been. I purposely didn't ask him what he'd done because I was still pretty much convinced he'd been up to something I didn't want to know about.

'Aren't you going to ask me where I've been?'

'No. Should I?'

'What's with you?'

'Nothing. Why?'

'You look funny. Feel okay?'

'Yeah, I'm okay,' but I was thinking about Marilyn again.

'Come over here, you big dope. Do you think . . .?' And I squirmed away because I knew what he was thinking, and I was thinking it, but I was ashamed of it. 'Hey, Gillian, Jesus . . . don't cry, there's nothing to cry about, everything's okay . . . hey . . . baby . . .' and there I was like a big fool, crying in his arms, admitting what I'd been thinking all afternoon.

'I told you. It's over. You don't have to worry about it any more. Now, come on out to the car.' He took my hand, led me down the steps, opened the car door, and started ripping newspapers off something in the back seat. It was a cradle, a beautiful, beautiful antique cradle, in dark burnished wood, with delicate carvings on it.

'Oh Chris . . .'

'There was an auction in Stockton today. I wanted to

239

surprise you. D'you like it?'

'Oh Chris! . . .' and I was crying again.

'Now what are you crying about?'

'Oh Chris . . .'

'You've already said that, now come on you silly girl. Give us a smile. There. Much better.'

'I'll help you get it out of the car.'

'No, ma'am. As long as you're still carrying what goes in the cradle, I'll carry the cradle. Just hold the doors open,' and he struggled up the steps holding the cradle.

'Don't hurt it,' and I held the doors open as wide as I could.

'You're too much,' and he grinned at me over his shoulder as he set it down in the hall.

'Chris? . . . You know something? You've changed.'

'So have you,' and we looked at each other for a long moment, and knew it was true.

32

The next couple of days were quiet. Sam was in school in the morning, and Chris was up in his studio most of the time, working on projects, busy with whatever it was he did up there. He'd come down for lunch and we'd have a quiet half-hour together before I picked Sam up at the playgroup. We were settling into a nice routine, and I felt as though I had never left, except for the fact that everything was better.

On Thursday, I looked up at Chris at lunch and told him I wanted to go downtown, shopping.

'What for?'

'A wedding dress.'

'You're kidding. Gillian, you don't mean it.'

'Yes I do. I want to get something new to wear. You know, something old, something new . . .'

'You've got something new: the baby. Does the maternity department carry wedding dresses these days?'

'Come on, Chris, be nice. I want to get something.'

'Have you thought of a colour? Like red maybe?'

'Chris! I shouldn't have told you.'

'No. You can do it. It's your business. It's your wedding, after all.'

'Well, it's yours too. But I want to look nice, and I don't have anything to wear.'

'What do you want to look nice for? Have you invited someone?'

'No, but I was going to talk to you about that too . . .'

'Oh no, Gillian, no way. You and I are going down to the justice of the peace, and we're getting married. No tourists. You can wear anything you goddam please, but you're not going to invite anybody. And I mean that.' And he looked as though he did.

'Okay, love. Okay. Don't get excited about it.'

'I'm not excited,' but he looked irritated and went back up to his garret while I cleaned up the lunch dishes.

After Sam was down for her nap in the afternoon I got dressed to go downtown and went up to the studio to tell Chris I was leaving.

'What's wrong with that?'

'What?'

'What you're wearing now?'

'Chris, I can't wear black to our wedding. It'd look like a bloody funeral for chrissake. Now come on . . . you said.'

'I know, I know. Go ahead and get yourself a veil while you're are it . . . with plastic cherries on it,' and I saw then that his good mood was back. He seemed to be finding the whole thing very funny. And as I closed the door behind me he started singing, 'Here comes the bride,' at the top of his lungs.

'Bug-off, Christopher,' but he just got louder.

I decided to make a real trip of it, parked the car in the Union Square Garage, and then headed for I. Magnin's. They were showing cruise clothes in all the windows, and once inside it felt more like New York than San Francisco. Everyone was all dressed up. It seemed a long way from Sacramento Street.

I went up in the elevator looking for the card that said 'Maternity' in the long line of descriptions of the different departments above the elevator doors. The elevator operator looked over at me, smiled and said 'Sixth.' I couldn't resist, so I looked back and smiled at her, and said, 'Bridal?' and her face froze. I laughed and said sixth would be fine.

'For a minute, there, I thought you meant it.'

I just laughed again as I stepped out . . . Oh lady, I do mean it. Yes I do.

The maternity department had as little charm as those places do, and I went through the racks finding nothing. The fabrics looked crummy, the colours were awful, everything had a bow just over the belly, or a high belt, or something that made me dislike it.

'May I help you?'

'I'm looking for something for my sister's wedding. It's an afternoon wedding, and it will be very small, so I don't want anything too formal.' That just about told her all she needed to know.

We looked and looked and came up with nothing.

242

Black was out, white was out, red was out, and I was pretty much out by the time we'd tried everything else on. 'How about a coat and dress? We got something in yesterday that would look very well on you. It's very tailored and light grey.'

Grey? For a wedding? And I really didn't need another coat.

But out came a marvellous soft grey dress with long sleeves and a perfectly straight shape, with buttons down the front, and a soft pointed collar, and wide cuffs; no belt, no bow over the belly, just two very large pockets set at a slant on either side. The buttons were covered in the same grey fabric, and the coat was perfectly plain and had the same straight, simple line, with a tiny gold chain belt in the back. It looked divine . . . with my grandmother's pearls, and black shoes . . . and . . .

'How much?'

'One forty-five.' Ouch, but what the hell, it was my wedding, and I could always use it again. I was getting a coat out of it after all.

'I'll take it.'

'Good. It looks wonderful on you. Your husband will like it.'

'Yes, he will.' He might. But a hundred and forty-five? I still had quite a lot of money saved up, so I explained it to myself all the way home as being a reasonable thing to do.

When I got home Chris and Sam were eating ice-cream in the kitchen.

'What'd you buy, Mommy?'

'A new dress.'

'Let me see it.'

'Not till Saturday. That's in two days.' And Chris started humming 'Here comes the bride' again. I went

243

upstairs and hung it in the back of my closet, feeling very pleased with myself. It was beautiful. The same kind of luminous grey as the fog. My wedding dress.

Early Friday morning, Chris jumped out of bed, gave me a shove and told me to get him some orange juice.

'Now?'

'Yes. Now! I have to be in Oakland by eight. We're shooting a film and I have to be there on time. Come on, lady, move it!'

'Okay,' and I rolled out of bed, not too pleased by the hour.

Chris left with his arms full of all sorts of boxes, and notes, and odds and ends that didn't look like much to me. He gave me a quick kiss and said he'd be home late and not to wait dinner for him. 'Now go back to bed.'

I hung out the door as he started the car, waved, and shouted a hearty 'Love you!' wondering if the whole neighbourhood was being awakened by my shouting, or his car coughing and gagging as it got started. Or his 'Love you too,' as he drove away. I went back to bed then for a little bit before getting up to feed Sam and get her to school.

The house seemed quiet without Chris when we left and Sam was in a grouchy mood. I thought she might be catching a cold, and decided to ask Chris to check on the heater in her bedroom. I didn't think it was working too well.

On the way back, I stopped off at the hardware store up the street from the house and decided to buy the paint for the baby's room. A lovely bright yellow. I figured that if I didn't buy it Chris would never get around to it. So I loaded it into the car and headed home.

When I got there the phone was ringing but it stopped

before I opened the door. Probably a wrong number. Chris's calls usually went through his answering service and nobody knew I was back yet.

The house was in order, so I went back upstairs to our room, opened my closet, and looked at the dress again. It looked so perfect, and as I stood there looking at it I decided to try it on again.

I whirled around in front of the mirror, wearing black shoes, my grandmother's pearls, and my alligator bag. I pulled my hair up off my neck and felt just like a bride. It was a far cry from my first wedding . . . a far cry. And I giggled at myself in the mirror. 'Gillian Forrester, my how you've changed!'

The phone rang again as I was preening in front of the mirror, and this time I got there in time to answer it.

'Mrs Matthews?' I didn't recognise the voice. Maybe someone from one of the shops looking for new customers. So I wound up my 'sorry, we don't need any' voice . . . 'this is the cleaning lady,' etc.

'Not till tomorrow. Yes?' I didn't see any point in volunteering my name. It couldn't be anyone we knew anyway.

'This is Tom Bardi. I'm a friend of Chris.'

'Yes?' I remembered hearing the name, but only vaguely.

'Mrs . . . uh . . . we were working on the same film over in Oakland this morning and . . .'

'Yes?' My God, was something wrong? 'Yes? Is anything wrong?'

'Chris fell off a rig, trying to get a shot, and, I'm so sorry to tell you this, like this, but . . . he's dead. He broke his neck when he hit. I'm calling you from St Mary's Hospital in Oakland . . . Are you all right? . . . Are you there?'

'Yes . . . I'm here.' I was leaden. There just wasn't

anything else for me to say.

'What's your name?'

'Gillian.'

'Gillian, are you all right? Are you sure? Look, can you come over here now?'

'No. Chris has the car.'

'All right, don't move. You just sit there and have a cup of coffee. I'll be over right away and I'll drive you back here.'

'Why?'

'Well, they want to know what to do with the . . . body.' The body? The body? The body! Chris, not 'the body'. Chris, Chris, and I started to whimper.

'Now, you just hang on. I'll be right over.'

I just sat there, on my bed, not moving, not even able to move my head or turn around. I just sat there in my new grey dress, looking down at my shoes, whimpering. And then I heard footsteps coming up the stairs, strong man's footsteps, taking the stairs two at a time . . . Chris! . . . It was a lie, it was a crank call, and he'd hold me and tell me it was a bad joke . . . Chris . . . and I looked up and there was a strange man in our room, looking down at me with a look of tenderness and embarrassment.

'I'm Tom,' and I just nodded my head.

'Are you all right?' and I nodded again, but I didn't mean it.

'Can I make you a cup of coffee?' I shook my head. I stood up, not remembering where I was supposed to go, or what I was supposed to do, but knowing this man was here for something.

'My God, you're pregnant . . . Jesus . . . Oh, I'm sorry.' I knew he was, he sounded as though he meant it, but I really didn't give a damn. I stood up and saw myself in the mirror, with Tom Bardi standing behind

246

me. I was still wearing my new dress, with all the tickets on it.

'I've got to change. I'll be ready in a minute,' and I started whimpering again. 'It's my wedding dress.' He looked at me for a minute as though he thought I was hysterical. He had a nervous, doubtful look about him like that was something he really couldn't handle.

'No, it's all right, I mean it. We were going to get married tomorrow.' I had to pull myself together to explain.

'Oh, I thought you were. I mean Chris said something about his wife . . . and a little boy named Sam . . . He never said anything about the baby though.'

'A little girl. Sam, I mean. Samantha . . . Gee, what am I going to do? I have to pick her up at school in a little while.'

'What school?'

'The Thomas Ellis School.'

'Okay, you get dressed and I'll call the school, tell them to hold on to her for a while. We won't be long . . . I mean . . .' and he turned around to walk downstairs. 'Where's the phone?' he shouted back.

'In the kitchen, behind the door.'

I put on my jeans and Chris's sweater again, grabbed my bag, and the dress lay on the unmade bed, half inside out, next to the T-shirt Chris had slept in . . . Jesus, oh good God, sweet Jesus . . . what have You done?

I clattered down the stairs in my wooden sandals and heard Tom hang up the phone.

'It's all set, they can keep her till four-thirty. We'll be back before that.' He looked uncomfortable again. 'Do you know what you want to do? I mean they want to know over there. What're you going to do with him?'

I hadn't thought of that. 'I don't know. Maybe I should call his mother . . .' Where the hell did she live

247

. . . ? Let me think a minute . . . Chicago . . . ? No . . . Detroit . . . ? No . . . Denver. That was it. I had met her once when she came to see Chris on her way someplace else. They weren't very close, and his father was dead.

I dialled long-distance. 'Denver Information, please.'

'I'm sorry, you can dial that yourself. Dial three-oh-three, then five, five, five . . .'

'Look, goddamit, will you please do it for me. My husband was just killed in an accident.'

'Oh . . . yes . . . Oh, I'm sorry. Just a moment, please.'

'Directory. What city please? May I help you?'

'Yes. Denver. Helen Matthews. I don't know the address.'

After a pause, she came back on the line. 'That's 663-7015.' I repeated it back to her. Why did I sound so calm, why did I sound so much like me? 663-7015 . . . 663-7015 . . . Now dial it, tell the nice lady, go ahead tell her, Chris Is Dead. That's right, Mrs Matthews, he's dead . . . Oh my God . . . I flicked the button on the phone up and down a few times. 'Operator? . . . Operator? . . .'

'Yes, ma'am. Do you want me to get that number for you now?'

'Yes. Please.'

'Station? Or person to person?'

'Station. No, person . . . no, oh anything . . . I don't care.'

'I'm sorry, but I have to know which.'

'Oh shit . . . make it person to person then. Helen Matthews, Mrs.'

She dialled, and the phone rang twice.

'Hello?'

'Hello. We have a person to person call for Mrs Helen Matthews.'

'This is she.' She sounded a little like Chris.

248

'Go ahead please.'

'Hello . . . Jane?'

'No, Mrs Matthews. This is Gillian Forrester. I'm a friend of Chris's. I don't know if you remember me. I met you last summer when you were here . . . I . . .'

'Yes, I remember. How are you?' She sounded a little puzzled.

'Fine, thank you. How are you?' Oh Christ, I couldn't get it out. And I looked over at Tom Bardi and knew how he had felt when he called me. I squeezed my eyes shut and sat down, holding the receiver with both hands to keep it from shaking.

'If you're looking for Chris, he isn't here. He's in San Francisco. Where are you? I'm afraid this is a very poor connection.' It was, and it wasn't going to get any better in a few minutes.

'I'm in San Francisco, too . . . that is . . . Mrs Matthews, Chris just had an accident. He's . . . dead . . . I'm sorry. I'm really sorry . . .' Oh Christ, don't go falling apart now, don't do that to her. 'Mrs Matthews, I'm sorry to do this to you, but the hospital wants to know what to do with, well . . . I thought I'd call and ask you what . . .' Oh God, she was crying. The nice old lady I met last summer was crying. 'Mrs Matthews? Are you all right?' Dumb question, and I looked up at Tom again. He was looking out the window, with his back to me, seeming to sag.

'Yes, I'm all right,' and she pulled herself together. 'I don't know what to tell you. His father is buried in New Mexico, where we used to live, and his brother is buried in Washington. He was killed in Vietnam.' Oh God, why did this have to happen to her? I had heard about the brother from Chris.

'Do you want me to bring him to Denver, Mrs Matthews?'

'No, I don't see any point in that. My daughter lives in Fresno. I think you'd better handle it in San Francisco. I'll fly down today. I have to call his sister first.'

'You can stay here with me. At the house' . . . his house . . . our house . . oh Jesus, what would she think of us living together? It was a little late to worry about that.

'No, I'll stay at a hotel with Jane, my daughter.'

'I'll pick you up at the airport. Call and tell me when you're getting in.'

'You don't have to, dear.'

'I want to . . . Mrs Matthews . . . I'm so awfully sorry,' and my voice broke again.

'I know you are, dear,' and there were tears in her voice again too.

I nodded, and we hung up.

Tom Bardi was watching me as I hung up and handed me a cup of coffee. 'Want something stronger?' I shook my head and took a swallow of the coffee. It was cold. 'We better get going.' I nodded and started towards the door.

'Oh, I want to make one more phone call. Please . . .' Peg. I had to tell Peg. Who else could I turn to? Who else had seen me cry and throw up and die over the years? Peg.

I dialled her direct, at her office.

'Miss Richards, please.'

'One moment please . . . Miss Richards' office.'

'I'd like to speak to her.'

'I'm sorry, Miss Richards is in a meeting.'

'Get her. Tell her it's Gillian Forrester. She'll take it.'

'Well, I'll have to see. Please hold.' Hold your ass, lady. Peg would come. And she did.

'Gillian? What's up? I'm in a meeting.'

'I know. Peg . . . he's dead.' And I broke down all over again.

'When?'

'This morning . . . accident . . . broken neck . . . goddam crane . . .' I could hardly get the words out.

'I'll take the eight o'clock plane tonight. At least I can spend the weekend with you. You okay?'

'No.'

'That's okay, you just hang in there till Aunt Peg gets there, then you can let go. I'll be there tonight.' Let's see, eight and five makes one a.m., minus the three-hour time difference. Peg would be there at ten. 'And listen, don't pick me up. I'll take a cab. Same address?'

'Yes.'

'Do you need anything else?'

'Just you. Oh Peg, thanks; thanks forever on this one.'

'Gotta go now, take it easy. Listen, do you have any Librium or something?'

'Yeah, but I don't want to.'

'Take it. You listen to Aunt Peg and take it,' but I knew I wasn't going to.

'Okay, thanks again . . . g'bye.'

'G'bye,' and we hung up.

I looked up at Tom Bardi still standing in the kitchen but beginning to fidget. 'Okay, let's go,' and he looked relieved. Maybe he thought I was going to call everyone I knew, and make him stand there, listening.

33

We drove to Oakland in silence. I had nothing to say. And I was grateful that Tom didn't try to talk. He just drove. Very fast. And I stared out the window, not crying, not thinking, not even feeling anything. I was just driving along in Chris's car, with a man named Tom Bardi, whom I'd never seen before today. It was strange, really strange, so I didn't think about it. I just sat.

The car veered suddenly, and I realised that we had swooped into the parking lot of St Mary's Hospital in Oakland. We stepped out of the car and Tom led the way into the emergency room.

Once inside, there was a little group of people, long-haired and blue-jeaned. They looked stunned, and huddled together as though to keep warm. The camera crew

Tom led me up to a desk and said something to the nurse in charge. She looked up, the only expression on her face a question, 'Mrs Matthews?'

'Yes,' I lied, because I didn't think she could handle the truth, and I knew I couldn't handle an explanation. What difference did it make anyway?

'Would you step this way, please?' and she led me into a little room with a red light lit up over the door, and a sign on the door that said 'Do Not Enter'. And there was Chris, dressed as he had been that morning, lying stretched out on a gurney, looking peaceful, one side of his face sandy, but no visible part of him bruised. They were wrong. He wasn't dead, he was just sleeping. I

252

brushed the sand off his face and smoothed his hair. I leaned down to kiss him and great horrible gulps of air got caught in my throat and made odd gurgling sounds. I leaned my face down to his and held him. But he felt strange, and his skin felt funny. The body of Christopher Caldwell Matthews. No longer Chris.

The nurse had been standing in the corner, watching, and I didn't give a damn. I forgot she was there. She walked up to me slowly, and held my elbow, propelling me very professionally towards the door. I kept looking back over my shoulder at Chris, watching to see if he'd move, or get up, or open an eye and wink. This was just one of those really ugly jokes, like Tom Bardi's phone call . . . Look, really, Nurse, I know he's just putting you on . . .

She kept holding on to my elbow, and moved me down the hall, back to the main desk again. 'Would you sign this, please? . . . And this?' She held out a ball-point pen. I signed Gillian Forrester twice, and turned around, not knowing where to go next. I looked up at her and asked what had to be done after that.

'Have you called a funeral home?'

'No, not yet.' He wasn't even cold yet.

'Well, there's a phone booth across the hall. If you look in the yellow pages, it might give you some idea.' That's it, find it in the yellow pages, let your fingers do . . . oh God.

Hobson's . . . Hobson's . . . that's the one . . . George Hobson's . . . 'put your loved ones in our hands' . . . I knew the guy who had done their ad campaign.

I looked their number up in the book in the phone booth and called.

'Hobson's Home,' in a mellow voice . . . oh Christ.

'This is Mrs Forrester. I'd like to speak to someone about . . .'

'Certainly, one moment please.'

'Yes?' A deep muted voice hit my ears. He had to be a fag. And I found out later that he was, when he minced across the lobby of Hobson's with a plastic grin, and a very tight black suit.

I told him the story. He said there was no problem. One of their cars would pick up Mr Matthews at three. Would that be all right? I said yes, it would be.

'And will you meet us here at three-thirty, Mrs Forrester, to make the arrangements?'

'Yes, that'll be fine.'

'Are you the the sister of the deceased?'

'No, I'm his wife.'

'Oh, I'm so sorry, I understood "Forrester",' and he was all unctuous apologies.

'That's right, Forrester. I'll tell the hospital you'll pick up Mr Matthews at three.' I didn't give one holy damn what he thought. I was Chris's wife, wedding or no wedding.

I told the nurse at the desk that a car from Hobson's would pick Chris up at three and then went back to tell Tom.

'Do you want to go back to the city now? I'll drive you in; someone else can take my car.'

'No. I'll wait. But you can go back now, if you want. There's no point in your waiting here too.'

'I'll stay.' It sounded very final. I was grateful, so I didn't protest.

'Do you want to lie down or something?'

'No, I'm okay.'

'Sure?'

'Sure. Thanks.' And I tried a smile for his benefit. He didn't smile back but walked over to the group of people who had seen Chris last and talked to them in a low voice. They all stood up, one by one, looked over at me, and

254

then away again, quickly, and shook hands with Tom. I saw him hand his keys to someone, and then they were gone. The silent mourners, gone.

'Tom, I can ride back in the car from Hobson's. I'd sort of like to do that.'

'No you can't. How do you think Chris would feel about that?' That was a hit below the belt, and I flinched.

'Okay.'

'Come on, there's a place to eat across the street. I'll take you over for a hamburger.'

'I couldn't . . .' I got nauseous just thinking about it.

'Then you can drink a cup of coffee. Come on.'

We sat, and drank coffee, and smoked, and the time passed, and we never said more than ten words to each other. This friend of Chris's whom I had never seen before was sitting there with me, the closest friend I had at that time. I needed him there, I clung to him, and barely even spoke to him.

The car from Hobson's finally came, a long maroon car with a man driving who looked like a chauffeur. It was a hearse. A hearse for Chris.

Chris came out on a narrow metal stretcher, covered with what looked like a green tarpaulin, and strapped on to the stretcher. They slid him into the back of the hearse and snapped the door shut, and the driver looked at me and said, 'Okay, want to follow me, or meet me there?'

'We'll follow,' I said before looking at Tom. I wanted to follow Chris.

I looked up at Tom and realised that I had been squeezing his hand the whole time we watched Chris being put in the car. My nails had dug into his hand and he had never said a thing. I don't think he noticed.

We got into Chris's car, and Tom started the motor . . .

255

'Watch the choke,' I told him, Chris's words . . . 'watch the choke' . . . the first day we'd been back . . . watch the choke, and I threw my arms around Tom Bardi, and cried and sobbed and choked.

'Ready to go?' The driver of the hearse wanted to know. Tom looked at me and I nodded. I lay back in the seat and wished I had taken the Librium Peg had suggested. But no, I wanted to 'handle' this on my own, no Librium. But thank God for Tom Bardi.

34

At Hobson's, I was led into a small office with elegant, pseudo-Louis XV furniture. Tom waited outside. The man who belonged to the voice on the phone came in. I had already seen him in the lobby. 'I'm Mr Ferrari. Mrs Forrester, isn't it?'
'Yes.'
'Now . . . when is the funeral?'
'I don't know yet.'
'Of course. We are going to put Mr Matthews in our Georgian Slumber Room, which I will show you after you look over these papers. Then I will introduce you to our cosmetician and we'll go downstairs to look at a casket. And after that there will be nothing left for you to do. Let's see, today is Friday, so I would imagine that the funeral will be on Sunday, or perhaps Monday?' Sympathetic alligator smile, and a pat on my hand . . . oh Christ, get your fucking hands off me. He sounded like a goddam social director on a Caribbean Cruise, 'and now . . .' shit.

'Oh yes, and Mrs Forrester, will you bring us a full suit of Mr Matthews' clothes some time this evening? Including shoes.' A suit? I wasn't even sure Chris had one.

'What for?' I had obviously shocked the man beyond all possibility heretofore known feasible.

'To lay him out.' And that smile again, coupled with an expression that sympathised with my stupidity.

'Lay him out? Oh, in the coff . . . no, that won't be necessary. I want it closed. He can wear what he has on.'

'Is he wearing a suit?'

'No, Mr Ferrari, he is not wearing a suit. He does not own a suit, and I like what he's wearing.' I began to snap back, and it made me feel better. 'I'll have to check with his mother about some of the details. She's coming in tonight.'

'From the East?'

'No, from Denver.' But don't worry, we can pay for it, Mr Ferrari. You'll get your money. That's what the papers were all about.

And he smiled at me, sure that Mr Matthews's mother would agree with him about the suit. Maybe she would. She was his mother after all.

'Now, shall we go downstairs and look at the caskets?'

We stepped out of the cloistered little office and I saw Tom, still sitting there. It was reassuring to see him still there.

'We won't be long,' I said, and Tom nodded. Mr Ferrari looked shocked. He was obviously prepared to give me the full show.

For some reason, in the elevator it dawned on me how I must look, in my jeans and sandals and Chris's old sweater. Poor Mr Ferrari. What one had to deal with these days, but I thought it was just as well. Maybe the bill wouldn't be so high. I didn't know how well Mrs Matthews stood financially and, while I could have paid for it with my savings, it would have left me pretty flat afterwards. Funerals could run into thousands.

Mr Ferrari opened a door and revealed a room full of caskets, displayed like cars in a showroom, on platforms, circled around the room, with crucifixes and without, with all sorts of adornments and hardware, lined with satin, velvet, and moire. And I saw Mr Ferrari winding up to give me the full speech. An Automobile Salesman at His Best.

'I'll take that one.'

'That one?'

'That one.'

'Very well, but wouldn't you like me to show you . . .'

'No. How much is it?'

He consulted a list and said, 'Three hundred and twenty-five dollars.'

'Fine,' and I turned and walked out of the room, pressing the elevator button before Mr Ferrari had either caught his breath or rejoined me.

Upstairs, I shook hands with Mr Ferrari and prepared to leave.

'Mr Matthews will be ready at seven this evening. You haven't seen the room yet.'

'I'm sure it'll be fine, Mr Ferrari.' I was exhausted and wanted to get out of the place.

'You're sure about the suit?'

'I'm sure. Thank you,' and with all my dignity, headed for the door, with Tom following me.

Once we got outside, he looked at me again. 'You okay?'

'Much better. Let's go pick up Sam,' and I gave him the address of the school. It was almost four-thirty and she'd be wondering what had happened.

At the school, Sam was drawing pictures in the office of one of the admissions people and looked perfectly happy.

'Where were you?'

'Busy. Let's go, sweetheart, it's time to go home.'

And she picked up her jacket and headed for the door, with her pictures all rolled up in one hand. After she was well out of the room, the admissions lady came around the desk to me and shook my hand. 'I'm so very sorry, Mrs Forrester.'

'Thank you.' I was going to have to get used to that. There would be a lot of 'I'm sorry's' in the next few days.

Tom was waiting in the car when Samantha and I came out.

'Who's that?'

'A friend of Uncle Chris.'

'Oh.' That was okay then, in her book.

Tom and she chatted all the way back to the house, which left my mind free to wander as we drove home. I was so tired I was numb.

'Tom, I want to stop at the florist on the way home. There's one just up the street from us. Do you have time?'

'Sure.'

'What do you want flowers for, Mommy? We've got enough at home.'

'I want to send some to somebody.' Oh God. It began to dawn on me that I'd have to tell her, what and how I didn't know. But I'd have to tell her something.

At the florist, I ordered two hundred dollars' worth of wild flowers in varied colours to be delivered to Hobson's by seven o'clock. I couldn't stand the thought of all white or salmon-coloured gladioli, not for Chris.

259

Outside, Sam and Tom were tickling each other in the car, and I gave a tired smile when I saw them. Tom had been unbelievable.

He drove us home and asked me if I wanted him to come in.

'You don't have to. I'm okay. But I could make you some dinner.'

'No. I'll go home.'

'Want me to drive you?'

'No. I live about six blocks away. I'll walk. I'll park the car for you.'

Sam and I stood in front of the house while he did, and he walked back towards us, looking as tired as I felt. He stopped for a moment in front of us, not knowing what to say.

'Tom . . . I don't know how to say it, but . . . thanks . . . You've been unbelievable . . . wonderful,' and tears started welling up in my throat again.

'So have you, Gillian, so have you.' He bent down and kissed my cheek, rumpled Sam's hair, and walked up the street with his head down. I think he was crying, but I wasn't sure because I was crying too.

'What are you crying for, Mommy? Do you hurt?'

'Yes, sort of.'

'Well, I'll take care of it, and you'll feel all better.'

'Thanks, sweetheart,' and we walked up the stairs to the empty house, hand in hand, the two of us alone again.

Mrs Matthews called while Sam was eating dinner. She said she'd get in at nine, but I didn't have to go to the airport. I told her I would and then set about finding a sitter for Sam. I called the only one of our neighbours whom I knew, and she said she'd be glad to. And, 'Oh, Gillian, I heard it on the news, and I'm so sorry,' so sorry, so sorry, there it was again.

'Thanks, Mrs Jaeger, thanks.' On the news? Christ.

Sam was as good as gold, took her bath, ate her dinner, and went to bed without any problems. She asked for Chris once and I put her off. I didn't want her to associate his going with the tears and unhappiness she'd see in the next few days. Better to tell her when I could handle it. When would that be? Anyway, not just then.

Mrs Jaeger came at eight and I drove to the airport for Mrs Matthews. I had remembered to change my clothes before going and wore something plain and black. My blue jeans and Chris's sweater lay piled on our still unmade bed, along with the grey dress.

35

I stood in the airport, waiting for the plane to come in. I looked around, wondering which of the people standing around might be Jane. Nobody looked the way I expected her to, so I stopped thinking about it, and stared out instead at the lights on the airfield. Half a dozen planes were lining up for take-off, and there were others coming in.

'United Airlines, Flight 402, from Denver, has arrived. Passengers will arrive at Gate 3 . . . Flight 402 . . .' She was one of the first people off and I recognised her right off, a smallish lady who must have been pretty once, with grey hair and a neat-looking black suit. She looked around, and past me. I don't think she recognised me at first.

'Mrs Matthews?'

'Gillian?'

'Yes.'

'Thank you for coming, dear. You needn't have,' and she looked around me, and over my shoulder as I was telling her it was quite all right, and all the things one is supposed to say.

'I don't see Jane. She said she'd meet me.' And then, as I looked around with her, she waved, and I saw a tall girl walking towards us . . . It was Chris transformed into a woman. It was the oddest feeling to look at that girl and see Chris, his walk, his shape, and, as she came closer, his eyes. It made me want to shudder, but I was fascinated, mesmerised by the apparition coming towards us. I couldn't take my eyes off her. She walked straight up to her mother and put her arms around her in a silent hug. And I was sorry I had come. I had no place with them. They needed each other, and I was a stranger there. I turned away, feeling awkward, and tried to think of what to say to Jane. 'I'm sorry'? No, not from me. Not me too. As I looked back at her, staring at the resemblance again, she let go of her mother and took a step towards me. And hugged me too.

'I know, Gillian. I know. I won't tell you I'm sorry. I know how you feel. Chris wrote to me last week.'

'He did? He didn't tell me a thing.' I was so surprised I didn't know what to say.

'He wouldn't have. Mom, why don't we get your bags,' and the three of us walked slowly towards the escalator to the baggage claim area.

We collected Mrs Matthews's things and I went to the parking lot to get the car.

'I'm sorry, it's not very roomy. Chris . . . I . . . well, we like it,' and there was an embarrassed silence.

Driving into the city there was very little said. There

was very little to say. And then, as though all at once all three of us felt we should be talking, we all started to talk at once, and then laughed nervously. We talked about San Francisco, the weather in Denver, flying, anything except Chris, and the accident.

'When is the baby due, Gillian?' Wow, talk about openers. That from Jane.

'Not for another two months. You have three, don't you?' She nodded, and while I tried not to look at Mrs Matthews, I hoped she hadn't noticed. Because, what we all forget, with our free-thinking friends, is that they have parents, and the great, liberated Christopher Caldwell Matthews had a mother who might not think illegitimate children were so cool. Chris hadn't thought so either, so I expected nothing short of horror from his mother. I could feel her looking at me then and chanced a quick glance and nervous smile in her direction. After all, I had only met her once.

She looked back at me, just as nervously, with a tiny smile, and her big sad eyes. 'I hope you won't mind me saying this, but I'm glad. My other son wasn't married either, and well, Chris . . .' and she trailed off. I wanted to kiss her, but couldn't while I was driving, so I looked back at her again, with a real smile this time.

'Do you want to stop . . . there . . . on the way in?'

'No, Mother, why don't you wait till tomorrow? Let's go straight to the hotel.'

'No. I want to go tonight, Jane. I want to see him . . .' and the last part of her words trailed off again.

'Ummmm . . . Mrs Matthews, I had the . . . uh . . . I had it closed . . . But it can be done the other way, if you like . . .' The other way . . . the other way . . . with Chris lying there, so still . . . for all to see, until we buried him.

'Oh.' It was such a small sound. 'Does he . . .? Was he very . . .?'

I cut her off; I didn't want to hear the words. 'No, he looks . . . fine.' I wanted to say 'beautiful', but I couldn't. He did look beautiful, the sleeping boy I had watched so often late at night, or early in the morning. All peaceful, the soul of a boy in the body of a man.

'I think Gillian was right, Mom. Let's leave it like that,' and Mrs Matthews just nodded.

After that the conversation lagged. There was nothing left to say, and we all sat deep in our own thoughts until we got to Hobson's. I pulled into their parking lot and parked the car. We all got out and I led the way in.

There was a pale – ghostly? – looking girl at the desk in the lobby, and Mr Ferrari was talking to a small group of people in a corner. He looked up as we walked in, nodded briefly, and looked as though he approved of my change of clothes. Schmuck.

I stepped up to the girl at the desk and my voice sounded hoarse again. 'Mr Matthews, the Georgian Room. Which way?'

'This way, please,' and she headed down the long hall, past other rooms, and I was afraid to look towards the open doors for fear that I'd see a body, and I didn't want to see that. She stopped at the last door on the left and we went in. And there it was, the dark wooden box I had picked out a few hours ago, and the flowers I had bought on Sacramento Street. They looked beautiful. They were red, yellow, and blue, with baby's breath spread through them. They looked so fresh and pretty, not heavy and dead. They were like Mozart, or Debussy. That was just what I had wanted.

There were two huge candles in bronze candelabra at either end of the casket, and a small prie-dieu just in front of it. Two settees and a few chairs against the wall. The lighting was dim; it looked so solemn, like a church.

It seemed like the wrong place for Chris. I could just hear him saying something like, 'Oh fuck off, Gill, what the hell is this?' But it had to be, and his mother looked as though she thought it was right.

'The flowers are lovely, Gillian. Did you do that?' And I nodded. She walked forward towards the casket then, and Jane squeezed my arm as Mrs Matthews knelt at the prie-dieu, and we stood back watching her, this woman who had lost two sons and a husband, all her men.

She got up after a moment and Jane took her place while Mrs Matthews sat on one of the settees and looked at her feet. I didn't have the courage to look at her any more, I just couldn't.

Jane rose and came towards me, leading her mother gently off the settee on the way. 'Come on, Mom, it's been a long day, and I told the hotel we'd be there by ten.'

As we walked down the hall I asked Jane where they were staying. 'The Sir Francis Drake.'

'I'll drop you there.'

In the car on the way over, Jane continued a normal conversation, while patting her mother's shoulder and occasionally giving her a squeeze.

'Mrs Matthews, I hate to bring this up now, but when do you think we should have the . . . funeral?' There. I'd gotten it out.

'Is Sunday too soon?'

'No. I don't think so. I think it might be better that way. Do you want to do it in church? I'm sorry to bring it up like this . . . so soon . . . but they want to know . . . at Hobson's, I mean . . .'

'Bastards.' It was Jane, sounding so much like Chris.

'Jane! They have a job to do just like everyone else.' Jane and I didn't add anything to that, but our sentiments ran in the same vein, and bastards was a nice word for it.

'Did Chris still go to church much?' Ouch.

'Not too often.' Better to lie a little than to say 'never'.

'I'm a Presbyterian, and his father was a Methodist. I don't think Christopher felt much one way or the other. He never leaned particularly to one side.' That was one way of putting it. In a way, it was the truth.

'There's a nice little Presbyterian church near our house. I could speak to the minister in the morning.'

'May I come with you?'

'Of course, I'm sorry. I didn't mean to take over, I just thought . . .'

'Gillian, you've been wonderful. Don't you worry about that.'

'I'll come and get you in the morning and we'll all go and see him together.'

Jane sounded as though she were grinding her teeth in the back seat. She really was like Chris. A church funeral for Chris. But it wasn't for Chris. It was for his mother, and for us. That's who funerals are for, a dirge for the living, not a celebration of the dead.

In front of the hotel we all hugged again, and they disappeared into the lobby, the tall fair girl who walked like Chris and the small lady in the black suit. She was only a little smaller than I, but she looked tiny to me, somehow, maybe because she was Chris's mother. I looked at my watch and decided to go back to Hobson's. Just for a minute. To be alone with Chris. Mrs Jaeger wouldn't mind waiting just a little bit longer. She'd understand.

I parked in the lot again and went in, relieved to see that Mr Ferrari was gone. The pale-looking girl was still at the desk, drinking coffee out of a styrofoam cup. It reminded me of the coffee at *Woman's Life*, and I walked down the hall thinking 'to her, this is just a job', and I couldn't help wondering what kind of person would want a job like that. The magazine had been throbbing with life, and people, and colour, and noise. Working in a place like this was as good as being dead yourself.

I reached Chris's room and walked in slowly. I sat in one of the chairs and thought for a while, leaning back and closing my eyes, resting, and thinking. Of little bits and pieces, short moments, and tiny words . . . Fifteen hours ago, Chris went clattering down the steps of the house, and now here I was in this quiet room filled with bright flowers, with Chris lying there . . . Maybe, maybe if I hold my breath and close my eyes, and count to 712, it will all go away, and I'll wake up. But I didn't. I gasped and opened my eyes, and it was all there, just the same except that I was out of breath, and the baby was kicking harder, infuriated by the momentary lack of oxygen.

I walked slowly towards the prie-dieu then, and knelt looking towards where Chris's head rested, though I couldn't see it. Tears ran down my face slowly, making plopping noises as they hit the velvet on the top of the prie-dieu. I think I prayed, but I'm not sure, and then I got up and left. Slowly, alone, wishing that I could feel that Chris was with me, near me. That's what you're supposed to feel, but I didn't. I felt as though Chris was shut up in that box. He was gone, and I was alone.

Chris's car was the only one left in Hobson's parking lot, and I started it, remembering about the choke. I drove home through the fog and got to Sacramento Street just before midnight, a little worried about Mrs Jaeger. I opened the door with my key and walked in, leaving my coat on the chair in the hall and heading towards the kitchen where I supposed she would be.

The kitchen light was the only one that was on.

'Mrs Jaeger? . . . Mrs Jaeger?' Maybe Sam had woken up and I went upstairs to see. When I reached the top of the stairs I saw that the light was on in our room, and I could see Peg through the open doorway, making my bed.

'Oh, Peg, you're a saint,' and I sagged in the doorway and just looked at her.

'No talk. Just get into bed. Here, sit down. I'll help.'

'Oh, Peg, you must be exhausted. It's three o'clock in the morning your time.'

'It's worse, your time, so no arguments. This is what I came out here for.'

'God, Peg, what am I ever going to do if I grow up one day and you're not around any more?'

'Oh shut up. None of that stuff.'

'What about Mrs Jaeger?'

'She left just before you got here. I didn't think she was going to trust me, but I talked so much, and so fast, and kept ushering her out the door at the same time, so she went. Where have you been?'

'I picked up Mrs Matthews at the airport, and then took them to Hobson's, and after that I dropped them off at the hotel, and then I . . . went back to Hobson's.'

'Went back to Hobson's? Hobson's being the local Frank Campbell's, I take it. What are you trying to do? Kill yourself and the baby?'

'Yes, I mean no. I mean yes, Hobson's is the local Campbell's, and no I'm not trying to kill myself or the baby. Peg, someone had to be there to pick her up.'

'There was no one else?'

'Chris's sister, but . . . Hell, I wanted to.'

'Good enough. Now, how about some hot chocolate, or something. And I brought you some pills from New York.'

'What kind of pills?'

'Cool-it pills. I called your obstetrician and he gave me a prescription for you.'

'Christ, Peg . . .'

'Did you take any Librium today?'

'Well, actually . . .' I shook my head.

'I figured.'

And I started looking around the room. Everything looked the way I had left it, except neater, and the stuff was cleared off the bed. The new grey dress was hanging on a hanger on the closet door.

'Peg . . . would you put that away, please? I don't want to see it.'

'Sure,' and it vanished into the closet.

'The funeral's Sunday, so you'll be able to get back to the office on Monday.'

'You giving me the bum's rush or something? I told them I'd be gone a week.'

Peg . . . Peg . . . unbelievable Peg who had held my head the first time I got drunk, who had always, always been there. And here she was, a few hours after I called, having travelled three thousand miles to be with me, and making my bed within five minutes of walking in the door. She was treating me like a patient, and she was the night nurse, flown out direct from New York. Just for me. It was the kind of friendship Chris couldn't understand, but thank God for Peg. There were one in ten million people like her, and I had been lucky enough to go to school with her.

She gave me the pill, and the hot chocolate, and I sat there thinking about Chris at Hobson's. 'Peg . . .'

'Try not to talk. Just tell me where you want me to sleep. Can I sleep in Sam's room?'

'Peg, you sleep here. I'll sleep in Sam's room.'

'No way. If you so much as put a foot on the floor,

I'll give you one of my world-famous left hooks!'

'You mean the one that almost got you kicked out of school?'

'The same,' and we giggled.

'Peg?'

'Yes?'

'You know . . . I . . . um . . .'

'I know . . .' and she turned out the light and I began to fall asleep as she was picking up the empty chocolate cup. She just seemed to fade away, and for a minute I tried to keep awake thinking that that looked like Peg Richards standing over me. But no, it couldn't be. Peg was in New York . . . Must be Chris . . . I'd have to remember to tell him in the morning. He'd think it was funny . . .

36

The sun was streaming into the room and I could hear voices downstairs . . . My God . . . what time is it? Eleven-forty-five. I jumped out of bed and went to the top of the stairs.

'Chris? . . . Sam? . . . Why'd you let me sleep this late? Today is . . .' Oh no, oh God no . . . I dropped back on to the top step and sat there with my face buried in my hands. Peg rushed up the steps, with Sam behind her, and she pulled me gently off the step and led me back to the bedroom.

'Whatsa matter with Mommy, Aunt Peg?'

'She's just very tired, Sam. Why don't you go back down and be a big girl and put the dishes in the sink?

That's a good girl,' and Sam clattered back downstairs. Peg sat me on the edge of the bed. And sat next to me, with an arm around my shoulders, while I started to sob and shake. 'Ohhhh Peg . . . ohhh.' We sat like that until Sam came back, looking puzzled and a little worried. I looked over at her and tried to smile a little for her, which made me cry more.

'Oh, Peg . . . I can't stop . . . I can't . . .'

'That's all right, Gill. You'll be okay. Why don't you go wash your face?'

'I was supposed to call Mrs Matthews. We have to go see the minister.'

'Jane called. She and her mother are coming by at one.'

'I'll pick them up.'

'No, they can take a taxi. Stop being a hero. You're being selfish, Gill. Think of the baby You loved him, so take good care of his child.' It was kind of a harsh thing to say, but it was like a splash of cold water. Peg was right.

'Peg . . . no more pills, please . . . huh?'

'We'll see. Listen, you've had a lot of calls. A guy named Tom Bardi, he wanted to know if there was anything he could do. I said we'd let him know. And Hilary Price, and Gordon Harte . . . and . . . let's see, oh, John Templeton . . . and . .'

'How do they know?' I looked at Peg and knew. 'You called them?'

'Just Gordon and John Templeton. Before I left. And your mother called. I think Gordon must have called her.'

'I don't want to talk to any of them . . . please.' I saw Peg watching me. 'I've got to call the minister. Where the hell is the phone book?' and I started scrambling around under the bed while the phone rang. I gave a horrible start as it rang next to me. 'You get it.'

Peg answered it and paused for a moment, listening. 'I'll have to see if she's in, Operator,' and she looked over at me as I shook my head frantically from side to side and waved a hand . . . no . . . no . . . I can't . . . She put her hand over the mouthpiece and whispered, 'It's Gordon. Do you want to talk to him?' I started to shake my head and then looked up at Peg for a long two seconds and reached for the phone. She handed it to me and ushered Sam out of the room again, closing the door behind them.

'Hello . . . Yes, this is she . . . Gordon? . . . Hello . . . Thanks for calling . . . Peg told me that . . . What?'

'I said I'd like to come out for a couple of days, if I can help.'

'No . . . no . . . Gordon, thanks, but I'd rather you didn't. It wouldn't . . . well, I don't think it's such a good idea.'

'How are you feeling, Gillian?'

'I don't know . . . I don't know. Today was going to be our . . .' and I started to cry all over again while Gordon tried to talk.

'I don't know what to say. I'm so sorry, Gill.' There it was, from Gordon this time – 'I'm so sorry.'

'I know you are.'

'Gillian, I know it's too soon for you to have thought about it, but why don't you come back to New York with Peg? There's nobody to take care of you out there.'

'No. I'm staying.' It was the most forceful thing I'd said in two days, except for my quick bout with Mr Ferrari, and this was one hell of a lot more important to me than whether or not Chris was wearing a suit. Nobody was going to tear me away from here. Not now. Not ever. NO!

'Well, don't put it out of your mind yet. Are you sure I can't do anything?'

'No . . . yes . . . I'll let you know if there is anything. There's nothing left to do. It's . . .' and I just went on crying. 'I can't talk any more . . . Thanks for the call . . . Thanks for everything.'

'Gillian, we're all with you. Please know that.' I nodded again and choked on another 'thanks' and hung up while he was still on the line.

I called the minister, and when Jane and Mrs Matthews arrived we went over and set it up with him. We'd have to do it at two-thirty. They couldn't do it sooner because of Sunday services. And I guess he had to eat lunch or something. We had missed our own lunch by the time we'd spoken to him, and we stood in a small group just outside the church wondering what to do next.

'Let's go back to the house.'

'Well, I'd like to go back to Hobson's for a while, Gillian.' It was Mrs Matthews speaking. Jane and Peg said nothing, and I offered to go back for the car. We walked slowly towards the house, Jane and Peg falling behind and talking in soft voices, Mrs Matthews and I discussing Bible passages for the funeral. We had sorrow as our bond, and our plans to hold us together. After this? Maybe the baby. He would be her grandchild, and maybe she would love him. Maybe he would look like Chris.

At the house, Sam saw us from the window and she and Mrs Jaeger waved. I could see Sam discussing something heatedly with Mrs Jaeger and suspected she wanted to come out.

'Let's get into the car, everybody, or Sam will get upset and want to come too.'

Everyone waved, and we got in as quickly as one pregnant woman and one older, less agile, woman possibly could.

On the way to Hobson's, no one spoke, and I parked once again in the same spot in their lot. We walked inside, still silent, and headed down the now familiar path towards the room where Chris was lying. I expected to find it empty and just as I had left it the night before, but we walked in to find Tom Bardi and the whole camera crew there, standing around, looking solemn, and in the process of signing the white and gold leaflet that Hobson's left out for guests to sign, to show that they had done their 'duty'.

Introductions were made, and there was a lot of shifting from one foot to the other, with no one knowing what to say. After a little bit they filed out, looking back at me again, and I saw that one of the girls was crying, and a boy had his arm around her, leading her out. Had she known Chris well? Had she been in love with him too? Had she slept with him? Did she feel sorry for me? I was curious, and felt guilty about it.

Tom stayed back for a few minutes, to talk to me.

'It was in the paper this morning.'

'What did it say?' I wanted it to say something nice.

'It was just a small news item, page eleven, not an obit, or anything like that.'

'I heard that it was on the news last night too.'

'Yeah . . .' and he nodded, and then he left.

I walked over to the little guest register to see what their names were, wondering which one was the girl. Just a lot of names. There were so many I didn't know. I was sorry I hadn't been there earlier. And then my eyes stopped halfway down the list . . . There it was. The tenth one down. Marilyn Lee, in a slanting, elaborate script. Marilyn Lee. She must be feeling like this too. Poor

274

Marilyn. I hoped that she had had a few minutes alone in here. The rivalry was over now. The two widows standing side by side.

'Who are all the flowers from, Gillian?'

'Flowers?' What flowers? And I looked around, realising that there were more than wild flowers in the room, at least a dozen more arrangements, some of them pretty, some funeralish and grotesque. I was surprised. I saw a little pile of invoice slips and cards on the table, and realised that this was one of Hobson's services. Yellow invoices describing each arrangement, and saying who it was from, with the sympathy card stapled on the back. White spider mums from some film company whose name I didn't recognise. White and yellow roses: Hilary Price. Mixed flowers on stand: John Templeton and the Staff. Spray of lilies of the valley: G. Harte . . . Gordon . . . and more, whose names I didn't know. Our friends, mostly my friends, and I reached out for Peg and started to cry again. Poor Mrs Matthews, that didn't make it any easier for her.

We sat for a couple of hours, and a few people drifted in and out, nodding to us, and one or two shook Mrs Matthews's hand and murmured the same 'I'm sorry' to her over and over again. How often had she heard that? For her husband, her other boy, and now for Chris.

Towards the end of the day, a neatly put together man in a dark suit stepped in, and for a moment I thought he might work for Hobson's. He looked so serious, so proper, but Mrs Matthews rose and said, 'Gillian, this is my son-in-law, Don Lindquist.' We shook hands and he put his arm around Jane after kissing Mrs Matthews.

How do you do's were exchanged, I introduced Peg, and then he stepped away from us and bowed his head near where Chris lay.

When he came back to our little group, he suggested he

take us all home, and then out for dinner later. I declined and Peg shot me a look, but I just couldn't face that scene.

'I drove up so I have the car.'

'Oh.' I would no longer be chauffeuring Jane and her mother around, which upset me a little. One of my jobs had been taken away from me, one of the things that was keeping me busy, helping me to keep my sanity . . . Oh.

After they left, Peg looked at me and stood up. 'Okay, kid, you're going home.'

'No, I'm not,' and I felt defiant. I was *not* leaving. 'You go home to Sam. It's late and the last two days have confused the hell out of her. Tell her I'll be home later.'

'That's just the point, Gillian. My going home to Sam is not going to unconfuse her. You come home too. You can come back later if you want.' Good old Peg, giving it the old honest heave-ho. Wham. She was right. I got up, put on my coat, and left with her, looking back at Chris's casket, 'just one more time'.

'Where've you been all day? Nobody plays with me. Just fat old Mrs Jaeger. I don't like Mrs Jaeger.' Sam was mad, she was feeling left out. 'And where's Uncle Crits?' She was mad at him too. We had all deserted her. And she started to cry. I took her in my arms and rocked her back and forth, taking as much comfort as I was giving.

'How about taking your bath with me?' and she cheered visibly, momentarily forgetting Chris, and she started up the stairs in a rush.

Peg said she'd cook dinner, so I headed upstairs, feeling relieved that I hadn't had to say more about Chris, and thinking that the hot bath would do me good too. I was feeling leaden again, and had had small cramps in my back all day. The baby was beginning to feel very low,

276

and I felt heavy as I walked up the stairs.

Sam was in high spirits at dinner, and the three of us laughed and giggled and told silly jokes to entertain Sam. And each other. I laughed too hard at everything, everything seemed so funny. It was a relief to be away from Hobson's, to be away from that dark wooden box, away from the yellow invoices with the sympathy cards, and the stuffy floral smell, and from Mrs Matthews and Jane and . . . it all went together. And the joke about the 400-pound canary was suddenly hysterical to me again, Sam and Peg and I each laughing till the tears ran down our faces.

We put Sam to bed and then walked out into the hall. 'Peg . . .'

'No,' and we looked defiantly at each other for an instant, and I came close to hating her briefly. She was not going to keep me from going back there. 'You're not going back, Gillian, you're not.'

'I am,' and she stood there between me and the stairs, and I wondered if one of her famous left hooks was going to come at me after all. And then we both looked so silly standing there I started to laugh again, and we both stood there, doubling over with giggles, like the time we unhooked the toilet seat in Miss MacFarlan's john and she fell in and we could hear her screaming as we ran all the way down the hall, then stopped breathless on the back stairs, laughing, and doubling over just like this.

'What's so funny?' Sam was back in our midst.

'Back to bed, young lady.' Peg shooed her back in while I got my coat and ran down the stairs. When Peg came out I was already at the front door, the car keys in my hand. 'See you later, Peg.'

'Okay, but if you're not back by eleven I'll call the police.'

'I'll be back by then,' and I blew her a kiss as I closed

the door and went back out in the fog. I could hear the foghorns, and I sat in the car for a few minutes just listening.

37

At Hobson's, the same pale girl was there, in the same dress, drinking the same coffee, reading the paper. At least she could read, and then I remembered something. 'Can I see that for a second?' and she looked up with a surprised rabbit look. No one ever asked her for anything except 'Which way to Mrs Jones?' or 'Where is the Greek Grotto Room?' She handed me the paper, and I turned to page eleven. Where the hell is it? Then there it was, in a small box, at the bottom of the page: 'In Safford Field, in Oakland, yesterday, Christopher Caldwell Matthews, age thirty-three, of 2629 Sacramento Street fell to his death from a crane while filming a documentary movie. He was rushed to St Mary's Hospital in Oakland, but had died on impact, of a broken neck.' That was all. They'd gotten it all in there, hadn't they? And people would read it and think, 'Gee, too bad,' or 'Crazy hippies,' or 'You never know about those movie people,' or . . . oh shit. 'Thanks,' and I gave her back her paper while she still looked surprised. I smiled at her, but that was too much for her. It wasn't in her Hobson's manual.

I walked back towards Chris's room, feeling as though I had been doing this all my life, like visiting a very old aunt in a nursing home. I felt as though Chris had always been there and I had always been coming to Hobson's to see him. It gave me a place to go to. But it was the dead Chris. The live Chris lived on his side of our rumpled bed, in the slippers that stood in opposite corners of the room, in the frazzled toothbrush that was still lying on the sink, in the studio I couldn't bring myself to go up to now . . . There was something sick about holding on to this dead Chris, but it seemed more alive to me than the live Chris just then. The live Chris would come back to me later in shooting moments, in flashes while I was doing dishes, or thought I heard him closing a door upstairs. That Chris would be with me always, but he was temporarily eclipsed by the Chris who was supposed to be lying in that box, being visited by people who signed the register.

Back in the Georgian Slumber Room, I looked at the register to see who had been there. There were two more names on the list, and I wondered if Marilyn had been back. I took off my coat and started picking up the flower petals that had fallen in the last few hours. I didn't want the room to look messy. We wouldn't want that. And I suddenly jumped, realising that there was someone else in the room. I wheeled around, feeling as though a ghost were behind me. It was Tom Bardi, sitting quietly in a corner, smoking a cigarette.

'Hi.'

'Hi,' and we sank back into our comfortable silence. I wanted to be alone with Chris. But it was better to have Tom there. With him in the room, I just sat, and looked, and fought off the constant desire to walk up to the box and look at it, wondering if Chris were really inside.

We sat and we sat, and smoked endlessly. No one came, no one walked by, nothing stirred.

'It's eleven-thirty. Don't you want to go home, Gill?'

'No . . . I'm . . . going to stay here tonight. It probably

sounds crazy to you, but it's a tradition . . . my family . . .
I want to.'

'Peg said she thought you would.'

'Peg? When? Did she call you?' And it began to be
clear.

He said 'no' too fast, shook his head too hard. I
knew he was lying. Peg had called, that was why Tom
Bardi had been sitting there when I arrived. He must
have jumped in his car and driven straight down, in
time to be sitting in the corner when I got there. Peg
had done it again. And so had Tom. What in hell would
I do without them? I would have resented their high-
handedness, except I needed it. I really needed it . . .
Two o'clock . . . three o'clock . . . five o'clock . . .

'Tom?' He was asleep, leaning over in a corner of the
settee. I had wanted to tell him that I was going to do
something, that he could leave if he wanted to, but I
had to do it. I was going to open the box. I wanted to
make sure it was really Chris, that he was wearing his
work clothes, that they hadn't snuck a suit on him after
all.

I tiptoed up to the dark wood box, lifted off the 'spray'
of roses his mother had ordered, and stepped back,
holding my breath. It was a hell of a thing to do, but I
had to do it. Now or never. Tomorrow would be too
late. The Matthews would be back, they would be
horrified, and after that he'd belong to all of them, and
to the minister, and to the people in the church. Tonight
he was still mine. Still Chris. Not 'Christopher Caldwell
Matthews, age thirty-three of 2629.' . . . And I was still
Gill. Not 'dearly beloved we are gathered here'. Why
do they only use that for weddings and funerals? Dearly
beloved . . . by whom? God? If he loved me so much why
had he done this to me? I remembered Gordon's 'Vaya

280

con Dios'. And Dios must have taken the wrong turnoff
somewhere. Back about Friday.

I stood there and looked back at Tom, still asleep . . .
okay, here goes. There was an ornate-looking key in a
lock, halfway down the side of the casket. It turned
easily and I tried to lift the lid. It was a heavy goddam
thing. But I got it up, and it rested upward, with its
grey velvet. I looked down, and there was Chris . . .
Chris . . . looking just as he had in the hospital on Friday,
except they'd taken the sand off his face. And there
was something wrong, something else . . . his hair!
They'd combed his hair all wrong. I went to my bag,
took out my comb, and combed it the way he wore it,
falling over his ears, a little scrambled in the front. I
leaned over and kissed the hair above his forehead, the
way I do to Sam after I do her hair. I tried to hold his
hand but it was stiff. Like a wax doll. He looked so pale.
I knelt at the prie-dieu and just watched, sure that I
had seen him move, or breathe. I sat and watched, and
then finally got up and put my arms around him. It
felt so odd, it didn't give, his body didn't bend any more,
that supple body, with the soft skin. The light began to
stream in and touch his face, and it was the same Chris
who had lain in bed next to me, the sleeping boy-man
I had watched so many mornings before, as the night
turned pale grey. My tears fell on to his hands, and on to
his shirt, and ran down my neck. Good tears. Not the
broken sobs of the past two days. I was crying for Chris,
not for me. I kissed him on the cheeks and on the eyes,
and on his hands, folded so strangely over his chest. I
put a tiny white flower next to him, and took the thin
gold chain from his neck. Maybe that was against the
law or something. But he always wore it, and I knew he
would not mind my having it. It was the same as a

wedding band . . . forever, until death do you part. I looked away as I lowered the lid. I didn't want to see his face disappearing as I closed it.

I looked over at Tom still asleep on the settee, and sat in one of the chairs. Morning continued to come, still grey, and we sat there, the three of us, Tom and Chris and I. I was glad I'd done it, because I had faced death, I had touched it, and kissed it. I had buried the dead Chris in that box, I had said good-bye to the dead Chris, and the live Chris began to come to life again. I would never see the body again, or touch that face, but I would see the smile, and hear the laugh, remember the shouts, and see his face when I got up in the morning and heard a familiar sound. Chris had come back to me, and would stay with me always, and I leaned my head back and fell asleep.

Something was shaking me, and I looked up into Tom Bardi's face, surprised, forgetting where I was.

'Want some coffee?'

'Yes, what time is it?'

'Eight-thirty. You must have been sleeping a long time. I sacked out hours ago myself.' Yes, a long time. He came back with two cups of steaming coffee in those styrofoam cups. We drank them and made small talk. The room was not so formidable in the daylight with sun beginning to stream in through the windows.

We finished the coffee, and Mrs Matthews arrived with Jane and Don, all of them looking very neat and dressed up, Mrs Matthews in another black suit, Jane in a navy blue coat dress, and Don in the same dark suit.

Tom said he'd drive me home, but we both had our cars, so we followed each other up towards the west end of the city, through the empty streets. It was still too early for any traffic on a Sunday. Mrs Matthews had told me to meet them in church, so there was no need for me to go back, and I was grateful to have a few hours at home. I had said good-bye to Chris and to Hobson's and I wondered who would be in the Georgian room tomorrow. I would never forget it. I would walk by years later and look down that hall, visible from the street, and wonder who was in the Georgian Slumber Room now.

Tom waved as I stopped in front of our house and he drove on. I meant to ask him in for a cup of coffee, but it was just as well. Peg and Sam were eating breakfast, and I stopped for a cup of coffee, feeling more tired than I had since Friday, but more peaceful, much quieter. After breakfast I went upstairs and lay on our bed, not sleeping, just lying there, grateful that Peg and Sam were in the garden and away from me. Today was a day I wanted to be left alone.

At one-thirty, Peg came up to see how I was doing, and poked her head in the door. 'You've got about half an hour,' and I was reminded of when Peg had been the maid of honour at my wedding. She grumbled and bitched, and complained about wearing 'that jackass veil you picked out, Gill, you bitch,' but she had ended up being the ringleader, and had been very brides-maidish about the whole thing, except when she burned her veil straight up the front, smoking a cigarette before we went up the aisle. Peg.

I did my hair, and got all ready, except for the dress. I hadn't really decided what to wear. The black dress that I had worn in New York looked so worn out, and my coat was a tweed which wasn't dark enough. My dark blue dress was too tight my charcoal dress had a huge egg stain down the front, courtesy of Samantha, and I had forgotten to send it to the cleaners after I got out to San Francisco, which left the 'wedding dress', the pale grey dress Chris hadn't even seen, hanging in the back of the closet where Peg had put it at my request on the night she arrived.

Twenty minutes later I stood in front of the mirror wearing the dress and coat, the black shoes, my grandmother's pearls, and my hair rolled into a neat bun at the base of my neck, looking just as I would have on my wedding day with Chris. It was a day and a lifetime too late for the wedding. And I reached into the collar of my dress to touch the gold chain I had taken from Chris's neck that morning . . . too late . . . much, much too late.

38

Mrs Matthews and the Lindquists were waiting in the minister's office behind the church. We met there, looking sombre, all of us dressed up, and each one engrossed in his or her own thoughts. We spoke to the minister for a few moments, and then he left and we heard the music start, softly, in the background. I had forgotten all about talking to the organist, and I didn't recognise what he was playing. It just sounded very sweet and sad. We walked into the church then, and I slipped into the first pew with Chris's family. Peg and Tom Bardi sat just behind us, and I looked around to see Peg, just once more. I reached back and she squeezed my hand, and then I noticed that there must have been seventy or eighty people scattered through the church. Not a great many,

I guess, nothing like the huge pompous funeral we had had for my grandmother, but a lot of people for Chris, for a man who really didn't see many people. A girl in a black dress and veil caught my eye, over to the left, and I looked again, knowing who I'd see. It was Marilyn. Our eyes met and held, no real kinship, no bond as there was with Chris's family. But we understood each other better than Chris's family would have understood either of us. Both of us stood alone now. Chris had moved on. And I turned back to look at the minister.

Chris lay in his casket, the flowers around it, front and centre.

'Dearly beloved . . . that he may rest in peace. Amen.' and we stood in silent prayer, as the organ played something that sounded like Bach, while I wished I had remembered to ask for Ravel. The pallbearers from Hobson's wheeled the casket down the aisle, and Mrs Matthews stepped out on Don's arm and walked behind it, slowly, looking still smaller than she had seemed before. Jane followed, and I fell into step behind her, wondering if Marilyn was going to follow me. I felt everyone watching us as we walked out, following us with their eyes, and heard a few sniffs, and a couple of loud sobs. They could do that; we couldn't. I knew Marilyn wasn't sobbing. It's always the people who knew the 'deceased' the least who can cry like that.

Outside, we climbed into Hobson's long maroon limousine, behind the hearse. I saw Peg get into Tom Bardi's car, and the procession began, down Sacramento to Gough, and then out on the highway to Daly City, which specialises in used car lots and cemeteries.

Jane and Don talked on the way out; Mrs Matthews and I said nothing. We sat next to each other, she looking down, while I looked out the window, realising that this was the same strip of road we'd travelled coming in from the airport a week ago, when Sam and I had come in from New York. A borrowed Volkswagen bus, and a maroon limousine. A thousand worlds apart, and only one short week.

At the cemetery, the minister reappeared, and we stepped forward towards the grave site, the four of us, and Peg and Tom, and five people I didn't know . . . and Marilyn. At first, I hadn't seen Marilyn. She stood a little apart, looking beautiful and tragic, the veil putting a soft grey cloud over her face, making her eyes look even larger than they were, the black dress beautifully cut. She had a wonderful grace about her, a certain style I guess. There was pride too in the way she stood. Dignity. She stood so alone, and yet she had come there for Chris, in spite of us. She looked straight at me, not showing any sign of emotion, but there. With Chris. Like us. I admired her for coming, and for the way she stood there. I guess, in her shoes, I would have done the same, but I would have looked embarrassed, or nervous. There was none of that about Marilyn.

The minister said the Lord's Prayer while we bowed our heads. And then silence. I jumped as his voice boomed out, 'Christopher Caldwell Matthews, we commit you to the earth, and into the hands of God,' and I added silently, 'Vaya con Dios.'

We returned to our various cars, and as we drove away I looked back and saw Marilyn, still standing there, straight and proud and alone, a widow, in a black veil.

39

The Lindquists left San Francisco right after the funeral, taking Mrs Matthews with them. She was going to stay in Fresno for a while. I promised to call when the baby was born, and then they were gone. When they dropped me off at home, I saw Tom Bardi's car out front. Inside, he, Peg, and Sam were talking, and they stopped when I came in.

'Hi, Mommy. Where's Uncle Crits?' It was a sad wail, and those two big eyes looked up at me, wanting an answer this time. Now or never. I took a deep breath.

'Sam, let's sit down for a minute.'

'Has he gone away like my real Daddy?'

'No. He hasn't.' I didn't want her to think that life was a series of men who went away, and came back to visit once in a while. Maybe it was, but not Chris, not this time. 'Sam, do you remember when Grandma Jean went to Heaven?'

'You mean Daddy's Mommy?'

'Yes,' and I saw Peg and Tom get up quietly and leave, and go into the kitchen, closing the door soundlessly behind them. I thought Peg was crying, but I wasn't sure. I was looking at Sam. I had to see this child, really see her, and tell her something that she could carry with her always, something of Chris.

'Well, darling . . . sometimes God loves people, specially much, and he feels they have done everything they had to do, and then he takes them up to Heaven with him.'

'Does he love everybody that much?'

'Yes, he loves everybody, but he lets some people stay here for a very long time. And other people, he takes up with him a little sooner.'

'Mommy . . . does he love you that much?' Her chin was beginning to quiver.

'Sam darling, nothing is going to happen to me.' I could see where her reasoning was leading. 'But he needed Uncle Chris to help with some things now. So now, Uncle Chris is in Heaven, with God, and Grandma Jean.'

'Will he ever come back to visit us?'

'Not the way you mean, Sam. But every time you think of Uncle Chris, that'll be like a visit. When you think of Uncle Chris, he'll always be with you. We can talk about him, and think about him, and go right on loving him. That's what forever means.'

'But I want him with us here.' That look . . . Oh God . . . that look . . .

'So do I, but this is how God wants it. We're going to miss him very much, but we have each other. And I love you very, very much.' She threw herself into my arms, and we were both crying. 'Sam, please don't be sad. Uncle Chris wouldn't want you to be sad. He isn't sad, and he doesn't hurt, and he still loves us . . .' We sat there rocking back and forth, her tears mingling with mine, and her tiny fingers squeezing the back of my neck, holding on for dear life. We rocked and rocked, and when she stopped, I looked down and saw that she had fallen asleep. My tiny wild Indian girl who had put three worms into the hands of Chris Matthews last week, who would have to live with the fact that he was gone. I sat looking at her in the darkening room, and lay her against the cushions on the couch, her face still streaked with tears.

I stood up and went to look down at the garden, took another deep breath, and went to find Tom and Peg. When I found them, they were still sitting in the kitchen, and looking a little red-eyed. They looked up at me, embarrassed, and Peg said, 'How about a drink?'

'I don't think it would help.'

'Where is she?'

'Asleep on the couch. I'm not going to wake her up for dinner. It's been a rough couple of days for her too. I hope she sleeps through.'

'Want me to carry her up to bed?'

'Thanks, Tom, that's a good idea. I think I'll go to bed too. I've had it.' I could hardly get up the stairs. Tom was walking ahead with Sam in his arms, hanging limp like a rag doll. And Peg walked behind me. I almost wanted to ask her to push, the top of the stairs looked too far away.

I lay back on my bed, still wearing the grey dress, and Peg came in to help me get undressed. 'I just can't, Peg.'

'I know. Just take off the dress. You just lie there for a while.'

I took off the new grey dress and lay down while she closed the shades and turned off the lights, and I was asleep as suddenly and as soundly as Sam had been.

I was being stabbed, someone was trying to murder me, or pummel me, they were tearing at my back, and slashing open my stomach, ripping at every muscle . . . My God, help me, somebody help me, please . . . I fought to wake up to get rid of the pain, to escape from the bad dream. I woke up limp, and exhausted, and turned to look at the clock next to the bed. I lifted my head to see, and the same pain seized me again, tearing through my back and reaching across my belly like hands tearing through my guts. It made me cry out, and Peg came in as I was trying to catch my breath, while the pain went away again.

'Gill? Something wrong? I heard you . . . Christ, you look awful.'

'I don't feel so great.' I tried to sit up and the pain ripped through me again, making me clutch at the sheet and squirm so as not to cry out.

'Don't move. I'll call the doctor. What's his name?'

'Morse. Number's on the pad in the kitchen . . . Tell him . . . I think I'm in labour . . . Tell him . . .' and another pain tore through me. I lay in bed fighting the panic and trying to ride with the pain, waiting for Peg to come back.

'He said to bring you to the hospital right away. Can you walk to the car?'

I tried to stand up but couldn't even sit up, and as I tried to roll over towards the side of the bed we saw that there was blood where I had been lying.

'Oh my God . . . Oh Jesus, Peg . . .'

'Now just take it easy, Gill. I called Tom, he's coming to stay with Sam. He can carry you down to the car.'

I lay back, hurting too much to talk any more. Peg blurred and faded away and came back again, and the pain kept hitting at me, and grabbing me and lifting me up and throwing me against what felt like sharp rocks. I wanted to hold Peg's hand but couldn't lie still enough. And then I saw Tom Bardi in the doorway. He was standing over me after that, and soon I was lifted out of bed, with the blanket, and set down again in Chris's car. I saw Tom and Peg exchange looks, and I think I must have fainted then because the next time I opened my eyes there were a thousand lights above me, a lot of noise, and people, and metallic sounds, and I felt woozy, as though I were floating just under the lights, and above the people, suspended between two worlds. I floated for a while and then . . . oh God . . . oh my God . . . they're tearing me apart . . . they're killing me . . . oh God . . . Chris . . . Peg . . . please stop them . . . I can't stand it, I can't, I can't . . . I can't . . . and everything went black.

I woke up in a strange room, feeling as though I were going to vomit. I looked over and saw Peg, and then it all faded again. It kept coming and going. I'd wake up and see Peg, and then she'd go away again. It kept coming and going. Somewhere in another world there was someone in a bed, with transfusions and tubes and all sorts of things happening to her. I could see it clearly, but I didn't know who she was. I wondered, but not enough to ask. I was too tired . . . too tired . . .

Oh Jesus, do my guts hurt. 'Peg? . . . what happened?' And I turned towards her to talk to her . . . my stomach . . . it's flat . . . the baby . . . 'Peg . . . Peg . . . the baby?' But I already knew. I knew what had happened. The baby was dead.

'Lie back, Gillian, you've been out of it for a long time.'

'I don't care.' Sobs shook me and made everything hurt worse.

After a while I asked what time it was. 'Two o'clock.'

'In the afternoon? . . . Jesus . . .'

'Yeah, Gill . . . and . . . it's Tuesday . . .'

'Tuesday? . . . My God!'

Nurses came and went, Peg came and went, and time passed. There was nothing left to rush for, or to think about. Sam was at home with Peg, and Mrs Jaeger, and

Chris and the baby were gone. Nothing mattered any more. Nothing and no one. Not Chris, not the baby, not Sam, not me. Not anything.

Peg must have made her phone calls again, because there were flowers from Hilary again, and Gordon, and 'John Templeton and the Staff'. It looked like an instant replay of the funeral. Only this time, I wasn't touched. I just didn't give a damn any more.

I also discovered that it's hospital practice to put a woman who has just lost a baby in the maternity wing along with everyone else. It's one of the most psychologically inhuman facts of modern medicine, but there it is. And there you are, hearing the babies being rolled down the hall, listening to them cry. And wishing you were dead.

I was informed of how much the baby had weighed, how long he had been, what his blood type was, and how long he had lived. Seven hours and twenty-three minutes. And I'd never even gotten to see him. It was a boy.

By the end of the week I was feeling stronger and they decided to let me go home on Sunday. I had to get back anyway. Peg had to leave.

'I'm staying another week.'

'No you're not. You've been out here long enough, taking care of me and my recurring disasters.'

'Stop being dramatic. I'm staying.'

'Look, Peg, I'll call an agency and get another mother's helper. I'm supposed to sit on my ass for three weeks. You don't expect to stay out for that long, do you?' Peg wavered then, and we agreed to compromise. She'd stay until the following Wednesday.

On Sunday, I went home. I was evicted along with a half-dozen starry-eyed girls holding their babies wrapped in pastel-coloured blankets. Peg picked me up with the car, and I grabbed my little overnight case from the nurse, got into the car, and all I could say was, 'Come on, Peg, let's get the hell out of here.' She stepped on the gas and we were off, towards Sacramento Street.

At home, everything was in perfect order. The superwoman efficiency of Peg Richards was visible everywhere. Sam was waiting for me at the door with a little bunch of flowers she'd picked in the garden. And it was so good to be back with her. I felt guilty because I had given her so little thought while I was in the hospital. I had almost stopped caring about her too. But there she was, sweet Sam.

Peg shooed me upstairs, put me to bed, brought me a cup of tea, and I felt like a queen. A sick queen, but nevertheless, *a queen*. There was absolutely nothing for me to do except lie there and be waited on.

I was still feeling very weak, and it was nice having Peg to run interference for me. The phone rang twice after I got home. Once it was Mrs Matthews, and the second time it was Gordon. Peg looked over at me both times, and I shook my head. Not yet. Everyone knew. That was good enough. I had nothing left to add. Mrs Matthews would only tell me how sorry she was, and I was sorry enough on my own, and also felt badly to have added to her grief. Gordon would only want to come out, or for me to go back to New York, and I didn't want to hear about it. I had chosen blue jeans and daisies . . . and I still wanted them. I didn't want to hear about New York, or the magazine, or anything else. It was all behind me, however things had turned out.

I looked through my mail and saw that Gordon had sent the picture of the three of us standing in front of the Rolls. I looked at it once and tossed it on the table next to my bed while Peg looked on. 'That was such a long time ago, Peg.' She nodded and put the picture back in the envelope.

The only good thing the hospital had done for me was that it had put a little more time between me and the brutal realities that had hit me so suddenly. For a while, I didn't have to wander around the house, touching things, looking at things, being reminded. Not right away. And now I had to rest, and there would be more time.

The next few days slid by, and on Wednesday Peg left with hugs and good-byes and the kind of thanks you can't even begin to say, and promises to call and write. She even said she'd come out for a week in the spring. Tom Bardi took her to the airport, and I began to wonder if there was more to that than just helping me. Their week and a half together had created the same kind of bond that happens on sea voyages. They had been isolated from their own worlds, and thrown together constantly, not on a pleasure trip, but by a series of disasters, and they had formed a circle around me, becoming enmeshed in it themselves. Maybe like after a sea voyage they would find nothing in common when they met again, if they met again. Peg didn't say anything before she left, so I was left to wonder.

Tom was of Chris's world, very much like him in his directness and no bullshit ways, yet he was simpler than Chris, and he seemed kinder; he didn't have Chris's ruthless honesty. Or his sparkle either, for that matter. But I suspected that he might have been easier to live with because of it. He was also less adept with words. And I noticed before Peg left that he looked at her with a kind of awe. It was something for me to think about anyway.

I had a mother's helper again by then. She was sleeping in Sam's room, and the entire routine rolled along, while I got my strength back, and some of the emotional pain began to dim. As I had told Sam, Chris was always with us. We talked about him, the memory of his face lit up my days, and the sound of his voice filled my dreams. I found myself sleeping most of the time, too much of the time. It was an easy escape, and in sleep there was always Chris. He was always waiting for me to fall asleep, ready to stretch out a hand and pull me to his side, away from the empty house . . . and the truth.

40

In March, I learned in a letter from John Templeton that Julie Weintraub had been in a coma for almost three weeks, and had then died quietly, never regaining consciousness. It was merciful, as her last days of lucidity had been filled with excruciating pain. To me, that seemed to close a whole volume of my life. Chris, the baby, Julie. All gone. My life was beginning to fill with ghosts. I was back on my feet by then, and spending a lot of time around the house, painting a little, being with Samantha, and letting time move on, without actually filling it. There seemed to be nothing to fill it with. I had gained back some of the weight I had lost, and was looking healthy from the long walks I took with Sam.

Tom Bardi dropped by a lot, brought small presents for

Sam, and had dinner with us occasionally. He hadn't a great deal to say, but he was a nice presence, and Sam and I enjoyed him. He almost never mentioned Peg, but whenever I did he seemed to shoot up straight in his chair and listen to hear everything I said. It was sweet to watch, and I wondered if Peg knew about it or if they both did, and I was just the last one to know for certain.

One day, I couldn't resist. 'Do you ever hear from Peg, Tom?'

'No,' and he blushed.

'Why don't you call her some time?'

'Call her?' He looked so shocked that I dropped the subject. They were grownups; Peg was one of the most straightforward people I'd ever known, and Tom looked like he could take care of himself, so I decided to shut my big mouth and mind my own business.

I had heard from Gordon twice before he left for France, empassioned pleas begging me to think of myself, and of him, and join him. But I didn't want to leave San Francisco. Or Chris.

I still hadn't done anything about clearing out Chris's things, and when I got too lonely I'd open his closet and look at the boots, and the jeans and sweaters, and his smell would put its arms around me and Chris would only be out for a little while. His studio remained untouched. I had been up there once to look for some papers, but not again. Everyone in the house knew that it was off limits. It was becoming a kind of shrine.

I wrote to Peg regularly and told her what we were doing, and she answered sporadically. I knew that she was getting tired of her job, and once she mentioned that she might come out. But she never brought it up again. She knew that my doors were always open to her, and I hoped she would come.

She began to prod me in her letters: '. . . You have to see some men . . . You should get a job . . . You should take a trip . . .' She never suggested going back to New York though. She knew better.

Sam's school year ended at the very end of May, and I sat with her at breakfast one morning, thinking that it had been five months since Chris had died. In a way, it seemed as though Sam and I had lived that way forever, and in another way, it seemed as though he had walked through the room that morning. I was keeping it that way, keeping Chris alive, to keep myself alive, to hang on.

It was lonely, but not the kind of lonely that I had suffered through in New York when I'd gone back. That had been a fierce, biting, rolling kind of thing; it was full of worry and alternatives, and constant frustration, though I may not have seen it that way at the time. It was a time full of anger. But the spring after Chris's death had no anger to it, nothing in common with those days, except for the fact that I was alone. There was an irrevocability to it, a quiet acceptance. My ship lay at anchor and I had nowhere to go. There was nowhere I wanted to go, except where I was. I was painting more, reading a lot, and becoming increasingly introspective. It was like becoming a nun. It was also a little bit like a dark tunnel; I was passing through it, and when I got to the end of it . . . if I got to the end of it . . . then I'd see.

Sam was due to visit her father in June, and I was thinking of going up to the mountains around Lake Tahoe, just to get away a little, but I hesitated. I was happy at home, with Chris's things all around me. Happy sleeping in his bed, happy in his sweaters and workshirts.

I had finally married Chris. But I had married a dead man, and was drifting along with him. I was almost as dead as he.

'Sam, the doorbell. Be a big girl and answer it for me. I'm upstairs, but ask who it is first,' and then Tom Bardi was racing up the stairs, two at a time, and he burst into the room.

'Peg is coming!'

'When?'

'Tomorrow.' He was grinning from ear to ear.

'She is? Are you sure? How do you know?' It seemed funny that I wouldn't have heard anything about it.

'She just called me,' and he looked irritated with me for doubting it. As though I could make it not true by my questions.

I hadn't heard anything, other than the vague hint in her last letter. That's funny.

'She's coming in tomorrow morning. Early. I'm going to pick her up.' I was tempted to ask if I could go too. After all I had known Peg all my life, and here was a stranger going out to get her. But I didn't say anything. Maybe Peg would like it better this way. She had called him, not me.

The phone rang then, and it was Peg.

'I'm coming out tomorrow.'

'I know.'

'Oh.'

'Tom's standing right here.'

'Say hi for me. Can I stay with you again?' And all my suspicions went down the drain. Or almost.

'Sure. I'd love it. How long do you think you'll be here?'

'Week, maybe two, maybe three. I'll see. I've got three, but really should go see Mother on the way back.'

'Great. Tom said he'd pick you up. Why don't you come over afterwards? Or . . . just see how it goes. See you tomorrow. Peg, I can't wait!' We said good-bye and hung up.

'Did she want to talk to me?'

'She had to run. She'll be here tomorrow, Tom.' He looked like a little boy, that same look Chris had had, the same look Samantha got.

Then Tom clattered back down the stairs and vanished, and the next time I saw him he was at my front door, standing behind Peg, and he looked as though he had found the pot of gold at the end of the rainbow. Peg threw herself into my arms, and we laughed and squealed and hugged, and Sam got into the act. It was a genuine homecoming.

'Welcome back. We've missed you.'

'Well, I see the place hasn't changed. Boy, it's nice to be back.' Tom took her things up to Sam's room and reappeared. We had lunch together, and sat around for a while, and then they went out for a walk and said they'd go to a movie. I went to bed early and didn't hear Peg come in.

Next morning she came down to breakfast, and she had that serious look on her face that meant she was going 'to talk to me'. Mother Peg. Lecture time. I braced myself with a cup of coffee and a grin. I really had missed Peg.

'Gillian.' She sounded very firm.

'Yes, Peg? Or should I call you "Margaret"? You sound like a Margaret this morning,' but she didn't smile back.

'Where's Sam?'

'Out with some friends. Why?'

'Because I want to talk to you, and I don't want Sam to hear this. Gill, when I said that the place looked the same yesterday, I didn't know how true that was. Jesus, Gill, his stuff is still all over the place, his papers, his clothes, his shirts, his toothbrush. What the fuck are you trying to do to yourself? You're twenty-nine years old. He's dead. You're not. I bet you haven't even touched his studio. Have you? Well, have you?' Christ, she had hit low. It was true, but how could she understand? How could she begin to understand? Peg had a warm heart and a full life of her own making, but she'd never been married, never had children, never lost the man she loved, or his child. She couldn't understand.

'Peg, you don't understand.'

'I do understand. I understand much better than you think, much better than you do even. I see it better than you do. And Tom says it too. He says you wear his clothes, talk about him as though he were still here. You don't do anything, you don't go out. Jesus, Gill, it's goddam creepy.'

'It is not creepy. It's how I want to live. And you make it sound as though I go around in drag in his clothes, goddammit. Get off my fucking back, will you?' I was getting mad because I didn't like the truth of what she was saying. She had no right.

'I have no right to talk to you like this . . . except I do. Because I love you, Gill. I can't stand to see you doing this to yourself. You've done some crazy things and I've always stood by you. You came back to New York, to have his baby, and I didn't say anything because I thought maybe you were right. I wouldn't have done it, but I could at least understand it. But this . . . this is different, this is sick. Please see that, oh please, Gill, see what you're doing to yourself . . . and to Sam. What the hell do you think this is doing to her?' And again I knew it was true, and I wound up to fight back, without looking up at Peg.

When at last I did look up, I saw that she was crying. For me, and for Samantha, and maybe even for Chris.

When I saw her crying, tears welled in my own eyes, and I laid my head down on the table, and cried, all those months of peace and adjustment, blown to hell in ten minutes. Because I had never adjusted. I had known peace because I had lived in a dream, and had never come face to face with the truth. Maybe I could have faced losing Chris if I had had the baby, but when I lost the baby there was nothing left. Nothing real. So I created my own dream world, and hung on to Chris. In those ten minutes the whole shell I had built around myself cracked wide open, and I sat there naked and raw, and bleeding, exposed to all the things I had hidden from in all those months, exposed to the truth. Chris was dead.

Peg let me sit there and cry it out, moving quietly around the kitchen. Just once she put her hand on my shoulder and said, 'I'm sorry, Gill,' and I managed to choke out, 'Don't be.' Because she was right, and she was right to say it. I had been wrong. Terribly, terribly wrong, and I had been doing something awful to Samantha in the bargain.

'Peg, will you help me?'
'How, baby?'
'Help me go through his stuff.'
She nodded. 'When?'
'Now.'
'Now?'
'Now. If I don't do it now, maybe I'll never do it. Maybe then I'd just live forever in this spider web I've spun for myself.'
'Okay. Let's go,' and for hours we sat there and sorted and made piles and divided up. It was just as though we

had done it the day after the funeral; it wouldn't have made any difference. The pain was all there. Intact.

I made a small pile for Mrs Matthews of things I thought she'd want to have. And another small pile for Jane. And I kept a few things out for myself, things I wasn't ready to give up, things that were Chris. But this time I put them in a box. I'd have them; I didn't have to hold them and smell them every night. I'd just know they were there.

The rest of the stuff we put in big piles in the down-stairs closet, ready to go to Goodwill.

At the end of the day I thought Sam might be coming home, so we stopped. There was nothing left to do on the first two floors anyway. We'd cleaned it out.

'Tomorrow, the studio.'

'You want Tom to help?'

'Yes.'

The next day the three of us went through the place, dividing and sorting. I gave a lot of things to Tom; they were the tools of his trade and he could use them. We worked like demons through the day, and at 6:07 p.m. the studio was no more. The earthly goods of Christopher Caldwell Matthews had been divided up and disposed of. End of an era.

41

After Peg's second week with me I was beginning to wonder. She made no mention of leaving, and I didn't want to bring it up and make her think I was pushing her out. She was spending a lot of time with Tom, and I wasn't seeing too much of her, but she looked happy, and San Francisco seemed to agree with her.

Sam and I were enjoying our last days together before she went off to be with her father for a month. And I was thinking about getting a job. As usual, Peg's visit had had an effect.

I was mulling over the wants ad one morning when Peg came in and stood in the doorway with that 'I've got to talk to you' look again.

'Come on, stop looking so official. Come and sit down. And don't give me hell about anything. I've been a good girl. I'm even looking at the want ads in the paper.'

'Christ . . . do I look like that?' and she laughed.

'Yes you do. What's up?'

'Well . . . Tom and I are getting married,' and she sat there, looking as though she were holding her breath.

'Peg! . . . Wow!' I jumped up and hugged her. 'When?'

'Tomorrow.'

'Do you have a licence?' The same words I had asked Chris not so very long ago.

'Yes.'

'Well, for chrissake! Couldn't you have said something?'

'I didn't know. Honest, Gill, I wasn't sure. I had this feeling after I went back to New York, but I never heard from Tom and I didn't know if he felt it too . . . and . . . oh shit.'

'Jesus, Peg, I can't believe it. Fairy tales do exist . . . for some people,' and we both looked away, both of us knowing that her dream had started with my nightmare.

Tom rang the doorbell then and I kissed him and said, 'Congratulations!' and he blushed furiously.

'She told you?'

'Told me what?' and he blushed even more, while Peg and I burst into whoops.

'She's putting you on, love. I told her.' He looked relieved.

Thomas Hugo Bardi and Margaret Allison Richards were married the next day, at City Hall, along with what looked like all the same funny old people who had been there the day Chris and I had gone down for our licence, which I still have.

Samantha and I stood by to watch the whole thing happen, along with a friend of Tom's, and we all went out to lunch in Sausalito after that.

After lunch, Tom picked up Peg's things at my house and they went off to his place for their honeymoon. After they left, I couldn't help thinking what a far cry it was from the little girl dreams we had all had in school. Peg had always sworn she'd elope with a professional cowboy or something of the sort. But none of our dreams had looked very much like this. Better this way, I thought. She has a better chance. They're going to be okay. I wondered if Peg's mother knew yet. The formidable Mrs Richards who was as unlike Peg as mustard is to caviar. She was going to have a few things to say.

By noon the next day they were back at my place for lunch, chatting with Sam, sitting at my kitchen table as though they had been married for the last seven years.

'What are you going to do about your stuff in New York?'

'Oh one of the girls at the office said she'd pack it up and send it. I don't really have a whole lot. And she can keep some of it, she's taking over my apartment,' which reminded me that the lease on Chris's house was up next month, and I had to sign the renewal paper. 'They were really nice at the office though. They said they figured that something like this would come up sooner or later. And they offered me a job in the Oakland buying office as a wedding present.'

'You're going to commute?'

'For that price, you better believe it!'

'What's your mother say? I forgot to ask you the other day.'

'Nothing I'd care to repeat, but she'll get over it.'

We sat around talking about nothing much for a while, and I thought about how nice it was to see them together. But it made me miss Chris again. It was all so closely linked. It was painful to see them, though I would never have admitted it to Peg. But I think she knew.

'Gillian?'

'Yes?'

'Why don't you go on a trip or something? And you know, I was thinking, it might do you good to move into a smaller place.'

'Hey, now wait a minute, Peg. Cool it. I cleaned out my house, and followed all your advice, but don't let it go to your head. It stops there. You just cool it. Why don't you start picking on Tom, henpeck him a little, show him how a wife behaves.'

'Now don't go getting all huffy. I mean it. At least you could go on a trip. You don't have a job yet, and Sam will be gone. Why don't you go to Hawaii, or something?'

'Because I don't like Hawaii. Richard and I went there before Sam was born and it rained the whole goddam time.

'Well, go someplace else then.'

'I'll think about it,' but I really didn't mean it. Cleaning out the house was one thing, leaving it was another.

Tom and Peg got up to leave, and they said they'd be

back some time tomorrow or the next day.

'Listen, you guys, you're on your honeymoon. You don't have to baby-sit with me.'

'No. We just like the coffee,' that from Tom, who patted my shoulder again as they left. I think they felt they had to take care of me. It was a nice thing to do. Maybe they felt they owed me a debt for bringing them together. Whatever it was, it was nice to have them around, they were nice to watch, but they kept giving me this lonely feeling as I'd watch them leave or look at each other in a funny way or hold hands when they didn't think I was looking. Chris had been gone a long time.

42

I had had a letter from Gordon telling me how well things were going for him and how much he liked Eze. He was thinking of having a show in Paris in the late fall, if all went well, and if his work kept up at the pace he was keeping. He was settled, had rented a tiny house with an incredible view, and a skylight, and he was learning to play boule.

He suggested that I might like to come and visit for a few days if I was in Europe for the summer, or I might want to spend a month with him, 'if that appeals', but I gathered from the tone of the invitation that he knew I wouldn't accept. I hadn't seen him in months, and it might as well have been years. I felt so much older, and different. Not wiser, just a little more tired, and yes, different.

I was in the midst of packing Sam's things for her visit with Richard, and was thinking that it was going to be nice to have Tom and Peg around. It wouldn't be quite so lonely. The house would be so empty without Sam, but it was better than having her commute on weekends or getting confused by constant visits had her father lived nearby. I wondered if she'd grow up with the same sense of unfamiliarity with her father that I had had with mine. Maybe that's the price you pay. Or just the price some fathers pay.

The phone was ringing . . . probably Peg.

'Hello?'

'*Allo? Allo? Oui? . . . Allo?*'

'Yes, I'm here . . . Hello.' Terrible connection; it sounded like little gnomes grinding rocks in a coal mine.

'*Madame Foe-ress-taire, s'il vous plaît. Nous avons un appel de la part de Monsieur Ahrte,*' and the aahhrte rolled in the operator's throat, reminding me of French teachers in school.

'*C'est elle-même.*' This is she.

'Gillian?'

'Yes. Gordon, what the hell are you doing calling me all this distance? You must be getting rich over there.'

'I'm sitting in front of the most exquisite sunset I've ever seen. I had to call you. I want you to come over.'

'For a sunset? I think I might miss it. You're too much. It's a long way off, Gordon. I want to stay here for a while.'

'Why don't you come over? And bring Sam. It would be marvellous for her.'

'Her father is picking her up in two days. She's all set for the summer, or one month at least. So I'm going to stay home and keep house.'

'For whom?'

'Me.'

'Gillian, please. Don't answer me now, think about it, please.'

'All right, I'll think about it.'

'No you won't, I can tell.' He was right.

'Really, I will. I'll write and let you know what I decide.' I'll write and tell you no.

'No. If you write, that means you're not coming. I'll call you in a few days. There's a flight out of Los Angeles that goes direct to Nice. I could pick you up there.'

'Christ, I haven't been there since I was a kid.'

'Well, it's time you came back . . . please.' There was that pleading tone in his voice again.

'Well, I'll think it over. How's everything else?'

'Wonderful. I'm happy here. You were right.' At least I had been right for someone. But that wasn't fair. It wasn't anyone's fault that Chris had fallen off a crane.

'How's Greg?'

'He was over here during spring vacation. Loved it, said he's coming back in July,' and there was something new in Gordon's voice. I could hear it in spite of the little gnomes hacking away at our transatlantic connection.

'Look, this is costing you a fortune. I'll talk to you soon.'

'Think about it, Gill . . . I need you.'

'Good-bye.'

'Bye . . . I'll call you at the end of the week.'

. . . I need you . . . I need you . . . How long had it been since a man had said that to me? Months? Longer? Had Chris ever really needed me, or just wanted me? And Gordon hadn't needed me before either. Not until the very end. How long since a man had needed me? Ever? . . . I need you . . .

*

I called Peg and told her, and her reaction was instantaneous. 'Go!' It was a command. But I had known she would say that. Why did I call her? To hear her tell me that? To hear her say 'Go!'?

'Don't be an ass. All I need is to go to the south of France and get all messed up with Gordon.'

'Messed up? What's messed up? He was good enough for you before. Do you have something better I don't know about? Shit, Gillian, I'd jump at the chance.'

'Don't let Tom hear you say that.'

'All right, all right, but if you don't go . . . baby, you're out of your mind,' and we hung up, equally irritated with each other. I was annoyed with Peg, and with myself for calling her. Now, I'd have to listen to her push and harp for the next few days, and then bitch at me all summer about not going.

Sam left with Richard and they flew to London. Before he left, he looked at me and I think he felt sorry for me. 'I'm sorry this has happened to you, Gill,' and he only knew the half of it.

'Thanks. So am I. But we're doing fine. Sam likes San Francisco.' Anything to get off the subject.

'You never go to Europe any more. Why don't you come over this summer, to pick up Sam? It would give you a chance to roam around again.'

'And recapture my youth?'

'I didn't say that.'

'No, but you thought it. I'll see.' Everyone was pushing Europe this season.

I told Sam I'd call her, and she looked tearful as they left. I remembered that same feeling from when I was a child, and it tore at my heart as they drove away while I stood on the steps waving.

*

I sat in the house, listening to the emptiness, looking at the toys she'd left in the living-room, wondering how people survive without children.

The phone rang again. I hoped it was Peg. It would be nice to have them over to put some life and voices back in the place.

'*Allo?*' Oh Christ. Gordon again. And I hadn't really given it any thought. Not yet. I needed time. Please, some time. Not yet . . . always not yet.

'Gillian? What's the word? But before you tell me, I want you to know that I'll understand if you don't come. I want you here, but I understand. I have no right . . .'

'I'm coming,' and I almost fell off my seat I was so surprised at myself.

'You are?' I wasn't the only one who was surprised.

'Yes. I just made up my mind. This minute, in fact.' I was still stunned.

'When are you coming?'

'I don't know. I really hadn't thought about it till this second. When's the next plane over?'

'Tomorrow.'

'Too soon.'

'All right. There's another one a week from tomorrow. That ought to give you time to get yourself together. When's Sam leaving?'

'She just left, about eight minutes ago.'

'All right, I'll meet you in Nice, a week from tomorrow. I'll be at the airport. And Gillian . . . darling . . . thank you. You'll love it here, you really will . . . Thank you.'

I murmured something in response and we hung up. What the hell had I done? I had given myself a vacation, nothing more. Oh, yes, much more. I had held out a hand and allowed myself to be needed again, because I needed Gordon too. It was a beautiful feeling. Chris . . .

Chris . . . darling, I'm sorry . . . but as I walked upstairs I remembered Chris. And Marilyn. The real Chris. He'd understand. He really would have.

'Peg? I'm going. I just talked to Gordon. I'm leaving a week from tomorrow.'

'Hallelujah! We'll be right over.' And they were, with a bottle of Spanish wine, which we finished in an hour, amidst great giggles and back pounding. They were 'proud' of me. Too proud. I felt as though I had betrayed Chris, and in a quiet moment I went out to the kitchen to get more ice. And get away from them.

Tom was right behind me and he was looking down at me as I fiddled with the ice tray. I was trying not to cry, and not to look back at him, when he grabbed my arm and pulled me out of my hiding place in the refrigerator.

'Gillian. He would have wanted it. He wouldn't have liked you like this.'

'I know. But I can't help it. I have to . . . I had to.'

'I know that. But now you have to stop. Love him, Gillian, remember him, remember what he was. But don't turn him into a ghost. He wasn't that kind of man. And you're not that kind of woman. Hang on to him. We all will. And maybe you'll never love anybody as much as you loved him, but I'll bet you never loved him alive as much as you love him dead.' It was true, it was true. I had had doubts and bad moments. But I did love him, and I looked up at Tom with tears running down my cheeks again, and feeling defiant. 'I did love him.'

'I know you did. But be brave, Gill. Don't settle for halfway. You never have before and he never did,' and I hung on to Tom and cried. It was almost over . . . don't settle for halfway . . . step out, walk ahead, move on, reach out . . . to love again . . . be brave enough . . . to go to Eze . . . brave enough for Gordon. Brave enough for Chris.

When we walked out of the kitchen, Peg looked up at us and said, 'Kissing in the kitchen, huh? Listen, Gill, I hate to ask you this, but . . . can we borrow the house while you're gone? We have to give up Tom's place. It's too small and it's driving me nuts. The lease is up this month and we should be able to find something else pretty soon.'

'Sure! You don't even have to ask. You can move in tomorrow.'

'Well, I think we can wait a week.' It was a nice feeling to know that there would be people living in the house while I was gone. Living people. Happy people. Our friends in Chris's house.

A week later, Tom and Peg drove me down to Los Angeles. I had insisted that I could fly down and just change planes, but they wanted to go down and see Tom's parents, and they wanted to see me off.

'How do I know you won't sit in Disneyland all summer and tell us you've been to France?'

'Don't you trust me?'

'No,' and she looked as though she might mean it. It was a nice trip down; we took turns driving, and the trip went quickly.

'Pan American Flight 115, departing from Gate 43 . . . final call for all passengers departing to Nice, France, on Pan American Flight . . .'

'That's it.'

'Yeah.' We stood around looking nervous, not knowing what to say. That same feeling we had had at Hobson's. God, how I hate good-byes.

312

'Peg, take care . . . I'll write . . . Tom . . .' and he squeezed me in a big bear hug and passed me on to Peg who hugged me too and looked shaken.

'Now get on that goddam plane before I fall apart, willyouforchrissake.' That was the old Peg.

'Good-bye, you two.'

Tom gave me one of his boy-man grins. 'We'll take good care of the house. And let us know when you're coming back so we can sweep up the dirt.' I nodded, and they waved, and I walked through the gate to Flight 115. I looked back and they were still there, watching, and holding hands.

43

It wasn't quite tourist season yet, so the flight was less than half full. It is a long flight, and most people prefer to break it up by stopping in New York. Most of the people looked European, and I sat alone, with three seats to myself, across the aisle from a man who was also travelling alone and who looked definitely American. He looked over at me a few times, and I thought he might try to start a conversation so I looked away.

I slept for most of the trip, and looked down at the clouds, thinking about Peg and how far we'd come together. Tom too. He had become one hell of a good friend, and it seemed fitting that he and Peg should end up together. Who would have believed all this a year ago? Who would believe anything the year before it happens?

*

'Excuse me, but aren't you Lillian Forrest? I think I met you in New York.' It was the man from across the aisle. I was tempted to say, 'No, the name's Jane Jones.'

'Gillian Forrester. You were close,' and I looked away again, hoping he'd be satisfied with having established who I was. I didn't ask him to reciprocate the information, for fear it would lead him into further conversation.

'You won't believe this, but I met you at a party you gave, oh way back in October it must have been, last year. In New York. Great party!'

'Thanks.'

'I was working for a bank in New York, and this chick says, "I've been invited to the greatest party, I mean this girl really knows how to give them." And she was right. Great party! Would you believe, after that she got married, and I got transferred to Los Angeles, and my sister had twins? I mean, all that since last fall,' and he looked at me, as though I really shouldn't believe it.

'Thanks, about the party, I mean. Sounds like you've had a busy year,' and I cringed, thinking I had encouraged him to expound further.

'Yeah. Sometimes I just sit back and think, "whoda believed it a year ago, here I am in Los Angeles." I mean it's a whole new world. A whole new life.'

'Mmm . . . I know what you mean. Who would believe?' and I turned away again, to look out the window, down at the clouds.

'You know something, Lillian, you look different. I almost didn't recognise you, except I never forget a face.' He stared at me for a moment. 'Yeah, you've changed. Something about the way you look. Not older, just different.' That's right, brother, 'different', but older; it's okay, you could have said it, because, baby, I earned it.

I turned away then, for the last time, and slept the rest of the way to Nice.

'Veuillez attacher votre ceinture de sûreté, et ne pas . . .' — please fasten . . . 'We will be arriving in Nice in approximately fifteen minutes; the local time is three-thirty-five and the temperature is seventy-eight degrees Fahrenheit. Thank you for flying Pan American. We hope you have enjoyed your flight, and wish you a pleasant stay in Nice. If you wish to make reservations for the trip home, please see our ticket agent in the main lobby of the terminal building. Thank you and good-bye . . . *Mesdames et messieurs, nous allons atterrir à Nice dans . . . Merci et au revoir.'*

The plane came to a bumpy stop on the runway and taxied in towards the terminal building, stopping just far enough away to allow a gangway to be rolled up next to the aircraft. I came down the stairs and looked around. No sign of Gordon. And then I remembered customs. *La douane.* He would be waiting on the other side. I felt surprisingly calm, only a little irritated that I hadn't at least had time to comb my hair properly before landing. I had slept till the last minute and had had to do all possible repairs from my seat. I felt rumpled; it had been a long trip.

The *douanier* looked North African, and stamped my passport and bags without a second glance. American passport. Abracadabra, like magic. They hate your guts, but at least they don't rip your luggage apart. Not like in the States.

'So long, Lillian . . . see you 'round.' My friend from across the aisle. Still no Gordon. Maybe he had been delayed by traffic, maybe. But what if? . . . Oh not

315

something else. Oh please, Lord, don't do this to me. You can't hate me this much . . . No, oh no . . . and as I began to panic I looked up and there he was. Taller than I had remembered, thinner, his beard looked fuller, his eyes bluer in the tanned face. He stood looking uncertain, as though he wasn't sure he ought to come and get me after all. All the last months stood between us, the story of it in his eyes, just as I knew it was in mine. We just went on standing there.

'Watch your step, madame, it's a very big step. Watch your step, sir.' There were two steep steps down from the customs area, and a guard was warning arriving tourists. You're right, it's a very big step monsieur. And Tom's words rang in my ears: 'Be brave, Gill. Don't settle for halfway . . .' I stepped down, slowly, carefully, deliberately, looking down at the steps to be sure of my footing. Always look to be sure of your footing. Look at those steps . . . one . . . two . . . and I was at his side.

He continued to look down at me for an endless moment, doubtful, as though he didn't dare believe. He pulled me to him, slowly, holding me gently in his arms.

'I'm back,' I whispered into his shoulder.

He closed his eyes then and pulled me closer. 'Now I know. I thought I'd lost you too.' After a moment we faced each other again, all our years reflected in our eyes, the people we had been, the people we had loved, the people we had lost in different ways . . . his wife . . . my husband . . . Juanita . . . Greg . . . Chris . . . they stood around us, and watched us go, hand in hand, going home.

To Love Again

Danielle Steel

To Bill, Beatrix and Nicholas,
with all my love.

And to Phyllis Westberg,
with love and thanks.

Chapter One

In every city there is a time of year that approaches perfection. After the summer heat, before the winter bleakness, before snow and rain are even dreamed of. A time that stands out crystal clear, as the air begins to cool; a time when the skies are still bright blue, when it feels good to wear wool again, and one walks faster than one has in months. A time to come alive again, to plan, to act, to be, as September marches into October. It is a time when women look better, men feel better, even the children look crisp again as they return to school in Paris or New York or San Francisco. And maybe even more so in Rome. Everyone is home again after the lazy months of summer spent clattering along in ancient taxis from the piazza to the Marina Piccola in Capri, or they are fresh from the baths in Ischia, the sun-swept days at San Remo, or even simply the public beach in Ostia. But in late September it is over, and autumn has arrived. A business-like month, a beautiful month, when it feels good just to be alive.

Isabella di San Gregorio sat sedately in the back seat of the limousine. She was smiling to herself, her dark eyes dancing, her shining black hair held away from her face by two heavy tortoise-shell combs as she watched passersby walking quickly through the streets. Traffic was as Roman traffic always is: terrifying. She was used to it, she had lived there all her life, except for her occasional visits to her mother's family in Paris and the one year she had spent in the States at twenty-one. The following year she had married Amadeo and become a legend of sorts, the reigning queen of Roman couture. She was by birth a

1

princess in that realm, and by marriage something more but her legend had been won by her talent, not only by acquiring Amadeo's name. Amadeo di San Gregorio had been the heir to the House of San Gregorio, the tabernacle of Roman couture, the pinnacle of prestige and exquisite taste in the eternal international competition between women of enormous means and aspirations. San Gregorio – sacred words to sacred women, and Isabella and Amadeo the most sacred words of all. He in all his golden, green-eyed Florentine magnificence, inheriting the house at thirty-one; she the granddaughter of Jacques-Louis Parel, the king of Paris couture since 1910.

Isabella's father had been Italian but had always taken pleasure in telling her he was quite sure that her blood was entirely French. She had French feelings and French ideas, French style, and her grandfather's unerring taste. At seventeen she had known more about high fashion than most men in the business at forty-five. It was in her veins, her heart, her spirit. She had an uncanny gift for design, a brilliance with colour, and a knowledge of what worked and what didn't that came from studying her grand-father's collections year after year. When at last in his eighties he had sold Parel to an American corporation, Isabella had sworn that she would never forgive him.

She had, of course. Still if he had only waited, if he had known if . . . but then she would have had a life in Paris and never met Amadeo as she had when she set up her own tiny design studio in Rome at twenty-two. It had taken six months for their paths to cross, six weeks for their hearts to determine what the future would be, and only three months after that before Isabella became Amadeo's wife and the brightest light in the heavens of the House of San Gregorio. Within a year she became his chief designer, a seat for which any designer would have died.

It was easy to envy Isabella. She had it all – elegance,

2

beauty, a crown of success that she wore with the casual ease of a Borsalino hat, and the kind of style that would still make an entire room stop to stare at her in her ninetieth year. Isabella di San Gregorio was every inch a queen, and yet there was more. The quick laughter; the sudden flash of diamonds set in the rich onyx eyes; her way of understanding what was behind what people said, who they were, why they were, what they were and weren't and dreamed of being. Isabella was a magical woman in a marvellous world.

The limousine slowed in a vast traffic snarl at the edge of the Piazza Navona, and Isabella sat back dreamily and closed her eyes. The blast of horns and invective was dimmed by the tightly sealed windows of the car, and her ears were too long accustomed to the sounds of Rome to be disturbed by the noise. She enjoyed it, she thrived on it. It was a part of the very fibre of her being, just as the mad pace of her business was part of her. It would be impossible to live without either one. Which was why she would never leave her business life entirely, despite her semi-retirement of the year before. When Alessandro had been born five years before, the business had been everything to her, the spring line, the threat of espionage from a rival house, the importance of developing a boutique line of ready-to-wear to export to the States, the wisdom of adding men's wear and eventually cosmetics and perfume and soap. All of it mattered to her intensely. She couldn't give it up, not even for Amadeo's child. This was her lifeblood, her dream. But as the years had gone by, she had felt an ever greater gnawing at her soul, a yearning, a loneliness when she returned home at eight thirty and the child was already asleep, tucked into bed by other hands than hers.

'It bothers you, doesn't it?' Amadeo had watched her as she sat pensively in the long grey satin chair set just so in the corner of the sitting room.

3

'What?' She had seemed distracted as she answered, tired, disturbed.

'Isabellezza – ' Isa-beauty. It always made her smile when he called her that. He had called her that from the first. 'Talk to me.'

She had smiled at him sheepishly and let out a long sigh. 'I am.'

'I was asking you if it bothers you very much not being here with the child.'

'Sometimes. I don't know. It's hard to explain. We have – we have lovely times together. On Sundays, when I have time.' A tiny tear had crept out of one of the brilliantly dark eyes, and Amadeo held out his arms to her. She had gone to them willingly and smiled through her tears. 'I'm crazy. I have everything. I . . . why doesn't the damn nurse keep him up 'till we come home?'

'*Alle dieci?*' At ten o'clock?

'It isn't, it's only . . .' She had looked at her watch in irritation and then realised that he was right. They had left the office at eight, stopped to see their lawyer at his home for an hour, stopped for yet another 'minute' to kiss their favourite American client in her suite at the Hassler, and . . . ten o'clock. 'Damn. All right, so it's late. But usually we're home at eight, and he's never awake.' She had glared at Amadeo, and he had laughed gently as he held her in his arms.

'What do you want? One of those children that movie stars take to cocktail parties when they're nine? Why don't you take off more time?'

'I can't.'

'You don't want to.'

'Yes, I do . . . no, I don't.' They had both laughed. It was true. She did and she didn't. She wanted to be with Alessandro, before she missed it all, before he was suddenly nineteen and she had missed her chance. She had seen it

4

happen to too many women with careers – they mean to, they're going to, they want to, and they never do. They wake up one morning and their children are gone. The trips to the zoo that never happened, the movies, the museums, the moments they meant to share, but the phones were ringing, the clients waiting. The great events. She didn't want that to happen to her. It hadn't mattered so much when he was a baby. But now it was different. He was four and he knew when he didn't see her for more than two hours in three days, he knew when she was never there to pick him up at school, or when she and Amadeo spent six insane weeks planning the next collection or the line for the States.

'You look miserable, my love. You want me to fire you?' To Amadeo's astonishment as well as her own she had nodded. 'Are you serious?' Shock registered in his eyes.

'Partly. There must be a way for me to work part of the time and be here a little bit more too.' She had looked around the splendour of their villa, thinking of the child she hadn't seen all day.

'Let's think about it, Bellezza. We'll work something out.'

And they had. It was perfect. For the past eight months she had been chief design consultant to the House of San Gregorio. She made all the same decisions she had always made, she had her hand in every pie. The unmistakable hand of Isabella was still recognisable in every design San Gregorio sold. But she had removed herself from the mechanics of the business, from the nitty-gritty of the everyday. It meant overburdening still further their beloved director, Bernardo Franco, and it meant hiring another designer to carry out the interminable steps between Isabella's concepts and the final product. But it was working perfectly. Now Isabella came and went. She

5

sat in on major meetings. She pored over everything with Amadeo during one marathon day each week. She stopped in unexpectedly whenever she had an appointment nearby, but for the first time she felt she was truly Alessandro's mother now too. They had lunch in the garden. She saw him in his first school play. She took him to the park and taught him nursery rhymes in English and funny little songs in French. She laughed with him, ran with him, and pushed him on the swing. She had the best of all possible worlds. A business, a husband, and a child. And she had never been happier in her life. It showed in the light that danced in her eyes, in the way she moved and laughed and looked when Amadeo came home. It showed in the things she said to her friends as she regaled them with tales of Alessandro's latest accomplishments: 'And my God, how that child can draw!' Everyone was amused. Most of all Amadeo, who wanted her to be happy. After ten years of marriage he still adored her. In fact, more than he ever had. And the business was thriving, despite the slight change of regime. Isabella could never absent herself totally. It simply wasn't her style. Her presence was felt everywhere. The sound of her echoed like a perfectly formed crystal bell.

The limousine stopped at the kerb as Isabella caught a last glimpse of people on the street. She liked what women were wearing this year. Sexy, more feminine. Reminiscent of her grandfather's collections in years before. It was a look that pleased her very much. She herself stepped from the car in an ivory wool dress, perfectly draped into a river of tiny, impeccably executed pleats. Her three long strands of enormous pearls hung from her neck at precisely the right depth of the softly draped neckline, and over her arm was a short chocolate mink jacket, a fur that had been designed just for her in Paris by the furrier once employed by Parel. But she was in too much of a hurry to slip it on.

She wanted to discuss some last-minute details of the American line with Amadeo, before meeting a friend for lunch. She glanced at the faceless gold watch on her wrist as a sapphire and a diamond floated mysteriously on its face, indicating only to the initiated the exact time. It was ten twenty-two.

'Thank you, Enzo. I'll be out five minutes before noon.' Holding the door with one hand, he touched his cap with the other and smiled. She was easy to work for these days, and he enjoyed the frequent trips in the car with the little boy. It reminded him of his own grandchildren, seven of whom lived in Bologna, the other five in Venice. He visited them sometimes. But Rome was his home. Just as it was Isabella's despite her French mother and her year in the States. Rome was a part of her, she was born there, she had to live there, she would die there. He knew what every Italian knew, that a Roman was meant to live nowhere else.

As she walked decisively across the sidewalk toward the heavy black door in the ancient facade, she glanced up the street as she always did. It was a sure way to know if Amadeo was in. All she had to do was look for the long silver Ferrari, parked at the kerb. The silver torpedo, she called it. And no hands touched that car, except his. Everyone teased him about it, especially Isabella. He was like a small child with a toy. He didn't want to share it. He drove it, he parked it, pampered it, and played with it. All by himself. Not even the doorman at San Gregorio, who had worked there for forty-two years, had ever touched that car. Isabella was smiling to herself as she approached the impressive black door. At times he was like a little boy; it only made her love him more.

'*Buon giorno, Signora Isabella.*' Only Ciano, the grandfatherly doorman in black-and-grey livery, called her that.

7

'*Ciao, Ciano, come sta?*' Isabella smiled widely at him, displaying teeth as beautiful as her much celebrated pearls. '*Va bène?*' It goes well?

'*Benissimo.*' The rich baritone rolled musically at her as he swept the heavy door open with a bow.

The door shut resoundingly behind her as she stood in the entrance hall for a moment, looking around. As much as the villa on the Via Appia Antica, this was her home. The perfect pink marble floors, the grey velvets and rose silks, the crystal chandelier that she had brought from Parel in Paris after long negotiation with its American owner. Her grandfather had had it made in Vienna, and it was almost beyond price. A sweeping marble staircase rose to the main salon above. On the third and fourth floors were offices done in the same greys and pinks, the colours of rose petals and ashes. It was a combination that pleased the eye as much as the carefully selected paintings, the antique mirrors, the elegant light fixtures, the little Louis XVI love seats tucked into alcoves here and there where clients could rest and chat. Maids in grey uniforms scurried everywhere, their starched white aprons making crisp little noises as they brought tea and sandwiches to the private rooms upstairs where clients stood through arduous fittings, wondering how the models survived entire shows. Isabella stood for a moment, as she often did, surveying her domain.

She slipped quietly into the private elevator, pressing the button for the fourth floor, as she began to go over the morning's work in her head. There were just a few things to take care of; she had settled most of the current business yesterday, to her satisfaction. There had been design details to work out with Gabriela, the chief designer, and administrative problems to discuss with Bernardo and Amadeo. Today's work wouldn't take her long at all. The door slid silently open and revealed the long grey carpeted

8

hall. Everything about the House of San Gregorio was downplayed. Unlike Isabella, who was anything but. She was obvious and splendid and eminently visible. She was a woman one saw and wanted to see, a woman one wanted to be seen by. But the House of San Gregorio was a showcase for beauty. It was important that what they had to show there was not overwhelmed by the house itself. It wasn't, it couldn't be. Despite the beauty of the seventeenth-century building that had once been the home of a prince, the wares of San Gregorio were too resplendent to be overwhelmed by anything or anyone. Isabella had created a perfect meshing of remarkable models, extraordinary designs, and incredible fabrics and brought them together with women who wore them well. She knew that somewhere, in the States, in Paris, in Milan, the women who wore their boutique line, their ready-to-wear, were not anything like the women who came to this address. The women who came here were special – countesses, princesses, actresses, literary figures, television person- alities, notables and nobles who would have killed or died for San Gregorio's designs. Many of them were women like Isabella herself – spectacular, sensual, superb.

· She walked silently towards a pair of double doors at the end of the long hall and pressed down on the highly polished brass handle. She appeared like a vision in front of the secretary's desk.

'Signora!' The girl looked up, startled. One never quite knew when Isabella would appear, or just what she would have on her mind. But today Isabella only nodded, smiled, and walked immediately toward Amadeo's office. She knew he was in. She had seen the car. And unlike Isabella, he rarely strayed to the other floors. He and Bernardo kept mainly to their upstairs offices. It was Isabella who prowled, who wandered, who appeared suddenly in the mannequins' room, in the corridors outside the private fitting rooms, in the main salon with the long grey silk runway, which had to be constantly replaced. That was a source of constant irritation to Bernardo, ever practical in his directorship of the house. It was on his shoulders that the budget fell. As president and chief of finance, Amadeo designed the budget, but Bernardo had to live with it, seeing that the fabrics and beads and feathers and wondrous little ornaments fell within the limits Amadeo had set for them. And thanks to Bernardo they always existed well within that budget. Thanks to Bernardo the house had been carefully and at times brilliantly run for years. Thanks to Amadeo's investments and financial acumen they had prospered. And thanks to Isabella's genius with design they had gloried as well as flourished. But it was Bernardo who bridged the world of design and finance. It was he who calculated, speculated, weighed, and pondered what would work, what wouldn't, what would cost them the success of the line, or what was worth the gamble. And thus far he had never been wrong. He had a flair and a genius that made Isabella think of a matador, proud, erect, daring, flashing red satin in the face of the bull, and always winning in the end. She loved his style and she loved him. But not in the way that Bernardo loved her. He had always loved her. Always. From the first day he had met her.

Bernardo and Amadeo had been friends for years and they had worked together in the House of San Gregorio before Isabella had appeared on the scene. It had been Bernardo who had discovered her in her tiny atelier in Rome. It had been he who had insisted that Amadeo come to see her work, meet her, talk to her, and perhaps even convince her to come to work for them. She had been remarkable even then, sensationally beautiful and incredibly young. At twenty-two she was already a striking woman, and a genius with design. They had arrived in her little studio that day to find her wearing a red silk shirt and a white linen skirt, little gold sandals and not much else. She looked like a diamond set in a valentine. The heat had been crushing, but even more so moments later when her eyes met Amadeo's for the first time. It had been then that Bernardo realised how much he cared too and that it was already too late. Amadeo and Isabella had fallen instantly in love, and Bernardo had never spoken up. Never. It was too late, and he would never have been treacherous to his friend. Amadeo meant too much to him; for years he had been like a brother, and Amadeo was not the kind of man one betrayed. He was precious to everyone, beloved by all. He was the one person you wanted to be like, not a man you'd want to hurt. So Bernardo didn't. He knew also that it saved him the pain of finding out that she didn't love him. He knew how much she loved Amadeo. It was the governing passion of her life. Amadeo actually meant more to her than her work, which in Isabella's case was indeed remarkable. Bernardo couldn't compete with that. So he kept his pride and his secret and his love and he made the business better; he learned to love her in another way, to love them both with a passion of his own, and a kind of purity that burned like a white fire within him. It created enormous tension between him and Isabella, but it was worth it. The results of their encounters, their rages, and their wars were always splendid: extravagantly beautiful women to parade down their runways . . . women who occasionally paraded into Bernardo's arms. But he had a right to that. He had a right to something more than his work and his love for Amadeo and Isabella. He burned with a kind of bright light all his own, and the women who drifted through the house, models or clients, were drawn to him by something they never quite understood, something never fully revealed, something Bernardo himself no longer consciously thought about. It was merely a part of him now, like his infallible sense of style, or his respect for the two people he worked with, who in their own way had become one. He understood perfectly what they were. And he knew that he and Isabella could never have been like that. They would have remained two, always two, always in love, always at war; had she even known his feelings, they would have met like colliding constellations, exploding in a shower of comets across the heavens of their world. But it was not like that with Isabella and Amadeo. It was gentle, tender, strong. They were soldered as one soul. To see Isabella look into Amadeo's eyes was to see her disappear into them, to move into a deeper part of herself, to see her grow and fly, her wings stretched wide. Amadeo and Isabella were as two eagles soaring across their private sky, their wings in perfect harmony, their very beings one, their unison complete. It was something Bernardo no longer even resented. It was impossible to resent a pair like that. They were beautiful to see. And now he had grown confortable with what was a fiery working relationship with a lady he loved from afar. He had his own life. And he shared something special with them. He always would. They were an indestructible, inseparable threesome. Nothing would ever come between them. The three of them knew that.

As Isabella stood outside Amadeo's office door for a moment, she smiled to herself. She could never see that door without thinking of the first time she had seen it and these halls. They had been different then. Handsome but not as strikingly elegant as they were now. She had made them something more, as Amadeo had made her something more. She grew in his presence. She felt infinitely precious, and totally safe. Safe enough to be what she was, to do what she wanted, to dare, to move in a world with no limits at all. Amadeo made her feel limitless, he had shown her that she was, that she could be everything she wanted to be and do everything she wanted to do, and she did it all with the power of his love.

She knocked softly on the door few people knew about. It led directly into his private office. It was a door only she and Bernardo used. And the answer came quickly. She turned the handle and walked in. For a moment they said nothing, they only looked as the same thrill swept through her soul that she had felt since she had first seen him. He smiled in answer. He felt it too. There was unfettered pleasure in his eyes, a kind of gentle adoration that always drew her to his arms like a magnet. It was the gentleness in him that she loved so much, the kindness, the compassion he always had. His was a different fire from hers. His was a sacred flame that would burn forever, held aloft for the sad and weary, a proud light, a beacon to all. Hers was a torch that danced in the night sky, so bright and beautiful that one almost feared to approach it. But no one feared to approach Amadeo. He was eminently welcoming. Everyone wanted to be close to him, although in truth, only Isabella was. And Bernardo too, of course, but differently.

'*Allora*, Isabellezza. What brings you here today? I thought we settled everything yesterday.' He sat back in his chair, one hand held out to her, as she took it.

'More or less. But I had a few more ideas.' A few. . . . He laughed at the word. A few with Isabella meant thirty-five, or forty-seven, or a hundred and three. Isabella never had a few of anything, not a few ideas, or a few jewels, or a few clothes. Amadeo smiled broadly as she bent for a moment to kiss his cheek and he reached out and touched her hand.

'You look beautiful today.' The light in his eyes bathed her in sunshine.

'Better than this morning?' They both laughed. She had been wearing a new cream on her face, her hair tied up

13

high on her head, a comfortable dressing gown, and his slippers.

But Amadeo only shook his head. 'No. I think I liked you better this morning. But . . . I like this too. Is it one of ours?'

'Of course. Would I wear anything not ours?' For a moment the dark eyes flashed into his green ones.

'It looks like one of your grandfather's designs.' He studied her carefully, narrowing his eyes. He had a way of seeing and knowing all.

'You're very smart. I stole it from his nineteen thirty-five collection. Not totally, of course. Just the flavour.' She grinned. 'And the pleats.'

He smiled at her in amusement and bent toward her again for a rapid kiss. 'The flavour is excellent.'

'It's a good thing we don't work together full time anymore, we'd never get anything done. Sometimes I wonder how we ever did.' She sat back in her seat, admiring him. It was impossible not to. He was the Greek god of a hundred paintings in the Uffizi in Florence, the statue of every Roman boy, long, lean, graceful, elegant; yet there was more. The green eyes were knowing, wicked, wise, amused. They were quick and certain, and despite the golden Florentine beauty of his genes, there was strength there as well, power and command. He was the head of the House of San Gregorio, he had been the heir to a fairly major throne, and now he wore the mantle of his position well. It suited him. He looked like the head of an empire, or perhaps a very large bank. The neatly tailored pin-striped suit accentuated his height and narrow figure, yet the broad shoulders were his own. Everything about Amadeo was his own. There was nothing fake or flawed about him, nothing borrowed, nothing stolen, nothing unreal. The elegance, the aristocratic good looks, the warmth in his eyes, the quick wit, the sharp mind, and the

14

concern he had for those around him. And the passion for his wife.

'What are you doing down here all dressed up today by the way? Other than sharing a "few" ideas with me, of course.' He smiled again as their eyes met, and Isabella broke into a smile.

'I'm having lunch with some ladies.'

'Sounds terrible. Can I lure you to a room at the Excelsior instead?'

'You might, but I have a date with another man after lunch.' She said it smugly, and laughter danced in her eyes, as well as his.

'My rival, Bellezza?' But he had no cause to worry and he knew it.

'Your son.'

'In that case, no Excelsior. *Peccata*.' A pity.

'Next time.'

'Indeed.' He stretched his legs out ahead of him happily, like a long, lazy cat in the sun.

'All right. Shut up. We have work to do.'

'*Ècco*. The woman I married. Tender, romantic, gentle.'

She made one of their son's horrible faces, and they both laughed as she pulled a sheaf of notes out of her handbag. In the sunlight in his office he saw the sparkle of the large emerald-cut diamond ring he had bought her that summer for their tenth anniversary. Ten carats, of course. What else? Ten carats for ten years.

'The ring looks nice.'

She nodded happily as she looked down at it. It looked good on her long graceful hands. Isabella wore everything well. Particularly ten-carat diamonds. 'It does. But you look nicer. I love you by the way.' She pretended to be flip, but they both knew she was not.

'I love you too.' They shared a last smile before plunging into work. It was better now. Better when they weren't

15

together every day. By the end of the afternoon he was always hungry for her and anxious to get home. And there was something special now about their meetings, their evenings, their lunches, their days. She was mysterious to him again. He found himself wondering what she was doing all day, where she was, what she was wearing, as the thought of her perfume filled his mind.

'You don't think the American line is too subdued? I wondered about that last night.' She squinted at him, not seeing him but the designs she and Gabriela had gone over the day before.

'I don't. And Bernardo was ecstatic.'

'Shit.' She returned her eyes to his with genuine concern. 'Then I'm right.' Amadeo laughed at her, but she didn't smile. 'I'm serious. I want to change four of the fabrics and add one or two of the pieces for France to that line. Then it'll work.' She looked certain, as she always did. And she was rarely wrong. That absolute certainty of hers had won them fashion awards for ten years. 'I want to bring in those purples, and the reds, and the white coat. Then it will be perfect.'

'Work it out with Bernardo and tell Gabriela.'

'I already did. Tell Gabriela, I mean. And Bernardo's new soap for the men's line is all wrong. It hung in my nose all afternoon.'

'That's bad?'

'Terrible. A woman's perfume should stay with you. The smell of a man should only come to you as you go to him and leave you with only a memory. Not a headache.'

'Bernardo will be thrilled.' For a moment he looked tired. Occasionally Isabella and Bernardo's wars exhausted him. They were essential to the business though, and he knew it. Without the fierce pull of Isabella and the stern anchor of Bernardo the House of San Gregorio would have been very different than it was. But as the axle that kept the two wheels from flying off in separate directions, he felt the strain on him was at times more than he enjoyed. But as a threesome they were a miraculous team, and all three of them knew it. And when all was said and done, somehow they always managed to stay friends. He would never understand it. With Isabella raging and calling Bernardo names that he had never even dreamed she knew, and Bernardo looking as though he might at last commit murder, he would then find them after hours in one of the private fitting rooms, drinking champagne and finishing a plateful of the day's sandwiches like two children at their own tea party after the grown-up guests have gone home. He would never be able to figure it out; he was just grateful that it worked that way. Now, with a sigh, he looked at his watch. 'Do you want me to call him in?' He never had to deliver messages for Isabella. She always delivered them herself. Straight from the hip. To the groin.

'You'd better. I have to be at lunch at noon.' She looked at the unreadable watch. That had been a present from him too.

'God. We're playing second fiddle to ladies' lunches now.' But there was laughter in his eyes. He knew that in Isabella's life that would never be true. Other than himself, and Alessandro, it was the business that Isabella lived for, that kept her breathing and kicking and eight hundred per cent alive.

Amadeo picked up the phone and spoke briefly to his secretary. She'd call Mr. Franco at once. Which indeed she did, and he came at once as always. He strode into the room like an explosion, and suddenly Amadeo could feel Isabella tense. She was already preparing for battle.

'Ciao, Bernardo.' Isabella smiled casually at him as he walked into the office in one of a hundred dark suits that he owned, all of which looked exactly the same to Isabella. He

17

wore the same gold pocket watch on each one of them, the same impeccably starched white shirts, and ties that were usually dark with tiny, tiny white dots. Or when he felt very outrageous, tiny red ones. 'I love your suit.' It was their standing joke. She always told him that his suits were excessively boring. But the simplicity of his suits was part of his style.

'Listen, you two, don't start today. I'm not in the mood.' Amadeo looked ominously at them, but as always his eyes laughed even when his lips did not. 'Besides, she has to be at lunch in forty minutes. We're only second best to her lunches now.'

'That figures.' Bernardo squeezed out a small smile and sat down. 'How's my godson?'

'Alessandro is perfect. The dining room curtains, however, are not.' Amadeo started to grin as Isabella told the tale. He loved the boy's mischievousness, the fire in the dark eyes so much like hers. 'When I was here yesterday, solving your problems for you' – she raised an eyebrow, waiting for Bernardo to take the bait, and was clearly disappointed when he did not – 'he borrowed my manicure scissors and "fixed" them, as he put it. He cut off roughly a metre which, he tells me, got in his way every time he drove his favourite truck along the window. He couldn't see the garden. Now he can see the garden. Perfectly, in fact.' But she was laughing too, as was Bernardo. When he smiled like that, twenty of his thirty-eight years fell away from him and he was barely more than a boy himself. But he had worked too long, and when he wasn't being amused by tales of Alessandro, he often looked austere. Much of the weight of the House of San Gregorio was on his shoulders and it often showed. He had worked hard and well for them, and it had taken its toll. Never married, childless, too much alone, and too often at work, late at night, early in the morning, on Saturdays, on holidays and holy days

18

and days when he should have been somewhere else, with someone else. But he lived for what he did, he wore his responsibilities like his dark suits; they were a part of him, like his hair, almost as dark as Isabella's and his eyes, the colour of the Roman summer sky. His was the face the models fell for. But they meant little to him. They amused him for an evening or two, not more. 'Your new soap doesn't work.' As usual she gave it to him straight, and Amadeo almost winced, waiting for the battle to begin.

Bernardo sat very still. 'Why not?'

'It gave me a headache. It's too heavy.'

'If someone cut my dining room curtain in half, I'd get a headache too.'

'I'm serious.' Her eyes levelled ominously into his.

'So am I. Our tests all show it's perfect. No one else felt it was too heavy.'

'Maybe they had bad colds and couldn't smell it.'

Bernardo rolled his eyes and burrowed back into his chair. 'For God's sake, Isabella, I just told them to go ahead on production. What the hell do you want me to do now?'

'Stop it. It's wrong. Just like the cologne was wrong at first, and the same reasons.' This time Amadeo closed his eyes. She had been right about that one too, but it had been a battle Bernardo had lost with pain. And fury. He and Isabella had barely spoken to each other for a month.

Bernardo's lips tightened, and he dug his hands into the pockets of his vest. 'The soap has to be strong. You use it with water. In the bath. You rinse it off. The scent goes away.' He explained it to her through narrowed lips.

'Capisco. I've used soap before. Mine doesn't give me a headache. Yours does. I want it changed.'

'Goddamn it, Isabella!' He slammed a fist on Amadeo's desk and glared at her, but she was unmoved.

She smiled victoriously at him. 'Tell them at the lab to work overtime on it, and you won't be held up in production by more than two or three weeks.'

'Or months. Do you know then what happens to the ads we've already run? They're wasted.'

'They'll be more so if you go ahead with the wrong product. Trust me. I'm right.' She smiled slowly at him then, and Bernardo looked for a moment as though he might explode.

'Do you have any other pleasant surprises for me this morning?'

'No, just have a few additions to the American line. I already talked to Gabriela about them. They don't present a problem.'

'My God, why not? You mean it will be easy? Isabella, no!' But suddenly he was smiling again. He had a vast capacity for fury and forgiveness.

'You'll let me know about the soap?' She homed in on him again.

'I'll let you know.'

'Good. Then that takes care of everything, and I don't even have to run off to lunch for another twenty minutes.' Amadeo grinned at her, and she ensconced herself on the arm of her husband's chair and gently touched his cheek with her hand. And as she did so the anniversary diamond caught the bright sunlight and dashed it in a shower of rainbow reflections against the far wall. She saw Bernardo watch it with a look of sudden displeasure and she looked amused. 'What's the matter, Nardo, one of your girl friends giving you a bad time again?'

'Very amusing. As it so happens, I've been chained to my desk for the last week. I'm beginning to feel like the house eunuch.' Amadeo's brows knit with a sudden frown. He was worried they were working him too hard, but Isabella knew that Bernardo's sudden look of woe

20

stemmed from something else. She knew him too well to believe he minded being overworked any more than she did. And she was right in thinking that he did not. They were all three tremendously overworked, and they loved it. Bernardo was only a trifle more compulsive than his two friends. But he was now looking genuinely disturbed as he glanced from Isabella's large diamond ring to her pearls. 'You're crazy to wear that, Isabella.' And then with a meaningful look at Amadeo: 'I told you that last week.'

'What's all this about?' Isabella looked from one to the other in amused consternation, and then her eyes settled on her husband's kind face. 'He's trying to get you to take back my ring?'

'More or less.' Amadeo looked suddenly very Italian as he shrugged.

But Bernardo was not enjoying their game. 'You know damn well that isn't what I meant or what I said. You know what happened to the Belloggios last week. It could happen to you.'

'A kidnapping?' Isabella looked stunned. 'Don't be ridiculous, Nardo. The Belloggio brothers were the two most important political men in Rome. They knew everyone and they wielded an extraordinary amount of power. The terrorists all hated them as capitalist symbols.'

'They also knew they were worth a bloody fortune. And their wives trotted around this town looking like an ad for Van Cleef. You don't think that had anything to do with it?'

'No.' Isabella looked undisturbed, and then she stared at Bernardo again. 'What's gotten into you? Why should you suddenly start worrying about that? Are you having trouble with your ulcer again? That always makes you peculiar.'

'Stop it, Isabella. Don't be childish. That's the fourth major kidnapping this year, and contrary to what both of you seem to think, not all kidnappings happening in Europe these days are political. Some of them just happen because people are rich and they let the whole damn world know it.'

'Ah, and so you think I walk around advertising what we've got. Is that it? My God, Bernardo, how incredibly vulgar.'

'Yes, isn't it, though?' His eyes suddenly blazed, as he grabbed a newspaper off Amadeo's desk. His eyes were on the pages as he leafed quickly through it and the other two watched him. 'Yes, terribly, terribly vulgar, Isabella. I'm so glad you wouldn't do anything as coarse as that.' And with that he flipped the paper open to a large photograph that showed them both walking into a large palazzo the night before. It had been a party to celebrate the opening of the opera, and Isabella was wearing a strikingly beautiful beige moiré evening dress with a matching coat, lined in a breathtaking blanket of sable, that fell all the way to her feet. And around her neck and on both wrists were ropes of diamonds that glittered in unison with the large rock on her hand. 'I'm glad you're so simple.' And then he looked ominously at Amadeo. 'Both of you.' The chauffeured Rolls Amadeo only brought out for state occasions was visible just behind them, and the small studs in the shirt under Amadeo's evening jacket glittered much like the small diamonds at Isabella's ears. They both looked at the photograph blankly as Bernardo glared accusingly at them from where he stood.

'We weren't the only ones there, you know.' Isabella said it softly. It touched her that he cared, and the subject wasn't entirely new. He had brought it up before, but now with the Belloggios being kidnapped and murdered there seemed a dogged determination about his concern. 'Darling, you really don't have to worry about us.'

'Why? Do you think you're so sacred? You think no one

22

will touch you? In these times if that's what you think, you're mad! Both of you!' For moment he seemed close to tears. He had known one of the Belloggios and gone to the funeral the week before. The kidnappers had, insanely, demanded fifteen million dollars and the release of half a dozen political prisoners. But the family had been unable to accede to their demands, and the government unwilling to. The results had been tragic. But although Isabella and Amadeo looked sympathetic, they remained unmoved. Bernardo was obviously seeing ghosts.

Isabella stood up slowly and walked to where Bernardo stood. She reached up, hugged him, and smiled. 'We love you. And you worry too much.' Amadeo was frowning, but out of concern for Bernardo, not fear for himself.

'You don't understand, do you?' Bernardo looked at them both in growing despair.

But this time it was Amadeo who answered as Isabella sat down in a chair with a sigh. 'We understand. But I think there's less reason for concern than you think. Look at us' – he waved humbly from Isabella to himself – 'We're no one. We're dress merchants. What can anyone want from us?'

'Money. What about Alessandro? What if they take him?' For an instant Amadeo almost shuddered. Bernardo had scored.

'That would be different. But he's never alone, Bernardo. You know that. The villa is closed. No one could get in. You needn't be so worried. He is safe, and we are safe.'

'You're wrong. No one is safe anymore. And as long as you both run around looking like that' – he waved unhappily at the newspaper picture again – 'you're courting disaster. I saw that this morning and I wanted to kick you both.' Amadeo and Isabella exchanged a quick look, and Bernardo turned away. They didn't understand.

They thought he was crazy. But it was they who were mad. Naive and simple and stupid. Bernardo wanted to shout at them both but he knew there was no point. 'Dress merchants' . . . the biggest couture house in Europe, one of the largest fortunes in Rome, two spectacular-looking people, a vulnerable child, a woman covered with jewels . . . dress merchants. He looked from one to the other again, shook his head, and walked to the door. 'I'll see about the soap, Isabella. But do me a favour, both of you.' He paused for a moment, looking agonised again. 'Think about what I said.'

'We will.' Amadeo said it softly as Bernardo closed the door. And then he looked at his wife. 'He may be right you know. Perhaps we should be more careful about you and Alessandro.'

'And about you?'

'I'm hardly an object of great interest.' He smiled at her. 'And I don't go around in diamonds and furs.'

She smiled at him for a moment and then pouted. 'You can't take back my ring.'

'I don't intend to.' He looked at her tenderly.

'Never?' She was a petulant child as she sat down on his lap and he grinned.

'Never. I promise. It's yours. And I'm yours. Forever.' He kissed her then, and she felt the same rising fervour in her that he had aroused in her since they'd met. Her arms went around his neck, and her mouth came down hard on his.

'I love you, *carissimo* . . . more than anything in this world . . .' They kissed again, and she felt tears sting her eyes when at last she pulled away. That happened sometimes. She was so happy, she wanted to cry. They had so much together, so much history, so many victories, not only the awards and the kudos, but the tender memories, the birth of their son, the days they had spent alone on an island in

Greece five years before when they felt the business was suddenly too much for them; it had been then that Alessandro had been conceived. A thousand moments stood out in her mind and made Amadeo infinitely precious to her once again.

'Isabellezza . . .' He looked down at her with a smile in his deep emerald eyes. 'You have made my life perfect. Have I told you that recently?'

She smiled back. 'You've done the same for me. You know what I'd like to do?'

'What?' Whatever it was, they would do it. There was nothing he would deny her. Others would perhaps say she was spoiled, indulged by her husband. But she wasn't. She equally spoiled him. It was something they did for each other. A reciprocity of generous loving that they both enjoyed.

'I'd love to go to Greece again.' Bernardo's words of warning were already forgotten.

'When?' He smiled again. He wanted to go too. It had been one of the most beautiful times of his life.

'In the spring?' She looked up at him, and he found her unbearably sexy.

'Shall we make another baby?' It was something he'd been thinking about for a while. This seemed a good time. They had only wanted one before Alessandro. But he was such a joy that lately Amadeo had been thinking of broaching the subject with Isabella again.

'In Greece?' Her dark eyes opened very wide, and her mouth seemed rich and full as he bent to kiss her again. After he did, she smiled at him. 'We don't have to wait until Greece, you know. People make babies in Rome all the time.'

'Do they?' He whispered it into her neck. 'You'll have to show me how.'

'*Ecco, tesòro.*' And then suddenly she laughed at him and

25

looked at her watch. 'But not until after lunch. I'm late.'

'How awful. Perhaps you'd best not go at all. We could go home to the villa and – '

'*Doppo* . . .' Later. And then she kissed him once more and walked slowly to the door, turning for an instant with her head cocked to one side as her hand touched the handle. She looked back over her shoulder at him with a question. 'Did you mean it?'

'About your not going to lunch?' He smiled, amused.

But she shook her head and laughed at him. 'No, you lecherous beast. I mean about the baby.' She said the last very gently, as though the idea meant something to her too.

But he was nodding his head as he looked at her. 'Yes, I did. What do you think, Bellezza?'

But she smiled at him mysteriously from the door. 'I think we should keep it in mind.' And then with a kiss she was gone as he stood watching the door. He wanted to tell her just once more that he loved her. But it would have to wait until tonight. He was surprised too at what he had just said about wanting another baby. He had thought about it but not yet put it into words. Now suddenly he knew that he meant it. And it didn't have to interfere with her career. Alessandro didn't, and they both had a great deal to give the child. In fact the more he thought about it, the more he liked the idea. He went back to his desk and picked up a sheaf of papers with a smile.

It was almost one o'clock when Amadeo finally stood up and stretched. He was pleased with the figures he had been pursuing. The American deals they had made that autumn were going to bring in a tidy price. Very salutary indeed. He was about to take himself for a solitary lunch of congratulation when he heard a soft knock on the door.

'*Si?*' He looked surprised. His secretary usually buzzed him, but she was probably already out to lunch. He turned

toward the door and saw one of the under secretaries
peeking timidly around the door.

'*Scusi, signore, mi dispiace* . . . I'm sorry but . . . ' She smiled
at him. He was so unbearably handsome that she never
quite knew what to say. She hardly ever got to talk to him
anyway.

'Yes?' He smiled back. 'Is there something I can do?'

'There are two men here to see you, sir.' Her voice
trailed off as she blushed.

'Now?' He dropped his eyes to the appointment book,
open on his desk. There was nothing penned in until three.
'Who?'

'They . . . it's about your car. The -- the Ferrari.'

'My car?' He looked surprised and confused. 'What
about it?'

'They – they said there was . . . an accident.' She waited
for an explosion but none came. He looked disturbed but
not angry.

'Was anyone hurt?'

'I don't think so. But they're here . . . just outside . . . in
Miss Alzini's office, sir.' He nodded gently and walked past
her through the outer office to find two men looking
awkward and embarrassed. They were wearing neat but
simple clothes, their hands were large and brown, their
faces red; he was not yet sure if it was from mortification or
the sun. And it was very clear that they were in no way
used to such surroundings. The shorter of the two seemed
afraid to even stand upon the carpet, and the taller clearly
wished that he might disappear instantly through the
floor. A butcher perhaps, maybe a baker, working men,
labourers perhaps. And when they spoke, their voices were
coarse but awed and respectful. They were aghast at what
had happened. They were beside themselves to learn that
the car was his.

'What happened?' He continued to look confused but

27

his voice was gentle and his eyes were kind, and if he felt any dismay about his car, he betrayed it not at all.

'We were driving; it was very crowded, your honour. You know, lunch.' Amadeo nodded patiently as he listened to the tale. 'A woman and a little girl were running across the street; we swerved so as not to hit them, and . . .' The shorter man grew redder still. '. . . we hit your car instead. Not too bad, but it hurt the car a little. We can fix it. My brother has a shop, he does good work. You'll be pleased. And we pay. Everything. We pay everything.'

'Of course not. We'll work it out between our insurance companies. Is there a great deal of damage?' He tried not to show the unhappiness he felt.

'*Ma* . . . We are so sorry. Not for all the world would we have hit your honour's car. A Fiat, a foreign car, anything, but not so fine a car as yours.' The taller man wrung his hands, and at last Amadeo even smiled. They were so absurd, standing there in his secretary's office, probably more demolished than his car. He found himself having to suppress a burst of nervous laughter and was suddenly glad that Isabella was not around to look mischievously at him with her mock-serious gaze.

'Never mind. Come, we'll go and look.' He led them to the tiny private elevator, inserted his key, and stood with them as they descended toward the first floor, the two men with heads bowed in humiliation and Amadeo attempting to engage them in some ordinary banter.

Even Ciano had gone to lunch when Amadeo stepped outside and looked up the street toward the car. He could see their car still double-parked beside it. It was a large, awkward, antiquated-looking car and might in fact have been heavy enough to inflict some serious damage. With a look of masked concern he strode up the street, the two men walking nervously behind him, clearly terrified by what he'd see. As he reached his car, walking along the sidewalk, he noticed that a third companion was still waiting in the ancient Fiat, looking unhappy as he saw Amadeo approach. He inclined his head in brief salutation, and Amadeo stepped around his car into the street to inspect its injured left side. Slowly his eyes swept along the side as he stooped over slightly, the better to see the damage they had done. But as he hovered there, bending over, his eyes suddenly narrowed in confusion; there was no damage, no dent, no injury to the beloved car. But it was too late to ask them further questions. As his eyes widened in surprise an object of immeasurable weight swept down brutally on the back of his neck, and sagging instantly, he was pushed and then pulled unceremoniously into the back of the waiting car. The entire matter took less than an instant and was neatly handled by Amadeo's two innocent-looking morning callers. The men slid calmly into the Fiat beside their friend, and it pulled sedately away from the curb. Within two blocks of the House of San Gregorio, Amadeo was neatly bound and trussed, a gag and blindfold secured, and his motionless form lay silently, barely breathing on the floor of the car as his kidnappers drove him away.

Chapter Two

The sun had just set with a bright flow of orange and mauve as Isabella stood resplendent in green satin in her living room. Delicate brass and crystal wall sconces cast a soft light around the room. She glanced at the deep blue Fabergé clock on the mantelpiece. She and Amadeo had bought it years before in New York. It was a collector's item, a priceless piece, almost as priceless as the emerald-and-diamond necklace carefully clasped around her neck. It had been her grandmother's and was said to have once belonged to Josephine Bonaparte. It held her long white neck in its delicate grasp as she spun slowly on one heel and began pacing the room. It was five minutes to eight, and they were going to be very late for the Principessa di Sant'Angelo's dinner. Damn Amadeo. Why tonight, of all nights, couldn't he be on time? The princess was one of the few people who actually unnerved Isabella. She was eighty-three years old with a heart of Carrara marble and eyes of steel, a long-ago crony of Amadeo's grandmother, and a woman Isabella frankly abhorred. She gave regular command performances, cocktails at eight, dinner precisely at nine. And they still had to drive halfway across Rome and then out into the countryside to the Palazzo Sant'Angelo, where the principessa held court in ancient yet startlingly beautiful ball gowns, brandishing her gold-handled ebony cane.

On edge, Isabella caught a glimpse of herself in a mirror over a delicately ornate French table and wondered if she should have done something different with her hair. She studied her reflection with dismay. Too simple, too severe.

She had swept her hair high on her head in a perfectly plain knot so as not to detract from the necklace and the matching earrings Amadeo had had made. The emeralds were exquisite, and her dress was precisely the same shade of green. It was from her own collection of that year, a perfect shaft of green satin which seemed to fall straight from her shoulders to the floor. Over it she would wear the white satin coat she had designed for it, with the narrow, tightly fitting collar and broad cuffs lined in an extraordinary fuchsia silk. But perhaps it was too striking, or maybe her hair looked too plain, or ... dammit where the hell was Amadeo? And why was he late? She glanced at the clock again and began to purse her lips as she heard a breathless, soft whisper from the door. Surprised, she turned and found herself staring into the wide brown eyes of Alessandro, in sleepers, hiding behind the living room door.

'Sh ... Mamma ... *vieni qui* ...' Come here.

'*Ma cosa fai?*' What are you doing? She was instantly drawn into the conspiratorial whisper, a broad grin spreading across her face.

'I escaped her!' The eyes were afire with the same flame as hers.

'Who?'

'Mamma Teresa!' Maria Teresa, of course. The nurse.

'Why aren't you sleeping?' She was already beside her son, kneeling carefully on her high heels. 'It's very late.'

'I know!' A giggle of pure five-year-old glee. 'But I wanted to see you. Look what I got from Luisa!' He held out a handful of cookies lovingly bestowed by the cook, the crumbs already squeezing through the chubby fingers, the chocolate chips nothing more than a brown blur in his hand. 'Want one?' He shoved one rapidly into his mouth before proffering the hand.

31

'You should be in bed!' She was still whispering, restraining her laughter.

'Okay, okay.' Alessandro gobbled another cookie before his mother had a chance to decline. 'Will you take me?' He looked at her with eyes that melted her soul, and she nodded happily. This was why she no longer worked eleven hours a day at the office, no matter how much she sometimes regretted not spending every waking moment at Amadeo's side. This was worth it. For that look, that shining mischievous smile.

'Where's Papa?'

'On his way home, I hope. Come on.' Alessandro slipped his clean hand carefully into hers, and they made their way down a long dimly lit parqueted hall. Here and there were portraits of Amadeo's ancestors and a few paintings they had bought together in France. The house looked more like a palazzo than a villa, and occasionally when they held very grand parties, couples waltzed slowly down the long mirrored hall to the strains of an orchestra.

'What'll we do if Mamma Teresa finds us here?' Alessandro looked up at his mother again with those melting brown eyes.

'I'm not sure. Do you think it would help if we cry?' He nodded sagely, then giggled, hiding his mouth with his still crumb-covered hand.

'You're smart.'

'So are you. How did you get out of your room?'

'Through the door to the garden. Luisa said she'd make cookies tonight.'

Alessandro's room was done in bright blues and filled with books and games and toys. Unlike the rest of the house it was neither elegant nor grand, it was simply his. Isabella let out a long elaborate sigh as she marched him towards the bed and grinned at the boy again. 'We made it.'

But it was more than Alessandro could stand. He collapsed on his bed with a small whoop of glee, pulling the rest of the cookies out of a pocket – he had only carried the excess in his hand. He set about gobbling them as Isabella urged him under the covers.

'And don't make a big mess.' But it was a useless caution, and she didn't really care. That's what little boys were about – cookie crumbs and broken wheels, headless soldiers and smudges on walls. She liked it that way. The rest of her life was silken enough. She liked the nubs and crumbs and textures of her times with her son. 'Will you promise to go to sleep as soon as you finish?'

'I promise!' He looked at her solemnly with admiring eyes. '*Tu sei bella.*'

'Thank you. So are you. *Buona notte, tesòro.* Sleep tight.' She kissed him on the cheek and then on his neck. He giggled.

'I love you, Mamma.'

'I love you too.'

As she stepped back into the hall she felt tears fill her eyes and felt foolish. To hell with the Principessa di Sant'Angelo. She was suddenly glad Amadeo had been late. *But good Lord, what time must it be now*? Her heels clicked rapidly as she hurried back to the living room for another look at the clock. It was eight twenty-five. How was that possible? What was going on? But she knew all too well what was probably going on. A last-minute problem, an urgent call from Paris or Hong Kong or the States. A fabric that couldn't be delivered, a textile mill on strike. She knew all too well how easily one could be delayed. Crises like that had kept her from Alessandro every night for far, far too long. Now she decided that it was probably wise to give Amadeo a call, meet him at the office, with his dinner jacket over her arm.

She walked back to her tiny pink silk boudoir and picked

up the phone. The number was part of her fingers, part of her soul as well as her mind. A last exhausted secretary picked up the phone. '*Pronto*. San Gregorio.'

'*Buona sera*.' She identified herself quickly and unnecessarily and asked the woman to find Amadeo and put him on the line. There was a pause, a rapid apology for the delay, and then a pause again as Isabella tapped her foot and began to frown. Maybe something was wrong. Maybe he'd driven that damned too-fast car of his into a tree. She suddenly felt too warm in the heavy green satin, felt her heart seem to stop as Bernardo took the phone.

'*Ciao. Cosa c'e?*' What's up?

'Where the hell is Amadeo, dammit? He's almost two hours late. He promised he'd come home early tonight. We're dining at the gargoyle's house.'

'Sant'Angelo?' Bernardo knew her well.

'Who else? Anyway where is he?'

'I don't know. I thought he was with you.' The words escaped him too quickly as his brow furrowed into a frown.

'What? Isn't he there?' For the first time Isabella was frightened. Maybe something really had happened to him with the car.

But Bernardo was quick to answer, and there was nothing unusual in his even tone. 'He's probably here somewhere. I've been slaving over that damn soap you don't like. I haven't been in his office since noon.'

'Well, go find him and tell him to call home. I want to know if I should meet him at the office or if he still wants to come here to dress. The old bitch will probably kill us. Now we'll never make it to dinner on time.'

'I'll go check.'

'Thanks. And, Bernardo? You don't think something's wrong?'

'Of course not. I'll find him for you in a minute.'

34

Without saying more, he hung up. Isabella stared uneasily down at the phone.

Her words rang in Bernardo's ears . . . *something wrong. Something wrong.* That was precisely what he did think. He'd been trying to find Amadeo himself all afternoon to discuss a new possibility with that bloody soap. They would need more money for testing, quite a lot of it, and he had wanted Amadeo's okay. But Amadeo had been out. All day. Since lunchtime. Bernardo had consoled himself with the thought that Isabella and Amadeo had probably disappeared for an afternoon rendezvous. They did it often, as only he knew. But if Amadeo wasn't with her, then where was he? By himself? With someone else? With another woman? Bernardo cast aside that thought. Amadeo didn't cheat on Isabella. He never had. But where was he then? And where had he been since noon?

Bernardo began to comb the offices, prowling all four floors. All he could discover was a young, trembling secretary, still pounding away at the typewriter on her desk, who explained that two men had come to see Amadeo to explain that they had accidentally smashed up his car. Signore San Gregorio had left then, she explained. Bernardo felt himself turn grey as he hurried out to the street and slipped nervously into his car. As he shoved the Fiat into gear and pulled away he saw the Ferrari where he had seen it since that morning, in its parking space at the curb. He slowed for a moment as he drove past it. There was no damage. It hadn't been touched. His heart began to race. He drove much too quickly toward Isabella and Amadeo's home.

True to his word, Bernardo had obviously found him. Isabella grinned to herself as she hurried across the living room to return to her boudoir to answer the phone. Idiot, he had probably forgotten the principessa and her dinner, as well as the time. She'd give him hell. But without much conviction. She was roughly as capable of giving Amadeo hell as she was of forbidding Alessandro his chocolate cookies. The vision of his chubby, crumb-covered smile came to mind again as she picked up the phone.

'Well, well, darling. A little bit late coming home tonight, aren't you? And what the hell are we going to do about the principessa?' She was already smiling, spoke before waiting for his first word. She knew it would be Amadeo.

But it wasn't. It was a strange man.

'*Pronto, signora.* I don't know what you are going to do about the principessa. The question is what are we going to do about your husband?'

'What?' Christ. A crank call. Just what she needed. And briefly she felt like an ass. A secret admirer perhaps? Despite their unlisted phone number, now and then some stranger called. 'I'm sorry. I think you have the wrong number.' She was about to hang up when she heard the voice again. This time it sounded more harsh.

'Wait! Signora di San Gregorio, I believe your husband is missing. Isn't that right?'

'Of course not.' Her heart was racing. Who was this man?

'He's late. Is that right?'

'Who is this?'

'Never mind that. We have your husband. Here . . .' There was a sharp grunt, as though someone had been pushed or struck, and then Amadeo was on the line.

'Darling, don't panic.' But his voice sounded tired, weak.

'What is this? Some kind of joke?'

'It's not a joke. Not at all.'

36

'Where are you?' She could barely speak as panic gripped her. Bernardo had been right.

'I don't know. It doesn't matter. Just keep your head. And know . . .' There was an endlessly painful pause. Isabella's whole body began to shake violently as she clutched the phone. '. . . know that I love you.'

They must have pulled the phone away from him then; the strange man's voice returned. 'Satisfied? We have him. Now do you want him back?'

'Who are you? Are you mad?'

'No. Only greedy.' There was a cacophony of laughter as Isabella desperately tried to steady her grip on the phone. 'We want ten million dollars. If you want him back.'

'You're crazy. We don't have that kind of money. Nobody does.'

'Some people do. You do. Your business does. Get it. You have the whole weekend to figure it out while we baby-sit for your husband.'

'I can't . . . for God's sake . . . listen . . . please . . .' But he had already hung up, and Isabella stood wracked by sobs in her boudoir. Amadeo! They had Amadeo! Oh, God, they were mad!

She didn't even hear the doorbell ring, or the maid run to answer it, or Bernardo's rapid footsteps as he ran toward her sobs.

'What is it?' He looked at her in horror from the doorway as she stood convulsed by what she had just heard. 'Isabella, tell me, what?' Was he hurt? Was he dead?

For a moment she couldn't speak and then, uncomprehending, she stared at him as tears poured down her face. Her voice was a pathetic croak when she spoke to Bernardo at last. 'He's been kidnapped.'

'Oh, my God.'

37

Chapter Three

An hour later Isabella was still sitting in her boudoir, ashen and shaking, clutching Bernardo's hand when they got the second call.

'By the way, we forgot to tell you, signora. Don't call the cops. If you do, we'll know. And we'll kill him. And if you don't come up with the money, we'll kill him too.'

'But you can't. There's no way – '

'Never mind that. Just stay away from the cops. They'll freeze your money as soon as the banks open, and then neither he nor you will be worth a damn.' They had hung up again, but this time Bernardo had listened too.

She was crying again after the call.

'Isabella, we should have called the police an hour ago.'

'I told you not to, dammit. The man is right. The police will watch us all weekend and then on Monday they'll freeze everything we've got so we can't pay the ransom.'

'You can't anyway. It would take a year to free up that kind of money. And the only one who could do it anyway is Amadeo. You know that.'

'I don't give a damn. We'll get it. We have to.'

'We can't. We have to call the police. There's no other way. If they do want that kind of money, you don't have it to give them, Isabella. You can't risk making them angry. You have to find them first.' Bernardo looked almost as pale as Isabella as he ran a desperate hand through his hair.

'But what if they find out? The man said – '

'They won't. We have to trust someone. For God's sake, we can't trust them.'

'But maybe they'll give us time to raise the money. People will help us. We could make some calls to the States.'

'Screw the States. We can't do that. You can't give them time. What about Amadeo while you try to come up with the money? What are they doing to him?'

'Oh, God, Bernardo! I can't think . . .' Her voice disappeared into a pale, childlike whine as Bernardo took her into his own trembling arms.

'Please, let me call.' It was only a whisper. And her answer was only a nod. But the police were there in fifteen minutes. At the back door, wearing old clothes, looking like friends of the servants, with old frayed peasants' hats in their hands. At least they had made the effort to conceal who they were, Isabella thought, as Bernardo ushered them inside. Maybe Bernardo was right after all.

'Signora di San Gregorio?' The policeman recognised her immediately. Isabella was looking frozen and regal as she sat glued to her chair still in the emeralds and the green satin gown.

'Yes.' It was barely audible. Tears once again drowned her dark eyes, and Bernardo took a tight grip on her hand.

'We are sorry. We know you are in much pain. But we must know everything. How, when, who last saw him, have there been earlier threats, is there anyone in your business or your household whom you have reason to suspect? No one must be spared. No kindness, no courtesy, no loyalty to old friends. Your husband's life is at stake You must help us.' They looked suspiciously at Bernardo, who met their gaze evenly. It was Isabella who explained that Bernardo had insisted on calling the police.

'But they said . . . they said that if we called . . . that . . .' She couldn't go on.

'We know.'

They made endless inquiries of Bernardo and sat

39

patiently with Isabella during two hours of unbearably painful interrogation. By midnight it was over. They knew all that there was to be told. Bitter firings in the business, intrigues and rivalries, forgotten enemies and grudge-bearing friends.

'And they've said nothing about when they want the money or where or how?' Isabella shook her head miserably. 'It is my suspicion that they are amateurs. Lucky ones perhaps, but nonetheless, they are not professionals. Their second call, to remind you not to call the police, shows that. Professionals would have told you that immediately,' the sombre senior officer said.

'I knew it myself. That was why I didn't let Signore Franco call you.'

'You were wise to change your mind.' The officer in charge spoke again, soothingly and with great compassion. He was the kidnap specialist on the Roman force. And regrettably, he had had a great deal too much experience in recent years.

'Will it help us if they're amateurs?' Isabella gazed at him hopefully, praying that he would quickly say yes.

'Perhaps. These matters are very delicate. And we will handle it accordingly. Trust us, signora. I promise you.' And then he remembered something he himself had forgotten. 'You were going somewhere this evening?' He glanced again at the jewels and the dress.

She nodded dumbly. 'We were going to a – a dinner . . . a party . . . Oh, what does it matter now?'

'Everything matters. Whose party?'

For a moment Isabella almost smiled. 'The Principessa di Sant'Angelo. Will you make inquiries of her too?' Oh, God, the poor gargoyle.

'Only if it becomes necessary.' The inspector knew that name. The most formidable dowager in Rome. 'But for the moment it will be wisest if you tell no one yourself. Do not

40

go out, do not tell friends. Tell people that you are ill. But answer the phone yourself. The kidnappers may not be willing to speak to anyone else. We want to know the rest of their demands as quickly as possible. You have a little boy?' She nodded mutely. 'He stays at home too. And the entire house will be ringed by guards. Discreetly, but definitely.'

'Do I keep the servants at home too?'

'No.' He gave a firm shake of the head. 'Tell them nothing. And perhaps one of them will give himself away. Let them out as usual. We will follow all of them.'

'You think it may be one of them?' Isabella looked ashen but hopeful. She didn't care who it was, just so they found Amadeo in time, before those lunatics did something to him, before they . . . she couldn't think of the words. She didn't want to. It couldn't happen. Not to Amadeo. Not to them. Tears began to fill her eyes again, and the inspector turned away.

'We will just have to see. And for you, I regret, it will be a very difficult time.'

'What about money?' But as soon as she had said it, she regretted the words. The inspector's face went suddenly hard. 'What about it?'

'Do we . . . shall we – '

'All of your accounts and those of your business will be frozen on Monday morning. We will notify your bank just before they open.'

'Oh, my God.' For a moment she looked at Bernardo in terror, and then in fury at him and the cop. 'How do you expect us to run our business?'

'On credit. For a while.' His face looked frozen as well. 'I'm sure that the House of San Gregorio will not have trouble doing that.'

'Then what you are sure of, Inspector, and what I am sure of are two different things.' She stood up quickly, her

41

eyes ablaze with their own angry light. She didn't give a damn about money for the business. She wanted to know that she could get her hands on it if she had to, for Amadeo, if the cops' ideas turned out not to work. Damn them, damn Bernardo, damn . . .

'We'll let you get some sleep.' For the first time in her life, she wanted to shout out loud at him 'Fuck you' but she didn't. She only clenched her teeth and her hands, and in a moment they were gone and she was alone with Bernardo in the room.

'You see, damn you! You see! I told you they'd do that. Now what the hell are we going to do?'

'Wait. Let them do their job. Pray.'

'Don't you understand? They have Amadeo. If we don't come up with ten million dollars, they'll kill him! Haven't you gotten that into your head?' For a fraction of an instant she thought she was going to slap him, but the look on his face said that she already had.

She raged, she stormed, she cried. And he slept in the guest room that night. But there was nothing either of them could do. Not on a weekend, and not with the accounts frozen, and probably not without.

She never went to bed that night. She sat, she waited, she cried, she dreamed. She wanted to break everything in the villa, wanted to wrap it all up and offer it as gifts . . . anything . . . anything . . . just send him home . . . please . . .

They had to wait another twenty-four hours for the next call. And it was more of the same. Ten million dollars by Tuesday, and it was now Saturday night. She tried to reason with them, that it was the weekend, that it was impossible to get money together when the banks and offices and even their business was closed. They didn't give a damn. Tuesday. They figured that gave her plenty of time. They would tell her the location later.

And this time they didn't let Amadeo come to the phone.

'How do I know he's still alive?'

'You don't. But he is. And he will be until you screw up. As long as you don't call the cops and you come up with the money, he'll be fine. We'll call you. Ciao, signora.' Oh, Jesus . . . what now?

She looked like a ghost by Sunday morning, her eyes darkly ringed, her face deathly pale. Bernardo came and went, attempting to keep up a semblance of normalcy, and making references to hearing from Amadeo on his trip. It was easy to believe the story that she was sick. She looked it. But none of the servants gave anything away. No one seemed to know the truth. And the police had found out nothing. By Sunday night Isabella felt sure she would go mad.

'I can't, Bernardo, I can't anymore. They're not doing anything. There has to be another way.'

'How? Apparently even my personal account will be frozen. I'm going to have to borrow a hundred dollars from my mother tomorrow. The police tell me I can't even cash a cheque at my bank.'

'They're going to freeze you too?' He nodded silently. 'Damn.'

But there was one thing they wouldn't have frozen by Monday. One thing they couldn't touch. She lay awake in her bedroom all Sunday night, counting, figuring, guessing, and in the morning she went to the safe. Not ten million but maybe one. Or even two. She took the long green velvet boxes in which she kept her jewellery to her room, locked the door, and spread everything out on her bed. The emeralds, the new ten-carat ring from Amadeo, a ruby necklace she detested for its garishness, her pearls, the sapphire engagement ring Amadeo had given her ten and a half years before, her mother's diamond bracelet, her grandmother's pearls. She made a careful inventory and

43

quietly folded the list. Then she emptied the contents of all the boxes into one large Gucci scarf and stuffed the heavy bundle into a big old brown leather bag. It would almost pull her shoulder off when she wore it, but she didn't give a damn. To hell with the police and their eternal watching and checking and waiting to see. The one man she knew she could trust was Alfredo Paccioli. Her family and Amadeo's had done business with him for years. He bought and sold jewellery for princes and kings, statesmen and widows, and all the great and near-great of Rome. He had always been her friend.

Isabella dressed silently, pulling on brown slacks and an old cashmere sweater; she reached for her mink jacket but cast it aside. She put on an old suede one, and on her head she wore a scarf. She barely looked like Isabella di San Gregorio. She sat quietly for a moment, thinking, wondering how to get there in spite of the guards. And then she realised that it didn't matter. She didn't have to hide from them. All she had to get was the money. And it was important that no one recognise her once she was inside. She buzzed Enzo in his apartment over the garage and told him that she wanted him at the back door in ten minutes. She wanted to take a little ride.

He was waiting with the car in ten minutes as she had requested, and stealthily she crept from the house. She didn't want Alessandro to see her, didn't want to answer the questions in his eyes. She had told him for the past four days that she was sick and didn't want to give him her germs so he had to keep busy and play with Mamma Teresa, his nurse, in his room or outside. Papa was on a trip; the school had called, and everyone was having a vacation. Thank God, he was only five. But she succeeded in avoiding him once again on her way out and was suddenly grateful for Maria Teresa's busy routine for the child. She couldn't have dealt with him just then, couldn't

44

have faced him without holding him too tight and bursting out in a fierce, frightened cry.

'*Va meglio, signora?*' Enzo gazed at her thoughtfully in the rearview mirror as they pulled away, and she only nodded tersely as her unmarked police escort discreetly pulled away from the kerb.

'*Si*.' She gave him the address of the shop next to Paccioli's, not very far from her own house of couture, and decided that she didn't give a damn if Enzo knew why she was going there. If he was one of the conspirators, then let him know that she was doing her best. The bastards. There was no one left she could trust. Not now. And not ever again. And Bernardo, damn him, how could he have been so right? She fought back tears again as they drove to the address. The ride took less than fifteen minutes, and she made a quick business of stopping briefly in two boutiques and then disappearing quickly inside Paccioli's. Like the House of San Gregorio, it was a discreet facade, in this case marked only by the address. She stepped into the silent beige womb and spoke to a young woman at a large Louis XV desk.

'I want to see Signore Paccioli.' Even in a scarf and no makeup, it was difficult to divest herself of her tone of command. But the young woman was unimpressed.

'I'm terribly sorry, but Mister Paccioli is in a meeting. Clients are here from New York.' She looked up as though expecting Isabella to understand. But she had missed her mark. And the anonymous brown leather bag on Isabella's shoulder was cutting into her skin.

'I don't care. Tell him it's . . . Isabella.'

The woman hesitated, but this time only for a moment. 'Very well.' There was something desperate about the woman, something frighteningly crazy about her eyes as she kept shifting her handbag higher up on her shoulder. For an insane moment the young woman prayed that this

45

oddly dishevelled stranger was not carrying a gun. But in that case there was all the more reason to summon Mr. Paccioli from inside. She walked down a long narrow hall, leaving Isabella alone with two blue-uniformed guards. And she returned in less than a minute, with Alfredo Paccioli walking hurriedly at her side. He was somewhere in his early sixties, almost bald, with a delicate white fringe that matched his moustache and somehow accented his laughing blue eyes.

'Isabella, *cara, come stai*? Shopping for something to show with the collections?'

But she only shook her head. 'May I speak to you for a moment?'

'Of course.' He looked at her more closely then and didn't like what he saw. Something was terribly wrong with her. As though she were very ill, or perhaps a little bit mad. What she did a moment later almost confirmed it as she silently yanked open the brown bag and pulled the silk-wrapped bundle out, spilling its contents on his desk.

'I want to sell it. All of it.' Then had she gone mad? Or was it a fight with Amadeo? Had he been unfaithful? What in God's name was wrong?

'Isabella ... dearest ... you can't mean it. But that – that piece has been in your family for years.' He gazed in horror at the emeralds, the diamonds, the rubies, the ring he had sold to Amadeo only months before.

'I have to. Don't ask me why. Please. Alfredo, I need you. Just do it.'

'Are you serious?' Had their business gone suddenly bad?

'Absolutely.' And he could see now that she was neither ill nor insane, but something was very seriously, desperately wrong.

'It may take a little time.' He lovingly fingered the exquisite pieces, thinking of finding each one a home. But it

46

was not a task that he relished. It was like selling family or auctioning off a child. 'Is there truly no other way?'

'None. And I don't have any time. Give me whatever you can for them now. Yourself. And don't discuss this with anyone. No one. It's a matter of . . . it's . . . oh, God, Alfredo, please. You must help me.' Her eyes filled suddenly with tears, and he reached out a hand as his eyes questioned hers.

'I'm almost afraid to ask.' Twice before something like this had happened. Once, a year before. And the second time only a week before. It had been horrible . . . terrible . . . and it hadn't worked.

'Don't ask. I can't answer you. Just help me. Please.'

'All right. All right. How much do you need?' *Ten million dollars. Oh, God.*

'You can't give me what I need. Just give me what you can. In cash.'

He looked startled and then nodded. 'I can give you' – he made a rapid calculation of the cash he had available at the time – 'perhaps two hundred thousand today. And perhaps the same again in a week.'

'Can't you give it all to me today?' She looked desperate again, and for a moment he wondered if she might faint on his desk.

'I can't, Isabella. We just made an enormous purchase in the Far East. All of our main assets are in stones right now. And quite obviously that's not what you want.' He glanced down at the small mountain of diamonds and then back into her eyes with a thought. Suddenly he felt as frightened as she. Her desperation was contagious. 'Can you wait a minute while I make some calls?'

'To whom?' Her eyes were instantly filled with terror, and he saw her hands shake again.

'Trust me. To some colleagues, some friends. Perhaps among us we can come up with some more money. And . . .

47

Isabella . . .' He hesitated, but he thought he had understood. 'It *must* be . . . cash?'

'Yes.'

Then he was right. Now his own hands shook. 'I'll do what I can.' He sat down next to her, picked up the phone, and called five or six friends. Jewellers, furriers, one somewhat shady banker, a professional gambler who had been a customer and become a friend. Among all of them he could come up with another three hundred thousand dollars in cash. He told her and she nodded. That gave her five hundred thousand. Half a million dollars. It was one twentieth of what they wanted. Five percent. His eyes sought hers with a look of sorrow. 'Won't that help?' He found himself praying that it would.

'It will have to. How do I get it?'

'I'll send a courier out immediately. I'll take what I think we need in jewels for the other jewellers.' She watched dispassionately as he took a few pieces. When he took the diamond, she bit her lip to hold back the tears. Nothing mattered – only Amadeo.

'This should do it. I should have the money here in an hour. Can you wait?'

She nodded tersely. 'Send your messenger out the back door.'

'I'm being watched?'

'No. I am. But my car is out front, and they may be watching who leaves here.' He asked no further questions. There was no need.

'Do you want some coffee while you wait?' She only shook her head, and he left her after gently patting her arm. He felt so helpless and he was. She sat in solitary silence for a little over an hour, waiting, thinking, trying not to let her mind drift back to the agonizingly tender moments they had shared. Thinking back to first times and last times, and funny times, to seeing him with tiny

48

Alessandro in his arms for the first time: to their first collection, which they presented with outrageous courage and delight; to their honeymoon; their first vacation; their first house; and the first time they had made love, and the last time only four days before . . . They tore at her heart in a way she couldn't bear. The moments and voices and faces crowded into her head as she attempted to push them away, as she felt panic rising in her soul. It was an endless hour until at last Alfredo Paccioli returned. The exact amount was in a long brown envelope. Five hundred thousand dollars in cash.

'Thank you, Alfredo. I will be grateful to you all my life.' And Amadeo's. It wasn't ten million. But it was a start. If the police were right, and the kidnappers were indeed amateurs, perhaps even half a million would look good to them. It would have to. It was all she had now that all the accounts were frozen.

'Isabella . . . is there – is there anything I can do?'

Silently she shook her head, opened the door, and strode out, hurrying past the young woman at the desk, who was pleasantly bidding her good day, and then as she heard her, Isabella stopped.

'What did you say?'

'I said, good morning, Mrs. di San Gregorio. I heard Mister Paccioli mention collections and I realised that you were . . . I'm sorry . . . I didn't recognise you at first . . . I

'You didn't.' Isabella turned on her fiercely. 'You didn't recognise me, because I was never here. Is that clear?'

'Yes . . . yes . . . I'm sorry . . .' Good God, the woman was truly mad. But there was something else about her too. Something . . . the bag . . . it didn't look so heavy now. She swung it over her shoulder as though it were suddenly light. What had she had in there that had been so important and so heavy?

'Did you understand me?' Isabella was still staring at

49

the receptionist, the exhaustion of three sleepless nights making her indeed look crazy. 'Because if you didn't, if you tell anyone, anyone that I was here, you will be out of a job. Permanently. I'll see to it.'

'I understand.' So she was selling her jewellery then. The bitch. The young woman nodded politely as Isabella hurried out the door.

Isabella had Enzo drive her straight home. She sat waiting for hours by the phone. She never moved. She just sat there in her bedroom, behind a locked door. An inquiry about lunch from Louis brought only a terse no. The vigil wore on. They had to call. It was Monday. They wanted the money by the next day. They would have to tell her where to leave it and precisely when.

But by seven that evening they still hadn't called. She had heard Alessandro clattering through the halls and the voice of Mamma Teresa admonishing him to remember that his Mother had the flu. And then all was silent again, until at last there came a fierce banging on the door.

'Let me in.' It was Bernardo.

'Leave me alone.' She didn't want him in the room if they should call. She wouldn't even tell him about the jewellery. He'd probably tell the police. And she'd had enough of that nonsense. She was taking care of it now. She could promise them a million dollars – half tomorrow, the other half by next week.

'Isabella, I have to talk to you. Please.'

'I'm busy.'

'I don't care. Please. I must . . . there's something I – I have to show you.' For a moment she heard his voice crack. And then she told him, 'Slip it under the door.'

It was the evening paper. Page five. *Isabella di San Gregorio was seen at Paccioli's today* . . . It described what she had worn, how she had looked – and almost every item she

50

had just sold. But how? Who? Alfredo? And then she knew. The girl. The eager little bitch at the desk. Isabella's heart dropped as she unlocked the door.

Bernardo was standing there, crying silently, staring at the floor.

'Why did you do that?'

'I had to.' But suddenly her voice was flat. If it was in the papers, then the kidnappers would know too. And they would know more: that if she was selling her jewellery, her accounts were probably frozen. They would know that she had told the police. 'Oh, no.'

They said nothing more to each other. Bernardo simply walked into the room and silently took his place by the phone.

The call came at nine. It was the same voice, the same man.

'*Capito, signora.* You squealed.'

'I didn't. Really.' But her voice had the frantic ring of untruth. 'But I had to get more money. We couldn't get enough.'

'You'll never get enough. Even if you didn't tell the cops, they'll know now. They'll come snooping around. Someone will tell them if you don't.'

'But no one else knows.'

'Bullshit. How dumb do you think we are? Listen, you want to say good-bye to your old man?'

'No, please . . . wait . . . I have money for you. A million . . .' But he wasn't listening, and Amadeo was already on the phone.

'Isabella . . . darling . . . everything's all right.'

Everything's all right? Was he crazy? But she didn't care if he was. He had never sounded so good to her, and her heart had never turned over, then soared as it did now. He was still there, somewhere; they hadn't hurt him. Maybe everything *would* be all right. As long as Amadeo was still there, somewhere, anywhere, it was all right.

'You've been a very brave girl, darling. How's Alessandro? Does he know?'

'Of course not. And he's fine.'

'Good. Kiss him for me.' She thought she heard his voice tremble then and she shut her eyes tightly. She couldn't cry. Not now. She had to be as brave as he thought she was. Had to be. For him. 'I want you ... always ... to know how much I love you,' he was saying. 'How perfect you are. What a good wife. You've never given me a single unhappy day, darling. Not one.' She was openly crying now and fighting back the sobs that clutched at her throat.

'Amadeo, darling, I love you. So much. Please ... come home.'

'I will, darling. I will. I promise you. And I'm right there with you now. Just be brave for a little while longer.'

'You too, my beloved. You too.' With that the connection was silently severed.

The police found him in the morning near a warehouse in a suburb of Rome, strangled and still very beautiful, and very dead.

Chapter Four

Police cars surrounded the limousine as Enzo guided it slowly into the heart of Rome. She had chosen a church near the House of San Gregorio, not far from the Piazza di Spagna. Santo Stefano. They had gone there when they were first courting and wanted to stop somewhere to rest for a moment after their long walks during lunch. It was ancient and simple and pretty and seemed more appropriate to her than the more elaborate cathedrals of Rome.

Bernardo sat beside her in the car as she stared unseeingly forward, looking only at the back of Enzo's head. Was it he? Was it someone else? Who were the betrayers? It didn't matter now. Amadeo was gone. Taking with him the warmth and the laughter, the love and the dreams. Gone. Forever. She was still in shock.

It had been two days since her visit to Alfredo Paccioli, when she had gone clutching her scarf filled with jewels. Two days. She felt leaden, as though she also had died.

'Isabella . . . bella mia.' Bernardo was gently touching her arm. Silently he took her hand. There was so little he could do. He had wept for an hour when the police called him with the news. And again when Alessandro had flown into his arms.

'They killed my Daddy . . . they . . . they . . .'

The child had sobbed as Isabella stood by, letting him find what solace he could from a man. He would have no man now, no father, no Amadeo. He had looked at his mother with such terror in his dark, unhappy eyes. 'Will they ever take you?' No, she had answered. No, never. As

53

she held him so tightly in her arms. *And they will never take you either*, tesòro. *You are mine.*

It had been more than Bernardo could bear as he watched them and now this. Isabella, frozen and icelike in black coat and hat and stockings and a thick black veil. It only enhanced her beauty, only made her seem more, rather than less. He had brought her back all the jewellery without saying a word. Today she was wearing only her wedding ring and the large anniversary solitaire she had got only a few months before. Was that all? Was it only five days since they had last seen him? Would he truly never return? Bernardo had felt like a five-year-old child himself as he had looked down on the face of Amadeo di San Gregorio, so still and peaceful in death. He looked more than ever like the statues, the paintings, the young graceful boys of long-ago Rome. And now he was gone.

Bernardo helped her quietly from the car and held her arm tightly as they stepped inside. Police and guards at every entrance, and armies of mourners seated inside.

The funeral was brief and unbearably painful. Isabella sat silently next to him, tears rolling relentlessly down her face beneath the black veil. Employees and friends and relatives were sobbing openly. Even the gargoyle was there, with her gold and ebony cane.

It seemed years before they returned to the house. Contrary to tradition, Isabella had let it be known that she would see no one at home. No one. She wanted to be left alone. Who knew which of them had betrayed him? But Bernardo knew now that it was unlikely to be someone of their acquaintance. Even the police had no clue. They assumed, probably correctly, that it had been 'lucky amateurs', greedy for a piece of the San Gregorio wealth. There were no fingerprints, no bits of evidence, no witnesses, there had been no more calls. And there wouldn't be, the police were sure of it. Except from the hundreds, maybe thousands, of cranks who would start their macabre games. The police manned her telephone now, waiting for the onslaught of minor madmen who took pleasure in haunting and taunting and teasing, confessing, and threatening, or breathing obscenities into the phone. They had told Isabella what she could expect. Bernardo cringed at the thought of it; she had been through enough.

'Where's Alessandro?' Bernardo sipped a cup of coffee after the funeral, thinking how unbearably empty the house seemed and ashamed to find himself grateful that if it had to be someone, it had been Amadeo and not the child. Isabella wouldn't have been able to make that choice. But to Bernardo it was clear. As it would have been to Amadeo. He would have gladly sacrificed himself to spare his only child.

'He's in his room with the nurse. Do you want to see him?' Isabella looked at him lifelessly over her cup.

'I can wait. I wanted to talk to you about something anyway.'

'What?' She wasn't easy to talk to these days, and she wouldn't let the doctor give her anything to help. Bernardo guessed accurately that she hadn't really slept in almost a week.

'I think you need to get away.'

'Don't be absurd.' She set her cup down viciously and stared at him. 'I'm fine.'

'You look it.' He stared back at her, and for a moment she gave in to the flicker of a smile. It was the first taste of the old tension between them in a week. It felt comfortable and familiar.

'All right, I'm tired. But I'll be fine.'

'Not if you stay here.'

'You're wrong. This is where I need to be.' *Near his things, his home . . . near . . . him . . .*

'Why don't you take a trip to the States?'

'Why don't you mind your own business?' She sat back in her chair with a sigh. 'I'm not going, Bernardo. Don't push me.'

'You heard what the police said. Cranks will be calling, bugging you. Already now the press won't leave you alone. Is this how you want to live? What you want for Alessandro? You can't even send him back to school.'

'Eventually he can go back to school.'

'Then go away until then. A month. A few months. What is there to stay for?'

'Everything.' She looked at him very deliberately as she slowly pulled off her hat and took the veil from her eyes. There was something frightening and determined about the way she looked at him now.

'What does that mean?'

'It means I'm coming back to work on Monday. Part time, but every day. Nine to one, nine to two. Whatever it takes.'

'Are you joking?'

'Not at all.'

'Isabella, you can't mean it.' He was shocked.

'I can and I do. Just who do you think will run the business now -- now that . . . he's gone?' She faltered for a moment on the words. But he bridled as soon as she had said them.

'I thought I could do that.' For a moment he sounded hurt and very tough. She looked away and then back at him.

'You could. But I can't do that. I can't sit here and abdicate. I can't give up what Amadeo and I shared, what he built, what we loved, what we made. He's gone now, Bernardo. I owe it to him. And to Alessandro. One day the business will be his. You and I will have to teach him what

56

he needs to know. You and I. Both of us. I can't do that just sitting here. If I did that, all I could do was tell him what it was like twenty years ago 'when your father was alive'. I owe him more than that, and Amadeo, and you and myself. I'm coming back on Monday.'

'I'm not saying you shouldn't come back. I'm just saying it's too soon.' He tried to sound gentle but he was not Amadeo. He couldn't handle her in Amadeo's gentle way, only with fire.

But this time she only shook her head, her eyes filling with tears again. 'It's not, Bernardo . . . it's not too soon at all. It's much . . . much . . . too late.' He put a hand over hers and waited until she caught her breath. 'What would I do here? Wander? Open his closets? Sit in the garden? Wait in my boudoir? For what? For a man . . .' A sob broke from her as she sat very still, her head held very high. '. . . a man . . . whom . . . I loved . . . and who is never again . . . coming . . . home. I have to . . . come back to work. I have to. It is a part of me, and it was a part of him. I will find him there. Every day. In a thousand different ways. In some of the ways that mattered most. I just . . . have to. That's all. Even Alessandro understands. I told him this morning. He understands perfectly.' She looked proud for a moment. He was such a good little boy.

'Then you're making him as crazy as you are.' But Bernardo didn't mean it unkindly, and Isabella only smiled.

'May I make him as crazy as I am, Bernardo. And as lovely as his father was. May I make him just as fine as that.' And with that she stood up, and for the first time in days he saw a real smile and only a glimmer of what had once been the sparkle in her eyes, only days before, only days. 'I need to be alone now. For a while.'

'When will I see you?' He stood up, watching her. Isabella was still there. Somewhere, sleeping, waiting, but she would come alive again. He was sure of it now. There was too much life in her not to.

'You will see me on Monday morning, of course. In my office.'

He only looked at her silently and then he left. He had a lot on his mind.

Chapter Five

Isabella di San Gregorio did indeed appear in the office on Monday morning, and every day after that. She was there from nine to two, inspiring awe, terror, admiration, and respect. She was everything Amadeo had always known she was. She was made of fire and steel, of heart and guts. She wore his hat now as well as her own, and a thousand others. She worked on papers in her room at home at night long after Alessandro went to sleep. She had two interests in her life now, her work and her child. And very little else. She was tense, tired, drawn, but she was doing what she had said she would do. She even sent Alessandro back to school – with a guard, with caution, with care, but with determination. She taught him to be proud, not afraid. She taught him to be brave, not angry. She taught him all that she herself was and still managed to give him something more. Patience, love, laughter, and sometimes they cried together too. Losing Amadeo had cost them both almost everything they had. But now it brought them closer and it made them friends. The only one whose friendship suffered was Bernardo. It was he who took the brunt of her sorrow and anxieties and fatigue. Instead of running more of the business, it seemed to him he ran less. He worked harder, longer, more, and yet she was trying to be everything, the root, the core, the heart and the soul of the House of San Gregorio. It left him drudgery. And bitterness. And anger. Which showed in every meeting between them now. The wars were constant, and Amadeo was no longer there to temper them. She was trying to be Amadeo as well as herself, and she was not sharing with him as she had with

Amadeo. She was still in command. It created more tension than ever between them. But at least the business hadn't suffered from the blow of Amadeo's passing. After a month, the figures were stable; after two months they were better than they had been the year before. Everything was better, except the relationship between Bernardo and Isabella, and the way Isabella looked. The phone rang constantly day and night, at home and in the office. The cranks had arrived, as promised. Threats, arguments, confessions, harangues, sympathy and accusations, obscenities and propositions. She no longer ever answered the phone. Three men covered it twenty-four hours a day at the villa, and another three covered the phone at the office. But still no clue had turned up to identify the kidnappers, and it was clear now that they would never be found. Isabella understood that. She had to. She also knew that eventually they would leave her alone. The cranks, the maniacs, the fools. All of them. One day. She could wait. But Bernardo disagreed.

'You're crazy. You can't go on living like this. You've already lost twenty pounds. You're practically scrawny.' He didn't mean it of course; she was always beautiful to him – but still she looked ill.

'That has nothing to do with the phone calls. It has to do with what I eat, or don't.' She tried to smile at him from across her desk, but she was too tired to argue anymore. They'd been at it all morning.

'You're jeopardising the child.'

'For chrissake, Bernardo, I'm not!' Her eyes raged at him now. 'We have seven guards on the house. One with Enzo in the car. Another at school. Don't be a horse's ass.'

'Wait, just wait, you bloody fool. Did I tell you that day, did I, about the way you two lived? Was I wrong?'

It was a bitter blow.

'Get out of my office,' Isabella shouted.

'Get out of my life!'

'*Va cagare!*' He slammed the door as he left. For a moment she was too stunned to go after him to apologise and she felt too tired even to try. She was so goddamn tired of fighting with Bernardo. She tried to remember if it had always been like that. Hadn't it been fun before too? Hadn't they laughed together at times? Or had they only laughed when Amadeo was there to coax them away from their battles? She couldn't remember anymore. She couldn't remember anything except the mountains of papers that lay on her desk – except at night. Then she remembered. Too much. She remembered Amadeo's soft sleeping sounds in the bed at night and his hands on the warm flesh of her thighs. She remembered the way he yawned and stretched when he awoke, the look in his eyes as he smiled at her over the morning paper, the way he smelled just after he had shaved and bathed, the way his laughter rang out in the hall when he chased Alessandro, the way . . . She lay with the memories every night. She took work home with her now, hoping to keep the visions at bay, hoping to lose herself in fabric orders and collection details, statistics and figures and investments. The nights were too long after Alessandro went to bed.

She shut her eyes very tightly and sighed as she sat in her office, trying to will herself back to work, but there was a soft knock at her door. Unwillingly she jumped, startled. It was the side door to Amadeo's office, the door he had always used. For a moment she felt herself tremble. She still had that mad feeling that he was going to come back. That it was all a bad dream, a terrible lie, that one of these evenings the Ferrari would slide down the gravel driveway, the door would slam, and he would call out to her, 'Isabellezza! I'm home!'

'Yes.' She stared at the door as the knock came again.

'May I?' It was only Bernardo, still looking strained.

'Of course. What are you doing in there?' He had been in Amadeo's office. She didn't want him in there. She didn't want anyone there. She used it to find refuge sometimes, for a moment, at lunch, or at the end of a day. But even she knew that she couldn't keep Bernardo out. He had a right to access to Amadeo's papers, to the books he kept on the wall behind his desk.

'I was looking for some files. Why?'

'Nothing.' The look of pain in her eyes was unmistakable. For a moment Bernardo ached for her again. No matter how impossible she was at times, no matter how they differed in their aspirations for the business, he still understood the magnitude of her loss.

'Does it bother you so much when I go in there?' His voice was different now than it had been a little while before when he had shouted and slammed the door.

She nodded, looking away for a moment and then back at him. 'Stupid, isn't it? I know you need to get things from his office sometimes. So do I.'

'You can't turn it into a shrine, Isabella.' His voice was soft, but his eyes firm. She was already doing that to the business. He wondered how long it would go on.

'I know.'

He stood uneasily in the doorway, not sure this was the time. But when? When could he ask her? When could he tell her what he thought? 'Can we talk for a minute, or are you very busy?'

'I have some time.' Her tone wasn't very inviting. She forced herself to gentle her voice. Maybe he wanted to apologise for what he had just said as he slammed out of her office a little while before. 'Is there something special?'

'I think so.' He sighed softly and sat down. 'There's something I haven't wanted to bother you with, but I think that maybe it's time.'

'Oh, Christ. Now what?' Who was quitting, what had

62

been cancelled, and what wasn't going to arrive? 'That goddamn soap again?' She'd heard enough, and every time they had to discuss it, it reminded her again of the day when . . . when Amadeo . . . that last morning . . . She averted her eyes.

'Don't look like that. It's nothing unpleasant. In fact' – he tried to convince her by smiling – 'it could be very nice.'

'I'm not sure I could stand the shock of something "very nice".' She sat back in her chair, fighting exhaustion and a pain in the small of her back. Nerves, strain, it had been there since . . . 'All right, out with it. Tell me.'

'Ecco, signora.' And suddenly he regretted not taking her to lunch. Maybe that would have been better, a few hours away, a good bottle of wine. But who could get her to go anywhere anymore? And moving three feet out of the building meant taking with them her army of guards. No it was better here. 'We've had a call from the States.'

'Someone has ordered ten thousand pieces, we're dressing the First Lady, and I just won an internationally coveted award. Right?'

'Well . . .' For a moment they both smiled. Thank God, she was mellower than she had been earlier that morning. He wasn't sure why, maybe because she needed him so much, or maybe she was just suddenly too tired to fight. 'It wasn't quite that kind of call. It was a call from Farnham-Barnes.'

'The omnivorous department store monster? What the hell do they want now?' In the past ten years F-B, as it was called, had been carefully devouring every major top-notch department store in the States. It was now a powerful entity to be reckoned with, and an account coveted by everyone in the trade. 'Were they happy or not with their last order? No, never mind. I know the answer to that, they want more. Well, tell them they can't have

63

more. You already know that.' Because of the number of stores in their chain, Isabella was careful to keep the reins well in hand. They could only have so much of her ready-to-wear line and a miniscule quantity of the designer line. She didn't want women in Des Moines, Boston, and Miami all wearing hundreds of the same dress. Even in ready-to-wear Isabella was careful and kept an iron control. 'Is that it?' She glared at Bernardo, already bridling, and he felt his upper lip grow stiff.

'Not exactly. They had something else on their minds. The parent company, something called IHI, International Holdings and Industries, which happens to own Farrington Mills, Inter Am Airlines, and Harcourt Foods, has been making discreet inquiries of us since Amadeo's . . . for the past two months.'

'What kind of inquiries?' Her eyes were black slate. Cold and hard and flat.

But there was no point beating around the bush any longer. 'They want to know if you'd be interested in selling out.'

'Are you crazy?'

'Not at all. For them it would be a brilliant addition to what they've done with F-B. They've acquired almost every major department store worth having in the States, yet they've maintained each one's identity. It's a chain without being a chain. Each store has remained every bit as exclusive as it was before, yet it benefits from being part of a much larger organisation, more extensive funding to draw on, greater resources. Business-wise, the system is brilliant.'

'Then congratulate them for me. And tell them to go screw. What do they think? That San Gregorio is some little Italian department store to add to their chain? Don't be absurd, Bernardo. What they're doing has nothing to do with us.'

64

'On the contrary. It could have everything to do with us. It gives us an international feeding system for all other lines, production facilities, mass marketing if we want it, for the colognes, the soap. It's a top-ranking operation and would fit in perfectly for all our main lines.'

'You're out of your mind.' She looked at him and laughed nervously. 'Are you actually suggesting that I sell to them? Is that what this is all about?'

He hesitated for only a fraction of a second and then nodded, fearing the worst. It was quick to come. 'Are you mad?' She was shrieking at him and rapidly got to her feet. 'Is that what that bullshit was about this morning? About how tired I look? How thin? What is it, Bernardo? Are they offering you an enormous fee if you can talk me into it? Greed, everyone is motivated by greed, like the . . . those . . .' She choked on the words, thinking of Amadeo's kidnappers, and turned away quickly to hide a sudden dew of tears. 'I don't want to discuss this.' She stood with her back to him, looking out of the window, unconsciously searching for Amadeo's car. It had already been sold.

Behind her Bernardo's voice was surprisingly quiet. 'No one is paying me a fee, Isabella. Except you. I know it's too soon for you to think about this. But it makes sense. It is the next obvious step for the business. Now.'

'What does that mean?' She wheeled to face him, and he was pained to see the tears still in her eyes. 'Do you think Amadeo would have done this? Sold out to some commercial monster in America? To a corporation? An F-B and an IHI, and a God-knows-what-else. This is San Gregorio, Bernardo. San Gregorio. A family. A dynasty.'

'It is an empire with an empty throne. How long do you really think you can manage this? You'll die of exhaustion before Alessandro comes of age. And not even that. You run the same risk that Amadeo did and so does Alessandro.

You know what's happening in Italy now. What about you? What if something happens to you? How constantly can you keep yourself guarded, every time you go in or out, or stand up or sit down.'

'For as long as I have to. It will die down. You actually think selling out is the answer? How can you even say that after what you've put into it, after what you've built with us, after . . .' Again the tears filled her eyes.

'I'm not betraying you, Isabella.' He fought for control. 'I'm trying to help you. There's no other answer for you except to sell out. They're talking about enormous sums of money. Alessandro would be an immensely rich man.' But he knew as he said it that that wasn't the key.

'Alessandro will be what his father was. The head of the House of San Gregorio. Here. In Rome.'

'If he's still alive.' The words were spoken softly, with a film of anger.

'Stop it! Stop!' She stared at him, her hands trembling, her face suddenly contorted into a hideous frown. 'Stop saying that! Nothing like that will ever happen again. And I won't sell out. Ever. Tell those people no! That's all, that's final. I don't want to hear the offer. I don't want you to discuss anything with them. In fact I forbid you to talk to them!'

Christ, women! 'Don't be a fool.' Bernardo shouted, 'We do business with them. And in spite of your asinine restrictions IHI is still one of our biggest accounts.'

'Cancel it.'

'I won't.'

'I don't give a damn what you do, damn you. Just leave me alone!'

This time it was Isabella who slammed out of the room and took refuge in Amadeo's office next door. Bernardo sat in hers for only a moment, then retreated to his own quarters down the hall. She was a fool. He knew she'd

66

never agree to it, but this sale was her best bet. Something was happening to her. Once, the business had added joy and zest and something wonderful and powerful to her life. Now he could see it destroying her. Every day in these offices made her more lonely, more bitter. Every day surrounded by guards made her more frightened, no matter how much she denied it. Every day dreaming of Amadeo broke off another piece of her soul. But she had the reins now. Isabella di San Gregorio was in control.

The next morning Bernardo called the president of IHI and told him Isabella had said no. After he did and thought mournfully of the opportunity Isabella had turned down, his secretary buzzed him on the intercom.

'Yes?'

'There's someone here to see you.'

'Now what?'

'It's about a bicycle. He said you told him to deliver it here.' Bernardo smiled tiredly to himself and let out another sigh. The bicycle. It was about all he was ready to handle after a difficult start to his day.

'I'll be right out.'

It was red, with a blue-and-white seat, and red, white, and blue streamers flying from the handlebars, a bell, a speedometer, and a tiny licence plate with Alessandro's name. It was a beautiful little bicycle, and he knew it would delight the child, who had been dying for a 'real bike' since the summer. Bernardo knew that Amadeo had planned to give him one for Christmas. He had ordered this one, a tiny silver astronaut suit, and half a dozen games. This was going to be a difficult Christmas, and with a glance at his calendar as he stood up, he realised that it was only two weeks away.

Chapter Six

'Mamma, Mamma . . . it's Bernardo!' Alessandro's nose was pressed to the glass; the Christmas tree sparkled behind him. Isabella put her arms around him and looked outside. She was smiling. She and Bernardo had set aside the wars a few days before. She needed him this year, desperately, and so did the child. She and Amadeo had both lost their parents over the last decade, and as only children they had nothing to offer Alessandro in the way of family, except themselves and their friend. As always Bernardo had come through. 'Oh, look . . . look! It's tremendous! He has a package . . . and look! More!' Bernardo did a hilarious pantomime, staggering under the weight of his bundles, all of them shoved into a huge canvas sack. He was wearing a Father Christmas hat with one of his dark suits.

Isabella was laughing too as the guard opened the door. '*Ciao, Nardo, come va?*' He kissed her lightly on the cheek and turned his attention instantly to the little boy. It had been a rough couple of weeks in the office. The IHI matter was definitely closed. Isabella had sent them a brutally succinct letter, and Bernardo had been livid to his very core. Other problems had cropped up; all finally had been handled and resolved. It had been a wearying time for both of them. But somehow, with the depressing threat of Christmas, they had both managed to put their differences aside. She handed him a glass of brandy as they all sat down next to the fire.

'When can I open them? Now? . . . Now?' Alessandro was hopping up and down like a little red elf in sleepers as

Mamma Teresa hovered somewhere near the door. The servants were all celebrating in the kitchen, with wine and the presents Isabella had given them the night before. The only members of the household not included in the celebration were the guards. They were treated as invisibles, and the safety of the entire household depended on their remaining on duty at all the entrances to the villa and just outside. The phone men were posted as usual in Amadeo's old study, and the crank calls raged on, doubled now, for some reason, during the holidays. As though what they had already been through hadn't been enough. There had to be more. And Bernardo knew it was taking its toll on her. She always knew about the calls, as though she sensed them. She trusted no one now. Something tender and giving that had been so much a part of her was slowly dying inside.

'When can I open them? When?' Alessandro tugged at Bernardo's sleeve. He pretended not to hear.

'Open what? That's just my laundry over there in that bag.'

'No, it's not . . . no, it's not! Mamma . . . please . . .'

'I don't think he'll make it till midnight, let alone Christmas Day!' Even Isabella was smiling as her eyes gently caressed the child. 'What about Mamma Teresa, darling? Why don't you give her her present first?'

'Oh, Mamma!'

'Come on.' She pushed a large package into his arms and he scampered off to deliver a handsome pink satin robe to her, the finest from Isabella's American line. From Isabella there had already been a handbag and a small elegant watch. This was a year to be good to everyone, all of those who had shown themselves so devoted to her and the child. At least she no longer suspected the members of her household. She believed, at last, that the betrayers had been people from outside. She had given Enzo a new coat, a warm, black cashmere to wear over his uniform when he chauffeured her around town, and an excellent new radio for his room. He could even get Paris and London on it, he had told her with pride that day. There had been presents for the entire household, and equally handsome, thoughtful ones for everyone at the office. But for Alessandro there had been the most special gift of all. He had not seen it yet, but Enzo already had it mounted and everything prepared.

He had just scampered back into the room. 'She says it's beautiful and she'll wear it all her life and think of me.' Alessandro looked happy with the effect the large pink bathrobe had had. 'Now me.'

Isabella and Bernardo laughed as they looked at him, with eyes so bright and opened so wide. For a moment it was as though nothing ugly had ever happened. For an instant the pain of the last months was not.

'All right, Master Alessandro. Go to it!' Bernardo waved grandiosely toward the large canvas bag, and the boy dived towards it and then into it with loud squeals of glee. Paper and ribbons instantly started flying, and in a moment he was wearing the silver astronaut suit, the feet of his red sleepers peeking through. He was laughing and giggling and slid rapidly across the highly polished wood floor to give Bernardo a kiss, before diving back for more. The games, new crayons, a large cuddly brown bear, and then the bicycle at last, pushed way to the back of the large canvas sack.

'Oh . . . oh . . . it's beautiful . . . Is it . . . is it a Rolls-Royce?' They both laughed as they watched him, already astride the new bike.

'Of course it's a Rolls. Would I give you anything less?' He was already weaving across the living room, aimed first at a Louis XV table, then at the wall, as the two people who loved him laughed till they cried. And then they all saw Enzo, smiling hesitantly from the door. His eyes questioned Isabella, and she nodded with a smile. She whispered something to Bernardo, and he raised his eyebrows and then laughed.

'I think I may have been outdone.'

'Not at all. He'll probably come to breakfast on the bicycle tomorrow morning. But this . . . I just wanted to give him something to make him less unhappy about being confined at home. He can't . . .' she hesitated painfully for a moment, '. . . he can't go to the playground anymore.' Bernardo nodded silently, put down his brandy, and rose. But the momentary sadness in Isabella's eyes was gone again, as she turned smilingly to the child. 'Go get Mamma Teresa and your coat.'

'Are we going out?' He looked intrigued.

'Just for a minute.'

'Can't I wear this?' He looked down happily at his astronaut suit, and Bernardo took a gentle swing at his behind.

'Go on, you can wear your coat over it.'

'Okay.' He said the American word with his own Roman accent and disappeared at full speed as Bernardo winced.

'I may have to replace the mirrors in your hall.'

'Not to mention the dining room table, all the cabinets between here and his room, and possibly the glass doors.' They both listened smilingly as the bicycle bell rang out from the long hall. 'It was just the right gift.' She also knew that it had been what Amadeo planned for him, and for a moment no one spoke. She looked at him searchingly then and let out a small sigh. 'I'm glad you could be here with Alessandro this year, Nardo . . . and with me too.'

Gently he touched her hand as the fire in the hearth crackled and blazed. 'I wouldn't have been anywhere

71

else.' And then he smiled at her. 'Despite the ulcers you give me at work.' But this was different. And now suddenly there was a different kind of electricity in the air.

'I'm sorry, I – I feel so much on my shoulders now. I keep thinking you'll understand.' She looked up at him, the beautifully etched face so pale and so perfectly set around the dark eyes.

'I do understand. I could help more, you know, if you'd let me.'

'I'm not sure I can. I have this insane urge to – to do it all myself. It's difficult to explain. It's all I have left, except Alessandro.'

'One day there will be more.' One day . . . but she only shook her head.

'Never again. There is no one like him. He was a very special man.' Tears rolled into her eyes again as she pulled her hand away and looked silently into the fire. And Bernardo looked away and sipped at his brandy again as he heard the bicycle bell chime and Alessandro come careering down the hall with Mamma Teresa in tow 'Ready?' Isabella's eyes were a little too shiny, but nothing in the face she turned to her child showed how great was her pain.

'Si.' The little face looked out impishly from the large plastic astronaut hat.

'Allora, andiamo.' Isabella stood up and led the way to the double doors leading into the garden. A guard was unobtrusively standing off to the side, and they all saw now that the garden was brilliantly lit. She looked down at the child, and she heard him catch his breath.

'Mamma! . . . !' It was a small but beautiful carousel, just the right size for a five-year-old child. It had cost her a fortune, but it was worth every bit of it when she saw the light in his eyes. Four horses danced gaily beneath a carved wooden tent painted red and white; there were bells and clowns and decorations. Bernardo thought he had never seen the boy's eyes so wide. Enzo helped him carefully into the saddle of a blue-painted horse with green ribbons attached to a golden halter with little silver bells. A switch was flicked on, and the carousel began to turn. Alessandro squealed with excitement and delight. The night was suddenly filled with carnival music as the servants came to the windows, and everywhere his audience smiled.

'*Buon Natale*!' Isabella called out to him and then ran to jump into the saddle of the next horse, a yellow one with a little red saddle edged in gold. They laughed at each other as the carousel spun slowly around. Bernardo watched them, feeling something very tender tear at his heart. Mamma Teresa turned away, wiping a tear from her eye, and Enzo and the guard shared a smile.

Alessandro rode round and round for almost half an hour, and them at last Isabella urged him back inside.

'It will still be there in the morning.'

'But I want to ride it tonight.'

'If you stay out here all night, Santa Claus won't come.'

Santa Claus? Bernardo smiled to himself. What didn't the child have? The smile faded. A father. That's what Alessandro didn't have. He helped the child down from the carousel and held his hand tightly as they walked back inside. He disappeared quickly to the kitchen as Bernardo and Isabella regained their seats by the fire.

'What a marvellous thing, Isabella.' The echo of the carnival chimes still rang in his head. And finally she was smiling as she hadn't in months.

'I always wanted one of my very own when I was a child. It's perfect, isn't it?' For a moment her eyes were almost as bright as the fire. For an instant he wanted to say 'So are you.' She was a remarkable woman. He hated her and loved her, and she was his dearest friend.

'Do you suppose he'll let us ride it with him if we're very, very nice?' She laughed with him and poured herself a small glass of red wine. And then as though she had forgotten something, she jumped to her feet and ran to the tree.

'I almost forgot.' She picked up two small boxes wrapped in gold and returned to the fire. 'For you.'

'If it's not a carousel of my very own, I don't want it.' And again they both laughed. But the laughter dimmed very quickly as he discovered what was inside. The first was a tiny immensely intricate calculator in its own silver case; it looked like a very elegant cigarette case and could be worn concealed in his vest.

'I had it sent from the States. I don't understand it. But you will.'

'Isabella, you're crazy!'

'Don't be silly. I should have got you a hot-water bottle for your ulcer, but I thought this might be more fun.' She kissed him fondly on the cheek and handed him the next box. But this time she turned away, staring into the fire. And when he had opened it, he fell silent as well. There was very little he could say. It was the pocket watch he knew Amadeo had treasured and had almost never worn because it was so sacred to him. It had belonged to his father, and on its back initials of three generations of San Gregorios were elaborately engraved. Beneath them, he suddenly realised, were his own.

'I don't know what to say.'

'*Niènte, caro.* There is nothing to say.'

'Alessandro should have this.' But she only shook her head.

'No, Nardo. You should.' And for an endless moment her eyes held his. She wanted him to know that no matter how great the friction between them at work, he was

74

precious to her, and he mattered. A great deal. He and Alessandro were all she had left now. And Bernardo would always be special to her. He was her friend. As he had been Amadeo's friend too. The watch was to remind him of that, that he was something more than simply the director of San Gregorio or the man she yelled at every day, twenty-seven times before noon. Away from the office he was someone important to her, a kind of family. He was a part of her other life. And the look in her eyes told him all that now as he watched her. His eyes seemed to hold hers for a very long time as though he were wondering about something, as though he were trying to resist a tidal wave over which he had no control.

'Isabella . . .' He sounded suddenly oddly formal, and she waited, knowing he was deeply moved by the gift. 'I – I have something to say to you. I have for a long time. It may be the wrong time. It probably is . . . I'm not sure. But I have to tell you. I must be honest with you now. It's . . . very important . . . to me.' He hesitated lengthily between words as though what he was saying was very difficult for him, and the look in his eyes told her it was.

'Is something wrong?' Her eyes suddenly filled with compassion. He looked agonised, poor man, and she had been so hard lately. What in God's name was he about to say? She sat very still and waited. 'Nardo . . . you look frightened, *caro*. You needn't. Whatever it is, you can say it to me. God knows we've been outspoken enough for all these years.' She tried to make him smile and he wouldn't, and for the first time in all the years he had known her, he thought her insensitive. My God, how could she not know? But it wasn't insensitivity, it was blindness. He knew it as he watched her, and then he nodded and put down his glass.

'I am frightened. What I have to tell you used to frighten

75

me a great deal. And what worries me now is that is might frighten you. And I don't want it to. That's the last thing I want.' She sat very still, watching him, waiting.

'Nardo . . .' She started to speak, holding out a long graceful white hand. He took it and held it fast in his own. His eyes never left hers.

'I will tell you very simply, Bellezza. There's no other way. I love you.' And then softly, 'I have for years.'

She seemed almost to jump at his words, as though a current had suddenly gone through her and shocked her entire body. 'What?'

'I love you.' He seemed less frightened this time and more like the Bernardo she knew.

'But Nardo . . . all these years?'

'All these years.' He said it proudly now. He felt better. At last it was out.

'How could you?'

'Very easily. You're a pain in the ass a lot of the time, but strangely enough that doesn't make you hard to love.' He was smiling and she laughed suddenly; it seemed to break some of the tension in the room.

'But why?' She stood up now and walked pensively toward the fire.

'Why did I love you or why didn't I tell you?'

'All of it. And why now? Why now, Nardo . . . why must you tell me now?' There were suddenly tears in her voice and her eyes as she leaned against the mantelpiece, staring into the fire. He walked softly toward her, stood next to her, and turned her face gently toward his so he could look into her eyes.

'I didn't tell you for all these years because I loved both of you. I loved Amadeo too, you know. He was a very special man. I would never have done anything to hurt him or you. I put away my feelings, I sublimated them. I put what I felt into the business, and maybe' – he smiled

– 'even into fighting with you. But now . . . everything has changed. Amadeo is gone. And day after day after week I watch you, lonely, destroying yourself, pushing yourself, alone, always alone. I can't bear it anymore. I'm there for you. I have been for all these years. It's time you knew that. It's time you turned to me, Isabella. And . . .' he hesitated for a long moment, and then he stood very still and said it, '. . . and it's time I got mine too. Time I was able to tell you that I love you, to feel you in my arms, to be Alessandro's stepfather, if you let me, and not just his friend. Maybe I'm mad to tell you all this, but . . . I – I have to . . . I've loved you for too long.' His voice was hoarse with the pent-up passion of years, and as she watched him tears wended their way slowly down her face, rolling mercilessly down her cheeks and on to her dress. He watched her and slowly let his hand go to her face and brush away the tears. It was the first time he had touched her that way, and he felt unbridled passion tear through his loins. Almost without thinking, he pulled her toward him and crushed his mouth against hers. She didn't fight him, and for an instant he thought he felt her kiss him back. She was hungry and lonely and sad and afraid, but what was happening was too much for her, and suddenly she pushed him firmly away. They were both breathless, and Isabella was wild eyed as she looked at her old friend.

'No, Nardo! . . . No!' She was as much fighting against what he had just told her as against his kiss.

But suddenly he looked even more frightened than she did, and he shook his head. 'I'm sorry. Not for what I've said. But for – for pushing you too quickly. . . . I . . . my God, I'm so sorry. It *is* too soon. I was wrong.'

But as she watched him she felt achingly sorry for him. It was obvious that he had suffered for years. And during all of the time she had never known and she was certain that Amadeo had been as ignorant as she. But how could she have been so stupid? How could she have not seen? She looked at him with compassion and tenderness and held out both hands. 'Don't be sorry, Nardo, it's all right.' But as a bright light of hope came into his eyes, she quickly shook her head. 'No, I don't mean it like that. I – I just don't know. It's too soon. But you weren't wrong; if that's what you feel, you should tell me. You should have told me a long time ago.'

'And then what?' For a moment he sounded bitter and jealous of his old friend.

'I don't know. But I must have seemed very stupid and cruel over the years.' She looked at him warmly, and he smiled.

'No? Just very blind. But perhaps it was better that way. Had I told you, it would have complicated things. It may do that now.'

'It doesn't have to.'

'But it might. Do you want me to leave San Gregorio, Isabella?' He said it honestly, and his voice sounded very tired. It had been a difficult evening for him.

But she looked at him now with fire in her eyes. 'Are you crazy? Why? Because you kissed me? Because you told me you loved me? For that you would leave? Don't do that to me, Nardo. I need you, in too many ways. I don't know what I feel right now. I'm still numb. I still want Amadeo night and day . . . about half of the time I don't understand that he's never coming home. I still expect him to . . . I still hear him and see him and smell him . . . There's no room for anyone else in my life, except Alessandro. I can't make you any promises now. I can barely hear what you're saying. I hear it, but I don't really understand it. Not really. Maybe one day I will. But until then all I can do is love you as I always have, as a brother, as a friend. If that's a reason for you to leave San Gregorio, then do it, but I will

78

never understand. We can go on as we always have; there is no reason not to.'

'But not forever, *cara*. Do you understand that?'

She looked pained as their eyes met. 'What do you mean?'

'Just what I said, that I can't go on like this forever. I had to tell you because I can't live with the secret of my feelings any longer, and there's no reason to. Amadeo is gone, Isabella, whether you recognise it or not. He's gone, and I love you. Those are two facts. But to go on forever, if you don't love me in quite that way, to go on working for you, because in truth I do work *for* you and not *with* you, especially now, to go on playing second fiddle forever, Isabella . . . I can't. One day I want to share your life with you, not exist on the fringe of it. I want to give you what there is of my life. I want to make you better and happier and stronger. I want to hear you laugh again. I want to share the victory of our collections and fabulous deals. I want to stand beside you as Alessandro grows up.'

'You will anyway.'

'Yes.' He nodded simply. 'I will. As your husband or as your friend. But not as your employee.'

'I see. Then what you're saying is that either I marry you or you quit?'

'Eventually. But it could take a very long time . . . if . . . I thought there were hope.' And then after a long pause, 'Is there?'

But she was equally long to answer. 'I don't know. I have always loved you. But not in that way. I had Amadeo.'

'I understand. I always did.' They sat in silence for a long time, watching the fire, each lost in thought, and gently once again he took her hand. He opened it, looked

79

into the delicate, finely lined palm, and kissed it. She did not withdraw her hand, but with sad eyes she only watched him. He was special to her, and she loved him, but he wasn't Amadeo. He never would be . . . never . . . and as they sat there they both knew. He looked at her long and hard as he took his hand from hers. 'I was serious before. Would you like me to quit?'

'Because of tonight?' She sounded tired and sad. It hadn't been a betrayal but it had been a loss. In a way she felt that she had just lost him as her friend. He wanted to be her lover. And there was no opening for the job.

'Yes. Because of tonight. If I've made it impossible for you to exist with me at the office now, I'll go. Immediately if you like.'

'I don't like. That would be even more impossible, Nardo. I'd go under in a week.'

'You'd surprise yourself. You wouldn't. But is it what you'd prefer?'

She shook her head honestly. 'No. But I don't know what to say to you about all this.'

'Then say nothing. And one day, if the time is ever right, a long time from now, I'll say it again. But please don't torment yourself or feel that this is hanging over your head. I won't leap out of doorways and take you in my arms. We've been friends for a long time. I don't want to lose that either.' Suddenly she felt relieved. Perhaps she hadn't lost everything after all.

'I'm glad, Nardo. I can't deal with an either-or situation at this point. I'm not ready. Maybe I never will be.'

'Yes, you will. But maybe never for me. I understand that too.'

She looked at him with a tender smile and leaned slowly toward him to kiss his cheek. 'And when did you get so smart, Mister Franco?'

'I always was; you just never noticed.'

'Is that so?' He was smiling and she was laughing, the whole atmosphere of the room had changed again.

'Yes, that's so. I happen to be the genius around the office these days, or hadn't you noticed?'

'Not at all. And every morning when I look in the mirror and say, "Mirror, mirror on the wall, who's the genius of them all . . . ?" ' But they were both laughing now and suddenly their faces were closer again and he could feel her soft breath on his cheek, and all he wanted to do was kiss her again, and he could see her mouth waiting for his, but this time he didn't do it, the moment passed, and in embarrassment Isabella laughed oddly, stood up, and walked away. No, it was not going to be easy at the office. They both knew that now.

'Look what Laura baked for Santa!' On his soft sleeper-clad feet, he had approached unheard. But they looked up now to see Alessandro carrying two plates covered with gingerbread that he deposited carefully on a little stool he placed next to the fire. He looked at them soberly and then picked up one large warm piece of the gingerbread, which he rapidly ate. And then he disappeared again, having broken the painful spell.

'Isabella . . .' He looked at her and smiled. 'Don't worry.' She only patted his arm, and they exchanged a smile as Alessandro returned, uneasily carrying two mugs of milk.

'Are you having a party or feeding Santa?' Bernardo grinned at him and sat down again.

'No. Nothing's for me.'

'All of this is for Santa?' Bernardo watched him with a broad grin, but the boy's face grew slowly serious, and he shook his head. 'Is it for me?' The head shook soberly again.

81

'It's for Papa. In case . . . the angels let him come home . . . just for tonight.' He looked again at the two places he had set near the fireplace and then kissed his mother and Bernardo good night. And five minutes later Bernardo left and Isabella went quietly to her room. It had been a very long night.

Chapter Seven

'How's the carousel holding up?' Bernardo stretched his legs in front of him as he and Isabella ended a private conference at the end of a long day. It was three weeks after Christmas, and they had been doing nothing but work. But at last things seemed to be settling into a routine again. It had even been almost ten days since they'd had a good fight. And he hadn't mentioned his Christmas 'confession' again. Isabella was relieved.

'I think he likes it almost as much as your bike.'

'Has he broken any of the furniture with it yet?'

'No, but he's certainly trying. Yesterday he set himself a race course in the dining room and only knocked over five chairs.' They laughed for a moment, and Isabella stood up and stretched. She was relieved that the holidays were over and she was pleased with the work they had done. With some effort they had both returned to their old relationship, and even Bernardo could see that she was in a peaceful mood. And then he saw her stiffen as she heard Amadeo's phone. 'Why are they ringing that office?'

'Maybe they couldn't get through to yours.' He tried to underplay it, although for a moment it had startled him too. But they both knew that the men who cleared her phone calls sometimes tied up all the lines. 'Do you want me to get it?'

'No. It's all right.' She walked quickly into Amadeo's office and was gone for only two minutes when Bernardo heard a scream. He ran in to find her white-faced and hysterical, with both hands to her mouth, staring at the phone.

'What is it?' But she didn't answer, and when she tried, all that came from her was a croak and then another scream. 'Isabella, tell me!' He was holding her by both shoulders and shaking her desperately as he searched her eyes. 'What did they say? Was it something to do with Amadeo? Was it the same man? Isabella . . .' He was seriously considering slapping her as the guard who haunted her outer office rushed inside. 'Isabella!'

'Alessandro! . . . They . . . said . . . they . . . have him! . . .' She fell, sobbing, into Bernardo's arms as the guard ran frantically for the phone, dialling her home number, but he couldn't get through.

'Call the police!' Bernardo shouted over his shoulder as he grabbed her coat and her handbag and rushed her through her own office and out the door. 'We're going to the house.' And then, stopping for a moment in the doorway, he looked hard at Isabella and held her by both arms. 'It's probably only cranks again. You know that, don't you? He's probably all right.' But all she could do was stare at him and shake her head frantically from side to side.

'Was it the same voice, the same man?' he asked.

She shook her head again. Bernardo motioned to the guard to follow him, and the three of them ran down all three flights of stairs and outside. They collected another guard on the way. Isabella's car was already waiting for her as it did at the end of every day. Enzo stared at them in confusion as the four of them hurtled into the car, one of the guards shoving Enzo aside as he slid over, taking command of the wheel.

'*Ma, che* . . .' Enzo began, but one look at Isabella told him what he didn't want to know. '*Cosa c'e*? What is it? *Il bambino*?'

No one answered him. Isabella continued to clutch

84

Bernardo, and they roared toward the villa on Via Appia Antica.

The driver barely waited for the electric gates to slide open. One of the guards was already out of the car before they came to a stop. He ran into the house, followed an instant later by Isabella, Bernardo, Enzo, and the last guard, all of them pounding frantically through the house. The first person Isabella saw was Luisa.

'Alessandro? Where is he?' She could speak now and she grabbed the frightened servant roughly with both hands.

'I . . . signora . . . he . . .'

'Tell me!'

The elderly cook began to cry, confused. 'I don't know. Mamma Teresa took him out an hour ago, I thought . . . What is wrong?' Then seeing Isabella hysterical before her, she knew. 'Oh, God, no. Oh, God! . . .' The air was filled with her long sorrowful scream. The sound cut into Isabella like a blade. All she could think to do was to stop it, cut it off. Unthinking, she reached back and slapped Luisa before Enzo could take the cook away. A moment later Bernardo's arm was around her waist and he was half steering, half dragging Isabella across the hall to her room. Just as they reached the door there was a commotion at the other end of the house. The sound of feet. The guards thundering through the house. And then, like music, the voice of Alessandro, and that of Mamma Teresa, as usual, unruffled, as she came in with the child. Isabella stared at Bernardo, wild-eyed, and ran into the hall.

'Mamma!' Alessandro began, then stopped. She hadn't looked like that since they had told him four months before that she had the flu, and that had been when . . . Looking at her, frightened, reminded, he ran toward her and began to cry.

Clutching him warmly against her, her voice wracked

85

by sobs, she looked at Mamma Teresa. 'Where were you?'

'We went for a ride.' The elderly nurse was beginning to understand what must have happened as she looked at Isabella and the phalanx of guards. 'I thought a change would do the boy good.'

'Nothing happened?' Mamma Teresa shook her head as Isabella looked back at Bernardo. 'Then it was only . . . another one of those calls,' she said. But she had believed them. It had been so like those others, those horrible threatening voices. And how had they got through? She felt herself swaying and dimly aware of someone removing the child from her arms.

Five minutes later she came to in her room with Bernardo and one of the maids standing over her, staring anxiously as she returned from unconsciousness.

'*Grazie.*' Bernardo nodded dismissal to the maid, handed Isabella a glass of water, and sat down at the edge of the bed. He looked almost as pale as Isabella. She sipped the water silently from a glass held in a trembling hand.

'Do you want me to call the doctor?'

She shook her head, and they sat for a moment, shaken, silent, stunned by what they had thought.

'How did they get through?' Isabella said finally.

'One of the guards says there is something wrong with the lines today. The intercept system on the phones at the office must have gone out for a few minutes. Or maybe they just missed the call. It could have rung in Amadeo's office for any reason. Even a crossed wire.'

'But why would they do that to me? Oh, God, Bernardo . . .' She closed her eyes and leaned her head back on the pillows for a moment. 'And poor Luisa.'

'Never mind Luisa.'

'I'll go to see her in a few minutes. I just thought – '

'So did I. I thought this was for real, Isabella. And what

86

if one day it is? What if someone takes him too?' He stared at her mercilessly as she closed her eyes and shook her head.

'Don't say that.'

'What will you do? Add another dozen guards to the retinue? Build a fortress just for you and the boy? Have a heart attack the next time you get a crank call?'

'I'm not old enough to have a heart attack.' She looked at him bleakly with an attempt at a smile, but Bernardo did not return it.

'You can't live like this any longer. And don't make me speeches about what you're doing for Amadeo, about taking his place. If he knew what you were doing, how you were living, locked in, here, in the office, keeping the child locked up. If he knew the risks you're taking with that boy just by continuing to live in Rome, he would kill you, Isabella. You know it yourself. Don't you dare ever try to justify this by telling me that you're doing it all for him. Amadeo would never forgive you. And maybe one day neither will Alessandro. You are giving him a childhood of terror, not to mention what you're doing to yourself. How dare you! How dare you!' Bernardo's voice had risen steadily as he spoke. He stalked around the room turning to glare at her, waving his hands. He ran one hand through his hair and then sat down again, regretting his own outburst, prepared for Isabella's wrath. But as he looked at her he was stunned to realise that this time Isabella hadn't told him to go to hell. She hadn't invoked the sacred name of Amadeo, hadn't told him that she knew she was right.

'What do you think I should do? Run away? Leave Rome? Hide for the rest of my life?' she said. But there was no sarcasm this time. Only the shadow of the terror she had just felt again.

'You don't need to hide for the rest of your life. But maybe you have to do something like that for a while.'

87

'And then what? Bernardo, how can I?' She sounded like a frightened, tired, little girl. Gently Bernardo reached for her hand.

'You have to, Isabella. You have no choice. They'll drive you mad if you stay here. Go away. For six months, a year. We'll work it out. We can communicate. You can give me orders, instructions, ulcers, anything, but don't stay here. For God's sake, don't stay here. I couldn't bear it if . . .' He shocked them both by dropping his head into his hands. He was crying. '. . . if something happened to Alessandro or to you.' He looked up at her then, the tears still flowing from his blue eyes. 'You're like my sister. Amadeo was my best friend. For God's sake. Go away.'

'Where?'

'You could go to Paris.'

'There's nothing there for me anymore. Everyone's gone My grandfather, my parents. And if these people can do this to me here, they'll do it to me just as easily in France. Why can't I just find a secluded place in the country here, maybe not that far from Rome? If no one knows where I am, it would be the same thing.'

But Bernardo looked at her angrily now. 'Don't start playing games. Get out, dammit! Now! Go somewhere. Anywhere. Not ten minutes out of Rome, not in Milano, in Florence. Get the hell out!'

'What are you suggesting? New York?' She had said it sarcastically, but the moment she had said it, she knew, and so did he. She paused for a long moment, thinking, as he watched her, hoping, praying. Silently she nodded yes. She looked at him soberly, thinking it all out, and then slowly she got up from the bed and walked to the phone.

'What are you doing?'

The look in her eyes said that she wasn't beaten, that she

hadn't given up. That there was still hope. She wouldn't stay away for a year. She wouldn't let them drive her away from her home, from her work, from where she belonged. But she would go. For a while. If it could be arranged. There was fire in her eyes again as she picked up the phone

Chapter Eight

A long lanky blonde, with her hair falling over one eye, sat in a tiny bright yellow room pounding away at a typewriter. At her feet a small brown cocker spaniel slept, and spread around the room were books, plants, and mountains of papers. Seven or eight coffee cups lay empty and overturned, having been checked out by the dog, and tacked over the window was a poster of San Francisco. She called it her view. It was clearly the den of a writer. And the framed covers of her last five books hung crookedly on the far wall, scattered among equally askew photographs of a yacht moored in Monte Carlo, two children on a beach in Honolulu, a president, a prince, and a baby. All of it related somehow to publishing, lovers, or friends, except for the baby, which was hers. The date on the photograph went back five years.

The spaniel stirred lazily in the winter heat of the New York apartment, and the woman at the typewriter stretched her bare feet and reached down absentmindedly to stroke the dog.

'Hang in, Ashley. I'm almost through.' She grabbed a black pen and made a few hasty corrections with a long slender hand, bare of rings. The voice in which she had spoken to the dog was decidedly southern. Savannah. It was a voice reminiscent of plantations and parties, elegant drawing rooms of the Deep South. It was the voice of gentility. A lady. 'Goddamn!' She grabbed at the pen again, crossed out half a page and scrambled frantically on the floor for two pages she hadn't seen in an hour. They were there somewhere. Reworked, taped, patched. And, of course, essential. She was rewriting a book.

At thirty she still had the same shape she'd had when she'd come to New York at nineteen to model, despite her family's violent protests. She'd hung in for a year, hating it, but admitting it to no one, except her beloved room-mate from Rome, who had come to the States for a year to study American design. Like Natasha, Isabella had come to New York for a year. But Natasha had taken a year off from college to try and make it on her own. It was not what her parents had had in mind for her. Rich in artistic southern ancestry and poor in cold cash, they wanted her to finish school and marry a nice southern boy, which was not what Natasha had in mind.

At nineteen all she had wanted was to get out of the South, get to New York, make money, and be free. And she had. She'd made money as a model and then as a free-lance writer. She'd even been free, for a while. Until she met and married John Walker, theatre critic. A year later they had had a child and a year after that, they'd had a divorce. All she had left was a great body, a sensational face, a talent for writing, and a fifteen-month-old child. And five years later she had written five novels and two movies, and in the literary world she was a star.

She had moved to a large comfortable co-op on Park Avenue, put her son in a private school, hired a housekeeper, invested her money - and Natasha Walker was having a ball. Having acquired success to add to her beauty, Natasha had it all.

'Mrs. Walker?' There was a soft knock on her door.

'Not now, Hattie, I'm working.' Natasha pushed the long blonde hair out of her eyes and began to sift through the pile of papers again.

'Are you sure? There's a phone call. I think it's important.'

'Take my word for it. It's not.'

'But they said it's from Rome.'

The door was opened before Hattie could add another word to her exhortation. There was no longer any need. Natasha marched across the kitchen, her bare feet long and slender on the bright yellow floor, her tight jeans showing her hip bones, the man's shirt she wore tied just beneath her small breasts.

'Why didn't you tell me it was Rome?' She looked reproachfully at the black woman with the soft, curly grey hair and then flashed her a quick smile. 'Don't worry about it. I know what a pain in the ass I am when I'm working. Just don't go in there. No clean coffee cups, no plant watering, nothing. I need the mess.' Hattie made a mock-frown at the familiar refrain and disappeared down a bright, sunny hall to the bedrooms as Natasha grabbed the phone. 'Yes?'

'Signora Natasha Walker?'

'Yes.'

'We have a communication to you from Roma. One instant, if you please.' Natasha sat very still and waited. She hadn't spoken to Isabella since she'd first heard the news. She had wanted to fly to Rome for the funeral. But Isabella hadn't wanted her to. She had asked her to wait. She had written, and waited, but for the first time in the eleven years of their friendship, there had been no answers, no news. It had been four months since Amadeo had been murdered, and she had never felt as cut off from Isabella since the day she had left the apartment they'd shared for a year and gone back to Rome. She hadn't written during those first few months either, but that was because she'd been so busy with her designing, and then so much in love. So much in love – Natasha could still remember the excitement in Isabella's letters when she had written to tell her: '. . . and he's marvellous . . . and I love him . . . so

92

handsome . . . so tall and blond and I'll work for him at San Gregorio, doing real couture . . .' The joy and the excitement had gone on for years. It had been a permanent honeymoon with those two. And then suddenly he was dead. Natasha had sat in shock and horrified silence when she'd heard the story on the six o'clock news.

'Signora Walker?'

'Yes, yes, I'm here.'

'We have your party.'

'Natasha?' Isabella's voice was strangely subdued.

'Why the hell haven't you answered my letters?'

'I . . . don't know, Natasha . . . I didn't know what to say.'

Natasha frowned and then nodded. 'I've been worried about you. Are you all right?' The concern in her voice travelled five thousand miles to greet Isabella, who brushed the tears from her eyes and almost smiled.

'I suppose so. I need a favour.' It was always like that with them. They could pick up where they had left off, not speak to each other for six months, then instantly be sisters again when they met or spoke. It was one of those rare friendships that could always be put down without cooling off.

'Name it,' Natasha said.

Isabella briefly explained what had happened with Alessandro that day – or what hadn't, but could have. 'I can't bear it anymore. Not like this,' she said. 'I can't take a chance with him.'

Thinking of her own child, Natasha felt a tremor just listening to the story. 'No one could. Do you want to send him to me?' Their sons were within four months of the same age, and Natasha was not one to be undone by an additional child. 'Jason would love it,' she added. 'He keeps bitching me about not having a brother. Besides, they're two of a kind.' A year before, when they'd all met to

93

go skiing in Saint Moritz, the two boys had amused themselves by cutting off each other's hair. 'I'm serious, Isabella. I think you should get him out of Rome.'

'I agree.' There was a fraction of a pause. 'How would you feel about having a room-mate again?' She waited, not knowing what Natasha would say, but her answer was instant. It took the form of a long, delighted, southern little-girl squeal. Isabella suddenly found herself laughing.

'I'd love it. Are you serious?'

'Very. Bernardo and I have come to the conclusion that there's no other way. Just for a while. Not permanently of course. And, Natasha' – she paused, wondering how to explain that she was not just getting away – 'it may be awkward. I'll have to stay hidden. I won't want anyone to know where I am.'

'That's going to be a bitch. You won't be able to set foot out of the apartment.'

'Do you really think people there would know my face?'

'Are you serious? Not the construction workers going to work on the subway maybe, but just about everyone else. Besides, if you do a disappearing act in Rome, it'll be in the papers all over the world.'

'Then I'll just have to stay hidden.'

'Can you live with that?' Natasha had her doubts.

'I have no choice. For the moment anyway. This is what I have to do.'

Natasha had always admired her sense of duty, her courage, her style.

'But you're sure you can stand living with me? I could stay somewhere else,' Isabella said.

'The hell you will. If you stay anywhere else, I'll never speak to you again! How soon are you coming?'

'I don't know. I've only just made the decision. It will take time to work it out at the office. I'm going to have

94

to continue to run San Gregorio from wherever I am.

Natasha let out a long slow whistle in answer. 'How the hell are you going to manage that?'

'We'll just have to work it out. Poor Bernardo, as usual, will wind up with the brunt of the work. But I can talk to him by phone every day if I have to, and we have a New York office for our representative there. I can call in without telling them I'm in New York. I think it can be done.'

'If it can, then you'll do it. And if it can't, you'll do it anyway.'

'I wish I felt as sure. I hate leaving the business here. Oh, Natasha . . .' She let out a long, unhappy sigh. 'It's been such an awful time. I don't even feel like me anymore.'

Natasha didn't say it, but Isabella didn't sound like herself either. The past four months had obviously taken a hell of a toll.

'I feel like a machine,' Isabella went on. 'I just manage to get through the days, killing myself in the office and playing with Alessandro when I can. But I keep . . . I keep thinking . . .' Natasha could hear her friend's voice crack at the other end of the line. 'I keep thinking he'll come home again. That he's not really gone.'

'I think that's what happens when somebody we love disappears suddenly like that. You don't have time to absorb it, to understand.'

'I don't understand anything anymore.'

'You don't have to.' Natasha's voice was gentle. 'Just come home.' There were tears in her own eyes now as she thought of her friend. 'You should have let me come to Rome four months ago. I'd have brought you back then.'

'I wouldn't have gone.'

'Yes, you would. I'm six inches taller than you are, remember?'

Suddenly Isabella laughed. It would be lovely to see

95

Natasha again. And maybe it would even be fun to go to New York. Fun! What an insane thing to think about after all that had happened in the past four months.

'Seriously, how soon do you think you can make it?' Natasha was already making rapid calculations and had started to scribble notes. 'Do you want to send Alessandro on ahead? Or do you want me to come and get him now?'

For a moment Isabella considered it but she said, 'No. I'll bring him with me. I'm not going to let him out of my sight.' As she listened Natasha began to wonder what kind of effect all this was having on the boy, but it was not the moment to ask and Isabella had already gone on. 'Remember, don't say anything to anyone about this. And Natasha ... thank you.'

'Go to hell, spaghetti face.'

Spaghetti face – Natasha's pet name for her, one Isabella hadn't heard in years. As she said good-bye she realised that for the first time in months she was laughing. She hung up the phone and looked up to see Bernardo, his face a study in anxiety and strain. She had forgotten he was there.

'I'm going.'

'How soon?'

'As soon as we can work it out at the office. What do you think? A few weeks?' She looked at him, her mind suddenly beginning to whirl. Was it even possible? Could it be done? Could she run the business from her hiding place with Natasha in New York?

But Bernardo was nodding. 'Yes. We'll get you out of here in the next few weeks.' And with that he took a pad of paper from the desk in her bedroom, and they began to map out a plan.

Chapter Nine

For the next three weeks, the phone calls flew between New York and Rome. Did Isabella want one phone line or two? Would Alessandro go to school? Was she bringing guards?

Isabella laughed and threw up her hands. Amadeo had once declared that Natasha could build a bridge, run a country, or win a war without so much as smudging her manicure. Now Isabella decided he had been right.

Two phones, Isabella decreed. She would decide later whether or not to send Alessandro to school. And no, there was no need for bodyguards. Park Avenue co-ops were veritable fortresses of security these days, and Natasha's was one of the most well guarded in New York.

Isabella's plans for departure were equally well guarded. No general had ever mapped a campaign as thoroughly or as secretly as she and Bernardo had planned for the escape of the San Gregorios. No one, not even the highest echelon of San Gregorio, knew her destination; most did not even know she was leaving at all. It had to be that way. Everything had to be a secret. For her sake and the sake of the child.

She would simply disappear. Rumour would whisper that she was hiding in the penthouse above her offices. Just Isabella, alone with the child. Meals were to be sent up, empty plates returned; laundry would come and go. There was in fact to be a tenant in that apartment; Livia, Amadeo's trusted secretary, had volunteered to closet herself there, making the appropriate noises, walking around on the creaky parquet floor. Everyone would know that someone was living there in hiding. How could anyone suspect that Isabella herself was in New York? It would work. At least for a while.

'Is everything ready?' Isabella looked up at Bernardo. He was slipping another stack of file folders into a large leather bag.

He nodded silently, and Isabella realised how drawn and tired he looked.

'I think I've got copies of every file we have,' she said. 'What about the exports to Sweden? Do you want me to sign some of that stuff now, before I go?'

She continued packing as Bernardo retreated to his office for the papers. Another leather briefcase. More files, more swatches, some of Amadeo's figures, financial sheets from their rep in the States. She had enough work to keep her busy for six months. There would be more, a constant flow of documents, files, reports, information. What could not be done by telephone, Bernardo would forward through Natasha's literary agent, addressed only to Mrs Walker. Isabella focused on the plan, the work to be done. To think why she was packing, to admit she was leaving, was more than she could bear.

Bernardo was back in a moment with the papers. Isabella uncapped the gold Tiffany pen that had been Amadeo's and signed her name.

'You know, I don't suppose this is the time or the place for it, but I still wish you'd consider that idea,' Bernardo said.

'What idea?' Isabella looked at him stupidly. She could hardly think anymore. She had too much on her mind.

'The IHI–F-B takeover. Maybe eventually in New York you could meet with them.'

'No, Bernardo. And I'm telling you that for the last time.' She didn't want even to argue about it anymore.

And now she didn't have the time. 'I thought you promised me you wouldn't bring that up again.'

'All right. All right.' In a way she was right. They had too much else to tackle right now. Later. They could always discuss it later when she had tired of trying to run the business from five thousand miles away. The thought stopped him. Who would have believed six months ago that Amadeo would be dead, Isabella in hiding, and he, Bernardo, alone? He felt a wave of desolation wash over him as he watched her lock the last case. He was remembering the summer they had all gone to Rapallo. Amadeo had counted Isabella's seventeen bags – table linens, sheets, bathing suits . . . hat boxes, one suitcase just for shoes. But this was not going to Rapallo. This was a whole other life – a life begun with two briefcases, one bag for Isabella's clothes, and another for Alessandro's.

'Alessandro will be heartbroken we're not taking his bike,' Isabella said suddenly, interrupting his thoughts.

'I'll send him one in New York. A better one.' God, how he was going to miss the child. And Isabella too. It would be strange not having her near. No shouting matches, no onyx eyes burning into his. His ulcer relied on her, and so did he.

'We'll be back very shortly, Nardo. I don't think I'll be able to stand this for very long.'

She stood up again, looking around her office, wondering what she'd forgotten, opening her file cabinet for a last time as Bernardo watched her, silent. She glanced over her shoulder at him with a tired half-smile. 'Listen, why don't you go home and get some sleep? It's going to be a long night.'

'Yeah, I suppose. I . . . Isabella . . .' There was an odd catch in his voice as slowly she turned around. 'I'm going to miss you. And the boy.' The look in his eyes was the first hint of his real feelings since Christmas.

99

'We'll miss you too.' Her voice was muffled as she held out her arms, and they hugged in the familiar room. How soon would she see it again? Or him? 'But we'll be back. Soon too! You'll see.'

'*Ecco.*' There were tears in his eyes, which he blinked back as she stepped aside. It was one thing to hide his feelings and quite another not to be near her at all. He already ached at the loss of her, but it was the only way. For her sake and the boy's.

'Now go home and get some sleep.'

'Is that an order?'

'Of course.' She grinned lopsidedly at him and slid into a chair. 'What a hell of a time of year to go to the Riviera.' She tried to look bored and nonchalant as he laughed from the door. That was the plan they had. He would drive her across the border into France, across the Riviera to Nice, where she would take a morning flight to London, and from there the change of guards and on to New York. Most likely she and Alessandro would be in transit for almost twenty-four hours.

'Is there anything I should bring tonight for Alessandro? Some cookies? A game?'

'Cookies are always a great idea, but maybe a blanket and a small pillow. And some milk.'

'Anything else? For you?'

'Just be there, Nardo. And pray we'll all be safe.' He nodded soberly, pulled the door open, and was gone. He prayed not only that she would leave safely, but that she would return safely, and soon as well. And that she would return to him.

Chapter Ten

'Mamma, can you tell me a story?'

Isabella perched on the edge of Alessandro's bed. A story . . . a story . . . she could barely think tonight, let alone weave elaborate tales.

'Please?'

'All right, let's see.' Her brow puckered into a frown as she looked at him, her long elegant fingers clasping his tiny white hand. 'Once upon a time there was a little boy. He lived with his mother, and – '

'Didn't he have a daddy?'

'Not anymore.'

Alessandro nodded, understanding, and settled into his bed. She told him of the place where the boy lived with his mother and all the friends that they had, people who loved them, and a few who did not.

'What did they do?' He was beginning to like the story; it had a believable ring.

'About what?' It was easy to distract her, she had a thousand things on her mind.

'What did they do about the people who didn't like them?'

'They ignored them. And you know what else they did?' She lowered her voice conspiratorially. 'They ran away.'

'They did? That's terrible!' Alessandro looked shocked. 'Papa always said it was wrong to run away. Except when you absolutely have to, like from a lion or a very bad dog.'

She wanted to tell him that some people were like dogs but she wasn't quite sure what to say. She looked down at him pensively; his hand was still in hers.

'What if running away made them safer? If it kept them from being bothered by lions and bad dogs? And what if they went to a wonderful place where they could be happy again? Wouldn't that be all right?' She found as she looked at him she had a great deal to say.

'I guess so. But is there a place like that? Where everyone is safe?'

'Maybe. But you're safe anyway, my darling. You know that. I won't ever let anything happen to you.'

He looked up at her worriedly. 'But what about you?' He still had nightmares about it. If they had got his Papa, couldn't they also take his Mamma? It was useless to tell him over and over again they could not. If not, why would they have a houseful of bodyguards? Alessandro was nobody's fool.

'Nothing will happen to me either. I promise you.'

'Mamma . . .'

'What?'

'Why don't we run away?'

'If we did, wouldn't it make you sad? There'd be no Mamma Teresa, no Enzo, no Luisa . . .' *No carousel, no bicycle, no Rome. No reminders of Amadeo . . .*

'But you'd be there!' He looked enchanted.

'Would that be enough?' She was amused.

'Sure!'

His gentle smile gave her the courage to continue the story, the tale of the little boy and his mother who found a new home in a new land, where they were magically safe and they had new friends.

'Did they stay there forever?'

She looked at him for a long moment. 'I'm not sure, I think they went home again. Eventually.'

'Why?' It seemed a ridiculous idea to him.

'Maybe because home is always home, no matter how difficult it is.'

'I think that's stupid.'

'Wouldn't you want to come home if you went away?' She looked at him in astonishment, surprised by what he had said.

'Not if bad things had happened there.'

'Like here?'

He nodded silently. 'They killed my Papa here. They're bad people.'

'Everyone didn't do it, Alessandro. Just one or two very bad men.'

'Then how come no one found them, to punish them, or hurt them, or spank them?' He looked at her woefully, and she pulled him gently into her arms.

'Maybe they will.'

'I don't care. I want to run away. With you.' He snuggled closer to her, and she felt the warmth of him in her arms. It was the only warmth she felt these days now that Amadeo was gone.

'Maybe one day – we'll run away to Africa together, and live in a tree.'

'Ooooohhh, I'd like that! Can we? Can we please?'

'No, of course not. Besides, you couldn't sleep in your nice cosy bed in a tree. Could you?'

'I guess not.' He gazed at her softly for a long moment, then smiled and patted her hand. 'It was a good story.'

'Thank you. By the way, did I tell you today how much I love you?' She was leaning toward him and whispering in his ear.

'I love you too.'

'Good. Go to sleep now, darling. I'll see you soon.'

Very soon. In seven hours. She tucked him tightly and closed the door softly as she walked into the long mirrored hall.

The evening was an agony of waiting. She sat in the living room, going over some papers and watching the

Fabergé clock crawl slowly toward eight. At eight o'clock dinner was served in the dining room, and she ate as always, quickly and alone. By twenty to nine she was back in her room again, staring out the window, at herself in the mirror, at the phone. She could do nothing until all was quiet. She didn't even dare go back to the hall. She sat there alone for three hours, thinking, waiting, looking outside. From her bedroom window she could see the carousel in the garden, the kitchen windows, the dining room, and the little study Amadeo had used to do paperwork at home. By midnight every window in the house had been darkened, except her own. She crept out stealthily to a locked closet at the end of the long hall, opened the door quickly, glanced inside and pulled out two large Gucci bags. There were a soft chocolate leather with the classic green and red stripe. She looked at them, wondering. How could you pack a whole lifetime into two bags?

Back in her room she locked the door, pulled the shades, and opened her closet, looking things over without making a sound. And then quickly she pulled trousers from the hangers, cashmere sweaters from the specially made silk-lined plastic bags. Handbags, stockings, underwear, shoes. It was easier now. Everything she wore these days was still black. It took her exactly half an hour to pack three skirts, seven sweaters, six black wool dresses, and one suit. Black loafers, five pairs of high heels, one pair of black suede-and-satin evening shoes. Evening shoes? She glanced into the closet again and carefully extracted one perfectly simple, long black satin dress. She was finished in less than an hour. She went to the safe. Everything was back in its box again as it had been since Bernardo brought it all back from Paccioli, having returned Alfredo's five hundred thousand dollars. The money she had never been able to deliver to the kidnappers. The jewellery she no longer wore. But she didn't dare leave it here. What if someone broke in? If someone stole it. If! She felt like a refugee fleeing her country during a war as she emptied the green velvet boxes into satin jewellery cases and stowed them in the secret compartment of a large black alligator Hermès handbag. She would wear that over her arm on the trip. At last she swung her suitcase to the floor and slipped from the room, locking it behind her. She carried an empty suitcase down the hall to Alessandro's room, locking his door from the inside. The child was asleep, snuggled deep in his covers, one hand clutching a teddy bear, the other hanging out of the bed. She smiled at him briefly and began to empty his dresser. Warm clothes, a snowsuit, mittens and woollen caps, play clothes to wear in the apartment, and games and a few of his favourite toys. She looked around, wondering what would be most precious as she made the choice. By one thirty she was ready, the suitcases next to her, the room dim in the soft light. Bernardo would be bringing the two suitcases she had packed in the office. She was ready.

The clock on her bedtable ticked relentlessly. She had decided to wake Alessandro at one forty-five. She knew that somewhere, outside, the two guards were waiting, prepared to travel, though they had no idea where. They had been carefully screened by Bernardo and had been told to concoct a story explaining their whereabouts for the day. They would be back in Rome by the next night after depositing Isabella and Alessandro in London, where they would catch their afternoon flight.

Isabella sat breathlessly, feeling her heart pound in her chest. What was she doing? Was she right to leave? Could she really leave everything in Bernardo's hands? And why was she leaving her home?

Soundlessly she opened the door again and stepped softly outside. The house was totally silent as she drifted slowly down the hall. She still had ten minutes before she went to wake Alessandro ten minutes to say goodbye. She found herself in the living room, glancing around in the moonlight, touching a table, staring at the empty couch. Here there had been countless parties with Amadeo, happy evenings, better days. She remembered the fuss she had made choosing the fabrics, the pieces they had bought in Paris, the clock they had lovingly brought back from New York. She wandered on then, past the dining room, to a smaller living room they had rarely used. Finally, silently, she stood in the doorway of the tiny study Amadeo had loved so much. Usually it was flooded with sunshine and daylight, filled with treasures and books and trophies and bright-flowering plants. She had made it a haven for him, and they had retreated there often, talking about business or laughing at Alessandro from the French doors that led out to the garden. It was here that they had watched him take his first steps, here that Amadeo had so often told her he loved her, here that he had now and then made love to her on the comfortable brown leather sofa and once or twice on the thickly carpeted floor. Here they had drawn the shades and the curtains, hidden and plotted and cavorted and lived – here in the room that was now so empty as she stared into it, barely daring to enter it, one hand resting on the door.

'Ciao, Amadeo, I'll be back.' It was a promise to herself, and to him, to the house, and to Rome. She crossed the carpet and stopped when she reached the desk. There was still a photograph of her there, in a silver frame that had been a gift from Bernardo. As she looked at it in the darkness she remembered the little golden Fabergé egg. She had given it to him for their anniversary, just before Alessandro was born. She fingered it gently, touched the leather on the desk, and then slowly turned. 'Ciao

Amadeo.' As she closed the door quietly behind her she whispered, 'Good-bye.'

She stood for a moment in the hallway, then walked quickly to Alessandro's room, praying he would wake easily and not cry. Briefly Isabella felt a pang. It seemed an act of cruelty to take the child without even letting Mamma Teresa say good-bye. She had cared for him lovingly, sometimes even fiercely, for all of his five years. She prayed that the woman would bear the shock of his disappearance courageously and somehow understand when she read Isabella's letter the next day.

She opened the door softly bent over him, holding him close to her, feeling his soft, purring breath on her neck.

'Alessandro, *tesòro*. It's Mamma. Darling, wake up.'

He stirred gently and shifted on to his side. She touched his face with a soft finger and kissed him on both eyes.

'Alessandro . . .'

He opened his eyes to look at her then and smiled sleepily. 'I love you.'

'I love you too. Come on, darling, wake up.'

'Isn't it night time still?' He looked at her strangely, glancing at the darkness outside.

'Yes. But we're going on an adventure. It's a secret. Just you and I.'

He stared at her with interest, eyes widening. 'Can I take my bear?'

She nodded, smiling, hoping he couldn't hear the rapid trip-hammer of her heart. 'I packed some of your toys and your games in a suitcase. Come on, sweetheart. Get up.' He sat up sleepily, rubbing his eyes, and she swung him up into her arms. 'I'll carry you.' She walked softly to the doorway, locked the door behind them, and hurried to her room, whispering to him that they mustn't talk, then sat him on her bed, removing his sleepers and dressing him in warm clothes.

'Where are we going?' He held out a foot as she put on his sock.

'It's a surprise.'

'To·Africa?' He looked delighted. On with the other sock. A blue T-shirt, blue corduroy overalls. A red sweater. His shoes. 'To Africa, Mamma?'

'No, silly. Some place better than that.'

'I'm hungry. I want a glass of milk.'

'Uncle Bernardo will have milk and cookies for you in the car.'

'Is he coming too?' Alessandro looked intrigued.

'Only part of the way. The only people going all the way on our adventure are you and I.'

'Not Mamma Teresa?' He pulled away from her, and Isabella stopped. She looked him in the eye and slowly shook her head.

'No, darling, she can't come with us. We can't even say good-bye.'

'Won't she be very sad at us and hate us when we come back?'

'No. She'll understand.' At least she hoped so.

'Okay.' He sat down on the bed again, picking up his teddy bear with one hand. 'I like going places better with you anyway.' They were whispering, and Isabella smiled.

'I like going places with you too. Now are we ready?' She looked around. Everything was put away or packed. Only his sleepers lay forlornly on her bed. On her desk was a note explaining to Mamma Teresa and the housekeeper that Mr Franco had decided it would be wiser for her and the child to go out of town. They could contact Mr. Franco immediately with any problems in the house. They were not to report her disappearance or speak to the press. 'Oh, we almost forgot something.' She smiled at him as he stifled a yawn. 'Got your teddy bear?' He picked up the bear as she helped him into his coat. 'All ready?' He nodded again and took a firm grip of her hand. Suddenly, at the door, she stiffened. She could hear the grinding of the electric gates, a slow churning of gravel, and then the hushed voices of Bernardo and the two men. A moment later there was a soft knock.

'Isabella, it's me.' It was Bernardo. Alessandro let out a giggle.

'This is fun.'

She opened the door to him and saw one of the guards at his side. 'Are you ready?'

She nodded, looking at him, her eyes very wide.

'I'll carry Alessandro. Giovanni will take the bags. This is it?'

'That's everything.'

'Fine.' They were speaking in whispers. She turned off the light. The headlights of the Fiat cast a shadowed glow in the hall. Silently he picked up Alessandro as the other man took the bags. Isabella was last. She closed the door. It was over. Her good-byes had been said. She was leaving her home.

Bernardo took the wheel with one of the guards next to him. The other sat next to Isabella and Alessandro in the back seat. She glanced over her shoulder once as they pulled away. The house looked as it always had. But it was only a house now. An empty house.

Chapter Eleven

'*Va bène?*' Isabella glanced over at Bernardo. They had been driving for hours, racing through the night. 'Aren't you tired?'

He shook his head. He was too nervous to think of his own weariness. The sun would be up in an hour, and he wanted to cross the border before daybreak. For the first time he regretted taking his Fiat and longed for Amadeo's Ferrari. As it was, he had been going ninety-five miles an hour, but he could have used some extra speed now. In normal hours the customs men might connect the name on her passport with her face and call the newspapers.

'How much longer?' Isabella said.

'Another hour. Maybe two.' The guard said nothing. Alessandro was sound asleep on her lap. Bernardo had passed him some milk and the cookies; he had munched them happily, had two sips of milk, and passed out.

It was almost sun-up when Bernardo finally ground to a halt. Two customs booths sat stolidly on either side of the border. One Italian, the other French. They inched to the gate on the Italian side and honked.

'*Buon giorno.*' Bernardo looked pleasantly at the uniformed guard and handed him five passports. The man in uniform stared disinterestedly at the car. He held the passports in his hand and then motioned to Bernardo to open the trunk. He hopped out of the car, unlocked it, revealing Isabella's four bags, two filled with papers, the other two with clothes.

'Just your belongings?' Bernardo nodded. 'You're going to France?'

'Yes.'

'For how long?'

'A couple of days.'

The official nodded, still holding the passports in one hand he began to open the first one, which belonged to one of the guards, as Bernardo prayed fervently that he wasn't a man who was abreast of the news. The name of San Gregorio was more familiar now than it had ever been. But they were both startled by a sudden honking as two trucks pulled up right behind the car. The customs man made an impatient gesture, and the first truck driver used an arm and a fist to express something crude. With that the officer slapped shut the passport, shoved them all at Bernardo, and waved them back into his car. 'Ècco. Have a good trip.' He marched off toward the truck driver with a look of repressed fury. Gratefully Bernardo started the car.

'What happened? What did he say?' Isabella was looking at him anxiously from the back seat. He smiled. 'He said have a good trip.'

'Did he say anything about my passport?'

'Nope. That jerk behind us did us a big favour. I'm so happy, I'd give him a kiss.' The two guards smiled in spite of themselves as they rolled quietly across the border and once again stopped. 'He made a rude gesture at the customs guy, and he lost interest in us,' Bernardo explained.

'Now what?' Isabella looked nervously at the man walking towards them in dark blue.

'The French customs man stamps our passports, and we're off.' Bernardo rolled down the window and once again smiled.

'Bonjour, messieurs, madame.' He smiled benignly at them, glanced appreciatively at Isabella and briefly at the child. Isabella found herself staring at the red trim on his uniform and wishing herself miles away. 'A holiday? Or business?'

'A little of both.' There was no other way to explain the two suitcases crammed with papers, in case they were inspected. 'My sister, our cousins, and my nephew. Family business.'

'I see.'

He took the passports from Bernardo. Isabella held Alessandro very tight.

'You will be staying long in France?'

'Only a few days.' It didn't matter what he told him; they would all be returning by different ways – and Isabella and Alessandro not at all.

'Anything in the trunk? Food? Plants? Seeds? Potatoes?'

Oh, Christ. 'No, only our luggage.' Bernardo made to step out but the guard waved his hand.

'Not necessary. *Merci.*' He went to the window, picked up his stamp, flicked through the passports, and endorsed their entry, without even looking at the names. '*Bon voyage.*' He waved them on as the gate opened, and Isabella smiled at Bernardo with tears in her eyes.

'How's your ulcer?'

'Alive and kicking.'

'So is mine.' They both laughed then as Bernardo stepped hard on the accelerator.

They were in Nice by mid-morning, and Alessandro had just begun to stir. His mother, like the others, had not slept all night

'Is this Africa? Are we here yet?' He sat up with a broad sleepy smile.

'We're here, darling. But this isn't Africa. It's France.'

'Is that where we're going?' He looked disappointed. He'd been to France before, several times.

112

'Want some more cookies?' Bernardo glanced at him as they sped on.

'I'm not hungry.'

'Neither am I.' Isabella was quick to second his sentiments, but ten miles from the airport Bernardo stopped at a small stand. He bought them fruit and then stopped and bought four cups of coffee and a container of milk.

'Breakfast, everyone!'

The coffee did wonders for all of them. Isabella combed her hair and freshened her make-up. Only the men looked as though they'd spent the night driving, with tired eyes and dark beards.

'Now where are we going?' Alessandro was wearing a white moustache of milk, which he wiped with the teddy bear's arm.

'To the airport. I'm going to put you and your Mummy on a plane.'

'Oh, goodie!' Alessandro clapped his hands with glee as Isabella watched him. It was extraordinary, not a murmur, not a regret, not a tremor or a good-bye. He had accepted their departure and their 'adventure' like something they'd been planning for weeks. Even Bernardo was a little startled. And still more so as they said good-bye at the airport.

'Take good care of your Mamma! I'll talk to you soon on the phone.' He looked at the child tenderly, praying that he wouldn't cry. But Alessandro looked him over disapprovingly.

'They don't have phones in Africa, silly.'

'Is that where you and your Mamma are going?'

'We are.'

Bernardo ruffled the boy's hair gently and watched nervously as passengers hurried toward the plane. 'Ciao,

Isabella. Please . . . take care.'

'I will. You too. I'll talk to you as soon as we get there.'

He nodded and then took her gently into his arms.
'Addio.' He held her longer than he should have, feeling a
lump in his throat.

But she only held him tightly and looked at him soberly
at last. 'Until soon, Bernardo.' She held him fiercely again
for one last moment, and then with the guards walking on
either side of her and the child in her arms, the long swirl of
mink coat disappeared. He hadn't wanted her to wear
that. Just something simple and black, one of her wool
coats, but she had insisted that she might need it in New
York. Isabellezza. He felt something terrible tremble
within him. What if he had lost her forever? But he didn't
let himself think of it further as he slowly wiped a tear away
and walked out of the airport whispering, 'Good-bye.' She
still had a long journey ahead of her, and he wanted to be
back in Rome by that night.

Chapter Twelve

The new bodyguards were waiting as Isabella stepped into the lounge at Heathrow Airport, holding Alessandro in her arms. She felt her heart leap as she watched them move toward her. They were tall, dark, and had the wholesome look of American football players.

'Mrs. Walker?' They were referring to Natasha and the password she and Natasha had agreed on.

'Yes.' She stared at them for a moment, not knowing what to say, but the taller of them handed her a letter, written in Natasha's hand. She opened it hastily, read what it said, and put it down:

You're almost home, spaghetti face. Kiss your little clown for me and relax.

Love, N.

'Thank you. What do we do now?' They pulled out their tickets and handed hers to her. They had been instructed not to say anything in front of Isabella's men. She opened the envelope and glanced at the time. She'd have to dismiss her two men now. She turned to them, spoke to them quickly in Italian, and they rose and shook her hand. They wished her good luck, hoped she would return quickly, and then they surprised her by stooping quickly to kiss Alessandro. Tears sprang to her eyes again as they left her. She had just lost the last reminder of home. They had been in and out of the house for so many months now, it was odd to think that now they would be gone. Like Alessandro, she was getting tired. It had been a long, draining night, and a nervous morning, wondering if she would find and recognise Natasha's men and what would happen if somehow she did not.

'We'd better go now.' The first man took her arm, and she found herself being propelled toward the gate, with Alessandro still in her arms.

As they boarded the plane she found herself waiting for something ghastly to happen – a bomb scare, an explosion, someone trying to grab Alessandro ... anything. It was like living in a nightmare; she had never felt so far from home. But the plane took off uneventfully, and at last they were in the air.

'Where are we going, Mamma?' Alessandro looked at her tiredly now, the wide brown eyes a little confused.

'To Aunt Natasha, darling. In New York.' She kissed him gently on the forehead, and with one hand in hers they both fell asleep.

She woke four hours later, when Alessandro climbed out of her arms. She gave a quick start, reached for him, then sat back with a smile. The two American bodyguards were still seated on either side. Alessandro was standing in the aisle staring at one of them.

'*Mi chiamo Alessandro, e lei?*'

The man looked at him, smiled, and put out both hands helplessly. '*No capito.*' He glanced at Isabella for help.

'He asked you your name.'

'Oh. Steve. And you're ... Alexandro?'

'Alessandro.' He corrected sedately, a mischievous gleam in his eyes.

'Okay, Alessandro. Have you ever seen one of these?' He pulled out an American fifty-cent piece, made it disappear, then promptly removed it from one of Alessandro's ears. The boy gave a delighted squeal and clapped his hands for more. A fifty-cent piece, a nickel, a quarter, then a dime appeared and disappeared while they struck up an awkward conversation, Alessandro chattering in

Italian and the large man communicating mostly in mime.

Again Isabella closed her eyes. It had all gone smoothly so far; all she had to do now was get through customs in New York and then back to Natasha's apartment, where she would take off all her clothes, sink into a tub of warm water, and hide for the rest of her life. She felt as though she'd been wearing the same clothes for the past week.

They had dinner, watched a movie and, except for two trips to the bathroom with Alessandro, they never left their seats. When they did, both guards casually came along. But Isabella was quick to notice that no one on the plane had shown an interest. Even the stewardesses seemed unimpressed. They were listed on the manifest only as I. and A. Gregorio, S. Connally, and J. Falk. Nothing exciting about that. Her long dark mink had drawn a look of approval from the chief steward, but even that was not remarkable. On the run between London and New York, they saw plenty of mink. Had they seen some of the jewellery carefully hidden at the bottom of her handbag they might have been more impressed.

'We'll be coming into New York in about half an hour,' the man named Steve leaned over to say. He spoke in a hushed, barely audible voice, and Isabella nodded her head. 'Mrs Walker will be waiting for you on the other side of customs. We'll go with you as far as her car.'

'Thank you.'

He looked at her cautiously, as soon as she looked away. He was almost certain he'd figured it out. They'd had a case like this two years before. A woman kidnapping back her children from their father, who had absconded with them to Greece. Something about the way she clung to the boy told him that something similar had happened to her. Damn shame to do that kind of thing to a kid too. He couldn't understand these rich people sometimes, yanking kids back and forth, like some kind of a game. But she

117

looked like a nice woman, in spite of the occasional look of panic and the frown that too often altered her face. She had probably been scared shitless that her husband would catch on to her and she'd never get the kid out of France. That was all they knew of her, that she had been arriving in London from Nice. He turned his head slightly to watch her again as the plane began to descend.

'Another potty stop, Alessandro? Customs might take a long time.' His mother rapidly translated, but the child shook his head. 'Okay. Have you ever been to New York before?' Again Isabella translated. Alessandro shook his head, adding that he had thought they were going to Africa anyway. The tall, broad-shouldered American laughed and quickly fastened the boy into the seat. But Alessandro was watching his mother now and reached for her hand. Isabella held it in her own and gazed absently at the lights on the ground. It was four thirty in the afternoon, New York time, but in early February, evening had already come.

How different it was this time. She had last been to New York two years before. With Amadeo. Generally he did the American trips without her. She had preferred going to England and France. But that last time they had come to New York together, and it had been like a dream. They had stayed at the St. Regis, dined at Caravelle, and Grenouille, and Lutece. They had gone to an enormous party for American designers, attended several black-tie dinners, taken long walks in the park. This time there would be no St. Regis, no Lutece, no quiet, shared moments. She had left him now. She couldn't even wander with her memories anymore, see him in all the familiar corners of their home. There were no familiar corners. No familiar people. Only Natasha and her child and Isabella's own. Nothing that had been a part of Amadeo's life was left to her, and she was sorry suddenly that she hadn't brought something along. Something of his, to look at and touch and remember – something to remind her of the laughter and loving in his eyes. *Isabellezza*. She could still hear him call her name.

'Mamma! Mamma!' Alessandro was tugging at her sleeve. They were already on the ground. '*Siamo qui*.' We're here.

The two men looked at her quickly. 'Shall we go?' The plane hadn't even come to a halt yet, but they were already in the aisle. The man named Steve was handing her coat to her, the other one had Alessandro in his arms. The moment the plane came to a full stop, they were propelling her into the passageway. She felt for a moment as though she were still flying, nearly lifted off the ground between them, as they hurried along. Minutes later, when they arrived at customs, the other passengers were still straggling slowly from the plane.

The customs officer motioned to Isabella to open the bags. She unlocked them, flicking all four open as the bodyguards and Alessandro stood by.

'Purpose of your visit?'

'A family trip.' The customs agent cast an eye at the men on either side.

Jesus, what if he realises . . . if he recognises my name . . .

'What are these papers?' He looked at the two overstuffed bags.

'Some work I brought along.'

'You're planning to work over here?'

'Just on some private matters. Family matters.' He glanced again at the two suitcases and then began to dig his way through her clothes. But there was very little of interest, in Alessandro's bag or hers.

'All right, go on.'

They had made it. *She* had made it. Now all they had to do was find Natasha, and they could go home. For a moment she stood there, staring blankly, wondering if something had gone wrong and then she saw her, running toward them, her long blonde hair flying, floating silkily over a lynx coat. She was running, coming toward Isabella, and then suddenly they were in each other's arms, holding each other close, with Alessandro between them. He protested and then squealed as Natasha nibbled his neck.

'Ciao, Alessandro. How've you been?' She took him quickly from Isabella into her long lanky arms, and then the two women stood facing each other as hoarsely Natasha spoke to her. 'Welcome home.' And then she turned back to Alessandro. 'Do you know how heavy you are, kiddo? How about letting him walk to the car?' But quickly Isabella shook her head. His feet had barely hit the ground since Rome. It would be too easy for someone to sweep him off his feet, to grab him; he had been in someone's arms since they began the trip.

'It's all right. I'll carry him.'

'I understand.' And then she looked at the two bodyguards. 'We're out here.' The small tightly knit group moved as one body toward the exit and then toward the car. A Rolls-Royce with a chauffeur, and licence plates with initials Isabella didn't have time to see. Before she could catch her breath, they were whisked into the leather interior, the door had closed, the bags were stored, the men had waved, and the chauffeur pulled away from the kerb.

It was only then that Isabella realised they weren't alone in the car. There was another man in the front seat. She looked suddenly as he turned his head toward them and smiled. He was handsome and blue eyed, with a young face and silvery hair.

'Oh.' Isabella made only one small sound as he turned. But Natasha was quick to pat her hand. 'It's all right

Isabella. This is my friend, Corbett Ewing.' He nodded and extended a hand.

'I didn't mean to frighten you. I'm awfully sorry.' They shook hands, and Isabella nodded stiffly. She hadn't expected to see anyone but the driver in the car. She looked at Natasha inquiringly, but Natasha only smiled and exchanged a look with Corbett. Then Isabella understood. 'How was the trip?' It was quickly obvious that he knew only that she had arrived from Rome. His look of casual ease as he sat there told her that he knew nothing of the potential terror of the trip. For an instant, but only that, she was annoyed at Natasha for bringing him along. She didn't want to have to make polite conversation all the way into New York. But it was also obvious that he had lent them the car, and perhaps Natasha had wanted him along. They seemed to understand each other, and Isabella realised that perhaps Natasha too had been cautious and needed his strength.

Isabella smilingly made the effort. She felt that she owed it to her friend. 'The trip was fine. But I think we're both . . . a little . . .' She suddenly faltered; she was so exhausted, she could barely find her words. '. . . we're both very tired.'

'I can imagine.' He nodded again, and after a few moments he turned to the front and spoke in low tones to his driver. But Isabella's fragile beauty hadn't escaped him before he turned away.

Chapter Thirteen

The Rolls-Royce limousine pulled up sedately in front of Natasha's building as the doorman and one porter rushed instantly to their aid. Isabella stepped out, holding Alessandro tightly by the hand, a look of bewilderment on her pale, ivory face. As she stood for a moment, looking up at the building and down the long tree-lined street, it dawned on her once again how very far from home she was. In another world, another lifetime. Only the day before she had worked at San Gregorio, and lived in the villa in Rome. And now she was here, at Natasha's on Park Avenue in New York. It was six o'clock in the evening, and crowds of New Yorkers were coming home from work. It was dark and the air was chilly, but everywhere about them was a kind of excitement, a cacophony of noises, a symphony of bright lights. She had forgotten how loud and how busy New York could be, somehow madder, even more exciting than Rome. As she stood briefly on the sidewalk, watching women in jewel coloured heavy wool coats and fur hats rush past, lost in the crowds of prosperous, energetic-looking men, she suddenly wanted to go somewhere, to go for a walk, get some air. She wanted to see them, to sniff out the town, and look in the shops. It didn't matter anymore that she had hardly slept at all in almost forty hours, that she had driven and flown halfway around the world. For a moment, just a moment, she wanted to come alive again, to be one of them. Natasha watched her as the doorman removed her luggage. And from where he stood on the sidewalk, Corbett was watching her too.

'Is everything all right, Isabella?'

She looked up at him carefully. 'Yes, fine. And . . . thank you so much for the ride.'

'Not at all.' And then he turned to Natasha. 'Will you two ladies be all right now?'

'Of course.' Natasha leaned toward him and kissed him on the cheek. 'I'll call you later.'

He nodded silently, watching them hurry inside and then, lost in his own thoughts, he climbed back into his car.

Natasha and Isabella marched rapidly through the lobby and crammed into the elevator en masse as a black-uniformed man in gold braid and white gloves manoeuvred the controls and the highly polished brass gate.

'Good evening, Mrs Walker.'

'Thank you, John. Good night.'

Natasha glanced at Isabella again as she fitted her key into the lock. 'You know, for a broad who's been travelling since God knows when this morning, you don't look half bad.' Isabella smiled in answer, and a moment later Natasha had opened the door, unleashing Ashley's barking excitement, Jason's frantic greeting, and Hattie's hello. The smells and sounds of the apartment overwhelmed Isabella as she came through the door. There was none of the palatial perfection of her villa on the Via Appia Antica, yet the apartment suited Natasha to perfection. Had Isabella designed a setting to show off Natasha's striking beauty, it would have been precisely what she saw now. The living room was enormous, ice-white with dollops of richly textured cream, smooth white fabrics, white leather, white walls, long mirrored panels, and much chrome. There were stark glass tables that seemed suspended in thin air, delicate lighting, a white marble fireplace, and plants that hung airily from the ceiling to the floor. The large handsome modern paintings were the only splash of bold colour in the room.

'Do you like it?'

'It's exquisite.'

'Come on. I'll give you a tour. Or are you too dead to move?' The southern drawl was as gentle as ever, like a gentle southern breeze on a warm summer night. As always it seemed incongruous with Natasha's rapid pace, her determined step, her colourful language. She seemed to embody everything New York, until you heard the soft drawl, saw the big wistful blue eyes and the long golden hair.

Isabella was suddenly smiling and she wanted to see more. Alessandro had already disappeared with Hattie and Jason, the little brown spaniel yipping at their heels.

They had just entered Natasha's bedroom. Natasha sprawled into a chair. 'You hate it? Be honest. I don't know what happened to me when I did this room.'

'I know what happened. It's a dream.' The rest of the apartment was starkly modern, but in her bedroom Natasha had gone totally wild. In the middle of the room was a richly ornate antique four-poster, draped in clouds of silky white, with cushions and ruffles and wonderful little lace pillows, and a dressing table from a Scarlett O'Hara dream. There were two blue-and-white love seats near a tiny fireplace, and near a window was a beautiful wicker chaise longue upholstered in pale blue.

'It's so wonderfully southern, Natasha. Like you.' And then the two of them laughed again, as they had an aeon ago when Natasha was nineteen and Isabella twenty-one.

'C'mon,' Natasha said, 'there's more.' The dining room was done in restrained modern splendour with an enormous glass table, chrome chairs, and sideboards of thick glass. But here again Natasha had gone silently mad. The ceiling was painted blue and had been endowed with large white summery clouds.

'It's like a trip to the beach, isn't it?' She had done the

entire apartment with panache and humour, and somehow it also managed to look both spectacular and welcoming at the same time. A warm, cosy den managed to combine both modern wonders and old, coppers, velvets, more modern art, and a brightly crackling fire.

They peered briefly into Natasha's office and the large friendly kitchen with the bright yellow floor. Then Natasha looked at her, smiling, her eyes dancing for a moment as she stepped to one side. 'And if you'll walk down that hall, Isabella, I have a surprise.'

A month before it had been an empty maid's room, crammed with boxes and old skis. But after Isabella's first phone call Natasha had set to work with a vengeance. Now, as she swung open the door, she almost crowed at the look in Isabella's eyes. She herself had bought yards of fabric, a delicate rose silk a decorator friend had just brought back from France. With staples and tacks and delicate trimming, she had covered the walls in soft pink. A tiny French desk stood in the corner with a perfect little chair covered in the same rose. Some bookshelves, some plants, a beautiful little Oriental carpet in pale greens woven with shades of raspberry and the same dusty rose as the walls. There were two beautiful brass lamps on the desk and the table, a file cabinet she'd found that was actually covered in wood, and a tiny settee that had been irresistible, covered in velvet with cushions of the rose silk.

'My God, it almost looks like my boudoir.' Isabella stared at her and almost gasped.

'Not quite. But I tried.'

'Oh, Natasha, you didn't. How could you?'

'Why not? The phone has two lines. The file cabinet is empty. And I'll share my typist with you if you're very, very nice.' There was everything. Everything she could have possibly wanted. And more than that: there was a look to it, of something familiar, something warm, something from home. There were tears in her eyes again as she stared at it.

'You are truly the most extraordinary woman I know.'

Natasha squeezed Isabella's shoulders and walked back out to the hall. 'Now that you've seen your office, I'll show you your bedroom, but it's not quite so grand.'

'How could it be? Oh, Natasha, you're amazing.' Isabella was still speechless as they marched back down the main hallway the way they had come. On the way they passed Jason's room, where the boys were already tearing apart Alessandro's suitcase while Hattie ran a bath.

'*Va bène, tesòro*?' she called out to Alessandro from the door.

'*Si, ciao!*' He waved happily at her and disappeared under the bed with Jason to go after the dog.

'You think your dog will survive?'

'Don't worry. Ashley's used to it. Here we are.' She opened the door and stepped in ahead of Isabella. The room was not as frilly as Natasha's nor as starkly modern as the rest of the house. It was warm and cosy and pleasant, done in rich bottle greens and antique French rugs. There were narrow glass tables and a dark green velvet chair. The bedspread was done in the same heavy velvet, and on the foot of the bed was a length of dark fur, folded neatly, like something from a baronial manor in a distant wintry land. A fire was burning in the marble fireplace. Dark red roses stood in a cut-crystal vase on a low table. In the corner was an armoire with magnificently panelled malachite doors.

'My God, that's a beauty. Where did you ever find that?'

'In Florence. Last year. Aren't royalties wonderful, Isabella? It's amazing what they can do for a girl.' Isabella sat down on the bed, and Natasha in the green velvet chair.

'Are you all right, Isabella?'

126

ı am.' She stared at the fire and for a moment she let her mind drift back to Rome.

'How was it?'

'Leaving? Difficult. Frightening. I was afraid every mile of the trip. I kept thinking something would happen. Someone would recognise us and find me out. I kept thinking . . . I worry about Alessandro . . . I suppose we couldn't have stayed in Rome.' For a moment, seeing Natasha so comfortable in her surroundings, she had longed for her own home in Rome.

'You'll go back.'

Isabella nodded silently in answer and then sought her friend's eyes. 'I don't know what to do without Amadeo. I keep thinking he'll come home. But he doesn't. He . . . it's hard to explain what it's like.' But she didn't have to. The pain of it was clearly carved in her heart, her soul, and her eyes.

'I suppose I can't really imagine,' Natasha said. 'But . . . you have to hold on to the good thoughts, the happy memories, the precious moments that make up a lifetime, and let the rest go.'

'How?' Isabella's eyes shot straight into hers. 'How do you forget a voice on a phone? A moment? An eternity of waiting, of not knowing, and then . . . How do you pick up the pieces, make it mean something again? How do you give a damn about anything, even your work?'

Before Natasha could answer, Alessandro and the puppy bounded in the door. 'He has a train! A real one! Just like the one Papa took me to see in Rome! Want to see it?' He was beckoning from the doorway, Ashley nibbling at his toes.

'In a minute, darling. Aunt Natasha and I want to talk for a while.'

Alessandro dashed off; Natasha watched him dart away. then answered the question.

'Alessandro, Isabella. Maybe that's all you hang on to for now. The rest will begin to fade in time. Not the good stuff, just the pain. It has to. You can't wear it for a lifetime, like five years ago's dress!'

Isabella laughed at the comparison. 'Are you suggesting I'm out of fashion?'

'Hardly.' The two women exchanged a smile. 'But you know what I mean.'

'Ècco. But, oh, Natasha, I feel so old. And there's so much I must do. If I can even manage to do it from here. God only knows how I'll cope with Bernardo from five thousand miles and over the phone.' She didn't want to explain the difficulties of their situation, but it all showed in her eyes.

'You'll do it. I'm sure.'

'And you don't mind too terribly much having a room-mate?'

'I told you. It'll be like old times.'

But not quite, and they both knew it. In the old days they had gone out together, to restaurants, to operas, to plays. They had seen friends, met men, given parties. This was a very different time. Isabella would be going nowhere, except if it seemed safe for her to do so. Maybe, Natasha thought, they could go for a walk in the park. She had already cancelled most of her engagements for the next three weeks. Isabella didn't need to see her running in and out, going to cocktails, benefits, and all the latest shows. It startled her when Isabella spoke.

'I made a decision when we arrived tonight.' For a moment Isabella looked at her with a hint of laughter lurking in her eyes.

'What's that?'

'I'm going out tomorrow, Natasha.'

'No, you're not.'

'I have to. I can't live caged up here. I need to walk, to

get air, to see people. I watched them tonight as we drove through the city and pulled up at your door. I have to see them, Natasha. I have to know them and feel them and watch them. How can I make sensible decisions about my business if I live in a cocoon?'

'You could make the right decisions about fashion if you were locked in a bathroom for ten years.'

'I doubt that.'

'I don't.' For a moment there was war in Natasha's blue eyes. 'We'll see.'

'Yes, Natasha, we will.'

But as she said it she came alive again, and although it worried her, Natasha was relieved as she wandered back to her bedroom. Isabella di San Gregorio was not gone at all. At first she'd been worried, she wasn't sure how much of her friend had survived the ordeal. Now she knew. There was still fight there, and anger, and bitterness, and fear. But there was fire and life, and the diamond glints were still shining in the brilliant onyx eyes.

Having ascertained that the boys were surviving, she walked back to Isabella's bedroom to offer her dinner after she bathed and changed her clothes, but she only smiled as she stood in the doorway. Sprawled out on the green velvet bedspread, Isabella was dead to the world. Natasha pulled the fur cover over her, whispered 'Welcome home,' turned off the lights, and softly closed the door.

Chapter Fourteen

Wrapped in a blue velvet robe with a tall mandarin collar, Isabella wandered sleepily into the hall. It was very early. A wintery dawn sun cast shimmering daggers across the skyscrapers of New York. She stood at the living room window for a moment, thinking of the city that lay at her feet – a city that drew the successful, the dynamic, the fiercely competitive, and those destined to win. A city for people like Natasha – and she had to admit, for herself. But it was not the city Isabella would have chosen; it lacked the decadence, the laughter, and sheer charm of Rome. Yet it had something else; it shone brightly like a river of diamonds, and she watched as it seemed to beckon to her.

She walked softly into the kitchen, opened the cupboards, and found the makings of what Natasha called coffee. It was not what she would have served at home. But once she had made it, it was pungent and familiar and reminded her of their life together twelve years before. Scents always did that for her – one fragrance, a distant aroma, and she could see again all that she had long ago seen: a room, a friend, a moment, a date with a long-forgotten man. But this was no time for dreaming. She glanced at the kitchen clock and knew that her day had begun. It was six thirty in the morning. And six hours later than that in Rome. With luck she would catch Bernardo in his office, before lunch, staggering under the weight of what lay on his shoulders now. She took the cup of coffee to her pretty little office and smiled to herself as she switched on a light. Natasha, sweet Natasha. How kind she was.

How much she had done. But the tenderness in her eyes rapidly faded as she prepared for the business at hand.

As the operator put through the connection to Italy, Isabella unzipped one of her two overstuffed bags, pulled out a thick pad and two brightly coloured pens. She had just enough time to sit down and take another sip of her coffee as the receptionist at San Gregorio answered the phone.

The operator asked for Bernardo, as nervously Isabella began to tap the soft carpet with the tips of her well-polished toenails. She was careful to keep silent so the girl at San Gregorio wouldn't have a clue as to the identity of the caller. She had time for only one hasty doodle, and then he was on the line.

'Yes?'

'*Ciao, bravo.* It's me.' *Bravo* . . . roughly translated: good guy, patient one. More than anyone the name suited him.

'It went well?'

'Perfectly.'

'How do you feel?'

'Tired. A little. Still a little in shock, I suppose. I don't think I realised till I got here just what it all means. You're just lucky I was too tired to get on the next plane for home.' She felt a wave of homesickness overwhelm her and suddenly she wanted to reach out to him.

'You're lucky. I'd have given you hell and sent you right back.' His voice sounded grave, but Isabella laughed.

'You probably would have. Anyway we're stuck with it now, this madness we've concocted. We'll just have to make the best of it for as long as I'm here. Now tell me, what happened? Everything smooth over there?'

'I just sent you a clipping from *Il Messaggero*. Everything has gone according to plan. You are now in residence, as reported, in our penthouse suite.'

'And everything else?'

131

'Mamma Teresa took it badly at first, but I think now she understands. She thought you should have taken her with you. But she seems resigned. How's the baby?' The baby . . . she and Amadeo hadn't called him that in two years.

'Delighted. Perfectly happy. In spite of the fact that we didn't get to Africa.' They both laughed again, and Isabella was grateful that years before they'd installed a special line. It was used only by Isabella, Amadeo, and Bernardo, and now it would guarantee them freedom. There were no extensions where anyone could listen from anywhere in the house. 'Anyway now tell me. What's cooking? Phone calls? Messages? New orders? Any last-minute problems with the summer line?' It was to be unveiled soon. It was a hell of a time for Isabella to disappear.

'Nothing drastic has happened, except with the red fabric you ordered from Hong Kong.'

'What about it?' Her toes tensed as they played with the phone line snaking beneath her desk on the floor. 'They told me last week there was no problem.'

'They lied to you. They can't deliver.'

'What?' Her voice would have carried throughout the apartment, except that she had the foresight to close the door. 'Tell those bastards they can't do that. I won't buy from them again. Oh, Christ . . . no, never mind. I'll call them – dammit, I can't. It's thirteen hours later than here. But I can call them in twelve hours. I'll call them tonight.'

'You'd better work out some alternatives. Isn't there anything we can use here in Rome?'

'Nothing. Unless we use the purple from last season instead of the red.'

'Will that work?'

'I'll have to talk to Gabriela. I don't know. I'll have to see how that fits with the rest of the line.'

132

She knew instantly that it would create a whole different look for them. She had wanted a summer of primary colours this year. Bright shining blues, sunny yellows, the Hong Kong red, and plenty of white. If they used the purple, she'd need greens, oranges, maybe some of the yellow, only a little red. 'It changes the whole balance,' she said.

'Yes. But can it be done?'

She wanted to scream at him, 'Yes, but not from here!' 'What I'd like to know is how you can tell me nothing drastic has happened? The Hong Kong red is drastic.'

'Why don't you replace it with something from the States?'

'They didn't have anything I wanted. Never mind. I'll work it out later. What else? Any other happy little titbits for me?'

'Only one.'

'They're not delivering the pale green?'

'They already did. No, this is good news.'

'For a change.' But despite the sarcasm in her voice, Isabella's face had come alive. She didn't know how she'd do it, how she'd manage to make major fabric and colour changes in so little time, from so far away, but it brought her back to San Gregorio as she spoke to him. No matter where she was, she still had her business, and if she had to move mountains, she'd make the changes on time. 'So what's the good news?'

'F-B bought enough of the perfume to float the sixth fleet.'

'That's nice.'

'Don't get so excited.' Bernardo sounded like himself again. Tired, angry, annoyed.

'I won't. I'm sick of those bastards and their offers to buy us out. And don't bother me with that bullshit while I'm here.'

'I won't. What do you want me to tell Gabriela?' The chief designer was going to get ulcers when she heard the news. Changes? What changes? How can we make changes now?

'Tell her to stop everything till I call back.'

'That means when?'

'In September, darling. I'm on vacation, remember? What the hell do you think it means? I told you, I'll call Hong Kong tonight. And I'll work out alternatives today. I know every colour, every piece of fabric we have in stock.' And Bernardo knew only too well that she did.

'I assume this will affect ready-to-wear too.'

'Not so much.'

'But just enough.' His ulcer gave a familiar twinge. 'All right, all right. I'll tell her to hold it. But for God's sake, call me back.' The old irritation was back between them again. Insanely, it felt familiar and good.

'I'll call you after I talk to Hong Kong. About one o'clock.' She said it matter-of-factly, already scribbling a river of tiny well-organised notes. 'What does my mail look like?'

'There's nothing much.'

'Good.' Amadeo's secretary was answering all her mail from the top floor. 'I'll talk to you tonight. Call me if anything happens today.' But at his end Bernardo knew he would not. He could save it all till that night.

'You'll have plenty to keep you busy.'

'Mmm . . . hmm . . . I will.' He knew her well enough to know that she had already covered two sheets of her pad. 'Ciao.'

They hung up as though they were both seated in their respective offices at opposite ends of the same floor, and in her brand new office Isabella tore off her notes and spread them out before her. She had exactly twelve hours to replace that Hong Kong red. Of course there was always the chance that she could badger them into sending it, if they had it, if they could. But she knew she couldn't risk depending on them. Not anymore. She made another hasty note to herself for Bernardo. She wanted to cancel the account in Hong Kong. She had seen better fabrics in Bangkok anyway. In what concerned San Gregorio, Isabella was not one to be understanding or to be pushed around.

'You're up bright and early.'

Isabella looked up in surprise as Natasha's tousled blonde head poked throught the door. 'What happened to the days when you used to sleep till noon?'

'Jason. I had to learn to work in the daytime and sleep at night. Tell me something, do you always look like this at seven o'clock in the morning?' She was staring admiringly at the pale blue velvet dressing gown.

'Only when I go to work.' She grinned at her friend and pointed at the notes on the desk. 'I just talked to Bernardo.'

'How goes it in Rome?'

'Terrific, except I have to re-do half the summer collections before I call him back tonight.'

'Sounds like my rewrites. Jesus. Before you get started, can I fix you some eggs?'

Isabella shook her head. 'I've got to do some work on this before I eat. What about the boys? Are they up yet?'

'Are you kidding? Listen . . .' She put her finger to her lips, and they both smiled as they heard a distant shriek. 'Hattie's getting Jason dressed for school.' She looked gently at Isabella, walked into the room, and sat down. 'What are we going to do about Alessandro? Do you want him to stay home?'

'I – I don't know . . .' The clouds returned to her dark eyes as she frowned back at Natasha. 'I had planned to, but . . . I don't know. I'm not sure what to do.'

'Has anyone realised yet that you've left Rome?'

'No. Bernardo says it went perfectly. According to *Il Messaggero*, I have taken refuge at the top of the house.'

'Then there's no reason why anyone would suspect who he is. Do you suppose you could convince him not to tell anyone his last name? He could go to school with Jason and say he's our cousin from Milan. Alessandro . . .' She thought a moment. 'What about your grandfather's name?'

'Parel?'

'Parelli?' Natasha grinned at her creation. 'I spend half my life making up names. Every time I start a new novel, I start staring at the labels on anything at hand and I must have every name-the-baby book ever made. Well, how about it? Alessandro Parelli, our cousin from Milan?'

'And what about me?' Isabella was amused by her inventive friend.

'Mrs. Parelli, of course. Just give me the word and I'll call the school. As a matter of fact . . .' She looked pensive. 'I'll call Corbett and ask him if he has time to take them on his way to work.'

'Wouldn't that be something of an imposition?' Isabella looked concerned, but Natasha shook her head.

'If it were, I'd do it myself. But he loves doing things like that. He's always helping me with Jason.' She looked away for a moment, lost in her own thoughts. 'He has this thing about being helpful . . . about people who need him.' Isabella watched her, wondering if Natasha needed him enough. She seemed so independent. She would have smiled to know that it was the same thought that always crossed Corbett's mind.

'Well, if he wouldn't mind very much, it would be lovely. That way they wouldn't see me at the school.'

'That's what I was thinking.' She gnawed at a pencil. 'I'll call him.' And she disappeared before Isabella could say more. But since she had met him on the way in from the airport, Isabella had been wondering what lay between the silver-haired man and her old friend. It seemed a nice relationship, and the understanding between them was something that Isabella watched with envy now. But how serious were they? From Natasha, she knew she would gain no insight, not until she was ready to talk.

Natasha went to call Corbett and returned to say he'd be there shortly. The boys were up and tearing about.

'My God, will he be able to stand it?' Isabella winced and Natasha grinned.

'You will know how truly crazy the man is when I tell you that he'll love it. Even at this hour of the day.'

'Obviously a masochist.' But Isabella was smiling as she searched Natasha's eyes, but there was no answer there.

Natasha looked at her sympathetically in the kitchen as she made toast.

'Can you sleep today?'

'Are you kidding?' Isabella looked at her, horrified, and they both suddenly laughed. 'What about your work?'

'You'll hear me pounding away in half an hour. But not' – she grinned at her impishly – 'in anything quite as fancy as that.'

Isabella laughed. Natasha, she knew, possessed a uniform for working – jeans, sweat shirts, and woollen argyle socks. Suddenly Isabella realised she could do the same. She was suddenly invisible, non-existent, unknown.

'All right, Mrs. Parelli from Milan, I'll go call the school.' Natasha disappeared and Isabella went back to find her son.

She found him in the bedroom playing with Ashley, a big smile on his face.

'What are you so happy about?' She swept him into her arms with a kiss.

'Jason has to go to school today. I'm staying home with his train.' But Isabella plopped him back on his bed.

'Guess what? You're going to school too.'

'I am?' He stared at her in dismay. 'I can't play with the train?'

'Sure you can. When you come home. Wouldn't it be more fun to go to school with Jason than to stay here alone all day while I work?'

He thought about it for a minute and cocked his head to one side. 'Nobody will talk to me. And I can't talk to them.'

'If you go to school with Jason, pretty soon you'll be able to talk to everyone, and a lot quicker than if you sit here speaking Italian to me. What do you think?'

He nodded his head thoughtfully. 'Will it be very hard?'

'No different from your school in Rome.'

'We get to play all the time?' He looked at her delightedly, and she smiled.

'Is that all you used to do?'

'No, we had to do letters too.'

'How awful.' His expression said that he agreed. 'Do you want to go?' She wasn't sure what she'd do with him if he said no.

'Okay. I'll try it. And if I don't like it, we can both quit. Jason can stay home with me.'

'Aunt Natasha will love that. And listen, I have something to tell you.'

'What?'

'Well, it's all part of the adventure. We have to keep it a secret that we're here.'

He looked at her and then he whispered, 'Should I hide in school?'

She tried to keep her face serious and gently took his hand. 'No, silly. They'll know you're there. But . . . we don't want anyone to know who we are.'

'We don't? Why not?' He looked at her strangely, and she felt the iron mountain fall back on her heart.

'Because it's safer. Everyone thinks we're still in Rome.'

'Because of – of Papa?' His eyes were large and sorrowful now as they looked into hers.

'Yes. We're going to say that our name is Parelli. And that we're from Milan.'

'But we're not from Milano. We're from Roma.' He glared at her, annoyed. 'And we're di San Gregorio. Papa wouldn't like it if we lied about that.'

'No, and I don't like it either. But it's all part of the secret, Alessandro. We have to do it this way, but only for a little while.'

'Then can I tell them my real name at school?'

'Maybe later. But not now. Alessandro Parelli. They'll probably never even use your last name.'

'They better not. I don't like that one.' For a moment Isabella almost laughed. They'd probably call him Alessandro Spaghetti, as Natasha had done to her when they met.

'It doesn't matter what they call you, darling. You know who you are.'

'I think it's silly.' He tucked his legs under him and watched his friend. Jason was carefully tying knots in the laces of his shoes, which he had carefully put on. But on the wrong feet.

'It's not silly, Alessandro. It's necessary. And I will be very, very angry with you if you tell anyone our real name. If you do that, we'll have to go away again, and we won't be able to be with Aunt Natasha anymore, or Jason.'

'Will we have to go home?' He looked horrified. 'I haven't even used his train.'

'Then do as I tell you. I want you to promise me. Alessandro, do you promise?'

'I promise.'

'Who are you?'

He looked at her defiantly. 'I am Alessandro . . . Parelli. From Milan.'

'All right, darling. And remember that I love you. Now hurry up and get dressed.'

They could already smell Hattie making bacon in the kitchen. And Jason was staring down in confusion at his oddly clad feet.

'You have them on the wrong feet, sweetheart.' Isabella stooped down to give him a hand. 'Guess what? Alessandro is coming to school with you today.'

'He is? Oh, wow!' She explained to him about Parelli and that they were cousins from Milan. And then she remembered to tell the same thing to Alessandro.

'I'm his cousin? Why can't I say I'm his brother?' He had always liked the idea.

'Because you don't speak English, silly.'

'After I learn, then can I say that we are?'

'Never mind that. Just get your pants on. And wash your face!'

Twenty minutes later Corbett buzzed from downstairs. The boys were respectably clad in corduroy pants and sneakers with shirts and sweaters, woollen hats and warm coats. They had gobbled a quick breakfast and were off. As the door closed behind them Natasha looked at her faded T-shirt and wiped her hands on her jeans.

'Somehow I always wind up wearing whatever he was last eating. Alessandro sure looked cute.'

'He wanted to tell them he was Jason's brother.' Isabella sighed as they walked away from the door.

'Do you think he'll be able to keep his name a secret?' For a moment Natasha was worried.

'Unfortunately in the last four and a half months he has learned a great deal about secrecy, discretion, caution, and and danger. He understands that the first three are necessary to avoid the last.'

'That's quite a lesson for a five-year-old boy.'

'It is as well for a thirty-two-year-old woman,' Isabella

said, and as she watched her Natasha knew she spoke the truth.

'I hope you keep that in mind, spaghetti face. I wasn't exactly thrilled with your announcement last night that you wanted to go out. Alessandro is one thing, he's an anonymous child. There is nothing even faintly anonymous about you.'

'There could be.'

'What did you have in mind, seeing a plastic surgeon for a new face?'

'Don't be absurd. There is a way of carrying oneself when one wants to be seen. Of "being there", of commanding attention, and saying "Here I am". If I don't want to be seen, I don't have to be. I can wear a scarf, a pair of slacks, a dark coat.'

'Dark glasses, a beard, and a moustache. Right. Look, Isabella. Do me a favour. I have very delicate nerves. If you're going to start wandering around New York, I may have a nervous breakdown. In which case I won't be able to finish my rewrite, my next advance won't come in, my royalties will dry up, my publisher will can me, and my child will starve.'

But Isabella only laughed as she listened to her. 'Natasha, I adore you.'

'Then be a good friend. Stay home.'

'I can't do that. For God's sake, Natasha, if nothing else I need air.'

'I'll buy you some. I'll have it sent to your room.' She smiled, but she had never been more serious. 'If you start roaming around New York, someone will see you. A reporter, a photographer, someone who knows fashion. Christ, maybe even a reporter from *Women's Wear Daily*.'

'They're not interested in me. Only my collections.'

'Who're you kidding, darling? Not yourself, and not me.'

'We'll talk about it later.'

With the question of Isabella's venturing out still unresolved between them, they left each other for their separate worlds: Natasha, lost among her unruly papers, her many half-filled coffee cups, and her visions and characters and imaginary world; Isabella to her pad covered with minutely detailed notes, her carefully kept files, her long lists of the fabrics they currently had in stock, her swatches, her samples, her perfect memory of the summer line. Neither of them even heard the children come home at three thirty, and it was another two hours later when they met, each of them stiff, hungry, tired, in the kitchen.

'Christ, I'm hungry.' For a moment Natasha's accent seemed even more southern. Isabella looked tired, and there were soft shadows under her eyes. 'Did you eat today?'

'I didn't think to.'

'Neither did I. How'd it go?'

It had been gruelling, but she had made a contingency plan for the entire couture collection. 'I think we'll make it. We may not even have to use what I did today. But I couldn't take the chance.' She would only know for sure when she called Hong Kong at midnight.

They smiled at each other over their coffee as Natasha closed her eyes for a minute and Isabella stretched tired arms. Today had been a new experience for her. No buttons to push, no secretaries to command, no elevator to charge in and out of, investigating problems on every floor. No image to carry off, no aura, no magic, no spell. She had worn a black cashmere sweater and a well-worn pair of jeans.

'What are you doing tonight?' she asked Natasha.

'Same as you. Staying home.'

'Because you want to, or because of me?'

Isabella wondered how patient Corbett would be with Natasha's self-imposed sentence. It really wasn't fair to him.

'Don't be silly. Because I'm goddamn exhausted. And believe it or not, because I like to stay home. Besides, you're a lot more amusing than any of the invitations I've had in weeks.'

'I'm flattered.' But Isabella wasn't fooled by the blustering speech.

'Don't be. I'm surrounded by morons and bores, and people who invite me because they want to say that they know me. Ten years ago I was just another model from Georgia, and suddenly I'm 'A Novelist', 'A Writer', someone to decorate a dinner party.'

Dinner parties! Isabella had not been to one in months, and then she had never gone alone. It was never just Isabella, but Isabella and Amadeo, together. *We*, not *I*.

We were a kind of magical team, she thought. The two of us, who we were, what we were, what we looked like together. Like asparagus and hollandaise. It's difficult when you can no longer have both. Not as spicy, not as sweet . . . not as interesting . . . not as . . .

Suddenly sad again Isabella looked at Natasha with admiration – her brave friend who 'decorated' dinner parties unescorted and seemed always to have marvellous times. 'I'm nothing without him,' she whispered. 'All the excitement is gone. Everything that I was . . . that we were – '

'That's nonsense, you know. It may be lonely, but you're still what you always were. Beautiful, intelligent, an extraordinary woman, Isabella. Even alone. You were two wholes added to each other that made two and a half, not two halves that made one.'

'We were more than that, Natasha. We were one that made one. Superimposed, entwined, meshed, soldered.

braided. I never quite knew where I began and he left off. And now I know . . . only too well . . .' She stared into her coffee, her voice whispery soft.

Natasha touched her hand. 'Give it time.'

But when Isabella looked up, her eyes were angry. 'Why should I? Why should I give it anything? Why did it have to happen to me?'

'It didn't happen to you, Isabella. It happened to him. You're still here, with Alessandro, with the business, with every part of you, your mind, your heart, your soul, still intact. Unless you let bitterness rob you, as you already think it has.'

'Wouldn't it do the same to you?'

'Probably. I probably wouldn't have the balls to do what you've done. To go on, to take over the business, to make it better, to keep running it even from over here. But that's not enough, Isabella. It's not enough . . . oh, God, baby, please . . . don't lose you.' Tears sprang up to her eyes as she looked at the dark-haired beauty, so tired, so suddenly bereft and alone. As long as she buried herself in her work all day, she wouldn't feel it. But sooner or later, even in the tiny maid's room office, the day had to end for her and she had to go home. Natasha understood.

Isabella stood up quietly, patted Natasha's shoulder, and walked silently back to her room. When she emerged again ten minutes later, she was wearing dark glasses, her mink coat, and another black wool hat. Natasha stopped short at the sight of her.

'Where the hell are you going?'

'Out for a walk.' It was impossible to see her eyes behind the glasses, but Natasha knew instantly that she had been crying.

For an instant the two women stood there, locked in battle without a single word. Then Natasha surrendered, overcome with sadness for her friend.

'All right. I'll go with you,' she said, 'but for chrissake, take off that coat. You look about as discreet as Greta Garbo. All you need is one of her hats.'

Tiredly Isabella grinned at her with a shrug that was pure Italian. 'This is all I brought with me, my only coat.'

'Poor little rich girl. Come on, I'll find you something.' Isabella trailed behind her as Natasha went to her closet and produced a red wool coat.

'I can't wear it. I . . . Natasha, I'm sorry . . .'

'Why not?'

'It's not black.' Natasha stared at her for a moment, not understanding, and then as she looked at her she knew. Before that she hadn't been sure.

'You're wearing mourning?' Isabella nodded. 'You can't just borrow the red coat?' The whole concept was new to her. The idea of wearing black dresses, black sweaters, black stockings. For an entire year.

'I'd feel awful.'

Natasha stared into her closet again and then muttered over her shoulder, 'Would you settle for navy blue?'

Hesitating for an instant, Isabella nodded and quietly took off the spectacular mink coat. Natasha pulled on a fox jacket, warm gloves, and a huge red fox hat. She turned to find Isabella smiling at her.

'You look marvellous.'

'So do you.'

It was amazing how she could do it. But she did. The navy blue coat was totally plain, and her black wool cap was hardly more exciting, but the ivory face and the deep set almond eyes were all she needed. She would have stopped traffic in the dead of night.

The two women left the apartment soundlessly. It was already dark outside. Natasha plunged ahead as the doorman swept open the door, and for a moment Isabella was startled by the bitter chill. She felt suddenly as though someone had punched her, hard, in the chest. She gasped for a moment and felt a crystalline haze of tears fill her eyes.

'Is it always like this in February? Somehow I only remember New York in the fall.'

'A blessed repression, my dear. Most of the time it's worse. Any place special you want to walk?'

'How about the park?' They were hurrying along Park Avenue. Natasha looked at her, shocked.

'Only if you're feeling suicidal. They have a quota to meet you know. I think it's something like thirty-nine muggings and two murders an hour.' Isabella laughed at her and suddenly felt her body come alive.

But it wasn't energy that spurred her feet forward, only tension and loneliness, and fatigue, and fear. She was so tired – of working, of travelling, of hiding, of missing him, and being brave. 'Try to be brave for just a little while longer.' She could still hear the words Amadeo had said to her when they had let him talk to her . . . that last night.

Her feet were already pounding the pavement. Natasha kept pace with her, but Isabella had forgotten she was there. '*Try to be . . . brave . . . brave . . . brave . . .*' It seemed to Isabella that they had covered miles when they finally stopped.

'Where are we?'

'Seventy-ninth Street.' They had gone eighteen blocks. 'You're not in bad shape, for an old broad. Ready to go home now?'

'Yes. But more slowly. How about walking somewhere more interesting?' They had passed block after block of buildings that looked like Natasha's, stone fortresses with awnings and doormen. Impressive but unexciting.

'We can walk over to Madison and look at the shops.' It was almost seven o'clock now. A dead hour when people were at home. That hour after work and before one went out for the evening. And it was really too cold for many

146

people to be window-shopping at night. Natasha glanced at the sky. There was a familiar chill in the air. 'I think it might snow.'

'Alessandro would love that.' They were walking slowly now, catching their breath.

'So would I.'

'You like snow?' Isabella looked at her in surprise.

'No. But it would keep you at home, without me having to run my ass off just to make sure you don't get out of line.'

Isabella laughed at her, and they walked on, past blocks of boutiques that housed delights from Cardin, Ungaro, Pierre D'Alby, and Yves Saint Laurent. There were art galleries and coiffures by Sassoon.

'Checking out the competition?' Natasha watched her, amused. Isabella was drinking it all in, her eyes sparkling with pleasure. She was a woman who loved every facet of her work.

'Why not? Their things are very pretty.'

'So are yours.'

Isabella executed a half bow as they strolled on. It was the Faubourg St.-Honoré of New York, a shimmering necklace of bright, priceless gems, strung together, enhancing each other, a myriad of treasures hidden in each block.

'You really love it, don't you?'

'What, New York?' Isabella looked surprised. She liked it. It intrigued her. But love . . . no . . . not yet. Even after her year there she had been glad to go back to Rome.

'No. Fashion. Something happens to you, just looking at clothes.'

'Aahhh . . . that.'

'Christ, I'd have gone nuts if I'd had to go on modelling.'

'That's different.' Isabella looked at her wisely, the keeper of secrets rarely bestowed.

'No, it's not.'

'Yes, it is. Modelling is like a lifetime of one-night stands. There are no love affairs, no tender lovers, no betrayals, no broken hearts, no marriages, or precious offspring. Designing is different. There is history, drama, courage, art. You love the clothes, you live with them for a while, you give birth to them, you remember their fathers, their grandfathers, the dresses of other collections, other times. There is a romance to it, an excitement, an . . .' She broke off, then laughed at herself. 'You must think I'm mad.'

'No. That's how I feel about the people in my books.'

'Nice, isn't it?' The two women looked at each other in perfect understanding.

'Very.'

They were almost home. As they rounded the corner on to Park Avenue Natasha felt the first flakes of snow.

'See, I told you. Not that I suppose that will keep you at home.' But there was no harm in this. They could walk like this in the evening. It hadn't been risky after all.

'No, it won't. I couldn't have stayed in the apartment. Not for very long.'

Natasha nodded quietly. 'I know.'

She also knew that Isabella would not be satisfied forever with a brief evening stroll.

Chapter Fifteen

'Mamma! *Guardi!* ... It snowed!'

And indeed it had. A foot-deep blanket covered the entire surface of New York. And from the cosy warmth of the apartment all four of them watched the swirling storm. It hadn't stopped since Natasha and Isabella had returned to the apartment the evening before.

'Can we go play in it?'

Isabella glanced at Natasha, who nodded and offered to lend them the appropriate clothes. School was of course closed. The city had come to a complete stop.

'We'll go after breakfast.' Isabella glanced at her watch. And after she called Bernardo in Rome. She had reached Hong Kong too late the previous evening and she hadn't dared call him that night. She absented herself from the boys quickly, closed the door to her office, and picked up the phone.

'Where were you last night? I figured you'd call me around four.'

'How charming. My manners are not as bad as that, Bernardo. That is why I waited till this morning.'

'Kindly signora.'

'Oh, shut up.' She was smiling, and in a good mood. 'The Hong Kong fabric is hopeless. We'll have to go with the alternate plans.'

'What alternate plans?' He sounded baffled.

'Mine of course. Did you tell Gabriela to hold everything?'

'Obviously. That's what you wanted. I practically had to pick her up from a dead faint on the floor.'

'Then you should thank me. In any case I worked out everything yesterday. Now, do you have pen and paper?'

'Yes, madame.'

'Good. I've got it all worked out. First the couture collection, then we'll do the rest. Starting with number twelve, the red lining is now yellow. The fabric number in our storeroom is two-seven-eight-three FBY . . . Fabia-Bernardo-Yvonne. Got that? Number sixteen, seventeen, and nineteen . . .' On she went until she had covered the entire line. Even Bernardo was stunned.

'How in God's name did you do that?'

'With difficulty. By the way, the additional pieces in the ready-to-wear collection won't cost that much more. By using fabric we've got in stock, we're saving a hell of a lot of money.'

Indeed they were, Bernardo thought with admiration. And she had spelled out every single bloody fabric. She knew every piece, every roll, the yardage available, the textures, the shades.

'And if thirty-seven in the couture line looks awful, tell her to skip it,' Isabella continued. 'We probably ought to just forget it and only leave it in as number thirty-six in the blue.'

'Which one is that?' He was overwhelmed. In a day she had done the work of a month. In one morning she had salvaged the entire summer line. Only in speaking to Gabriela again the previous evening had he realized how potentially disastrous the absence of the fabric from Hong Kong could have been.

'Never mind which one that is. Gabriela will know. What else is new?'

'Today, nothing. Everything's quiet on the home front.'

'How nice for you. In that case I'm taking a vacation today.'

'You're going out?' he sounded horrified

'Only to the park. It's snowing. Natasha and I just promised the boys.'

'Isabella, be careful.'

'Obviously. But believe me, there won't be another soul.'

'Why don't you just let Allessandro go with Natasha? You stay home.'

'Because I need some fresh air, Bernardo.'

He began to speak, but she cut him off.

'Bernardo, I love you. Now I have to go.'

She was curt, cheerful, and unnerving as she blew him a kiss and hung up the phone. He didn't like it. He didn't like it at all. There was a little too much spunk in her voice again. And at this distance he had no control. He just hoped that Natasha was smarter than Isabella and wouldn't let her go out for more than an occasional brief stroll after dark. Then he laughed to himself. There was one way to keep her out of trouble, and that was to heap more work on her, like the massive endeavour of the day before. It was inconceivable that she had actually done it.

'Are you ready?' Isabella looked at the two little boys bundled up like snowmen, Jason in a red snowsuit, Allessandro in a bright yellow spare.

They were off to the park instantly, and within half an hour the boys were sliding down little hills on Jason's sled. Slipping, whooshing, squealing along, laughing, and throwing snow. After the sledding they got into a snowball fight, and quickly Isabella and Natasha joined the fun. Only a few brave souls had been hardy enough to come out in the cold.

The four weathered it for almost two hours, and then happy and sodden they were ready to go home.

'Hot baths for everyone!' Natasha shouted as they came in the door. Hattie had hot chocolate and cinnamon toast waiting and a fire going in the den. The snowstorm continued for another day, and the boys didn't have to go to school all week as businessmen snowshoed to their offices and housewives resurrected skis to get to the store.

But for Isabella the holiday was a brief one, and after the day of sledding she returned to her office in the back of Natasha's apartment with a fresh batch of problems from Rome. Two of the more important alternate fabrics had been accidentally destroyed by a flood in the storeroom the week before. Their number-one model had quit and everything had to be fitted again. Minor problems, major headaches, disasters and victories, a month filled with a blessed mountain of work in which Isabella could hide, except for the evening walks with Natasha. They had now become a ritual without which Isabella thought she couldn't live.

'How long are you going to go on like this?' They had just stopped for a light on Madison Avenue. Isabella had been peering into boutique windows, examining the spring displays. It was March, and the last snows had finally come and gone, though it was still wintry cold and there was almost always an icy wind.

Her question caught Natasha by surprise. 'What do you mean? Go on like what?'

'Living like a hermit, baby-sitting for me? Do you realize you haven't been out once in the evening during the five weeks we've been here? Corbett must be ready to kill me by now.'

'Why should he?' Natasha looked baffled as she stared at her friend.

But Isabella was amused at her feigned innocence. She had long since understood. 'Certainly he must expect a little more of your time.'

'Not as a rule, thank you. We keep our lives very much

to ourselves.' Natasha looked faintly amused. But this time it was Isabella who stared.

'What the hell do you mean?' She wasn't angry at Isabella, just confused.

But Isabella answered with a slow smile. 'I don't expect you to be a virgin, you know, Natasha. You can be honest with me.'

'About what?' And then suddenly Natasha was grinning. 'About Corbett?' For a long moment she laughed until tears came to her eyes. 'Are you kidding? Oh, Isabella . . . did you think? . . . Oh, Jesus!' And then she looked at her friend, amused. 'I can't imagine anything less appealing to me than getting involved with Corbett Ewing.'

'Are you serious? You're not involved with him?' Isabella looked stunned. 'But I had assumed . . .' And then she looked even more puzzled. 'But why not? I thought that you two – '

'Maybe you thought, but Corbett and I never thought. We've been friends for years and we'll never be anything more. He's almost like a brother and he's my very best friend. But we're both two basically very high-powered people. As a woman, I'm not gentle enough for Corbett, not fragile or helpless enough. I don't know, I can't explain it. He always says I should have been a man.'

'How unkind.' Isabella looked disapproving.

'Doesn't Bernardo say unkind things to you?'

Isabella smiled in answer. 'At least every day.'

'Exactly. It's like brother and sister. I can't imagine anything different with Corbett.' She grinned to herself again, and Isabella shrugged, feeling a little silly.

'I must be getting old, Natasha. All my perceptions are off. I truly assumed right from the beginning . . .' But Natasha just grinned and shook her head. And Isabella was pensive for a long moment as they walked along. She

153

was suddenly thinking of Corbett Ewing in a very different light.

They didn't speak again until they approached the building and Natasha noticed Isabella smiling as they walked along.

'You should have gone to the opera ball, you know,' Isabella said. 'It would have been fun.'

'How do you know?'

'We have a marvellous one in Rome.'

'I mean how do you know there was one here and that I was invited to it?'

'Because I'm an excellent detective and the invitation didn't quite burn.'

Suddenly there were tears in Natasha's eyes. Her lies, her 'sacrifice', had been a disservice to her friend. 'All right,' she said, throwing her arm around Isabella's shoulders and hugging her briefly. 'You win.'

'Thank you.' Isabella marched into the building with a look of victory and an awesome glint in her eye.

Chapter Sixteen

Isabella turned the light off in her office. It was eight o'clock in the evening and she had just made her last call to rome. Poor Bernardo, it was two in the morning for him, but the summer collection had just opened and she had to know how it had gone.

'Exquisite, *cara*,' he had said. 'Everyone declared it a marvel. No one understands how you could do it with the pressure you've been under, with the difficulties, with everything.' While she listened to him, her eyes had glowed.

'It didn't look too peculiar with all those new colours instead of the red?' Working this way, on paper, from a distance was a little bit like being blind.

'No, and the turquoise lining in the white evening coat was sheer genius. You should have seen the reaction of the Italian *Vogue*.'

'*Va bène.*' She was happy. He had given her every detail until at last there was nothing left that she didn't know. 'All right, darling, I guess we've done it. I'm sorry I woke you. Now go back to bed.'

'You mean you don't have any other projects for me at this hour? No frantic instructions about your new ideas for the fall?' He missed her, but his need was fading. It had been good for both of them – her escape had been an escape for him too.

'*Domani.*' Tomorrow. For a moment her eyes clouded over. The fall . . . would she have to design the collection from here then? Would she never be able to go home? Two months. It had already been two months since she had come to the States. Two months of hiding and running her business from five thousand miles, on the phone. Two months of not seeing the villa, not sleeping in her own bed. It was already April. The month of sunshine and gardens and the first burst of springtime in Rome. Even in New York the weather had been a little warmer as she had strolled every evening to the edge of the park and a few times to the East River to catch the parade of joggers and sturdy-looking little boats. The East River was not the Tiber, and New York wasn't her home. 'I'll call you in the morning,' she told Bernardo. 'And by the way, congratulations on the soap.'

'Please. Don't even mention it.' It had taken four months to do the research, another two to put it on the market. But at least it had paid off. They had just received an order for half a million dollars from F-B, of course.

Bernardo was describing the orders, but she wasn't listening. The soap. Even that reminded her of her last day with Amadeo. That fateful day when she had argued with Bernardo and then left them to run off to lunch. It had been almost seven months. Seven long, lonely, work-filled months. She dragged her attention back to Bernardo.

'What's it like in New York now by the way?' he was asking.

'Still cold, perhaps a bit warmer, but everything is still very grey. They don't see spring here until May or June.'

He didn't tell her that the garden at the villa was in full bloom. He had been there to check on things only a few days before. Instead he said, '*Bène, cara.* I'll talk to you tomorrow. And congratulations!'

She blew him a kiss and they hung up. *Congratulations.* In Rome she would have watched with terror and fascination as they opened the show. She would have stood by, breathless, suddenly unsure of the colours, the fabrics, the look, unhappy with the jewellery, the music, and the models' perfectly done hair. She would have hated every moment, until the first *mannequin* stepped on to the grey silk runway. Then, after it had begun, she would have felt the thrill of it as she did each season. The sheer excitement, the beauty, the madness of the high-fashion world. And when it was over, she and Amadeo would have winked at each other secretly from across the murderously jammed room and then found each other later for a long, happy kiss. The press would have been there, and there would have been rivers of champagne. And parties in the evening. It was like a wedding and a honeymoon four times a year.

But not this year. Tonight she was in blue jeans, in a tiny one-room office, drinking coffee, and very much alone.

She closed the door to her office and glanced at the kitchen clock as she walked past. She heard the boys in the distance and wondered why they weren't in bed. Alessandro had learned English, not perfectly, but enough to be understood. When he wasn't, he shouted to compensate for it, as though otherwise he might not be heard. The odd thing was he rarely spoke it. It was as though Alessandro needed his Italian as a reminder of home, of who he really was. She smiled to herself as she walked past their room. They were playing with Hattie, had the television going, and Jason had just set up his train.

She had missed her walk tonight. She had been too nervous, waiting to call Bernardo, wondering what had happened at the opening of the collections that day. And she was growing tired of the familiar route now anyway, even more so now that Natasha didn't always come along. She had picked up her life again, and in the evenings Isabella was often alone. Natasha was going to be out again that evening. A benefit ball.

Pausing at her own doorway, Isabella stopped for a moment and then walked slowly to the end of the hall to Natasha's door. It was nice to see her looking pretty again, wearing bright colours, doing something elegant or surprising with her long blonde hair. It brought fresh life to Isabella, so tired of looking in the mirror and seeing her own face, her dark hair pulled back, and the constant sobriety of her austere black clothes on her ever thinner form.

She knocked softly once and smiled as Natasha muttered, 'Come in.' She had long tortoise-shell hair-pins clenched in her teeth, and her hair was already swept in a swirl of loose Greek curls, which cascaded softly from a knot on the top of her head.

'That looks pretty, madame. What are you going to wear?'

'I don't know. I was going to wear the yellow one until Jason checked it out.' She groaned again as she jabbed in another of the long pins.

'Don't tell me, fingerprints?' Isabella glanced at the discarded yellow silk.

'Peanut butter with his left hand. Chocolate ice cream with his right.'

'Sounds delicious.' She was smiling again.

'Yeah, maybe, but it looks like hell.'

'What about this one?' Isabella went into her closet and came out with something familiar and pale blue. She had thought of Natasha when she bought the fabric. It was the same colour as her eyes, a kind of lavender with a bluish hint.

'That? It's gorgeous. But I never know what to wear with it.'

'What about gold?'

'Gold what?' Natasha looked at her quizzically as she finished her hair.

'Sandals. And a touch of gold in your hair.' She was staring at her as she did the models at their fittings for the collections in Rome. Eyes narrowed, feet wide apart, seeing something different than what actually was. Creating her own magic with a woman, a dress, an inspiration.

'Wait! You're going to spray my hair gold?'

Natasha shrank at the frilly white dressing-table, but Isabella ignored her and disappeared. She was back in a minute with a needle and some very fine gold thread.

'What's that?'

She threaded the needle as Natasha stared.

'Sit still.' She wove it in airily with a deftly moving hand, clipping thread, making the ends disappear, and working miracles with the needle again until it was done, creating only an impression, as though mixed in with Natasha's own hair she had grown little shimmering wisps of gold.

'There.'

Natasha stared at her reflection in astonishment and grinned.

'You're amazing. Now what?'

'A little of this.' She set down a box of powder, transparent, translucent, shimmering with tiny flecks of gold. The impression it created was one of dazzling beauty, a shining lustre to an already lovely face. Then she disappeared into Natasha's closet and came out with gold sandals with low heels. 'You'll look like a goddess when I'm through.'

Natasha was beginning to believe her as she strapped her own forgotten sandals to invisibly stockinged feet.

'Nice stockings. Where'd you get them?' Isabella looked down with interest.

'Dior.'

'Traitor.' Then, thoughtfully, 'Don't apologize. They look nicer than ours.' She made a mental note to say something to Bernardo. It was time they did something new and different about theirs. 'Now . . .' She pulled the dress out of its plastic case and grunted with satisfaction as

159

she dropped it perfectly without disturbing a hair on Natasha's head. She zipped her up in businesslike fashion and walked around to the front, tucking, smoothing, approving. The dress was one of hers. She had done it for their spring line, only three years before. For jewellery she picked from among her own things a ring of pale mauve amethysts, edged with diamonds and set in gold. There was a pair of tiny, delicately fashioned ear-rings, and a bracelet as well. It was a remarkable set. 'Where did you ever get it?'

'Amadeo bought it for me in Venice last year. They're nineteenth century, I think. He said the stones are all imperfect, but the setting is remarkably fine.'

'Oh, Jesus, Isabella. I can't wear this. Thank you, but, darling, you're nuts.'

'You bore me. Do you want to look lovely or don't you? If not, you might as well stay here.' She closed the necklace around Natasha's throat. It fell to precisely the right depth of the necklace, sparkled dazzlingly from the pale mauve chiffon folds. 'Here, put these on yourself.' She held out the ear-rings after closing the bracelet on Natasha's wrist. 'You look marvellous.' Isabella gazed at her in sheer delight.

'I'm scared stiff. What if I lose them, for chrissake? Isabella, please!'

'I told you, you bore me. Now go out and have a good time.'

Natasha glanced in the long mirror and smiled at Isabella and her own reflection. The doorbell rang almost instantly, and a stockbroker in a dinner jacket arrived to claim his date. Isabella went to her room and waited until she heard the door close again. There had only been a soft knock before Natasha left with him, and a hastily whispered thanks.

And with that, Isabella was left with the sounds of the

boys again, and the whoosh and whistle of Jason's little toy train.

She looked at her watch half an hour later, and went to kiss them both in their bed. Alessandro looked at her strangely. '*Non esce più, Mamma?*' You don't go out any more?

'No, darling. I'd rather stay here with you.' She turned out the lights for them and went to lie down on the fur throw on her bed. '. . . *non esce più, Mamma? . . . No, caro. Mai.*' Never. Maybe never again.

She tried to sleep as she gazed at the fire, but it was useless. She was still too nervous, too excited, too on edge after the day of waiting for news of the collections in Rome. And she hadn't had any air all day long. Hadn't walked. Hadn't run. With a sigh at last she turned over, looked into the fire, and then stood up. She went to find Hattie, in her room watching television, her hair in curlers and a copy of *Good Housekeeping* near her bed. 'You'll be home for a while?'

'Yes, Mrs Parelli. I'm not going out.'

'I'm going for a walk then. I'll be back very soon.'

Isabella closed the door again and returned to her own room. The borrowed navy blue coat hung in her closet now, and she no longer needed the wool hat. She shrugged quickly into the coat and picked up her bag, glancing around the room for a moment as though she were afraid to leave something behind. What? Her handbag? Her compact? Long white kid opera gloves? She looked down sombrely at the jeans that she wore, and for an instant a pang of jealousy shot through her. Natasha. Lucky Natasha. With her benefits and her gold sandals and her beaux. Isabella smiled to herself when she thought back to their conversation about Corbett.

She should have known Corbett was not Natasha's type. He couldn't be handled easily enough. She looked at herself in the mirror then, angrily, and whispered, 'Is that what you want?' She didn't, of course. She knew she didn't. Not a stockbroker in horn-rimmed glasses. 'Ah, then it's a beautiful one you want.' She accused herself as she softly closed the door. 'No! No!' was her answer. But what did she want then? Amadeo, of course. Only Amadeo. But as she thought it, a brief vision of Corbett flashed into her head.

That night she walked further than she ever had, her hands jammed into her pockets, her chin tucked into the collar of the coat. What was it she wanted? Suddenly she wasn't sure. She wandered more slowly past the now too familiar shops. Why didn't they change the windows more often? Didn't anyone care? And didn't they know that they were still using last year's colours? And why wasn't it spring? She found fault with all of it as she pushed the vision of Natasha repeatedly out of her head. Was that it then? Was she only jealous? But why shouldn't Natasha have a good time? She worked hard. She was a good friend. She had opened her home and her heart to Isabella as no one ever had. What more could she possibly want from her? To keep her locked at home the way she herself was?

Suddenly, in spite of herself, she knew the answer only too well. It wasn't Natasha's imprisonment she wanted, but some freedom of her own. That was all. She dug her hands further into her pockets, jammed her chin even further down, and walked on endlessly until, for the first time, she was downtown. No longer in the cosy, residential safety of the sixties; or the distinguished sobriety of the seventies; or even the decorous boredom of the eighties; not to mention the dubious, shabby gentility of the nineties, where she had now and then strayed; but the other way this time, past the bustling fifties, its restaurants, its excited diners, its screeching taxis, and its far larger shops. Past department stores with overdone windows, and Tiffany's with its glittering goodies, Rockefeller Center with its still hopeful skaters, and St Patrick's with its lofty spires. She walked all the way down to Forty-second Street, to the office buildings, the less fashionable stores, and the drunks. Everything seemed to be careering past her at a speed that reminded her of Rome. At last she turned back towards Park Avenue, and past Grand Central Station, she stood looking straight up Park. Lined on either side of her were skyscrapers, towering monuments of glass and chrome, where fortunes were aspired to, ambitions fulfilled. It took her breath away as she stared at them; the tops of the buildings seemed to lead straight to heaven. Slowly, thoughtfully, Isabella walked home.

She felt as though she had opened a new door that night and there was no way she could close it again. She had been crouching, hidden in a maze, locked behind an apartment door, pretending that she was living in a village far from the city's excitement. But she had seen too much that night, felt the nearness of power, success, money, excitement, ambition. By the time Natasha came home, she had made up her mind.

'What are you still doing up, Isabella? I thought you'd have been asleep for hours.' She had seen the light in the living-room and wandered in, puzzled.

Isabella shook her head briefly, smiling a little at her friend. 'You look wonderful tonight, Natasha.'

'Thanks to you. Everyone loved the gold in my hair; they couldn't figure out how I'd done it.'

'Did you tell them?'

'No.'

'Good.' She was still smiling. 'One has to have a few secrets after all.'

Natasha watched her, worried. Something had changed tonight. There was something about the way Isabella sat there, about the way she looked, and the way she smiled. 'Did you go out for a walk tonight?'

'Yes.'

'How was it? Did anything go wrong?' Why did she look like that? There was something peculiar about her eyes.

'Of course not. Why would anything go wrong? It hasn't yet.'

'And it won't. As long as you're careful.'

'Ah, yes.' She looked wistful. 'That.' She suddenly raised her head with a look of power and grace that suggested that she should have been the one wearing the gold threads in her hair. 'Natasha, when are you going out again?'

'Not for a few days. Why?' Dammit. She was probably lonely and bored. Who wouldn't have been? Particularly Isabella. 'As a matter of fact I was thinking of staying home for the rest of the week, with you and the boys.'

'How dull.'

That was it then. Natasha should have known. She had got too swept up in it all again, taken Isabella too much at her word.

'Not at all, silly. In fact' - she yawned prettily - 'if I don't stop running around like this, I'm going to roll over and die.' But Isabella was laughing at her, and Natasha didn't understand.

'What about the film premiere you were supposed to attend day after tomorrow?'

'What film premiere?' Natasha widened her eyes and looked spectacularly dumb, but Isabella only laughed more.

'The one on Thursday. Remember? The benefit for the heart foundation or whatever it is!'

'Oh, that. I thought I wouldn't go.'

'Good. I'll use your ticket.' She sat back and almost crowed.

'What? I hope you're kidding.'

'No, I'm not. Want to get me a ticket?' She grinned at Natasha and crossed her legs under her on the couch.

'Are you nuts?'

'No. I walked downtown tonight, and it was wonderful. Natasha, I can't do this anymore.'

'You have to. You know you have no choice.'

'Nonsense. In a city the size of this one? No one will know me. I'm not saying I'm going to start parading around, going to fashion shows, and having lunch. But some things I can do. It's insane to hide like this here.'

'It would be insane not to.'

'You're wrong. At something like your film premiere I can slip in and slip out. After the cocktails, the gathering. I can just watch the movie and the people as I come and go. What do you think? That I can design clothes for women of fashion without setting foot out of my house and getting a feeling for what's working, what isn't, what they like, what looks good on them, without even seeing what's being worn? I'm not a mystic, you know. I'm a designer. It's a very down-to-earth trade.'

But the speech wasn't convincing, and Natasha only shook her head.

'I can't do it. I can't. Something will happen. Isabella, you're mad.'

'Not yet. But I will be. Soon. If I don't start getting out. Discreetly. With caution. But I can't go on like this for much longer. I realised that tonight.' Natasha looked woebegone, and Isabella patted her hand.

'Please, Natasha, no one even suspects that it's not I at the top of the house in Rome.'

'They will if you start showing up at film premieres.'

'I promise you, they won't. Will you get me the ticket?' She suddenly wore the pleading eyes of a child.

'I'll think about it.'

'If you don't, I'll get it myself. Or I'll go somewhere else

165

Somewhere out in the open, where I'm sure to be seen.' For a moment her dark eyes glinted viciously, and Natasha's own blue ones suddenly blazed.

'Don't blackmail me, dammit!' She jumped to her feet and paced around the room.

'Then will you help me? Please, Natasha . . . please . . .'

At the sound of her friend's words Natasha turned slowly to face her again, looked at the haunted eyes, the narrow, pale face, and even she had to admit that Isabella needed more than the apartment and an occasional walk up Madison Avenue in the dark. 'I'll see.' But Isabella was tired of the game now; her eyes caught on fire and she jumped to her feet.

'Don't bother, Natasha. I'll take care of the matter myself.' She marched towards the back of the house. In a moment Natasha heard her close her door. Slowly she turned off the lights in the living-room and looked at the city outside. Even at two in the morning, it was alive, busy, bustling; there were trucks, taxis, people; there were still horns and voices, excitement and turmoil outside. It was why people flocked to New York, why they couldn't stay away. She herself knew that she needed what it gave her, needed to feel its tempo beating like the pulse in her veins. How could she deny it to Isabella? But perhaps in not denying it to her, if the kidnappers found her again, she could cost Isabella her life. On silent feet Natasha walked slowly down the hall. She stood outside Isabella's doorway and then gently knocked. The door opened quickly, and the two women stood there, silent, face to face. It was Natasha who spoke first.

'Don't do it, Isabella. It's too dangerous. It's wrong.'

'Tell me that when you have lived like this, in terror, in hiding, for as long as I have. Tell me you'd be able to go on.'

But Natasha couldn't tell her that. No one could.

166

'You've been very brave, Isabella, and for such a long time.'

'*Brave . . . for just a little while longer.*' The echo of Amadeo's words caught Isabella unexpectedly and lodged in her throat. With tears in her eyes she shook her head. 'I haven't.'

'Yes, you have.' They were still whispering. 'You've been brave and patient and wise. Can you be for a little while longer?'

Isabella almost cried out at the words as frantically she shook her head from side to side, whispering to Amadeo, as well as her friend. 'No. No, I can't.' And then she stood very straight, very tall, and looked at Natasha boldly, the tears suddenly gone. 'I can't be brave for a little while longer. I've done this for as long as I can.'

'And Thursday?'

Isabella looked at her, smiling slowly. 'The premiere? I'll be there.'

Chapter Seventeen

'Isabella! . . . Isabella! . . .' There was a frantic knocking as Natasha stood in front of her door.

'Wait a minute! I'm not ready yet. Just a second . . . there . . .' She slipped into her shoes and clipped on her ear-rings, glanced at herself quickly, and pulled open the door. Natasha was waiting, dressed for the evening in a beige Chinese evening coat lined in the palest peach satin. The trousers she wore under it were mocha-brown velvet, all the colours brought together in brown-and-peach brocade shoes. And she was wearing coral ear-rings that peeked through her blonde hair. Isabella looked her over admiringly and smiled in pleasure as she approved. 'My dear, you look marvellous. And it's not even one of mine! Where did you get that sensational outfit?'

'In Paris last year.'

'Very handsome.'

But suddenly it was Natasha who looked and approved, startled into silence as she saw the familiar figure standing regally in the centre of the room.

It was the old Isabella, and for a moment Natasha was breathless, under the spell. This was Isabella di San Gregorio as she had once been. Amadeo's woman and the brightest star in all of Rome.

It was not only what she wore, but the way she wore it, and the angle of the long, ivory neck, so delicately carved, the sweep of her perfectly combed and knotted dark hair, the shape of her tiny ears, the depth of the remarkable black eyes. But now Natasha gasped at what she was wearing, so simple and so stark. One totally plain stretch of black satin which fell from her shoulders to her toes. A tiny V at the neckline, the smallest of cap sleeves, and the richness of the heavy black satin, which exposed only the tips of black satin shoes. Her hair was swept into a knot, her arms totally bare, and her only jewellery was a pair of large onyx ear-rings set in diamonds, as bright as her shining eyes.

'My God, it's gorgeous, Isabella!' It was perfectly simple, perfectly plain. 'It must be one of yours.'

Isabella nodded. 'My last collection, before . . . we left home.' There had been a long pause. *Before Amadeo disappeared.* It was from the same collection as the green satin dress she had worn that night, waiting for him to come home.

'What are you wearing over it? Your mink coat?' Natasha was hesitant. The coat was sure to draw attention. Yet, even in totally plain black satin, Isabella was a woman everyone would see.

But Isabella was shaking her head, this time with a tiny look of pleasure, the hint of a smile.

'No, I have something else. Something from the collection we opened this week. Actually,' she said over her shoulder as she fumbled in the closet for a moment, 'this is only a sample, but Gabriela sent it to me to show me how well it worked. That was the box you picked up at your agent last week. In the collection we lined it in turquoise, to be worn over purple or green.' And as she spoke she emerged from the closet again, wearing a creamy white satin coat. With the black beneath it she looked even more striking than before.

'Oh, God.' Natasha looked as though she'd seen a ghost.

'You don't like it?' Isabella was stunned.

'I love it.' Natasha closed her eyes and sat down. 'But I think you're crazy. You're crazy. You'll never be able to pull this off.' She opened her eyes again, staring at Isabella ın the remarkable white coat and the strikingly simple black gown. The whole outfit was so simple and so beautiful that it shrieked of haute couture. And one look at her face, so pale and so revealing, and the game would be over. The whereabouts of Isabella di San Gregorio would be instantly known. 'Is there any even faintly human chance I can talk you out of this?' Natasha stared at her glumly.

'None.' She was in command again. The princess of the House of San Gregorio in Rome. She glanced at the watch she had left on the table, then back at her friend. 'You'd better hurry, Natasha, you'll be late.'

'I should be so lucky. And you?'

'Just as I promised. I'll stay here until precisely nine-fifteen. I'll get into the limousine you rented for me, go straight to the theatre, have the driver check with the ushers if the movie has started, and if it has done so, on schedule at nine-thirty, I'll hurry inside. I'll sit in the aisle seat you reserved for me and depart the instant the house-lights come on at the end.'

'The instant *before* the house-lights come on. *Don't* wait for the credits, or for me. Just get the hell out. I'll come home later, after the dinner.'

'*Ècco.* And when you get back, I shall be here, and we can celebrate a perfect evening.'

'Perfect? A thousand things could go wrong.'

'But nothing will. *Va, cara.* You'll be late for the cocktail.'

Natasha stood as though paralysed. Isabella was smiling at her. She didn't seem to understand anything, how great a risk she was running, how easily she could be recognised, the furor it would cause if her residence in New York became known.

'Does Bernardo know what you're up to?'

'Bernardo! Bernardo is in Rome. And this is New York.

Here I am only a face in the fashion magazines. Not everyone keeps up with fashion, my dear. Or didn't you know?'

'Isabella, you're a fool. You don't just design dresses for French countesses and rich women from Rome and Venice and Milan. You have an entire American line, men's wear, ready-to-wear, cosmetics, perfumes, soaps. You are an international commodity.'

'No. I'm a woman. And I can't live like this anymore.'

They had been over it one hundred and three times in the past two days, and Natasha's arguments were wearing thin. The best she'd been able to do was come up with a reasonably safe plan. And with luck it would work if Isabella came late enough, left early enough, and sat quietly in her seat in between. Maybe, just maybe, it would be all right.

'So are you ready?' Isabella was looking at her sternly, as though urging a reluctant debutante to attend her first dance.

'I wish I were dead.'

'Don't be foolish, darling.' She kissed Natasha's cheek softly. 'I'll see you there.'

Without another word Natasha stood up to go; she paused for a moment in the doorway, shook her head, and then left as Isabella sat down again, smiling to herself and impatiently tapping one black satin shoe on the floor.

Chapter Eighteen

The limousine Natasha had rented was waiting in quiet black splendour outside the door. It was precisely nine fifteen. Isabella walked out to the kerb. The air on her face felt wonderful, and for once she didn't even mind the cold. The driver closed the door behind her with a thud as Isabella settled herself carefully on the seat, the white coat spread around her like a coronation robe.

They drove decorously through Central Park and then headed downtown to the theatre, as Isabella silently watched the other cars pass by.

Oh, God, she was out at last. In silks and satins, in perfume and evening clothes. Even Alessandro had looked at her with excitement and squealed with glee as he kissed her goodnight carefully, holding both hands, as instructed, in mid-air. 'Just like with Papa!' he had shouted.

But it wasn't just like with Papa. For a moment Isabella's thoughts flew back to Rome. The days of going to parties in the Ferrari, of rushing home from the office to chatter and dress for a ball, her mind still in a work-battered daze, of Amadeo singing in the shower as she laid out his dinner jacket and disappeared into her dressing-room to emerge in grey velvet or blue brocade. It was foolish, an 'empty life', someone had once told her, but it was also their world. They had conquered it together and they enjoyed it, sharing their laughter and their success with amusement and pride.

It was different now. The seat next to her was empty. There was no one but the driver in the long black car. No one to talk to when she got there, no one to laugh with when at last she got home, no one to shine for and smile at Her head had been just a little higher because he had been there.

Her face was suddenly very sober as they halted outside the theatre. The driver turned in his seat to look at her.

'Mrs Walker mentioned something about my going in to see if the movie has already started.'

He left her in the limousine and went to see if all was ready.

She felt her heart begin to race a little, as it had at her wedding when, in a cloud of white lace and veiling, she had been Amadeo's bride. But it was foolish to feel like that now. She was only going to a movie. And this time she was wearing black. And she was no longer Amadeo's bride, but his widow. It was too late to hesitate though. The chauffeur had already returned to help her from her car.

In the darkened theatre Natasha was frantic. A party of seven had taken over the first seven seats along the aisle, and all her excuses – 'I'm sorry, would you mind terribly? My cousin . . . she has a terrible cold . . . here in a minute . . . coming late . . . may not feel well and have to go . . .' – were useless. No one heard her, the group was too unwieldy and too large. A fat man from Texas – 'in oil, darlin'' – in a dinner jacket and a Stetson had had too much to drink. 'Bad kidneys, darlin', you know.' It had been impossible to move him from his seat on the aisle. Beside him were his white-brocaded wife, their hosts, and next to them the financial editor of *The Times* of London, yet another very social couple, and at last Natasha with her spare seat. She wanted to kill Isabella. The plan had been lunacy from the start. Isabella would have to climb over everyone; it was going to be impossible to keep her from being seen. She sat glowering, waiting for the film to start, hoping Isabella would develop smallpox or at least typhoid, maybe even malaria, on her way to the car.

'You look happy tonight, Natasha. What happened to you, they cancel your new book?'

'I should be so lucky.' She glanced across the empty seat at Corbett Ewing.

'You look mad as hell.' He glanced with amusement at the man in the white dress Stetson in the aisle seat. 'Problems with Texas?' Corbett Ewing looked at her with dancing blue eyes and a broad grin.

'I was trying to save the seat for a friend.'

'Aha! So you're in love again. Goddamn it, every time I go out of town, I seem to miss my chance.'

Natasha smiled. But he suddenly realised that she was concerned. And as he watched her he understood who the friend had to be. As he thought of her he felt his heart race.

'Where've you been?' Natasha tried to make idle chitchat but the worry was still in her eyes.

'Tokyo mostly. Then Paris, London. And last week Morocco. God, that's a beautiful place.'

'So I hear. How's business?' With Corbett that was like asking the White House chef, 'How was lunch?' Corbett was constantly brewing some of business and industry's major deals.

'All right. How's your book?'

'Finished, finally. I've decided that I'm not really a writer. Just a rewriter. I spend six weeks cooking them up and six months boiling them down.'

'Actually, that's about how it works with me.' They both fell silent for a time, watching the crowds.

And then, without any notice, Corbett moved into the empty seat. Natasha looked at him, startled, and gestured to him to move back.

'I can't see there.' He looked at her sweetly.

174

'Corbett...will you please move!' Her voice was urgent. but his smile only widened as he shook his head.

'No, I won't.'

'Corbett!' But at that moment the lights suddenly dimmed. Natasha went on urging him in the darkness, and behind them a row of dowagers complained.

'Ssshhh!'

At precisely that moment the usher's flashlight appeared at the end of the aisle. Natasha looked up, startled. At least Isabella was right on time. She was standing in momentary confusion, staring down at the man in the white hat.

'Hi, darlin', you must be Natasha's cousin. Now isn't that a nice coat.' It was spoken in a loud stage whisper as the dowagers came alive again, and the Texan introduced Isabella to his wife. Isabella murmured pleasantly and glanced down the row of seats. Natasha signalled to her, and Isabella nodded, progressing slowly over seven pairs of feet and knees.

'I'm sorry...oh...sorry...terribly sorry.' She had reached Natasha, who only pointed silently to the empty seat...Isabella nodded, glanced at Corbett, climbed over both of them, settled her coat around her and sat down. The movie was just beginning and the theatre was very dark, but as she sat there she turned to Corbett, and they exchanged a smile. At first she was too excited to watch the movie; instead she found herself staring up and down the long dark aisles. What did they look like, who were they, what were they wearing, and could they possibly understand how good it felt to be out? She was smiling to herself in the darkness, staring happily at the back of elaborate hair-dos and well-barbered heads. At last she let her eyes be drawn by the movie and sat happily, almost childlike, enjoying what was happening on the screen. How long had it been since she'd even been to a movie? She thought for a moment. Early September, with Amadeo. Seven months...

175

she heard herself utter a small happy groan. The film itself was delightful, and she was enchanted by its beauty and the humour of the two stars. She watched, engrossed, until the curtain went down slowly and the house-lights began to come up.

'Is it over?' Isabella glanced at Corbett in confusion, not satisfied that the story had been resolved. But he was smiling at her, amused, and pointed at the words on the screen almost hidden by the gold tassels of the heavy curtain still swinging closed.

'It's only intermission.' And the smile deepened. 'It's nice to see you, Isabella. Let's go to the lobby for a drink.'

But as Isabella nodded, Natasha's hand was instantly on her arm, and her eyes held Corbett's with a dark frown.

'I think she should stay here.'

He paused for an instant, looking with interest at Isabella and then with concern at his old friend. He wanted to tell her to relax a bit, that he was neither a masher nor a rapist, but this wasn't the place nor the time. He turned again to Isabella. 'Would you like me to bring something back?' But Isabella only shook her head, smiling politely, and sat down again in her seat.

As soon as he had left, Natasha moved closer, wishing once again that she hadn't agreed to let Isabella come.

Isabella only smiled at her and patted her hand. 'Don't look so worried, Natasha. Everything is fine.' She was getting the chance she had so desperately wanted. To watch the people, to look at the gowns, to hear the laughter, to be 'there'. And suddenly Natasha saw her standing, looking slowly around.

She hissed at her fiercely. 'Sit down.'

But Isabella was Isabella, and before Natasha could stop her, she had begun to slide slowly in the opposite direction, towards the other aisle. 'Isab – . . . goddamn . . .' She whispered to herself through clenched teeth, standing up quickly, apologising, avoiding toes in elegant slippers, and trying to stay close to Isabella. But the instant they had joined the throng in the aisle, Isabella seemed to be swept from her on a current of people who swirled between then, laughed gaily, tried not to spill drinks, and tugged at Natasha's long sleeves.

'Natasha! Darling! I missed you at – '

She muttered quickly, 'Later,' and pressed on. But she was a good distance behind Isabella now, cascading into the lobby with the others, where a crowd pressed around the makeshift bar.

'Changed your mind?' It was Corbett Ewing, suddenly towering above Isabella as she looked up at him with a smile.

'Yes, thank you.'

'Would you like a drink?'

'No, I – ' Far behind her Natasha was suddenly staring, a look of panic in her eyes. She waved frantically to Corbett, who only waved back.

Natasha did not return the smile but gazed frantically at Isabella. She had to get to her. She motioned to her to turn around. Isabella did so, puzzled, wondering if there was something special she should see. It was Natasha who saw the danger approaching, in the form of two reporters, one from *Women's Wear Daily* and the other from the People section of *Time*. The woman from *WWD*, spiderlike in a black jersey dress, had stared at Isabella for a moment, knit her brows, and then was attempting to move closer, having whispered something to the man she had in tow. Meanwhile Isabella was smiling at Corbett and casting Natasha an embarrassed look.

Natasha was still not able to get near her. She wanted to kick them, bite them, shove them aside. She had to get to Isabella, before the two reporters, before . . .

It was too late. A double flash exploded in Isabella's eyes. She wheeled suddenly, frightened, briefly blinded by the lights. She grabbed at Corbett's arm just as Natasha reached her and pulled her to her side.

Corbett was still standing there, startled, his drink in his hand, his powerful body blocking the reporters who had momentarily been shoved aside. Natasha grabbed his arm then, shouting above the din.

'Get her out of here for God's sake! Now.' She grabbed his drink from him, and both his arms were around Isabella like a fortress as another flash of light went off in her face. Before she knew what had happened, he had propelled her half-way across the room. Dimly Isabella heard the murmur that had gone up in the lobby. Corbett held her arm tightly, and they ran out of the lobby to his Rolls-Royce. Isabella had not said a word, but as she ran with him something told him that this was not new to her. They barrelled into the car. As the door was still closing Corbett was shouting, 'Get us the hell out of here.' It was only then that the reporters came hurtling after them through the door. Corbett grinned. Football in college still paid off now and then. And he had to admire Isabella. She had come the distance with him, without ladylike pretensions about high heels or falling or what she might be doing to her dress. She sat on the seat now, without speaking, trying to gather her wits and catch her breath. They had already turned the corner, and the reporters were left gaping at the kerb.

'Are you all right?' Corbett turned to her now, opening a compartment and pulling out a brandy decanter and one glass.

'How convenient.' And then, smiling faintly, 'Yes. I'm fine.'

'Does this happen to you often?' He handed her the glass, and she took it.

178

'Not in a while.'

He looked at Isabella and noticed the hand that trembled as she held her glass. At least she was human, despite the composure. She was no longer even out of breath. 'Natasha didn't tell me where I should take you. Do you want to go home? Or would it be safer at my place?'

'No, our place will be fine. And I apologise for – for the ugly scene.'

'Not at all. My life is extremely dull by comparison.' He gave the address to the chauffeur. But he was suddenly unnerved by what he had seen of Isabella. Despite the composure, there was a look of despair on her face. 'I don't mean to make light of it. It must be very unnerving. Is that why you left Italy? Or is this something that only happens to you here?' His voice was gentle as he settled back next to her on the seat.

'No. This . . . it happened at home too. I – I'm sorry but I can't explain. It's very awkward. I'm only very sorry to have spoiled your evening. You can just drop me off and go back.'

But that was not at all what Corbett Ewing had in mind. There was something rare and strange about this woman that touched his heart. Something hidden, something remarkable and oblique. She had regal bearing, beauty, he could see in her eyes that there was humour and wit, but there was also something else, something buried, something more. Pain, sorrow, loneliness, he had seen it now, with her dark, smouldering look. He sat very quietly for a moment, then as they turned into the park he spoke easily again.

'How's my friend Alessandro?' They exchanged a smile, and Corbett was pleased to note that the mention of the boy seemed to unbend her.

'He's very well.'

'And what about you? Bored yet?' He knew that she

179

rarely left the apartment, except for brief walks with Natasha. He didn't understand it, but it seemed to be all she did. But now she shook her head vehemently with a smile.

'Oh, no, not bored! I've been so busy!'

'Have you?' He looked intrigued. 'Doing what?'

'Working.'

'Really? Did you bring your work with you?' She nodded. 'In what line?'

For an instant she was stumped. But she came up with an answer quickly. 'With my family. In . . . art.'

'Interesting. I'm afraid I can't claim anything as noble as my line of work.'

'What do you do?' Obviously something very successfully, she thought, as her eyes gently wandered over the wooden-and-leather interior of the new Rolls.

'A number of things, but mostly textiles. At least that's what I prefer. The rest I leave to the people I work with. My family began with textiles a long time ago and that's what I've always liked best.'

'That's interesting.' For a moment there was a light in Isabella's eyes. 'Are you particularly involved in any one kind?' She was dying to know if she bought from him but she didn't dare ask. Perhaps she could glean the information from something he said.

'Wools, linens, silks, cottons. We have a line of velvets that upholsters most of this country, and of course man-made fibres, synthetics, and some new things we're developing now.'

'I see, but not dress fabrics then.' She looked disappointed. Upholstery wasn't her bag.

'Yes, of course. We do garment fabrics too.' Garment. She cringed at the hideous word. Garment. Her dresses weren't garments. That was Seventh Avenue. What she did was haute couture. He couldn't decipher the look in her eyes but he was amused just the same. 'We probably even made the fabric for the dress you have on.' He allowed a rare burst of pride to show in his voice, but she looked at him then, haughty, the princess from Rome.

'This fabric is French.'

'In that case I apologise.' Amused, he backed down. 'Which brings to mind something far more important. You never told me your last name.'

She hesitated only for an instant. 'Isabella.'

'That's all?' He smiled at her. 'Just Isabella, the Italian friend?'

'That's right, Mister Ewing. That's all,' She looked at him long and hard, and he nodded slowly.

'I understand.' After what he had glimpsed at the theatre, he knew she had been through enough. Something very difficult had happened to this woman, and he wasn't going to pry. He didn't want to frighten her away from him.

They pulled up at that moment in front of Natasha's door, and with a small sigh Isabella turned to him and proffered her right hand. 'Thank you very much. And I'm terribly sorry to have spoiled your evening.'

'You didn't. I was just as happy to get out of there. I always find benefits a bore.'

'Do you?' She looked at him with interest. 'Why is that?'

'Too many people, too much small talk. Everyone is there for the wrong reasons, to see their cronies and not to benefit whatever cause. I prefer seeing my friends in small gatherings where we can hear each other talk.'

She nodded. In some ways she agreed with him. But in other ways evenings like that one were in her blood.

'May I see you inside, just to make sure no one is lurking in the halls?'

She laughed at the suspicion, but gratefully inclined her head.

'Thank you. But I'm quite sure I'm safe here.'

As she said it something told him that that was why she had come to America. To be safe.

'Let's just make sure.' He walked her to the elevator and then inside. 'I'll just take you up.'

Isabella said nothing until the elevator stopped, and then suddenly she felt awkward; he had been so incredibly nice.

'Would you like to come in for a moment? You know, you could wait for Natasha until she comes home.'

'Thank you, I'd like that.' They closed the door. 'Why didn't she come back with us, by the way, instead of staying to play *Meet the Press*?' That had puzzled him as he had run with Isabella, thinking of what Natasha had just said.

Isabella sighed as she looked at him. She could at least tell him that much. 'I think she felt it would be wiser if no one knew I was with her.'

'That's why you came in late?' She nodded, and he said, 'You lead a very mysterious life, Isabella.' He smiled, not asking further questions, as they sat down on the long white couch.

The rest of the evening passed quickly. They chatted about Italy, about textiles, about his home. He had a plantation he had bought in South Carolina, a farm in Virginia, and a house in New York.

'Do you keep horses in Virginia?'

'Yes, I do. Do you ride?'

She grinned at him over their brandies. 'I used to. But it's been a long time.'

'You and Natasha will have to bring the boys down there sometime. Would you have time for that before you go back?'

'I might.' But as they began to speak of it Natasha marched through the door. She looked wilted and exhausted and she looked Isabella straight in the eye.

'I told you you were crazy to try it. Do you have any idea what you've done?' Corbett was startled for a moment at the look on her face and the vehemence of her tone. But Isabella did not appear to be ruffled. She motioned to Natasha to sit down.

'Don't get so excited. It was nothing. They took some pictures. So what?' She tried to conceal her own worry and held out a warm hand.

But Natasha knew better. She turned her back in fury, and then stared at Corbett and then Isabella, as she pulled up the satin tunic and sat down.

'Do you have any idea who they were? *Women's Wear*, *Time* magazine. The third one was the Associated Press. And I think I might even have caught a glimpse of the society editor from *Vogue*. But the fact is, you ass hole, that it wouldn't have mattered if it was a twelve-year-old boy with a Brownie. Your game is up.'

What game? What was happening? Corbett was intrigued. He looked at both women and was quick to speak.

'Should I go?'

Natasha answered him before Isabella could. 'It doesn't matter, Corbett. I trust you. And by tomorrow morning the whole world will know.'

But Isabella was angry now. She stood up and walked around the room. 'That's absurd.'

'Is it, Isabella? You don't think anyone remembers you? You think in two months everyone has forgotten you? Do you really feel that safe? Because if you do, you're a fool.'

Corbett said nothing. He only watched Isabella's face. She was frightened, but determined, and she had the look of someone who had taken her chances, lost the first hand, and was not going to give in or quit. He wanted to comfort her, to tell her he'd protect her, to tell Natasha to settle down. His voice was deep and gentle when at last he spoke.

'Maybe nothing will come of it.'

Natasha only glared at him furiously, as though he had been part of the original plot. 'You're wrong, Corbett. You don't know how wrong you are. By tomorrow it will be in all of the papers.' She looked unhappily at Isabella. 'I'm right, you know.'

Isabella stood very still and spoke very softly. 'Maybe not.'

Chapter Nineteen

Corbett Ewing sat in his office, staring at the morning paper in despair. True to Natasha's predictions, it was all in the news. He was reading *The New York Times*. 'Isabella di San Gregorio, widow of the kidnapped and subsequently murdered couturier, Amadeo di San Gregorio . . .' It went on to explain once again every possible detail of the kidnapping and its eventual unhappy outcome. More interestingly it described in intricate detail how she had disappeared and it had been thought that she had taken refuge in a penthouse atop her couture house in Rome. There was a brief line, questioning if she had in fact been in the States all along, or if she had slipped away after the successful opening that week of San Gregorio's spring line. The article went on to mention that it was not known where she was staying and that discreet enquiries of prominent people in the fashion world had turned up nothing. Either they were co-operating in keeping her whereabouts secret or they didn't know. Signore Cattani, the American representative of San Gregorio in New York, said that he had heard from her more frequently than usual in recent months, but that he had no reason to believe that she was in New York and not Rome. There was also a mention of the fact that she had been seen at the film premiere escorted by a tall, white-haired man, that they had made good their escape together in a black chauffeured Rolls. But his identity had been uncertain. The reporters' interest had centred on their shock at seeing Isabella, and although one of the reporters had been under the impression that he was indeed a familiar face, no

185

one had actually thought to check him carefully, and all they had of him in the photographs was his back as they ran.

Corbett sighed, set down the paper, sat back in his chair, and swivelled slowly around. What did she know of him? What had Natasha said? He wished that, of all the women in the world, she were anyone but who she was. He sat, looking dejected, glancing at the paper, and then at his hands. Slowly his thoughts turned from his own worries to hers. Isabella di San Gregorio. It had never dawned on him before.

Natasha's cousin from Milan! He smiled to himself at the story and then smiled more broadly as he put together the rest of the pieces and remembered the whole silly game . . . he had told her he was in textiles . . . she had told him her family was in art. Yet she knew something about fabrics. And the way she bridled when she had told him that the satin for her outfit was surely not his but had been bought in France! He understood everything better now: the secrecy, their flight from the benefit, and Isabella's eyes filled with fear, as though she had lived that scene only too often, as though she had been haunted by it for much too long. Poor woman. What she must have gone through. He found himself also wondering how she managed to run her business from New York.

One thing was certain: Isabella di San Gregorio was a remarkable woman, a woman with talent and beauty and soul, but he wondered now if he would ever get to know her. If he even had a chance. He realised that there was only one answer, and it had to come from her. That night he would tell her. He couldn't take a chance of her finding out later and having it taint what he felt for her, what he wanted to help her do. If she'd let him. If she'd even speak to him again.

With a long sigh of resignation Corbett Ewing stood up

and left his desk. He looked far up Park Avenue to where he knew Isabella hid, in Natasha's apartment, with her child and Natasha's, and then he sat down again and picked up the phone

Isabella was still talking to Bernardo in Rome. He had first got the news at noon. His secretary had brought him the afternoon paper, which he read in horror, his eyes flaming, but without saying a word. He had called Isabella at six in the morning, and at seven, and now again, just after ten.

'All right, goddamn it! So what! I did it! There's no changing that now. I'll go back into hiding. No one will know if I'm still here. I can't bear it any longer. I work night and day. I eat with the children. I take short walks after dark. No people, Bernardo. No one to look at and laugh with and talk to. No one intelligent to talk business with. The only excitement in my evenings is provided by Jason's electric train.' Her voice pleaded with him, but Bernardo didn't want to hear.

'All right, go ahead, make a spectacle of yourself. Expose yourself. But if something happens to you or Alessandro, don't come crying to me, because it'll be your own goddamn fault.' And then suddenly he took a long breath and slowed down. At the other end he could hear Isabella crying softly into the phone. 'All right, all right, I'm sorry . . . Isabella, please . . . but I was so frightened for you. It was such a foolish thing to do.' He lit a cigarette and then stubbed it out.

'I know.' She sobbed again and then tiredly wiped her eyes. 'I just felt I had to. I really didn't think anyone would see me or that there would be any harm.'

'Do you understand differently now? Do you realise how visible you are?'

She nodded miserably. 'Yes. I used it love it. Now I hate it. I'm a prisoner of my own face.'

'It's a beautiful face, and I love it, so stop crying.' His voice was gentle.

'So what do I do now? Come home?'

'Are you crazy? It would be worse than last night. No. You stay there. And I'll try telling them that you only left here after the collection and you're coming back to Europe. I'll hint to them something about France. That will make sense to them because of your mother's family there.'

'They're all dead.' She sniffed loudly and blew her nose.

'I know that. But it makes sense that you'd have ties there.'

'You think they'll believe it?'

'Who cares? As long as they don't see you out in public again, you're safe. No one seems to know where you're staying. Did Natasha leave the party with you?' He prayed for a moment that one of them had been smarter than that.

'No. A friend of hers took me home. She left separately.'

'Good.' He paused for a moment, trying to sound off-handed. 'And by the way, who was the man in the photograph?' That was all he needed. For her to get involved with someone over there.

'He is a friend of Natasha's, Bernardo. Relax.'

'He won't tell anyone where you are?'

'Of course not.'

'You're too trusting. I'll get busy here with the press. And Isabella, please . . . for God's sake, *cara*, use your head and stay home.'

'*Capisco, capisco.* Don't worry. Now I understand. Even here I'm a prisoner. More so even than I was in Rome.'

'One day that will be over. You just have to be patient for a while. It's only been seven months since the kidnapping, you know. In a few months, in a year, it will be old news.' Old news . . . she was thinking that she would be old news by then too.

'Yeah. Maybe. And Bernardo . . . I'm sorry to give you so much trouble.' She suddenly felt like a very naughty child.

'Don't worry. I'm used to it. I'd be lost without it by now.'

'How's your ulcer?' She smiled into the phone.

'Doing beautifully. I think it's growing bigger and stronger every hour.'

'Stop that. Take it easy, please, will you?'

'Yeah. Sure. Now get to work on those problems with the ready-to-wear for Asia, and if you get bored, you can start on the summer line.'

'You're too good to me.'

'*Ecco*. I know. I'll call you later if anything else comes up. Nothing should if you keep your door closed and stay home.'

'*Capisco*.' They said ciao and hung up. At her end Isabella felt resentful. Why should she have to stay home, and what right did he have to tell her not to trust Corbett? She stepped out of her office, wandered into the kitchen, and found Natasha pouring herself a cup of coffee and looking grim.

'Did you have a nice chat with Bernardo?'

'Yes, lovely. But do me a favour, not you too.' Natasha had been quick to storm into her room at seven, with the newspaper in her hand and a look of fury still on her face. 'I don't think I can take any more today. I made a mistake. I was over-confident. I shouldn't have gone out last night, but I did. I had to. I couldn't stand it anymore. But I realise now that I have to stay in the background at least for a while.'

'What's he going to tell the press?'

'That I was here for a few days and that I'm going to live in France.'

'That ought to keep them scouting around Paris for a

day or two. And you, what are going to do?'

'What I have been doing. My work and not much else.'

'At least one nice thing happened out of all that ruckus last night.' She watched Isabella intently.

'What?' Isabella looked blank.

'You ran into Corbett again.' Natasha paused, watching her face. 'And may I say that you made quite a hit.'

'With Corbett? Don't be silly.' But as she turned away Natasha was sure she saw her blush.

'Do you like him?' There was a long silence. 'Well?'

But slowly Isabella turned to her with a warm light in her eyes. 'Natasha, don't push.'

She nodded. 'I think he might call you.' Isabella nodded silently in answer, but her heart did a little leap as she went back to her office and closed the door.

Chapter Twenty

Isabella was still in her room, dressing for dinner, when Corbett arrived. From behind her closed door, as she listened, she heard the delighted shrieks of Jason and in a moment the equally pleased giggles of her own son. She smiled to herself. It wouldn't do him any harm to see a man for a change. It had been too long since he had been around Bernardo, and unlike her own home, Natasha didn't have any men working in her household. Alessandro had contact with only females, which lately had made him miss his father all the more.

Isabella zipped up the black wool dress she was wearing, smoothed her black stockings, and slipped into black suede shoes. She put on black enamel and pearl ear-rings and ran a hand over her dark, severely worn hair. She grinned to herself as she flicked the light off. The swan had turned into an ugly duckling again. But it didn't matter. She wasn't trying to woo Corbett Ewing, and like Alessandro, it would do her good to have a male friend.

When she walked quietly into the living-room, she found him besieged by both boys, who had just opened two large packages that had yielded identical firemen's hats equipped with flashing lights and sirens with two firemen's coats to match.

'Look, we're firemen now!' They donned their equipment and zoomed around the room. Alessandro was obviously delighted to see Corbett again, and the shrieking from the sirens was appalling, as Natasha winced.

'Lovely gift, Corbett. Remind me to call and thank you tomorrow morning at six o'clock.'

He started to answer and then saw Isabella standing across the room. He rose quickly, looked at her nervously, and walked towards her to take her hand. 'Hello, Isabella. How are you?' But her eyes told him how she was. She was tired. Exhausted. But he found himself struck by her beauty again. She would have been surprised to hear it, but he decided that she looked even more so in the stark black wool, without the magnificence of satins and the striking white coat. 'You must have had quite a day.' He rolled his eyes sympathetically, and she smiled as she followed him into the room and sat down on the couch.

'Oh, I survived it. One always does. What about you?'

'For me it was easy. All they knew about me was that I had white hair. The only thing they didn't say was that I was an elderly gentleman –' He started to say more but the boys cut him off.

'Look, look, it squirts water!'

'Oh, no!' Jason had discovered that there was a little pipe fitted somewhere into the hat that could be filled with water and subsequently used to douse all of one's friends.

'Corbett, I may never speak to you again!' Natasha groaned and announced to the boys that it was time for bed.

'No, Mommy . . . Aunt Isabella . . . no . . . please!' Jason looked at them pleadingly, but Alessandro simply moved in closer to Corbett's knees. He was staring at him with interest while Jason continued to play with the hat. Isabella had never seen him so quiet, and from a little distance she watched. Corbett had noticed it too and he turned to smile at him and casually put an arm around the small shoulders.

'What do you think of all this, Alessandro?'

'I think it is . . .' He groped for the right English, 'very fun. I like very much the hat.' He stared up at Corbett admiringly and grinned.

'I thought they were pretty good too. Would you like to come and see a real firehouse with me sometime?'

'For firemans?' He looked at Corbett and then at his mother with awe. 'You go too?' Isabella nodded, noticing that Alessandro now spoke in English to her too.

'Of course. I meant both of you. What do you say?'

'*Si!*' But that was too much for him. He spent the next five minutes rattling frantically to his mother in Italian. There were lengthy discussions about how wonderful American firemen must be, what they wore, how big their trucks were, and whether or not they really used a brass pole.

'*Non so . . . non so . . . aspetta . . .* wait, we'll find all that out!' Isabella was laughing with him, and she watched with amusement as he shifted his seat from next to hers on to Corbett's knee.

'We will go soon?'

'I promise!'

'Very good.' He clapped his hands and took off in hot pursuit of Jason, and moments later they were banished to their room, despite begging, pleading, protests, and outraged comments that it was too early for firemen to go to bed. When at last they were gone, the room was strangely quiet.

Corbett watched Isabella once again. 'You have a lovely boy.'

'I'm afraid he's a little eager for male company, as you probably observed.' But after what Corbett had undoubtedly read in the papers that day, there was no need to hide the truth. 'In Rome he had one of my business associates who is his godfather. Here he has' – she looked at Natasha – 'only us. It's not quite the same thing. But you needn't feel obliged to take him to a firehouse. The gifts you brought are marvellous. You've done more than enough.'

'Don't be silly. I'd love it. Natasha can tell you. Jason is one of my best friends.'

'Fortunately,' she confirmed it, 'since his charming father never shows up.' She and Isabella had discussed that often in the past two months. But Jason seemed happy anyway, and having another child around was doing both boys a lot of good. It made up for other lacks, other losses, as neither of their mothers could.

'I'll work it out for some time this week. Maybe this weekend, if you're all free.' But as he said it Isabella looked at him and laughed.

'Oh, yes, we're quite free.'

Corbett was glad that she was laughing. After what he had read that day, he was not sure how she still could. But as he watched her he realised how very strong she was. She was bruised, she was lonely, but she was undaunted, and there was still laughter there, and fire, and a certain indestructible joy. He smiled at her openly and then raised an eyebrow.

'Tell me, Isabella,' he said, 'would you like to hear some more from me about textiles tonight? Or shall we just discuss art?' He was laughing at her now too. In a moment they were all laughing, and the atmosphere in the room was easy and free.

'I'm sorry. I couldn't help it. But what you told me was very interesting. Even if we do buy most of our satins in France.'

'That's your mistake. But the least you could have done was tell me that you were in fashion or something related to the trade.'

'Why? I was enjoying what you had to tell me. And you were absolutely right about everything except synthetics. I hate using them in couture.'

'But you do use them in ready-to-wear, don't you?'

'Obviously. I have to, for durability, and the price.'

'Then I'm not so far off.' They launched into an intricate discussion of chemicals and colours. Quietly Natasha left them. When she returned, the conversation had moved on to Asia, the difficulties of doing business there, the climate, the financial arrangements, problems of exchanges, open markets, all highly specialised terms, until at last Hattie announced dinner and Natasha yawned.

'I adore you both, but you're boring the hell out of me.'

'I'm sorry.' Isabella was quick to apologise. 'It's just very nice to have someone to talk to about business for a change.'

'I'll forgive you.'

Corbett smiled at his hostess.

The three of them had a delightful evening. They made their way to lemon soufflé and then finally espresso as Hattie passed a small silver platter covered with mints.

'I shouldn't.' Natasha sounded like Scarlett O'Hara as she plopped four of the tiny candies into her mouth.

'Neither should I.' Isabella hesitated, but then shrugged. 'But why not? According to Natasha and Bernardo, I'm going to be in hiding for the next ten years anyway, so I might as well get enormous and fat. I can let my hair grow to my ankles . . .'

Natasha quickly interrupted, 'I didn't say ten years. I said one.'

'What difference does it make? One year? Ten? Now I know how people feel when they're sentenced to prison. It never seems real until you've living it, and once you are, it's difficult to believe it will ever stop. It just goes on and on and on until one day it's over, and by then it probably doesn't matter any more.' She looked serious as she stirred her coffee and Corbett watched.

'I don't know how you stand it. I'm not sure I could.'

'Apparently I don't stand it very gracefully or I'd never have indulged in that fiasco last night. Thank God for you,

Corbett, or I would have been thrown to the wolves, and by now I wouldn't even be able to stay here at Natasha's. I'd have to be hiding alone with Alessandro some place else.' The three of them were considerably sobered by the thought.

'I'm glad I was there then.'

'So am I.' She looked at him openly, and slowly she smiled. 'I'm afraid I was very foolish. But also very lucky. Thank you again.' She had come to her senses, but he was shaking his head.

'I didn't do anything. Except run like hell.'

'That was enough.' For a moment their eyes met across the table, and he looked at her with a warm smile. Reluctantly they left the dining-room and returned to the living-room to sit by the fire. They chatted about Natasha's books, the theatre, travel, and events in New York, and for a moment Natasha looked worried seeing a look of longing come into Isabella's eyes. Corbett understood quickly, and for a moment they were all quiet. And then Natasha stood up lazily and turned her back to the fire.

'Well, you two. I think I'm going to be rude for a change. I'm tired.' But she knew also that Corbett had wanted to speak to Isabella alone. Surprised, Isabella waited for Corbett to suggest that he should go, but he didn't. He stood to kiss Natasha, and then they were alone.

He watched her briefly as she looked absently into the fire, the glow lighting her face softly, the light reflecting in her large dark eyes. He wanted to tell her how lovely she looked, but knew instinctively that he could not.

'Isabella . . .' His voice was whisper-soft, and she turned her face towards his. 'I'm awfully sorry about last night.'

'Don't be. It was inevitable, I suppose. I only wished that it could be different.'

196

'Natasha's right, you know. Eventually, it will be.'

'But not for a very long time.' The laughter had faded, and she looked at him wistfully. 'In some ways I've been spoiled.'

'Is that sort of thing important to you, like last night?'

'Not really. But people are. What they're doing, what they look like, what they think. It's very difficult suddenly living without them in my own tiny world.'

'It needn't be quite as tiny as this.' He glanced around the softly-lit living-room and turned his eyes to hers with a smile. 'There are ways for you to get out without being seen.'

'I tried that last night.'

'No, you didn't. You walked right into the bull-ring, dressed like the matador, and when everyone noticed you, you were surprised.'

She laughed at the comparison. 'I hadn't thought of it quite that way.'

He laughed softly too. 'I'm not sure if I said just the right thing. But you can get out of here. You can go for drives in the country. For long walks. There's no need to lock yourself up here entirely. You need it. You need to get out.'

She stretched unhappily, trying to quell the yearning in her heart.

'Will you let me take you out sometime? With Alessandro perhaps? Or alone?'

'That would be very nice.' She sat very still for a moment and looked into his eyes. 'But you don't have to, you know. You're very kind.'

He wouldn't take his eyes from hers. He shook his head softly, then looked away. 'I understand more than you think I do. I lost my wife a long time ago. Not as shockingly as you lost your husband. But it was intolerably painful in its own way. I thought I would die without her in the beginning. One loses all that is familiar, all that matters, everything that really counts. The one person who knows how you think, how you laugh, how you cry, how you feel, the person who remembers the favourite jokes of your childhood, the worst fears, the person who knows it all, who has the key. Suddenly you're left alone and you're certain that no one will ever understand again.'

'And do they?' Isabella watched him, fighting back tears. 'Does someone else learn the language, understand the secrets; does anyone ever really care again?' She was thinking, *Will I ever care again?*

'Eventually I'm sure there is always someone. Maybe the secrets aren't quite the same, maybe they laugh differently, or they cry more, or their needs are differently geared to yours. But there are other people, Isabella. As much as you don't want to hear it, it's something you should know.'

'Have there been for you? Anyone who could replace her?'

'In some ways no. But I haven't really been open to it, not unlike you. What has happened though is that I've learned to live with it. It doesn't hurt every day. But then again I didn't lose my home, my country, my whole way of life as you have right now.'

She sighed softly. 'The only two things I haven't lost are my business and my child. Which is why I'm here. There was a false alarm about Alessandro, and I decided that I couldn't live that way any more.'

'But you still have those two things, and no one can take them from you. Not the business and not the child. They are both safe here with you.'

'Alessandro is, but I worry about the business a great deal.'

'I don't think you have to. From what I've read of it, it seems to be quite secure.'

'For now. But I can't run it this way forever. You of all people must understand that.'

He did, better than he wanted to tell her. After what she had just told him, he couldn't say more. He felt a weight settle on his shoulders as he warmed his hands at the fire.

'Eventually there are changes you can make. You can open a larger office here. You can divide your administration in such a way as to allow you to run it from anywhere. But only if you have to. And this probably isn't the right time.'

'I plan to go back to Rome.'

He nodded sagely in answer, saying nothing. Then softly: 'In time I'm sure you will. And in the meantime you're here. I'd like to help you make the most of that. The one thing that saved me when Beth died was my friends.'

Isabella nodded her understanding; she knew that only too well.

'Corbett . . .' She looked at him with tears suddenly shining in her eyes. 'Do you ever get over the feeling that any day now she's coming home? I don't think anyone understands it. But I keep feeling that, as though he were only on a trip.'

He smiled gently and nodded. 'In some ways he is. I believe that one day we'll all meet again. But now we have this life to make better. We have to make the most of it while we're here. But in answer to your question, yes, I used to feel that Beth was only out for a while, for a few hours, away for a couple of days, visiting, shopping, somewhere. I'd hear the elevator, or a door would close in my apartment, and I'd think "She's home!" And a minute later I'd feel even worse than before. Maybe it's a game that we play with ourselves to keep from knowing the truth. Or maybe it's just hard to break old habits. Someone comes home every day and you think that they will forever. The only thing that changes in the end is eventually that someone no longer comes home. What it does is make you very grateful for what you have, while you have it, because now you know how brief and ephemeral it sometimes is.' They sat quietly again for a while as the ashes in the fire dimly glowed.

'Seven and a half months is not very long. But it's long enough to be very lonely and to realise that you really are on your own.'

'It frightens me sometimes. No, that's not true. It terrifies me.'

'You don't look very terrified to me.' She looked calm, pulled together, and able to handle almost everything, and he was sure that in the last seven and a half months she had. 'Just don't let people push you. Go at your own pace.'

'I don't have a pace. Except in my work. That's the only life I have now.'

'Now, only for now. Don't forget that. It's not forever. Remind yourself of that every day. If it gets unbearably painful, tell yourself that it is only right now. When I lost Beth, a friend told me that – a woman. She said that it was a little bit like having a child. When you're in labour and it gets unbearable, you think it will go on forever, that you'll never survive. But it isn't forever, it is only a few hours. And then it's over, finished, behind you. You've done it, you've arrived.'

She smiled at the comparison. She had had a hard time when Alessandro was born. 'I'll try to remind myself.'

'Good.'

And then she looked at him questioningly. 'Do you have children, Corbett?'

But he shook his head. 'Only those I borrow occasionally from friends.'

'That may not be such a bad arrangement.' She grinned at him. 'You may feel that way, especially after you've gone to the firehouse with Jason and Alessandro.'

'I'll enjoy it.' Now what about you?'

'What about me?'

'Would you like to go for a drive tomorrow?'

'Aren't you working?' She looked startled.

'It's Saturday. Are you?'

'I'd forgotten. And I was going to but' – she looked warmly at him – 'I'd love to go for a drive. In broad daylight?'

'Of course.' He looked momentarily victorious.

'There are curtains in the backseat of my car. We can draw them until we get a little way out of town.'

'How mysterious.' She was laughing again, and Corbett stood up as she held out her hand. 'Thank you, Corbett.' He was going to tease her about being formal, but decided that it would be wiser not to. He shook her hand then and walked to the door.

'I'll see you tomorrow, Isabella.'

'Thank you.' She smiled again as the elevator reached them. 'Good night.'

This time when he left her he was smiling, but a tremor of fear ran through him when he remembered all that he hadn't said.

Chapter Twenty-One

The next day they drove into Connecticut for the day, hidden deep in the secrecy of his curtained Rolls, chatting about business again, this time about her grandfather's couture house in Paris and then once again about Rome.

'How do you know so much about all this?' She looked at him intently as they drove beneath trees that were just beginning to show leaves.

'It's no different than any business. Whatever the commodity you deal in, the concepts are often the same.' The idea intrigued her. She had never even thought of applying what she knew of her business to anything else.

'Are you involved in a great many undertakings?' But she already knew from his extensive knowledge that he was. She thought it strange how close-mouthed he was about business – most men were so eager to talk about nothing else.

'Yes.'

'Why don't you tell me more about them?'

'Because they would all bore you. Some of them even bore me.' She laughed with him and stretched happily as they got out of the car.

'If you only knew how long it's been since I've walked on grass and seen trees. And finally, finally, there's a little green here. I thought it was going to be grey forever.'

He smiled at her gently, 'See. it's the same thing. Nothing is forever, Isabella. Nothing good, and nothing bad. We both know that by now. You can't chop down a tree because it isn't yet in bloom. You have to wait, nurture

202

it, love it. In time it revives again.' He wanted to tell her, 'So will you.'

'Perhaps you're right.' But she was too happy to think of the past now. She just wanted to breathe deeply and enjoy the country and her first taste of spring.

'Why didn't you bring Alessandro?' He looked down at her.

'He and Jason had a date with some friends in the park. But he told me to be sure and remind you about the firehouse.' She wagged a finger at him, laughing. 'I told you so!'

'I've already arranged it. For Tuesday afternoon.'

'You're a man of your word then.'

He looked at her seriously. 'Yes, Isabella, I am.'

But she knew that already. Everything about him suggested the man of honour, someone you could rely on and trust with the secrets of your heart. She hadn't met anyone like him in years; it had been even longer since she had opened up to anyone as she had to him. Her only confidants had been Amadeo, Bernardo, and Natasha. But she had lost Amadeo, and she and Bernardo, well, she and Bernardo were not talking about personal matters anymore. There was too much distance between them, and, too, she was feeling herself withdraw from him and he from her. So she was left with Natasha, and now Corbett. It was amazing how in a few short days she had come to trust him and all that he said.

'What were you thinking?'

'That it's strange how comfortable I feel with you. Like an old friend.'

'Why is that so strange?' They stopped at a fallen tree and sat down. His long legs were stretched out before him, crossed at the ankles; his broad shoulders were encased in fine English tweed. He looked amazingly young, despite the prematurely white hair.

203

'It's strange only because I don't know you. Not really, not who you are.'

'Yes, you do. You know all the essentials about me. Where I live, what I do. You know that I've been Natasha's friend for years. You know other things. I've also told you a great deal.' He was referring to Beth, his lost wife. Isabella nodded quietly and then looked up at the trees, her long neck arched skyward, her hair hanging down her back. He was smiling at her; for a moment she looked like a child on a swing.

He was intrigued by her, by her great beauty, and her diamond-sharp mind, the delicate elegance combined with the rare strength and the power of command. She was all contrasts and rich shadings, with mountains and valleys and textures that he loved. 'Why do you always wear black, Isabella? I've never seen you wear a colour, except that night; the coat you wore was white.'

She looked at him simply. 'For Amadeo. I'll wear black like this for a year.'

'I'm sorry. I should have known that. But people don't do that any more in the States.' He looked upset, as though he had said something he shouldn't have, but Isabella smiled.

'It's all right. It doesn't upset me. It's a custom, that's all.'

'You even wear black at home.' She nodded. 'You must look marvellous in colours though – dove colours, and pale peach, and bright blues, and magenta – with your dark hair . . .' He looked dreamy and boyish. She laughed.

'You should be a designer, Corbett.'

'Sometimes I am.'

'Like with what?' Her eyes grew serious as she straightened her head to look at him more closely. He was an interesting man.

204

'Oh, I picked out some designs for an airline once.' He was afraid to say much more

'Was it successful?'

'The airline?'

'No, the design. Did it look well?'

'I thought so.'

'You used your textiles?' He nodded, and she seemed to approve.

'That was good business. I try to use interchangeable things once in a while between my ready-to-wear and my couture. It's not always easy though because of the fabrics. But I do it when I can.'

'Where did you learn all this?' He was fascinated, and she smiled.

'My grandfather. He was a genius. The one and only Jacques-Louis Parel. I watched him, I listened, I learned from him. I always knew I'd be a designer. After I spent a year here, I set up my own design studio in Rome.' That was how she had met Amadeo, how it had all begun.

'Congenital genius then.'

'Obviously.' With a grin she picked a tiny wildflower.

'And humility too.' He put an arm easily around her shoulder and stood up then. 'How about some lunch?'

'Can we go somewhere?' She looked delighted, but he quickly shook his head.

'No.' For a moment her eyes fell.

'I was stupid to ask.'

'We'll come back this summer. There's a nice restaurant just over that hill. But in the meantime, Isabella, I made some provisions.'

'You did?'

'Of course. You didn't expect me to starve you, did you? I have a little more sense than that. Besides, I get hungry too, you know.'

'You brought a picnic?'

'More or less.' He held out a hand to her, and she got up from the log, dusting off her black skirt and pulling the black blazer closer around her as they walked back to the car. Corbett drove to a nearby lake, stopped, and unpacked a large leather bag. The picnic consisted of pâté, Brie, French bread and caviar, cookies and pastries and fruits.

She looked at it all delightedly, spread out on the little table he had popped out of a compartment on the back of the front seat. 'My heavens, this is gorgeous. The only thing missing is the champagne.'

He bowed from his seat and looked mischievously at her. 'You spoke too soon.' He opened the bar again and withdrew a large bottle resting in a bucket of ice. He set out two glasses.

'You think of everything.'

'Almost.'

She played with Alessandro through a rainy Sunday and was grateful that it hadn't rained the day before. On Monday she worked for fifteen hours, and on Tuesday she spent the day making calls to Hong Kong and Europe, to Brazil, and to Bangkok.

She was in the kitchen in bare feet and blue jeans, sipping coffee, when the doorbell rang. She looked up startled. It was ten minutes too early for it to be the boys. Hattie was marketing, and Natasha had told her she'd be gone all day. With a puzzled look Isabella went to the front door and looked through the tiny peep-hole and then grinned. It was Corbett, also wearing an old sweater and jeans.

'How could you forget something so important? It's firehouse day, of course!'

Isabella looked embarrassed. 'I forgot.'

'Are the boys here? If not, I'll have to take you. The firehouse will never forgive me if we don't show up. I'll just say you're my niece.' His eyes wandered over Isabella appreciatively, suddenly noticing the long thin legs and the narrow hips.

'The boys will be home in five minutes, and they'll be thrilled. And how are you?'

'I'm fine. What are you two up to? Working as usual?'

'Of course.' Isabella looked at him grandly and then beckoned him back towards her office door. 'Would you like to see the beautiful office Natasha gave me when I arrived?' She was like a little girl showing off her room. And he followed her willingly and whistled when he stepped inside. 'Isn't it lovely?'

'It certainly is.' Her work was spread out on the table, mountains of papers, and the floor was covered with neat stacks of designs. 'This must take some getting used to. I imagine you have a little more space in Rome.'

'Just a bit.' She smiled to herself, thinking of the enormous offices she and Amadeo had shared on the fourth floor. 'But I'm managing.'

'It looks like you are.'

At that moment the boys arrived, with whoops at discovering that he was there. Ten minutes later they had left again, with Corbett, and they didn't return for another two hours.

'How was it?' Isabella was waiting for them when they got home, and they told her in every detail. Alessandro announced to her excitedly that there really was a brass pole, calling it over his shoulder as Hattie finally dragged him off for a bath. 'And more to the point,' she said to Corbett when they were alone, 'how are you? Exhausted?'

'A little. But we had a wonderful time.'

'What a good sport you are. Would you like a drink?'

'Please. Scotch and water on a lot of rocks.'

'Very American.' She cast him a look of mock disapproval and went to Natasha's white marble bar. 'What should I be drinking?'

'Cinzano, Pernod, or maybe kir.'

'I'll remember that next time. But frankly, I prefer Scotch.' She handed it to him, and he grinned. 'Where's Natasha?'

'Dressing for dinner and a gallery opening.'

'And you, Cinderella?'

'The usual. I'm going out for my walk.'

'You're not afraid to do that, Isabella?' He looked at her with sudden concern.

'I'm very careful.' She didn't even stroll back on Madison Avenue anymore. 'It's not very exciting, but it helps.' He nodded.

'May I join you tonight?'

She answered quickly. 'Sure.'

They waited until he had finished his drink and Natasha had left for the evening before they went out. They covered her usual route and a bit more, jogging part of the way and strolling the rest of the way home. She always felt better once she'd done that. As though her body were crying out for exercise and fresh air. It still wasn't enough, but it was better than nothing.

'Now I know how those poor little dogs feel, locked up in apartments all day.'

'I feel that way in my office sometimes.'

'Yes.' She looked at him reproachfully. 'But you can get out.'

He seemed to be thinking about something then as they returned to the apartment, but the boys set upon them quickly, in their pyjamas now, with freshly washed hair, and the moment was lost. Isabella watched him with them for half an hour as they wrestled and played. Corbett seemed to be having a good time. He had a lovely way with children, as he did with everyone. But it pleased her to see the children with him. He was their only man. Hattie finally arrived on the scene though and despite frantic protests took them both off to bed.

'Do you want to stay for dinner?'

'I'd love it.'

In the kitchen they ate a cosy dinner that Hattie had left for them to serve themselves -- fried chicken and corn on the cob – and dripped butter over their plates. After dinner they wandered to the back of the house and settled down in Natasha's pleasant little den. Isabella put on some music, and Corbett comfortably stretched his long legs.

'I'm awfully glad I went to that benefit last week. Do you know I almost didn't go?'

'Why not?'

'I thought I'd be bored.' He laughed at the thought of it, and Isabella did too.

'Were you?'

'Hardly. And not for an instant since then.'

'Neither have I.' She smiled at him easily and was surprised when he took her hand.

'I'm glad. I'm so sorry for what you've been through. I wish I could change all that.' But he couldn't, and he knew it. Not yet.

'Life isn't easy sometimes, but as you said, we always survive.'

'Some do, some don't. But you're a survivor. So am I.'

She nodded, agreeing. 'I think my grandfather taught me that. No matter what happened, what went wrong, he picked himself up and did something better immediately afterwards. Sometimes it took him a little time to catch his breath, but he always managed to do something spectacular. I admire that.'

'You're a great deal like him,' he said, and she smiled her thanks. 'Why did he finally sell the business?'

'He was eighty-three and tired and old. My grandmother was dead, and my mother had no interest in the business. I was the only one left. And I was too young. I couldn't have run Parel then. Though I could now. Sometimes I dream of buying it back and merging it with San Gregorio.'

'Why haven't you?'

'Amadeo and Bernardo always insisted that it didn't make sense.'

'Does it? To you?'

'Maybe. I haven't totally ruled it out.'

'Then maybe one day you'll buy it.'

'Maybe. One thing's for sure: I'll never sell out what I have.' She was referring to San Gregorio.

'Was there a question of that?' He looked away as he asked her.

'Not for me. Never. But my director, Bernardo Franco, keeps trying in that direction. He's a bloody fool. I'll never sell.'

Corbett nodded knowingly. 'I don't think you should.'

'One day the business will belong to Alessandro. I owe him that.' Again Corbett nodded, and the conversation turned to other things -- music and travel, the places they had lived as children, and why Corbett had never had a child.

'I was afraid I wouldn't have time for one.'

'And your wife?'

'I'm not really sure she was the type. In any case she agreed with me, and we never had one, and now it's a little too late.'

'At forty-two? Don't be absurd. In Italy men much older than you have children all the time.'

210

'Then I'll run out and have one immediately. What do I do? Put an ad in the paper?'

Isabella smiled at him from the opposite end of the tiny couch. 'I shouldn't think you'd have to do anything as drastic as that.'

He smiled softly. 'Maybe not.' And then, not even knowing how it happened, she saw him draw closer, put his hands on her shoulders. She felt herself drift into his arms. The music was playing in the distance and there was a pounding in her ears as Corbett kissed her and she clung to him as to a life raft in a heavy surf. He kissed her gently and she felt it deeply as she sensed her whole body reach out for him until she pulled away with a little lurch.

'Corbett! No!' She startled herself but was quickly comforted by the look in his eyes. It was a look of gentle loving from a man she trusted, with whom she felt totally safe. 'How did that happen?' Her eyes were misted with tears of confusion and, perhaps, a touch of joy.

'Well, let's see, I slid along the couch here, then I put my hand here . . .' He was laughing at her kindly, and she couldn't do anything but laugh too.

'That was terrible, you shouldn't do that, Amadeo – ' Suddenly she stopped. There was no Amadeo. Quick tears rose to her eyes. But he took her back in his arms and held her close to him as she cried.

'No, Isabella, don't. Don't look behind you, darling. Think of what I told you. The pain won't go on forever. This is very, very new.'

But he was grateful as he held her that Amadeo had been gone for almost eight months. It was long enough for her to be ready, to at least consider someone else.

'But I shouldn't, Corbett.' She pulled away from him slowly. 'I can't.'

'Why not? If it's not something you want too, then we won't even talk about it again.'

'It's not that, I like you . . .'

'Is it too soon? We'll go slowly. I promise. I don't want you to be unhappy, not ever again.'

She smiled at him gently then. 'That's a lovely dream. Nothing is forever, remember? Nothing good, and nothing bad.'

'No, but some things are for a very long time. I would very much like that with you.'

Without knowing why she said it, she found herself saying, 'So would I.'

He smiled at her then. They drank brandy, listened to the music, and sat on the floor like children. It was easy to be with him, and she was happy, happier still when he kissed her again. This time she didn't argue, and she didn't want him to stop. Finally he glanced at his watch, looked at her warmly, and stood up.

'I think, my darling, it's time for me to go home.'

'So early? It can't be more than ten o'clock.'

He shook his head. 'It's almost one thirty, and if I don't get out of here now, I'm going to attack you.'

'Rape?' She said it with amusement. She was back in control.

'We could start with that. It has a nice ring, don't you think?' His blue eyes were twinkling wickedly, and she laughed.

'You're impossible.'

'Maybe, but I'm mad about you.' He reached a hand out to her and pulled her up. 'Do you know that, Isabella? I haven't felt like this for years.'

'And before that?' She was still playing. She was so happy suddenly that she wanted to fly.

'Oh, before that I fell in love with a girl named Tillie Erzbaum. She was fourteen and had a fabulous chest.'

'How old were you?'

He considered it thoughtfully. 'Nine and a half.'

'Then you're forgiven.'

'Thank God.'

They walked slowly to the door and he kissed her again as they said goodnight.

'I'll call you tomorrow.' She smiled at him happily. 'And what about our walk? May I join you tomorrow?'

'I think that might be arranged.'

When she woke up the next morning, she was horrified at what she'd done. She was a widow. In her heart she was still a married woman. What was she doing kissing him all night on the den floor? Her heart pounded each time she thought of it, and she felt sorrow mixed with unfamiliar guilt. When he called her, she hid in her office and told Natasha in a brusque voice through the door that she was too busy to take calls from anyone, even him. But it wasn't his fault, she reasoned, as she tried fruitlessly to lose herself in her work. It wasn't his fault at all. She had been as eager as he for those kisses, as surprised as he at her responses, and much more so at what she felt stirring deep in her soul. But Amadeo . . . Amadeo . . . It was true then. Amadeo was not coming back again.

'Where are you going?' Natasha looked at her in surprise as she hurried towards the front door.

'I'm going for my walk early. I have too much work to do tonight.' She glanced nervously at Natasha, and her voice was sharp.

'All right. You don't have to get so uptight about it. I just asked.'

She was back at five o'clock, but still shaken, still nervous, still shocked at what she'd done. Then, suddenly, as she came up in the elevator she realised that she was being a fool. She was a grown woman, she was lonely, and he was a very attractive man. So she had kissed him. So what? But when she opened the door to the apartment, she jumped when she saw him standing in the middle of the room. As usual the children were playing around his legs, and Natasha was sprawled out on the couch, surrounded by books and papers, trying to chat with Corbett in spite of the din.

'Hi, Isabella. How was your walk?' Natasha called out.

'Fine.'

'I hope it did something for you. You were in one rotten mood when you left.'

She nodded, and Corbett grinned. But there was nothing too familiar, nothing possessive or uncomfortable about the look in his eyes.

'Did you have a rough day?'

She nodded again, trying to smile at him, and she relaxed a little at the continued look of comfortable friendship in his eyes. Maybe she had made too much of it. Maybe he wouldn't pursue it after all. It had been the brandy, the music, but it could still be forgotten; it wasn't too late. And then she found herself smiling and sprawled like Natasha in a chair. Natasha was yelling for Hattie while the boys and Corbett played. Hattie appeared a moment later, and Natasha waved the boys away.

'Jesus, I love them, but sometimes they drive me nuts.'

Corbett relaxed in a chair, let out a sigh, and grinned. 'Don't you two ever play rough with them? They've got more energy than brand-new box springs.'

'We read them stories.' Natasha looked at him in amusement. 'And play games.'

'Then buy them a punching bag or something. No, come to think of it, I guess they don't need one. They have me.'

His eyes met Isabella's, this time with a more pointed look. 'You already went for your walk?'

She nodded. 'Yes.'

'Okay. Then show me what you did in your office today. You promised yesterday, remember?' And before she could object, he had taken her hand and pulled her to her feet. Not wanting to make a scene in front of Natasha, she walked quickly to her office. Corbett closed the door.

'Corbett, I –'

'Wait a minute before you say anything. Please.' He sat down in a chair and looked at her kindly. 'Why don't you sit down?'

She did so, like an obedient schoolgirl, relieved only that he hadn't swept her expectantly into his arms.

'Before you tell me what you're thinking,' he went on, 'let me tell you what I already know. I've been through this. I know what it's like. And it's awful, so at least let me share what I learned. If I'm not entirely crazy, I left here last night and you were as happy as I was. But sometime – maybe last night, maybe this morning, maybe not even till tonight, though I doubt that – you started thinking. About your husband, about what used to be, about still being married. You felt guilty, frightened, crazy.'

Isabella stared at him in amazement, not saying a word, but her eyes very wide.

'You couldn't even understand why you'd done it, you could barely remember who I was. But let me tell you, darling, that's natural. It's something you have to go through. You can't run away from it now. You're lonely, you're human, you didn't do anything terrible or wrong. And if you had been the one who'd been kidnapped, your husband would be going through exactly the same thing right now. It takes about this long to feel again, to thaw out, and then you've got all the same feelings you've ever had before and no one to share them with. But now you've got me. You can either try it, very, very slowly, or you can run like hell and hide in your guilt and your feelings of still being married for the rest of your life. That's not an ultimatum. You may just not want me. I may not be the right one. If that's what you're thinking, I'll understand it. But don't run away from what you feel, Isabella . . . You can't go back.' He stopped then, almost breathless, and Isabella looked at him, stunned.

'But how did you know?'

'I went through it. And the first time I kissed a woman I felt as though I had defiled Beth's memory, as though I had betrayed her. I was torn apart. But the difference was that I didn't give a damn about that woman. I was just lonely and horny and tired and sad. I care about you, though. I love you. And I hope to hell you can care about me.'

'How do you understand everything like that?' She looked at him in amazement from across the room. And he smiled at her lovingly, easily, straight from the heart.

'I'm just very smart.'

'Ah, and humble!' She was suddenly smiling again, and enjoying teasing him.

'In that case, we happen to be evenly matched. Is that why you went out walking without me?'

'I wanted to run away from you. To have finished my walk before you got here.'

'That was smart.' But he didn't look hurt by it, nor did he look amused. He simply understood.

'I'm sorry.'

'Don't be. Do you want me to leave now? It's all right, Isabella, I'll understand.'

But she shook her head and held out her hand. He walked to her and took it, looking down into the bottomless black eyes.

'I don't want you to go. I feel stupid now. Maybe I was

wrong.' She clung to him as the children did, and gently he took her hands and knelt beside her, holding them in his own.

'I told you we'd go slowly. I'm not in a rush.'

'I'm glad.' And with that she put her arms softly around his neck and hugged him, childlike. They held each other that way for what seemed like a very long time, and this time it was Isabella who moved her hand slowly, touched his chin and his eyes and his lean, handsome face. It was she who took the first step this time and whose lips sought his, gently at first then hungrily. And it was she who trembled when they stopped.

'Take it easy, darling.'

But she was smiling again. 'What was it you said about rape?'

'If you rape me, I'll punch you.' He looked like offended virtue itself as she laughed. Then he was smiling again. 'Want to go for a drive?' he looked hopeful, but he didn't want to push.

'You brought the car?'

'No, I was planning to steal one. Of course I did. Why?'

'Then I'd love it.' She paused. 'What will we tell Natasha?'

'That we're going out for a drive. Is that so wrong?'

She looked at him sheepishly. 'I still feel guilty.'

But he smiled gently at her. 'Don't worry about it. Sometimes so do I.'

They bid Natasha a casual au revoir and went out for a drive, down to Wall Street, to the Cloisters, and then through the park. Settled against the plush upholstery, sitting close to him, she felt protected from the world.

'I don't know what happened to me today,' she said.

'Don't worry about it, Isabella. It's all right.'

'I suppose so. Do you suppose I'll ever be sane again?' She looked at him, smiling, half in jest, half in truth.

217

'I hope not. I like you like this.'

She smiled at him tenderly. 'I like you too.'

But Isabella knew that she more than liked him two weeks later when Natasha was away for the weekend with the boys.

'You mean they just left you?' He looked infinitely sorry for her when he came by on Saturday afternoon for tea. He had planned to sit with her for a few hours and maybe go for a walk, and he had been hoping that perhaps Natasha was going out. He enjoyed his time alone with Isabella, but it was even more precious to him because it was so rare. They were always surrounded by children, or Natasha, or even Hattie, the maid. 'Where did they go?'

Isabella smiled in amusement as she handed him a cup of Earl Grey. 'Just to some friends of Natasha's in Connecticut. It'll do the boys good.'

He nodded slowly, but it wasn't the boys he was thinking of as gently he reached for her hand. 'Do you realise how quiet it is here, and how seldom we're alone?'

She sat there thinking, and slowly her mind drifted back to Rome. She had had so much space in her home there, so much room to herself, so many hours of her own time. 'I wish you had known me then.' She said it dreamily as he watched her eyes.

'When, Isabella?'

'In Italy . . .' She said it softly and then looked up at him with a soft blush. 'But that doesn't make any sense, does it?' In Italy, in the good days, she had been married. Corbett would have had no place in her life.

But he understood what she was thinking. It was normal that now and then she should long for her home. 'Do you have a wonderful house there?'

She smiled and nodded, and then told him about

Alessandro's Christmas carousel as her eyes danced. She looked so lovely as she told him that he put down his cup and took her in his arms.

'I wish I could take you back there . . . take you home, if that's what you want.' And then he spoke very softly. 'But maybe one day home will be here?' But she didn't really think so; she couldn't imagine spending the rest of her life anywhere except Rome. 'Do you miss it awfully?'

She shrugged and smiled. 'Italy is . . . just Italy. There's nothing like it anywhere in the world. Crazy people, crazy traffic, good spaghetti, wonderful smells . . .' As she said it she found herself thinking of the narrow back streeets not far from San Gregorio, of women nursing babies in doorways and children running out of church, of the birds singing in the tree-tops in her garden . . . just thinking of it brought tears to her eyes.

And as he watched her Corbett felt sympathy for her tear at his heart. 'Do you want to go out for dinner tonight, my love?' It was the first time he had called her that and she smiled, but slowly she shook her head.

'You know I can't.'

But he thought for a moment. 'Perhaps you can.'

'Are you serious?'

'Why not?' His eyes danced with mischief now. He had a plan. 'There's a funny little Italian restaurant I used to go to, way downtown. No one "respectable" ever goes there.' He grinned. 'We could probably dash in for a quick dinner, and no one would have any idea who you were. And it's so Italian that it's bound to feel like home.' For a moment he wondered if that would make things worse, but he had a feeling that wouldn't be the case, and he was going to see to it that she had a marvellous time.

Like a fellow conspirator he waited in the living-room while she got dressed. She emerged giggling, in black slacks and sweater, with a black Borsalino fedora pulled low over one eye.

'Do I look mysterious?' She was laughing, and so was he.

'Very much so!'

He even had the Rolls parked a few doors away, and they slipped unnoticed into the restaurant, where they gorged and Isabella chatted happily with their waiter as they drank inexpensive Roman wine.

'Promise you won't tell Natasha! She'd kill me for this.' Her eyes sparkled, and he agreed.

'I couldn't tell her. She'd probably kill me first.' But he didn't feel nervous about Natasha. He knew that Isabella was safe, and when they had had their fill of pasta and the simple red wine, they drove slowly home with a brief detour through the park. 'Happy?' She nodded and settled her head against his shoulder. She had put her hat on the seat beside her, and her raven hair lay softly against his coat. He touched it gently, and then her cheek with his hand. And his eyes never seemed to leave her as he and Isabella went slowly inside.

'Do you want to come in for coffee?' She looked at him invitingly, but it wasn't coffee either of them had in mind.

He nodded and followed her inside, but once in the hallway, Isabella never bothered to put on the lights. She found herself instantly in Corbett's arms and in the darkness felt herself throbbing with a passion that she had long since forgotten, as Corbett pressed his mouth down on hers. Breathlessly they walked hand in hand to the bedroom, and without turning on the lights, Corbett undressed her and she him, and their bodies joined at last. It seemed hours later when she turned on a small light and smiled at him as he lay in her bed. She looked around the room at the debris of their clothes, and she started to laugh.

'What's so funny, my darling?'

'We are.' She looked down at him and then kissed him softly on the neck. 'You can't trust us at all. My room-mate goes away for the weekend, and what do we do? We run out for dinner and then we come home and make love.'

He pulled her slowly back to him again. '. . . and then we do it again . . . and again . . . and again . . .'

Chapter Twenty-Two

April and May sped past them very quickly. When the weather permitted, they went walking every evening, or they went on drives. Sometimes they took Alessandro to the country and watched the look of wonder in his eyes as he played in grass, and built castles on still deserted beaches. And once or twice they took Natasha with them. For the first few weeks she had tried to pretend that she didn't know what was happening, but at last she had asked. And Isabella had nodded girlishly as she laughed and admitted that she and Corbett were in love.

She was obviously immensely happy, and whenever Natasha saw Corbett, so was he. But it was also clear to Natasha that aside from Isabella's delight about her romance she still had major worries with her work.

It was a warm, balmy evening when Corbett arrived at the house with a hansom cab to take Isabella for a drive. She laughed when she saw it, and they rode around in it for two hours.

'So how was work today, sweetheart?' He pulled her closer to him and looked down into the dark eyes.

'Terrible. Bernardo is giving me trouble again.'

'The new line?'

'No, that's already settled. We open next week. It's everything else. Plans for the winter, cosmetics, fabrics, I don't know. He's impossible right now.'

'It could be that there's too much on his shoulders with you over here.'

'What are you suggesting?' She looked at him tiredly. 'That I go home?'

'Hardly. I've always thought though that there are things you could change.'

'I know, but I can't now. Not while I'm here.' The way she said it made her think of Rome again, which was something she hated to admit to Corbett now. They had clung to each other as though it would be forever, but sooner or later she would have to go home. And Corbett's business would always keep him in the States. *Nothing is forever*, she thought to herself, and then pushed the words from her mind.

'Well, don't worry about it. Things will probably settle down in a few days.'

But they didn't. For the next two weeks, matters only got worse. Blow-up after blow-up after argument after fight. Isabella was sick of it. She told Bernardo that one morning on the phone. He seemed to have separated himself from her and seemed, in fact, better able to handle his feelings for her.

Oh, Bernardo, she thought to herself more than once. *If only it could be you I love. Life would be so much simpler.*

'Be sensible for chrissake and sell out.'

'Ah, no, that again! Listen, Bernardo, I thought we settled that before I left!'

'No, we did not. You just refused to listen to reason. Well, I've had it up to here. Gabriela is doing the work of ten people, you change the goddamn fabrics every time we turn around, you don't understand a thing about marketing cosmetics, and I get stuck cleaning up after you every goddamn time.'

'Is that right, then why don't you have the balls to quit like a man instead of telling me to sell out? Maybe the problem is with you, and not with the business! It's you who makes the problems between us all the time, you who

223

won't do what I tell you. Why don't you do what I ask you to do for a change instead of shoving F-B down my throat everytime I open my mouth?'

The rage of Italian continued from Isabella's office. 'I won't listen to this anymore. And if you don't stop it, I'm coming home,' she shouted. 'The hell with all that garbage about danger. You're running my business into the goddamn ground.' It wasn't a fair accusation and she knew it, but the level of frustration between them had surged tidal-wave high. She had been in the States for five months and the charm of doing business this way was beginning to wear very thin.

'Do you have any idea of what you're doing, Isabella? Have you ever even listened to the F-B people? No. Of course not. You would rather sit on your ass over there and insult me and hang on to your business and your ego and save face.'

'The business is perfectly solid and you know it.'

'Yes, I know it. But the fact is I can't do it alone anymore, and you still can't come home. Circumstances, Isabella, circumstances. Your grandfather ran into circumstances too, and he was smart enough to sell out.'

'I never will.'

'Of course not.' She could hear the acid in his voice. 'Because you're too proud to, despite that fact that F-B and IHI and Ewing have all been begging me for you to sell out. Well, in point of fact not lately,' he went on, 'but I know damn well all I have to do is pick up the phone and call them and you'd have yourself a deal.'

There was no answer to what he'd said to her. Isabella was shocked nearly speechless.

'Who?'

'What are you talking about?' She wasn't making sense suddenly, and he was confused.

'I'm asking you who's been offering to buy us.' Her voice had the ring of cold steel.

'Are you crazy? I've been telling you since last October and you ask me who?'

'I don't give a damn. Tell me now. Slowly.'

'Farnham-Barnes.' He spoke to her as though she were retarded.

'And who else?'

'No one. What's wrong with you? F-B. F-B. F-B. And they belong to IHI.'

'And what was that other name?'

'What? Ewing? He's chairman of the board of IHI. The offer originally came from him.'

'Oh, my God.'

'What is it?'

'Nothing.' She was shaking from head to foot.

The picnics. The walks, the dinners – the firehouse . . . they flashed before her eyes – what a fine joke on her. It was a love affair – his love affair with the House of San Gregorio.

'Should I call them?'

'No. Do you understand me? Never! Cancel our dealings with F-B as of today. Call them, or I'll do it myself!'

'You are crazy!'

'Listen to me, Bernardo, I am not crazy and I've never been more serious in my life. Call F-B and tell them to drop dead. Now, today. *Finito.* No more offers, no more orders. Nothing. And get yourself ready. I'm coming home this week.' She had just decided. The nonsense had gone on for long enough. 'If you still think it's necessary, hire two guards, but that's all. I'll call you and let you know when I'm arriving.'

'Are you bringing Alessandro?' Bernardo was shocked. She was speaking in a voice that he hadn't heard in years.

Maybe never. She was suddenly ice and daggers, and he was glad he wasn't in the same room with her or he'd have feared for his skin.

'I'm not bringing Alessandro. He can stay here.'

'How long will you be here?' He didn't even argue. He knew there was no point. Isabella was coming home. *Punto.* Period. *Finito.* And maybe she was right. It was time.

'For as long as I have to be to whip you and everyone else there back into line. Now call Farnham-Barnes.'

'You're serious?' He was truly shocked now.

'I am.'

'*Capito.*'

'And tell them to get the penthouse ready. I'll stay there.' Without further ado she hung up on him.

'How dare you!' Isabella marched into the tiny room and stood glaring at Natasha.

'What?'

'How dare you!'

'How dare I what?' Natasha looked at her in sudden terror. Isabella stood before her, trembling from head to foot, her face white as paper, and her hands clenched at her sides.

'You set me up!'

'Isabella? You're not making sense!' Had she cracked up then? Was the strain of the business too much for her? But as Natasha watched her, it was clear that she had something very definite on her mind. She sat down suddenly, eyeing Natasha, an evil smile of fury hovering on her face.

'Let me tell you a little story then,' Isabella said. 'Perhaps after that we'll both understand. Last October, after my husband died – you know, Amadeo – perhaps you remember him? Well, he died, the victim of a brutal kidnapping . . .'

Natasha stared at her. If this was madness, it was calculated madness, cold and furious, with every word dipped in bitterness. Frightened, she watched her. There was nothing to do now but let her go on.

'He left me with his business, a large and successful couture house in Rome. We also do ready-to-wear, cosmetics, lingerie, I won't bore you with the list. I took over the business, worked my ass off, and vowed to myself and Amadeo that I would keep the business strong, until one day our son could take over, in twenty-five or thirty years. But lo and behold, my right-hand man, Bernardo Franco, first proposes marriage.' Natasha was shocked, but Isabella pressed on. 'And then announces to me that an American business named Farnham-Barnes wants to buy me out. No, I tell him. I'm not selling. But he pushes and he pushes and he tries and he tries. Unsuccessfully. I won't sell. So, miraculously, one day a phone call comes, telling me that my son has been kidnapped too. Only, fortunately, it is a hoax. And my son is fine. Bernardo then tells me that my life and the child's are not safe in Rome. I must leave, he tells me. So I call my friend Natasha Walker in New York, whom, as it so happens, he has screwed once or twice when she was in Rome.' Natasha began to argue, but Isabella held up a hand. 'Let me go on. I then call my friend Natasha, who invites me to stay with her. An elaborate plan is concocted to keep me safe and to run the business from Natasha's apartment in New York. Wonderful. Bernardo tries once again to get me to sell to F-B and I won't. I fly to America, with my son, and my friend Natasha picks us up at the airport, with a friend in a very pretty Rolls-Royce. I then live with Natasha, I run my business, Bernardo drives me crazy, and every time he has the opportunity he bugs me to sell out. I still hold my ground. But I become friends with the man at the airport, Mister Corbett Ewing. Conveniently "my friend",' – she dripped venom on the words – 'Natasha, invites me to join her at a film premiere. I go, and whom should I be sitting next to, but Mister Corbett Ewing, who only happens to be the chairman of the board of IHI, which owns Farnham-Barnes, which wants to buy me out. Happy coincidence, no? I spend three months being pumped about my business, being courted, being primed by this monster, this. user, this villain, who wants to buy my business and will apparently do anything to do it, including pretending to be in love with me, playing up to my child, and using my "friends". Natasha, of course, invites him over night and day and is thrilled when we "fall in love". And what happens, then, my dear, do you get a commission from Corbett when he marries me and convinces me to sell to him?'.

Natasha looked at her in astonishment and slowly stood up. 'Do you mean what you're saying?'

Isabella was like ice now. 'Every word. I think Bernardo arranged the hoax about Alessandro to get me out of the way, he used you to send me over here, and you saw to it that Corbett Ewing got close to me! It was all very handsomely done, but it's useless, because I will never sell out. Never! Not to Corbett, not anyone, and I think what you all did is disgusting! Do you hear me, damn you? Disgusting! You were my friend!' There were tears of rage and disappointment in her eyes now, and Natasha dared not approach.

'Isabella, I did nothing. Nothing! It was you who wanted to come here. You who wanted to go to that damned premiere. I didn't want you to do it. What do you think, that I tipped off the press? Oh, Jesus!' She sat down again and ran a hand through her tangled hair.

'I don't believe you. You're lying, like Bernardo. Like *him*.'

'Look, Isabella, please. I know this is difficult, and the

way you tell it, everything fits, but it just happened that way, no one planned it, certainly not Corbett.' There were tears running down her face now. 'He loves you, I know that. He was distraught when he found out who you were after the premiere. He came here the day after to tell you; he talked about it with me. He was afraid that something like this might happen. But he didn't tell you. I don't know why, but something happened that night that made him change his mind. He was afraid of losing you before he had a chance, and he hoped that if it ever came out, by then you might understand.'

'Understand what? That he slept with me to steal my business? I understand that perfectly.'

'For chrissake, listen to me.' Natasha was sobbing and holding her head in both hands. 'He loves you, he didn't want to lose you. When he found out who you were, he told his men at F-B to drop their offer and never ever mention his name.'

'Well, Bernardo just did.'

'Was it a new offer, or was he still referring to the old one?'

'I don't know, but I'll inform myself about it when I go to Rome. Which brings up my only further question. You say you're my friend – well, I have no one to turn to no matter what I think the truth is – will you keep Alessandro for me while I go home?'

'Of course. When are you leaving?' Natasha looked shocked.

'Tonight.'

'For how long?'

'A month, two months. As long as it takes me. I don't know. And keep that bastard away from my child while I'm gone. When I return, I'll work out another arrangement. If I am not going back to Rome permanently, I'll find a place of my own.'

'You don't have to do that, Isabella.' Natasha had crumpled on to her bed, crushed.

'Yes, I do.' She started to leave the room, then stopped for a moment. 'Thank you for keeping Alessandro for me.' She loved Natasha. They had been through much together. No matter what the truth was.

Natasha was still crying. 'I love him, and I love you. What are you going to say to Corbett?'

'Just what I told you.'

She called him then, and he was there an hour later, looking scarcely better than Natasha had when she was through.

'Isabella, all I can tell you is that I tried to tell you so many times. But something always intervened.' He looked at her, heartbroken, from a seat half-way across the room. He didn't dare to come near her. 'I'm horrified it came out this way.'

'You had to push and pump and prime and find out and dig inside my head for all you could learn about the house. Well, do you know enough now? It won't do you a bit of good, you know. I'm not selling, and I had Bernardo cancel all our dealings with Farnham-Barnes as of today.'

'There has been no offer from F-B to San Gregorio in over three months.'

'I'll have to check that out. But it makes no difference. You were smart enough not to make offers while you were "courting" me, maybe you figured that I was smart enough to find you out. But then what? What did you have in mind, Corbett, to marry me and charm me out of San Gregorio? You never stood a chance.'

'What are you going to do now?'

'I'm going back to Rome and kick everyone's ass right back into line.'

'And then what? Come back here to hide again? Why

230

don't you bring the business with you? That's the only thing that makes any sense.'

'Never mind what I do with my business. You've already said and done enough.'

'Then I'll go now. But you must know one thing, Isabella. What happened between us was real, it was honest, I meant every bit of it.'

'It was a lie.'

'I wasn't. I love you.'

'I don't want to hear it!' She stood up and smiled at him viciously. 'Nothing lasts forever, Corbett. Remember? Not even a lie. You used me, dammit! You took my heart and my body and my vulnerability, and you used me, just to add another notch to your corporate belt. San Gregorio. Well, you got me, but you won't get the rest.'

'I can't say I never wanted the rest. Before I met you, I did. But not after that. Never for an instant after that.'

'I will never believe you.'

'Then I'll say goodbye.'

She watched as he walked unhappily out of the room. But she was already in her room packing when he waved his car away and walked alone, rapidly, head bent, back to his office.

Chapter Twenty-Three

The plane touched down at Leonardo da Vinci Airport at 11.05 the next morning. Bernardo and two guards were waiting as she came out of customs, and the greeting she gave Bernardo showed affection as well as strain. She looked exhausted, having not slept a wink on the flight. It had been painful leaving Alessandro, awkward leaving Natasha, and all she had wanted to do was get away.

She had cried halfway to Rome. He had betrayed her. They had all betrayed her. Bernardo, Amadeo, Corbett, Natasha. All the people she trusted. All the people she loved. Amadeo, by dying; Bernardo by his efforts to make her sell out; and Corbett – she couldn't bear thinking of it. She wondered how she would begin again, how she would even function anymore.

As she came through customs with two small suitcases she looked tiredly into Bernardo's eyes. It was hard to believe that she hadn't seen him in five months. It felt more like five years.

'Ciao, Bellezza.' He thought as he looked at her that the five months she'd spent in New York hadn't been very kind. She looked frail, thin, and ravaged, and there were deep circles carved under her eyes. 'Do you feel well?' He was worried.

'Only tired.' For the first time in twenty-four hours she smiled.

He could sense the strain in her all the way into Rome. She was unusually reticent as she gazed silently and painfully out the window of the limousine.

'Nothing has changed much.' He tried to make small

talk. He didn't want to talk business in front of the guards.

'No, but it's warmer.' She remembered how cold it had been the night of her flight.

'How's Alessandro?'

'He's fine.'

Isabella longed to see the villa but she knew she wasn't ready to. Not yet. And she had business to do at the house. It made more sense for her to stay there. There was more to it, though she could only barely admit it to herself. Having given her body to Corbett, she hadn't wanted to return to the bed she and Amadeo had shared. Now she had betrayed him too. And for what? A ruse. A lie.

She felt her heart patter softly as they pulled up in front of the heavy black door. She wanted to cry out, but all she did for a moment was stare at it. Then she was out of the car and striding into the House of San Gregorio as though she had never been gone. No one had been warned of her coming, but she knew it would be all over Rome by that night. She didn't give a damn. Let them haunt her, let them set off flashbulbs in her face; she didn't give a damn about that either. Nothing would ever bother or surprise her, not anymore. Out of long habit she inserted her key in the elevator and pushed the fourth-floor button as Bernardo watched her, stricken, unhappy.

Something dreadful had happened to her, he realised. She was dead inside. That pale, ivory face he loved so well was like a mask. He had never seen her like this, not even during those awful hours when they had waited, not during the funeral or even on her flight into exile. The Isabella he had known for years was no more.

From the end of the fourth-floor hall she walked to the door of the stairs to the penthouse, Bernardo following up the short flight of stairs. It was then that she finally sat down, that she took off the black fedora she had worn, and seemed to relax.

'*Allora, va bène, Bernardo?*'

'I'm all right, Isabella. What about you? You've been gone for five months and you come home and act like I have leprosy.'

Maybe you do, she thought. She said only, 'Did you call F-B?'

He nodded. 'It made me ill, but I did. Do you know what that will do to our figures?'

'We'll make it back by next year.'

'What happened yesterday?' He didn't dare argue with her now. She looked too tired, too frail.

'I learned something very interesting.'

'And what was that?'

'That a friend of Natasha's, whom I also thought had become my friend, had been using me. To buy the business. You may recognize the name, Bernardo. Corbett Ewing. I wasn't amused.'

Bernardo looked at her, shocked. 'What do you mean, "using" you?'

She spared him the details. 'I never realised who he was. But Natasha knew, of course. And you did. I have no idea if you all concocted this thing together. I have no way of knowing; there is no way I ever will know. I'm not sure if that's why you insisted that I get out of Rome. It doesn't matter anymore, Bernardo. I'm home now. It's really Ewing who's the villain. The matter has been settled. I'm not selling. And I've made a decision that I should have made awhile ago. It has taken me some time.'

Bernardo wondered what was coming. His ulcer twinged miserably, and he waited for her news.

'I'm moving the main part of the business back with me, to the States.' It had been Corbett's suggestion. But, remarkably, he'd been right.

'What? How?'

'I haven't worked that out yet. The couture will stay

234

here. Gabriela can run it. I can fly over several times a year. That end of the business doesn't need my constant supervision. The rest of it does. Otherwise it's impossible, it's too much of a strain on you . . . and on me.' She smiled again, but weakly, and watched Bernardo as he absorbed the shock. 'We'll work it out together while I'm here. But I want you to come with me. No matter what has happened, I need you. You've always been my friend and you're too good to lose.'

'I'll have to think about it. This comes as a bit of a shock. I don't know, Isabella . . .' But with her words she was only confirming what he already knew. He was only her friend and employee. She would never let him be more. And he realised something else. He was glad. She would always have been too much for him to handle as a lover. She was going on about her plans.

'I can't live over here any more, not with Alessandro. You were right about that. I can't take that chance. There's no reason why we can't run the entire inter-national end from New York. And' – she hesitated again 'I've decided to take Peroni and Baltare with me, if they'll go. Of our four under directors they're the only two who speak English. The other two will have to go. But we can talk about the rest later. And I'll say one thing.' She sighed softly and looked around. 'It's nice to see something familiar for a change. I've been damn tired of being so far from home.'

'But you've decided to stay there. Are you sure?'

'I don't think I have a choice.'

'Maybe not. What about the villa?'

'I'll close it and keep it. That belongs to Alessandro. He may come back here to live one day. But it's time I set up a home for him over there. And it's time I stopped hiding. It's been nine months since Amadeo died, Bernardo. It's enough.'

He nodded slowly, trying to understand it. Nine months. And how much had already changed.

'What about Natasha? I gather then that you two have had a falling-out?'

'You gather correctly.' She didn't volunteer more.

'You really think that Ewing was trying to push you?'

'I'm as sure as I'll ever be. Perhaps you know more about that than I do. I'll never know that either.'

It was shocking. She trusted no one now. She was suddenly bitter and cold. It made him uncomfortable and it frightened him.

What he saw in the next three weeks did nothing to change his mind.

Isabella made her announcements to the directors and checked every inch of the House of San Gregorio, going from room to room to office to stock room to desk to file, on every floor. Within three weeks she knew everything that was happening and all that she wanted to know. The two under directors she'd asked to join her in New York had agreed to do so, and she had decided to hire two American under directors to work with them there. The rest of the staff was being shuttled and divided. Gabriela was immensely pleased. She would be almost autonomous now in the couture end, overseen only by Isabella, who trusted her completely. But it was there that Isabella's trust stopped. She was suspicious, untrusting, and the greatest change of all was that she didn't even fight with Bernardo anymore. She was no longer an easy woman to work for, and she was suddenly a woman whom everyone feared. Her axe could fall anywhere. Her black eyes saw everything, her ears heard it all. She seemed to have got over her suspicions of him – but she was distrustful of everyone else.

'Well, Bernardo, where do we stand?'

She watched him over lunch in her office. For only a moment he wanted to touch her hand. He wanted to free her from this hideous spell, to assure himself that she was still human, to reach out to her. But he wasn't sure if anyone could anymore, not even he. The only time her voice warmed was on the phone with Alessandro; she had promised him in her phone call that morning that she was coming home soon.

'We stand remarkably well, Isabella.' Bernardo let the moment pass with a small sigh. 'Considering the kind of changes we're making. I'd say you've done splendidly. We ought to be able to set up offices in New York in another month.'

'That means late July, early August. It'll do.' And then came the final question. The one he'd been dreading for weeks. 'And you?'

He hesitated for a long moment, and at last he shook his head. 'I can't.' She stopped eating, put her fork down, and stared. For an instant she looked like the old Isabella, and he was almost relieved.

'Why not?'

'I've thought about it. But it would never work.' She waited in silence while he went on. 'You're ready to run it by yourself. You understand the business as well as I do, better in fact than even Amadeo did. I don't know if you realise that.'

'That's not true.'

'Yes, it is.' He smiled at her, and she was touched. 'And I wouldn't be happy in New York. I want to be in Rome, Isabella.'

'And do what?'

'Something will come along. The right thing. In time. I might even take a long vacation, go somewhere, spend a year in Greece.'

'You're crazy. You couldn't live without the business.'

237

'Everything has to come to an end.'

She looked at him thoughtfully. 'Nothing is forever.'

'Precisely.'

'Will you think about it for a while longer?'

He almost agreed to it and then he shook his head again. It was pointless. It was over. 'No, *cara*, I won't. I don't want to live in New York. As you said when you got here, it's enough.'

'I wasn't referring to you.'

'I know that. But it's time for me now.' Suddenly, as he looked at her, there were tears in her eyes. The drawn, tired face with the big black eyes crumpled. He moved to sit next to her on the leather couch and took her in his arms. '*Non piange, Bellezza. Isabellezza . . .*' Don't cry.

Isabellezza . . . At the sound of the word she turned her head and broke into sobs.

'Oh, Bernardo, there is no Isabellezza anymore.'

'There will always be. For me. I will never forget those times, Isabella. Nor will you.'

'But they're over. Everything's changed.'

'It has to change. You're right to change it. The only thing you're wrong to change is you.'

'But I'm so confused.' She stopped for a moment to blow her nose in his handkerchief as he gently ran a hand over her dark hair.

'I know you are. You don't trust anyone anymore. It's natural after what happened. But now you have to put it away. You have to stop before you let it destroy you. Amadeo is gone, Isabella. But you can't let yourself die too.'

'Why not?' She looked like a heartbroken little girl as she sat next to him and blew her nose again.

'Because you're too special, Bellezza. It would break my heart if you stayed like this, angry, unhappy, distrustful of

238

everyone. Please, Isabella, you have to open up and try again.'

She didn't tell him that she had done that and been hurt more than she ever had before.

'I don't know, Bernardo. So much has changed in the last year.'

'But you'll see. You'll find in time that some of them have been good changes too. You're making the right decision taking the business to America.'

'I hope so.'

'What are you doing about the villa, by the way?'

'I'll start packing up next week.'

'You're taking everything with you?'

'Not all of it. Some things I'll leave here.'

'Can I help you?'

Slowly she nodded. 'It would make it much easier. I've – I've been afraid to go back.'

He only nodded and smiled as she blew her nose for a last time.

Chapter Twenty-Four

The car turned into the gravel driveway and came to a halt
outside the familiar front door. Isabella looked at it
thoughtfully for a moment before she stepped out. The
house looked larger to her somehow, and the grounds
seemed strangely quiet. For a moment it was like returning
from a long trip. She expected to glimpse Alessandro's face
at the window and then a minute later see him come
bounding out to meet her, but he didn't. No one came.
Nothing stirred.

Bernardo stood soundlessly behind her as she began to
walk slowly towards the house. In the five weeks that she
had been in Rome, she had never come out here. In a way,
in her heart, she hadn't really been back. She had come to
Rome to minister to her business. But this was something
different, something private, a piece of the past. And she
herself had known that she wasn't ready to see it. Now that
she was back again, she was grateful that she wasn't alone.
She glanced over her shoulder then with a soft smile,
remembering Bernardo. But the dark eyes weren't smiling;
they looked unhappy and distant as she looked around her
and then rang the bell. She had her key with her but she
didn't want to use it. It was like visiting someone else now.
Someone she had once been.

Bernardo watched as a maid opened the door and
Isabella stepped inside. He had warned them. Signora di
San Gregorio was coming home. The information was met
with trepidation and excitement: with Alessandro?
Forever? There had been a flurry of planning – what rooms
to open, what meals to prepare. But Bernardo had been

quick to dispel the illusions. She won't be staying there, and she will be alone. Alessandro was still in America. And then he had dealt the last blow. She'll be closing the house.

But it wasn't the same anymore anyway. The central figures of the household were already gone. Mamma Teresa had left in April, understanding at last that her charge would be gone for too long. Bernardo had spoken to her openly, the risks were too great. He would be gone for a year maybe, perhaps a little less, or probably more. She had gone to a family in Bologna, with three daughters and two little boys. She had never quite recovered from the way Isabella had left her, without even warning her that she was taking Alessandro away from her, in the dark of night, leaving his bed empty and his room locked, and the woman who had protected and loved him far behind. Luisa had taken a job for the summer in San Remo, with people for whom she had worked once before. And Enzo had retired; his room in the garage was empty. The three stars of the household had long since tearfully gone. Now there were only the lesser lights to help Isabella.

Bernardo had ordered countless boxes, which had been left in the front hall. Isabella saw them as soon as she entered. Silently she stood and looked at them, but her eyes drifted away from them. She seemed to be waiting – for familiar noises, for sounds she had heard there, for voices that were no more. Bernardo watched her, hanging carefully back. She put down her light linen jacket and began to walk slowly down the long hall. Her footsteps rang out emptily. Had it only been five months since the night she'd fled with Alessandro? Five months since she had crept down that hall, collecting suitcases and Alessandro in his red sleepers, whispering 'sshhh' and promising adventure? '*Are we going to Africa, Mamma?*' She smiled to herself and wandered into the living-room. She glanced at the blue Fabergé clock that she had looked at so ıntently that night she had waited for Amadeo, when they were expected for dinner at the Principessa's house – the night he had been so late, the night he had disappeared. She sat down heavily on the chaise longue near the window, staring emptily at Bernardo.

'I don't even know where to begin.' Her eyes were full and heavy, and he nodded, understanding.

'It's all right, Bellezza. We'll do it slowly, room by room.'

'It will take years.' She looked out to the garden. The carousel she had given Alessandro for Christmas was shrouded in canvas, its chimes and music silent. Tears came to her eyes, but she smiled.

Bernardo watched her, remembering that night, as he was. He fumbled in his pocket and pulled something out that he held in his hand.

'I never gave you this last Christmas. I was afraid it would make you too unhappy if I gave you a gift.' Christmas with Amadeo had always been an extravaganza, jewellery and funny objects, little treasures and remarkable books she had coveted, tiny wonders she had always loved. There had been no way Bernardo could have made that up to her, and he had been afraid to even try. But he had gone to Alfredo Paccioli and he had bought her something that now, five months later, he held out to her. 'I felt awful afterwards not giving you anything.' Silently he felt for the now familiar pocket watch that had been Amadeo's. He always wore it.

He handed her the small package. She took it, her eyes filling, and sat down again with a very small smile.

'You don't need to give me presents, Bernardo.' But she took it and opened it, then she looked up at him, speechless with emotion. It was a large gold ring with the seal of San Gregorio carefully engraved in it, impeccably carved in a smooth face of black stone. It was onyx, and its proportions were perfect on her long slender hand. She slipped it on

242

above her wedding ring, her eyes wide and mist-filled again.

'Bernardo, you're crazy . . .'

'No, I'm not. Do you like it? He smiled at her from where he stood, looking very young to her, almost like a boy.

'It's perfect.' She gazed at the ring again.

'If you like it half as much as I do my pocket watch, I'll be happy.'

Without saying more, she rose and went to him. They hugged each other for a moment, and he felt her heart beating as he held her close.

'Thank you.'

'*Va bène, Bellezza*. Sshhh. No, don't cry. Come on, we have work to do.' They pulled apart slowly, and he took off his jacket and unclasped his cuff links as she watched. 'Where do we start?'

'My bedroom?'

He nodded, and hand in hand they walked determinedly down the hall. She was dividing everything into three categories. The things she would leave in the house under dustcovers, to be retrieved by her one day perhaps, or put to use in the house if Alessandro ever opened it again, if as a grown-up he came back to Rome. The things she would pack and send to America. And precious objects that couldn't be left there, but would have to be put in storage. Of those, she decided, there were few. Things were either worth taking with her or could be left here at the house. Things like the grand piano, and some of the large antique furniture that had been in Amadeo's family for years, but of which neither of them had ever been very fond. Most of the rugs she was leaving in storage. They may not fit in her new rooms. The curtains would stay on the windows they were made for. The sconces and the chandeliers would stay. She didn't want to leave holes and gaping openings in the house. When Alessandro came back one day, she wanted it to still look like a home, not a barracks that someone had ransacked, preparing for flight.

'*Allora.*' She looked at him. '*Avanti!*'

He smiled at her, and they began to pack. First her bedroom, then Alessandro's, then her boudoir; then finally they stopped for lunch. The sacred shrine was being dismantled, the boxes were piling up endlessly in the hallway, and Isabella was satisfied as she looked around. It was a good opportunity to weed out her favourite things from the ones she didn't really care about. Bernardo had watched her carefully, but there had not been a single tear since they had started. She was in command of herself again.

They sat in the garden, eating lunch. 'What are you going to do about the carousel?' Bernardo said. He was munching on a prosciutto and tomato sandwich. Isabella poured them both a glass of white wine.

'I can't take it. I don't even know where I'll be living. We may not have a garden.'

'If you do, let me know. I'll have it packed up.'

'Alessandro would love that.' She looked at Bernardo. 'Will you come to visit us?'

'Of course I will. Eventually. But first' – he looked victorious – 'I'm going to Greece.'

'You've decided then?'

'It's all settled. I rented a house last week on Corfu, for six months.'

'And after that?' She took another sip of wine. 'Maybe you should come to New York and look it over.'

He shook his head. 'No, Bellezza, we both know we've made the right decisions. I'll do something here.'

'For one of my rivals?' Her look of concern was only half serious, but again he shook his head.

'You don't have any, Isabella. And I couldn't bear to work for second best after you. I've already had five offers.'

244

'Jesus, have you? From whom?' He told her, and she was derisive.

'They make garbage, Bernardo. No!'

'Of course, No! But something else may come up. There's been one offer that intrigues me.' He told her. It was the largest designer of men's wear in Italy, who also did private fittings in London and France.

'Wouldn't that bore you?'

'Maybe. But they need someone to run it. Old man Feleronio died in June, the son lives in Australia and is a doctor, the daughter knows nothing about the business. And,' he looked at her mischievously, 'they don't want to sell it. They want someone to run it for them, so they can go on living like kings. Eventually I think they'll sell, but maybe not for another five or ten years. It would give me a lot of freedom to do what I want.' He smiled at her.

'Go ahead, say it. Something you never had with me.'

'I wouldn't have respected you as much if you'd taken a back-seat. And there's no reason for you to, you know more about this business than anyone in Europe.'

'And the States,' she added proudly.

'And the States. And if you do half as good a job teaching Alessandro, San Gregorio will go on for the next hundred years.'

'Sometimes I worry about that. What if he doesn't want it?'

'He will.'

'How can you know?'

'Do you ever talk to him about it? He sounds more like fifteen than five. He may not quite have your eye for design and colour, but the workings of it, the genius, the machinery of San Gregorio, it's already in his blood. Like Amadeo. Like you.'

'I hope so.' She made a mental note to talk to him about it more when she got back. 'I miss him terribly,' she said,

245

and I think he's getting angry. He wants to know when I'm coming home.'

'When are you?'

'In another month. It's just as well. Natasha took a house in East Hampton for the summer. He can be at the beach there while I finish here and then when I look for an apartment in New York.'

'You're going to be awfully busy. You have to find temporary office space — the boys are going to be arriving over there two weeks after you do — not to mention finding permanent space, an architect to do it, a place for you and Alessandro to live – '

'While *you* sit on your ass in Greece!'

He grinned at her. 'I've earned it, you monster.'

'Come on,' she said, 'let's go back to work.'

They worked until eleven o'clock that evening, dividing treasures in the living-room, packing what they could, and leaving the rest for the professional packers. Red labels marked what was going with her, blue ones what was staying in Rome, green ones what was going into storage. Then there were the left-overs, the inevitable throwaways that surface in everyone's life when they move. Even for Isabella, with her Louis XV and her marble and her Fabergé, there were still broken toys, things that she hated, books she didn't want to keep, and dishes that were cracked.

Bernardo dropped her off that night at the House of San Gregorio and picked her up again the next day. For the next three weeks they stopped work early, arriving back at the villa by two o'clock and leaving after midnight. By the fourth week the job was done.

Isabella stood for a last, lonely moment, amid the mountain of boxes stacked up neatly in the living-room and the hall. A sea of red labels, the treasures she was sending to New York. The house suddenly echoed strangely; the lights were off. It was after two o'clock in the morning.

'Are you coming?' Bernardo was already waiting in the driveway.

'*Aspetta!*' she shouted. Wait. Even as she thought. For what? Was he coming? Would she hear his footsteps? The man who'd been gone for ten months. She whispered softly in the darkness. 'Amadeo?'

She waited, listening, watching, as though he might come back to her and tell her his disappearance had all been a joke. That she should stop everything and unpack. There hadn't really been a kidnapping . . . or there had been, but it was someone else they had killed. She stood there, trembling, alone, for a minute that seemed like an hour. Then, tears streaming from her eyes, she closed the door softly and locked it. She held the door-knob for a last time, knowing that she would never be back.

Chapter Twenty-Five

'You'll come to see me? You promise?' She was clinging to Bernardo at the airport. They had both been crying. Now he dabbed at her eyes with his handkerchief and brushed roughly at his own.

'I promise.' He knew how nervous she suddenly was about running the business alone in New York. But she was staffing it wisely. Peroni and Baltare were unimaginative but solid. Isabella didn't need anyone with imagination, she had enough for them all. 'Kiss Alessandro for me,' he said.

She was crying again. 'I will.' It had been an unbearable week of goodbyes. At the villa. At the house. With Gabriela, whom she would see on her next trip to Rome in three months. But still there was the constant pain of leaving, and now Bernardo. In some ways it was like leaving as she had six months before. But this time it was in broad daylight, from the Rome airport, the two body-guards looked bored, and there had been no more crank calls. It was finally over. Even Bernardo had agreed that she would be safe now being seen in New York. It was no secret that the business was moving, and there would be photographs and phone calls from the press. But the police had assured her that she was no longer in any real danger. She had to be reasonable, and perhaps a little careful with Alessandro, but no more so than anyone in her position. She had learned the lesson well. Painfully well.

She kissed him for a last time, and he smiled at her, once again through his own tears.

'*Ciao, Isabellezza.* Take care.'

'Ciao, Nardo. I love you.'

They hugged one last time, and she got on to the plane. Alone this time, without bodyguards, in first class, with her name on the manifest. Her eyes were streaming with tears.

She slept for three hours, then submitted to a brief dinner, taking some papers from her briefcase and smiling at the prospect of seeing Alessandro. She hadn't seen him in two months.

When the plane landed in New York, she went quickly through customs, without fear this time. She remembered the last time she'd come into New York, exhausted, terrified, her jewellery hidden in her handbag, the bodyguards beside her, and her child in her arms. Today the customs officers dismissed her with a wave, and she muttered a quick 'thank you', passing through the gate, her eyes combing the airport.

Then she saw them, Natasha and the children, waiting, and she ran towards them and took Alessandro in her arms.

'Mamma! . . . Mamma!' The whole airport was filled with his clamouring. She held him tightly in her arms.

'Oh, darling, how I love you . . . oh, and you look so brown. Bernardo said to kiss you.'

'Did you bring my carousel?' His eyes were wide and happy, a reflection of her own.

'Not yet. If we find a house with a garden, I'll have them send it, but you're almost too big for it, you know.'

'Carousels are for babies.' Jason looked at them disgustedly, all that kissing and hugging. That kind of stuff wasn't appropriate for a man. But Isabella kissed him anyway, and tickled him, and he suddenly laughed.

'Wait till you see what I've brought you two!' There were shrieks of excitement and more laughter, and Isabella looked up at Natasha. Her face sobered, but she smiled gently. 'Hello.'

For an instant Natasha hesitated, and then they went into each other's arms. 'I've missed you, too, you know.'

'So have I. It was horrible not having a roommate.' They both laughed again. Natasha knew as they walked along together that she was no longer angry. The light of anguish had somewhat dimmed in her friend's eyes.

'I almost dropped dead when you said you were moving the business. What did they say in Rome?'

'The same thing. The only one who thought it was wonderful was Bernardo. He knew I was right to do it. It's going to be a mad-house for a while. I have a million things to do.' She groaned just thinking of it.

'I'll help you.'

'Aren't you staying out in East Hampton?' They all looked brown and healthy from their month in the sun.

Natasha nodded. 'Yes, but I can leave the boys with Hattie.'

Isabella nodded slowly. 'All right.' She had some fences to mend with Natasha. The business with Corbett didn't matter so much anymore. Maybe Natasha's intentions had been good. But it didn't matter. Isabella didn't want to know. The subject was closed between them. This time there was no Rolls, only the ordinary limousine Natasha sometimes rented, with the driver who had taken Isabella to the disastrous premiere in April. Isabella smiled at him. It seemed a thousand years before.

They went back to the apartment. The boys opened their packages, shouting and laughing, trying on sweaters and funny hats, throwing pieces of new games, and playing with their toys.

At last Isabella smiled shyly at Natasha, holding out a package. 'This one is for you.'

'Come on, Isabella. Don't be silly.'

'Never mind. Open it.' It was the cream of the new

winter couture collection, which had opened in June. It was a soft blue cashmere dress with a matching blue coat. Natasha held it up in front of the mirror, looking awed.

'It's gorgeous.'

'It matches your eyes.' From the folds of more paper Isabella extracted the scarf and a matching hat. 'You can wear it to lunch with your publisher.'

'Like hell I will. Why waste it on him?'

'Then you can wear it to lunch with me. At Lutece.'

For a moment Natasha stared at her silently. 'You're going out again?'

Isabella nodded. 'It's all right now. It's time.' Corbett had been right, she thought, her imprisonment hadn't lasted forever. Only ten months, though it seemed like a lifetime to her.

In the morning Natasha and the boys went back to East Hampton and Isabella went to work. Not on the phone to Rome this time, but with four real estate agents, who dragged her from one end of Park Avenue to the other, along the side streets, and up and down Fifth. In a week she had temporary office space, had hired five bilingual secretaries, rented mountains of office equipment, and ordered phones. It was barely more than adequate but it was a beginning.

At the end of the second week, she found what she was looking for. Atop one of the tallest skyscrapers in the city, two floors for the House of San Gregorio with a view of the entire city of New York.

Finding the apartment had taken her longer, but at the end of another two weeks of searching, she stood in a penthouse on Fifth Avenue, looking out at the view. There was the sweep of Central Park beneath her, the Hudson River in the distance, and the skyline of the city to her left, facing south. The apartment itself was spacious and lovely. There were four bedrooms – one for herself, one for

Alessandro, a guest room, and one she could use as a den – two maids' rooms, a huge dining-room with a fireplace, a double living-room, and a large hallway and foyer that reminded her vaguely of the house in Rome.

The real estate agent had watched her intently. 'You like it?'

'I'll take it.' There was an army of doormen and porters, even more than there were in Natasha's building twelve blocks south.

The next day Natasha came in from East Hampton to see it. 'My God, Isabella, look at that view.' Isabella stood proudly on her new terrace. There would even be room for the carousel, if it would survive the winter snows in New York. 'When do you move in?'

'Well, I called the movers yesterday. The ship gets in tomorrow. I was thinking of next Saturday. I have to get it over with, so I can get back to work.' Her henchmen from Rome had been arriving, and everyone was eager to settle down and dig in.

But Natasha looked suddenly unhappy. 'So soon?' Isabella nodded. 'That's awful. I'm going to miss you. And Jason says he'll be afraid to sleep alone in his room.'

'He can come to visit every weekend.' Isabella smiled at her.

'I feel as though I'm getting divorced again.'

'You're not.'

In the heat of the September afternoon the two women looked at each other, and Isabella finally decided to broach the painful subject. She owed it to her friend.

'I owe you an apology, Natasha.'

Natasha knew instantly what Isabella was speaking of, but she shook her head and looked away. 'No, you don't.'

'Yes. I don't understand what really happened. I was angry at Corbett. But I was wrong to lash out at you. I don't know if you tried to help him or not, but it doesn't matter. If you did it was out of good intentions. I know that. And I'm sorry for what I said.'

But Natasha looked at her intently now. 'You're wrong about him.'

'I'll never know that.'

'You could talk to him, let him tell you. You could at least give him that chance.'

Isabella only shook her head.

'Nothing lasts forever. Nothing good. Nothing bad. Corbett told me that in the beginning. He was right.'

'He still loves you.' Natasha spoke the words softly.

'Have you seen him then?' Isabella sought her friend's eyes, and Natasha nodded.

'He understands what happened. Maybe better than you do. He was afraid of that happening from the first. The only mistake he made was not telling you in the beginning.'

'It doesn't make any difference now. It's over.'

Unhappily Natasha knew that Isabella meant it. It was over for Isabella. But not for Corbett or the boy. But Natasha said nothing, and Isabella spoke no more of Corbett until that afternoon.

She was telling Alessandro about the apartment.

'You mean I can have my carousel?'

'Absolutely. I already called Rome.'

'Mamma! . . . Mamma! Wait till Corbett sees it.' His eyes glowed, and for an instant everything stopped.

Isabella looked at him strangely, then shook her head. 'He won't see it, darling.'

'Yes, he will! He's my friend.' Defiance blazed in Alessandro's dark eyes. No one had said anything to him, but he had sensed a rift between his Mamma and his friend. Alessandro didn't like it. Not at all. He could tell in the way Corbett now spoke of his mother. As if he were afraid of her. As if she were dead. 'I will invite him over to see it.' He looked up at her, challenging, but her voice grew hard.

'No, Alessandro, you won't.'

'I will. I promised him this summer.'

'Did you? When?'

'When I saw him at the seaside. He was in East Hampton too.'

With that Isabella turned on her heel and marched off to find Natasha. Once again she found her in her office, with a cup of coffee in her hand, reading a fresh page. Isabella slammed the door hard behind her. Natasha jumped at the sound, then stared at her friend as though she'd lost her mind.

'What's the matter?' The look on Isabella's face was strangely familiar, but before Natasha could place it, Isabella began to rage.

'Why didn't you tell me? He was there in East Hampton all summer, hanging around Alessandro, trying to get to me again!'

Natasha stood up, hands on her hips. This time she wasn't giving an inch. 'Alessandro needs him, Isabella. And Corbett is *not* trying to get to you. Stop being so paranoid, for chrissake. What is it with you? You think everyone wants to steal your goddamn business, everyone is using you or your child.'

'They are, goddammit! They took my husband too.'

'"They" did. "*They*". People who were crazy, who wanted money. But that's over, Isabella. Over! No one is trying to hurt you now.'

'I don't give a damn. I don't want that man near him.'

'You're wrong. But tell him that, don't tell me.'

'But you knew it! You knew how I felt when I went back to Rome.'

'I thought you'd come to your senses, that you'd get over it.'

'I never will. I already came to my senses. The minute Bernardo mentioned his name. I don't want that man near Alessandro again.' With that she slammed out of Natasha's office, went to her own room, and with a trembling hand, picked up the phone.

He was quick to come on the line. 'Isabella? Is something wrong?'

'Very much so. And I want to see you. Now! Can you see me?'

'I'll be there in half an hour.'

'Fine. I'll meet you downstairs.' She didn't want Alessandro to see him. She watched the clock in her bedroom, and in twenty-five minutes she went down. Four minutes later the Rolls pulled up in front of the door. Corbett was alone in the car, driving. He got out and opened the door for her. She slipped into the car with him, but when he began to turn on the ignition, she quickly waved the hand wearing her new ring from Bernardo.

He noticed it and understood instantly what it was. He wanted to tell her that it was pretty, that she looked beautiful, that he still loved her, but she didn't give him the chance.

'Don't bother, Corbett. I'm not going anywhere with you. But I didn't want to speak to you upstairs where Alessandro could hear us.'

His face tensed with worry. 'What's wrong?'

'I want you to stay away from him. Is that clear to you? I want you out of his life, entirely, permanently, and completely. I've had enough of your games – working on my friends, my associates, my business, and now my child. The other you had a right to do; how you conduct your business affairs is up to you. But when you use me personally, or my son, Corbett, then you are engaging in a war you can only lose. If you come near him again, if you send him gifts, if you try to see him or call him, or if you let him call you, *I* will call the police and my lawyer. I will sue you for harrassment. I'll have *your* business, and I'll see you in jail. Molesting a minor, attempted kidnap, rape, call it anything you want to, but stay the hell away from my child!' She was screaming so loudly that the doorman would have heard her, if Corbett had not had the foresight to roll up the windows.

He looked at her for an instant, disbelieving what he was hearing. Then anger overcame him. 'Is that what you think I'm doing, Isabella?' he asked. 'Using the boy to get to you again? Is that what you think? Is it? How pompous, how arrogant, how incredibly stupid you are! I told you months ago that you should keep your business, I told you my offers had been withdrawn. I fell in love with you, and to tell you the truth I felt damn sorry for you. Locked up like an animal, afraid of everyone, trusting no one. You've had a bad break in life, Isabella. And so has the child. He lost his father; he's as lonely as you are. And you know what? I love him. He's a wonderful little boy. And he needs me. He needs a lot more than just you! You're a bloody machine. Your business, your business, your business! I'm sick of hearing about it. Now leave me alone and get the hell out of my car!'

Before she could answer him, he had jumped out, gone around the front of the Rolls, and was holding the door open for her, as, astounded, she stepped out.

'I trust I made myself clear to you.' She glared at him icily.

'Absolutely,' he said. 'Goodbye.' He got back in his car again, and before she had got back into the building, he was gone.

Chapter Twenty-Six

The apartment was looking lovely, the offices were working with the usual frenzy, and the carousel had just arrived. It was the end of September, and Jason and Natasha had come to the penthouse to try it out. Alessandro was jumping up and down, laughing and squealing, and Jason had decided that it wasn't 'bad at all'.

'Oh, God, I love it, Isabella. I want one too.' The two women smiled at each other, watching the children ride round and round. The first breeze of autumn had broken the spell of summer, and Isabella was stretched out on the terrace, outside her new home, pleased with her accomplishment.

The walls of the bedrooms had been covered in fabrics, there were wonderful curtains, and rugs on every floor. The bathrooms had already been done in marble when she bought it, but she had changed all the fixtures. Opening on to the terrace there were exquisite French doors.

'You're a genius,' Natasha said, looking admiringly around her.

'No. I'm a designer. Sometimes that helps.'

'How's the new collection coming?'

'Slowly.'

'So is the new book.'

'It takes me time to settle down every time I change location. But at the rate they're going on the new office space, I won't have to worry about that again till next year. It's taking them forever.'

'Baloney. How long have they been at it?' She grinned at Isabella. 'Two weeks?'

Isabella smiled back at her. 'Six.'

'Patience, patience!'

'A virtue for which I have never been known.'

'You're learning.' She had learned a great deal of that in the last year. 'How does it feel to go out again?'

'Heavenly.' And then she sobered. 'But a little strange. I keep waiting for it to happen. The awful. The inevitable. The press to flash lights in my face, and then the threats, the crank phone calls.'

'And does it?'

Isabella shook her head, smiling slowly. 'No, only the reporters from *Women's Wear* who want to know what I'm eating or what I'm going to wear. But it takes a long time to forget the nightmare, Natasha. A very, very long time.' At least she no longer waited for Amadeo to come home at night. It had taken a year. 'Which reminds me.' She turned her thoughts to something light. 'I want you to join me for dinner tomorrow night. Are you busy?'

'Of course not. The man I spent my energies on all summer just went back to his wife. The bastard.'

Isabella grinned, and they said it together: 'Nothing lasts forever.'

Natasha said, 'Shut up and tell me where we're going.'

The soft pink lighting warmed the familiar faces, faces one usually saw in fashion magazines or on the covers of *Fortune* or *Time*. Movie stars, moguls, publishers, authors, heads of corporations. The very good at what they did, and the very rich because they were. The tables were placed close together, the candles on the pink tablecloths danced in the soft breeze from the garden, and everyone's diamonds seemed to be glittering, as shining faces talked and laughed. Lutece had never been lovelier.

They ordered caviar to begin with, and filet mignon and poached salmon for each of them. A half bottle of red wine for Isabella, and a half of white for Natasha's fish. The salad was hearts of palm and endive, and there were big beautiful strawberries for dessert. Isabella was looking comfortable and happy, when suddenly Natasha noticed her dress.

'What's the matter?' Isabella watched her, but her friend just sat and stared.

'For a whole year you look like a nun or a scarecrow and suddenly you don't and I didn't even notice.'

Isabella only smiled. The period of official mourning was over, and tonight, for the first time, she was dressed in the palest mauve and white. The underdress was a perfectly stark, white gaberdine of her own design, and over it she had worn a soft mauve cashmere tunic, with the amethyst-and-diamond ear-rings she had once lent to Natasha.

'Do you like it? It's new.'

'Same collection as my blue marvel?' Isabella nodded as Natasha leaned towards her to confess, 'I turned up the air conditioning the other day just so I could wear it around the house.'

'Don't worry. It'll be cold enough for it soon.' Isabella shuddered, already thinking of the long New York winter that would seem to go on forever.

'You look beautiful,' Natasha said. Still there was a glimmer of something very lonely in her friend's deep, onyx eyes. 'I'm glad it's over, Isabella.' She was immediately sorry she had said it, because in some ways she knew it was not. It would never be. The loss of Amadeo would always weigh on Isabella's heart.

'I can't believe that it's been a year.' Isabella looked up from her coffee then, a wistful look in her eyes. 'In some ways it seems as though he's been gone forever. In other ways it seems only yesterday. But it's easier for me here than it was in Rome.'

'You made the right decision.'

Isabella smiled again. 'Time will tell.'

They chatted on for another hour, and then they each went home, Natasha to what now seemed to her like an empty apartment, and Isabella to her new penthouse. She undressed quietly, put on her nightgown, went to kiss Alessandro, already sound asleep in his bed, and peacefully slipped into her own bed and turned off the light. It was six o'clock the next morning when she was awakened, startled, by the sound of the phone.

'Hello?'

'Ciao, Bellezza.'

'Bernardo! Do you know what time it is? I was sleeping. Are you bored already?' Bernardo had left for Corfu shortly after her own return to New York.

'Bored? *Sei pazza*. You're crazy. I love it.' His voice sobered quickly. 'Isabella, darling . . . I had to call. I have to go to Rome.'

'Already?' She laughed at him. 'Going back to work already? That was quick.'

'No, it's not that.' There was a pause as Bernardo steeled himself to tell her. He wished he were there with her, not thousands of miles away on an island, staring helplessly at his telephone. 'I got a call yesterday. I waited till they called me back this morning, until they were sure.'

'Who, for chrissake?' She sat up and yawned sleepily. It was Saturday and she had wanted to sleep till noon. 'You're not making sense.'

'They got them, Isabella.'

'Who got what?' She was frowning now, and her blood froze suddenly as she understood. 'The kidnappers?'

'All of them. There were three. One of them talked too much. It's all over, Isabella. It's all over, *cara*.'

Listening to him, she was suddenly crying and shaking her head. 'It was over last year,' she said. She didn't know

260

if she was happy or sad now. It didn't make any difference anymore. Amadeo was gone. And catching the men who had killed him would not bring him back.

'We have to go to Rome. The police called me back this morning. They've got special permission to speed it up. The trial will be in three weeks.'

'I'm not going.' She stopped crying. Her face was deathly white.

'You have to, Isabella. You have to. They need your testimony.'

'Nardo . . . no! *Non posso. Non posso!* I can't.'

'Yes, you can. I'll be there with you.'

'I don't want to see them.'

'Neither do I. But we owe it to Amadeo. And to ourselves. You can't stay away, Isabella. What if something happens, if they are set free? Can you let this happen to someone else?'

At his words the events of a year ago rushed over her again. He had lied to her then, goddamn Corbett. It did go on forever. It would never be over. Never! She was crying again into the phone.

'Isabella, stop it. It's almost over now.'

'It isn't.'

'I promise you, *cara*. It is. Just this one last thing, and then you can put it behind you forever. The police asked me to call you, they thought it would be less of a shock if you heard it from me,' he went on. 'They don't think the trial will take more than a week. You can stay at the house.'

'I'm not coming.'

His voice was firm now. 'Yes, Isabella. You are.'

When she hung up, she sat in her bed. Seeing visions she had blotted from her mind for the last year – of waiting in the living-room in her green evening dress, watching the clock on the mantelpiece; of Alessandro and his handful of

261

cookies that night. And then the phone call, the visit to Alfredo Paccioli to sell her jewellery, Amadeo on the phone telling her to be brave. She squeezed her eyes closed, trying not to scream. With a trembling hand, she reached for the phone again, dialled Natasha's number.

By the time a sleepy Natasha answered, Isabella was hysterical.

'What? Who is this? Isabella! What's the matter? Darling, talk to me . . . Isabella? . . . Please . . .' Natasha said.

'They've caught them . . . the kidnappers . . . and I have to . . . go to the trial . . . in Rome . . .'

'I'll be right over.'

Her face buried in her pillows, Isabella fled the visions and dropped the phone.

Chapter Twenty-Seven

They drove from the airport straight to the House of San Gregorio, speeding through Rome. It was that miraculous time of the year again, still sunny and warm, yet with cool breezes and blue skies and no clouds. Mid-October. It had once been her favourite time of year. She sat in the car in stony silence, wearing a grey suit and a matching grey hat. Bernardo could barely see her eyes beneath the brim, cast down towards her hands folded tightly in her lap.

'It starts tomorrow, Bellezza. You were right to come.'

She looked at him tiredly then, and he cringed at the pain he saw so sharply etched in her eyes. 'I'm tired of doing what's right. What does it matter now?'

'It matters, *bella*. Trust me.'

She took his hand in hers. After all this time, all the arguments and accusations, she did.

There were a few photographers waiting for her at the door, but Bernardo steered her through, and they passed rapidly through the house, to the penthouse, where he set her bags down, and poured them each a glass of wine.

'How was the trip?'

'It was all right.'

'And Alessandro?'

'Mad at me for leaving, but he's fine.'

'Did you tell him why you were coming?'

She nodded slowly. 'Yes, I did. I wasn't going to, but Natasha said I owed it to him to tell him. So he wouldn't be afraid anymore.'

'What did he say?'

She looked startled. 'He was happy. But he didn't see why I had to go. Neither do I.' She sipped at the wine again and looked at Bernardo, tanned and looking years younger after his month at Corfu.

'You did and you know it. What about the office?'

'Everything's fine.' For the first time she smiled at him as she pulled off the grey hat.

'What about you?' He looked at her sharply.

'What's that supposed to mean?'

'Are you seeing anyone? It's been over a year now. It's time you went out.' He had finally come to accept what would never be between them and cherish what they had.

'Mind your own goddamn business.' She looked away at the rooftops of Rome.

'Why should I? You don't mind yours. What about Corbett Ewing?'

'What about him?' Her eyes shot back to him, startled. 'How much do you know about us?'

'I figured it out eventually. Your violent reaction about F-B, and the way you sounded that day, when I mentioned Ewing to you on the phone. I've never heard you angrier.'

She nodded slowly. 'I have never been so angry. But I thought he'd seduced me on purpose, just to get his hands on San Gregorio.'

'Is that what you think now?'

She shrugged. 'It doesn't matter anymore. I haven't seen him at all.'

'Did he seduce you?' Bernardo's voice was very soft.

'That's none of your business.' Then she softened. 'For a little while I thought we were in love. But I was wrong, that's all. It would never have worked anyway.'

'Why not?'

264

'Because – oh, dammit, Bernardo, I don't know. Maybe we're too different. Maybe I'm married to the business now. Besides, it'll never be like it was with Amadeo. And I don't want to break my heart, or anyone else's, finding that out.' She looked at him sadly. He shook his head.

'So you waste yourself, is that it? At thirty-three you close the door. You lose Amadeo, and you give up.'

'I haven't given up. I have Alessandro and the business.' She stared at him defiantly, but he wasn't buying it.

'That's not much of a life. Did you at least give Ewing a chance to tell you what happened, to find out if what you think is true?'

'I told you, it doesn't matter. And yes, I saw him once when I got back from Rome.'

'And what happened?'

'Nothing. I told him to stay away from Alessandro. I found out that while I was here Natasha had let him see the child.' She sighed softly and smiled a bitter smile. 'I told him that if he came near us again, I'd call my lawyer and the police and have him arrested for molesting Alessandro – something like that.'

'Are you crazy? What did he say?'

'He told me to get the hell out of his car.'

'He was right. I'd have kicked you out. For God's sake, Isabella, what were you thinking of?'

'I don't know . . . Myself . . . Amadeo . . . something. I told you, it's over. It wouldn't have worked out.'

'Not if that's the way you've been behaving.' He poured himself another glass of wine.

'Natasha sees him of course. They're old friends.'

'Did she tell him about the trial?' Bernardo was looking at her strangely, but she only shrugged.

'I don't know. Maybe. In any case it was in the papers again the day before I left New York. Page nine this time; we're finally shrinking in importance again. I'll tell you.

265

I'll be damn glad when the only place I see my name is in the fashion section.'

'That'll come. After this week it'll all be over. Now get some sleep. I'll pick you up in the morning.' He kissed her cheek gently and left her sitting there, sipping the last of her wine.

Chapter Twenty-Eight

'*Va bène?*' Bernardo looked at her worriedly as she stepped out of the car. She had worn a black dress today, but no black stockings this time. It was a long-sleeved black wool dress, with alligator shoes and matching handbag, and her hat was discreet and small. She wore only her pearls and the ring Bernardo had given her the last time she'd left Rome.

'Are you all right, Isabella?' he asked. She was so pale that for a moment he was afraid she would faint on the courthouse steps.

'*Va bène.*' I'm fine.

He took her arm. In an instant the barrage began. Photographers, television cameras, microphones, madness. It was reminiscent of that whole ugly time. She clutched his hand tightly, and a moment later they were inside the courthouse, waiting in a tiny room adjoining the judge's chambers. He had made it available just for her.

They sat for what felt to Isabella like hours before a uniformed guard came in and beckoned to her.

Holding tightly to Bernardo, her legs feeling wooden, she followed him into the courtroom, averting her eyes from the long table where the defendants sat, trying not to look at them, not wanting to see. Bernardo could feel her trembling as she sat down.

The testimony was long and laborious: Amadeo's secretary, the doorman, and finally two San Gregorio employees who had seen the two men come in. The story about the car was explained, and Bernardo could see one of the men squirm. More testimony from the coroner, two minor officials, and then finally it was over; court would not reconvene after lunch. Due to the painful nature of the trial, and in consideration of Signore di San Gregorio's widow, the proceedings would be adjourned until the next morning.

The judge ordered the bailiffs to remove the accused. As they stood up, ready to be escorted away, Bernardo heard Isabella gasp.

They were ordinary men in plain clothing, men she had never seen, but suddenly they were there, before her, the men who had snuffed out Amadeo's life. Bernardo held her arm tightly. Isabella had turned whiter still.

'It's all right, Isabella, it's all right,' he said, feeling helpless to soothe her. She needed something more than even he could give her. 'Come on, let's go now.'

Blindly she let herself be led. In a moment they were being mobbed again on the front steps.

'Signora di San Gregorio, did you see them? . . . How did they look . . . Do you remember? . . . Can you tell us? . . .' A hand snatched off her hat. She was running and crying, protected by two guards and Bernardo, until at last they reached the car. She threw herself into his arms, sobbing all the way back to the house. He got her upstairs quickly and helped her to the couch.

'Do you want me to call a doctor?'

'No . . . no . . . but don't leave me . . .' she began as the telephone rang. She sat bolt upright with a look of terror in her eyes. She couldn't go through it again, couldn't bear it. 'Tell them to stop putting calls through.' But Bernardo had already answered it and was speaking in low tones. She could not hear what he was saying. Finally he looked at her, smiled, and nodded his head. And then, without explaining further, he handed her the phone and left the room.

268

'Isabella?' At first she didn't recognise the voice. Then her eyes grew wide.

'Corbett?' But it couldn't be.

But the voice answered, 'Yes,' adding, 'and don't hang up on me. Or at least not just yet.'

'Where are you?' Her face was expressionless; it sounded as though he were here with her, in the same room.

'I'm downstairs, Isabella, but you don't have to see me. If you want, I'll go away.'

'But why?' And why now of all times?

'I came to steal the business. Remember me?'

'Yes, I remember you. I – I owe you an apology . . . for what I said to you in the car.' She was smiling into the phone.

'You don't owe me anything. Not an apology, not the business, not anything. Nothing but ten minutes of your time.'

An idea occurred to her then, and she was astonished. Bernardo! Had he asked Corbett to come? 'Did you fly to Rome to see me, Corbett?'

He nodded his head and answered her. 'Yes. I knew what you must be going through. I thought that maybe you needed a friend.' Then, 'Isabella, may I come upstairs?'

A moment later she opened the door for him. She did not speak. Her eyes were dark and tired and empty. Slowly she put out her hand.

'Hello, Corbett.'

It was like the beginning. He shook her hand solemnly and followed her into the room.

'Would you like a glass of wine?'

She was smiling now as she looked at him, and it took everything he had not to take her in his arms. He shook his head and looked around the room. 'Is this your office?'

'No, it's an apartment we keep for important guests.'

And then she looked at him unhappily and sat down with her head bowed. 'Oh, Corbett, I wish I weren't here.' He sat down next to her and watched her.

'I'm sorry you have to go through this, but at least they caught them. At least now you won't wonder what happened to them and if they'll ever strike again.'

'I suppose so. But I thought I had put it all away.'

He only shook his head. He didn't want to tell her that you never really can. You can't erase a memory. Or deny an irreparable loss. You could dull it, you could heal it, you could fill the void with something else. 'Isabella' – he paused for a moment – 'may I be there with you tomorrow?'

She looked at him, horrified. 'At the trial?' He nodded. 'But why?' Was he curious then? Was that it? Was he like all the others? Was that why he had come? She looked at him suspiciously, and he took her hand.

'I want to be there with you. That's why I came.'

This time she nodded, understanding, as her fingers tightened slowly in his grasp.

Chapter Twenty-Nine

The next morning she stepped out of the car with a guard ahead of and behind her, and with Corbett and Bernardo on either side. Together, they ploughed through the mob, her head bowed, her face hidden by a black hat with a brim. Moments later they were in the courtroom and the judge had entered and called Alfredo Paccioli, the jeweller, to the stand.

'And Signora di San Gregorio brought you her jewellery? All of it?'

'Yes,' Paccioli murmured.

'What did you give her in exchange for it? Did you give her anything?' The attorney was pressing, and again Paccioli said yes.

'I gave her all the cash I had in the office at the time. And I got another three hundred thousand dollars from merchants I know. I also promised to get her an equal amount the following week.'

'And what did she say?'

Corbett felt Isabella stiffen next to him, and he turned slightly to watch her. Her face was so pale, it was almost white.

'She said it wasn't enough, but she took it.'

'Did she tell you why she needed the money?'

'No.' Paccioli paused, unable to go on. When he spoke again it was almost a whisper. 'But I suspected. She she...looked...ravaged...broken...frightened...' He had to stop then as tears washed his florid face. His eyes met Isabella's. She was crying too.

271

The judge called a recess.

The testimony continued agonizingly for another three days. At last, on the fifth morning, the judge looked at her regretfully and asked her to take the stand.

'You are Isabella di San Gregorio?'

'I am.' Her voice was a tremulous whisper, her eyes almost larger than her face.

'Are you the widow of Amadeo di San Gregorio, who was abducted from his office on September seventeenth and murdered on –' The attorney checked the correct date. He supplied it, and Isabella nodded miserably.

'I am. Yes.'

'Can you tell us, in orderly fashion, what happened on that day? The last time you saw him, what you did, what you heard?'

Step by step she went through it: her arrival at the house that morning, the business they had discussed, Bernardo's warning, how she and Amadeo had been touched but had cast the warning aside. She looked briefly at Bernardo. There were tears in his eyes, and he looked away.

With anguish Corbett watched the proceedings, willing her to have the strength to go on. For days now he had watched her and listened, taken her back to San Gregorio each afternoon, and talked with her until night. But he had said nothing of an intimate nature, never touched her, except gently with his eyes. He had come to Rome as her friend, knowing that these days would be most painful, that in reliving it, at last she would be free. But knowing also that it might break her, that even if she survived it, she might want nothing from him. He had come anyway, he had been there, as he was there for her now.

'And when did you realise that your husband was late?'

'At . . . I don't know . . . perhaps seven-thirty.' She told of

272

being interrupted by Alessandro. And then, in agony, she explained further of calling Bernardo, of waiting, of suddenly being afraid. And then the phone call. She began to describe it, but she broke down and couldn't go on. She gasped for a moment, fighting for air and composure, but suddenly the tears were flowing from her eyes.

'They – they said they had . . . my husband.' It was a word strangled between a gasp and a scream. '. . . that they would kill him . . . and . . . they let me talk to him, and he said . . .'

Bernardo looked at the judge unhappily, but he only nodded. It was best if she got it over with all at once. They had to go on.

'And then what did you do?'

'Bernardo . . . Signore Franco arrived. We talked. Later that night we called the police.'

'Why later? Had the kidnappers told you not to?'

She took a deep breath and went on. 'Yes, later. But at first I was afraid that if I called the police, my accounts would be frozen and I wouldn't be able to come up with the money at all. And they were frozen, of course.' She sounded bitter as she said it.

'Is that why you tried to sell your jewellery?'

She looked at Paccioli, seated in the back of the courtroom, and nodded. He was crying openly. 'Yes. I would have done anything . . . anything . . .'

Corbett's jaw tightened, and he and Bernardo exchanged an anguished glance.

'And then what happened? After you got the money? Did you deliver it to the kidnappers, although it was less than they had asked?'

'No. I was going to. I was going to tell them. It was Monday night, and they wanted the money by Tuesday. But . . .' She began to tremble again. '. . . but they called . . . It was . . . it was . . .' A look of horror crossed her face, and her eyes searched out Corbett and Bernardo. '*Non posso!* I can't go on!'

No one moved. The judge spoke to her gently and urged her to finish if she could. She waited a moment, sobbing, while the bailiff brought her some water. She took a small sip and went on.

'It was in the papers that I had been to Alfredo. Someone told them.' And as she said it she remembered the face of the girl. 'The kidnappers knew then that my accounts had been frozen. That we'd called the police.' She sat very still and closed her eyes.

'And what did they tell you the next time you spoke to them?'

She whispered, with her eyes closed. 'That they'd kill him.'

'Was that all they said?'

'No.' She opened her eyes again, as though seeing a vision, as though she herself were now very far away. The tears streamed down her face. She looked up at the ceiling. 'They said that I could . . .' Her voice was fading as she looked back again. '. . . say goodbye to Amadeo . . . And . . . I did. He told me . . . he told me . . . to be brave for a little while, that everything would be . . . all right . . . that he loved me . . . I told him I loved him . . . and then . . . .'

She stared blindly into the courtroom.

'And then they killed him. The next morning the police found him dead.'

She was lifeless as she sat there, recalling the moment, the feeling, and the last sound of Amadeo's voice, which seemed to fade as her own voice died away. Silently she looked at the three men accused of his murder, and still crying, she shook her head. The judge quickly signalled to Bernardo. Her part in the trial was over. He wanted her removed.

274

Bernardo got quickly to his feet, having understood, and Corbett followed him and the attorney to the stand, where they reached out to Isabella, who looked at them, uncomprehending. 'They killed him . . . they killed him . . . Bernardo . . .' Her voice was a hideous wail in the courtroom . . . 'He's dead!'

Her scream had carried outside the courtroom. As Corbett and Bernardo assisted her towards the doors, they burst open, and the photographers were unleashed into the courtroom.

'Come on, Bernardo!' Corbett was suddenly all action as he swept Isabella out in his arms. 'Stay away from her, you bastards.' Bernardo and two guards were ploughing ahead, as the judge shouted for order and deputies attempted to have the press removed. The courtroom was a shambles, and Isabella was crying, and the crowd watched them, stunned.

Somehow they reached her car at last, the doors closed, and the three of them pressed together in the back seat as the car sped away, the press still shouting, cameras clicking.

Isabella collapsed on Corbett's chest.

'It's over, Isabella. It's over, darling . . . it's over.' He said it to her again and again as, stricken, Bernardo watched. He regretted ever telling her to make the journey. He had been wrong, but Corbett's eyes didn't reproach him, even when they reached the fresh crowd of press waiting for them at San Gregorio.

Bernardo stared at them in horror as Isabella began to shed fresh tears. Corbett glanced at the crowd and quickly told the driver, 'Don't stop here. Keep going.' He looked at Bernardo. 'We'll take her to my hotel.'

Bernardo nodded savagely, thinking that the only intelligent thing he'd done lately was call Corbett Ewing and ask him to come.

They were in his suite at the Hassler five minutes later, and Isabella stared at them with a ravaged face.

'It's all over now,' Corbett said. 'You'll never have to go through anything like this again.'

She nodded slowly, like a child who has just seen her entire family die in a fire.

Bernardo looked at her sorrowfully. 'I'm sorry, Bellezza.'

But she was more herself again as she watched him, and she learned forward to kiss his cheek. 'It doesn't matter. Perhaps now it really will be over. What will happen to those men?'

'If they live long enough to get out of the courtroom, they'll be found guilty, and I assume they'll be sentenced for life.' Bernardo said it viciously, and Corbett nodded; he agreed. But he stood up then and walked quickly towards the phone. He spoke into it softly and returned a moment later to consult the other two.

'I think we should leave for New York on the next plane. Can you leave, Isabella? Or do you have business to do?' She shook her head numbly and then looked up at him.

'What about my things?'

But Bernardo was on his feet now. 'I'll go get them.'

Corbett nodded. 'Fine. Can you meet us at the airport in an hour?' Bernardo nodded in answer, stood up, and looked down at Isabella.

'Is that all right with you?'

'The trial is finished?' They both nodded. The essential testimony had been given and there had never been any real doubt about the outcome. It was a capital offence. The men who had taken Amadeo and killed him would be punished.

'It's finished, Isabella. You can go home now.'

Home. Bernardo had called New York her home. For the first time, she realised that it was. She didn't belong in

276

Rome any more. Not after today, after this week, after what had happened. Her eyes sought Corbett's after Bernardo had left them and Corbett had locked the door. She watched him as he closed his suitcase and then returned for a moment to sit at her side.

'Thank you for being here. I . . . it was so awful . . . I thought I was going to die . . . All that kept me going was knowing that I had to say it, had to finish it, and get it out . . .' She looked at him again. 'And I knew I could do it as long as you were there.' And then she had to ask him. 'Did Natasha send you?'

But he shook his head slowly. He wasn't going to hide anything anymore. 'Bernardo called me.'

'Bernardo?' She looked shocked and then she nodded her head. '*Capisco.*'

'Are you angry?'

Her voice was very gentle as she smiled at him. 'No.'

This time he smiled too. He looked at her for a long moment, sitting close to her on the couch. 'There are some things we need to talk about, but right now let's get to the airport and get on that plane. Do you have your passport? If Bernardo misses us, he can always send your luggage on the next flight.'

'My passport is in my handbag.'

'Let's go then.' He held a hand out to her, and they both stood up. The limousine was already waiting downstairs. There were no paparazzi. They had no interest in Corbett Ewing at the Hassler. They were too busy at San Gregorio.

Bernardo met them at the airport an hour later, five minutes before they had to catch their plane. Isabella clung to him tightly for a last moment. '*Grazie, Nardo, grazie.*' He held her tightly for a moment and then pushed her towards the plane.

'I'll see you in March!' were his last words to her, as Corbett waved to him and they boarded.

As Rome shrank beneath them Corbett watched her silently, staring out over the wing. Finally she turned to him and slipped her hand into his. But he couldn't wait any longer. He gazed at her with a worried look in his eyes. 'Is it too soon to tell you I love you?' His voice was a whisper that barely reached her ears.

The smile spread to her eyes slowly as she looked at him.

'No, darling, it was never too soon.' They kissed long and hungrily as the stewardess waited to serve them champagne. She poured the bubbling wine into their glass, and Isabella picked up hers and looked long and hard into Corbett's eyes. Then softly she whispered to him as she lifted her glass, 'Forever, my love' . . . as long as forever may be.

Summer's End

Danielle Steel

To Bill, Beatrix, and Nicholas,
cherished people of my soul

SUMMER'S END

The summer came
  like a whisper
    dancing
    in her hair,
wishing he would
      care
    and dream
    and stop
      the carousel
    until he heard
    her truth
until he brought
  her youth
back
    laughing
      to her eyes,
she wanted him
    to realize
    she loved him
      still
    until
too late . . .
  but time
    would never
      wait,
  would never be . . .
    and she was free
for sand castles
  and dreams,
the summer schemes
  so sweet
    so sweet
    so new,
      so old . . .
the story told,
  the heavens
    blend
the love lives on
    'til
      summer's end.
                d.s.

Chapter One

Deanna Duras opened one eye to look at the clock as the first light stole in beneath the shades. It was 6:45. If she got up now, she would still have almost an hour to herself, perhaps more. Quiet moments in which Pilar could not attack, or harass; when there would be no phone calls for Marc-Edouard from Brussels or London or Rome. Moments in which she could breathe and think and be alone. She slipped out quietly from beneath the sheets, glancing at Marc-Edouard, still asleep on the far side of the bed. The very far side. For years now, their bed could have slept three or four, the way she and Marc kept to their sides. It wasn't that they never joined in the middle any more, they still did ... sometimes. When he was in town, when he wasn't tired, or didn't come home so very, very late. They still did – once in a while.

Silently she reached into the closet for the long, ivory, silk robe. She looked young and delicate in the early morning light, her dark hair falling softly over her shoulders like a sable shawl. She stooped for a moment looking for her slippers. Gone. Pilar must have them again. Nothing was sacred, not even slippers, least of all Deanna. She smiled to herself as she padded barefoot and silent across the thick carpeting and stole another glance at Marc, still asleep, so peaceful there. When he slept, he still looked terribly young, almost like the man she had met nineteen years before. She watched him as she stood in the doorway, wanting him to stir, to wake, to hold his arms out to her sleepily with a smile, whispering the words of so long ago, *'Reviens, ma chérie. Come back to bed, ma Diane. La belle Diane.'*

She hadn't been that to him in a thousand years or more. She was simply Deanna to him now, as to every-

9

one else. 'Deanna, can you come to dinner on Tuesday? Deanna, did you know that the garage door isn't properly closed? Deanna, the cashmere jacket I just bought in London got badly mauled at the cleaner. Deanna, I'm leaving for Lisbon tonight (Or Paris. Or Rome).' She sometimes wondered if he even remembered the days of *Diane*, the days of late rising and laughter and coffee in her garret, or on her roof as they soaked up the sun in the months before they were married. They had been months of golden dreams, golden hours – the stolen weekends in Acapulco, the four days in Madrid when they had pretended that she was his secretary. Her mind drifted back often to those long-ago times. Early mornings had a way of reminding her of the past.

'*Diane, mon amour*, are you coming back to bed?' Her eyes shone at the remembered words. She had been just eighteen and always anxious to come back to bed. She had been shy but so in love with him. Every hour, every moment had been filled with what she felt. Her paintings had shown it too, they glowed with the lustre of her love. She remembered his eyes, as he sat in the studio, watching her, a pile of his own work on his knees, making notes, frowning now and then as he read, then smiling in his irresistible way when he looked up. '*Alors*, Madame Picasso, ready to stop for lunch?'

'In a minute, I'm almost through.'

'May I have a look?' He would make as though to peek around the easel, waiting for her to jump up and protest, as she always did, until she saw the teasing in his eyes.

'Stop that! You know you can't see it till I'm through.'

'Why not? Are you painting a shocking nude?' Laughter lighting those dazzling blue eyes.

'Perhaps I am, monsieur. Would that upset you very much?'

'Absolutely. You're much too young to paint shocking nudes.'

'Am I?' Her big green eyes would open wide, sometimes taken in by the seeming seriousness of his words. He had replaced her father in so many ways. Marc had become the voice of authority, the strength on which she relied. She had been so overwhelmed when her father had died. It had been a godsend when suddenly Marc-Edouard Duras had appeared. She had lived with a series of aunts and uncles after her father's death, none of whom had welcomed Deanna's presence in their midst. And then finally, at the age of eighteen, after a year of vagabonding among her mother's relatives, she had gone off on her own, working in a boutique in the daytime, going to art school at night. It was the art classes that kept her spirit alive. She lived only for that. She had been seventeen when her father had died. He had died instantly, crashing in the plane he loved to fly. No plans had ever been made for her future; her father was convinced he was not only invincible but immortal. Deanna's mother had died when she was twelve, and for years there had been no one in her life except Papa. Her mother's relatives in San Francisco were forgotten, shut out, generally ignored by the extravagant and selfish man whom they held responsible for her death. Deanna knew little of what had happened, only that 'Mommy died'. Mommy died – her father's words on that bleak morning would ring in her ears for a lifetime. The Mommy who had shut herself away from the world, who had hidden in her bedroom with a bottle, promising always 'in a minute, dear' when Deanna knocked on her door. The 'in a minute, dears' had lasted for ten of her twelve years, leaving Deanna to play alone in corridors or her room, while her father flew his plane or went off suddenly on business trips with friends. For a long time it had been difficult to decide if he had disappeared on trips because her mother drank, or if she drank because Papa was always

11

gone. Whatever the reason, Deanna was alone. Until her mother died. After that there had been considerable discussion about 'what in hell to do'. 'For God's sake, I don't know a damned thing about kids, least of all little girls.' He had wanted to send her away, to a school, to a 'wonderful place where there will be horses and pretty country and lots of new friends'. But she had been so dist. aught that at last he had relented. She didn't want to go to a wonderful place, she wanted to be with him. *He* was a wonderful place, the magic father with the plane, the man who brought her marvellous gifts from faraway places. The man she had bragged about for years and never understood. Now, he was all she had. All she had left, now that the woman behind the bedroom door was gone.

So he kept her. He took her with him when he could, left her with friends when he couldn't, and taught her to enjoy the finer things in life: The Imperial Hotel in Tokyo, the George V in Paris, and The Stork Club in New York, where she had perched on a stool at the bar and not only drank a Shirley Temple but met her as a grown woman. Papa had led a fabulous life. And so had Deanna, for a while, watching everything, taking it all in, the sleek women, the interesting men, the dancing at El Morocco, the weekend trips to Beverly Hills. He had been a movie star once, a long time ago, a race driver, a pilot during the war, a gambler, a lover, a man with a passion for life and women and anything he could fly. He wanted Deanna to fly too, wanted her to know what it was to watch over the world at ten thousand feet, sailing through clouds and living on dreams. But she had had her own dreams that were nothing like his. A quiet life, a house where they stayed all the time, a stepmother who did not hide behind 'in a minute' or an always locked door. At fourteen she was tired of El Morocco, and at fifteen she was tired of dancing with his friends. At sixteen she had managed to finish school, and desperately wanted to go to Vassar or Smith. Papa insisted it would be a bore. So she painted instead, on sketch pads and canvases she took with her wherever they went. She drew on paper tablecloths in the South of France, and the backs of letters from his friends, having no friends of her own. She drew on anything she could get her hands on. A gallery owner in Venice had told her that she was good, that if she stuck around, he might show her work. He didn't of course. They left Venice after a month, and Florence after two, Rome after six, and Paris after one, then finally came back to the States, where Papa promised her a home, a real one this time, and maybe even a real-live stepmother to go with it. He had met an American actress in Rome – 'someone you'll love,' he had promised, as he packed a bag for the weekend at her ranch somewhere near L.A.

This time he didn't ask Deanna to come along. This time he wanted to be alone. He left Deanna at the Fairmont in San Francisco, with four hundred dollars in cash and a promise to be back in three days. Instead he was dead in three hours, and Deanna was alone. Forever this time. And back where she had started, with the threat of a 'wonderful school'.

But this time the threat was short-lived. There was no money left. For a wonderful school or anything else. None. And a mountain of debts that went unpaid. She called the long-forgotten relatives of her mother. They arrived at the hotel and took her to live with them. 'Only for a few months, Deanna. You understand. We just can't. You'll have to get a job, and get your own place when you get on your feet.' A job What job? What could she do? Paint? Draw? Dream. What difference did it make now that she knew almost every piece in the Uffizi and the Louvre, that she had spent months in the Jeu de Paume, that she had watched her father run with the bulls in Pamplona, had danced at El Morocco and stayed at the Ritz? Who gave a damn? No one did. In three months she was moved in with a cousin and then with another aunt. 'For a while, you understand.' She understood it all now, the loneliness, the pain, the seriousness of what her father had done. He had played his life away. He had had a good time. Now she understood what had happened to her mother, and why. For a time she came to hate the man she had loved. He had left her alone, frightened, and unloved.

Providence had come in the form of a letter from France. There had been a small case pending in the French courts, a minor judgement, but her father had won. It was a matter of six or seven thousand dollars. Would she be so kind as to have her attorney contact the French firm? What attorney? She called one from a list she got from one of her aunts, and he referred her to an international firm of lawyers. She had gone to their offices at nine o'clock on a Monday morning, dressed in a little black dress she had bought with her father in France. A little black Dior, with a little black alligator bag he had brought her back from Brazil, and the pearls that were all that her mother had left her. She didn't give a damn about Dior, or Paris, or Rio, or anything else. The promised six or seven thousand dollars was a king's ransom to her. She wanted to give up her job and go to art school day and night. In a few years she'd make a name for herself with her art. But in the meantime maybe she could live on the six thousand for a year. Maybe.

That was all she wanted when she walked into the huge wood-panelled office and met Marc-Edouard Duras for the very first time.

'Mademoiselle . . .' He had never had a case quite like hers. His field was corporate law, complex international business cases, but when the secretary had relayed her call, he had been intrigued. When he saw her, a delicate child-woman with a frightened beautiful face, he was fascinated. She moved with mystifying grace, and the eyes that looked into his were bottomless. He ushered her to a seat on the other side of the desk, and looked very grave. But his eyes danced as they talked their way through the hour. He too loved the Uffizi, he too had once spent days at a time in the Louvre; he had also been to São Paulo and Caracas and Deauville. She found herself sharing her world with him and opening windows and doors that she had thought were sealed forever. And she had explained about her father. She told him the whole dreadful tale, as she sat across from him, with the largest green eyes he had ever seen and a fragility that tore at his heart. He had been almost thirty-two at the time, certainly not old enough to be her father, and his feelings were certainly not paternal. But nonetheless he took her under his wing. Three months later she was his wife. The ceremony was small and held at city hall; the honeymoon was spent at his mother's house in Antibes, followed by two weeks in Paris.

And by then she understood what she had done. She had married a country as well as a man. A way of life. She would have to be perfect, understanding – and silent. She would have to be charming and entertain his clients and friends. She would have to be lonely while he travelled. And she would have to give up the dream of making a name for herself with her art. Marc didn't really approve. In the days when he courted her, he had been amused, but it was not a career he encouraged for his wife. She had become Madame Duras, and to Marc that meant a great deal.

Over the years she gave up a number of dreams, but she had Marc. The man who had saved her from solitude and starvation. The man who had won her gratitude and her heart. The man of impeccable manners and exquisite taste, who rewarded her with security and sable. The man who always wore a mask.

She knew that he loved her, but now he rarely expressed it as he had done before. 'Shows of affection are for children,' he explained.

But that would come too. They conceived their first child in less than a year. How Marc had wanted that baby! Enough to show her once more how much he loved her. A boy. It would be a boy. Because Marc said so. He was certain, and so was Deanna. She wanted only that. His son. It had to be; it was the one thing that would win her his respect and maybe even his passion for a lifetime. A son. And it was. A tiny baby boy with a whisper in his lungs. The priest was called only moments after the birth and christened him Philippe-Edouard. In four hours the baby was dead.

Marc took her to France for the summer and left her in the care of his mother and aunts. He spent the summer working in London, but he came back on weekends, holding her close and drying her tears, until at last she conceived again. The second baby died too, another boy. And having Marc's child became her obsession. She dreamed only of their son. She even stopped painting. The doctor put her to bed when she became pregnant for the third time. Marc had cases in Milan and Morocco that year, but he called and sent flowers and, when he was at home, sat at her bedside. Once more he promised that she would have his son. This time he was wrong. The long-awaited heir was a girl, but a healthy baby, with a halo of blonde hair and her father's blue eyes. The child of Deanna's dreams. Even Marc resigned himself and quickly fell in love with the tiny blonde girl. They named her Pilar and flew to France to show her to his mother. Madame Duras bemoaned Deanna's failure to produce a son. But Marc didn't care. The baby was his. His child, his flesh. She would speak only French; she would spend every summer in Antibes. Deanna had felt feeble flutterings of fear, but she revelled in the joy of motherhood at last.

Marc spent every spare moment with Pilar, showing her off to his friends. She was always a child of laughter and smiles. Her first words were in French. By the time she was ten she was more at home in Paris than the States – the books she read, the clothes she wore, the games she played had all been carefully imported by

Marc. She knew who she was: a Duras, and where she belonged: in France. At twelve, she went to boarding school in Grenoble. By then the damage was done; Deanna had lost a daughter. Deanna was a foreigner to her now, an object of anger and resentment. It was *her* fault they didn't live in France, *her* fault Pilar couldn't be with her friends. *Her* fault Papa couldn't be in Paris with Grand-mère who missed him so much. In the end they had won. Again.

Deanna walked softly down the steps, her bare feet a whisper on the Persian runner Marc had brought back from Iran. Out of habit she glanced into the living room. Nothing was out of place; it never was. The delicate green silk of the couch was smoothed to perfection; the Louis XV chairs stood at attention like soldiers at their posts; the Aubusson rug was as exquisite as ever in its soft celadon greens and faded raspberry-coloured flowers. The silver shone; the ashtrays were immaculate; the portraits of Marc's enviable ancestors hung at precisely the right angle; and the curtains framed a perfect view of the Golden Gate Bridge and the bay. There were no sailboats yet at this hour, and for once there was no fog. It was a perfect June day, and she stood for a moment, looking at the water. She was tempted to sit down and simply watch. But it seemed sacrilege to rumple the couch, to tread on the rug, even to breathe in that room. It was easier to simply move on, to her own little world, to the studio at the back of the house where she painted ... where she fled.

She walked past the dining room without looking in, then soundlessly down a long corridor to the back of the house. A half flight of stairs led to her studio. The dark wood was cold on her feet. The door was stiff, as always. Marc had given up reminding her to have something done about it. He had come to the conclusion that she liked it that way, and he was right. It was difficult to open, and it always slammed rapidly closed, sealing her into her own bright little cocoon. The studio was her own precious world, a burst of music and flowers tenderly tucked away from the stifling sobriety of the rest of the house. No Aubussons here, no silver, no Louis XV. Here, everything was bright and alive – the paints on her palette, the canvases on her easel, the soft yellow of the walls, and the big, comfortable, white chair that embraced her the moment she relinquished herself into its arms. She smiled as she sat down and looked around. She had left a terrible mess the morning before, but it suited her; it was a happy place in which she could work. She flung back the flowered curtains and pushed open the french doors, stepping on to the tiny terrace, the bright tiles like ice beneath her feet.

She often stood here at this hour, sometimes even in the fog, breathing deeply and smiling at the spectre of the bridge hanging eerily above an invisible bay, listening to the slow owl hoot of the foghorns. But not this morning. This morning the sun was so bright that she squinted as she stepped outside. It would be a perfect day to go sailing, or disappear to the beach. The very idea made her laugh. Who would tell Margaret what to polish, who would respond to the mail, who would explain to Pilar why she could not go out that night? Pilar. This was the day of Pilar's departure. Cap d'Antibes for the summer, to visit her grandmother and her aunts, uncles, and cousins, all down from Paris. Deanna almost shuddered at the memory. After years of enduring those stifling summers, she had finally said no. The eternal charm of Marc's family had been insufferable, politesse through clenched teeth, the invisible thorns that ripped through one's flesh. Deanna had never won their approval. Marc's mother made no secret of that. Deanna was, after all, an American, and far too young to be a respectable match. Worst of all, she had been the penniless daughter of an extravagant wanderer. It was a marriage that added nothing to Marc's consequences, only to her own. His relatives assumed that was why she had snared him. And they were careful not to mention it – more than twice a year. Eventually Deanna had had enough, and had stopped making the pilgrimage to Antibes for the summer. Now, Pilar went alone, and she loved it. She was one of *them*.

Deanna leaned her elbows on the 'errace wall, and propped her chin on the back of one hand. A sigh escaped her unnoticed as she watched a freighter glide slowly into the bay.

'Aren't you cold out here, Mother?' The words were as chilly as the terrace tiles. Pilar had spoken to her as though she were an oddity, standing there in her bathrobe and bare feet. Deanna cast a look at the ship and turned slowly around with a smile.

'Not really. I like it out here. And besides, I couldn't find my slippers.' She said it with the same steady smile and looked directly into her daughter's brilliant blue eyes. The girl was everything Deanna was not. Her hair was the palest gold, her eyes an almost iridescent blue, and her skin had the rich glow of youth. She was almost a head taller than her mother, and in almost every possible way the image of Marc-Edouard. But she did not yet have his aura of power – that would come later. And if she learned her lessons well from her grandmother and aunts, she would learn to mask it almost as viciously as they did. Marc-Edouard was not quite as artful; there was no need to be, he was a man. But the Duras women practiced a far subtler art. There was little Deanna could do to change that now, except perhaps keep Pilar away, but that would be a fruitless venture. Pilar, Marc, the old woman herself, all conspired to keep Pilar in Europe much of the time. And there was more to Pilar's resemblance to her grandmother than mimicry. It was something that ran in her blood. There was nothing Deanna could do, other than accept it. She never ceased to marvel, though, at how acutely painful the disappointment always was. There was never a moment when she didn't care, when it mattered less. It always mattered. She always felt Pilar's loss. Always.

She smiled now and looked down at her daughter's feet. She was wearing the absentee slippers. 'I see you've found them.' Deanna's words teased, but her eyes wore the pain of a lifetime. Tragedy constantly hidden by jokes.

'Is that supposed to be funny, Mother?' There was already warfare in Pilar's face, at barely seven-thirty in the morning. 'I can't find any of my good sweaters, and my black skirt isn't back from your dressmaker.' It was an accusation of major importance. Pilar flung back her long, straight, blonde hair and looked angrily at her mother.

Deanna always wondered at Pilar's fury. Teenage rebellion? Or merely that she didn't want to share Marc with Deanna? There was nothing Deanna could do. At least not for the moment. Maybe one day, maybe later, maybe in five years she'd get another chance to win back her daughter and become her friend. It was something she lived for. A hope that refused to die.

'The skirt came back yesterday. It's in the hall closet. The sweaters are already in your suitcase. Margaret packed for you yesterday. Does that solve all your problems?' The words were spoken gently. Pilar would always be the child of her dreams, no matter what, no matter how badly the dreams had been shattered.

'Mother! You're not paying attention!' For a moment Deanna's mind had wandered, and Pilar's eyes blazed at her. 'I asked you what you did with my passport.'

Deanna's green eyes met Pilar's blue ones and held them for a long moment. She wanted to say something, the right thing. All she said was, 'I have your passport. I'll give it to you at the airport.'

'I'm perfectly capable of taking care of it myself.'

'I'm sure you are.' Deanna stepped carefully back into her studio, avoiding the girl's gaze. 'Are you going to have breakfast?'

'Later. I have to wash my hair.'

'I'll have Margaret bring you a tray.'

'Fine.' Then she was gone, a bright arrow of youth that had pierced Deanna's heart yet again. It took so little to hurt. The words were all so small, but their emptiness stung her. Surely there had to be more. Surely one did not have children merely to have it end like this? She wondered sometimes if it would have been this way with her sons. Maybe it was just Pilar. Maybe the pull between two countries, and two worlds, was too great for her.

The phone buzzed softly on her desk as she sighed and sat down. It was the house line, no doubt Margaret asking if she wanted her coffee in the studio. When Marc was away, Deanna often ate alone in this room. When he was at home, breakfast with him was a ritual, sometimes the only meal they shared.

'Yes?' Her voice had a soft, smoky quality that always lent gentleness to her words.

'Deanna, I have to call Paris. I won't be downstairs for another fifteen minutes. Please tell Margaret that I want my eggs fried, and not burned to a crisp. Have you got the newspapers up there?'

'No, Margaret must have them waiting for you at the table.'

'*Bon. À tout de suite.*'

Not even 'good morning', no 'how are you? How did you sleep? ... I love you.' Only the papers, the black skirt, the passport, the – Deanna's eyes filled with tears. She wiped them away with the back of her hand. They didn't do it deliberately, they were simply that way. But why didn't they care where *her* black skirt was, where *her* slippers were, how *her* latest painting was coming. She glanced over her shoulder wistfully as she closed the door to her studio behind her. Her day had begun.

Margaret heard her rustling the papers in the dining room and opened the kitchen door with her customary smile. 'Morning, Mrs Duras.'

'Good morning, Margaret.'

And so it went, as ever, with precision and grace. Orders were given with kindness and a smile; the newspapers were carefully set out in order of importance; the coffee was immediately placed on the table in the delicate Limoges pot that had belonged to Marc's mother; the curtains were pulled back; the weather was observed; and everyone manned his station, donned his mask, and began a new day.

Deanna forgot her earlier thoughts as she glanced at the paper and sipped coffee from the flowered blue cup, rubbing her feet along the carpet to warm them from the chill of the tile on the terrace. She looked young in the morning, her dark hair loose, her eyes wide, her skin as clear as Pilar's, and her hands as delicate and unlined as they had been twenty years before. She didn't look her thirty-seven years, but more like someone in her late twenties. It was the way she lifted her face when she spoke, the sparkle in her eyes, the smile that appeared like a rainbow that made her seem very young. Later in the day, the consummately conservative style, the carefully knotted hair, and the regal bearing as she moved would make her seem more than her age. But in the morning she was burdened with none of the symbols – she was simply herself.

She heard him coming down the stairs before she heard him speak, calling back gaily to Pilar in French as the girl stood with wet hair on the second-floor landing. It was something about staying out of Nice and making sure she behaved herself in Antibes. Unlike Deanna, Marc would be seeing his daughter again in the course of the summer. He would be back and forth between Paris and San Francisco several times, stopping off in Antibes for a weekend, whenever he could. Old habits were too hard to break, and the lure of his daughter was too great. They had always been friends.

'*Bonjour, ma chère.*'

Ma chère, not *ma chérie*. My dear, not my darling, Deanna observed. The *i* had fallen from the word many years since. 'You look pretty this morning.'

'Thank you.' She looked up with the dawn of a smile, then saw him already studying the papers. The compliment had been a formality more than a truth. The art of the French. She knew it well. 'Anything new in Paris?' Her face was once again grave.

'I'll let you know. I'm going over tomorrow. For a while.' Something in his tone told her there was more. There always was.

'How long a while?'

He looked at her, amused, and she was reminded once again of all the reasons she had fallen in love with him. Marc was an incredibly handsome man, with a lean, aristocratic face and flashing blue eyes that even Pilar's couldn't match. The grey at his temples barely showed in the still-sandy-blonde hair. He still looked young and dynamic, and almost always amused, particularly when he was in the States. He found Americans 'amusing': It amused him when he beat them at tennis and squash, at bridge or backgammon, and particularly in the courtroom. He worked the way he played – hard and fast and well, and with extraordinary results. He was a man whom men envied and over whom women fawned. He always won. Winning was his style. Deanna had loved that about him at first. It had been such a victory when he first told her he loved her.

'I asked you how long you'd be away.' There was a tiny edge to her voice.

'I'm not sure. A few days. Does it matter?'

'Of course.' The edge to her voice.

'Have we something important?' He looked sur-

23

prised; he had checked the book and hadn't seen anything there. 'Well?'

No, nothing important, darling ... only each other.
'No, no, nothing like that. I just wondered.'

'I'll let you know. I'll have a better idea after some meetings today. There's a problem apparently on the big shipping case. I may have to go directly to Athens from Paris.'

'Again?'

'So it would seem.' He went back to the papers until Margaret set his eggs in front of him then glanced at his wife again. 'You're taking Pilar to the airport?'

'Of course.'

'Please see to it that she's properly dressed. Mother will have a stroke if she gets off the plane again in one of those outrageous costumes.'

'Why don't you tell her yourself?' Deanna fixed him with her green eyes.

'I thought that was more your province.' He looked unmoved.

'What, discipline or her wardrobe?' Each of them thankless tasks, as they both knew.

'Both, to a degree.' She wanted to ask to what degree, but she didn't. To the degree that she was capable of it? Was that what he meant? Marc went on. 'I've given her some money for the trip, by the way. So you won't have to.'

'How much?'

He glanced up sharply. 'I beg your pardon?'

'I asked how much money you gave her for the trip.' She said it very quietly.

'Is that important?'

'I think so. Or are discipline and wardrobe my only departments?' The edge of eighteen years of marriage coloured her tone now.

'Not necessarily. Don't worry, she has enough.'

'That's not what I'm worried about.'

'What are you worried about?' His tone was suddenly not pleasant, and her eyes were like steel.

'I don't think she should have too much money for the summer. She doesn't need it.'

'She's a very responsible girl.'

'But she is not quite sixteen years old, Marc. How much did you give her?'

'A thousand.' He said it very quietly, as though he were closing a deal.

'Dollars?' Her eyes flew wide. 'That's outrageous!'

'Is it?'

'You know perfectly well it is. And you also know what she'll do with it.'

'Amuse herself, I assume. Harmlessly.'

'No, she'll buy one of those damn motorcycles she wants so much, and I absolutely refuse to allow that to happen.' But Deanna's fury was matched only by her impotence and she knew it. Pilar was going to 'them' now, out of Deanna's control. 'I don't want her to have that much money.'

'Don't be absurd.'

'For God's sake, Marc...'

The telephone rang as she began her tirade in earnest. It was for Marc, from Milan. He had no time to listen to her before he left. He had a meeting to attend at nine-thirty. He glanced at his watch. 'Stop being so hysterical, Deanna. The child will be in good hands.' But that was a whole other discussion right there, and he didn't have time. 'I'll see you tonight.'

'Will you be home for dinner?'

'I doubt it. I'll have Dominique call.'

'Thank you.' They were two tiny, frozen words. She watched him close the door. A moment later she heard his Jaguar purr out of the driveway. She had lost another war.

She broached the subject again with Pilar on the way to the airport. 'I understand your father gave you quite a lot of money for the summer.'

'Here we go. What is it now?'

25

'You know damn well what it is now. The motor-cycle. I'll put it to you very simply, love. You buy one and I'll have you hauled home.'

Pilar wanted to taunt her with 'how will you know?' but she didn't dare. 'O.K., so I won't buy one.'

'Or ride one.'

Or ride one.' But it was a useless parroting, and Deanna found herself, for the first time in a long time, wanting to scream.

She glanced at her daughter for a moment as she drove and then looked straight ahead again. 'Why does it have to be this way? You're leaving for three months. We won't see each other. Couldn't it be pleasant be-tween us today? What's the point of this constant hag-gling?'

'I didn't start it. You brought up the motorcycle.'

'Do you have any idea why? Because I love you, be-cause I give a damn. Because I don't want you killed. Does that make any sense to you?' There was despera-tion in her voice, and finally anger.

'Yeah, sure.'

They rode on in silence to the airport. Deanna felt tears sting her eyes again, but she would not let Pilar see them. She had to be perfect, she had to be strong. The way Marc was, the way all his damned French relatives pretended to be, the way Pilar wanted to be. Deanna left her car with the valet at the kerb, and they followed the porter inside, where Pilar checked in. When the clerk handed back her passport and ticket, she turned to her mother.

'You're coming to the gate?' There was more dismay in her voice than encouragement.

'I thought that might be nice. Would you mind?'

'No.' Sullen, and angry. A goddamn child. Deanna wanted to slap her. Who was this person? Who had she become? Where had the sunny little girl who loved her gone? They each held tightly to their own thoughts as they walked towards the gate, collecting appreciative glances as they went. They were a striking pair. The dark beauty of Deanna in a beautifully cut, black wool dress, her hair swept into a knot, with a bright red jacket over one arm; Pilar in her youthful blaze of blonde, tall and slender and graceful in a white linen suit that had met with her mother's approval as she came down the stairs. Even her grandmother would approve – unless she found the cut too American. Anything was possible, with Madame Duras.

The plane was already boarding when they arrived, and Deanna had only a moment to hold the girl's hand tightly in her own. 'I mean it about the motorcycle, darling. Please . . .'

'All right, all right.' But Pilar was already looking past Deanna, eager to be on the plane.

'I'll call you. And call me, if you have any problems.'

'I won't.' It was said with the assurance of not-quite-sixteen years.

'I hope not.' Deanna's face softened as she looked at her daughter, then pulled her into a hug. 'I love you, darling. Have a good time.'

'Thanks, Mom.' She favoured her mother with a brief smile, and a quick wave, as her golden mane flew into the passageway. Deanna suddenly felt leaden. She was gone again. Her baby . . . the little girl with the curly blonde hair, the child who had held her arms out so trustingly each night to be hugged and kissed . . . Pilar. Deanna took a seat in the lounge and waited to see the 747 begin its climb into the sky. At last she rose and walked slowly back to her car. The valet tipped his cap appreciatively at the dollar she handed him and wondered about her as she swung her legs gracefully into the car. She was one hell of a good-looking woman; he couldn't quite guess how old she was: twenty-eight? thirty-two? thirty-five? forty? It was impossible to tell. Her face was young, but the rest of her, the way she moved, the look in her eyes, was so old.

*

27

Deanna heard him coming up the stairs as she sat at her dressing table, brushing her hair. It was twenty after ten, and he hadn't called her all day. Dominique, his secretary, had left a message with Margaret at noon: Monsieur Duras would not be home for dinner. Deanna had eaten in the studio while she sketched, but her mind had not been on her work. She had been thinking of Pilar.

She turned and smiled at him as he came into the room. She had actually missed him. The house had been strangely quiet all day. 'Hello, darling. That was a long day.'

'Very long. And yours?'

'Peaceful. It's too quiet here without Pilar.'

'I never thought I'd hear you say that.' Marc-Edouard smiled at his wife as he slid into a large blue-velvet chair near the fireplace.

'Neither did I. How were your meetings?'

'Tiresome.'

He was not very expansive. She turned in her seat to look at him. 'You're still going to Paris tomorrow?' He nodded, and she continued to watch him as he stretched his long legs. He looked no different than he had that morning and seemed almost ready to take on another day. He thrived on the meetings he called 'tiresome'. He stood up and walked towards her with a smile in his eyes.

'Yes, I'm going to Paris tomorrow. Are you quite sure you don't want to join Pilar and my mother in Cap d'Antibes?'

'Quite sure.' Her look was determined. 'Why would I want to do that?'

'You said yourself that it was too quiet here. I thought perhaps . . .' He put his hands on her shoulders as he went to stand behind her for a moment. 'I'm going to be gone all summer, Deanna.'

Her shoulders stiffened in his hands. 'All summer?'

28

'More or less. The Salco shipping case is too important to leave in anyone else's hands. I'll be commuting
back and forth between Paris and Athens all summer. I
just can't be here.' His accent seemed stronger now
when he spoke to her, as though he had already left the
States. 'It will give me plenty of opportunity to check
up on Pilar, which should please you, but not any opportunity to be with you.' She wanted to ask him if he
really cared, but she didn't ask. 'I think the case will
take the better part of the summer. About three
months.'

It sounded like a death sentence to her. 'Three
months?' Her voice was very small.

'Now you see why I asked if you'd like to go to Cap
d'Antibes. Does this change your mind?'

She shook her head slowly. 'No. It doesn't. You won't
be there either, and I think Pilar needs a break from
me. Not to mention . . .' her voice drifted off.

'My mother?' Marc asked. She nodded. 'I see. Well
then, *ma chère*, you will be here all alone.'

Dammit, why didn't he ask her to go with him, to
commute between Athens and Paris. For a wild moment
Deanna thought of suggesting it to him, but she knew
he wouldn't let her go. He liked to be free when he
worked. He would never take her along.

'Can you manage alone?' he said now.

'Do I have a choice? Do you mean I could say no
and you wouldn't go?' She turned her face up to his.

'You know that's not possible.'

'Yes, I do.' She was silent for a time and then shrugged
with a small smile. 'I'll manage.'

'I know you will.'

*How do you know dammit? How do you know? What
if I can't? What if I need you? . . . What if . . .*

'You're a very good wife, Deanna.'

For a brief second she didn't know whether to thank
him or slap him. 'What does that mean? That I don't

29

complain very much? Maybe I should.' Her smile hid what she felt and allowed him to dodge what he chose not to answer.

'No, you shouldn't. You are perfect the way you are.'

'*Merci, monsieur.*' She stood up then and turned away so he would not see her face. 'Will you pack yourself, or do you want me to pack for you?'

'I'll do it myself. You go to bed. I'll be there in a while.'

Deanna watched him dart around his dressing room, then disappear downstairs, to his study, she assumed. She had turned off the lights in the bedroom and was lying very still on her side of the bed when he returned.

'*Tu dors?* Are you asleep?'

'No.' Her voice was husky in the dark.

'*Bon.*'

Good? Why? What did it matter if she were asleep or not? Would he talk to her, tell her that he loved her, that he was sorry he was going? He wasn't sorry and they both knew it. This was what he loved to do, gad about the world, plying his trade, enjoying his work and his reputation. He adored it. He slid into bed, and they lay there for a time, awake, pensive, silent.

'Are you angry that I'm going away for so long?'

She shook her head. 'No, not angry, sorry. I'll miss you. Very much.'

'It will pass quickly.' She didn't answer, and he propped himself up on one elbow to study her face in the dark room. 'I'm sorry, Deanna.'

'So am I.' He ran a hand gently across her hair and smiled at her, and she turned her head slowly to look at him.

'You're still very pretty, Deanna. Do you know that? You're even prettier than you were as a girl. Very handsome in fact.' But she didn't want to be handsome, she wanted to be his, as she had been so long ago. His *Diane*. 'Pilar will be beautiful one day, too.' He said it with pride.

30

'She already is.' Deanna said it dispassionately, without anger.

'Are you jealous of her?'

He almost seemed to like the idea, and Deanna wondered. Maybe it made him feel important. Or young. But she answered him anyway. Why not? 'Yes, sometimes I'm jealous of her. I'd like to be that young again, that free, that sure of what life owes me. At her age it's all so obvious: you deserve the best, you'll get the best. I used to think so too.'

'And now, Deanna? Has life paid you its debt?'

'In some ways.' Her eyes held a certain sadness as they met his. For the first time in years he was reminded of the eighteen-year-old orphan who had sat across from him in his office wearing the little black Dior dress. He wondered if he had truly made her unhappy, if she really wanted more. But he had given her so much. Jewels, cars, furs, a home. All the things most women wanted. What more could she possibly want? He looked at her for a very long time, his eyes questioning, his face creased with a sudden thought. Was it possible that he really did not understand?

'Deanna . . .?' He didn't want to ask, but suddenly he had to. There was too much in her eyes. 'Are you unhappy?'

She looked at him squarely and wanted to say yes. But she was afraid. She would lose him; he would leave her, and then what? She didn't want to lose Marc. She wanted more of him.

'Are you unhappy?' He repeated the question and looked pained to realise what the answer was. She didn't have to say the words. Suddenly it was clear. Even to him.

'Sometimes I am. And sometimes not. Much of the time I don't give it much thought. I miss . . . I miss the old days though, when we first met, when we were very young.' Her voice was very small as she said it.

'We've grown up, Deanna, you can't change that.' He

31

leaned towards her and touched her chin with his hand, as though perhaps he might kiss her. But the hand fell away, as did the thought. 'You were such a charming child.' He smiled at the memory of what he had felt. 'I hated your father for leaving you in that mess.'

'So did I. But that was just the way he was. I've made peace with all that.'

'Have you?' She nodded. 'Are you quite sure?'

'Why shouldn't I?'

'Because I sometimes think you still resent him. I think that's why you continue to paint. Just to prove to yourself that you can still do something on your own, if you ever have to.' He looked at her more closely then, his forehead wrinkling into a frown. 'You won't ever have to, you know. I'll never leave you in the condition that your father did.'

'I'm not worried about that. And you're wrong. I paint because I love it, because it's a part of me.' He had never wanted to believe that, that her artwork was part of her soul.

He didn't answer for a time but lay looking up at the ceiling, turning things around in his mind. 'Are you terribly cross that I'm going away for the summer?'

'I told you, I'm not. I'll simply paint, relax, read, see some of my friends.'

'Will you go out a great deal?' He sounded worried, and she was amused. He was a fine one to ask about that.

'I don't know, silly. I'll let you know if I'm asked. I'm sure there'll be the usual dinner parties, benefits, concerts, that sort of thing.' He nodded again, saying nothing. 'Marc-Edouard, are you jealous?' There was laughter in her eyes, and then she laughed aloud as he turned to look into her face. 'Oh, you are! Don't be silly! After all these years?'

'What better time?'

'Don't be absurd, darling. That's not my style.' He knew that was true.

'I know that. But, *on ne sait jamais*. One never knows.'

'How can you say something like that?'

'Because I have a beautiful wife, with whom any man in his right mind would be crazy not to fall in love.' It was the most elaborate speech he had made to her in years. She showed her surprise. 'What? You think I haven't noticed? Deanna, now you are being absurd. You are a young and beautiful woman.'

'Good. Then don't go to Greece.' She was smiling up at him again, like a very young girl. But he didn't look amused now.

'I have to. You know that.'

'All right. Then take me with you.' There was an unaccustomed note in her voice, half teasing, half serious. He didn't answer for a long time. 'Well? Can I go?'

He shook his head. 'No, you can't.'

'Well, then I guess you'll just have to be jealous.' They hadn't teased like this in years and years. His going away for three months had produced an assortment of very odd feelings. But she didn't want to push him too far. 'Seriously, darling, you don't have to worry.'

'I hope not.'

'Marc! *Arrête! Stop it*!' She leaned forward and reached for his hand, and he let her take it in hers. 'I love you . . . do you know that?'

'Yes. Do you know as well that I love you?'

Her eyes grew very serious as they looked into his. 'Sometimes I'm not so sure.' He was always too busy to show her he loved her, and it wasn't his style. But now something told her that she had hit home, and she was stunned as she watched him. Didn't he know? Didn't he realise what he had done? The wall he had built around himself, surrounded by business and work, gone

33

for days or weeks, and now months, and his only ally Pilar? 'I'm sorry, darling. I suppose you do. But sometimes I have to remind myself of it.'

'But I do love you. You must know that.'

'Deep inside I think I do know.' She knew it when she recalled the moments they had shared, the landmarks in a lifetime, which tell the tale. Those were the reasons why she still loved him.

He sighed. 'But you need a great deal more. Don't you, my dear?' She nodded, feeling at once young and brave. 'You need my time as well as my affection. You need ... *enfin*, you need what I don't have to give.'

'That's not true. You could have the time. We could do some of the things we used to. We could!' She sounded like a plaintive child and hated herself for it. She sounded like the child who had hounded her father to take her along. And she hated needing anyone that much. She had sworn long ago that she never would again. 'I'm sorry. I understand.' Her eyes lowered and she withdrew.

'Do you understand?' He was watching her very closely.

'Of course.'

'Ah, *ma Diane* ...' His eyes were troubled as he took her in his arms. She didn't notice; her own were too filled with tears. He had said it at last. *'Ma Diane ...'*

Chapter Two

'You have enough money in the bank for the entire time I'll be gone. But if you need more, call Dominique at the office, and she'll transfer it. I told Sullivan I want him to look in on you at least twice a week. And ...'

Deanna looked at her husband in surprise. 'You told Jim to look in on me? Why?' Jim Sullivan was Marc-Edouard's American partner, and one of the few Americans he truly liked.

'Because I want to make sure that you're well, happy, and have everything you need.'

'Thank you, but it seems silly to bother Jim.'

'He'll enjoy it. Show him your latest paintings, have him for dinner. I trust him.' He looked at his wife with a smile. And she smiled back.

'You can trust me too.' In the eighteen years of her marriage, she had never cheated on Marc. She wasn't going to start now.

'I do trust you. I'll call as often as I can. You know where I'll be. If anything comes up, just call. I'll get back to you as soon as possible, if I'm not in.' She nodded quietly at his words, and then let out a small sigh. He turned to look at her in the silence of the Jaguar. For a moment there was worry in his eyes. 'You'll be all right, Deanna, won't you?'

Her eyes found his. She nodded. 'Yes. I'll be fine. But I'll miss you terribly.'

He was already looking back at the road. 'The time will go quickly. If you change your mind, you can always join Mother and Pilar in Cap d'Antibes.' He smiled at his wife again. 'Not that you will.'

'No, I won't.' She smiled back.

'*Têtue, va.* Stubborn one. Perhaps that's why I love you.'

35

'Is that why? I've often wondered.' There was a teasing sparkle in her eyes now as she studied the handsome profile next to her in the car. 'You'll take care of yourself, won't you? Don't work too terribly hard.' But it was a useless admonition, and they both knew it.

'I won't.' He smiled at her tenderly.

'You will.'

'I will.'

'And you'll enjoy every minute of it.' They both knew that was true too. 'I hope the Salco case comes out in your favour.'

'It will. You can be quite sure of that.'

'Marc-Edouard Duras, you are unbearably arrogant. Has anyone told you that yet today?'

'Only the woman I love.' He reached for her hand as he took the turnoff for the airport, and she touched his fingers gently with her own. It made her think of the night before and the rare meshing of their bodies that she cherished so much. *Ma Diane* ... 'I love you, darling.' She pulled his hand to her lips and gently kissed the tips of his fingers. 'I wish we had more time.'

'So do I. We will one of these days.'

Yes ... but when? She carefully put his hand back on the seat and left her fingers intertwined with his.

'When you come back, do you suppose we could go somewhere together, for a holiday?' She watched him, her eyes wide, childlike. She still wanted him, wanted to be with him, to be his. After all these years she still cared. Sometimes it still surprised her how much she did.

'Where would you like to go?'

'Anywhere. Just so we're together.' And alone.

He looked at her for a long moment as they pulled up outside the terminal, and for an instant Deanna thought she saw regret in his eyes. 'We'll do that. As soon as I get back.' Then he seemed to catch his breath. 'Deanna, I ...'

She waited, but he said no more; he only put his

arms around her and held her close. She felt her own arms go around him and hold him close. She squeezed her eyes tightly shut. She needed him more than he knew. There were tears sliding slowly down her face. He felt her trembling in his arms and pulled away to look at her with surprise.

'*Tu pleurs?*' You're crying?

'*Un peu.*' A little. He smiled, it had been so long since she had answered him in French. 'I wish you didn't have to go.' If only he'd stay, if they had some time without Pilar ...

'So do I.' But they both knew that was a lie. He pulled the keys out of the ignition and opened the door, signalling for a porter.

Deanna walked sedately beside him, lost in her own thoughts, until they reached the first-class lounge where he generally hid while waiting for a plane. She settled into a chair next to his and smiled at him. But he was already different, already gone, the moment in the car all but forgotten. He checked the papers in his brief-case and looked at his watch. He had ten minutes left, and he suddenly seemed impatient to leave.

'*Alors,* is there anything we forgot to discuss in the car? Any message for Pilar?'

'Just give her my love. Will you stop there before you go to Athens?'

'No, I'll phone her tonight.'

'And me too?' She watched the seconds tick by on the enormous clock on the wall.

'And you too. You're not going out?'

'No, I have some work I want to finish in the studio.'

'You should do something amusing, so you don't feel alone.'

I won't, I'm used to it. Again, she didn't say the words. 'I'll be fine.' She crossed one leg over the other, looking down at her lap. She had worn a new lavender silk dress and the purple jade earrings encircled by diamonds that he had brought her from Hong Kong, but he hadn't noticed. His mind was on other things.

'Deanna?'

'Hm?' She looked up to find him standing next to her, his briefcase in his hand and the familiar smile of victory in his eyes. He was off to the wars now, gone again, free. 'Is it time to go?' *Already? So soon?* He nodded, and she stood up, dwarfed by his considerable size, but the perfect companion beside him. They were a strikingly good-looking couple. They always had been. Even Madame Duras, his cold-eyed mother, had acknowledged it – once.

'You needn't walk me to the gate.' He already seemed distracted.

'No, but I'd like to. Is that all right?'

'Of course.' He held the door for her, and they stepped back into the bustle of the terminal, instantly lost among an army of travellers burdened with suitcases, gifts, and guitars. They arrived too soon at the gate, and he turned to look down at her with a smile. 'I'll call you tonight.'

'I love you.'

He didn't answer but bent to kiss the top of her head, then strode into the passageway to the plane, without a backward look or a wave. She watched until he disappeared, then slowly turned and walked away. *I love you.* Her own words echoed in her head. But he hadn't answered. He was already gone.

She slid into the car waiting at the kerb, and with a sigh turned the key and drove home.

She went quickly upstairs to change her clothes, and was buried deep in her own thoughts in the studio all afternoon. She sketched absently, and had just gone out on the terrace at last for some air, when Margaret knocked softly on the studio door. Deanna turned in surprise, as the housekeeper hesitantly entered the room.

'Mrs Duras ... I – I'm sorry ...' She knew how Deanna hated to be disturbed there, but now and then she had no choice. Deanna had disconnected the studio phone.

'Is something wrong?' Deanna looked distracted, standing there with her hair loose over her shoulders and hands tucked into the pockets of her jeans.

'No. Mr Sullivan is downstairs to see you.'

'Jim?' And then she remembered Marc-Edouard's promise that Jim would look in on her. He certainly hadn't lost any time. Always devoted to his associate's subtle commands. 'I'll be right down.'

Margaret nodded. She had done the right thing. She knew that Deanna wouldn't have wanted him upstairs in the studio. She had shown him into the icelike green living room and offered him a cup of tea, which he'd declined with a grin. He was as different from Marc-Edouard as two men could be, and Margaret had always liked him. He was rugged, American, and easygoing, and somewhere in his eyes was always the promise of a rich Irish smile.

Deanna found him standing at the window, looking out at the summer fog drifting in slowly over the bay. It looked like puffs of white cotton being pulled by an invisible string, floating between the spires of the bridge, and hanging in midair over the sailboats.

'Hello, Jim.'

'Madam.' He executed a small bow and made as though to kiss her hand. But she waved the gesture away with a gurgle of laughter and offered her cheek, which he unceremoniously kissed. 'I must admit I prefer that. Kissing hands is an art I've never quite mastered. You never know if they're going to shake with you, or expect to be kissed. Couple of times I damn near got my nose broken by the ones who planned to shake.'

She laughed at him and sat down. 'You'll have to get

Marc to give you lessons. He's a genius at it. It's either the Frenchman in him or a sixth sense. How about a drink?'

'Love it.' He lowered his voice to a conspiratorial whisper. 'Margaret seemed to think I should have tea.'

'How awful.'

She was laughing again, and he watched her appreciatively as she opened a small inlaid cabinet and withdrew two glasses and a bottle of Scotch.

'Drinking, Deanna?' He said it casually but he was surprised. He had never seen her drink Scotch. Maybe Marc-Edouard had had a good reason after all for suggesting he come by. But she was already shaking her head.

'I thought I'd have some ice water. Were you worried?' She looked at him with amusement as she returned with his glass.

'A little.'

'Don't worry, love. I haven't hit the bottle yet.' Her eyes seemed suddenly wistful as she took a sip from her own glass and set it down carefully on a marble table. 'But it's going to be a mighty long summer.' She sighed and looked up at him with a smile. Gently, he reached over and patted her hand.

'I know. Maybe we can go to the movies sometime.'

'You're a sweetheart, but don't you have anything better to do?' She knew he did. He had been divorced for four years and was living with a model who had moved out from New York a few months ago. He adored that type, and they always loved him. Tall, handsome, athletic, with Irish-blue eyes and ebony black hair, barely salted with grey. He was the perfect contrast to Marc-Edouard in every possible way, easygoing when Marc was formal; All-American, unlike Marc's totally European manner; and surprisingly unassuming, in contrast to Marc-Edouard's barely concealed arrogance. It had always struck Deanna as odd that Marc had chosen Jim as his partner, but it had been a wise choice.

Marc's own special brilliance was matched by Jim's; their stars just shone differently, and they moved in their own very separate orbits. The Durases rarely saw Jim socially. He was busy with his own life, and his collection of models, now dwindled to one – for the moment. Jim never stayed with one woman long.

'What are you up to these days?'

He smiled at her. 'Work, play, the usual. You?'

'Fiddling around in my studio, also the usual.' She played it down as she always did.

'What about this summer? Have you made any plans?'

'Not yet, but I will. Maybe I'll go see some friends in Santa Barbara or something.'

'God.' He made a horrible face, and she laughed.

'What's wrong with that?'

'You'd have to be eighty years old to enjoy that. Why don't you go down to Beverly Hills? Pretend you're a movie star, have lunch at the Polo Lounge, have yourself paged.'

'Is that what you do?' She laughed at the idea.

'Of course. Every weekend.' He chuckled and set down his empty glass, glancing at his watch. 'Never mind. I'll get you organised in no time, but now' – he looked regretful – 'I have to run.'

'Thank you for stopping by. It was kind of a long afternoon. It's strange with both of them gone.'

He nodded appreciatively, suddenly sobered. He remembered the feeling from the time when his wife and their two boys had first moved out. He had thought he'd go nuts, just from the silence.

'I'll call you.'

'Good. And Jim' – she looked at him for a long moment – 'thanks.'

He rumpled her long dark hair, kissed her forehead, and departed, waving at her as he slid into his black Porsche, thinking that Marc was crazy. Deanna Duras was one woman he'd have given almost anything to get his hands on. Of course he was too smart to play with that kind of fire, but he still thought Duras was nuts. Christ, he never even realised what a little beauty she was. Or did he? Jim Sullivan wondered to himself as he drove away, and Deanna softly closed the door.

She glanced at her watch, thinking that it was nice of Jim to come by and wondering how soon Marc would call her. He had promised to call her that night.

But he never did. Instead, there was a telegram in the morning:

Off to Athens. Wrong time to call. All well. Pilar fine.

Marc

Brief and to the point. But why hadn't he called? 'Wrong time to call,' she read again. *Wrong time. Wrong time . . .*

The telephone broke into Deanna's thoughts as she read Marc's telegram again. She already knew it by heart.

'Deanna?' The bright voice jarred her out of her reverie. It was Kim Houghton. She lived only a few blocks away, but her life couldn't have been more different. Twice married, twice divorced, eternally independent and merry and free. She had gone to art school with Deanna, but she was a major creative force in advertising now, because she had never been a very good artist. And she was Deanna's only close woman friend.

'Hi, Kim. What's new in your life?'

'Not much. I was in L.A. being nice to one of our new clients. The bastard is already talking about pulling the account. And it's one of mine.' She mentioned the name of a national chain of hotels, for which she handled the advertising. 'Want to have lunch?'

'I can't. I'm tied up.'

'Doing what?' Suspicion crept into her voice. She always knew when Deanna was lying.

'A charity luncheon. I have to go.'

'Dump it. I'll be your charity. I need some advice, I'm depressed.' Deanna laughed. Kimberly Houghton was never depressed. Even her divorces – two of them – hadn't depressed her. She had rapidly moved on to more fertile terrain. Usually in less than a week. 'Come on, love, let's go somewhere for lunch. I need a breather from this place.'

'So do I.' Deanna looked around the blue silk-and-velvet splendour of her bedroom, trying to fight off a feeling of gloom. For an unguarded moment her voice sagged into the phone.

'What does that mean?' Kim asked.

'It means, you nosy pain in the ass, that Marc is away. Pilar left two days ago, and Marc left yesterday morning.'

'Jesus, can't you enjoy it? You don't often get a breather like that, with both of them gone. If I were you I'd run around the living room stark naked and call in all my friends.'

'While I was still naked, or after I got dressed?' Deanna threw her legs over the side of the chair and laughed.

'Either way. Listen, in that case, forget about lunch. How about dinner tonight?'

'That's a deal. That way I can do some work in the studio this afternoon.'

'I thought you were going to a charity lunch.' Deanna could almost see Kim grinning. 'Gotcha.'

'Go to hell.'

'Thank you. Dinner at seven at Trader Vic's?'

'I'll meet you there.'

'See ya.' She hung up, leaving Deanna with a smile. Thank God for Kim.

'You look gorgeous. New dress?' Kimberly Houghton looked up from her drink when Deanna arrived, and the two women exchanged the smile of old friends.

43

Deanna was indeed looking lovely in a white cashmere dress that clung to all the right places and set off her dark hair and enormous green eyes.

'You don't look so bad either.' Kim had the kind of body men loved, rich and generous and full of promise. Her blue eyes danced, and her smile dazzled everyone it took in. She still wore her hair in the short cap of blonde curls she had worn for the last twenty years. She didn't have the startling elegance of Deanna, but she had irresistible warmth and a certain way with clothes. She always looked as though she ought to have ten men at her heels, and she usually did. Or at least one or two. Tonight she was wearing a blue velvet blazer and slacks with red silk shirt, unbuttoned dangerously low to reveal ample cleavage and a single diamond dangling enticingly on a narrow gold chain that fell neatly between her full breasts. An 'eye catcher' – as though she needed any help.

Deanna ordered a drink and settled on to the seat, dropping her mink coat on a chair. Kim was neither interested in it nor impressed. She had grown up in that world and had no desires for money or mink, only for independence and good times. She always made sure she had a great deal of both.

'So what's new? Enjoying your freedom?'

'More or less. Actually, this time I'm finding it a little hard to get used to.' Deanna sighed and took a sip of her drink.

'Jesus, as much as Marc travels, I'd think you'd be used to it by now. Besides, a little independence is good for you.'

'Probably. But he'll be gone for three months. That seems like forever.'

'Three months? How did that happen?' Kim's voice suddenly lost its champagne brightness, and a question appeared in her eyes.

'He has a big case going between Paris and Athens. It doesn't make sense for him to come home in between.'

44

'Or for you to go over?'

'Apparently not.'

'What does that mean? Did you ask?' It was like answering to a mother. Deanna smiled as she looked at her friend.

'More or less. He's going to be busy, and if I go over I'll be stuck with Madame Duras.'

'Screw that.' Kim had heard all the early stories of Marc-Edouard's indomitable mother.

'Precisely, though I didn't put it quite that way to Marc. So, *voilà*, I'm by myself for the summer.'

'And hating every minute of it after only two days. Right? Right.' She answered her own question. 'Why don't you go somewhere?'

'Where?'

'Jesus, Deanna, anywhere. I'm sure Marc wouldn't mind.'

'Probably not, but I don't like to travel alone.' She had never had to. She had always travelled with her father, and then with Pilar and Marc. 'Besides, where would I go? Jim Sullivan said Santa Barbara would be a bore.' She looked forlorn as she said it, and Kimberly laughed.

'He's right. Poor little rich girl. How about Carmel with me, tomorrow? I have to go down to meet with a client over the weekend. You could come along for the ride.'

'That's silly, Kim, I'd be in your way.' But for a moment, she had liked the idea. She hadn't been to Carmel in years, and it certainly wasn't far away, just a two-hour drive from the city.

'Why would you be in my way? I'm not having an affair with this guy for chrissake, and I'd enjoy the company. By myself, it would be a drag.'

'Not for long.' She looked pointedly at her friend, and Kim laughed.

'Please, my reputation!' She smiled broadly at Deanna then tilted her head to one side, shaking the halo

45

of soft blonde curls. 'Seriously, will you come? I'd love it.'

'I'll see.'

'No. You'll come. Settled? Settled.'

'Kimberly ...' Deanna was starting to laugh.

'I'll pick you up at five-thirty.' Kim grinned a victorious grin.

Chapter Three

Kim honked twice as she pulled up in front of the house, and Deanna glanced through her bedroom window before picking up her bag and running down the stairs. She felt like a girl again, off on a weekend adventure with a friend. Even Kim's car didn't look like something a grown-up would drive. It was an ancient MG painted bright red. Deanna appeared in the doorway a moment later, wearing grey slacks and a grey turtleneck sweater, and carrying a large brown leather bag.

'Right on time. How was your day?'

'Ghastly. Don't ask.'

'All right. I won't.' Instead, they spoke of everything else: Carmel, Deanna's latest painting, Pilar and her friends.

Finally, they lapsed into comfortable silence. They were almost in Carmel when Kimberly glanced over at her friend and saw the wistful look in her eyes.

'Penny for your thoughts.'

'Is that all? Hell, they ought to be worth at least five or ten cents.' She tried to laugh away her own thoughts, but Kim wasn't fooled.

'All right. I'll give you a dime. But let me guess. Thinking about Marc?'

'Yes.' Deanna's voice was quiet as she looked out at the sea.

'Do you really miss him that much?' Their relationship had always puzzled Kim. It had seemed to her at first like a marriage of convenience, yet she knew it was not. Deanna loved him. Maybe too much.

Deanna looked away. 'Yes, I miss him that much. Does that seem silly to you?'

'No. Admirable maybe. Something like that.'

'Why? Admirable has nothing to do with it.'

Kim laughed and shook her head. 'Sweetheart, eighteen years with one man looks more than admirable to me. It's goddamn heroic.'

Deanna grinned at her friend. 'Why heroic? I love him. He's a beautiful, intelligent, witty, charming man.' And making love with him the night before his departure had renewed something in her heart.

'Yes. He is.' Kim kept her eyes on the road as she said it, but she found herself wondering if there was more. If there was a side of Marc Duras that no one knew, a warm side, a loving side, another dimension to the man of unlimited beauty and charm. A human side that laughed and cried and was real. That would make him a man worth loving, to Kim.

'It's going to be a very long summer.' Deanna let out a small sigh. 'Tell me about this client of yours. Someone new?'

'Yes. He insisted on having this meeting in Carmel. He lives in San Francisco, but has a house here. He was on his way up from L.A. and thought this would be a more pleasant place to discuss the account.'

'How civilised.'

'Yes. Very.' Kim smiled at Deanna.

It was almost eight o'clock when they pulled up in front of the hotel. Kimberly climbed out of the MG with a shake of her curls and a glance at Deanna, pulling herself out of the car with a groan.

'Think you'll survive? I'll admit, this isn't the smoothest possible chariot for travelling.'

'I'll live.' Deanna looked around at the familiar surroundings. In the early days of their marriage, she and Marc had often come down to Carmel on weekends. They had wandered in and out of the shops, had cozy, candlelit dinners, and walked for miles on the beach. There was a bittersweet feeling to being here again, this time without him.

The hotel was tiny and quaint, with a French provincial façade and gaily painted window boxes filled with bright flowers. Inside, there were low wooden beams, a large fireplace framed by copper pots, and Wedgwood-blue wallpaper with a tiny white design. It was the kind of hotel Marc would have enjoyed; it looked very French.

Kimberly signed the register at the front desk then handed the pen to Deanna. 'I asked for adjoining rooms. O.K. with you?' Deanna nodded, relieved. She liked having a room to herself and hadn't really wanted to share one with Kim.

'That sounds fine.' She filled in her name and address on the card, then they followed the porter to their rooms.

Five minutes later Deanna heard a knock at the door.

'Want a Coke, Deanna? I just got two out of the machine down the hall.' Kim sprawled her long generous frame across Deanna's bed and held out an icy-cold can.

Deanna took a long sip and then let herself into a chair with a smile and a sigh. 'It feels so good to be here. I'm glad I came.'

'So am I. It would have been boring without you. Maybe we can even find time for the shops tomorrow when I'm through with business. Or would you rather go back to the city tomorrow afternoon? Do you have plans?'

'Absolutely none. And this is heaven. I may never go back. The house is like a tomb without Marc and Pilar.'

Kimberly thought it equally tomblike with them, but she didn't say anything to her friend. She knew that Deanna loved the house and that the security of her family meant a great deal. She had met Deanna at art school, shortly after the death of Deanna's father had left her penniless and alone. She had seen her struggle to make it on the little money she earned at her job. She had been there too when Marc began to court

49

Deanna, and she had seen Deanna come to rely on him more and more, until she felt helpless without him. She had watched Marc sweep her friend under his wing, tenderly, irresistibly, and with the determination of a man who refused to lose. And she had seen Deanna nestle there for almost two decades, safe, protected, hidden, and insistent that she was happy. Perhaps she was. But Kim was never sure.

'Any place special you want to go for dinner?' Kim drained the last of her Coke as she asked.

'The beach.' Deanna looked longingly through the window at the sea.

'The Beach? I don't know it.' Kim looked vague, and Deanna laughed.

'No, no. It's not a restaurant. I meant I wanted to go for a walk on the beach.'

'Now? At this hour?' It was only eight-thirty, and just barely dusk, but Kim was hungry to begin her evening and have a look around. 'Why don't you save that until tomorrow after my meeting with the new client?' It was obvious that Kim was not lured by surf and white sands. But Deanna was.

She shook her head resolutely and put down her Coke. 'Nope. I can't wait that long. Are you going to change before we go out?' Kim nodded. 'Good. Then I'll go for a walk while you dress. I'll just wear what I have on.' The cashmere sweater and grey slacks still looked impeccable after the drive.

'Don't get lost on the beach.'

'I won't.' Deanna smiled sheepishly at Kim. 'I feel like a kid. I can't wait to get out and play.' *And look at the sunset, and take a deep breath of the sea air ... and remember the days when Marc and I walked down that beach hand in hand.* 'I'll be back in half an hour.'

'Don't rush. I'm going to take a nice hot bath. We're in no hurry. We can have dinner at nine-thirty or ten.' Kim would make reservations in the staid, Victorian dining room of the Pine Inn.

'See you.' Deanna disappeared with a wave and a smile, pulling on her jacket and carrying a scarf in her hand. She knew it would be windy on the beach. When she stepped outside the fog was already rolling in.

She walked along the main street of Carmel, weaving her way between the few straggling tourists who had not yet taken refuge at dinner tables or in their hotels, their children chattering at their heels, their arms filled with booty from the shops, their faces smiling and relaxed. It reminded her of the time she and Marc had come here with Pilar. Pilar had been an exuberant nine, and she had joined them on one of their sunset strolls on the beach, collecting bits of driftwood and shells, running ahead of them and then back to report her discoveries, as Deanna and Marc talked. It seemed an aeon ago. She reached the end of the street and suddenly stopped to look down the endless expanse of alabaster beach. Even Marc had admitted that there was nothing like it in France. The perfectly white sand and the rich swell of waves rolling in towards the shore with sea gulls drifting slowly by. She took a deep breath as she looked at the scene again, watching the tide roll inexorably in. There was a lure to that beach, a lure like none she had ever known. She pocketed the scarf and slipped her shoes off, feeling the rush of sand between her toes as she ran towards the shore, stopping short of the water's edge. The wind ripped through her hair. She closed her eyes and smiled. It was a beautiful place, a world she had left buried in memory for too long. Why had she stayed away for so long? Why hadn't they been back here before? With another deep breath, she set off down the beach, one shoe in each hand, and her feet aching to dance in the sand like a child.

She had walked a long way before she stopped to watch the last rim of gold on the horizon. The sky had turned to mauve and a thick bank of fog was moving in towards the shore. She stood watching it for an interminable time, then walked slowly up towards the dunes where she made a seat for herself amid the tall grass and pulled her knees up under her chin as she looked out to sea. After a moment she rested her head on one knee and closed her eyes, listening to the sea and feeling a rush of joy in her soul.

'It's perfect, isn't it?'

Deanna jumped at the unexpected voice at her side. She opened her eyes to see a tall, dark-haired man standing beside her. For a moment she was frightened, but his smile was so kind that it was impossible to feel threatened while in the warm embrace of those eyes. They were a deep blue-green like the sea. He had the build of a man who might have played football in college. His hair was as dark as Deanna's and ruffled by the wind. He was looking down at her intently.

'I like it best at this time of day,' he said.

'So do I.' She found it easy to answer him and was surprised that it didn't annoy her when he sat down beside her. 'I thought I was alone on the beach.' She glanced shyly into his face, and he smiled.

'You probably were. I came up behind you. I'm sorry if I startled you.' He looked at her again with that same open smile. 'My house is just behind here.' He nodded over his shoulder to an area shrouded by wind-contorted trees. 'I always come out here in the evenings. And tonight I just got in from a trip. I haven't been here in three weeks. I always realise then how much I love it, how much I need to walk on this beach and look at that.' He looked straight ahead, out to sea.

'Do you live here all year round?' Deanna found herself conversing with him as though he were an old friend, but he had that way about him, it was impossible to be ill at ease.

'No, I come down on weekends whenever I can. And you?'

'I haven't been here in a long time. I came down with a friend.'

'Staying in town?'

She nodded, and then remembering, looked at her watch. 'That reminds me, I have to get back. I got carried away by my walk on the beach.' It was already nine-thirty and the last light of day had fled as they talked. She stood and looked down at him, smiling. 'You're lucky to have this anytime you like.'

He nodded in answer, but he wasn't really listening, he was looking intensely at her face, and for the first time since she'd noticed him next to her, Deanna felt an odd rush of warmth in her cheeks and was aware of her embarrassment when he spoke.

'Do you know, you looked like a painting by Andrew Wyeth, sitting there in the wind? I thought that when I first saw you sitting on the dune. Are you familiar with his work?' He had a look of great concentration in his eyes, as though measuring her face and the thickness of her hair. But she was already smiling.

'I know his work very well.' It had been her passion when she was a child, before she had discovered that Impressionism was much more her style. 'I used to know every piece he had done.'

'Every piece?' The sea-coloured eyes were suddenly teasing but still warm.

'I thought so.'

'Do you know the one of the woman on the beach?' She thought for a moment and shook her head. 'Would you like to see it?' He stood next to her, looking like a bright-eyed, much-excited boy, only the manly spread of his shoulders and the few strands of grey in his hair belied the look in his eyes. 'Would you?'

'I – I really have to get back. But, thank you ...' She trailed off in embarrassment. He didn't seem to be the kind of man one ought to be afraid of, but nevertheless he was only a stranger who had appeared on a beach. It struck her then that she was really a little bit mad to be talking to him at all, standing there alone in the dark. 'Really, I can't. Perhaps some other time.'

'I understand.' The fire dampened a little in his eyes,

but the smile was still there. 'It's a beautiful piece though, and the woman in it looks a great deal like you.'

'Thank you. That's a lovely thing to say.' She was wondering how to leave him. He seemed to have no immediate intention of returning to his house.

'May I walk you back up the beach? It's a little too dark now for you to be wandering around on your own.' He grinned at her, squinting into the wind. 'You might get accosted by a stranger.' She laughed in answer and nodded as they walked down the shallow dune back towards the sea. 'Tell me, how did you become so fond of Wyeth?'

'I thought he was the greatest American painter I had ever seen. But then,' she looked apologetically into his eyes, 'I fell in love with all the French Impressionists. And I'm afraid I forgot about him. Not forgot, really, but I fell a little bit out of love.'

They walked along comfortably, side by side, the only two people on the beach, with the surf pounding beside them. She laughed suddenly then. It was so incongruous, discussing art with this stranger, walking in the sand in Carmel. What would she tell Kim? Or would she tell Kim at all? For a moment she was inclined to tell no one about her new friend. It was just a moment's encounter at dusk on a quiet beach. What was there to tell?

'Do you always fall out of love that easily?' It was a silly thing to say, the sort of thing strangers say to each other for lack of something better. But she smiled.

'Generally not. Only when French Impressionists are involved.'

He nodded sagely. 'That makes sense. Do you paint?'
'A bit.'

'Like the Impressionists?' He seemed to know the answer already, and she nodded. 'I'd like to see your work. Is it shown?'

She shook her head, looking out at the waves capped

54

iridescently by the first light of the moon. 'No, not any more. Just once, a long time ago.'

'Did you fall out of love with painting too?'

'Never.' She looked down at the sand as she spoke and then back at him again. 'Painting is my life.'

'Then why don't you show?' He seemed puzzled by her reaction, but she only shrugged. They had reached the place where she had walked on to the beach.

'This is where I get off.' They stood in the moonlight, looking into each other's eyes. For the madness of one moment she wanted to be held in those strong, comfortable arms, wrapped in his Windbreaker with him. 'It was nice talking to you.' Her face was strangely serious as she spoke.

'My name is Ben.'

She hesitated for a moment. 'Deanna.'

He held out his hand, shook hers, and then turned away and walked back down the beach. She watched him, the broad shoulders, the strong back, and the wind in his hair. She wanted to shout 'Goodbye,' but the word would have been lost in the wind. Instead, he turned, and she thought she saw him wave at her once in the dark.

Chapter Four

'Where the hell have you been?' Kim was waiting for her in the lobby with a look of concern, when Deanna returned. She smoothed her tangled hair back from her face and smiled at her friend. Her cheeks were pink from the wind, her eyes shining. The word *radiant* flashed into Kim's mind as Deanna began a rush of explanation.

'I'm sorry. I walked farther than I thought. It took me ages to get back.'

'It sure did. I was beginning to worry.'

'I'm sorry.' She looked remorseful, and Kim's face softened into a smile.

'All right. But Jesus, let the kid loose on a beach and she vanishes. I thought maybe you'd run into a friend.'

'No.' She paused for a moment. 'I just walked.' She had missed it. Her chance to tell Kim about Ben. But what was there to say? That she had met a stranger on the beach with whom she had discussed art? It sounded ridiculous. Childish. Or worse, stupid and improper. And she found that when she thought of it, she wanted to keep the moment for herself. She would never see him again anyway. Why bother to explain?

'Ready for dinner?'

'I certainly am.'

They walked the two blocks to the Pine Inn, glancing into shop windows, chatting about friends. Theirs was always an easy exchange, and the silence left Deanna to her own thoughts. She found herself wondering about the unknown Wyeth Ben had suggested he had. Did he really or was it only a poster? Did it matter? She told herself not.

'You're mighty quiet tonight, Deanna,' Kim said as they finished their dinner. 'Tired?'

'A little.'

'Thinking about Marc?'

'Yes.' It was the easiest answer.

'Will he call you from Athens?'

'When he can. The time difference makes it difficult.' And it made him seem terribly far away. In only two days he already seemed part of another lifetime. Or maybe that was just the effect of being in Carmel. When she was at home, with his clothes and his books or on his side of the bed, he felt much nearer. 'What about your client tomorrow? What's he like?'

'I don't know. Never met him. He's an art dealer. The Thompson Galleries. As a matter of fact, I was going to ask you if you wanted to come to the meeting. You might like to see his house. I hear he has a fabulous collection in what he calls his "cottage." '

'I don't want to get in your way.'

'You won't.' Kimberly looked at her reassuringly, and they paid the cheque. It was already eleven-thirty and Deanna was glad to climb into her bed.

When she slept, she dreamed of the stranger named Ben.

The phone rang beside her bed as she lay on her back, sleepily wondering if she should get up. She had promised to go with Kim, but she was tempted to go back to sleep. And then take another walk on the beach. The lure of that bothered her. She knew why she wanted to go back, and it was a strange, uncomfortable feeling the way he lingered in her mind. She would probably never see him again. And what if she did? What then? The phone rang again, and she reached over to answer it.

'Rise and shine.' It was Kim.

'What time is it?'

'Five after nine.'

'God. It feels more like seven or eight.'

'Well, it isn't, and our meeting's at ten. Get up, and I'll bring you breakfast.'

57

'Can't I order room service?' Deanna had grown used to travelling with Marc.

'The Ritz this ain't. I'll bring you coffee and a Danish.'

Deanna realised suddenly how spoiled she'd become. Not having Margaret and one of her perfect breakfasts was becoming a hardship. 'All right. That'll be fine. I'll be ready in half an hour.'

She showered and did her hair and slipped into a cashmere sweater of a rich cornflower blue, which she pulled on over white slacks. She even managed to look fresh and alive by the time Kim knocked on her door.

'Jesus, you look gorgeous.' Kim handed her a steaming cup of coffee and a plate.

'So do you. Should I wear something more business-like? You look awfully grown-up.' Kim was wearing a beige gabardine suit with a persimmon silk blouse and a very pretty straw hat, and a little straw bag clutched under her arm. 'You look very chic.'

'Don't look so surprised.' Kim smiled and collapsed in a chair. 'I hope this guy is easy. I don't feel like arguing business on a Saturday morning.' She yawned and watched Deanna finish the coffee in her cup.

'Who am I supposed to be by the way? Your secretary or your chaperone?' Deanna's eyes sparkled over her cup.

'Neither, you jerk. Just my friend.'

'Won't he think it a little strange that you bring along your friends?'

'Too bad if he does.' Kim yawned again and stood up. 'We'd better go.'

'Yes, ma'am.'

The drive took only five minutes, with Deanna reading the instructions to Kim. The address was on a pretty street, the houses all set back from the road and hidden by trees. But she saw when they got out of the car that it was a small, pleasant house. Not elaborate, and far from pretentious. It had a windswept, natural look to it. A small black foreign car was parked outside, something convenient, not handsome. None of the evidence suggested that the promised art collection would be impressive or rare. But the inside of the house told a different tale, as a small tidy woman in a housekeeper's apron opened the door. She had the look of someone who came once or twice a week, efficient rather than warm.

'Mr Thompson said to wait for him in his den. He's upstairs on the phone. To London.' She added the last words with disapproval, as though she thought it a shocking expense. But not nearly as great an expense, Deanna thought, as the paintings on the walls. She looked at them with awe as they followed the housekeeper to the den. The man had a magnificent collection of English and Early American paintings. None of them were what Deanna would have collected herself, but they were a joy to behold. She wanted to linger so she could study each piece, but the woman in the apron marched them quickly and firmly into the den, glared at them long and hard, muttered, 'Sit down,' then disappeared back to her chores.

'My God, Kim, did you see what he has on his walls?'

Kimberly grinned, readjusting her hat. 'Beautiful stuff, isn't it? Not my cup of tea, but he has some awfully good pieces. Though they're not all really his.' Deanna raised an eyebrow in question. 'He owns two galleries. One in San Francisco, and one in L.A. I suspect he borrows some of these from his galleries. But what the hell, it's beautiful work.'

Deanna nodded in rapid agreement and continued to look around. They were seated in a room with a wide picture window that looked out at the sea. A simple pine desk, two couches, and a chair. Like the exterior of the house and the modest car, it was functional rather than impressive. But the art collection amply made up for that. Even here, he had hung two very fine, perfectly framed black-and-white sketches. She leaned closer to peer at the signatures then turned to look at a painting that hung behind her, the only ornament on a totally bare, white wall. Even as she turned to look, she felt herself gasp. It was the painting. The Wyeth. The woman on the dune, her face partially hidden as she rested it on her knees. And even Deanna could see that the woman was startlingly like her. The length and colour of her hair, the shape of her shoulders, even the hint of a smile. She was surrounded by a bleak, damp-looking beach and accompanied only by the passing of one lonely gull.

'Good morning.' She heard his voice behind her before she could comment on the painting. Her eyes met his in surprise. 'How do you do, I'm Ben Thompson. Miss Houghton?' There was an unspoken question in his eyes, but she quickly shook her head and pointed to Kim, who stepped forward with an extended hand and a smile.

'I'm Kimberly Houghton. And this is my friend, Deanna Duras. We heard so much about your collection that I had to bring her along. She's an amazingly gifted artist herself, though she won't admit it.'

'No, I'm not.'

'See!' Kim's eyes danced as she took in the good-looking man who stood before them. He looked to be somewhere in his late thirties, and he had extraordinarily beautiful eyes.

Deanna was smiling at them both and shaking her head. 'Really. I'm not.'

'How do you like my Wyeth?' He said it straight into Deanna's eyes, and she felt a little pull at her heart.

'I ... it's a very, very fine piece. But you already know that.' She found herself blushing when she spoke to him. She wasn't sure what to say. Should she admit having met him before? Should she pretend that there had been no meeting? Would he?

'Do you like it though?' His eyes held hers, and she felt herself grow warm under his gaze.

'Very much.' He nodded, pleased. And then she understood. He would say nothing about the night before on the beach. But she found herself smiling as they sat down. It was a strange feeling, having this secret between them, stranger still to know that she had met the 'new client' before Kim.

'Ladies, some coffee?' They both nodded, and he stepped into the hall to call to the housekeeper. 'One medium, two black.' As he came back into the room, he grinned at them. 'They'll either all be medium or all black. Mrs Meacham doesn't approve. Of anything. Coffee. Visitors. Or me. But I can trust her to clean the house when I'm gone. She thinks all this stuff is crap.' He waved airily around the room, a gesture encompassing the Wyeth and both sketches as well as the pieces they had seen on their way in. Kim and Deanna both laughed.

When the coffee arrived, all three cups were black. 'Perfect. Thank you.' He smiled boyishly at the housekeeper as she left the room. 'Miss Houghton ...?'

'Kimberly, please.'

'Okay, Kimberly, you've seen the ads we ran last year?' She nodded. 'What did you think?'

'Not enough style. Not the right look. Not aimed at the right marketplace for what you want.'

He nodded, but his glance kept wandering back to Deanna, who was still drinking in the Wyeth behind him. His eyes betrayed nothing as he watched her, and his words showed that he knew what he wanted from Kim. He was quick, funny, astute, and very business-like, and their meeting was over in less than an hour. She promised to give him some fresh ideas within two weeks.

'Will Deanna be consulting on the account?' It was hard to tell if he was teasing. Deanna shook her head rapidly and held up a hand, laughing.

'Good God, no. I have no idea how Kim comes up with any of her wizardly ideas.'

'Blood, sweat, and a lot of black coffee.' Kimberly grinned.

'What do you paint?' He was looking again at Deanna, with the same gentle eyes she had seen on the beach the night before.

Her voice was very soft as she answered. 'Still lifes, young girls. The usual Impressionist themes.'

'And mothers with young babies on their knees?' The eyes were always teasing, but unrelentingly kind.

'Only once.' She had done a portrait of herself and Pilar. Her mother-in-law had hung it in the Paris apartment and then ignored it for the next dozen years.

'I'd like to see some of your work. Do you show?' Again no betrayal of the night before, and she wondered why.

'No, I don't. I haven't shown in years. I'm not ready.'

'Now that's crap, to use your housekeeper's word.' Kimberly looked first at Ben Thompson and then at Deanna. 'You should show him some of your work.'

'Don't be silly.' Deanna felt awkward and looked away. No one had seen her work in too many years. Only Marc and Pilar, and now and then Kim. 'One day, but not yet. Thank you anyway though.' Her smile thanked him for his silence as well as his kindness. It was strange that he too should wish to remain mute about their meeting on the beach.

The conversation drew to a close with the usual amenities and a brief tour of his collection, conducted beneath the buzzardlike gaze of the housekeeper as she swept. Kimberly promised to call him the following week.

There was nothing unusual in his farewell to Deanna. No inappropriate pressure of her hand, no message in his eyes, only the warmth that she had already seen, and the smile he left them as he closed the door.

'What a nice guy,' Kim said as she started the little MG. The engine grumbled, then came to life. 'He's going to be a pleasure to work with. Don't you think?'

Deanna just nodded. She was lost in her own thoughts until Kim screeched to a halt outside their hotel.

'Why the hell don't you let him see your work?' Deanna's reticence always annoyed Kim. She had been the only one in art school who had really had a notable talent, and the only one who had buried her light under a bushel for almost twenty years. The others had all tried to make it and eventually failed.

'I told you. I'm not ready.'

'Bull! If you don't call him yourself, I'm going to give him your number. It's time you did something about that mountain of masterpieces you keep standing around in your studio, facing the wall. That's a crime, Deanna. It just isn't right. Jesus, when you think of the garbage I painted and busted my ass to sell –'

'It wasn't garbage.' Deanna looked kindly at her. But they both knew it hadn't been very good. Kim was much better at planning campaigns, headlines, and lay-outs than she had been at her art.

'It *was* garbage, and I don't even care any more. I like what I do. But what about you?'

'I like what I do, too.'

'And what's that?' Kimberly was becoming frustrated now, and her voice betrayed her feelings. It always wound up that way when they talked about Deanna's work. 'What *do* you do?'

'You know what I do. I paint, I take care of Marc and Pilar, I run the house. I keep busy.'

'Yes, taking care of everyone else. What about *you*? Wouldn't it do something for you to see your work shown in a gallery, hung somewhere other than your husband's office?'

'It doesn't matter where they're hung.' She didn't dare tell Kim that they weren't even there any more. Marc had hired a new decorator six months before, who had declared her works 'weak and depressing' and taken them all down. Marc had brought the canvases home, including a small portrait of Pilar, which now hung in the hall. 'What matters to me is painting it, not showing it.'

'That's like playing a violin with no strings for Chrissake. It doesn't make sense.'

'It does to me.' She was gentle but firm, and Kim shook her head as they got out of the car.

'Well, I think you're crazy, but I love you anyway.' Deanna smiled as they walked back inside the hotel.

The rest of their stay went by too quickly. They browsed in the shops, had dinner once more at the Pine Inn. On Sunday afternoon Deanna took one more walk on the beach. She knew where he lived now, knew it when she glimpsed the house hidden behind the trees. She knew how near she was to the Wyeth. She walked on. She did not see him again, and she was annoyed at herself for even wondering if he'd be on the beach. Why should he be? And what would she say if he were? Thank him for not letting Kimberly know they had met? So what? What did it matter? She knew she'd never see him again.

Chapter Five

When the phone rang, she was already in her studio, sitting back from the canvas trying to evaluate her morning's work. It was a bowl of tulips dropping their petals on a mahogany table, against a background of blue sky, glimpsed through an open window.

'Deanna?' She was stunned to hear his voice.

'Ben? How did you get my number?' She felt a warm blush rise to her cheeks and was instantly angry at herself for the way she felt. 'Kim?'

'Of course. She said that if I didn't show your work, she'd sabotage our account.'

'She didn't!' The blush deepened as she laughed.

'No. She just said that you were very good. Tell you what, I'll trade you my Wyeth for one of yours.'

'You're crazy. And so is Kim!'

'Why don't you let me judge for myself? Do you suppose I could come by around noon?'

'Today? Now?' She glanced at the clock and shook her head. It was already after eleven. 'No!'

'I know. You're not ready. Artists never are.' The voice was as gentle as it had been on the beach.

She stared into the phone. 'Really. I can't.' It was almost a whisper.

'Tomorrow?' Not pushy, but firm.

'Ben, really ... it's not that. I ...' She faltered and heard his laugh.

'Please. I'd really love to see your work.'

'Why?' She instantly felt stupid for the question.

'Because I like you. And I'd like to see your work. It's as simple as that. Doesn't that make sense?'

'More or less.' She didn't know what more to say.

'Are you busy for lunch?'

'No, I'm not.' She sighed sadly again.

'Don't sound so forlorn. I promise not to throw darts at your canvases. Honest. Trust me.'

Oddly, she did. She trusted him. It was something about the way he spoke, and the look she remembered in his eyes. 'I think I do. All right then. Noon.'

No one going to the guillotine had ever spoken as resolutely. Ben Thompson smiled to himself as he hung up.

He was there promptly at noon. With a bag of French rolls, a sizeable wedge of Brie, and half a dozen peaches, as well as a bottle of white wine.

'Will this do?' he asked as he spread his riches out on her desk.

'Very nicely. But you really shouldn't have come.' She looked dismayed as she eyed him over the table. She was wearing jeans and a paint splattered shirt, her hair tied in a loosely woven knot. 'I really hate being put on the spot.' Her expression was troubled as she watched him, and for a moment he stopped arranging the fruit.

'You're not on the spot, Deanna. I really did want to see your work. But it doesn't matter a damn what I think. Kim says you're good. You know you're good. You told me on the beach that painting was your life. No one can ever play with that. I wouldn't try to.' He paused, then went on, more softly, 'You saw some of the pieces I love in the cottage in Carmel. That's something I care about. This is something you care about. If you like my Wyeth, it makes me happy, but if you don't it doesn't change a bit of its beauty for me. Nothing I see will change what you do, or how much it matters. No one can ever touch that.'

She nodded silently, then slowly walked towards the wall where twenty paintings were propped, hidden and ignored. One by one, she turned them around, saying nothing and looking only at the oils as she turned them. She did not look at him until at last he said, 'Stop.' She glanced up in surprise and saw him leaning against her desk with a look in his eyes she didn't understand.

'Did you feel anything when you saw the Wyeth?' He was searching her face and holding her eyes.

She nodded. 'I felt a great deal.'

'What?'

She smiled. 'First, surprise, to realise that I was in your house. But then, a kind of awe, a joy at seeing the painting. I felt pulled by the woman, as though she were someone I knew. I felt everything I think Wyeth wanted to tell me. For a moment, I felt spellbound by his words.'

'As I do by yours. Do you have any idea how much you've put in those paintings, or how really beautiful they are? Do you know what it means to be reached out to and pulled at time after time after time, as you turn them around? They're incredible, Deanna. Don't you know how good they are?' He was smiling at her. She felt her heart pound in her chest.

'I love them. But that's because they're mine.' She was glowing now. He had given her the ultimate gift, and she knew he meant every word. It had been so long since anyone had seen what she painted – and cared.

'They're not only yours. They are you.' He walked closer to one of the canvases and silently stared. It was a painting of a young girl leaning over her bath – Pilar.

'That one is my daughter.' She was enjoying it now. She wanted to share more.

'It's a beautiful piece of work. Show me more.'

She showed him all of them. When it was over, she almost crowed with pleasure. He liked them, he loved them! He understood her work. She wanted to throw her arms around his neck and laugh.

He was opening the bottle of wine. 'You realise what this means, don't you?'

'What?' She was suddenly wary, but not very.

'That I will hound you until you sign with the gallery. How about that?'

She smiled broadly at him, but she shook her head. 'I can't.'

'Why not?'

'That's not for me.' And Marc would have a fit. He would think it commercial and vulgar – though the Thompson gallery had a reputation for anything but vulgarity, and Ben's family had been reputable in the art world for years. She had looked him up when she got back from Carmel. His grandfather had had one of the finest galleries in London, and his father in New York. Ben Thompson had carte blanche in the art world, even at thirty-eight years of age. She had read that too. 'Really, Ben, I can't.'

'The hell you can't. Listen, don't be stubborn. Come to the gallery and look around. You'll feel a lot better when you see what's there.' He suddenly looked very young as he said it, and she laughed. She knew what was there. She had researched that, as well. Pissarro, Chagall, Cassatt, a very small Renoir, a splendid Monet, some Corots. Also a few carefully hidden Pollocks, a Dali, and a de Kooning that he seldom showed. He had the best. As well as a few well-chosen, unknown, young artists, of whom he wanted her to be one. What more could she ask? But what would she tell Marc? *I had to. He asked me. I wanted ...*

'No.' He just wouldn't understand. And neither would Pilar. She would think it an obnoxious, show-offy thing to do. 'You don't understand.'

'You're right there.' He held out a piece of French bread and Brie. Twenty-two paintings spread around the room. And he had loved them all. She beamed as she took the bread from him.

'I've got thirty more in the attic. And five over at Kim's.'

'You're nuts.'

'No, I'm not.'

68

He handed her a peach. 'Yes, you are. But I won't hold it against you. How about coming to an opening we're having tomorrow night? That won't do any harm, will it? Or are you even afraid to do that?' He was goading her now, and she wasn't sure she liked it.

'Who said I was afraid?' She looked very young as she bit into the juicy peach, then smiled.

'Who had to? Why else would you not want to show?'

'Because it doesn't make sense.'

'You don't make sense.' But by then they were both laughing and into their third glass of wine. 'I like you anyway,' he announced. 'I'm used to dealing with crazies like you.'

'I'm not crazy. Just stubborn.'

'And you look exactly like my Wyeth. Did you notice it too?' His eyes pulled at her again. He put down his glass. She hesitated for a moment, then nodded.

'I did.'

'Only I can see your eyes.' He held them for a long moment, then glanced away. They were precisely the eyes he always knew the woman in the painting would have. 'You have beautiful eyes.'

'So do you.' Her voice was like a soft breeze in the room, and they were both reminded of their walk in Carmel.

He said nothing for a while; he only sat silently, looking at her paintings. 'You said that was your daughter. Is that really true?' He looked at her again, wanting to know more.

'Yes. She's almost sixteen. Her name is Pilar. And she is very, very pretty. Much more so than she looks in the painting. I've done several of her.' She thought wistfully of the one Marc's decorator had rejected into the hall. 'Some of them are quite good.' She felt free with him now, free to like her own work.

'Where is she now? Is she here?'

'No.' Deanna looked at him for a long moment. 'In the South of France. Her ... my husband is French.'

69

She wanted to tell him that Marc was away too, that he was in Greece, but it seemed treasonous. Why would she tell him? What did she want of this man? He had already told her that he liked her work. What more could she ask? She wanted to ask him if he was married. But that seemed wrong too. What did those things matter? He was here for her work. No matter how kind those deep, sea-green eyes were.

'You know' – he looked regretfully at his watch – 'I hate to say this, but I have to get to work. I have a meeting at three in the office.'

'Three?' Her eyes flew to the clock. It was already two forty-five. 'Already? How did the time go so fast?' But they had looked at a great deal of her work. She stood up with a regretful look in her eyes.

'You'll come tomorrow night? To the vernissage?' His eyes told her that he wanted her to come. She wasn't sure why.

'I'll try.'

'Please, Deanna. I'd like that.' He touched her arm briefly, and then with a last appreciative smile around the room, he stepped outside the studio and loped down the stairs. 'I'll find my way out. See you tomorrow!' His words faded as she sank into the comfortable white chair and looked around the room. There were four or five canvases of Pilar, but none of Marc. For one totally frantic moment she couldn't remember his face.

Chapter Six

Deanna parked the dark blue Jaguar across from the gallery and slowly crossed the street. She still wasn't sure if she should go, if it was wise. If it made sense. What if Kim were there? It would make her feel foolish. What if ... but then she thought of his eyes and pushed open the heavy glass door.

There were two black-jacketed bartenders standing nearby, alternately pouring Scotch and champagne and a pretty young woman was greeting the guests, who all looked either well heeled or artistic. Deanna saw quickly that it was the show of an older man's work. He stood surrounded by his friends, looking victorious and proud. The paintings were well displayed and had the flavour of Van Gogh. And then she saw Ben. He was standing at the far corner of the room, looking very handsome in a navy blue pin-striped suit. His eyes followed her inside and she saw him smile and grace-fully extricate himself from the group where he stood. He was standing next to her in a moment.

'So you came, did you? I'm glad.' They stood there for a moment, looking at each other, and she felt her-self smile. It was a smile she couldn't have repressed. She was happy to see him again. 'Champagne?'

'Thank you.' She accepted a glass from the extended hand of one of the bartenders, and Ben took her gently by the elbow.

'There's something I want to show you in my office.'

'Etchings?' She felt herself blush. 'How horrible, I shouldn't have said that.'

'Why not?' He was laughing too. 'But no, it's a tiny Renoir I bought last night.'

'My God, where did you get it?' She was following him down a long beige-carpeted hall.

'I bought it from a private collection. A wonderful old man. He says he never liked it. Thank God. I got it at an incredible price.' He unlocked his office door and stepped rapidly inside There, propped against the far wall, was a lovely delicate nude in the distinctive style that needed no glance at the signature. 'Isn't she pretty?' He eyed the painting like a new child of whom he was unbearably proud, and Deanna smiled at the light in his eyes.

'She's wonderful.'

'Thank you.' He looked at Deanna very hard then, as though there was something more he wanted to say, but he didn't. Instead, he looked around with a smile that invited her to do the same. There was another Andrew Wyeth above his desk, this one well known.

'I like that one too. But not as well as the other.'

'Neither do I.' Their thoughts were instantly back to Carmel. The silence was interrupted by a knock on the door. The young woman who had been greeting guests at the entrance was beckoning to Ben from the hall. 'Hi, Sally. What's up? Oh, this is Deanna Duras; she's going to be one of our new artists.'

Sally's eyes instantly opened wide. She approached with a handshake and a smile. 'What good news!'

'Now wait a minute!' Deanna glanced at Ben with an embarrassed smile. 'I never said that.'

'No, but I'm hoping you will. Sally, tell her how wonderful we are, how we never cheat our artists, never hang paintings the wrong way round, never paint moustaches on nudes.'

Deanna was laughing now and shaking her head. 'In that case, this isn't the gallery for me. I've always wanted to see a moustache on one of my nudes and haven't had the courage to do it myself.'

'Let us do it for you.' Ben was still smiling as he led them back into the hall and began to question Sally. There had already been three buyers at the show, and she had come back to discuss the price of one of the

72

paintings with him. The artist wanted more.

'I'll tell him we'll make it up on another piece. He already agreed to the price on that one. God bless Gustave – he's given me all my grey hair.'

'Not to mention mine.' Sally pointed at a virgin-blonde head and disappeared back into the crowd as Ben began to introduce Deanna to the guests. She felt surprisingly at home as she wandered through the gallery, meeting artists and collectors. And she was surprised that she didn't see Kim. She mentioned it to Ben when he joined her.

'Isn't she here? I thought she would be.'

'No. Apparently, she's tearing her hair out over a new ad for yogurt. Frankly, I'd just as soon she not get us confused. Better she get the yogurt out of her head before she starts in on art. Wouldn't you say?' Deanna laughed as he handed her another glass of champagne. 'You know,' he continued, 'I enjoyed yesterday enormously. Your work is extraordinarily good. And I'm not going to stop badgering you until you say yes.'

Deanna smiled at him over the champagne. Before she could protest, they were interrupted by several more collectors who wanted Ben's ear. He had his hands full with them until almost nine o'clock.

Deanna drifted slowly around the gallery, watching prospective buyers and admiring Gustave's work. She had stopped before one of his paintings when she heard a familiar voice just behind her. She turned in surprise. ·

'Studying the technique, Deanna?'

'Jim!' She looked into the laughing Irish eyes. 'What are you doing here?'

'Don't ask. Collecting culture, I guess.' He waved vaguely towards a group of people at the door. 'They dragged me here. But only after several stiff drinks.'

'An art lover to the core.' She wore her usual warm smile, but somewhere within her was an uncomfortable stirring. She hadn't wanted to see Jim Sullivan here.

73

She had come to see Ben ... or had she? Was she here only to see the gallery? She wasn't really sure, and perhaps Jim would know. Perhaps he'd see something different in her face, in her eyes, in her soul. Almost defensively, she reached for a familiar subject. 'Have you heard from Marc?'

He eyed her warily for a moment. 'Have you?'

She shook her head. 'I got a telegram the day after he left that he hadn't been able to call because it was the wrong time, and then I went to Carmel for the weekend. With Kim,' she added quickly and unnecessarily. 'He might have tried to call me then. I suppose he's in Athens by now.'

Sullivan nodded and gazed back towards his friends. Deanna followed his gaze, and her glance fell immediately on a stunning, chestnut-haired girl gowned in shimmery silver. Jim's model – she had to be.

'He must be,' Jim was saying. 'Well, love, I've got to run.' Almost as an afterthought, as he kissed her cheek, he pulled away to look at her again. 'Do you want to join us for dinner?'

Instantly, she was shaking her head. 'I – I can't ... I have to get home ... really. But thank you.' Damn. Why did she feel so uncomfortable? She had nothing to hide. But he hadn't seemed to notice anything different about her. And why should he? What was different?

'You're sure?'

'Positive.'

'All right. I'll call you.' He kissed her quickly on the cheek and rejoined his friends. A moment later, they were gone. She stared absently after them. He hadn't answered her about whether or not he'd heard from Marc. Instead, he had countered her question with his own, asking her if she had heard from him. She wondered why.

'You look awfully serious, Deanna. Thinking of signing up with us?' There was teasing in Ben's whis-

74

pered tones, and she turned to him with a smile. She hadn't noticed him come up to her.

'No. But I was thinking that I ought to go home.'

'Already? Don't be silly. Besides, you haven't eaten.' He looked at her for a moment. 'Can I interest you in some dinner? Or would your husband object?'

'Hardly. He's in Greece for the summer.' Their eyes met and held. 'And dinner would be lovely.' Why not? She smiled and forced Jim Sullivan from her mind.

Ben signalled to Sally that he was leaving, and unnoticed by the last stragglers, they passed through the glass door and into the cool summer fog. 'Sometimes this reminds me of London,' he said. 'I used to visit my grandfather there as a child. He was English.'

She laughed at the anonymity he assumed. 'Yes, I know.'

'Did you bring your own car?' Ben asked. She nodded at the dark blue Jaguar. 'My, my. I'm impressed. I drive a little German car no one here has ever heard of. It runs on practically no gas and gets me where I want to go. Would you be ashamed to be seen in something so simple, or shall we take yours?' For a moment she was embarrassed to have come in Marc's car, but she always drove it when she went out in the evening. It was a matter of habit.

'I'd much rather go in yours.'

'To L'Étoile?' He said it hesitantly, testing the waters.

'I think I'd like some place more like your car. Quiet and simple.' He smiled his approval, and she laughed. 'I suspect that you have a horror of ostentation, except in art.'

'Exactly. Besides, my housekeeper would quit if I showed up one day in a Rolls. She already thinks all that "crap" on the walls is an outrage. I once hung a beautiful French nude, and she took it down as soon as I left Carmel. I found it wrapped in a sheet when I got back. I had to take it back to the city.' She laughed as he unlocked his car and held the door for her.

He took her to a little Italian restaurant tucked into a side street near the bay, and they talked about art through most of the evening. She told him of her years of floating around Europe and the States with her father, devouring the museums wherever they went, and he told her of learning about art from his grandfather and then his father, watching great auctions in London and Paris and New York. 'But I never thought I'd go into the business.'

'Why not?'

'I wanted to do something more interesting. Like ride in rodeos or be a spy. I planned to be a spy at least until I was nine, but my grandfather insisted it wasn't respectable. Sometimes I'm not so sure our business is either. Actually, when I went to college I wanted to be one of those men who detects fakes in art. I studied for a while, but the forgeries always fooled me. I hope I do better now.'

Deanna smiled. From the look of the gallery and the house in Carmel, she felt sure he did.

'Tell me,' he said abruptly, 'how long have you been married?'

She was surprised at the suddenly personal question. He had asked her none so far. 'Eighteen years. I was nineteen.'

'That makes you ...' He went through the ritual on his fingers, and she laughed.

'A hundred and three, in November.'

'No.' He frowned. 'Isn't it a hundred and two?'

'At least. What about you? Have you ever been married?'

'Once. Briefly.' His eyes retreated from hers for a moment. 'I'm afraid I wasn't very good at detecting fakes there either. She took me for a beautiful ride, and I had a wonderful time. And then it was over.' He smiled and met her glance again.

'No children?'

76

'None. That's the only thing I've regretted. I would have liked to have had a son.'

'So would I.'

There was a hint of wistfulness in her voice that made him watch her as he said, 'But you have a lovely daughter.'

'I also had two boys. They both died right after they were born.' It was a weighty piece of information to pass across a dinner table to a relative stranger, but he only watched her eyes. He saw there what he needed to know.

'I'm sorry.'

'So was I. And then, stupidly, it was a sort of blow when Pilar was born. In French families baby girls are not greeted with applause.'

'You wanted applause?' He looked amused.

'At least.' She smiled back at last. 'And a brass band. And a parade.'

'One can hardly blame you. She was the third?' he asked. Deanna nodded. 'Are you very close?' He imagined they would be and was surprised to hear they were not.

'Not just now, but we will be again. For the moment she is terribly torn between being American and French. That kind of thing can be hard.'

'So can being fifteen.' He remembered with horror his sister at the same age. 'Does she look like you?' He hadn't been able to tell from the distant glimpses in Deanna's paintings.

'Not at all. She is the image of her father. She's a very pretty girl.'

'So is her mother.'

For a moment Deanna said nothing, then she smiled. 'Thank you, sir.'

The conversation drifted back then to art. He stayed away from painful and personal subjects, but sometimes she wondered if he was even listening. He seemed to be watching her all the time and saying other things with his eyes. It was midnight when at last they were encouraged to leave.

'I had a marvellous evening.' She smiled at him happily as he drew up alongside the parked Jaguar.

'So did I.' He said nothing more. As she started her car, he backed away with a wave. She saw him in her rearview mirror, walking back to his own car, his hands in his pockets and his head pensively bowed.

She was already in bed, with the lights out, when the telephone rang. But the rapid whir of the lines told her it was long distance.

'Deanna?' It was Marc.

'Hello, darling. Where are you?'

'In Rome. At the Hassler, if you need me. Are you all right?' But the connection was poor. It was very hard to hear.

'I'm fine. Why are you in Rome?'

'What? I can't hear you ...'

'I said why are you in Rome?'

'I'm here on business. For Salco. But I'll see Pilar this weekend.'

'Give her my love.' She was sitting up in the dark and shouting to make herself heard.

'I can't hear you!'

'I said give her my love.'

'Good. Fine. I will. Do you need money?'

'No, I'm fine.' For a moment all she heard was static and gibberish again. 'I love you.' For some reason she needed to tell him that and to hear him say the same. She needed a bond to him, but he seemed an interminable distance away.

'I love you, Marc!' And for no reason she could understand, she found that there were tears in her eyes. She wanted him to hear her, she wanted to hear herself. 'I love you!'

'What?'

And then they were cut off.

She quickly dialled the overseas operator and asked her for Rome. But it took another twenty-five minutes to put through her call. The operator at the Hassler answered with a rapid, *'Pronto'*, and Deanna asked for Signore Duras. They rang his room. No answer. In Rome, it was already ten o'clock in the morning. 'We are sorry. Signore Duras has gone out.'

She lay back in the dark and thought of her evening with Ben.

Chapter Seven

Marc-Edouard Duras walked along the Via Veneto in Rome, glancing into shop windows and occasionally casting an admiring glance at a pretty girl wandering past. It was a brilliantly sunny day, and the women were wearing T-shirts with narrow straps, white skirts that clung to shapely legs, and sandals that bared red enamelled toes. He smiled to himself as he walked, the briefcase under his arm. It didn't make sense really, this brief sojourn in Italy, but after all, why not? And he had promised ... *Promised*. Sometimes he wondered how he could promise so easily. But he did.

He paused for a moment, an aristocratic figure in an impeccably tailored grey suit, waiting for the machine-gun spurt of Roman traffic to hurtle past him, casting itself hurly-burly in all directions, sending pedestrians scurrying in flight. He smiled as he watched an old woman wave a parasol and then make an obscene gesture. *Ecco, signora.* He bowed slightly to her from the opposite side of the street, and she made the same gesture to him. He laughed, glanced at his watch, and hurried to a table in a café. Beneath a brightly striped umbrella he could take refuge from the sun and continue to admire the energy and ecstasy that were the very essence of Rome. *Roma* – it was a magical city. Perhaps the promise had been worth keeping after all. For an instant, but only that, the abortive conversation with Deanna crept into his mind. It had been almost impossible to hear her, and he was relieved. There were times when he simply couldn't deal with her, couldn't reach out to her, couldn't bear to imagine the pain in those eyes or hear the loneliness in her voice. He knew it was there, but it was sometimes more than he could handle. He could cope with it in San Francisco, in the context of his ordinary routine, but not when he was in the throes of a professional crisis abroad, or when he was at home in France, or ... here, in Rome. He shook his head slowly, as though to brush away the memory of her voice, and found himself gazing longingly up the street. He couldn't think of Deanna now. Couldn't. No. Not now. His mind was already a thousand miles away from her as his eyes sifted through the crowd: a pretty blonde, a tall brunette, two very Roman-looking men in light linen suits with thick dark hair, a tall Florentine-looking woman, like something in a Renaissance painting, and then he saw her. Striding gaily down the street with her own inimitable gait, the endless legs seeming to dance across the sidewalk as a brilliant turquoise skirt caressed her thighs. She wore the palest mauve silk shirt, delicate sandals, and a huge straw hat that almost hid her eyes. Almost. But not quite. Nothing could hide those eyes, or the sapphire lights that seemed to change with her every mood. They changed from the brilliance of fire to the mystery of the deep blue sea. A rich chestnut mane swept her shoulders.

'*Alors, chéri.*' She stopped only inches from him, and sensuous lips offered a smile for his eyes alone. 'I'm sorry I'm late. I stopped to look at those silly bracelets again.' He stood to greet her, and for once the chill reserve of Marc-Edouard Duras was clearly shattered. He wore the face of a boy, and one who was very much in love. Her name was Chantal Martin, and she had been a model at Dior. Their top model, in fact, for six-and-a-half years.

'Did you buy the bracelets?' His eyes caressed her neck, and as she shook her head, the chestnut hair danced beneath the hat he had bought her only that morning. It was frivolous, but delightful. And so was she. 'Well?'

Her eyes laughed into his. She shook her head again. 'No, again I didn't buy them.' Unexpectedly, she tossed a small package into his lap. 'I bought you that instead.' She sat back, waiting for him to open it.

'*Tu me gâtes, petite sotte.*' You spoil me, silly little one.

'And you don't spoil me?' Without waiting for an answer, she signalled for a waiter. '*Senta! ... Cameriere! ...*' He approached instantly, with a look of pleasure, and she ordered a Campari and soda. 'And you?'

'Inviting me to drinks, too?' She never waited for him to take matters in hand. Chantal liked to run her own show.

'Oh, shut up. What'll you have?'

'Scotch.' She ordered it the way he liked it, and he watched her eyes for a long moment as they sat beneath the umbrella. The beginnings of the lunchtime crowd swirled colourfully around them. 'Will you always be this independent, my love?'

'Always. Now open your gift.'

'You're impossible.' But that was precisely what had always fascinated him about her. She was impossible. And he loved it. Like a wild mare running free on the plains of Camargue. They had gone there together once, the land of the French cowboys and the beautiful, wild, white horses. He had always thought of her that way after that. Untamed, just a fraction out of reach, yet more or less his. More or less. He liked to think it was more rather than less. And it had been that way between them for five years.

She was twenty-nine now. She had been twenty-four when they met. It was the first summer that Deanna had refused to join him in France. He had felt odd to spend a summer without her; it had been awkward to explain to his family, insisting that she hadn't felt well enough to travel that year. No one believed it, but they had only said so behind his back, wondering if she were leaving Marc-Edouard or merely had a lover in the States. They would never have understood the truth – that she hated them, that she felt ill at ease, that she had wanted to stay at home, to be alone, to paint, because she detested sharing Marc with them, detested the way he was when he was with them, and detested even more watching the way Pilar became like them. It had been a shock for Marc-Edouard when she refused to come, a shock that left him wondering what it would mean now that she would no longer spend the summers with his family in France. He had decided to send her something beautiful, along with a letter asking her to change her mind. Remembering the eighteen-year-old wistful beauty who had sat in his office that day so long ago, he had gone to Dior.

He sat through the entire collection, making notes, watching the models, carefully studying the clothes, trying to decide which ones were most her style, but his attention had incessantly wandered from the outfits to the models, and in particular, one spectacular girl. She had been dazzling, and she had moved in a way that spoke only to him. She was a genius at what she did, whirling, turning, beckoning – to him alone, it seemed – and he had sat breathless in his seat. At the end of the show he had asked to see her, feeling uncomfortable for a moment, but barely longer. When she walked out to meet him in a starkly narrow, black jersey dress, her auburn hair swept up on her lovely head, those remarkable blue eyes alternately clawing and caressing, he had wanted to seize her and watch her melt in his embrace. He was a rational man, a man of power and control, and he had never felt that way before. It frightened him and fascinated him, and Chantal seemed very much aware of the power she had. She wielded it gracefully, but with crushing force.

And instead of buying Deanna a dress, Marc had bought Chantal a drink, and another, and another. They had finished with champagne at the bar of the hotel George V, and then much to his own astonishment, he heard himself ask her if she would let him take a room. But she had only giggled and gently touched his face with one long, delicate hand.

'*Ah, non, mon amour, pas encore.*' Not yet.

Then when? He had wanted to shout the words at her, but he hadn't. Instead he had courted her, cajoled her, showered her with gifts, until at last she acquiesced, demurely, shyly, in just the way that turned his heart and soul and flesh to fire beneath her touch. They had spent the weekend in an apartment he had borrowed from a friend, in the posh surroundings of the Avenue Foch, with a miraculously romantic bedroom, and a balcony looking out on gently whispering trees.

He would remember for a lifetime every sound and smell and moment of that weekend. He had known then that he would never have enough of Mademoiselle Chantal Martin. She had woven herself like thread beneath his skin, and he would never be quite comfortable again except with her. She drained him and enchanted him, and made him almost mad with a desire he had never felt before. Elusive, exotic, exquisite Chantal. It had gone on for five years. In Paris, and Athens, and Rome. Wherever he went in Europe, he took her and of course presented her in hotels and restaurants and shops as 'Madame Duras'. They had both grown used to it over the years. It was simply a part of his life now, and hers. A part of which his partner, Jim Sullivan, was acutely aware, and his wife, thank heaven, was not. Deanna would never know. There was no reason to tell her. It took nothing away from her, he told himself. She had San Francisco and her own little world. He had Chantal, and a much wider one. He had everything he wanted. As long as he had Chantal. He only prayed that it would go on for a lifetime. But that was a promise Chantal would never make.

'*Alors, mon amour*, your present, your present, open it!' Her eyes teased and his heart soared. He pulled open the box. It was the diver's watch he had admired that morning, saying it would be fun to have for their trips to the beach and his stays in Cap d'Antibes.

'My God, you're mad! Chantal!' It had been monstrously expensive, but she waved his objections away with a disinterested hand. She could afford it now that she was no longer at Dior. Three years before she had retired from the runway and opened her own modelling agency. She wouldn't let him set her up in an apartment in Paris to do nothing except her hair and nails and wait for him. She refused to be dependent on anyone, least of all him. It irritated him sometimes, and frightened him as well. She didn't need him, she only loved him, but at least of that he was sure. No matter what she did when he was in the States, she loved him. He was certain of it. And the perfection of their time together cemented that belief.

'Do you like it?' She eyed him coyly over her Campari.

'I adore it.' He dropped his voice. 'But I love you more.'

'Do you, m'lord?' She arched an eyebrow, and he felt a rising at his crotch.

'Do you require proof?'

'Perhaps. What did you have in mind?' She eyed him evilly from beneath her hat.

'I was planning to suggest lunch out in the country somewhere, but perhaps ...' His smile matched hers.

'Room service, darling?'

'An excellent idea.' He waved to the *cameriere* and quickly paid their bill.

She stood up languidly, letting her body sway gently against his for a tantalizing instant, then began to weave her way through the crowded tables, casting a glance at him over her shoulder now and then. He could hardly wait to get her home. He wanted to run back to the hotel, holding fast to her hand, but she walked at her own pace, in her own style, knowing that she had Marc-Edouard Duras precisely where she

85

wanted him. He watched her, amused. In a very few moments he would have her precisely where he wanted her. In his arms, in bed.

In their room he began unbuttoning her blouse with alarming speed, and she brushed him away playfully, making him wait before she'd let him reveal what he was so hungry for. She fondled him with one hand and nipped gently at his neck, until at last he found the button to her skirt and it dropped to the floor, leaving her in transparent pink lace. He almost tore at the blouse now. In a moment she stood naked in front of him as he softly moaned. She undressed him, quickly and expertly, and they fell together on the bed. Each time they made love was better than the time before, and ever reminiscent of the first. It left him sated, yet still hungry, eager to know that they would soon be joined again.

She rolled over in bed, lying on one elbow, her hair tousled but still beautiful. She watched him silently, smiling. Her voice was a husky whisper near his ear as her fingers played slowly across his chest and down towards his stomach. 'I love you, you know.'

He looked at her intently, his eyes searching hers. 'I love you too, Chantal. Too much perhaps. But I do.' It was a remarkable admission for a man like Marc-Edouard Duras. No one who knew him would have believed it. Least of all Deanna.

Chantal smiled and then lay back with her eyes closed for a moment, and there was concern in his eyes. 'Are you all right?'

'Of course.'

'You'd lie to me, though. I know it. Tell me seriously. Are you all right, Chantal?' A look of almost frantic worry crossed his face. She smiled.

'I'm fine.'

'You took your insulin properly today?' He was all fatherly concern now, the passion of the moment before forgotten.

86

'Yes, I took it. Stop worrying. Want to try your new watch in the bathtub?'

'Now?'

'Why not?' She smiled happily at him, and for once he felt totally at peace. 'Or did you have something else in mind?'

'I always have something else in mind. But you're tired.'

'Never too tired for you, *mon amour*.' And he was never too tired for her. The years between them vanished as he made love to her again.

It was three o'clock in the afternoon when they lay quietly side by side again. 'Well, we've taken care of this afternoon.' She smiled mischievously at him, and he grinned in answer.

'You had other plans?'

'Absolutely none.'

'Want to do some more shopping?' He loved to indulge her, to spoil her, to be with her, admire her, drink her in. Her perfume, her movements, her every breath excited him. And she knew it.

'I could probably be lured back to the shops.'

'Good.' The trip to Rome had been for her anyway. He was going to have to work hard that summer, and Athens would be dull for her. He knew how she loved Rome. And he always made a point of bringing her. Just to please her. Besides, he was going to have to leave her for the weekend.

'What's wrong?' She had been watching him very closely.

'Nothing. Why?'

'You looked worried for a moment.'

'Not worried.' But it was best to get it over with. 'Just unhappy. I'm going to have to leave you for a couple of days.'

'Oh?' Her eyes iced over like a winter frost.

'I have to stop off in Antibes to visit my mother and Pilar before we go to Greece.'

She sat up in bed and looked at him with annoyance. 'And what do you plan to do with me?'

'Don't make it sound like that, darling. I can't help it. You know that.'

'Don't you think Pilar is old enough to withstand the shock of knowing about me? Or do you still find me so unpresentable? I'm no longer the little mannequin from Dior, you know. I run the biggest modelling agency in Paris.' But she also knew that in his world that didn't count.

'That's not the point. And no, I don't think she's old enough.' In what concerned Pilar he was oddly stubborn. It irritated Chantal a great deal.

'And your mother?'

'That's impossible.'

'I see.' She threw her long legs over the side of the bed and stalked across the room, grabbing a cigarette on her way, turning to look at him angrily only when she had reached the window at the opposite side. 'I'm getting a little bored with being dumped in out-of-the-way places while you visit your family, Marc-Edouard.'

'I'd hardly call Saint-Tropez an "out-of-the-way place."' He was beginning to look annoyed, and his tone showed none of the passion of the hours before.

'Where did you have in mind this time?'

'I thought maybe San Remo.'

'How convenient. Well, I won't go.'

'Would you rather stay here?'

'No.'

'Do we have to go through this again, Chantal? It's getting very tedious. What's more, I don't understand. Why has this suddenly become an issue between us, when for five years you have found it perfectly acceptable to spend time on the Riviera without me?'

'Would you like to know why?' Suddenly her eyes blazed. 'Because I'm almost thirty years old, and I'm still playing the same games I was playing with you five years ago. And I'm just a little tired of it. We play make-believe games of "Monsieur and Madame Duras" halfway around the world, but in the places that matter – Paris, San Francisco, Antibes – I have to hide and slink around and disappear. Well, I'm sick of it. You want an exclusive arrangement. You expect me to sit in Paris and hold my breath for half the year, and then come out of mothballs at your command. I'm not going to do that any more, Marc-Edouard. At least not for much longer.' She stopped, and he stared at her, stunned. He didn't dare ask if she were serious. For a terrible instant, he knew that she was.

'What do you expect me to do about it?'

'I don't know yet. But I've been giving it a lot of thought lately. The Americans have a perfect expression, I believe: "Shit or get off the pot." '

'I don't find that amusing.'

'I don't find San Remo amusing.'

Christ! It was useless. A small sigh escaped him, and he ran a hand through his hair. 'Chantal, I can't take you to Antibes.'

'You *won't* take me to Antibes. There's a difference.'

And what's more, she had added San Francisco to the list of her complaints. That startling bit of information hadn't escaped him either. She had never even wanted to go to the States before.

'May I ask what brought all this on? It can't just be your thirtieth birthday. That's still four months away.'

She paused, her back to him, as she looked silently out the window, and then slowly she turned to face him again. 'Someone else just asked me to marry him.'

Time seemed to stand still. Marc-Edouard stared at her in horror.

Chapter Eight

'Deanna?' The phone had rung before she'd gotten out of bed. It was Ben.

'Yes.'

She sounded sleepy, and he smiled. 'I'm sorry. Did I wake you?'

'More or less.'

'What a very diplomatic answer! I'm calling to bug you a little more. I figure that sooner or later I'll wear down your resistance and you'll sign with the gallery just to get me off your back. How about lunch?'

'Now?' She was still half asleep and turned towards the clock wondering how late she had slept, but Ben was laughing at her again.

'No, not at eight o'clock in the morning. How about twelve or one? In Sausalito?'

'What's there?'

'Sunshine. A condition we're not always blessed with on this side of the bridge. Have I sold you?'

'More or less.' She laughed into the phone. What the hell was he doing, calling her at eight o'clock in the morning? And why lunch so soon? They had had dinner the night before, and lunch in her studio the day before that. She was beginning to wonder if she had found a new friend, an ardent potential dealer for her work, or something else. She wondered if it were wise to see him again quite so soon.

'Yes, it is.'

'What is?' She was confused.

'You're wondering if it's a good idea to have lunch with me. It is.'

'You're impossible.'

'Then we'll have lunch in the city.'

'No, Sausalito sounds nice.' She had accepted without

thinking further and found herself smiling at the ceiling as she spoke into the phone. 'I'm an easy sale at this hour of the day. No defences yet, no coffee.'

'Good. Then how about signing with the gallery before coffee tomorrow?'

'I may hang up on you, Ben.' She was laughing, and it felt wonderful to start the day off with laughter. She hadn't done that in years.

'Don't hang up on me till we settle lunch. Do you want me to pick you up around noon?'

'That'll do.' What'll do? What was she doing having lunch with this man? But she liked him. And lunch in Sausalito sounded like fun.

'Wear your jeans.'

'O.K., see you at noon.'

He pulled up in front of her house at exactly 12:02. He was wearing a turtleneck sweater and jeans, and when she climbed into the car, she saw that there was a basket on the seat, draped in a red-and-white cloth. The neck of a bottle poked its way out at one side. Ben opened the door for her and put the basket on the backseat.

'Good morning, madam.' He smiled broadly as she slid in beside him. 'I thought maybe we'd have a picnic instead. O.K.?'

'Very much so.' Or was it? Should she be having a picnic with this man? The head of Madame Duras told her no, while the heart that was Deanna's wanted an afternoon in the sun. But surely there were other things she could do, and she had the terrace outside her studio if she really wanted sun.

Ben glanced at her as he started the car and saw the faint pucker between her brows. 'Do we have a problem?'

'No.' She said it softly as he pulled away from the kerb. She found herself wondering if Margaret had seen them.

He amused her with stories about some of the gallery's more colourful artists as they drove across the splendour of the Golden Gate Bridge. He fell silent then for a moment. They were both looking out at the view.

'Pretty, isn't it?' he asked. She nodded with a smile. 'May I ask you an odd sort of question?'

She looked surprised for a moment. 'Why not?'

'How is it that you and your husband live here, instead of France? From what I know of the French they don't, as a rule, like living very far from home. Except under duress.'

She laughed. What he had said was true. 'There's a lot of business to be done here. And Marc isn't here that much anyway; he travels most of the time.'

'Lonely for you.' It was a statement, not a question.

'I'm used to it.'

He wasn't quite sure he believed her. 'What do you do when you're alone?'

They spoke in unison with a burst of laughter: 'Paint.'

'That's what I thought.'

'What ever made you come down to Carmel?' He seemed to be riddled with questions. So far they were all easy to answer.

'Kim. She insisted that I needed to get away.'

'Was she right?' He glanced over at her as he took the turnoff that led into the military preserve on the other side of the bridge. 'Did you need to get away?'

'I suppose I did. I'd forgotten how lovely Carmel is. I hadn't been there in years. Do you go every weekend?' She wanted to turn the questions back to him. She didn't really like talking to him about Marc.

'I go whenever I can. It's never often enough.'

She noticed then that they had taken a narrow country road and were driving past deserted bunkers and military buildings. 'Ben, what is this?' She looked around herself with curiosity. They might have stumbled on to a stage set for a movie depicting the years after a war. The barracks on either side of the road were crumbling and boarded up, and there were wild flowers and weeds climbing on to the road.

'It's an old army post from the last war. For some reason they hang on to it, though it's empty now. There's a beautiful beach down here at the end. I come here sometimes, just to think.' He looked over at her with a smile, and once again she was aware of how comfortable it was just to be with him. He had all the makings of a good friend. They fell into an easy silence as he drove the rest of the way.

'It's eerie, isn't it? It's so pretty and there's no one here.' His was the only car there when they stopped just before they reached the beach. She hadn't seen another car since he'd turned off the main road.

'There never is. And I've never told a soul about it. I like coming here by myself.'

'Do you do that sort of thing often? Like walk on the beach in Carmel by yourself?' she asked. He nodded, reaching over for the basket in the back seat. He was looking very closely at her.

'I never thought I'd see you again after that night on the beach.'

'Neither did I. It was strange, walking along, talking to you about art. I felt as though we'd known each other for years.'

'So did I, but I thought it was because you looked so much like the Wyeth.' She smiled and lowered her eyes. 'I wasn't quite sure what to say the next day when I found you in my den. I didn't know whether or not to acknowledge that we'd met.'

'What made you decide not to?' She looked back into his eyes with a very small smile.

'The ring on your left hand. I thought it might be awkward for you if I did.'

It was like him, Deanna realised, perceptive and thoughtful. She saw him frown a little, and sit back in his seat.

'Would it be awkward for you if people knew we were having lunch?' he asked.

'I don't see why.' But there was more bravado than truth in her face, and he saw it.

'What would your husband say, Deanna?'

The words were unbearably soft, and she wanted to tell him that she didn't give a damn, but she did. The bitch of it was that she did care. A lot.

'I don't know. The question has never come up. I don't have lunch with men very often.'

'What about art dealers who want to show your work?' Ben smiled at her. They had not moved from the car.

'No, least of all with art dealers. I never have lunch with them.'

'Why not?'

She took a deep breath and looked him in the eye. 'My husband does not approve of my work. He thinks it's a nice hobby, a pastime, but "artists are hippies and fools".'

'Well, that certainly takes care of Gauguin and Manet.' He thought for a moment. When he spoke, she felt as though his eyes were burning straight into her soul. 'Doesn't that hurt? Doesn't it force you to deny an essential part of yourself?'

'Not really. I still paint.' But they both knew that her denial was a lie. She had been forced to give up something she wanted very much. 'I suppose marriage is a kind of exchange,' she went on. 'Everyone compromises something.' But what did Marc compromise? What had he given up? She looked pensive and sad, and Ben looked away.

'Maybe that's what I had all wrong when I got married. I forgot the compromises.'

'Were you very demanding?' Deanna watched him with surprise.

'Maybe I was. It was so long ago, it's hard to be sure.

94

I wanted her to be what I had always thought she was ...' His voice drifted off.

'And what was that?'

'Oh' – he looked up with a wry little smile – 'faithful, honest, pleasant, in love with me. The usual stuff.' They both laughed then, and he grabbed the picnic basket and helped Deanna out of the car. He had brought a blanket too and spread it out carefully for her on the sand.

'Good God, did you make this lunch?' She looked at the goodies he was pulling out of the basket. There was crab salad, pâté, French bread, a little box of pastries, and more wine. There was also a smaller basket filled with fruit and richly sprinkled with cherries. She reached for a cluster and hung it over her right ear.

'You look lovely in cherries, Deanna, but have you tried grapes?' He handed her a small bunch. She laughed and draped them over her left ear. 'You look as though you should be climbing out of a horn of plenty ... it's all very *Fête Champêtre.*'

'Isn't it though?' She leaned back, looking up at the sky with a broad smile. She felt terribly young and irrepressibly happy. It was easy being with him.

'Ready to eat?' He looked down at her, a bowl of crab salad in one hand. She looked startlingly beautiful, reclining easily on the blanket with the fruit peeking through her dark hair. Seeing his smile, she remembered the cherries and the grapes. She pulled them away from her ears and sat up on one elbow.

'To tell you the truth, I'm ravenous.'

'Good. I like women with healthy appetites.'

'And what else? What else do you like?' It wasn't an appropriate question, but she didn't care. She wanted to be his friend. She wanted to know more, and to share.

'Oh, let's see ... I like women who dance ... women who type ... women who can read – and write! Women

95

who paint ... women with green eyes.' He stopped, staring down at her again. 'And you?' His voice was barely audible.

'What kind of women do I like?' She laughed at him.

'Oh, shut up. Here, have something to eat.' He handed her the loaf of French bread and the pâté, and she broke off the heel and slathered it handsomely with the delicate meat.

It was a perfect afternoon; the sun was high in the sky and there was a gentle breeze as the water lapped softly at the beach. Now and then a bird would fly by. Behind them the deserted buildings stood staring sightlessly. It was a world of their own.

'You know' – she glanced around and then back at him – 'sometimes I wish I painted things like this.'

'Why don't you?'

'You mean like Wyeth?' She smiled at him. 'It's not me. We each do what we do, very differently.' He nodded, waiting for her to say more. 'Ben, do you paint?'

He shook his head with a rueful grin. 'Not really. I used to try. But I'm afraid it's my lot in life to sell art and not to make it. I did create one piece of art though.' He looked dreamy again as he stared out at the bay. The summer wind played with his hair.

'What was it?'

'I built a house. A small one, but it was damn pretty. I built it myself with a friend.'

'How amazing!' She was impressed. 'Where?'

'In New England. I was living in New York then. It was a surprise for my wife.'

'Did she love it?'

He shook his head and turned to look at the bay again. 'No. She never saw it. She left three days before I was going to take her up to see it for the first time.' Deanna sat in silence for a moment, stunned. They had both had their disappointments in life.

'What did you do with it?'

'Sold it. I hung on to it for a while, but it was never

much fun. It always hurt a little too much. And then I moved out here. And bought the house in Carmel.' He looked over at Deanna, his eyes soft and sad. 'But it was nice to know I could do it. I don't think I ever felt as good as the day I finished that house. What a feeling! It really was an accomplishment.'

She smiled softly, listening. 'I know,' she said, after a moment. 'I felt that way when I had Pilar. Even though she wasn't a son.'

'Does that really matter so much?' He seemed annoyed.

'It did then. It meant a great deal to Marc, to have a boy. But I don't think he really cares any more. He adores her.'

'I think I'd rather have a daughter than a son,' Ben said.

Deanna looked surprised. 'Why?'

'They're easier to love. You don't have to get hung up with images and macho and all that crap that doesn't mean anything. You can just love them.' He looked as though he regretted not having a child, and she found herself wondering if he'd ever remarry.

'No, I won't.' He wasn't looking at her when he said it.

'Won't what?' She was confused. He had a way of answering questions she hadn't asked. Except in her own head.

'Get married again.'

'You're incredible. Why not?' She was still amazed that he had known what she was thinking.

'There's no point. I have what I need. And now I'm too busy with the galleries. It wouldn't be fair, unless it were someone as involved in them as I. I was less entranced by my business ten years ago. Now I'm in it up to my neck.'

'But you want children. Don't you?' She had understood that much.

'I also want an estate outside Vienna. I can live without that too. And what about you?'

'I already have a child. Do you mean do I want more?' She didn't understand.

'No, or maybe that too, but do you think you'll ever remarry?' He looked at her openly, with his deep, green eyes.

'But I am. Married, I mean.'

'Happily, Deanna?'

The question was painful and direct. She started to say yes, then stopped. 'Sometimes. I accept what I've got.'

'Why?'

'Because he and I have a history behind us.' She found herself not wanting to say Marc's name to Ben. 'You can't replace that, or deny it, or run out on it. We have a past.'

'A good one?'

'At times. Once I understood the rules of the game.' She was being brutally honest, even with herself.

'Which were?' His voice was so unbearably soft, it made her want to reach out to him and not talk about Marc. But Ben was her friend now. And she had a right to no more than that. Only his friendship. It was just as well that they were speaking of Marc. 'What were the rules?'

She sighed and then shrugged. 'A lot of "Thou shalt nots". Thou shalt not defy the wishes of thy husband, thou shalt not ask too many questions, thou shalt not want a life of your own, least of all as a painter ... But he was very good to me once. My father left me stranded and penniless and scared when he died. Marc bailed me out. I don't think I wanted quite as much bailing as he gave me, but he did. He gave me comforts and a home, a family and stability, and eventually he gave me Pilar.' She had not mentioned love.

'Was it all worth it? Is it now?'

She tried to smile. 'I guess so. I've stuck around; I like what I've got.'

'Do you love him?'

The smile faded slowly. She nodded.

'I'm sorry, Deanna. I shouldn't have asked.'

'Why not? We're friends.'

'Yes.' He smiled at her again. 'We are. Want to go for a walk on the beach?' He was on his feet, his arm extended to help her up. Their hands touched briefly before he turned and made rapid strides towards the shore, beckoning to her to catch up. She walked slowly, thinking of what they had said. At least everything was clear, and she did love Marc. At least now she wouldn't get into trouble with Ben. For a moment or two she had feared it; there was something about him that she liked very much.

He handed her seashells and walked in the water up to his knees, having discarded his sandals hours before. He looked like a tall, happy boy playing in the surf, and she smiled as she watched him.

'Want to race?' He looked at her mischievously as he came back to her side, and she accepted the challenge with amusement. If Pilar could see her mother now, racing with a man on the beach, as though they were children. But she felt like a girl, pounding along the damp sand, breathless and wind-tousled. She stopped at last, laughing and out of breath, shaking her head as he thundered past.

'Give up?' He shouted the words back to her. When she nodded, he loped back across the beach and came to a halt next to where she had sunk down on the sand. The sun had set off glints of red in her dark hair. He let himself down next to her, and they sat together, looking out to sea and catching their breath. After a moment she looked up at him, knowing what she would see: those sea-coloured eyes, waiting for hers.

'Deanna ...' He waited an interminable time, looking at her, and then leaned slowly towards her, whispering the words into the windswept darkness of her hair. 'Oh, Deanna, I love you ...'

As though he couldn't stop himself, he felt his arms go around her and his mouth close gently on hers, but her arms were as quickly around him and her mouth as hungry as his own. They sat there for a long time, holding each other and touching each other's faces, gazing into each other's eyes, with no more words between them than those he had spoken first. They didn't need words; they had each other in a world where time had stopped. It was Ben who pulled away at last, saying nothing, only standing up, quietly, slowly, reaching a hand out for hers. Together, hand in hand, they walked back down the beach.

They didn't speak again until they were back in the car. Ben sat there for a time, looking troubled.

'I should tell you I'm sorry, Deanna, but I'm not.'

'Neither am I.' She sounded as though she were in shock. 'But I don't understand it.'

'Maybe we don't have to. We can still be friends.' He looked at her then with an attempt at a smile, but there was none in her eyes, only the glimmer of something haunted.

'I don't feel betrayed. At least not by you.' She wanted him to know that much.

'By yourself?'

'Perhaps. I think I just don't understand.'

'You don't have to. You were very clear about your life when we talked about it before. There's nothing for you to understand, or explain.' His voice was so unbearably gentle. 'We can forget. I'm sure we will.'

But she didn't want to, and that was what astonished her most. She didn't want to forget at all.

'Did you mean what you said?' She meant his 'I love you', but she could see that he understood. 'I feel that way too. It's really a little crazy.'

'Isn't it just!' He laughed aloud this time and gently kissed her cheek. 'Maybe it's even very crazy. But however we feel, I won't destroy your life. You have what you need, and you don't need me rocking your boat now. I suspect that it's taken you the last eighteen years to come to terms with that life.' It was true, and she knew it. 'I promise, Deanna. I won't hurt you.'

'But what will we do?' She felt like a child, lost in his arms.

'Nothing. We'll be big kids, both of us. And good friends. Does that sound all right to you?'

'I suppose it has to.' But there was relief in her voice too, as well as regret. She didn't want to cheat on Marc. It meant a lot to her to be faithful.

He started the car, and they drove slowly home, saying little on the way back. It was a day she would not quickly forget. It seemed an eternity before they stopped at her house.

'Will you come to lunch in my studio now and then?' She sounded so forlorn that it made his pain more acute, but he smiled.

'Anytime. I'll call you sometime soon.'

She nodded and slipped out of the car. She heard him drive away before she had a chance to look back.

She walked slowly up the stairs to her bedroom, and lay down on the bed; then, glancing at the phone, she saw a message from Marc. Margaret had taken the call that afternoon. She cringed as she read it. PLEASE CALL MR DURAS. She didn't want to call now, didn't want to hear him. Not now. But she knew she had to. She had to force herself back to her life and away from the dream on the beach.

It took her half an hour to steel herself to make the call. At last, she dialled the overseas operator for Rome and asked for Marc's room at the Hassler.

This time he was in.

'Marc? It's me.'

'Yes. Hello.' He sounded strange and cold.

'Deanna.' She thought for a moment that he didn't

101

understand who it was. Then she realised the time. It was two A.M. in Rome. He had undoubtedly been fast asleep.

'Yes, yes, I know. I was asleep.'

'I'm sorry. We were cut off the last time we talked, and Margaret left a message. I thought perhaps it was important.' But suddenly she felt awkward with him. He didn't sound as though he'd been asleep.

'Right. Where were you?' God, why did he sound so cold? Why now? She needed a reason to hang on. A reason not to fall in love with Ben. A reason to stay faithful.

'I was out. Shopping.' She hated the lie, but what could she tell him? I was kissing Ben Thompson on the beach? 'Is everything all right in Rome?'

'Fine. Look' – he seemed to hesitate for a moment – I'll call you back.'

'When?' She had to know. She needed to hear him, needed to keep his voice in her head. Surely that would dull the pain of what she couldn't have. 'When will you call me?'

'Tomorrow. This weekend. I'll call, don't worry. *D'accord?*'

'Yes, all right, fine.' But she was cut to the quick by his tone. 'I love you.' The words were a tentative plea. He didn't seem to hear it.

'So do I. *Ciao.*' And then, without saying more, he hung up, as Deanna sat staring blindly at the phone.

Deanna ate alone in her studio that night, then stood for half an hour on the little tiled terrace, watching the sun set over the bay. She could have seen it with Ben, if she hadn't sent him away. Why had she? So she could feel virtuous when she called Marc halfway around the world? She felt tears slide down her cheeks. When she heard the doorbell ring, she jumped. She decided not to answer, and then wondered if it might be Kim, coming to see how she was. Kim would have recognised the lights in the studio and known she was hiding. She wiped the tears away with the tail of her shirt and ran barefoot down the back stairs. She didn't even think to ask who it was, she simply opened the door, looking like a tired, rumpled little girl, in jeans and bare feet, with her hair falling into her eyes. She looked up, expecting to see Kim and stood back in surprise when she saw who it was. It was Ben.

'Is this a bad time?' he asked. She shook her head. 'Can we talk?' He looked as troubled as she felt, and he was quick to come inside when she nodded yes.

'Come up to the studio. I was up there.'

'Working?' He searched her eyes, and she shook her head.

'Thinking.'

'Me too.'

She closed the door softly behind them. He followed her up the stairs, and she motioned him to her favourite chair. 'Coffee, or wine?'

'Neither, thanks.' He looked suddenly very nervous, as though he wondered why he had come. Then he sat back in the chair, closed his eyes, and ran a hand through his hair. 'This is crazy, I shouldn't have come.'

'I'm glad you did.'

'In that case' – he opened his eyes and smiled tentatively at her – 'so am I. Deanna, I – I know this is crazy ... but dammit I love you. And I feel like an irrational kid. I shouldn't even be here. I have absolutely nothing intelligent to say, except what I told you today on the beach.' His voice dropped to a whisper and he lowered his eyes. 'Just that I love you.'

The room was very still for a long moment as she watched him, her eyes filling with tears. He heard her sigh. 'I love you too.'

'You know what I came here to tell you?' he asked. 'That I'll accept anything. A moment, an evening, a summer. I won't stand in your way after that. I'll let go. But I can't bear to see us lose what we might have.' He looked at her then. Her face was wet with tears that dripped slowly on to her paint-splattered shirt, but she was smiling at him and holding out a hand. He took it firmly in his and pulled her towards him. 'Doesn't that sound crazy to you?'

'Yes. Very. And at the end of the summer?'

'We let go.'

'And what if we can't?'

'We'll just have to. I will because I know it will be for your peace of mind. What about you?'

'I suppose I could too.' Her arms went around him. 'I don't care what happens then, I just love you.'

He was smiling broadly as he held her close. It was what he had wanted to hear. He felt suddenly free and excited and alive.

'Will you come home with me, Deanna? My place is a mess, but I want to share it with you, show you my treasures. I want to show you the things I care about, give you my life, show you my galleries and how they work. I want to walk on the beach in Carmel with you, I want to ... oh, Deanna, darling, darling, I love you!'

They were both laughing now as he swept her into his arms and carried her down the stairs. For a moment Deanna was grateful that it was Margaret's night off, but she didn't dare think for longer than that. Only a moment, which was more thought than she spent on Marc. She was Ben's now. Ben's for the summer.

Chapter Nine

'Good morning.' She heard Ben's voice softly in her ear. She opened one eye. The room was unfamiliar. She was staring at a pale-yellow wall. Someone had thrown wide the shutters on the large windows that looked out at the bay, and sun streamed into the room. There were trees just outside his window, and she could hear birds singing. It was a splendid, hot summer day, more like September than June.

Deanna let her eyes wander across the pale-yellow wall, and quickly she was entranced by a watercolour of a beach, and then by a smaller pastel, and an oil. The artwork was all very subtle and sunny, not unlike Ben himself. She propped herself up on one elbow with a yawn and a stretch and a smile. He was looking down at her with the face of new love.

'I've been waiting for you for an hour. I thought you'd never get up!' He suddenly sounded less like a lover than a small boy, and she laughed.

'I think I was a trifle tired.' She smiled again and slid back into the sheets, with one hand on his thigh. It had been a long, delicious night in his arms, and they hadn't fallen asleep until dawn.

'Is that a complaint?'

'Uh-uh.' She let her lips drift up his leg and then stop at his hip, where she kissed the pale, tender white skin where a small vein throbbed. 'Good morning, my love.' She smiled at the life she saw stirring, and Ben pulled her gently back into his arms.

'Have I told you yet this morning how much I love you?' He was looking tenderly into her eyes, and there was something in his face she had dreamed of and painted but never seen. It was a kind of passion, a kind of unfettered love. It was something that she had long ago longed for and ceased to believe could exist. 'I love you, Deanna ... I love you ...' His words melted away on her lips as he kissed her for the first time that morning and let his body slide slowly over hers. She protested faintly but with laughter and squirms as he pressed her close to him. 'You have an objection?' He looked amused and surprised; he didn't look as though he would be swayed by whatever she said.

'I haven't even brushed my teeth! Or combed my hair ... or ...' Her words kept fading, swept away by his kisses, as she giggled and ran her hands through his uncombed hair. 'Ben ... I have to ...'

'No, you don't. I love you like this.' He seemed sure.

'But I ...'

'Shhh ...'

'Ben!' But this time she forgot about her teeth and her hair; she was too happy right where she was, swept away, adrift on a sea of delight as his whole body seemed to enter her soul.

'Sleepy, darling?' His voice was a whisper when they finally spoke. Almost two hours had passed, and she was curled happily in his arms, one leg braided between his.

'Mm-hmm ... Ben?'

'Yes?' His voice was so soft on the warm, summer morning.

'I love you.' Hers was almost the voice of a child.

'I love you, too. Now go to sleep.'

And she did, for another two hours. When she opened her eyes, he was standing at the foot of the bed, dressed and holding a tray. She woke up in surprise. He was wearing a businesslike, striped blue suit. 'What are you doing?' Confused, she sat up in bed and ran a hand through her hair. Suddenly she felt very naked and unkempt, as the sweet smell of their lovemaking drifted up from the bed. 'How long have I slept?'

'Not very long. I'd look like that too except I have a

luncheon at the gallery. I cancelled one yesterday and if I cancel this one too, Sally will quit. But I won't be gone long.' He placed the tray on her knees as she sat back against the pillows in the large double bed. 'I hope that'll do.' There were croissants, fruit, café au lait, and one carefully poached egg. 'I wasn't sure what you like for breakfast.' He looked very young again as he smiled.

Deanna looked at the breakfast in astonishment and then at him. What could she say? He had appeared in her life on a beach in Carmel, and now he was making her poached eggs and croissants for breakfast and apologising for not knowing what she liked. They had made love all through the night and for most of the morning; he had told her he loved her, and she him; she didn't even feel guilty for waking up in his bed and not her own – the bed she had shared for eighteen years with Marc. She didn't even give a damn about Marc this morning. She felt happy and young and in love, and all she wanted was what she had with Ben. She looked up at him with a rapturous smile and a sigh as she picked up a croissant.

'I warn you, sir, if you spoil me rotten, I will be unbearable in less than a week.'

'No, you won't.' He said it with certainty and amusement. Suddenly he seemed very grown-up once again.

'Yes, I will.' She closed her eyes blissfully as she ate the roll. 'I'll come to expect croissants every morning, and poached eggs, and café au lait ...' She opened her eyes again. They were very bright and very full of mischief. 'I'll even expect you to stay home from the office every day, just so we can make love.'

'No, you won't.'

'Oh, no? Why won't I?'

'Because tomorrow it's your turn to make breakfast for me. This is a democracy, Deanna. We live here together; we take turns. We spoil *each other*. We make *each other* poached eggs.' He leaned down to kiss her one last time. 'And I like mine fried.'

'I'll make a note of that.' She grinned at him.

He stood up. 'I'll remind you.'

'O.K.' She went on eating her breakfast, perfectly happy and at ease. She felt as though they had lived together for months if not years. It did not seem strange at all to have him smile happily at her naked breasts as she sipped café au lait from a bright-yellow mug. Everything between them was comfortable and easy and real. It was a far cry from the formality and rituals in her own home. And she found that she liked Ben's way better. The yellow mug in her hand had a feel of solidity. It felt strong, not like the prissy blue-flowered Limoges from Marc's mother.

'What are you doing today?'

'I think first of all I'll take a bath.' She wrinkled her nose, and they both laughed.

'I love you just like that.'

'You're a piggy.' She held her arms up to him though, and he kissed her again. When he pulled away, he rolled his eyes with regret.

'God, maybe I'll have to cancel that lunch after all.'

'There's later. Or' – she started to ask him if they would see each other that night, but she could already see the answer in his eyes.

'No "or", Deanna. I'll be finished at the gallery at five. I thought we could go somewhere quiet for dinner. Maybe somewhere in Marin?'

'I'd love it.' She sat back against the pillows with a broad smile, but she noticed that there was a shadow of concern in his eyes. 'Something wrong?'

'Not for me. But I – I was wondering how you feel about – about going out. I don't want to create any difficult situations for you.' He had to remind himself that she had another life. That she would never be entirely his. That she was on loan. Like a masterpiece from a foreign museum, not something he could own and keep on his gallery wall. It would make her infinitely more precious in the time that they'd share. 'Won't it create a problem for you if we go out?' He looked at her very openly, his green eyes tender and wide.

'It doesn't have to. It will depend on what we do, where we go, how we behave. I think it could be all right.' He nodded, saying nothing, and she held out a hand. He took it silently and sat down again on the bed.

'I don't want to do anything that will hurt you later.'

'You won't. Now stop worrying. Everything will be fine.'

'I mean it though, Deanna. I would hate it if you suffered for this afterward.'

'Don't you think we both will?'

He looked up in surprise. 'What do you mean?'

'I mean that this is going to be the most beautiful summer of my life, and hopefully yours. When it ends, when we both go back to our own lives, don't you think that we'll suffer?'

He nodded and looked down at the graceful hand he held tightly in his own. 'Do you regret what we decided?'

Deanna threw back her head and laughed a silvery laugh before kissing him tenderly on the cheek. 'Not for a moment.' And then she grew serious again. 'But I think we'd be crazy if we expected not to suffer later. If it's worth a damn, if it's beautiful, if we really care ... then we will. We'll have to accept that.'

'I do. For myself. But –'

'But what? You don't want me to hurt too? You don't want me to feel it? Or to love you? Don't be crazy, Ben. It's worth it.'

'I understand that. I agree. But I also want to be discreet. I don't want to create problems for you with Marc.' She almost cringed at the sound of his name.

Ben leaned towards her again, kissed her quickly, then stood. 'I think we've said enough for one morning.' He hated to think of what would happen at the end of the summer, but it was hard to believe that time would come. Their moments together had just begun. 'Where will you be at five?' He looked at her over his shoulder from the door. 'Here?'

She shook her head. 'I'd better go home.'

'Shall I pick you up there?' He looked dubious for a moment.

'I'll meet you here.'

He nodded, smiled, and was gone. She heard the little German car drive away a moment later, as she walked around the room, and then sat naked on the edge of the bed and crossed one leg. She was smiling to herself. She wanted to sing. She felt wonderful, and she was in love. What a lovely man he was, how gentle and how careful and how wise. And he amused her too; he loved to laugh, loved to tell silly stories and endless funny tales. He had spent hours the previous night telling her stories of his youth, showing her albums of photographs of himself as a child, and his parents and sister and their friends, many of them famous artists and actors and playwrights and writers. The albums still lay spread out on the floor.

He had a comfortable little house, very different from the cottage in Carmel. The place in Carmel was larger and wore the same bland, sandy colours as the beach, whites, beiges, greys, dust-coloured woods, and soft off-white wools. The city house was a tiny 'bijou' nestled high on Telegraph Hill and crammed full of paintings and books. There were two deep, red-leather couches in a living room walled with handsomely bound volumes, mostly about art. The walls were a soft beige that enhanced the two paintings he'd hung; the floors were of old burnished wood, and the rug was Oriental but not as fine as the ones Marc had brought back for her years before from Iran. Ben's little home was not a showplace; it was warm and lovely and a place he clearly liked to be, to spend evenings with his artists or his friends. There was an often used fireplace with brass andirons he had found in France and a bass fiddle propped up in one corner. He had a small piano and a guitar, a handsome, old English desk and a bronze bust of Cézanne. Throughout, there was a kind of friendly scramble, a kind of elegant wear and tear. Some of the objects were of value, but most were only of value to him and the people who loved him. The living room was very Ben, as was the pretty little yellow bedroom that looked east over the bay, and that was as bright as the morning sun. It boasted a tiny terrace filled with an array of bright flowering plants, and two comfortable, faded canvas chairs. Other than that there was a kitchen and one extra room, in which Ben housed his work – a few rare paintings, many files, another desk. The additional room allowed him to work at home, and like his car, was useful but not luxurious. As Deanna looked around, she realised again that he was an odd mixture of comfort and style, and he always seemed to happily marry the two in a way that was uniquely his. Deanna slipped into his blue-and-black silk bathrobe and wandered out on to the terrace. She sat down on one of the faded canvas chairs. It had once been a bright parrot green, now sun-bleached to a very pale lime. She stretched her legs out for a moment, turning her face to the sun and thinking of him, wondering where he was – already at the gallery? Having lunch? Signing cheques with Sally? Talking to Gustave? She liked the way he led his life, what he did, how he handled the people around him – how he handled her. She found that she even liked the idea of taking turns making breakfast – a democracy, he'd called it. It was just a very pleasant way to live. She let the robe fall slightly open, and smiled as she felt the bright warmth of the sun. In a while she would go home to her studio and paint. But not yet. She was too happy sitting in the sun like a cat, thinking of Ben.

'*Grazie Signore ... Signora Duras.*' The concierge at the Hassler bowed formally to Chantal and Marc as they checked out of the hotel and Marc endowed him with a more than healthy tip. A car was already waiting for them outside the hotel. Their bags had been stowed in the trunk, and the driver waited to take them to the airport.

Chantal was strangely quiet as they rode to the airport. At last Marc pulled his gaze from the windows and allowed himself to seek out her eyes.

'You're sure that's what you want to do?'

'Absolutely.'

But it worried him. She had never been this obstinate before. She had insisted that she was not going to hide in San Remo or some other town on the Riviera. She wanted to go back to Paris and wait for him there, while he visited his family in Cap d'Antibes. So that she could steal a weekend with her lover, the man who had asked her to marry him? The implied threat had not been lost on Marc. He felt a surge of murderous jealousy.

'Just what exactly are you planning to do with yourself all weekend?' There was a decided edge to his voice, but she returned his gaze evenly as the car raced through the traffic.

'I'll go into the office. I can't leave everything on Marie-Ange's shoulders. It's bad enough that whenever we travel I have to dump everything in her lap. As long as I have the time, I might as well go in and see what's happening there.'

'I'm impressed by your devotion to your business. That's new, isn't it?' It was rare for him to be sarcastic with Chantal.

But her tone matched his. 'No, it's not. You're just

not around to see it very often. What exactly did you think I was going to do?'

'Your bit of news yesterday did not go unnoticed, Chantal.'

'I said someone asked me. I did not say I accepted.'

'How comforting. One would assume, however, that he didn't ask you on the basis of two luncheons and a tea party. I would assume that you know each other rather well.'

Chantal didn't answer. She merely looked out the window, as secretly Marc-Edouard raged. Dammit, what did she expect of him? He couldn't be with her more than he already was, and he could hardly propose marriage. He had Deanna.

But Chantal's voice was oddly soft as she answered him. 'Don't worry about it.'

'Thank you.' He sighed, and his shoulders seemed to sag as he took her hand. 'I love you, darling. Please, please try to understand.'

'I do try. More than you know.'

'I know it's difficult for you. It is for me too. But at least don't establish a competition between you and Pilar and my mother. That just isn't fair. I need to see them too.'

'Perhaps, so do I.' There was something so sad in her voice that he didn't know what more to say. Had he been a less rational man, he might have decided to throw reason to the winds, and taken her with him, but he simply couldn't.

'Darling, I'm sorry.' Gently, he slipped an arm around her shoulders, and pulled her closer to him, and there was no resistance. 'I'll try to think this thing out. All right?' She nodded and said nothing, but a tear hovered on the end of her lashes, and he felt something tear at his heart. 'It's only for a few days, I'll be home on Sunday night, and we can have dinner at Maxim's, before we leave for Athens.'

'When are we leaving?'

'Monday or Tuesday.'

She nodded again. He held her close all the way to the airport.

Deanna turned her key in the door and stopped for a moment, listening for Margaret. There was no one at home. It was still Margaret's day off. Could it be? Hadn't weeks passed? Or months or even years? Had she only gone with Ben the night before to make love with him for the very first time? Had it only been eighteen hours since she'd left the house? Her heart pounded as she closed the door behind her. It had been so peaceful at his place as she bathed and got dressed. She had watched two little birds play on the terrace, and she had listened to one of his records while she made the bed. She'd grabbed a plum from a large basket of fruit in the kitchen as she left, feeling as though she had lived there for years, as though it were hers as well as his. Now, suddenly, she was here again. In Marc's house, in the home of Monsieur and Madame Duras. She glanced at a photograph of them in a silver frame, taken during their first summer in Cap d'Antibes. Could that have been her? Standing awkwardly with a glass of white wine in her hand, while Marc chatted with his mother beneath her gigantic straw hat. How awkward she felt again just looking at it, how awkward she felt in this room. She stood at the entrance to the pale-green silk living room with the Aubusson rug, thinking that just looking at it made her feel cold. But this was her home. This was where she belonged, not in that tiny house on the hill where she had just spent the night with a strange man. What on earth was she doing?

She slipped her feet out of her sandals, walked barefoot into the chilly green room and sat down carefully on the couch. What had she done? She had cheated on Marc for the first time in eighteen years, and it had all seemed so natural, so normal. For one entire night it was as though she didn't even know Marc, as though she were married to Ben. She reached for a small photograph of Pilar in another silver frame and saw that her hand was shaking. Pilar was in tennis clothes; the photograph had been taken in the South of France. Deanna stared at it almost blindly. She didn't even hear the persistent ringing of the bell. It was two or three minutes before she realised that there was someone at the door. She jumped up, startled, and put down the photograph of Pilar. Her mind raced as she walked to the door. Who was it? Who knew? And what if it was Ben? She didn't feel ready to see him now. It was wrong what they had done. She had to tell him, she had to stop, now before it was too late, before her orderly life came apart at the seams ... before ...

'Who is it?'

A voice informed her that there was a package. Reluctantly, she opened the door and saw the delivery boy. 'But I didn't order ...' Then she knew. They were flowers from Ben. For a moment she wanted to turn them away, send them back, pretend that the night before hadn't happened and never would again. Instead, she held out her arms and took the bundle inside, where she pulled off the card and held it for a moment before reading what it said:

Hurry home, my darling. I'll meet you at five.

I love you,
Ben

I love you, Ben. Her eyes ran over the words and filled with tears. *I love you, Ben.* It was already too late. She loved him too.

She ran upstairs to her room and packed a small bag. Then she went to the studio. That's all she would take. Just one or two canvases, some paints, she'd make do for a while. She didn't have to stay for more than a few days. That was all.

She left a number for Margaret and explained that

she was staying with a friend. By five-thirty she was back at his house. She parked the Jaguar half a block away and walked hesitantly towards the door. What in hell was she doing? But he'd heard her on the front steps. Before she rang, he opened the door with a bow and a smile and a sweep of one arm.

'Come in. I've been waiting for hours.' He closed the door softly behind her. For a moment she stood there, her eyes tightly shut against tears. 'Deanna? Are you all right, darling?' There was concern in his voice, but she nodded. Slowly, he put his arms around her. 'Are you afraid?'

She opened her eyes and hesitantly nodded her head.

But Ben only smiled and held her very close as he whispered into her hair, 'So am I.'

Chapter Ten

'O.K., kid, off your ass. It's your turn.' Ben poked her gently in the small of her back, and Deanna groaned.

'It is not. I made breakfast yesterday.' She smiled into the pillow and hid her face.

'Do you know that I love you, even if you are a liar? I made breakfast yesterday and two days before that and four days just before that. In fact I think you owe me three in a row.'

'That's a lie!' She was giggling.

'The hell it is. I told you, this is a democracy!' He was laughing too and trying to turn the naked body he loved so that he could see her face.

'I don't like democracy!'

'Tough. I want coffee and French toast and eggs.'

'What if I won't do it?'

'Then tonight you sleep on the terrace.'

'I knew it. I should have brought Margaret.'

'A ménage à trois? It sounds lovely. Can she cook?'

'Better than I can.'

'Good. We'll have her move in today.' He rolled over in bed with a satisfied smile. 'Meanwhile, get off your dead ass and feed me.'

'You're spoiled rotten.'

'And I love it.'

'You'll get fat.' She sat on the edge of the bed looking at his far-from-overweight body. 'Besides, eggs aren't good for you, they have carbohydrates or cholesterol or chromosomes or something, and ...' He pointed towards the kitchen, a mock scowl lining his face, and Deanna stood up. 'I hate you.'

'I know.'

Laughing, she vanished into the kitchen. They had been together for two weeks – a moment; a lifetime.

117

They shared the cooking and the chores. A funny little old lady came in twice a week to clean, but Ben liked doing things for himself, and Deanna found that she enjoyed sharing those things with him. They went marketing, cooked dinners, polished the brass, and pulled weeds from among the flowers on the terrace. She watched him pore over catalogues of upcoming auctions, and he watched her sketch, or work in pastels or oils. He was the first person she had allowed to see her work in progress. They read mystery books and watched television and went for drives; they walked on the beach once at midnight, and twice went down for the night to his house in Carmel. She went to another opening at his gallery and on a visit to a new artist, masquerading as his wife. It was as though nothing had come before and nothing would come after – they had only the time and the life that they shared.

Deanna set down the tray with his breakfast and the paper. 'You know something? I like you. I really do.'

'You sound surprised. Were you afraid democracy would wear you out?'

'Maybe.' She sat down with a small, happy shrug. 'I haven't taken care of myself or anyone else, in a practical way, in a long time. I'm responsible for everyone, but I don't think I've made breakfast in years. Or done any of the things that we've done.'

'I don't like being dependent on other people, like maids. Basically, I like a very simple life.'

She grinned to herself, remembering the three lavishly expensive paintings he had bought the day before in L.A., but she knew that what he was saying was true. Opulence wasn't his style. He had seen too much of it as a child, in the home of his grandparents and then his father. He was happier with the little house on the hill in San Francisco and the unpretentious cottage in Carmel.

He leaned over to kiss the tip of her nose, then sat back against his pillows again with the breakfast she

118

had made still waiting on the tray. 'I love you, Deanna.' He was smiling wickedly. 'Now when are you going to sign with the gallery?'

'Are you back at that again? *That* is what this is all about. You just want me to sign with the gallery. I knew it! I knew it!' She laughed as he ducked the pillow she aimed at his head. 'The things some people will do to sign new artists!'

'Well? Did it work?'

'Of course not! You'll have to do better than that!'

'Better?' He looked at her ominously and put aside the breakfast tray. 'What exactly do you mean by "better", why I ...' He closed his mouth over hers and reached for her body with his hands. 'Better ...?' They were both laughing now. It was half an hour later before they had untangled themselves and caught their breath. 'Well, was that *better*?' Ben asked.

'Much.'

'Good.' He looked up at her happily from where he lay on the bed. 'Now will you sign?'

'Well ...' She lay her head on his chest and looked at him with a small yawn. 'Maybe if you'd just run through that again ...'

'Deanna!' He rolled over and covered her body with his own, holding her throat menacingly in both hands. 'I want you to sign with me!' His voice boomed.

She smiled sweetly, 'O.K.'

'What?' He sat up, a look of astonishment on his face.

'I said O.K. O.K.?'

'Did you mean it?'

'Yes. Do you still want me? For the gallery, I mean.' She grinned, and looked at him questioningly. Maybe it had been only a game all along.

But he was looking at her as though she were crazy. 'Of course I still want you, you lunatic! You're the best new artist I've gotten my hands on in fifteen years!'

She rolled over again and looked at him with a

feline little smile. 'And just whom have you "gotten your hands on" in the last fifteen years?'

'You know what I mean. I mean like Gustave.' They both laughed at the thought. 'Are you serious, Deanna? Will you sign?' She nodded. 'You don't have to, you know. I love you even if you never let me show your work.'

'I know. But I've been watching you work for weeks, and I can't stand it. I want to be part of it too. I want my own show.'

He laughed. 'Your own, eh? No other artists. All right, you've got it. When?'

'Whenever it works for you.'

'I'll check the calendar with Sally. Maybe in a few weeks.' He dug into his breakfast with a broad smile. He looked as though she had just given birth to his son.

'Should I make you something else?' She was watching him devour the ice-cold French toast.

'All you have to do is bring me your paintings and let me show them. From now on I'll make breakfast. Every day. No ... five times a week. You do weekends. How's that?'

'Wonderful. I knew there were benefits to giving in.' She pulled the covers back to her chin. 'Ben? Do you think I'm doing the right thing?'

He knew what was coming. The doubts were written all over her face. But he was not going to let her back away. 'Shut up. If you start that, we'll do the show next week. You're good enough. You're terrific. You're fabulous. For God's sake, Deanna, you're the best young artist in this town, probably in L.A. too. Just shut up and let me do the show. All right?'

'All right.'

For a time she was very quiet, thinking about Marc. How could she tell him she had finally decided to show? Or did he even have to know? He had told her years ago to put her dreams about art away, that Madame Duras could not be some kind of 'hippie painter.' But she wasn't, dammit, and what right did he have to . . .

'What are you thinking?' Ben was still watching her.

'Nothing much.' She smiled. 'I was just thinking about the show.'

'Are you sure? You looked as though you were about to be beaten up.'

She sighed, then looked at him again. 'I felt as though I was. I was trying to think of . . . of what to tell Marc.'

'Do you have to?' Ben sounded momentarily strained.

'I probably should. I suppose it sounds crazy to you now, but I don't want to be dishonest with him. No more than I have to.'

'It does sound crazy, but I understand what you mean. He won't be pleased about a show, will he?'

'No, he won't. But I think I ought to tell him.'

'And if he says no?' Ben looked hurt and Deanna lowered her eyes.

'He won't.'

But they both knew he would.

Marc quietly let himself into the apartment. It was the second weekend he had gone away without Chantal. But his weekends in the South of France with his family were sacred. She had always understood that before. Why was she giving him problems about it now? She had barely been speaking to him on Friday when he had left. He set his bag down in the hall and looked around. She wasn't home. But it was already after nine o'clock. Where the hell was she? Out? Out with whom? He sighed a long tired sigh as he sat down on the couch. He glanced around. She hadn't left him a note. He looked at his watch again, and this time he reached for the phone. It would be noon in San Francisco, a good time to report to Deanna about Pilar. He dialled the call direct and waited for the phone to ring. He hadn't spoken to her in a week. He had been too busy to call, and the one time he had, Margaret had told him she was out.

'Hello?' Deanna answered the phone breathlessly as she came up the studio stairs. Ben had just dropped her off. She had promised to come home and pick out twenty-five of her favourite paintings. That would keep her busy for days. 'Yes?' She still hadn't caught her breath and at first she hadn't even noticed the whir of a long distance call.

'Deanna?'

'Marc!' She stared at the phone in astonishment, as though he were a ghost from the past.

'You needn't sound that surprised. It hasn't been that long since we've spoken.'

'No, no, I'm sorry. I just ... I was thinking of something else.'

'Is anything wrong?'

'No, of course not. How's Pilar?' She sounded vague to him as though she were at a loss for what to say. 'Have you seen her lately?'

'Just today. I just got back from Antibes. She's fine. She sends you her love.' It was a lie, but one he told often. 'And my mother sends her love too.'

Deanna smiled at this last. 'Pilar's all right?' Suddenly, speaking to Marc again reminded her of her duties. With Ben, she only thought of him and herself. She thought of her paintings and his galleries, their nights together, their good times. She was a woman again, a girl. But Marc's voice returned her to her role as mother. It was as though for a time she had forgotten.

'Yes, Pilar is fine.'

'She didn't buy the motorcycle, did she?'

There was a long moment of silence. Too long.

'Deanna...'

'Marc, did she?' Deanna's voice rose. 'Dammit, she did! I know it.'

'It's not really a motorcycle, Deanna. It's more, more

122

a ...' He looked for the words, but he was tired, and where the hell was Chantal? It was nine forty-five. 'Really, you have no need to worry. She'll be fine. I saw her drive it. She is extremely careful. Mother wouldn't allow her to ride it if she were not.'

'Your mother doesn't see her drive it away from the house. She has no more control over her than I do, or you. Marc, I told you explicitly ...' Tears began to sting her eyes. She had lost to them again. She always lost. And this time it was something dangerous, something that might ... 'Goddammit, Marc, why don't you ever listen to me?'

'Calm yourself. She'll be fine. What have you been up to?'

There wasn't a damn thing she could do. And she knew it. The subject of Pilar and the motorcycle was closed. 'Not much.' Deanna's voice was like ice.

'I called once; you were out.'

'I've started painting in a studio.'

'Can't you work at home?' Marc sounded irritated and confused.

Deanna closed her eyes. 'I found a place where it's easier for me to work.' Her heart started to race as she thought of Ben. What if Marc could read her mind? What if he knew? What if someone had seen them together? What if ...

'With both of us gone, I can't understand why you don't paint at home. And what is this sudden new frenzy for your work?'

'What "frenzy"? I'm painting as much as ever.'

'Deanna, I really don't understand.' But the tone in which he said the words suddenly hit her like a slap in the face.

'I enjoy my work.' She was goading him and she knew it.

'I don't really think you need call it "work".' He sighed into the phone and looked at his watch.

'I call it work because it is. I'm having a show at a

gallery next month.' Her voice rang with defiance, and she felt her heart race faster and faster. He didn't answer.

Then: 'You're what?'

'Having a show at a gallery.'

'I see.' There was a nasty tone of amusement in his voice, and for a moment she hated him. 'We're having a bohemian summer, are we? Well, maybe it will do you good.'

'Maybe it will.' *Bastard ... he never understood!*

'Is it necessary to prove your point by having a show? Why not dispense with that? You can work in your other studio, and let it go at that.'

Thank you, Daddy. 'The show is important to me.'

'Then it can wait. We'll discuss it when I get back.'

'Marc ...' *I'm in love with another man ...* 'I'm going to do the show.'

'Fine. Just let it wait till the fall.'

'Why? So you can talk me out of it when you come home?'

'I won't do that. We'll talk about it then.'

'It won't wait. I've already waited too long.'

'You know, darling, you're too old for tantrums and too young for menopause. I think you're being very unreasonable.'

She wanted to hit him, except that for a moment she also wanted to laugh. It was a ridiculous conversation, and she realised that she sounded a great deal like Pilar. She laughed and shook her head. 'Maybe you're right. Tell you what: You win your case in Athens; I'll do what I need to do with my art, and I'll see you in the fall.'

'Is that your way of telling me to mind my own business?'

'Maybe so.' She was suddenly braver than she had been in years. 'Maybe we both just have to do what we need to do right now.' *Oh God, what are you doing? You're telling him ...* She held her breath.

124

'Well, in any case, you need to listen to your husband, and your husband needs to go to bed, so why don't we just relax about all this for a while? We'll talk again in a few days. All right? Meanwhile, no art show. *C'est compris? Capisce?* Understood?'

She wanted to grit her teeth. She wasn't a child, and he was always the same. Pilar got the motorcycle, Deanna did not get the art show, and we'll all discuss it 'when I have time.' His way, always *his* way. But not any more. 'I understand, Marc, but I don't agree.'

'You don't have a choice.'

It wasn't like him to be so obvious. Deanna realised that he must be very tired. He must have noticed it too. 'Never mind,' he said. 'I'm sorry. We'll talk another time.'

'Fine.' She stood silently in her studio, waiting, wondering what he would say.

He said *'Bonsoir.'*

And he was gone. Good night. And this time she hadn't bothered to tell him she loved him. 'No art show.' The words rang in her head. No art show. She sighed heavily and sank into her chair. What if she defied him? What if she had the show anyway? Could she do that to him? To herself? Was she brave enough to just go ahead and do what she wanted? Why not? He was away. And she had Ben. But it wasn't for Ben. It was for herself. She looked around the room for a long moment, knowing that her lifetime was facing those walls, hidden on canvases no one had seen and would never see unless she did what she knew she had to do now. Marc couldn't stop her, and Ben couldn't make her do it. She had to do it now. Had to. For herself.

As Marc set down the phone, he looked at his watch again. It was almost ten, and the call to Deanna had done nothing to soothe his nerves. Dammit. He had told her about the motorcycle, and he hadn't meant to. And her bloody art show. Why the hell didn't she give up on that nonsense? And where the hell was Chantal? Jealousy was beginning to gnaw at his insides again as he poured himself a Scotch. When he heard the bell, he went to the door and opened it an inch. It was the little old man from next door. Monsieur Moutier. He was sweet, Chantal said, and he was taken care of by a daughter and a maid. He too had once been a lawyer, but now he was eighty years old. He had a soft spot for Chantal. Once he had sent her flowers.

'*Oui?*' Marc looked at him questioningly, wondering if the old man was ill. Why would he come to their door at this hour? 'Is something wrong?'

'I ... no. I ... *je regrette*. I wanted to ask you the same thing. How is mademoiselle?'

'Very well, thank you, except that as far as I can see she's a little bit late getting home.' He smiled at the elderly gentleman wearing the black smoking jacket and needlepoint slippers doubtless made by his daughter. 'Would you like to come in?' Marc stepped aside, wanting to get back to his Scotch, but the old man shook his head.

'No, no ...' He looked sorrowfully at Marc. He understood only too well. The man who always travelled, who was never there. He had been that way too. His wife had died, and he had learned too late. 'She is not late, monsieur. They took her to the hospital last night.' He gazed at Marc as the shock registered on his face.

'Chantal? My God! Where?'

'The American Hospital, monsieur. She was in some kind of shock. The ambulance driver said –'

'Oh, my God!' Marc glanced at the old man in terror and then ran inside to grab his jacket from a chair. He returned instantly and slammed the door to the apartment, as the old man stepped aside. 'I have to go.' Oh, my God ... Oh, Chantal ... Oh, no ... Then she wasn't out with another man. Having raced down the stairs, his heart hammering in his chest, Marc ran into the street and hailed a cab.

Chapter Eleven

The taxi pulled up at 92 Boulevard Victor Hugo in Neuilly in the quiet outskirts of Paris. Marc thrust some franc notes into the driver's hand and raced inside. It was well past visiting hours, but he walked purposefully towards the information desk and inquired for Mademoiselle Chantal Martin. Room 401, admitted with insulin shock, present condition satisfactory. She can go home in two days. Marc stared at the nurse, dismayed. Without discussing the matter further, he took the elevator to the fourth floor. A nurse sat sternly at her station and observed him as he disembarked from the elevator.

'*Oui*, monsieur?'

'Mademoiselle Martin.' He tried to sound commanding but he felt suddenly frightened. How had it happened and why? He felt a sudden surge of guilt for having gone to Antibes. 'I must see her.'

The nurse shook her head. 'Tomorrow.'

'Is she asleep?'

'You may see her tomorrow.'

'Please. I – I came all the way from –' He was about to say the South of France, then had a better idea. He flipped open his wallet. 'From San Francisco, in the United States. I caught the first plane after I heard.' There was a long pause.

'Very well. Two minutes. And then you go. You are ... her father?' Marc only shook his head. It was the final blow.

The nurse led him to a room not far away. Inside, a dim light burned. She left Marc-Edouard at the door. He hesitated for a moment on the threshold before stepping softly inside.

'Chantal?' His voice was a whisper in the dark room.

She was lying in her bed, looking very pale and very young. In her arm there was an intravenous tube, attached to an ominous-looking bottle. 'Darling . . .' He approached, wondering what he had done. He had taken on this girl and only given her half his life. He had to hide her from his mother, his child, his wife, sometimes even from himself. What right did he have to do this to her? His eyes were too bright as he stood at her side and gently took her free hand. 'Darling, what happened?' A sixth sense had already told him that the insulin shock was no accident. Chantal had the kind of diabetes one didn't fool around with. But as long as she took her insulin, ate well and slept enough, she'd be all right.

Her eyes closed and tears filtered through her lashes. '*Je m'excuse.* I'm so sorry . . .' Then after a pause: 'I took too much insulin.'

'On purpose?' As he watched her nod, he felt as though someone had delivered a blow to his heart. 'Oh, my God. Chantal, darling . . . how could you?' He watched her in sudden terror. What if she had died? What if . . . ? He couldn't bear losing her, couldn't bear it. Suddenly, the full force of it struck home. He reached for her unencumbered hand and pressed it hard. 'Don't ever, ever do that again!' His voice rose desperately. 'Do you hear me?' She nodded again. And then there were tears pouring down his face as well. He sat down at her side. 'I would die without you. Don't you know that?'

There was no answer in her eyes. No, she didn't know it. But it was true. He himself knew it for the first time. Now there were two of them. Deanna and Chantal. Two of them he owed a lifetime to, and he was only one man. He couldn't live with himself if he put Deanna out of his life. And he couldn't live without Chantal The weight of it struck him like an axe. He saw her watching him. He was almost grey. 'I love you, Chantal. Please, please don't ever do anything like this again. Promise me!' He squeezed harder on the delicate hand.

'I promise.' It was a whisper in the sudden electricity of the room. Fighting the sobs that were rising in his chest, Marc-Edouard folded her gently into his arms.

By the end of the day, Deanna had chosen eleven paintings. It was going to be hard work selecting the rest. She set the eleven to one side and then walked back to the main part of the house. She was still thinking of her talk with Marc. She wondered if she would have defied him about the show if he hadn't let Pilar buy the motorcycle. It was strange how those things worked. Their marriage was filled with petty revenges. She walked up the stairs to her bedroom and peered into the closet. What would she need? Another bathrobe, some jeans, the champagne-coloured suede skirt that she was sure Ben would like. What was she doing here, in Marc's bedroom planning her life with another man? Was she being menopausal or childish, as he'd suggested, or merely crazy? The phone rang as she stared into her closet, wondering. She didn't even feel guilty any more, except when she talked to Marc. The rest of the time she felt as though she belonged with Ben. The phone rang again and again. There was no one she wanted to talk to. She felt as though she had already moved out. But reluctantly, she picked it up.

'Hello?'

'Can I come get you? Are you ready to come home?' It was Ben. And it was only four-thirty.

'So early?' She smiled into the phone.

'You want some more time to work?' As though her work mattered, as though it were important, as though he understood.

But she shook her head. 'Nope. I'm all through. I picked out eleven today. For the show.'

Her voice was strong, and he smiled. 'I'm so proud of you I can hardly stand it. I told Sally today, about the show. We're going to run a beautiful ad.'

Oh, Jesus, not an ad. What about Kim? She felt as though she were gasping for air when she spoke again. 'Do you have to do an ad?'

'You let me handle my business, and you handle yours. Speaking of which, I'd like to handle ...' His voice was very soft in the phone, and Deanna blushed.

'Stop that!'

'Why?'

'Because you're in your office, and I'm – I'm here.'

'Well, if that's all that's stopping you, let's both get the hell out of those repressive places. I'll pick you up in ten minutes. Are you ready?'

'Desperately.' She couldn't wait to get out of the house. Every moment she spent in it was oppressive.

'Desperate enough to go all the way to Carmel?'

'I'd love it.' Then: 'What about your housekeeper?'

'Mrs Meacham? She'll be off.' It was disagreeable to be hiding like that, but he knew Deanna felt that she had no choice. She still wasn't free. 'Anyway, never mind Mrs Meacham. I'll pick you up in ten minutes. And by the way, Deanna,' he paused while she waited, wondering what he would say; he sounded very solemn. Then his voice dropped again, and she almost could see him smile. 'I love you.'

She smiled happily and closed her eyes. 'So do I.'

The weekend in Carmel was heavenly. The Fourth of July. They spent all three days wandering on the beach, lying in the sun, looking for shells, and collecting driftwood, and once or twice braving the still-icy ocean for a quick swim.

She was already smiling to herself as he lay down next to her on the blanket, shivering from the sea. She had been soaking up the sun and improving her deep-honey tan.

'What are you smiling about, sleeping beauty?' His body was cool and damp next to hers, and his skin felt delicious as she turned and ran her fingers down his arm.

'I was just thinking that this is all rather like a honeymoon. Or a very good marriage.'

'I wouldn't know. I've never had either one.'

'Didn't you have a honeymoon?'

'Not really. We spent it in New York. She was an actress and she was in something off Broadway, so we spent a night at the Plaza in New York. When the play folded, we went up to New England.'

'Did the play have a long run?' She looked admiring, with her big, innocent, green eyes. Ben smiled.

'Three days.' They both laughed, and Ben moved on to his side, so he could look at Deanna. 'Were you happy with Marc before I came along?'

'I thought I was. Sometimes. Sometimes I was terribly lonely. We don't have a relationship like this. In a way we're not really friends. We love each other, but ... it's very different.' She remembered their last conversation when he had told her not to show her work. He was still the voice of authority. 'He doesn't respect me the way you do – my work, my time, my ideas. But he needs me. He cares. In his own way he loves me.'

'And you love him?' His eyes searched her face. She didn't answer immediately.

'I thought we weren't going to talk about things like that. This is *our* summer.' There was reproach in her voice.

'But it's also *our* life. There are some things I need to know.' He was strangely serious.

'You already know them, Ben.'

'What are you saying?'

'That he's my husband.'

'That you won't leave him?'

'I don't know. Do you have to ask me that now?' Her eyes held an autumnal sorrow. 'Can't we just have what we know we can have, and then –'

'And then, what?'

131

'I don't know yet, Ben.'

'And I promised I wouldn't ask. But I find that increasingly difficult.'

'Believe it or not, so do I. My mind drifts to the end of the summer, and I ask myself questions I can't answer. I keep hoping for an act of God, a miracle, something that will take the answers out of our hands.'

'So do I.' He smiled at her then and leaned over to kiss her lips again and again. 'So do I.'

Chapter Twelve

'Ben?' He smiled to himself as Deanna's voice reached him from his spare room. It was late on a Sunday night, and they were just back from another weekend in Carmel.

'What? Need some help?' All he heard was a shout and a gurgle of laughter. She had been in there for over an hour. He climbed out of bed and went to see what was going on. As he opened the door to the spare room, in which he often worked, she was staggering to hold up a tenuously piled stack of canvases which had started to slide off a mountain of boxes propped against the wall.

'Help! It's an avalanche.' She peeked out at him, a small paintbrush clenched in her teeth, and both arms held aloft, trying to keep the pile of paintings from crashing to the floor. 'I came in here to sign a few that I noticed I had forgotten to sign, and ...' She shoved the paintings aside as he lifted them from her arms. Then, his hands still filled with the mountain of her work, he bent his head to kiss the tip of her nose.

'Take the paintbrush out of your mouth.'

'What?' She looked at him with an expression of absentminded pleasure. She was still thinking about two of the paintings she knew she had to sign.

'I said' – he put the paintings carefully aside, and reached for the brush with one hand – 'take that thing out of your mouth.'

'Why? This way I have my hands free to look for ...' But he silenced her almost immediately with a kiss.

'That's why, you dummy. Now, are you coming to bed?' He pulled her close to him, and she nestled against him with a smile.

'In a minute. Can I just finish this?'

'I don't see why not.' He sat down in the comfortable old chair at his desk and watched her ferret through the stack again looking for unsigned canvases. 'Are you as excited as I am, madam, about the show?' It was only four days away. Thursday. He was finally going to launch her into the art world. She should have been showing for years. He looked at her with pleasure and pride, as she stuck the end of the brush through her hair to free her hands once again. There was a huge smile on her face. It not only played with her mouth, it danced in her eyes.

'Excited? Are you kidding? I'm half crazy. I haven't slept in days.'

He suspected it was true. Every night when they went to bed, he looked sleepily into her eyes after their hours of lovemaking, and the last thing he remembered was always that smile. And suddenly in the mornings she was wide awake now. She jumped up and got him breakfast, then disappeared into the spare room where she had put all her work. She had brought her treasures to him, to keep until the show. She didn't even want them in the gallery until the day before the opening.

Now she signed the last one and turned to him with a grin. 'I don't know if I'll make it till Thursday night.'

'You will.' He glowed as he watched her. What a beautiful woman she was. She seemed even prettier lately, her face had a soft, luminous beauty, and her eyes a kind of passionate fire. There was a tenderness and a burning about her all at once, like a velvet flame. And their time together had a magic about it, like nothing he had ever known. The little cottage in Carmel fairly hummed with her presence, filling the rooms with flowers, bringing back huge pieces of driftwood which they lay against as they toasted their feet near the fire on 'their' dune just outside. She filled his dreams and his arms and his days. He could no longer imagine a life without her.

'What are you thinking?' She tilted her head to one side, and leaned against the stack of her paintings.

'About how much I love you.'

'Oh.' She smiled, and her eyes softened as she looked into his eyes. 'I think about that a lot.'

'About how much I love you?' He smiled and so did she.

'Yes. And about how much I love you. What did I ever do before you came along?'

'You lived excessively well and never made your own breakfast.'

'It sounds awful.' She walked towards him, and he pulled her down on to his lap.

'That's just because you're excited about the show and you can't sleep. Wait another month, or two ...' He paused painfully; he had been about to say a 'year', but they didn't have a year. Only another five or six weeks. 'You'll get tired of making breakfast. You'll see.'

She wanted to see. She wanted to see for a lifetime, not a month. 'I'll never get tired of this.' She buried her face in his chest, feeling warm and safe like a child. They were both brown from their weekend in Carmel, and her feet were still sandy as they brushed along the floor. 'You know what I think?'

'What?' He closed his eyes and smelled the fresh scent of her hair.

'That we're very lucky. What more could we have?'

A future, but he didn't say it. He opened his eyes and looked at her as she sat in his lap. 'Don't you ever want another child?'

'At my age?' She looked stunned. 'Good Lord, Pilar is almost sixteen years old.'

'What does that have to do with anything? And what do you mean "at your age"? Lots of women have babies in their thirties.'

'But I'm thirty-seven. That's crazy.'

He shook his head. Deanna was looking somewhat

stunned. 'It's not too old for a man, why should it be too old for a woman?'

'That, my darling, is very different indeed. And you know it yourself.'

'I do not. I'd love to have our child. Or even two. And I don't think you're too old.'

A baby? Now? She looked at him in astonishment, but he was perfectly serious. His arms were still around her.

'Do you mean it?'

'I do.' For a long moment he watched her eyes and wasn't sure what he saw. Confusion, amazement, and also sorrow and pain. 'Or are you not supposed to have any more children, Deanna?' He had never asked. There was no reason to. She shook her head.

'No, there's no reason why I can't, but ... I don't think I could go through it again. Pilar was a gift after the two boys. I don't think I'd want to do it again.'

'Do they know why those things happened?'

'Just flukes, they said. Two inexplicable tragedies. The odds of that happening twice in one family are minute ... but it did.'

'Then it wouldn't again.' He sounded determined, and Deanna pulled away.

'Are you trying to talk me into having a baby?' Her eyes were very large and her face very still.

'I don't know. Maybe I am. It sounds like it, doesn't it?' He smiled and hung his head. Then he looked up. 'Do you think that's what I was doing?'

She nodded, suddenly very serious. 'Don't.'

'Why not?'

'I'm too old.' *And I already have a child. And a husband.*

'That is the only reason I categorically will not accept! That's nonsense!' He sounded almost angry this time, and she wondered why. What did it matter whether or not she was too old for a child?

'Yes, I am. I'm almost forty years old. And even this

136

is pretty crazy. I feel like a kid again. I'm acting like I'm seventeen, not thirty-seven.'

'And what's wrong with that?' He searched her eyes, and she surrendered.

'Absolutely nothing. I love it.'

'Good. Then come to bed.' He picked her up in his arms and deposited her in the next room, on his large comfortable bed. The quilt was rumpled from where they had lain when they came back from Carmel, and there was only one small light on in the room. The soft colours looked warm and pretty, and the big vase of daisies she had picked Friday afternoon on the terrace gave the bedroom a country air. She did something special to his house, she gave it a flavour that he had longed for, for years. He had never really known what was missing, but now that he had her, he knew. What had been missing was Deanna, with her green eyes and dark hair piled on to her head, with her bare legs peeking out of his bed, or sitting cross-legged with her sketch pads on his desk surrounded by the flowers. Deanna, with her stack of paintings and her paintbrushes stuck into all his coffee cups, with the shirts that she 'borrowed' and splattered with paint, and with the countless thoughtful gestures – the ties she had cleaned, the suits she put away, the little presents she bought, the books she brought him that she knew he would love, the laughter and the teasing and the soft eyes that always understood. She had drifted into his life like a dream. And he never wanted to wake up. Not without Deanna at his side.

'Ben?' Her voice was very small next to him in the dark.

'What, love?'

'What if I get bad reviews?' She sounded like a frightened child, and he wanted to laugh, but he didn't. He knew how great her fear was.

'You won't.' He put his arms around her again, beneath the quilt. It had been a present from an artist's wife to his mother, years ago, in New York. 'The reviews will be wonderful. I promise.'

'How do you know?'

'I know because you're very, very good.' He kissed her neck and trembled at the feel of her naked flesh against his legs. 'And because I love you so much.'

'You're silly.'

'I beg your pardon?' He looked at her with a grin. 'I tell you I love you, and you think I'm silly. Listen here, you ...' He pulled her closer and covered her mouth with his, as they disappeared in unison beneath the quilt.

She woke at six the next morning and instantly disappeared into the spare room. She had remembered a painting that shouldn't be there. Then she thought of another that was probably not in the right frame. After coffee she remembered two more without signatures, and so it went for the remaining four days. She was in a frenzy of nervousness over the show. Through it all Ben smiled and loved and cajoled. He took her to dinner, dragged her to a movie, made her join him at the beach; he forced her to go swimming, kept her up late at night making love. On Thursday he took her out to lunch.

'I don't want to hear it.' He held up a hand.

'But, Ben, what if –'

'No. Not a word about the show until tomorrow.'

'But...'

'No!' He put his finger to her lips, and she moved it aside with a fresh burst of worry. But he only laughed. 'How is the wine?'

'What wine?' She looked around, distracted, and he pointed to her glass.

'The wine you're not drinking. How is it?'

'I don't know, and what I wanted to ask you is ...'

He put both fingers in his ears, and she started to laugh at him. 'Ben! Stop it!'

'What?' He smiled happily at her across the table. She was laughing.

'Listen to me! I wanted to ask you something about tonight!'

He started to hum gently, his fingers still in his ears. Deanna couldn't stop laughing. 'You're horrible and I hate you!'

'No, you don't. You can't keep your hands off me, and you want to drag me away with you so you can attack me. Right?'

'Actually, now that you mention it . . .' She grinned and took a sip of her wine, and they teased throughout lunch. He had taken the afternoon off. The paintings were all hung to perfection for Deanna's show. Sally was in control at the gallery, and he thought it a good idea to stay with Deanna, before she changed her mind or came apart at the seams. And he had a surprise for her that afternoon. He looked at his watch as they walked back to the car after lunch.

'Deanna, do you mind if I stop at Saks?'

'Now?' She looked surprised. 'No, that's all right.'

'It won't take me long.' He parked in front of the store with an abstracted smile. 'Want to come in?'

'No, I'll wait.'

'Sure?' He didn't push; he knew she didn't want to be alone today, not even for a short time.

'All right. I'll come.' It had been an easy sale, and he walked happily beside her into the store. 'What do you have to do?'

'Pick up a dress.' He said it with absolute self-confidence and complete nonchalance.

'A dress?'

'For Sally. She said she wouldn't have time. So I told her I'd get it and bring it to the gallery tonight in time for her to change. By the way, what are you wearing?' She had been so busy with her signatures and her frames that he wasn't even sure she'd given it any thought.

'I don't know. I thought I'd wear my black dress.'
She had brought two or three dinner dresses from the
house. They were hanging in his closet, along with her
jeans, her paint-splattered shirts, several pairs of gabardine slacks, and half a dozen turtleneck cashmere
sweaters. He liked the way her clothes looked next to
his.

'Why don't you wear the green dress?'

'Too dressy.' She was ten thousand miles away when
she spoke. 'Listen, do you know which critics are
coming?' Her eyes rushed into his.

'I don't think it's too dressy.' He looked amused.

'Did you hear what I asked you?' Distress was creeping into her voice.

'No. Now, what about the green dress?'

'Screw the green dress, I wanted to ask you –' He
kissed her hard on the mouth and left her breathless as
they got off the elevator on the second floor. 'Ben!'
But there had been no one around to see what he'd
done. 'Will you listen to me?'

'No.' He was already greeting the saleswoman. She
brought the dress out. 'Perfect.' He smiled at her again
and looked at Deanna. 'What do you think?'

'Hm?' She was hopelessly vague, but her attention
was suddenly arrested by the dress. It was an almost
mauve, heather-blue wool with a high neck, long
sleeves, and no back. And it had a beautifully cut
matching coat. 'That is pretty, isn't it? Is that Sally's
dress?' She took a step forward to touch the thin wool.
It was a French fabric and French design and must
have cost her a fortune. 'That's a beauty.' The saleswoman and Ben exchanged a smile of the eyes. 'Maybe
I should wear the green after all.'

'I don't think so. Why don't you just wear that?' He
had a look of innocence which totally confused
Deanna.

'Wear Sally's dress? Don't be silly.'

'You could lend her your green.'

'Darling, I love you, but I think you're quite mad.'
She smiled at the saleswoman and started to walk away,
but Ben gently took her arm and whispered in her
ear.

'I think you're crazy too, now go try on your new
dress.'

She looked at him in astonishment. 'Are you kidding?' He shook his head. 'It's for me?'

He nodded with a satisfied smile. 'Do you like it?'

'I ... oh, Ben, I can't. It's gorgeous!' She turned to
look at it again, and her eyes grew wide. It was exquisite, but probably also monstrously expensive. And
Ben had done that for her? The man who drove an
anonymous German car, and would rather eat spaghetti than caviar? The man who took pride in not
having a maid but only a cleaning lady once or twice
a week, when his grandfather had lived surrounded by
an army of servants, and his father had retired to a
palazzo near Rome? This man had bought her that
dress? It was the sort of thing she would have hesitated
even to charge to Marc. 'Good Lord!'

'Shut up and go try it. I want to see!'

She did, and he saw. It was perfect. The cut, the
style, the colour. She looked regal, coming towards him,
the coat draped over her arm. Her tan set off the rich
heather-blue, and her bare back and shoulders were
perfectly sculpted into the dress. 'What'll you wear
with it?'

'Diamond earrings and black silk sandals. And my
hair up.'

'Oh, God, I can't stand it.' He grinned with such
pleasure that even the saleswoman laughed.

When she put it on that night, he was sitting on the
bed. They smiled at each other, and he zipped up what
there was to zip in the back. She clipped the diamond
earrings on her ears and smoothed her hair up high on
her head. She looked perfect, and for a moment it took

his breath away. Then, with a smile, he gently took off the diamond earrings.

'What are you doing?'

'Taking these off.'

She looked puzzled. 'Why? Don't you like them?' Maybe it was because they had been a present from Marc. 'I don't have any others here that would do.'

'Never mind.' He reached into his pocket and took out a little blue silk bag. He opened it and took out two large and very beautiful pearls. There was a tiny diamond beneath each pearl, and the earrings looked very old and fine. 'I want you to wear these.'

'Oh, Ben.' Deanna looked at them with astonishment, then raised her eyes to his. 'What have you done?' The dress, the earrings, the show. He was giving her so much. Everything . . .

'The earrings were my grandmother's. I want you to have them, Deanna. This is a very special night.' There were tears in her eyes when she looked up at him again. Tenderly, he took her face in his. 'I want this to be the most beautiful night of your life. This is the beginning of your life in the art world, Deanna. And I want everyone to know just how good you are.' There was more love welling up in his eyes than she had ever seen, and her heart trembled as she put her arms around him.

'You are so good to me.'

'We're good to each other, and that's a very special gift.'

'I can't keep the earrings.' She couldn't. Not unless she stayed with Ben. But in another month she would have to go back to Marc.

'Yes, you can keep the earrings. I want you to have them. No matter what.'

He understood. He always understood. And somehow it made things worse. The tears spilled over and ran sadly down her face. Sobs began to shake her shoulders.

'Darling, don't.'

'Oh, Ben . . . I can't leave you.'

'You don't have to. Not yet. Let's just enjoy what we have.'

He hadn't sounded that philosophical since the beginning, and she wondered if finally he had accepted what would have to be. 'I love you.' Her voice was strained. She clung to him, and he closed his eyes.

'I love you too. Now, how about going to this opening of yours?'

He pulled away to look at her, and she nodded. Gently, he took one of the earrings and clipped it to her ear. And then, stopping at her mouth for a kiss, he clipped on the other. 'You look exquisite. And I'm so proud that this opening is yours.'

'I keep thinking I'm going to wake up, and it all will have been a dream. I'll wake up on the beach in Carmel, feeling like Rip Van Winkle, and Kim will still be waiting for me at the hotel. But every time I feel that way, I look around, and you're real.' She looked at him in astonished delight, and he laughed.

'Very much so.' He laughed again as he slipped a hand into her dress. 'And I would very much like to prove it to you, my darling. But I'm afraid we don't have time.' He held out an arm to her with a small bow. 'Shall we?'

She took his arm. 'But of course.'

'Are you ready?' They had just pulled up in front of the gallery.

'Oh, God, no!' Her arms went out to him, and her eyes were wide, but he held her close for only a moment, then swept her inside. There was a photographer waiting, and there were already a considerable number of guests. The art critics were there in force, and she even saw Kim, developing a cosy relationship with one of the gentlemen of the press. Sally hovered near, agog at the beautiful heather-blue dress.

All in all the evening was a smash. The gallery sold seven of her paintings. For a moment she felt as though she were parting with old friends. She didn't want to give up her paintings, but Ben teased her about it as he introduced her to the admirers of her work. Ben was wonderful with her: he was always nearby, yet never too close, supportive but not obvious. He was Benjamin Thompson III, gallery owner extraordinaire. No one would have known about their affair. He was as discreet as he had been that first morning with Kim, and Deanna knew she had nothing to fear. For a moment that day she had been afraid of what Marc might hear. One never knew who came to these shows, who would see, or what they would guess. But no one guessed anything that night, not even Kim, who had sent a huge bouquet of flowers to the house. She felt personally responsible for the match between Deanna and Ben – from a professional standpoint, of course, as she was not aware of any other. She had wondered, though, if Deanna had told Marc of the opening. But later in the evening Deanna told Kim that she had.

'What did he say?'

'Not very much. But he wasn't pleased.'

'He'll get over it.'

'I suppose he will.' But Deanna had not said more on the subject. She didn't tell Kim that Marc had forbidden her to have the show and hung up on her in the end. He had told her it was vulgar and pushy, but for the first time in their marriage she had stood her ground. It was too important to her for her to give in this time. *He* hadn't given in to her wishes about Pilar and the motorcycle. Why should she give in about her art?

'My heavens, what are you frowning about, darling?' Ben spoke softly, so no one else would hear, and Deanna drifted back from her own thoughts.

'Nothing. I'm sorry. I ... it's just ... so much has happened.'

'You can say that again. Sally just sold two more of your paintings.' He looked as happy as a boy, and Deanna wanted to throw her arms around him in a hug. Instead, she just caressed him with her eyes. 'Can I interest you in a celebration dinner?'

'Only if it's pizza.' She grinned at him, knowing his preferences.

'Not this time, madam. The real thing.'

'Hamburgers?'

'Go to hell.' Without further ceremony, he put an arm around her shoulders and kissed her cheek.

It was not an inappropriate thing for a gallery owner to do on the night of an artist's first success, but as Kim watched them she suddenly found herself wondering if there was something more. Deanna had just whispered something in Ben's ear, in answer to which, Kim had heard him say with a gentle smile, 'I'm glad you liked them.' Deanna had touched the pearls at her ears and happily walked away. As Kim watched, an idea came to her for the very first time.

Chapter Thirteen

'O.K. I'm ready. Tell me the truth.' Deanna sat in the bed in the yellow bedroom with her eyes closed, her hands clenched, a pillow held over her head.

'You look like you're waiting for the earthquake.' Ben looked at her and laughed. He was perched on the bed, next to her, the paper in his hand. 'What would you like me to read to you, darling? The stock market? The comics? Oh, I know!'

'Will you read it to me, dammit. I can't stand it another minute more.' She gritted her teeth, and he laughed again, turning to the reviews of her show. But he already knew what he would read. He had been in the business for too long to be very surprised. He generally knew what was in store. And as he glanced over the article, he knew he had been right again.

'O.K., now? Are you ready?'

'Benjamin! Read it dammit!' She said it through tensely clenched teeth and looked terrified as he started to read.

'... a luminous, delicate style that shows not only years of study and devotion to her work, but the kind of talent we too seldom see ...' His voice droned on as her eyes flew wide and she pulled the pillow away from her head.

'You made that up!' She grabbed for the paper. He held it out of her reach and went on reading, until he had come to the end of the piece.

'I don't believe it.' She looked as though she were in shock. 'It can't be.'

'Why not? You're good. I told you that. I know it, they know it, the people who bought your paintings know it. Everyone knows it except you, you big, silly, dopey, humble ...' He had reached out for her and was tickling her.

'Stop it! I'm famous! You can't tickle me now!' But she was giggling too hard to stop him. 'Stop it! I'm a star!'

'Yeah? And who made you a star? Who told you that you had to have a show? Who begged you? Who wanted to show your work the first time he saw it? Huh? Tell me, tell me.' They were both laughing now, and she was tangled into his arms, her pale pink silk nightgown creeping up towards her waist. He stopped for a moment, and looked at her, lying in his arms. She had never looked as beautiful, as delicate, and he wanted to hold her that way forever. He wanted to stop time.

'What's the matter, darling?' She had seen the look in his eyes and was watching him warily. 'Is something wrong?'

'On the contrary. You are incredibly beautiful.'

'And entirely yours.' She slid her body on to his and smiled happily at him as she settled her mouth on his for a long tender kiss. In less than a minute the pink silk nightgown lay on the floor. It was noon before they climbed out of bed. Deanna yawned sleepily as she stood at the door to the terrace, still naked, with her hair falling down her back like an ebony stream. He watched her from the bed, wanting her to stay there forever.

'You know, I think you're destroying my career.' He kept his eyes on her as she turned to him again. She looked so fragile and so young. Her looks belied the toughness he knew lay within. There was a certain steel in her, or she would never have survived the loneliness of her years with Marc.

'Why am I destroying your career? I thought I was going to make you a fortune with my brilliant paintings.' She looked imperiously over her shoulder.

'You would if I'd ever go to the office. It's a good thing I told Sally not to expect me in today. Do you know I've never done anything like this in my life?' But he didn't look unhappy with his new life-style as he wrapped himself in a towel, threw her his robe, and followed her out on to the terrace where they sat comfortably in the two green canvas chairs. 'You make me lazy and happy and horny and young.'

'Which is precisely what you do to me.' She leaned towards him and they kissed. 'I feel about twenty-one. Maybe twenty-two.'

'Good. Then let's get married and have twelve kids.'

She glanced at him again, and for a moment she almost thought he was serious. 'That would certainly give us some fresh problems to think about. Wouldn't it?' She tried to keep her tone light. She didn't want to talk about that with him again. She couldn't. It wasn't right. Instead, she asked, 'What are we doing this weekend?'

She held her face up to the sun and closed her eyes contentedly. It was lovely being with him, living with him, going to Carmel and staying in town, waking up in the morning and falling asleep at night beside him. She felt as though they had been together for the last hundred years, not merely seven weeks. Was it already that? Had their lives soldered together that quickly? It was remarkable how much had happened and how rapidly.

'Do you want to go down to Carmel, or are you tired of that?'

'I'll never be tired of that. It is the most perfect, peaceful place to be.'

'I'm glad.' He reached over and took her hand. 'That's how I feel too. But I keep thinking that you might like to do something more exotic.'

'Like what?' She was amused at the idea. Athens? She forced her mind back from thoughts of Marc.

'I don't know. We could go down to Beverly Hills. I

haven't been down there in weeks.' He usually went just for the day and was back in time for dinner. 'Or one of these days we could even go to New York.' He was never very far from his work – other galleries, other dealers, auctions, artists. In his own way, his passion for his profession wasn't so different from Marc's. The differences were that he included her and that it was a passion which she shared as well. 'In any case, my darling, what is your pleasure this weekend?'

'I told you. Carmel.' She opened her eyes with a warm, happy smile.

'Then Carmel it is.'

'And that reminds me ...' She put her head back with a frown. 'There are some things I want to pick up at the house.' She hadn't been there in days. Now and then she wondered what Margaret must be thinking. She had explained that she was working in a friend's studio and that it was easier to sleep there most of the time. But her occasional morning stops at the house to rumple her bed after Margaret had had the night off wouldn't fool anyone, least of all a woman who had worked for her for years. But what could she say? I'm in love with another man? So she simply kept her peace and avoided the old woman's wily, blue eyes.

It was two in the afternoon when Ben dropped her a block from the house. She wanted to look at the mail and sign a few cheques. She had to pay Margaret and leave her more money for food, not that she ever ate at home any more. Her heart and her stomach all lived somewhere else. She didn't even work in her own studio any more. She did all her painting at Ben's, including the painting she had been working on secretly, whenever he wasn't at home.

Deanna let herself in and called out to see if anyone was home. But Margaret wasn't there. Why should she be? Deanna never was, and there was little to do. There was the usual stack of bills and uninteresting invitations, no letter from Pilar, and nothing from Marc. He didn't write to her. He called. There was no mail for him either. Whenever he was away, Dominique came to the house three times a week and collected his mail to send by pouch, along with official papers.

She walked slowly up to her room, the mail in one hand and the other holding the banister, and stopped at the head of the stairs. It was depressing to be back here. It was like being forced to give up a dream, to grow old again, away from the man who talked about marriage and twelve kids. She smiled to herself at the thought and sighed when she heard the phone. She decided not to answer it, but then wondered if it might be Ben, stopping at a pay phone while he waited. It was as though no one else existed any more, only the two of them. She couldn't imagine that it would be anyone but him.

'Yes?' There was a smile in her voice when she answered.

'*Allo?*' Oh, *Jesus*, it was Marc. '*Allo?*'

'Marc?'

She was buying time.

'Obviously. And I'd like you to explain this nonsense about the show. Dominique just called me.'

'How convenient.'

'I told you what I thought. And what you've done is in very poor taste.' He sounded livid.

'On the contrary, I can assure you it was all in very good taste.'

'That, my dear, is debatable. You know perfectly well I forbade you to have the show. And the publicity! For God's sake, Deanna, it makes you sound like some sort of hippie.'

'It most certainly does not.' Her back stiffened at the thought. 'The reviews made me sound like a serious artist. And it could just be that I am.'

'I thought we had resolved that quite a while ago.'

'Maybe you did, but I didn't.' Damn him. He didn't understand. He never had.

'I see. In any case, I hope this gala new you isn't planning to indulge in conspicuous events like this every day.'

'Hardly. I'll be lucky if I show every five years.'

'In that case, I'm sorry I missed this one.'

'No, you're not.' She was furious now and she would not play his game.

'I beg your pardon?'

'I said you're not sorry you weren't here. I'm sick and tired of your hypocrisy. How dare you belittle my work.'

'Deanna?' He was shocked.

'I'm sorry, I ...' *God, what was happening?* She couldn't keep her stuffing inside any more. It was as though she had to let everything out. 'I don't know, Marc ... I think I'm tired.'

'I think you must be. Was this a bad time to call?' His voice dripped sarcasm and ice. He didn't like her attitude at all. She should have been made to go to Cap d'Antibes for the summer.

'No. I was just leaving for Carmel.'

'Again?'

'Yes. With Kim.' *Oh, God, not again.* She hated lying to him. 'It's not as though I have a lot to do, you know, when you're gone.' She knew that would keep him at bay.

'Well, it won't be for much longer.'

'How long?' She closed her eyes and held her breath. *Make it long, oh, please, don't let him come home ...*

'About a month.'

Deanna nodded silently. She and Ben had one month left. That was all.

They sped off on the familiar road to Carmel half an hour later. Deanna was unusually quiet as they drove. Ben glanced at her, beautiful and troubled with the breeze whipping through her hair.

'Anything wrong?' he asked. She shook her head.

151

'Bad news at home just now?'

'No.' After a long hesitation, she looked at the countryside speeding past and spoke again. 'He called.'

'How was it?' *Did you ask for a divorce . . . ?*

'As usual. It made me angry. He was furious about the show. His secretary called Paris especially to tell him.'

'Does it matter?' he asked. She shrugged. 'Do you still care so much if you make him angry?'

She turned to look at him then. 'In some ways he's like my father. Marc has been my authority figure for years.'

'Are you afraid of him?'

'I never thought so, but perhaps I am. I just thought I respected him. But . . . oh, who knows . . .'

'What's the worst thing he could do to you?'

'Leave me – or that's what I used to think.'

'And you don't feel that way any more?'

She shook her head. 'No.' In an odd way, she almost wished he would leave her. It would make everything so simple, but then of course there would be Pilar. Pilar would never forgive her. Deanna's brows knit, and Ben touched her hand.

'Don't worry so much. It'll all work out.'

'I wish I knew how. Ben, I – I don't know what to do.' She did. But she didn't want to do it. Lose him, or leave Marc. 'And . . . I also have an obligation to Pilar.'

'Yes, and an obligation to yourself. Your first obligation is to yourself, your second to your child. After that, it's all up to you.'

Deanna nodded, saying nothing for a while. She looked less troubled than she had at first. 'It's strange. I forget he exists most of the time. For eighteen years he has been the hub of my life, and suddenly in a month and a half it's as though he's gone and I've never known him. I feel like someone new. But he does exist, Ben. He calls and he's real and he expects me to talk to him, and somehow I can't.'

'Then don't talk to him for now.'

Jesus, he doesn't understand. And God, don't let him get possessive. Please, not yet . . .

But Ben went on, 'Why don't you just relax and enjoy what is. Later you can worry about what will be.'

'And that's what you do, is it?' She slid a hand on to his neck and kissed his cheek. She had seen the worry in his face, the fear in his eyes, the concern when he thought she wasn't looking. 'You don't worry at all, do you?'

'Me?' He shook his head, with a look of such assurance that she laughed.

'You're lying. You're as worried as I am. So don't make me any speeches. I used to think you were so cool that it never got to you. Well, I know better now.'

'Oh, yeah?' He looked at her, laughter and bravado mingled in his eyes. But he was terrified about what would happen in the fall. It was the one thing he could not bring himself to face.

'Well, at least he said he wouldn't be home for a month.'

'A month?'

Deanna nodded silently, and they drove on.

Chapter Fourteen

'Come on, sleepyhead. Get up. It's almost ten.' She opened one eye, groaned at him, and turned over. He patted her behind, then leaned over her with a kiss. 'Come on. You have an appointment with a prospective buyer today. You have to be at the gallery by eleven.'

'And what about you?' She spoke to him from the depths of her pillow.

'I'm going now. Darling, will you get up?'

'No.'

He sat down again next to her. 'Deanna, are you all right?' She had been frequently exhausted in the last two weeks since the show.

'I'm fine.' But she didn't feel it. Her head was heavy, and her body felt dipped in cement. It was so much easier to stay in bed, to sleep the day away, and drowse.

'How come you're so tired these days?' He was looking down at her with considerable concern.

'I think it must be old age.'

'Apparently. I just hope success won't prove to be too much for you, because it looks like you might just turn out to be very successful.' He chatted with her over his shoulder as he went out to the kitchen. 'Do you want toast?'

The idea did not appeal to her. She shook her head as she closed her eyes again and buried her head in the pillow. 'No, thanks!' But he reappeared a moment later with coffee, and for the first time in years that did not appeal to her either.

'Deanna? Are you really all right?'

'I'm fine. I'm just tired.' And sick with apprehension about Marc's return. It had to be that. It was draining her to the core, thinking about him, and Pilar. It was stupid letting them spoil these last weeks with Ben, but she couldn't help it. 'Really, darling, I'm all right. You don't need to worry.' She smiled brightly at him and took a sip of the coffee, but as the warm fumes rose into her face she almost gagged. She turned visibly pale and set down the cup.

'You are sick!' It was an accusation filled with fear.

'I'm not, so stop it. I'm fine, I'm wonderful, I'm healthy, and I adore you.' She reached out her arms for him with a bright smile, and he held her close. He didn't want anything to happen to her, he was suddenly terrified of losing her. He thought about it ten thousand times a day. She could get sick, have an accident, drown in the surf at Carmel; she could die in a fire ... *She could go back to Marc.*

'Who is this buyer we're meeting with today?'

'His name is Junot. He's either Swiss or French, I'm not sure which.'

French? Maybe he knew Marc. But before she could speak, Ben already had the answer.

'No. He just got to town this week, and he liked your work when he walked past the gallery. Nice and simple. O.K.?'

'Perfect, you mind reader.'

'Good. Then I'll see you there at eleven.' He looked at her again, forcing a smile. He waved as he closed the door. They both had it now, and he knew it. The clutches. She had nightmares and held him desperately tight as they fell asleep, and now this exhaustion and malaise. They were both suffering the same terrors, wondering what the end of the summer would bring, and already fearing their loss. They had two more weeks. Maybe even three if Marc were delayed. He was bringing Pilar home with him. But what then? Neither of them had any of the answers. Not yet. And the miracle they both wanted had not yet occurred.

Deanna was at the gallery promptly at eleven, wearing a cream-coloured silk suit with an ivory silk blouse.

Her shoes and bag were in the same vanilla colours. She wore her mother's pearls and the earrings Ben had given her just before her show. The prospective buyer, Monsieur Junot, looked awed. He made all the appropriate gestures, offers, and radiated charm. He bought not one of her paintings, but two of her best. She and Ben shook hands gleefully after he left. The sale had totalled almost eight thousand dollars, nearly half of which would, of course, go to Ben. He took the standard dealer's 40 per cent. Some dealers even took fifty. But she had still done handsomely in the past weeks. Since the show she had made almost twelve thousand dollars.

'What'll you do with it all?' Ben watched her in amusement. She was gazing happily at the cheque.

'Be independent,' she said suddenly, remembering what Marc had said before he left. That that was why she still painted, so she could be independent if she ever had to be again. Maybe he was right. It wasn't the only reason, certainly, but the feeling that she now had something of her own made her feel brand new.

'Want to prove your independence and take me to lunch?' Ben was looking at her with an admiring gaze, but though she looked remarkably pretty, he could still see in her eyes that she was not quite herself. 'How about it? Lunch?' He was dying to go out with her, to be with her, to take her home, to be alone with her, to enjoy every minute they still had. It was becoming an obsession. But she was shaking her head.

'I'd love to. But I can't. I'm having lunch with Kim.'

'Damn. All right, I won't ask you to break it. But when I leave here at five today, madam, you're all mine.'

'Yes, sir.' She looked up at him with pleasure.

'Promise?'

'That'll be an easy promise to keep.'

'All right, then.'

He walked her to the door of the gallery, bestowed a

small gentlemanly kiss on her cheek, and watched as she crossed the street to the Jaguar. What an elegant woman she was. And she was his. He smiled with pride as he went back inside.

'So, how's my favourite artist today? The new Mary Cassatt.' Kim had on a broad smile as Deanna slipped into her seat. They met, as usual, at Trader Vic's. Deanna hadn't been there in almost two months.

'Would you believe we just sold two more paintings this morning?'

'I believe it. Thank God Thompson knew when to push. I never thought I'd see the day you'd give in.' But she also knew that a lot of it had to do with Marc's absence. Deanna would never have agreed to the show, if Marc had been there to squelch it. 'Anyway, I'm delighted you did, and it's about time.' Kim signalled to the waiter and ordered champagne, despite Deanna's laughter and protests. 'Why not? We've barely seen each other since Carmel for chrissake. And we have a lot to celebrate.'

Deanna laughed to herself. More than Kim knew.

'So, other than the fact that you're now a famous artist, what's new?' Kim's eyes searched hers, but Deanna only smiled. 'You look like the cat that swallowed the canary.'

'I don't know why.'

'Bull! I think that maybe I know why.' She had seen it that night at Deanna's opening, but at first she hadn't been sure. 'Well, are you going to tell me, or am I going to die of suspense?'

'You mean I have a choice?'

'Never mind that. Come on, Deanna, be nice ... tell me.'

Kim was playing but Deanna was suddenly serious. 'It sounds as though you already know. Jesus, I hope it's not that obvious.'

'It's not. I just suddenly began to wonder, that night.

At the opening. But I don't think anyone else would have known.' Their eyes met at last, and Deanna was silent for a time.

'He's incredibly special, Kim. And I love him. Very much.'

Kim let out a slow sigh and waited. 'He seems like a very nice man. Is it serious?' she asked. Deanna nodded, and Kim sipped her champagne.

'I'd like to say I don't know. But I do know.' Her eyes filled with tears. 'I have to go back to Marc. Ben knows it too. I can't start all over again, Kim. I can't. I'm too old. I'm almost forty, and ...' Her voice was barely a whisper. 'I have a life with Marc. I've always loved him. And ... and there's Pilar ...' But Deanna couldn't go on. Her eyes were brimming, and she had to blow her nose.

Kim wanted to put her arms around her and come up with a magical solution. They both knew there was none.

'There's no other way?' Deanna shook her head. 'How does Ben feel?'

Deanna took a deep breath. 'As panic stricken as I. But I just can't walk out and start all over again. I can't ...' She sounded desperate as she whispered at Kim. 'I'm too old.'

'If that's all that's stopping you, you know damn well you're not. Hell, women remake their lives at sixty when their husbands die. At thirty-seven, you'd be crazy to throw something away you really want.'

'But it's not right. And I *am* too old, dammit, Kim. He wants children for God's sake, and I have a daughter who's almost grown.'

'All the more reason. Pilar will be gone. If you want more children, now's the time.'

'You're as crazy as he is.' Deanna tried to smile, but it was not an easy subject. She felt as though the next two weeks were already vanishing beneath her eyes.

'Are you happy with Ben, Deanna?'

'I've never been as happy in my life. And I can't understand it. I've lived with Marc for almost twenty years; we know each other, and suddenly ... Oh, Kim, I can barely remember what Marc looks like, how he sounds. It's as though my whole life is with Ben. At first I felt guilty; I thought I was horrible for doing what I did. Now I don't even feel badly. I just love him.'

'And you think you'll be able to give that up?' Kim looked at her with sorrow for what she knew was happening to her friend.

'I don't know. Maybe we can still see each other. Maybe ... Kim, I just don't know.'

Neither did Kim, but she suspected that Ben Thompson wouldn't put up with sharing her for very long. He didn't seem like that kind of man.

'Will you tell Marc?'

Deanna shook her head. 'Never. He would never understand. He'd be heartbroken. I – we'll just have to see. Ben has to go to New York in September for a few weeks. That'll give me time to see how things stand.'

'If I can do anything, Deanna ... if you need a shoulder or a hand – I'm always there for you, babe. I hope you know that.'

'I do.'

The two exchanged a smile and went on to other things, but long after Kim left her, she was haunted by Deanna's face, and what she had seen.

And when she had left Kim, Deanna had slowly driven home. She had to check the mail and pay her bills. She wasn't meeting Ben again till five. They'd go some place quiet for dinner, and then maybe for a walk, or to a movie, do the kind of things people did who didn't have children, or pressures, or too little time. She wanted to spend these two weeks as they had spent the two months before, simply, quietly – together. It was what Ben wanted too.

'Mrs Duras?' Margaret was waiting for her as she

turned her key in the door. She was wearing a look of tension which, at first, Deanna did not understand.

'Margaret? Are you all right?' She thought the older woman looked pale. As she reached the hall table, she realised that the housekeeper was still staring. 'Margaret? Is something wrong?' Her voice was more insistent this time, and she looked long and hard at the woman in the dark blue uniform. Could she know about Ben? Had she seen them? 'What is it?'

'There have been two calls ...' Margaret trailed off, not knowing what more to say. She wasn't really sure. She had no right to worry Mrs Duras but she had had a feeling.'

'From Mister Duras?' Deanna stood up very straight. 'From Madame Duras, his mother.'

'What did she say?' There was a frown in Deanna's eyes now. 'Was anything wrong?'

'I don't know. She only spoke to the operator in Paris. But she wants you to call back. Right away.'

'In Paris? You mean Antibes.' To Margaret, Deanna knew, it was one and the same. The housekeeper shook her head emphatically.

'No. It was Paris. They left a number.' Margaret ferreted the message from the pile and handed it to Deanna. She was right. It was Paris. It was the number of the house on the rue François Premier. Something was wrong. Perhaps the old lady was ill and wanted Pilar sent home early. Marc! Something had happened to Marc! A thousand catastrophes leaped into her head as she ran up the stairs to the bedroom phone. It would be just after midnight in Paris. Too late? Should she wait until morning?

The overseas operator put the call through quickly, and the familiar purring of the French phone was instantly in her ears. For years it had sounded to her like a busy signal, but now she was used to it and she knew. 'It may take them a minute to answer, I'm awfully sorry.'

'That's quite all right.' The operator sounded Californian and unhurried and Deanna smiled. Then she heard her mother-in-law's voice on the line.

'*Allo? Oui?*'

'*Mamie?*' The term of affection had never come easily to Deanna. After nearly twenty years she was still tempted to call her mother-in-law Madame Duras. '*Mamie?*' It was not a very good connection, but Deanna could hear, and she raised her own voice to make herself heard. Madame Duras sounded neither sleepy, nor pleasant. She never did. 'It's Deanna. I'm awfully sorry to call so late, but I thought that ...'

'Deanna, *il faut que tu viennes.*' Oh, Jesus, not in French, with a connection like that! But the older woman went on in a rush of French. Deanna could barely hear.

'Wait, wait. I can't hear you. I don't understand. Please say it in English. Is something wrong?'

'Yes.' The word was a long mournful wail, and then there was silence while Deanna waited. What had happened? It was Marc. She knew it! 'Pilar. ... She had ... an accident ... on the *moto*—'

Deanna felt her heart stop. 'Pilar?' She was shouting into the phone now, and she didn't hear Margaret come into the room. 'Pilar?' The connection was fading, and she shouted louder. '*Mamie?* Can you hear me? What happened?'

'Her head ... her legs ...'

'Oh, God! Is she all right?' The tears were pouring down her face and she was desperately trying to control her voice. '*Mamie?* Is she all right?'

'*Paralysées. Les jambes.* Her legs ... paralysed. And her head ... We don't know.'

'Where is she?' Deanna was shrieking.

'At the American Hospital.' The old woman was sobbing now.

'Have you called Marc?'

'We can't find him. He's in Greece. His *société* is

trying to locate him. They think he will be here tomorrow. Oh, please, Deanna . . . you will come?'

'Tonight. Right now.' Her whole arm was trembling as she looked at her watch. It was ten minutes to four. She knew there was a flight at seven-thirty. Marc took it all the time. With the time difference, she would be there at four-thirty Paris time, the next day. 'I'll be there . . . in the afternoon . . . I'll go directly to the hospital. Who is her doctor?' She hastily scribbled his name. 'How can I reach him?' Madame Duras gave her his home number.

'Oh, Deanna. The poor child . . . I told Marc that the *moto* was too big for a child. Why didn't he listen? I told him . . .'

So did I. *'Mamie*, is anyone with her?' It was the first thing that had come to her mind. Her baby was alone in a hospital in Paris.

'We have nurses, of course.' That sounded more like the Madame Duras Deanna knew.

'No one else?' There was horror in her voice.

'It is after midnight here.'

'I don't want her alone.'

'Very well. I'll send Angéline down now, and I shall go in the morning.' Angéline, the oldest maid on the face of the earth. Angéline. How could she?

'I'll be there as soon as I can. Tell her I love her. Goodbye, *Mamie*. I'll see you tomorrow.'

Desperate, Deanna flashed the operator. 'Doctor Hubert Kirschmann, person to person. It's an emergency.'

But *Docteur* Kirschmann was not answering his calls. And a call to the American Hospital did not yield a great deal more. Although still critical, Mademoiselle Duras was resting comfortably, she was conscious, and there was a possibility that they might operate in the morning. It was too soon to tell. She had been flown in from Cannes only that evening, and if Madame would

be good enough to call the *docteur* in the morning ...
Oh, go to hell. Pilar was not able to take phone calls,
and there was nothing more Deanna could do. Except
get on a plane.

She sat very still for a moment, fighting back tears,
holding her head in her hands, until a sudden sob
escaped her, wrenching its way free from her heart.
'Pilar ... my baby. Oh, my God!' The blue uniform
was around her then, and Margaret's comforting arms
held her tightly.

'Is it very bad?' Her voice was a whisper in the too
silent room.

'I don't know. They say her legs are paralysed, and
there's something wrong with her head. But I couldn't
get intelligent answers from anyone. I'm going to take
the next plane.'

'I'll pack a bag.'

Deanna nodded and tried to marshal her thoughts.
She had to call Ben. And Dominique. Instinctively, her
fingers dialled Dominique at the office. The voice she
disliked was quick to answer the phone. 'Where is Monsieur Duras?'

'I have no idea.'

'The hell you don't. Our daughter just had an accident, and they can't find him. Where is he?'

'I ... Madame Duras, I'm very sorry ... I'll do my
best to locate him by morning and have him call you.'

'I'm leaving for Paris tonight. Just tell him to be
there. And call his mother. Pilar is at the American
Hospital in Paris. And for God's sake, do me a favour,
will you please, Dominique, and find him?' Her voice
trembled on the words.

'I'll do my best. And I'm really very sorry. Is it
serious?'

'We don't know.'

She called the airline and the bank. She glanced at
what Margaret had put in her bag and quickly dialled

Ben before he left the gallery. She had an hour before she had to leave for the airport. He was quick to come on the line.

'I have to leave town tonight.'

'What did you do this afternoon? Rob a bank?' His voice was full of mischief and laughter; he was looking forward to the evening ahead. But he was quick to sense that something was wrong.

'Pilar had an accident. Oh, Ben ...' And then the tears came, sobbing, aching, frightened, and angry at Marc for letting her have the bike.

'Take it easy, darling. I'll be right there. Is it all right if I come to the house?'

'Yes.'

Margaret opened the door to him seven minutes later. Deanna was waiting in her room. She was still wearing the suit she had worn at lunch and the earrings Ben had given her. She was wearing those to France. He looked at her quickly as he walked in, and took her into his arms. 'It's all right, baby, it's all right. She'll be all right.'

She told him then about the paralysed legs.

'That could be just a temporary reaction from the fall. You don't know the details yet. It may not be nearly as bad as it sounds. Do you want something to drink?' She was dangerously pale, but she shook her head. All he saw was her face and the heartbreak written there. She began to cry again and took refuge once more in his arms.

'I've been thinking such awful things.'

'Don't. You don't know. You just have to hang in till you get there.' He looked at her again with a question. 'Do you want me to come?'

She sighed and gave him a glimmer of a smile. 'Yes. But you can't. I love you for asking though. Thank you.'

'If you need me, call, and I'll come. Promise?' he asked. She nodded.

'Will you call Kim and tell her where I've gone? I just tried to reach her and she's out.'

'She won't find it suspicious if I tell her?' He looked worried, but he was worried about Deanna, not Kim.

'No.' Deanna smiled. 'I told her about us today at lunch. She had already guessed, don't ask me how. At the opening. But she thinks you're a very special man. I think she's right.' She reached out to him again and held him close. It would be the last time for a while that she could do that, hold him and be his. 'I wanted a chance to go home again ... just to be there ... it gives me so much peace.' She meant his house, not her own, but he understood.

'You'll be home again soon.'

'Promise?' Her eyes found his.

'Promise. Now come on, we'd better go. Do you have everything you need?' he asked. She nodded and closed her eyes again. For just a fraction of a moment she had been dizzy. 'Are you all right?'

'I'm fine.' She followed him down the stairs and hugged Margaret as she left. They had an hour to get to the airport. Forty-five minutes later she would be on the plane. Twelve hours after that, she'd be in Paris – with her baby. Pilar.

During the drive to the airport Deanna found herself silently praying that she'd find her alive.

Chapter Fifteen

'*Quoi? Oh, mon Dieu!* Dominique, are you sure?'

'Absolutely. I also spoke to your mother. And the doctor.'

'What's his name?' She passed the information on to Marc as he gestured frantically for a pen. Chantal handed him hers. 'When did they operate?'

'This morning, Paris time. Three hours ago, I believe. She's a little better, they think, but she hadn't yet regained consciousness. They're mainly worried about her skull, and ... and her legs.'

The tears had started to pour slowly down Marc-Edouard's cheeks as he listened to Dominique. I'll send a wire. I'll be there tonight.' He flashed the concierge. His orders were terse. 'This is Duras. Get me on a plane. Paris. Immediately.' He hung up and wiped his face, looking strangely at Chantal.

'It's Pilar?' she asked. He nodded. 'Is it very bad?' She sat down on the couch next to him and took his hands.

'They don't know. They don't know ...' He couldn't bring himself to say the words, or to tell her that the motorcycle had been a gift from him, as the sobs began to convulse him.

Deanna got off the plane at Charles de Gaulle Airport in a cloud of exhaustion, terror, and nausea. She had spent the night staring straight ahead and clenching her hands. She called the hospital from the airport, but there was no news. Deanna hailed a taxi just outside the airport and sat silently as they sped along. She had given the driver the address of the American Hospital and told him only, '*Aussi vite que possible.*'

In true Gallic style, he took her at her word. The

trees at the roadside were barely more than a green blur in the corners of Deanna's eyes as she stared straight ahead of her, watching the driver's manoeuvres as he lunged and careened past every obstacle in sight. She could feel every pulse in her body, every throb of her heart ... hurry ... hurry ... *VITE!* It seemed hours before they reached the Boulevard Victor Hugo and screeched to a halt in front of the big double doors. Deanna reached quickly into her wallet for the francs she had exchanged from dollars at the airport. Without thinking she handed him a hundred francs, and flung open the door.

'*Votre monnaie?*' He looked at her questioningly, and she shook her head. She didn't give a damn about the change. Her lips were a tight, narrow line lost somewhere in the ivory agony of her face. He had understood from the first, when she had given him the address of the American Hospital. He had known. 'Your husband?'

'*Non. Ma fille.*' Once again her eyes filled with tears.

The driver nodded in sympathetic chagrin. '*Désolée.*' He picked her small brown-leather valise off the seat and opened his door. He stood there for a moment, holding it, looking at her, wanting to say something more. He had a daughter too, and he could see the pain in Deanna's eyes. His wife had looked like that once, when they had almost lost their son. He silently handed the bag to Deanna. Her eyes held his for only a fraction of a second, then she turned and strode rapidly into the hospital.

There was a sour-looking matron sitting at a desk.

'*Oui, madame?*'

'Pilar Duras. Her room number?' *Oh, God, just her room number, please. Don't let them tell me ... don't ...*

'Four-twenty-five.' Deanna wanted to let out a long anguished sigh. Instead, she only nodded curtly and followed the sign. There were two men and a woman on the elevator, going to other floors. They had the look of businesslike Europeans, maybe they were friends of patients, maybe husbands or wives, but none of them looked particularly shaken or upset. Deanna watched them enviously as she waited for her floor. The long, fear-filled plane ride was taking its toll. It had been a long sleepless night, and her thoughts had ricocheted from Pilar to Ben. What if she had let him come with her? She found herself longing for his arms, his warmth, his comfort, his support, and the gentleness of his words.

The elevator doors opened on four, and hesitantly she stepped out. There was a bustle of nurses, and in a few sedate little cliques she noticed elderly distinguished men; doctors. But suddenly, Deanna felt lost. She was six thousand miles from home, looking for a daughter who could even be dead. Suddenly, she wasn't even sure if she could speak French any more, or if she would ever find Pilar in that maze. Tears stung her eyes. She fought off a wave of dizziness and nausea, then slowly made her way to the desk.

'I'm looking for Pilar Duras. I'm her mother.' She didn't even try it in French. She just couldn't. She only prayed that someone would understand. Most of the nurses were French, but someone would speak English. Someone would know ... someone would make it all better – would take her to Pilar, would show her that she wasn't really that badly hurt ...

'Duras?' The nurse seemed troubled as she looked up at Deanna, and then frowned at a chart. Everything inside Deanna turned first to jelly, then to stone. 'Oh, yes.' She met Deanna's eyes and nodded, wondering suddenly if the desperately pale woman trembling in front of her was ill. 'Madame Duras?'

'Yes.' Deanna couldn't manage more than a whisper. Suddenly every moment of the trip had caught up with her. She just couldn't any more. She even found herself wishing for Marc.

'Madame Duras, are you all right?' The young woman in the white uniform had a heavy accent but her English was fluent. Deanna only stared at her. Even she wasn't quite sure. She felt very odd, as though she might faint.

'I have to ... I think ... May I sit down?' She looked around vaguely, and then watched in fascination while everything around her first turned grey, then shrank. It was like watching a slowly fading screen on a disgruntled television, as slowly ... slowly ... the picture just faded away. At last, all she heard was a hum. Then she felt a hand on her arm.

'Madame Duras? Madame Duras?' It was the same girl's voice, and Deanna felt herself smile. She had such a pleasant young voice ... such a pleasant ... Deanna felt unbearably sleepy. All she wanted to do was drift away, but the hand kept tugging at her arm. Suddenly, there was something cool on her neck, and then her head. The picture returned to the screen. A dozen faces surrounded her, all looking down. She started to sit up, but a hand immediately restrained her, and two young men spoke urgently to each other in French. They wanted to transfer her to emergency, but Deanna rapidly shook her head.

'No, no, I'm fine. Really. I've just had a very long flight from San Francisco, and I haven't eaten all day. Really, I'm just terribly tired and ...' The tears welled up in her eyes again. She tried to will them away. Dammit, why did they want to take her to emergency? 'I have to see my daughter. Pilar ... Pilar Duras.'

The words seemed to stop them. The two young men stared at her, then nodded. They had understood. In a moment, with a hand at each elbow, she was on her feet, while a young nurse helped her straighten her skirt. Someone brought a chair, and the first nurse brought her a glass of water. A moment later the crowd had dispersed. Only the young nurse and the older one remained.

'I'm awfully sorry,' Deanna said.

'Of course not. You are very tired. You have had a long trip. We understand. In a moment we will take you to see Pilar.' The two nurses exchanged a glance, and the older one nodded almost imperceptibly.

'Thank you.' Deanna took another sip of water and handed back the glass. 'Is Doctor Kirschmann here?' The nurse shook her head.

'He left earlier this afternoon. He was with Pilar all night. They performed surgery, you know.'

'On her legs?' Deanna felt herself trembling again.

'No. Her head.'

'Is she all right?'

There was an endless pause. 'She is better. Come, you will see for yourself.' She stood aside to help her up, but Deanna was steady now and furious with herself for the time she had just wasted.

She was led down a long peach-coloured hall and stopped at last at a white door. The nurse looked long and hard at Deanna, then slowly opened the door. Deanna took a few steps inside and felt the air freeze in her lungs. It was as though she could no longer breathe.

Pilar was wrapped in bandages, and covered with machinery and tubes. There was a severe-looking nurse sitting quietly in one corner, and at least three monitors were feeding out mysterious reports. Pilar herself was barely visible through the bandages, and her face was badly distorted by the various tubes.

But this time Deanna did not faint. She dropped the valise where she stood and advanced into the room with a firm step and a smile, as the nurse who had brought her in watched. She exchanged glances with the nurse on duty in the room. The woman approached, but Deanna didn't notice. She continued to make her way towards the bed, praying for strength and fighting back tears with a heartbreaking smile.

'Hi, baby, it's Mommy.' There was a soft groan from

170

the bed, and the eyes of her child followed her steps. It was easy to see that Pilar knew her and understood. 'Everything's going to be just fine. Just fine ...' She stood next to the bed and reached for Pilar's one undamaged hand, and gently, almost so lightly as not to touch her, she took the hand in both of hers, lifted it to her lips, and kissed the fingers of her little girl. 'It's all right, my darling, you're going to be fine.'

There was a gruesome sound from the girl in the bed.

'Shh ... you can talk to me later. Not now.' Deanna's voice was barely more than a whisper, but it was firm.

Pilar shook her head. 'I ...'

'Shhh ...' Deanna looked distressed, but Pilar's eyes were too full of words.

'Is it something you want?' Now Deanna watched, but there was no answer in the eyes. Deanna glanced at the nurse. Could she be in pain? The nurse approached, and together they watched and waited as Pilar tried again.

'Gl ... ad ... youuu ... came.' It was a threadlike, fragile whisper from the bed, but it filled Deanna's heart with passion and tears. Her eyes filled. She forced herself to smile while she went on holding Pilar's hand.

'I'm glad I came too. Now don't talk, baby. Please. We can talk later. We'll have a lot to say.'

This time Pilar only nodded yes, and then at last, closed her eyes for a while. The nurse told Deanna when they stepped into the hall that except for when they operated and she had been given an anaesthetic, Pilar had been awake the entire time, as though she were waiting for someone, for something, and now it was easy to see why.

'Your being here will make an enormous difference, you know, Madame Duras.' Pilar's nurse spoke impeccable English and looked terribly crisp. Deanna was relieved at her words. Pilar *had* been waiting for her. She still cared. It was stupid that at a time like this that should matter, but it did. She had feared that even in direst circumstances, Pilar might still reject her. But she had not. Or had she really been waiting for Marc? It didn't matter. Deanna walked softly back inside the room and sat down.

It was more than two hours before Pilar woke, and she only lay there watching her mother, her gaze never leaving Deanna's face. At last after their eyes had seemed to hold for hours, she thought she saw Pilar smile. Deanna approached the bed again and gently took the girl's hand once again.

'I love you, darling. And you're doing just fine. Why don't you try to get some more sleep?'

But her eyes said no. They stayed open again for an hour, watching, only watching, staring into her mother's face, as though drinking it in, as though she were reaching out with the words she couldn't find the strength to say. It was another hour before she spoke again.

'Doggie ...' Deanna looked puzzled, and Pilar tried again. 'Did ... you ... bring my ... doggie?' This time Deanna could not stop herself from crying. Doggie, the treasure of the years when she'd still been a child. Doggie, so old and dirty and bedraggled, and finally retired to a remote shelf somewhere in the house. Deanna had never been able to throw it out. Doggie brought back too many memories of Pilar as a child. Now Deanna watched her, wondering if she still knew where she was, or if she had drifted back to some distant place, to childhood, and Doggie.

'He's waiting for you at home.'

Pilar nodded with a tiny smile. 'O.K. ...' The word was feather soft on her lips as she drifted back to sleep.

Doggie. It brought Deanna back a dozen years as she sat in the narrow chair and let her own thoughts wander back to when Pilar had been three, and four, and five, and nine ... and then too soon twelve, and now almost sixteen. She had been so sweet when she was little, so tiny and graceful, the little girl with the golden curls and blue eyes. The delicious things she had said; the dances she sometimes had done for her parents when she played; the tea parties she'd held for her dolls; the stories she'd written, the poems, the plays; the blouse she had made Deanna one year for her birthday from two chartreuse kitchen towels ... and Deanna had worn it, very seriously, to church.

'Madame Duras?' Deanna was jolted back from a great distance at the sound of the unfamiliar female voice. She looked around, startled, and saw a new nurse.

'Yes?'

'Do you not wish to rest? We can make you a bed in the next room.' Her face was very gentle, and the eyes were wise and old. She patted Deanna's arm with her hand. 'You have been here for a very long time.'

'What time is it now?' Deanna felt as though she had been living in a dream for hours.

'Nearly eleven.'

It was two P.M. in San Francisco. She had been away from home for less than twenty-four hours, but it felt more like years. She stood up and stretched.

'How is she?' Deanna looked intensely at the bed.

The kindly nurse hesitated for a moment. 'The same.'

'When is the doctor coming back?' And why the hell hadn't he been there in the five hours that Deanna had been at Pilar's side? And where was Marc, dammit? Wasn't he coming? He'd whip these morons into shape and then things would start to move. Deanna glared at the monitors, irritated at the hieroglyphics they wrote.

'The doctor will be back in a few hours. You could get a little rest. You could even go home for the night. We have given Mademoiselle another injection. She will sleep now for quite a while.'

Deanna didn't want to leave, but it seemed as though it might be time to put in her appearance at her mother-in-law's house. She could find out if they had located Marc and see what was happening with this doctor. Who was he? And where? And what did he have to say? The only thing Deanna knew now was that Pilar was critical. Deanna felt desperately helpless, sitting there for hours, waiting for an explanation, or a sign, something to herald encouragement or good news ... someone to tell her it was nothing. But that would have been difficult to believe.

'Madame?' The nurse watched her sorrowfully.

Deanna looked almost as wan as Pilar as she picked up her bag. 'I'll leave a number where I can be reached, and I'll be back soon. How long do you think she'll sleep?'

'At least four hours, perhaps even five or six. But she will not be awake before three. And I promise ... if there is a problem, or if she wakes and wants you, I will call.'

Deanna nodded and jotted down Marc's mother's number. She looked agonizingly into the nurse's eyes. 'Call me immediately if ... I should come.' She couldn't bring herself to say more but the nurse understood. She clipped Deanna's number to the chart and smiled into Deanna's very tired eyes.

'I will call. But you must get some sleep.'

Deanna could never remember feeling so tired in her life, but the last thing she planned to do was sleep. She had to call Ben. Talk to the doctor. Find out about Marc. Her mind raced and she felt dizzy again. She steadied herself against the wall, but this time she did not faint. She merely stood for a long moment, looking at Pilar. Then, with eyes flooded with tears, she left the room, her suitcase in one hand, her coat over her arm, and her heart dragging behind her.

She found a taxi at a stand across the street from the hospital and sank back into the seat with a sigh so loud it was almost a groan. Every inch of her was tired and painful and sore, every fibre in her body was tense and exhausted, and her mind never seemed to stop its constant whirring: Pilar as a baby ... Pilar last year ... Pilar at seven ... Pilar in her room. In school. At the airport. With a new hairdo. Her first stockings. A red bow. It was a never ceasing film she had been watching all day, sometimes with the sound track, sometimes without, but it was a vision she couldn't escape, even as the cab sped through Paris to the rue François Premier.

It was an elegant neighbourhood, conveniently located near Christian Dior. The street was as pretty as any in Paris, quite close to the Champs Élysées. When she was younger, Deanna had often escaped in the afternoon to look at the shops and have an espresso at a café before returning to the austerity of life at her mother-in-law's, but now all thought of those days slipped from her mind. She rode blindly along, exhaustion enveloping her like a blanket drenched in ether.

The driver was smoking a Gauloise *papier maïs* and singing an old song. He was too happy to notice the gloom in the backseat, and when he stopped at the address, his eyes met Deanna's with a lure and a smile. She didn't notice. She simply handed him the money and got out. The driver only shrugged and drove away as she plodded towards the door. It had not gone unnoticed that her mother-in-law had not been at the hospital all evening. The nurse said she had been with Pilar for two hours in the morning. Two hours? That was all? And left her in that appalling condition all alone? It proved everything Deanna had always thought. Madame Duras had no heart.

She rang the doorbell with two quick, sharp jabs, and the heavy wooden outer door swung open before her. She stepped over the high threshold and closed the door behind her, making her way quickly to the tiny elegant çage. She always felt as though there ought to be a canary in that elevator and not people, but today her thoughts were far from flip as she pressed the button for the seventh floor. It was the penthouse; Madame Duras owned the entire floor.

A faceless maid in a uniform was waiting at the door,

175

when Deanna stepped out. *'Oui, madame?'* She looked Deanna over with displeasure, if not disdain.

'Je suis Madame Duras.' Deanna's accent had never been worse, and she didn't give a damn.

'Ah, bon. Madame is waiting in the salon.' How sweet. Pouring tea? Deanna felt her teeth grind as she marched behind the maid towards the living room. Nothing was unusual, nothing was out of place. No one would have believed that Madame Edouard Duras's granddaughter lay, possibly dying, in a hospital two miles away. Everything appeared to be in perfect order, including Madame Duras, as the maid escorted Deanna into the room. Her mother-in-law was wearing dark green silk and an impeccable coiffure, her step was firm as she walked towards Deanna with an extended hand. Only her eyes betrayed her concern. She shook hands with Deanna and kissed her on both cheeks, looking with dismay at the expression on her daughter-in-law's face.

'You've just come?' Her eyes glanced immediate dismissal to the maid, who instantly fled.

'No. I've been with Pilar all evening. And I've yet to see the doctor.' Deanna pulled off her jacket and almost fell into a chair.

'You look very tired.' The older woman watched her with a face set in stone. Only the wily, old eyes suggested that someone did indeed live behind the granite of her face.

'Whether or not I'm tired is beside the point. Who the hell is this Kirschmann and where is he?'

'He is a surgeon and he is known all over France. He was with Pilar until late this afternoon, and he will see her again in a few hours. Deanna' – she hesitated, then said more gently – 'there is simply nothing more he can do. At least not for the moment.'

'Why not?'

'Now we must wait. She must get her strength. She must . . . live.' Her expression showed pain at the word,

176

and Deanna ran a hand across her eyes. 'Would you like something to eat?'

Deanna shook her head. 'Just a shower and a little rest. And' – she looked up with an expression of agony in her face – 'I'm sorry to just march in like this. I haven't said any of the appropriate things like "good to see you", "how are you", but Mamie, I'm sorry, I just can't.'

'I understand.'

Did she? Deanna wondered. But what did it matter now if she did or not.

'I do think you should eat, my dear,' Madame Duras was saying. 'You look very pale.'

She felt very pale too, but she simply wasn't hungry. She couldn't have eaten, no matter what. Not tonight. Not after seeing Pilar limp and broken in that bed, asking for Doggie, and too weak to hold her mother's hand.

'I'll just shower and change and get back. It's liable to be a long night. By the way, have you heard from Marc?' Her brows knit as she asked. Her mother-in-law nodded.

'He'll be here in an hour.'

An hour ... One hour. After more than two months, Deanna felt nothing inside except what she felt for Pilar.

'He's coming in from Athens. He's very upset.'

'As well he might be.' Deanna looked his mother straight in the eye. 'He bought her the motorcycle. I begged him not to.'

Madame Duras instantly bridled. 'Deanna, he cannot be blamed. I'm sure he feels quite badly enough.'

'I'm sure he does.' She looked away, then stood up. 'He'll be landing in an hour?'

'Yes. Will you go to meet him?'

Deanna started to say no, but something inside her wavered. She was thinking of Pilar, and how the child looked ... how it would be for Marc walking in, as she had, and seeing her for the first time. It seemed cruel to let him walk into that alone. Pilar was his baby, his treasure, his child. She was also Deanna's, but to Marc, Pilar was almost a goddess. She couldn't let him face it as she had. She had to meet him at the plane.

'Do you have his flight number?' His mother nodded. 'Then I'll go. I'll just wash my face. I won't bother to change. Can you call a taxi?'

'Certainly.' The elder Madame Duras looked pleased. 'I'll be more than happy to. Fleurette will make a sandwich for you.' Fleurette, little flower. The name of the immensely rotund cook Madame Duras employed had always struck Deanna funny, but not tonight. Nothing was funny any more. She nodded curtly at her mother-in-law and hurried down the hall. She was just about to turn into the guest room when she noticed the painting in a dark passage. Left there, unwanted, unloved, unadmired, forgotten. It was the portrait of herself and Pilar. Madame Duras had never been very fond of it. Now, without thinking further, Deanna decided that this time she'd take it home, where it belonged.

In the familiar guest room, she looked around. Everything was a polite shade of sandy beige, in damask or silk, and the furniture was all Louis XV. It was a room that had always seemed cold to Deanna, even when she had slept in it on her honeymoon with Marc. She ran a comb through her hair and tried to make herself think of Marc. What would it be like to see him again? To see his face, touch his hand ... after Ben. Why was it that Ben seemed more real to her now, or was he only a dream? Had she once more been swallowed alive by this beige-silk world, never to return? She wanted desperately to call Ben but she didn't have time. She had to get to the airport in time to catch Marc as he left the gate from the plane, or she'd miss him entirely. She wondered if there were any way to leave a message that she was coming, but she knew from experience that such messages always went astray. A man with a thin, thready voice would stand in a corner of the airport whispering to himself, 'Monsieur Duras ... Monsieur Duras,' as Marc marched unknowingly by. And if he did get it, it might frighten him too badly about Pilar. She could at least spare him that.

The maid knocked on the guest-room door and told her the taxi was waiting. As she spoke the words, she handed Deanna a small package. Two ham sandwiches and part of a chicken. Perhaps Monsieur would be hungry too. Hungry? Jesus, who could eat?

Unlike the earlier ride from the airport which had seemed interminable, this one seemed much too short. She found herself nodding slowly off to sleep in the backseat as they raced along into the night, her thoughts jumping in disjointed confusion from Pilar to Ben to Marc. It seemed only moments later that the cab screeched to a halt.

'Voilà.'

She muttered an absentminded 'merci' to the driver, paid the fare and a handsome tip, and hurried inside, smoothing her skirt again as she ran. She was beginning to feel as though she hadn't changed her clothes in a week, but she didn't really care how she looked, she had too many other things on her mind. She glanced at the big board that listed the flight numbers and the gates and started out at a run in the direction of the gate from which she knew he'd come. The flight had just landed. It would be only a minute or two before the passengers would deplane. She had just enough time to make it. First-class passengers always debarked first, and Marc always travelled first class.

She darted in and out between other travellers, almost stumbling over someone's bags. But she reached the area just as the first passengers were coming through customs, and with a sigh backed off into a corner to watch. For a mad moment she wanted to surprise him, to show him that she cared, despite her betrayal of the summer. But even in this ghastly time of agony over Pilar, she wanted to hold out something to Marc, to make it easier for him. She would simply walk up beside him with a touch of the hand and a smile. She could still do that for him, she could give him a moment of pleasure in the midst of so much pain. She pulled her jacket closer around her and looked down at the cravat on her ivory silk shirt. Seven or eight people had already walked past her, but there was still no sign of Marc.

Then suddenly she saw him, tall and thin and narrow and neat, impeccably orderly and well tailored, even after the flight. She noticed with surprise that he looked less distraught than she had feared. Obviously, he did not yet understand how serious things were, or maybe ... And then, as she took a step from her hiding place, Deanna felt her heart stop.

He was turning, with a slow, soft smile, the smile that called her *Diane* and not Deanna. She saw him reach out and take a young woman's hand. She was yawning sleepily, and he let his hand drift to her shoulder as he pulled her close. The woman said something and patted his arm. Deanna watched them in speechless stupefaction, wondering who the girl was, but not even really caring. What she had seen was the missing piece in the puzzle, the answer to so many years of questions in her life. This was no casual acquaintance, no girl he had picked up on the flight. This was someone he was comfortable with, familiar with, someone he knew well. The way they walked and spoke and moved and shared told Deanna everything.

She stood riveted to the floor in the corner, with her hand raised in horror to her barely open mouth, and watched them walking away from her down the concourse until she could no longer see them. Then, her head down, running, seeing no one, and wanting desperately not to be seen, she ran towards the exit and hailed a cab.

Chapter Sixteen

Feeling panic-stricken and out of breath, Deanna gave the cab driver the address of the hospital. She lay her head back against the seat and closed her eyes. She could hear her heart pounding in her ears. All she wanted was to get away, to put as many miles between herself and the airport as she could. There was a momentary feeling of madness, of being swept along by a wave, of having walked into someone else's bedroom and found him undressed, of having discovered what she had never been meant to see. But had she? Was it truly that? What if it was only a woman with whom he had shared the ride on the plane? What if her assumptions were crazy, her conclusions insane? No, there was more to it than that. She had known it the moment she had seen them. In her heart of hearts, she had simply known. But who was she? And how long had it been happening? A week? A month? A year? Was that what had happened this summer or was it something more? Much, much more ... ?

'*Voilà,* madame.' The driver turned to her with a backward glance at his meter. Deanna could barely hear. Her mind was running in fourteen directions at once. During the whole agonizing ride from the airport she hadn't thought even once of Ben. It didn't occur to her that she had done the same, all she knew was that she had seen her husband with another woman, and she still cared. Very much. She was blinded by the surprise and the pain.

'Madame?' The driver started at her as she looked again at the meter, glassy-eyed, vague.

'*Je m'excuse.*' She quickly handed him the money and got out, looking around. She was back at the hospital, but how had she gotten there? When had she told him that address? She had planned to go back to the apartment to collect her wits, but instead she had come here. It was just as well. Marc would be going home to drop off his things and see his mother, and then would finally come to Pilar. Deanna had bought a little more time. She was not yet ready to see him. Every time she thought of him, standing there, she saw the pretty young head leaning close to his, her hand on his arm, their eyes linked as he slipped an arm around her shoulders. And she looked so damn young. Deanna's eyes filled with tears as she pushed her way through the heavy glass doors and back into the hospital lobby. She took a deep breath. It already had a familiar smell. Without thinking, she felt her hand push the elevator button for the fourth floor. She had become a robot, an automated body without a mind: she could feel herself functioning, but she couldn't understand it. All she could think of was that face, next to Marc's. And he had looked so happy, so young...

'You'll be all right?' Marc looked at her with tired eyes as he picked up his coat. Chantal was lying on the bed.

'I will be fine. You have enough to think about without worrying about me.' But she knew that he hated it when she was tired. The doctor had warned him after her brush with death that she mustn't wear herself out. Ever since, Marc had been treating her like an overprotective papa with a delicate child. He wanted her to get lots of rest, eat well, and take care of herself so that the diabetes would never get out of hand and the dire possibilities the doctor had warned them of would never occur. 'Will *you* be all right?' She held her arms out to him. She hated to see him go, hated to know how little she could do for him. But she knew that she couldn't go to the hospital with him. Deanna would be there. It was one thing to insist upon being taken to Cap d'Antibes, to make a stand when everything was well, but it would have been madness for her to go with him now. This wasn't the time. Chantal understood that. Her timing had always been excellent. 'Will you call me and tell me how she is?' There was real concern in her eyes, and Marc was instantly grateful.

'As soon as I know anything. I promise. And darling ...' He sat down and held her close. 'Thank you. I – I couldn't have made the trip without you. This has been the most difficult night of my life.'

'She'll be all right, Marc-Edouard. I promise you.' He held her very tightly. When he pulled away, he wiped his eyes and cleared his throat.

'*J'espère.*' I hope.

'*Oui, oui. Je le sais.*'

But how could she know it? How did she know? And what if she were wrong?

'I'll be back later for my bag.'

'You'll wake me if I'm asleep?' It was a kittenish smile that lurked in her eyes, and he laughed.

'*On verra.*' But he had already left her, his mind was somewhere else. They had only gotten in from the airport ten minutes before, but already he felt as though he had lingered too long. He slipped into his raincoat.

'Marc-Edouard!' He stopped and turned at the sound of her voice. He was already at the door.

'*N'oublie pas que je t'aime ...*' Don't forget that I love you.

'*Moi aussi!*' The door closed soundlessly on his words.

He drove Chantal's tiny Renault to the hospital and parked down the street. He should have taken a taxi, but he didn't want to waste another moment. He wanted to be there. At her side. Seeing what had happened. Trying to understand. Coming back on the flight, he had run it over and over and over in his mind. The why and the how and the when, none of it making any sense. There were moments when it seemed as though nothing had happened, as though they were just going back to Paris as always after his business meetings in Greece ... and then suddenly it would all come crystal clear again and he would remember Pilar. He would never have been able to keep himself together on the flight back had it not been for Chantal.

The lobby was quiet. Dominique had already given him Pilar's room number when they spoke on the phone, and he himself had succeeded in getting through to Dr Kirschmann before he left Athens. It had been too soon to know anything. The damage to her skull was considerable, to her legs perhaps permanent; her spleen had been ruptured, one kidney bruised. She was, all in all, a very sick girl.

Marc felt his chest go tight as he entered the elevator and pressed four. His mind was a blank as the elevator ascended. Then, with a whir, the doors opened and he stepped out. He felt lost for a moment, powerless and afraid, as he glanced around him, wondering where to find his child. He saw the head nurse at the desk and sombrely approached her.

'Pilar Duras?' The nurse began to give him directions to the room. He held up a hand. '*D'abord*, how is she?'

'Critical, monsieur.' The nurse's eyes were grave.

'But any better than she has been?' In answer: only a shake of the head. 'And Dr Kirschmann? He's here?'

'He was and he has left again. He'll be back in a while. He's keeping a very close watch on the situation. She is completely monitored ... We're doing all that we can.'

This time Marc only nodded. He cleared his throat and dabbed at his eyes with his handkerchief as he marched purposefully down the hall. He had to pull himself together, show Pilar that everything would be all right, he would make her better, he would give her his strength. Chantal was forgotten, all that he had in his mind was his little girl.

The door was ajar, and he glanced inside. The room seemed to be filled with machines. There were two nurses, one in a sterile, green operating-room suit and the other in white. Their eyes searched his face. Soundlessly, he stepped inside.

'I am her father.' The whispered words had a ring of authority, and they both nodded as his eyes swept the room. He instantly found her, dwarfed by the bed and the tubes and the monitors that jumped with precision at her every breath. For a moment he felt a chill seize him as he looked at her face. She was a very pale grey and she looked like no one he knew, until he stepped closer and recognised the distorted features of his child. The tubes and the pain and the bandages had almost totally changed her, but it was his Pilar. He watched her for a long moment as she lay there with her eyes closed, and on silent feet he came nearer and ever so delicately reached out and touched her hand. The hand stirred only slightly. She opened her eyes. But there was no smile, and only the faintest look of recognition.

'Pilar, *ma chérie, c'est Papa.*' He had to fight back tears. He said nothing more, he only stood there, staring at her, holding her hand, and watching until once again she closed the brilliant blue eyes. He felt as though all the air in the room had been sucked away, it was so difficult to think and see and breathe. How could this happen? How? And to his child? He felt his knees tremble, and for a moment he thought he would be sick, but he went on standing, watching, and touching the pale little hand. Even her nails were a strange mottled colour, she was barely getting enough air. But he stood there, and he stood there, never moving, never speaking, only watching his child.

Silently, from her seat in the corner, Deanna watched him. She had said nothing when he entered the room, and he hadn't seen her, concealed as she was by the mammoth machines.

It was almost twenty minutes later when at last he found the familiar face and those eyes ... watching him with a look of despair. He looked surprised when he saw her, as though he didn't understand. Why had she said nothing? Why did she just sit there? When had she come? Or was it simply that she was in shock? She looked ravaged, almost as pale as Pilar.

'Deanna ...' It was the merest whisper.

Her eyes never left his face. 'Hello, Marc.'

He nodded and let his gaze drift back to Pilar. 'When did you get here?'

'At five o'clock.'

'You've been here all night?'

'Yes.'

'Any change?'

There was silence. Marc looked at her again, the question repeated in his eyes.

'She seems to be a little worse. I went out for a little while, earlier ... I had to ... I went to your mother's house to drop off my bag. I was only gone for about two hours, and ... and when I came back, she seemed to be having a great deal of trouble breathing. Kirschmann was here then. He said that if she's not better in a few hours, they'll want to operate again.' She sighed and lowered her eyes. It was as though she had lost them both in those two hours. Pilar and Marc.

'I just got in.'

Liar. You didn't. You got in two hours ago. Where did you go? But Deanna said nothing at all.

They stayed that way for almost an hour, until finally the nurse asked them to step outside, just for a few minutes; there were some dressings that had to be changed. Slowly Deanna stood up and left the room. Marc had hung back for a moment, reluctant to leave his child. Deanna's mind wandered back to the scene at the airport. It was suddenly all so strange. She hadn't

186

seen him in two months, yet they had barely said hello. She couldn't play the game of the happy reunion. Suddenly it was too late. But he wasn't playing it either, or perhaps he was just too distraught over Pilar.

She wandered down the hall, solemnly, her head bowed, thinking of bits of prayers she had known as a child. She had no time now to waste on Marc; all her energies had to be spent on Pilar. She heard his steps just behind her, but she didn't turn; she merely kept walking, foot after foot after foot, down the hall until she reached the end, and stood staring blankly out a window with only a view of a nearby wall. She could see him standing behind her as she gazed at the reflection in the glass.

'Deanna, can I help?' He sounded tired, subdued. She shook her head slowly. 'I don't know what to say.' His voice caught as he began to cry. 'I was wrong to give her the ... to ...'

'It doesn't matter now. You did it. It's done. It could have happened in any of ten thousand ways. She had an accident, Marc. What difference does it make now whose fault the accident was, who gave her the motorcycle, who ...' Deanna's own voice was shaky.

'*Mon Dieu* ...' She watched him drop his face into his hands and then she saw him straighten and heard him take a deep breath. 'My God, if only she'll come out of it all right. What if she can't walk?'

'Then we'll teach her to live the best way she can. That's what we owe her now. Our love, our help, our support, in whatever she has to face ...' *If only we get that chance*. For the first time in almost twenty years, Deanna felt a hideous wave of terror ... *What if?*

Deanna felt his hands on her shoulders, then he turned her slowly around. His eyes were the eyes of Pilar, and his face was that of a very old, tired man.

'Will you ever forgive me?'

'For what?' Her voice was distant and cold.

'For this. For what I've done to our child. For not listening to you when I should have. For —'

'I came to pick you up at the airport tonight, Marc.'

Something in her eyes told him that she had died, and he felt something inside him freeze. 'You must have just missed me.' But there was a question in his voice. He searched her face.

'No. I left. I ... it explained a great deal to me, Marc. I should have known. A long time ago. But I didn't.' She smiled a tiny smile, then shrugged. 'I suppose I've been a fool. And may I congratulate you. She looks not only pretty, but young.' There was bitterness as well as sorrow in her voice.

'Deanna,' the hands on her shoulders tightened, 'you're coming to some very strange conclusions. I don't think you understand.' But it all sounded lame. He was too tired and upset to come up with a worthwhile story. He felt his life coming down around his ears. 'It was a nerve-racking flight, and this has been an incredible day, you know that yourself. The young lady and I began to talk and really —'

'Marc, stop. I don't want to hear it.' She simply knew. That was all. And she didn't want reassurances in the form of lies. 'Please. Not tonight.'

'Deanna ...' But he couldn't go on. Another time he might have been able to, but not then. He simply couldn't concoct an appropriate tale. 'Please.' He turned away then; he couldn't look at the pain in her eyes. 'It really isn't what you think.' But he hated himself for the words. It was what she thought, every bit of it. And now he felt traitorous, denying Chantal. Whichever way he turned, he was damned now. 'It isn't.'

'It is, Marc. It was as clear as day. Nothing you could tell me now would change that. Nothing would take away what I saw, what I felt, what I knew.' It had been like an arrow, straight to her heart. 'You must have thought me very stupid for all these years.'

'What makes you think it has been years?' *Dammit,* how did she know?

'The way you moved together, the way you walked, the way she looked at you. It's difficult to achieve that kind of ease in a very short time. You looked more married with her than you ever did with me.' But suddenly she wondered. Hadn't she looked just as married with Ben? And in a very short time. Still, as she had ridden back from the airport that evening, she had known – the absences, the distance, the constant trips, the phone number in Paris that appeared too often on their bill, the few odd stories that had never quite fit. And tonight, the look in his eyes. If it hadn't been that girl, it had been someone. For years. She was sure.

'What do you want me to say?' He faced her again.

'Nothing. There is nothing left to say.'

'Are you telling me it's over? That you'd leave me because you saw me at the airport with a girl? But that's insane. Deanna, you're mad.'

'Am I? Are we so happy together? Do you enjoy my company, Marc? Do you long to come home when you're away? Or is it that we have a deep and meaningful relationship, that we respect each other's needs and virtues and feelings? Maybe it's that we're so blissfully happy with each other, after all these years –'

'Maybe it's that I still love you.' As he said it, his eyes filled with tears, and she turned her head.

'It doesn't matter if you do.' It was too late now. They had each gone their separate ways.

'What are you saying, Deanna?' He was suddenly grey.

'I'm not entirely sure. First let's get through this with Pilar. After that we can talk about us.'

'We'll make it. I know we will.' He looked at her with determination, and she felt fatigue wash over her like a wave of cement.

'What makes you think so? Why should we make it?'

'Because I want to.' But he didn't sound totally sure.

'Really? Why? Because you like having a wife as well as a mistress? I can hardly blame you. That must be a very cosy arrangement. Where does she live, Marc? Over here? That must work out perfectly.' And that was why he hadn't wanted her to join him on the trip to Greece.

'Deanna, stop it!' He reached out and grabbed her arm, but she pulled away.

'Leave me alone.' For the first time in her life, she hated him, what he was, what he did to her, and all that he didn't understand, and for one painful, blinding moment she found herself longing for Ben. But was Marc really so bad? Was she any different, any better? Her mind was in a whirl. 'I don't want to discuss this with you tonight. We have enough on our minds. We can discuss it when Pilar is out of the woods.'

He nodded, relieved. He needed time. He had to think. He'd find the right words to say. He would set things right.

Almost at that instant the nurse beckoned to them both from down the hall, and their own problems were forgotten as they hurried towards her.

'Is there any change?' Marc was the first to ask.

'No. But she's awake. And she's asking for both of you. Why don't you talk to her a little, but be careful not to wear her out. She needs the little strength that she has.'

Deanna noticed a subtle change in Pilar as they entered the room. Her colour was no better, but her eyes seemed more alive. They seemed to wander nervously from one face to another, looking for someone, searching, darting here and there.

'Hello, sweetheart. We're right here. Papa's here now too.' Deanna stood very close to her and ever so gently stroked her hand. When she closed her eyes, she could imagine that Pilar was still a very small child.

'That ... feels ... nice ...' Pilar's gaze drifted to her father and she tried to smile, but her breathing was laboured and she closed her eyes from time to time. 'Hi, Papa ... How ... was ... Greece?' She seemed much more aware of current events than she had been earlier, and suddenly she also seemed more restless. 'I'm ... thirsty ...'

Deanna glanced at the nurse, who shook her head and made a sign with her finger: 'No.'

'Water?'

'In a little while, sweetheart.' Deanna went on talking in a soothing voice while Marc stood near her, agonized. He seemed to have lost his power to speak, and Deanna could see from his full eyes and trembling lip that he was waging a constant battle with tears.

'*Ça va?*' At last he had spoken, and again Pilar tried to smile.

She nodded gently. '*Ça va.*' But how could anything be O.K. in the condition she was in? Then, as though she understood what he was going through, she looked pointedly at him and fought to find the words. 'I ... was going ... much too fast ... My fault, Papa ... not yours ...' She closed her eyes and squeezed Deanna's hand. 'I'm sorry.'

The tears now ran freely down Marc's face. Quietly he turned away. Pilar's eyes remained closed.

'Don't worry, darling. It doesn't matter whose fault. But your mother was right.' He glanced at Deanna.

'Mommy ... ?' Her voice seemed to be growing weaker.

'Shh. Don't talk ...'

'Remember the little playhouse I used to have ... in the garden? I keep dreaming ... of that ... and my little dog. Augustin.'

He had been a funny little terrier, Deanna remembered, who had been replaced by a pug, and then a cat, and then a bird, until finally there were no more pets. Marc-Edouard did not like animals in his house.

'Where ... did you send ... Augustin?' They had given him to a family in the country.

'He went to the country. I think he was very happy.' Deanna pattered on, but now her eyes sought Marc's. What did this mean? Was she better or worse? She was reminded suddenly of the tiny baby boy who had moved so much in her arms in the few hours before he died. Philippe-Edouard. Was this the same, or was this a sign that she was improving? Neither of them knew.

'Mommy? ... could I have ... Augustin back? ... You ask Papa ...' It was the voice of the child now. Deanna closed her eyes and took a quick breath.

'I'll talk to Papa.'

Marc's eyes were suddenly filled with fear. He looked at Pilar, and then Deanna. 'We'll get you a dog, *chérie* ... You'll see. A wonderful little dog with floppy ears and a very waggly tail.' He was looking for anything he could find in his head, just to find the words to put in his mouth.

'But I want ... Augustin.' The voice was plaintive now, and the nurse signalled them away. Pilar had drifted off again and she didn't notice them leaving the room.

This time they paced up and down the hall, at first saying nothing. Without thinking, Deanna reached for Marc's hand. 'When the hell is Kirschmann coming back?'

'They said soon. Do you think she's worse?'

Deanna nodded. 'She seems nervous, fidgety, anxious.'

'But she's talking. That might be a hopeful sign.'

'Maybe it is,' Deanna said. But there was terror in both their hearts. As they paced the hall, his arm slipped around her shoulders, and she didn't fight him away. Suddenly she needed him there, as he needed her. He was the only person who understood, who could share what she felt, who *knew*.

'Marc?' He looked at her with anguished eyes, but she only shook her head. Tears poured down her face, and silently he took her into his arms. He had nothing to say, no words of comfort, only his tears to add to hers.

They walked the long hall again, end to end, seven or eight more times, and finally sat down on two straight-backed chairs. Deanna's eyes were glazed with fatigue. She stared at the hem of her much creased cream skirt.

'Do you remember when she was five and we got her that dog?' She smiled to herself as she remembered. They had hidden the little puppy in a boot and left him in Pilar's closet, ordering her to immediately open the door and pick up her clothes. And there he had been, peeking out of the boot. Pilar had squealed with delight.

Marc smiled to himself too, with the memory. 'I will always remember her face.'

'So will I.' Deanna looked up at him, smiling through her tears and reached for his handkerchief to blow her nose. It was strange. Only an hour before they'd been fighting and she'd been hinting at divorce. But it didn't matter now. Their marriage was no longer what mattered, only their child. Whatever pain had passed between them, they still shared Pilar. At that precise moment Marc was the only person who had any idea what she felt, and she was the only living soul who shared his terror with him. It was as if they held each other very tightly and didn't let go, and kept moving and kept talking and hoping and praying ... then Pilar would still be there, she couldn't die. Deanna looked up at Marc again, and he patted her hand.

'Try to relax.'

She sighed again and put a hand over her eyes, but before she could speak, the nurse was at their side.

'Doctor Kirschmann would like to see you. He's in with her now.'

They leaped to their feet and almost ran to the room, where he stood at the foot of the bed, alternately watching the girl and the machines. It seemed hours before they walked out to the hall.

'*Docteur?*' Marc was the first to speak.

He looked grieved. 'I want to give her a little more time. If things aren't looking better in an hour, we'll take her back to the operating room and see what we can do.'

'What do you think?' Marc wanted words from him, promises, guarantees.

'I don't know. She's holding on. I can't tell you more than that.' He could have told them how good her chances were, but they weren't, so he didn't volunteer the odds. 'Do you want to sit with her for a while?'

'Yes.' Deanna spoke first and reclaimed her post near Pilar's head. Marc joined her.

They stood there like that for almost an hour, while Pilar slept, making strange sounds, now and then stirring, and seeming to fight for breath. Marc rested one hand on the bed, feeling the little frail body near him, his eyes never leaving her face. Deanna held her hand and waited. For something ... for hope. The hour was almost over when at last she woke.

'Thirsty ...'

'In a little while, darling.' Deanna's words were a gentle whisper caressed by a smile. She touched the girl's forehead with an infinitely light hand. 'In a while, my love. Now sleep. Mommy and Papa are here, darling. Sleep ... you're going to feel so much better, very soon.'

And then Pilar smiled. It was a real smile, despite the tubes, and it tore at Marc's and Deanna's hearts.

'I feel ... better ... now.'

'I'm glad, *chérie*. And you'll feel much better tomorrow. Mommy is right.' Marc's voice was as soft as a summer breeze. Once again Pilar smiled and closed her eyes.

It was only a moment later when the doctor stepped back in and nodded for them to go out.

He whispered to them as they left. 'We'll prepare her for surgery now. You can step back in in just a moment.' He turned, and they went outside. Deanna felt breathless now too, as though like Pilar she had to fight for air. The hallway was at the same time too cold and too stuffy, and she had to hold on to Marc for support. It was four o'clock in the morning, and neither of them had slept in two days.

'She said she felt better.' Marc held out the slim hope and Deanna nodded. 'I thought her colour was a little better too.'

Deanna was about to say something but Dr Kirschmann reappeared, coming down the length of the hall.

'*Merde*. He ought to be spending his time with Pilar, dammit. Not looking for us.' Marc began to walk towards him, but Deanna stopped. She already knew and clutched Marc's arm. She knew, and she could walk no further. The world had just ended. Pilar was dead.

Chapter Seventeen

The sun was just coming up as they left the hospital. It had taken more than an hour to sign the papers and make the arrangements. Marc had decided that he wanted the funeral held in France. Deanna didn't care. One of her babies was buried in California, the other in France. It didn't matter to her now. And she suspected that Pilar herself would have preferred it. Dr Kirschmann had been sympathetic and kind. There had been nothing for him to do. She had been much too far gone when they brought her in from the South of France. The blow to her head had been too severe, and he marvelled only that she hadn't died in the moments after the accident. 'Ahh ... motorcycles!' he said as Marc visibly cringed.

They had been offered coffee, which they had refused, and finally they were through. Marc took her arm and guided her gently towards the street. She felt as though her brain had ceased to function within the last hour. She couldn't think, couldn't move, couldn't even feel. She had gone through all the formalities mechanically, but she felt as though she too had died.

Marc walked her to the little blue Renault and unlocked the door.

'Whose car is this?' It was a strange question to ask on a morning like that, but her eyes stared at him almost blindly as she spoke.

'It doesn't matter, get in. Let's go home.' He had never felt so tired, or so lost, or alone. All his hopes had been dashed, all his joys, all his dreams. It didn't even matter to him now that he had Deanna, and Chantal. He had lost Pilar. The tears rolled slowly down his face again as he started the car, and this time he let them flow unchecked. He didn't care.

In her seat Deanna put her head back and closed her eyes, feeling a knot in her chest and a lump in her throat. There was a lifetime of crying lodged there, but for the moment it wouldn't come out.

They drove slowly through Paris, as street cleaners swept and the sun shone too brightly on the pavement. It should have been a day of rain and heavy mist, but it wasn't, and the bright sun made the horror seem a lie. How could she be gone on a day like this? But she was ... she was – gone. The thought kept running through Marc-Edouard's head – gone – while Deanna stared unseeingly out of the window.

The maid was already at the door when they reached the Duras apartment, still draped in her bathrobe. She had heard the elevator and come running to know. Marc-Edouard's face said it all. Silently she began to cry.

'Shall I wake Madame?'

Marc shook his head. There was no point, waking her now. The bad news could wait.

'Some coffee, monsieur?'

This time he nodded and softly closed the door as Deanna stood by, feeling lost. He looked at her for a moment, wiped his eyes, and held out a hand. Without saying more, she took it, and they walked slowly to their room.

The shades were drawn, the shutters were closed, the bed was turned down, but somehow Deanna did not want to go to bed. She couldn't face it, couldn't bear lying there and thinking, couldn't bear knowing that Pilar was dead. Marc-Edouard sank into a chair and put his face in his hands. Slowly the sobs came again. Deanna went to him and held his shoulders in her hands, but there was nothing more she could do. At last he cried himself out, and she helped him to the bed.

'You should try to sleep.' She whispered it to him as she had to Pilar.

'And you?' His voice was hoarse when he spoke.

'I will. Later. Didn't you bring a bag?' She looked around the room in surprise. None of his things was there.

'I'll get it later.' He closed his eyes. Picking up his bag meant seeing Chantal. He would have to tell her about Pilar. As he would have to tell his mother. And their friends. He couldn't bear it. Telling them would make it real. The tears seeped out of the corners of his eyes again. Finally, he drifted to sleep.

Only Deanna drank the coffee when it came. She took her cup to the salon, where she sat alone, looking out over the rooftops of Paris, thinking of her child. She felt peaceful as she sat there, thinking, looking at the gilt-edged morning sky. Pilar had been so many things, and not often easy in recent years, but eventually she would have grown up. They would have been friends ... *Would have been.* It was hard to imagine. She felt as though Pilar were right there, nearby, and in no way lost. It was inconceivable to her that they would no longer talk, or laugh, or argue, that Pilar would no longer fling that long golden hair like a mane, or flash those blue eyes to get whatever she might want, that Deanna's slippers would no longer be borrowed, her lipstick wouldn't be gone, her favourite robe wouldn't disappear along with her best coat ... As she thought of it, the tears finally came in great waves. She knew, finally, that Pilar was no more.

'Deanna?' It was the old woman, standing in the centre of the room, looking like a statue in an icy-blue robe. 'Pilar?'

Deanna shook her head and closed her eyes. Madame Duras steadied herself on a chair.

'Oh, my God. Oh, *bon Dieu ... bon Dieu.*' And then, looking around, tears rolling down her cheeks: 'Where is Marc?'

'Asleep, I think. In bed.' Her mother-in-law nodded

and silently left the room. There was nothing she could say, but Deanna hated her once more for not even trying. It was her loss too, but she owed Deanna the words at least.

On tiptoe Deanna walked back to their room. She was afraid to wake Marc and she opened the door very quietly. He was still sleeping, snoring softly. This time, as she watched him, he no longer looked young. His whole face seemed to sag with grief and even in sleep Deanna could see that he wasn't at peace.

She sat for a time, watching him, wondering what would happen, what they would do. A great deal had changed in a day. Pilar. The woman she had seen him with at the airport. She realised now that was probably where he had gotten the car and where he had left his bag. She wanted to hate him for it, but now she didn't care. She suddenly realised she had to call Ben. A glance at Marc's watch told her that it was past eight-thirty. It would be midnight in San Francisco. He might still be up, and she had to call him now, while she could.

She ran a hand over her hair, put her jacket on again, and grabbed her handbag. She would make the call half a block away at the post office where Parisian residents without telephones made their calls. She didn't want his number on her mother-in-law's bill.

She felt numb as she rode downstairs in the tiny elevator and then walked the half block to the *poste*. She could not move her feet quickly and she couldn't slow her steps either; she just kept moving at the same pace, like a machine, until she reached the post office phone booth and closed the door.

The number rang only twice, and the connection had been rapidly made. She felt herself tremble as she waited, and then she heard his voice. He sounded sleepy, and she realised then that he had already been in bed.

'Ben?'

'Deanna? Darling, are you all right?'

'I ...' And then the words stopped. She couldn't say more.

'Deanna?'

She was trembling violently, still unable to speak.

'Oh, darling ... is it ... ? How bad is she? I've been thinking of you every minute, ever since you left.' The only sound Deanna made in answer was a short convulsed sob. 'Deanna! Please, sweetheart, try to calm down and talk to me.' But suddenly a ripple of fear raced up his back. 'My God, is she ... Deanna?' His voice was suddenly very soft.

'Oh, Ben, she died this morning.' For another endless moment she couldn't speak after she said the words.

'Oh, God, no. Darling, are you alone? Where are you?'

'In the post office.'

'Oh, for God's sake, what are you doing there?'

'I wanted to call you.'

'Did ... is he in Paris too?'

'Yes.' She tried to catch her breath again. 'He got here last night.'

'I'm so sorry. For both of you.'

She sobbed again. With Ben she could let herself go, she could reach out to him and show him how badly she needed him. With Marc she always kept up a front. She had to live what he expected, be what he thought she should be.

'Do you want me to come over? I could take the first plane out in the morning.'

And do what? she wondered. It was too late for Pilar. 'I'd love you to, but it doesn't make much sense. I'll be home in a couple of days.'

'Are you sure? I don't want to be a problem, but I'll come over right away if it'll help. Would it?'

'Very much.' She smiled through her tears. 'But it's better not to.'

'And ... everything else?' He tried not to sound concerned or upset.

'I don't know. We'll have to talk.'

He knew she was talking about Marc. 'Well, don't worry about all that now. Just get through this, and then we can worry about the rest. Is it ... are you going to have it here?'

'The funeral?' She wanted to die when she said the word. Her hand shook terribly. She tightened her grip on the phone. 'No, Marc wants it here. It doesn't matter. I think Pilar probably would have preferred it too. In any case I'll be home in two or three days.'

'I wish I could spare you all that.'

'It ...' but she couldn't go on for a moment, '... doesn't matter. I'll be all right.' But would she? She wasn't so sure. She had never felt this shaky in her life.

'Well, remember, if you need me I'll come. I won't go anywhere for the next few days without leaving a number, so you can always reach me. O.K.?'

'O.K.' She tried to smile as she said it, but the effort made her cry more. 'Can you ... could you call ...'

'Kim?'

'Yes.' It was a sad little croak.

'I'll call right away. Now I want you to go home and get some rest. Darling, you can't keep pushing. You have to rest. Go get some sleep. And as soon as you come home, we'll go to Carmel. No matter what. I don't care what happens after that, but you're coming to Carmel with me. We'll walk on the beach, and we'll be together.'

She was sobbing violently now. They would never be together again. She'd never walk on that beach again, or any other. She would be trapped in this nightmare forever, alone.

'Deanna, listen to me,' Ben was saying. 'Will you think of Carmel through all this, and try to remember that I love you?'

She nodded sadly, still unable to get out the words.

'My love, I'm with you every moment. Be strong, my darling. I love you.'

'I love you too.' But her voice was only a whisper as she hung up the phone, then walked to the counter and paid the woman at the desk for the phone call – and passed out cold on the floor.

Chapter Eighteen

'Where on earth have you been?' Marc was sitting in the living room looking rumpled and haggard when she returned. 'You were gone for hours.' It was an accusation. He was staring at her, red-eyed, over a cup of coffee. She looked scarcely better, in fact considerably worse. 'Where were you?'

'I went for a walk. I'm sorry. I needed some air.' She put her handbag down on a chair. 'How is your mother?'

'You can imagine. I called the doctor half an hour ago, and he gave her a shot. She probably won't wake up until noon.'

For a moment Deanna envied her. What an easy way out. She didn't voice the thought. Instead, she asked, 'And you?'

'We have a lot to do today.' He looked at her mournfully and then noticed the smudges on her skirt. 'What happened? Did you fall?'

She nodded and looked away. 'I must have been tired. I stumbled. It's nothing.'

He came to her then and put an arm around her. 'You should really go to bed.'

'I will. But what about the arrangements?'

'I'll take care of it. You don't have to do anything.'

'But I want to ...' She suddenly felt out of control again, as though she never had any say.

'No. I want you to get some sleep.' He led her to the bedroom and sat her on the bed. 'Shall I call the doctor for you?' She shook her head, then lay down, looking up at him with heartbroken eyes that tore at him. 'Deanna ...'

'What about your friend?'

He stood up and turned away. 'Never mind that.'

'Maybe now isn't the time, but sooner or later we'll have to talk about it.'

'Perhaps not.'

'What does that mean?' She stared at him very hard. He turned to face her.

'It means that it's not your affair. And that I will do my best to settle it.'

'Permanently?'

He seemed to hesitate a long time, and then he quietly nodded, his eyes never leaving hers. 'Yes.'

Chantal heard his key turn in the lock as she climbed out of the shower. She hadn't dared call the house on the rue François Premier, and her last anonymous call to the hospital had brought only the information that Pilar was the same. She had intended to call again as soon as she had coffee, but Marc-Edouard arrived first, looking as though he hadn't slept all night. Chantal looked up and smiled from the bathroom doorway. The pale yellow towel was drying her leg.

'*Bonjour, mon chéri.* How's Pilar?' She stood up with a serious expression, holding the towel in one hand. There was something in his eyes that suddenly frightened her. He closed them and covered them for a moment with one hand. It seemed a very long time before he looked at her again.

'She – she's gone. At four o'clock this morning.' He sat down heavily in a chair in the living room, and Chantal came to him quickly, pulling a pale pink robe off a hook on the bathroom wall.

'Oh, Marc-Edouard ... oh, darling, I'm so sorry.' She knelt beside him and pulled him gently into her arms, encircling his shoulders and holding him tight like a child. '*Oh, mon pauvre chéri*, Marc-Edouard. *Quelle horreur* ...'

This time he didn't cry, he only sat with his eyes closed, feeling relieved to be there.

She wanted to ask him if something else was wrong.

It was an insanely stupid question, given what had happened that morning, but he seemed odd to her, different, strange. Perhaps it was only exhaustion and the shock. She let go of him only long enough to pour him a cup of coffee, and then sat down again at his feet, her body curled on the white rug, the pink bathrobe concealing only the essentials and leaving long silky legs bare. He was staring at her as she lit a cigarette. 'Is there anything I can do?'

He shook his head. 'Chantal, Deanna saw us last night. She came to the airport to pick me up, and she saw us both get off the plane. And she knew. Everything. Women are uncanny that way. She said she knew by the way we moved that we had known each other for a long time.'

'She must be a very intelligent woman.' Chantal studied him, wondering what he would say next.

'She is, in her own quiet way.'

'And? What did she say?'

'Not too much. Yet. Too much has been happening, but she's an American. She doesn't take this kind of thing well. None of them do. They believe in eternal fidelity, the perfect marriage, husbands who wash the dishes, children who wash the car, and everyone goes to church together on Sunday and lives happily ever after until they're all a hundred and nine.' He sounded bitter and tired.

'And you? Do you believe that?'

'It's a nice dream anyway. But not very real. You know that as well as I do.'

'*Alors*, what do we do? Or, more exactly, what do you do?' She didn't want to ask, 'her or me', but it amounted to that and they both knew it.

'It's too soon to know, Chantal. Look at what has just happened. And she is in terrible condition; it's all bottled up inside.'

'It's still fresh.'

He nodded agreement and looked away. He had

come here to say goodbye to Chantal, to end it, to explain that he couldn't do this to Deanna – they had just lost their only child. But as he looked at her, as he sat next to her, all he wanted was to reach out and pull her into his arms, to run his hands over her body, to hold her close, now and forever, again and again. How could he let go of what he loved and needed so much?

'What are you thinking about, Marc-Edouard?' She could see the look of torment on his face.

'About you.' He said it very softly, looking down at his hands.

'In what way?'

'I was thinking,' he looked up into her eyes again, 'that I love you, and that right now I want more than anything to make love to you.'

She sat watching him for a long moment, then she stood up and held out a hand. He took it and followed her silently into the bedroom. She smiled as he slipped the pink robe off her shoulders.

'Chantal, you will never know how much I love you.'

For the next two hours he showed her in every way he knew how.

Chapter Nineteen

The funeral was brief and formal and agonizing. Deanna wore a plain black woollen dress and a little black hat with a veil. Marc's mother was dressed all in black with black stockings. Marc himself wore a dark suit and black tie. It was all done in the most formal of French traditions in a pretty little church in the *seizième arrondissement*, and the 'Ave Maria' was sung by the parish-school choir. It was heartbreaking, as the children's voices soared over the notes, and Deanna desperately tried not to hear. But there was no avoiding any of it. Marc had done it all *à la française* – the service, the music, the eulogy, the little country cemetery with yet another priest, and then the gathering of friends and relatives at the house. It was an all-day enterprise, with endless rounds of handshaking and regrets, explanations and shared sorrows. To some it was undoubtedly a relief to mourn that way, to Deanna it was not. Once more she felt that Pilar had been stolen from her, only now it really didn't matter any more. This was the very last time. She even called Ben collect from the house.

'I'm sorry. I won't stay on long. I just needed to talk to you. I'm at the house.'

'Are you holding up?'

'I don't know. I think I'm numb. It's all like a circus. I even had to fight them about an open coffin. Thank God, at least that battle I won.'

He didn't like the sound of her voice. She sounded nervous, tired, and strained. But it was hardly surprising under the circumstances. 'When are you coming back?'

'Sometime in the next two days, I hope. But I'm not sure. We'll discuss it tonight.'

'Just send me a wire when you know.'

She heaved a small sigh. 'I will. I guess I'd better get back to the ghoulish festivities now.'

'I love you, Deanna.'

'So do I.' She was afraid to say the words, lest someone walk into the room, but she knew he'd understand.

She went back to the fifty or sixty guests who were milling around her mother-in-law's rooms, chatting, gossiping, discussing Pilar, consoling Marc. Deanna had never felt as much a stranger as now. It seemed hours since she had seen Marc. He found her at last in the kitchen, staring out a window, at a wall.

'Deanna? What are you doing out here?'

'Nothing.' Her big sorrowful eyes looked into his. He was actually looking better. And day by day she seemed to look worse. She wasn't feeling well either, but she hadn't mentioned that to Marc, or the fact that she had fainted twice in the past four days. 'I'm just out here catching my breath.'

'I'm sorry it's been such a long day. My mother wouldn't have understood if we'd done it differently.'

'I know. I understand.'

Suddenly, looking at him, she realised that he understood too, and that he could see what a toll it was taking on her. 'Marc, when are we going home?'

'To San Francisco?' he asked. She nodded. 'I don't know. I haven't given it any thought. Are you in a hurry?'

'I just want to get back. It's ... harder for me here.'

'*Bon*. But I have work I must complete here. I need at least another two weeks.'

Oh, God, no. She couldn't survive two more weeks there under her mother-in-law's roof – and without Ben. 'There's no reason why I should stay, is there?'

'What do you mean? You want to go home alone?' He looked distressed. 'I don't want you to do that. I want you to go home with me.' He had already thought about it. It would be too hard for her to face the house alone: Pilar's room, all her things. He didn't want that. She'd have to wait for him.

'I can't wait two weeks.' She looked frantic at the idea, and he noticed again how exhausted and overwrought she was.

'Let's just see.'

'Marc, I have to go home.' Her voice trembled as it rose.

'All right. But first, would you do something for me?'

'What?' She looked at him strangely. What did he want? All she wanted was to get away.

'Will you go away with me for two days? Anywhere, for a weekend. Someplace quiet, where we both can rest. We need to talk. We haven't been able to here, and I don't want you to go back until we do talk. Quietly. Alone. Will you do that for me?'

She waited for a long moment and looked at him. 'I don't know.'

'Please. It's all I ask. Only that. Two days, and then you can go.'

She turned away to stare out at the rooftops again. She was thinking of Ben and Carmel. But she had no right to rush home to him just to make herself feel better. She owed something to their marriage, even if it was only two days. She turned to look at Marc and slowly nodded. 'All right. I'll go.'

Chapter Twenty

'*Merde alors!* What do you expect of me? My daughter dies three days ago, and you want me to announce to Deanna that I want a divorce? Doesn't that seem a little hasty to you, Chantal? And has it occurred to you that you're taking unfair advantage of this situation?' He felt torn between two women, two worlds. Once again he felt an odd kind of pressure from Chantal, a kind of emotional blackmail that told him there would be tragedy if Chantal suffered a loss. Both women wanted him to make a choice, a painful choice. He'd realised that all the more this week. Deanna seemed as though she would be only too happy to leave him right now. She had yet to forgive him for what she had seen at the airport the night of Pilar's death. But he didn't want to lose Deanna. She was his wife, he needed her, he respected her, he was used to her. And she was his last link to Pilar. Leaving Deanna would be like leaving home. But he couldn't give up Chantal either – she was his excitement, his passion, his joy. He looked at Chantal now with exasperation and ran a hand through his hair. 'Can't you understand? It's too soon!'

'It's been five years. And now she knows. And maybe it isn't too soon. Maybe it's the best time right now.'

'For whom? For you? Dammit, Chantal, just be a little bit patient. Let me sort things out.'

'And how long will that take? Another five years, while you live there and I live here? You were supposed to go back in two weeks, and then what? What about me? I sit here waiting for two months until you return? *Et alors?* I was twenty-five when we met, now I'm nearly thirty. And then I'll be thirty-five, and thirty-seven and forty-five. Time passes quickly. Especially like this. It goes much, much too fast.'

He knew that was true, but he was simply not in the mood. 'Look, could we just put this away for a while? Out of simple decency, I'd like to let the woman recover from the loss of her daughter before I destroy her life.' For a moment he hated Chantal. Because he did care, because he didn't want to lose her – and because that gave her the upper hand.

And she knew it. 'What makes you think your leaving her would destroy her life? Maybe she has a lover.'

'Deanna? Don't be ridiculous. In fact I think you're being absurd about this whole thing. I'm going away for the weekend. We have a lot of things to discuss. I'll talk to her, I'll see how things are. And in a while I'll make the right move.'

'What move is that?'

He sighed imperceptibly and suddenly felt very old. It had come to this. 'The one you want.'

But as he hailed a cab two hours later to go back to his mother's apartment where Deanna was waiting, he found himself wondering. Why did Chantal have to pull this on him? First the arguments over Cap d'Antibes, then that terrible night he had returned to find her gone – perhaps forever – when she had stopped taking her insulin. And now this. But why? Why now? For an odd reason he did not understand, it made him want to rush back to Deanna and protect her from a world that was about to be very cruel.

They left for the country in the morning. Deanna was strangely quiet as they drove out of town. She sat lost in her own thoughts. He had wanted to take her some place neutral, where there wouldn't be a cascade of memories of Pilar. They both had enough of that to deal with at his mother's house. A friend had offered his country house, near Dreux.

He glanced over at Deanna distractedly and then shifted his concentration back to the road, but he found himself thinking of Chantal again. He had spoken to her that morning before they left:

'Will you tell her this weekend?'

'I don't know. I'll have to see. If I drive her to a nervous breakdown, it won't do any of us any good.' But Chantal had sounded petulant and childish. Suddenly, after so many years of patience, she was getting out of hand. Still she had been the mainstay of his life for the past five years. He couldn't give her up. But could he so easily give up Deanna? He glanced over at her again. Her eyes were still closed and she hadn't said a word. Did he love her? He had always thought so, but after the summer with Chantal he wasn't as sure. It was impossible to know, to figure it out, to understand – and damn Chantal for pushing him now. He had promised Deanna only two days ago that he would end the relationship with Chantal, and now he had made the same promise to his mistress about Deanna.

'Is it very far?' Deanna's eyes fluttered open, but she did not move her head. She felt weighed down by the same exhaustion that had plagued her for days.

'No. It's about an hour. And it's a pretty house. I haven't stayed there since I was a boy, but it was always lovely.' He smiled at her. There were circles under her eyes. 'You know, you look awfully tired.'

'I know. Maybe this weekend I'll get some rest.'

'Didn't you get some sleeping pills from my mother's doctor?' He had told her to the last time the man had come to the house.

She shook her head. 'I'll work it out for myself.' He made a face, and for the first time, she smiled.

They arrived before she spoke again. It was indeed a beautiful place, an old stone house of considerable grandeur and proportion, almost in the style of a château, surrounded by magnificently manicured gardens. In the distance were fruit orchards that stretched for miles.

'It's pretty, isn't it?' He said it tentatively, and their eyes met.

'Very. Thank you for arranging this.' Then as he reached for the bags, she spoke again, barely audibly. 'I'm glad we came.'

'So am I.' He looked at her very cautiously, and they both smiled.

He carried the bags into the house and set them down in the main hall. The furniture was mostly English and French Provincial, and everything in the rooms was faithful to the seventeenth century when the house had been built. Deanna wandered down the long halls, looking at the beautifully inlaid floors and glancing out the tall windows into the gardens. She stopped at last at the end of the corridor, in a solarium filled with plants and comfortable chairs. She sat down in one and stared silently out at the grounds. It was a while before she heard Marc's footsteps echoing down the hall.

'Deanna?'

'I'm in here.'

He entered the room and stood in the doorway for a while, looking outside and occasionally glancing at his wife.

'*C'est joli, non?*' He spoke absentmindedly, and her eyes reached up to his. 'It's pretty.'

She nodded. 'I understood. Marc?' She didn't want to ask, but she had to. And she knew he wouldn't be pleased. 'How's your friend?'

For a long time he didn't answer. 'I don't know what you mean.'

'Yes, you do.' She felt nausea rise in her as she searched his eyes. 'How have you decided to handle it?'

'Don't you think it's a little too soon to discuss it? We just got out of the car.'

She smiled at him. 'How French. What did you have in mind, darling? That we spend the weekend being charming and then discuss it on the way home Sunday night?'

'That was not why I brought you here. We both needed to get away.'

She nodded again, her eyes filling with tears. 'Yes. We did.' Her mind immediately sped back to Pilar. 'But we have to talk about this too. You know, I suddenly wonder why we've stayed married.' She looked up at him again. He came into the room and slowly sat down.

'Are you mad?'

'Maybe I am.' She looked for her handkerchief and blew her nose.

'Deanna, please ...' He glanced at her, then looked away.

'What? You want to pretend that nothing has happened? Marc, we can't.' Too much had happened over the summer. She had had Ben, and now she knew Marc had someone too. Only in Marc's case, it probably had gone on for years.

'But this is not something for you to worry about now.'

'What better time? We're both already in such pain, we might as well lance the whole boil. If we don't, it'll go on throbbing and hurting forever, while we try to make believe it's not there.'

'Have you been so unhappy for so long?'

She nodded slowly, turning to look outside. She was thinking of Ben. 'I never realised, until this summer how terribly lonely I've been, how constantly alone ... how little we do together, how little we've shared. How little you understand what I want.'

'And what is it you want?' His voice was very low and soft.

'Your time, your affection. Laughter. Walks on the beach ...' She said the last without thinking and then turned her head towards him in surprise. 'I want you to care about my work, because it's important to me. I want to be with you, Marc. Not all by myself at home. What do you think will happen now, with Pilar gone? You'll travel for months, and what will I do? Sit there and wait?' The very thought of that existence made her tremble inside. 'I can't do it any more. I don't want to.'

'Then what do you suggest?' He wanted her to say it, wanted her to ask for the divorce.

'I don't know. We could call it a day, or if we decide to stay married, then things would have to be different, especially now.' Jesus, what was she doing? If she stayed with him, she couldn't have Ben. But this was her husband, the man she had lived with for eighteen years.

'You're telling me you want to travel with me?' He looked annoyed.

'Why not? She travels with you, doesn't she?' Deanna had finally figured that out. 'Why couldn't I?'

'Because ... because it's unreasonable. And impractical. And – and expensive.' And because then he couldn't take Chantal.

'Expensive?' Deanna raised an eyebrow with a small, vicious smile. 'My, my. Does she pay her own way?'

'Deanna! I will not discuss this with you!'

'Then why did we come here?' Her eyes were fierce in the narrow white face.

'We came here to rest.' They were the words of a monarch, her king. The subject was now closed.

'I see. Then all we have to do is get through the weekend, be polite, and go back to Paris pretending nothing happened. You go back to your little friend, and in two weeks we go back to the States and go on as always. And just how long will you stay there this time, Marc? Three weeks? A month? Six weeks? And then you'll be gone again, and for how long, and with whom, while I sit all alone in that goddamn museum we live in, waiting for you to come back. Alone again dammit. Alone!'

'That's not true.'

'Yes it is, and you know it. And what I'm telling you now is that I've had enough. As far as I'm concerned, those days are over.' She stood up suddenly then and was about to leave the room, but when she got to her

215

feet, she felt faint. She stopped for a moment, looking down and holding on to her chair.

He watched her, at first saying nothing, then with concern in his eyes. 'Is something wrong?'

'No. Nothing.' She straightened herself and glared at him from where she stood. 'I'm just very tired.'

'Then go and rest. I'll show you our room.' He gently took her elbow until he was sure that she was steady on her feet, then led the way down the long hall to the other end of the house. They had taken over the master bedroom, a splendid suite done in silks the colour of raspberries and cream. 'Why don't you lie down for a while, Deanna.' She was looking steadily worse. 'I'll take a walk.'

'And then what?' She looked up at him miserably from the bed. 'Then what do we do? I can't do this any more, Marc. I can't play the game.'

He was tempted to say 'What game?' to deny it all. He said nothing, and Deanna went on, looking directly into his eyes as she spoke. They looked troubled and a little too full.

'I want to know what you feel, what you think, what you're going to do. What's going to be different for me, other than the fact that we no longer have Pilar. I want to know if you're going to go on seeing your mistress. I want to know all the things you think it's rude to say. Say them now, Marc. I need to know.'

He nodded silently and walked to the other side of the room, looking out the window towards the gently rolling hills. 'It's not easy for me to talk about those kinds of things.'

'I know.' Her voice was very soft. 'Half the time we've been married, I've never been sure if you loved me.'

'I always did.' He spoke without turning around, and all she could see was his back. 'I always will love you, Deanna.'

She felt tears sting her eyes. 'Why?' She could barely say the word. 'Why do you love me? Because I'm your wife? Out of habit? Or because you really care?' But he didn't answer, he only turned to her with a look of intense pain on his face.

'Must we do this? Now ... so soon after Pilar's ... death?' Deanna didn't speak. His whole face had trembled as he spoke of Pilar. 'Deanna, I – I just can't.'

Without another word he strode out of the room, and she next saw him, with his head bent, walking in the garden. Her eyes filled with tears again as she watched him. The past few days felt like the end of her life. For a moment she didn't even think of Ben. Only Marc.

He did not return to the house for an hour, and when he did, he found her asleep. There was still a look of exhaustion around the black-circled eyes. For the first time in years, she was wearing no makeup, and in contrast to the raspberry silk bedspread he thought her face looked almost green. He wandered back into the main hallway and into a study beyond. For a moment he sat there, staring at the phone. And then, as though he had to, he started to dial.

She answered on the third ring. 'Marc-Edouard?'

'*Oui.*' He paused. 'How are you?' What if Deanna woke up? Why had he called her?

'You sound odd. Is something wrong?'

'No, no. I'm just very tired. We both are.'

'That's understandable. Have you talked?' She was relentless. It was a side of Chantal he had never known.

'Not really. Only a little.'

'I suppose it's not easy.' He could hear her sigh.

'No, it's not.' He paused. There were footsteps in the hall. 'Look, I'll call you back.'

'When?'

'Later.' And then: 'I love you.'

'Good, darling, so do I.'

He hung up with a trembling hand as the footsteps approached. But it was only the caretaker, come to see that they were comfortably settled. Satisfied, the man went away, and Marc sank slowly into a chair. It would never work. He couldn't keep up the charade forever. Calling Chantal, pacifying Deanna, flying back and forth between California and France, hiding and excusing, and showering them both with guilt-inspired gifts. Deanna was right. It had been almost impossible for years. Of course Deanna hadn't known then, but now that she did, it made everything different. It made him feel so much worse. He closed his eyes, and his mind went immediately back to Pilar, to the last time he had seen her. They had walked on the beach. She had teased him and he had laughed, and he had made her promise to be careful with the motorcycle. Again, she had laughed ... The tears flooded his throat again, and suddenly the room was filled with the sound of his sobs. He didn't even hear Deanna come in, catlike, on stockinged feet. She went to him slowly and held his shivering shoulders in her arms.

'It's all right, Marc. I'm here.' There were tears on her face as well, and he could feel the warm wetness through his shirt as she rested her cheek on his back. 'It's all right.'

'If you only knew how I loved Pilar ... Why did I do it? Buy her that damned machine! I should have known.'

'It doesn't matter now. It was meant to be. You can't do this to yourself for the rest of your life.'

'But why?' His words shook with pain as he turned to look at his wife. 'Why her? Why us? We already lost two boys, and now the only child we had. Deanna, how can you bear it?'

She squeezed her eyes shut. 'We don't have any choice. I thought – I thought I would die myself when the two babies died ... I thought I couldn't go on another day. Each day I just wanted to give up, to hide in a corner. But I didn't. I went on ... somehow. In part, because of you. In part, because of myself. And then we had Pilar, and I forgot that kind of pain. I thought – I thought I'd never feel that way again. But now I remember what it's like. Only this time it's so much worse.' She lowered her head, and he reached out and took her in his arms.

'I know. If you knew how I wish now that we had had those sons. We have – we have no more children.' Deanna nodded silently, feeling more than ever the pain of his words. 'I would do anything to – to have her back.'

They sat there for a long time, holding each other. At last they went outside for a walk. It was dinnertime when they came back.

'Do you want to go into the village to eat?' He looked at her with an expression of grief and fatigue, but she shook her head.

'Why don't I make something here? Is there any food?'

'The caretaker said his wife left us some bread and cheese and eggs.'

'How about that?' He nodded indifferently. She took off the sweater she had worn on their walk, set it on a large Louis XIV chair, and headed for the kitchen.

She was back in twenty minutes with scrambled eggs, toast and Brie, and two cups of steaming black coffee. She wondered if they'd feel better after they ate, if it really made any difference. All week long, people had told them to eat, as though that would help. But she didn't care any more if she ever ate. She had made the dinner for Marc and because it gave them something to do. Neither of them seemed to want to talk, although there should have been a great deal to say.

They ate in silence. After the meal they drifted apart, she to the long halls and galleries to study the collection of paintings, Marc to the library. At eleven o'clock they went to bed in silence, and in the morning he got out of bed as soon as she stirred. It was eleven before either of them spoke. Deanna had just gotten up and was feeling queasy as she sat on a dressing-room chair.

'*Ça ne va pas?*' He looked at her with a frown of worry.

'No, no. I'm fine.'

'You don't look it. Should I get you some coffee?' The very idea made her sick. She shook her head almost in desperation.

'No, really. Thanks.'

'Do you think something is wrong? You haven't looked well in days.'

She tried to smile, but it was a futile attempt. 'I hate to say this, darling, but neither have you.'

He only shrugged. 'You don't suppose you have an ulcer, Deanna?' She had had one after the death of their first little boy, but it had never recurred. She shook her head.

'I don't have any pain. I'm just exhausted all the time, and now and then I feel sick. It's just fatigue,' she went on, forcing a smile. 'It's no wonder. Neither of us has had much sleep. We're both fighting staggering time changes, long trips, the shock ... I suppose it's a wonder we're still on our feet. I'm sure it's nothing.'

But Marc wasn't sure he agreed. He saw her sway for a moment when she stood up. Emotions could do strange things to one. It made him think of Chantal again as Deanna disappeared into the shower. He wanted to call her again, but she wanted reports, she wanted to hear news, and he had none to give her, except that he was spending a weekend with his wife – and they both felt like hell.

In the shower Deanna stood with her face turned up and the water racing down her back. She was thinking of Ben. In San Francisco it was two in the morning; he would still be asleep. She could see his face so clearly in his bed, the dark hair tousled, one hand on his chest, the other resting somewhere on her ... No, he was probably in Carmel, and she found herself thinking of their weekends there. How different it was from these days with Marc. It was as though she and Marc had nothing left to say. All they had was the past.

She turned the shower off at last and stood thinking for a moment, looking out the open windows into the garden as she dried herself with thick raspberry-coloured towels. This house was a far cry from Carmel. A château in France, and a cottage in Carmel. Raspberry silks, and comfortable old wools. She thought of the cosy plaid blanket on Ben's country bed as she caught a glimpse of the ruffled silk bedspread in the other room. It was like the contrast between her two lives. There, the simple, easy reality of life with Ben in his 'democracy' where they took turns making breakfast and putting the garbage outside the back door; and here, only the eternal empty splendour of her life with Marc. She ran a brush through her hair and let out a long sigh.

In the bedroom beyond, Marc was reading the paper with a frown. 'Will you join me in church?' He looked over the paper as she emerged from the bathroom, her robe firmly closed, and stood in front of the wardrobe. She nodded and pulled out a black skirt and a sweater. They were both wearing formal *deuil*, the solid black mourning still common in France. The only things she omitted were the black stockings, which her mother-in-law wore.

Deanna looked strangely plain in the unalleviated black, with her dark hair pulled severely into a bun at the nape of her neck. Once again she wore no makeup. It was as though she no longer cared.

'You look terribly pale.'

'It's just the contrast with all this black.'

'Are you sure?' He stared at her for a moment before they left the house, but she only smiled. He acted as though he was afraid she were dying, but maybe he was afraid of that too. They had both lost so much.

They drove in silence to the tiny country church of Sainte Isabelle. Deanna slipped quietly into the pew at Marc's side. The church, tiny and pretty and warm, was filled with peasants, and a few weekenders like them, down from Paris. She suddenly remembered that it was still summer, not quite the end of August. In the States it would soon be Labor Day, heralding the fall. Her sense of time had vanished in the past week. She could not keep her mind on the service. She thought of Carmel, and of Ben, of Marc, and then Pilar; she thought of long walks in the country as a child, and then she stared fixedly at the back of someone's head. It was stuffy in the small church, and the sermon droned on and on. Finally, gently, she touched Marc's arm. She began to whisper that she was too warm, but suddenly his face swam before her eyes, and everything went dark.

Chapter Twenty-one

'Marc?' She reached out to him as he and another man carried her to the car.

'Quiet, darling, don't talk.' His face was a pale, perspiring grey.

'Put me down. Really, I'm all right.'

'Never mind that.' He thanked the man who had helped him carry her to the car, and once more clarified their directions to the nearest hospital.

'What? Don't be crazy. I only fainted because it was so hot.'

'It was not hot, it was quite cool. And I won't discuss it.' He slammed the door on her side and got in behind the wheel.

'Marc, I will *not* go to the hospital.' She put a hand on his arm. Her eyes implored him, but he shook his head. She was a pale, opaque kind of grey. He started the car.

'I'm not interested in what you will "not" do.' His face was set. He didn't want to go to a hospital again, didn't want to hear those sounds, or smell those odours around him. Never ... never again. He felt his heart race. What if it were serious? What if she were very ill? What if ... He glanced at her again, trying to mask his fear, but she was looking away, staring out at the countryside. He glanced at her profile and then down at her shoulders, her hands, everything draped in so much black. Austere. It seemed symbolic of everything happening to them now, everything they said. Why could they not escape it? Why wasn't this simply a weekend in the country, from which they would return relaxed and happy to find Pilar with that dazzling smile on her face. He looked over at Deanna once more, and let out a sigh. The sound dragged her eyes back from the road.

'Don't be so silly, Marc. Really, I'm perfectly all right.'

'*On verra.*' We'll see.

'Would you rather we just go back to Paris?' Her hand trembled as she rested it in his, and he looked sharply at her again. Paris – and Chantal. Yes, he wanted to go back. But first he had to know that Deanna was all right.

'We'll go back to Paris once you've seen a doctor.' She was about to protest again, but a wave of dizziness swept over her. She put her head back on the seat. He looked at her nervously and stepped on the gas. She didn't argue, she didn't have the strength.

It was another ten minutes before they pulled up in front of a small efficient-looking building with the sign HÔPITAL SAINT GÉRARD. Without a word, Marc got out of the car and came quickly to her side, but when he held open the door, Deanna made no move to get out.

'Can you walk?' There was terror in his eyes again. What if this were the beginning of a stroke? Then what would he do? She'd be paralysed and he'd have to stay with her always. But that was madness, he *wanted* to stay with Deanna, didn't he? His pulse raced as he helped her out of the car.

She was about to tell him again that she was all right. By now they both knew she was not. She took a deep breath and stood up with a tiny smile. She wanted to prove to him that she'd make it, that this was only nerves. For a moment, as they walked into the hospital, she felt better, and wondered why they had come. For a minute she even walked in her usual smooth, easy strides. Then, as she was about to boast of it to Marc-Edouard, an old man was rolled past on a gurney. He was ancient and wrinkled, foul smelling, his mouth open, his face slack. She reached a hand out to Marc and passed out on the floor.

He gave a shout and collected her in his arms. Two

nurses and a man in a white coat came running. In less than a minute they had her on a table in a small, anti-septic-smelling room, and she was awake again. She looked around for a moment, confused. Then she saw Marc, standing horrified in the corner.

'I'm sorry, but that man ...'

'That's enough.' Marc approached slowly, holding up one hand. 'It wasn't the old man, or the temperature in the church.' He stood next to her, very tall, very grim, and suddenly very old. 'Let's find out what it was – what it is. *D'accord?*' She didn't answer as the doctor nodded to him, and he left.

He haunted the corridor, looking strangely out of place and glancing at the phone. Should he call her? Why shouldn't he? What difference did it make? Who would see? But he didn't feel like it now. His thoughts were with Deanna. She had been his wife for eighteen years. They had just lost their only child. And now, perhaps ... He couldn't bear the thought. He passed the phone once more, without even stopping this time.

It seemed hours before a young woman doctor came to find him.

And then he knew. And knew he could tell Deanna the truth. Or he could tell her a lie – a very small lie. He wondered if he owed it to her to tell her, to tell her that he *knew* – or if, instead, Deanna owed something to him.

Chapter Twenty-two

Deanna sat up straight in her bed, looking paler than the whitewashed wall behind her head. 'You're wrong. It's a lie!'

Marc was staring at her and wearing a very small smile. He was completely calm. 'It most certainly is not. And six months from now, my darling, you'll have a very hard time convincing anyone of that, I'm afraid.'

'But I can't be.'

'And why not?' His eyes searched her face.

'I'm too old to be pregnant, for chrissake.'

'At thirty-seven? Don't be absurd. You will probably be able to have a child anytime in the next fifteen years.'

'But I'm too *old*!' She was shrieking it at him and she looked near tears. Why had they not told her first, given her time to absorb the shock before she had to face Marc? But no, that was not the way of things here, in France, where the patient was always the last to know anything. And she could well imagine the scene Marc would have made: a determined man, an *important* man who must be informed of Madame's condition first; he did not wish his wife to be upset, and they had just been through so much, such tragedy . . .

'Darling, please don't be foolish,' Marc was saying. He stood up and walked to the side of the bed, where he gently rested his hand on her head, and ran it slowly down the long silky black hair. 'You're not too old at all. May I sit down?' he asked. She nodded, and he sat down on the edge of the bed.

'But . . . two months?' She looked at him with eyes filled with despair. She had wanted it to be Ben's. She had thought of it too, for the first time just before she fell asleep. It had dawned on her, and she had argued with the thought, but as she drifted off to sleep she suddenly wondered – the dizziness, the nausea, the constant desire for sleep. All she had been able to think of was Ben. She didn't want it to be Marc's. She looked at him now in disappointment and pain. Two months pregnant meant it was Marc's, not Ben's.

'It must have happened that last night before I left. *Un petit au revoir.*'

'That is not funny.' Tears filled her eyes. She was far from pleased. Now he understood even more than she knew. But now he understood that there was not only another man, but someone she loved. It didn't matter. She would forget him. She had something important to do in the next months. She owed Marc his son. 'I don't understand.'

'Darling, don't be naive.'

'I haven't gotten pregnant in years. Why now?'

'Sometimes that's how those things happen. In any case it makes no difference. We're getting a whole new chance – another family, a child.'

'We've already had a child.' She looked like a petulant little girl as she sat cross-legged in her hospital bed, wiping away tears with the palm of her hand. 'I don't want any more children.' *At least not yours.* Now she knew the truth too. If she had truly loved him, she would have wanted his baby. And she didn't. She wanted Ben's.

Marc was looking embarrassingly pleased and painfully patient. 'It's normal to feel that way at first. All women do. But when it comes ... Remember Pilar?'

Deanna's eyes flashed into his. 'Yes, I remember Pilar. And the others. I've done that, Marc. I won't do it again. For what? For more heartbreak, more pain? For you to not be there for another eighteen years? At my age, you expect me to bring up a child alone? And another half-breed, another half-American, all French?

You want me to go through that again, competing with you for the allegiance of our child? Dammit, I won't do it!'

'You most certainly will.' His voice was quiet and as solid as steel.

'I don't have to!' She was shouting at him now. 'This isn't the Dark Ages! I can have an abortion if I want to!'

'No, you can not!'

'The hell I can't!'

'Deanna, I won't discuss this with you. You're upset.' She was lying in her bed now, crying into the pillow. 'Upset' was barely adequate for what she felt. 'You'll get used to the idea. You'll be pleased.'

'You mean I don't have a choice, is that it?' She glared at him. 'What'll you do to me if I get rid of it? Divorce me?'

'Don't talk nonsense.'

'Then don't push me around.'

'I'm not pushing, I'm happy.' He looked at her with a smile and held out his arms, but there was something different in his eyes. She didn't come to him. After a moment he took her hands and brought them one after the other to his lips. 'I love you, Deanna. And I want our child. Our baby. Yours and mine.'

She closed her eyes and almost cringed as he said it. She had been there before. But he said nothing; he only stood up and took her in his arms, then stroked her hair briefly. Then he pulled away. She watched him leave, looking pensive and distracted.

Alone in the dark, she cried for a while, wondering what she should do. This changed everything. Why hadn't she known? Why hadn't she guessed? She should have figured it out before, but she'd only missed it once, and she thought that was nerves, there had been the opening of the gallery, her constant love-making with Ben, then the news of Pilar, the trip ... She thought it was just a matter of a couple of weeks.

228

But two months? How could that be? And Jesus, it meant she had been pregnant by Marc the whole time she had been with Ben. Allowing that baby to stay in her now was like denying everything she'd had with Ben and tearing out her heart. This baby was a confirmation of her marriage to Marc.

She lay awake in her bed all night long. The next morning Marc-Edouard checked her out of the hospital. They were driving straight back to Paris, his mother's, before he left the next day for Athens. 'And this is it. I'll be gone for five or six days. After that, I'll have it all wrapped up in Greece. A week from now we'll leave Paris, go home, and stay there.'

'What does that mean? I stay there, and you travel?'

'No. It means I stay there as much as I can.'

'Five days a month? Five days a year? Something like that?' She stared out the window as she asked. She felt as though she had been condemned to a replay of her first eighteen years as his wife. 'When will I see you, Marc? Twice a month for dinner, when you're in town, and don't have to have dinner somewhere else?'

'It won't be like that, Deanna. I promise.'

'Why not? It always has been before.'

'That was different. I've learned something now.'

'Really? What?' She looked bitter as she watched him drive, but his voice was soft and sad when he spoke and he kept his eyes on the road.

'I've learned how short life can be, how quickly gone. We had learned that together before, twice, but I had forgotten. Now I know. I have been reminded again.' Deanna hung her head and said nothing. But he knew he had hit his mark. 'After Pilar, after the others, could you really have this one aborted?'

She was shocked that he had read her thoughts, and she didn't answer for a long time. 'I'm not sure.'

'*I'm* quite sure. It would destroy you.' The tone of his voice frightened her. Maybe he did know. 'The guilt, the emotional pain, you'd be finished. You'd never be able to think or live or love, or even paint again. I guarantee it.' The very idea terrified her. And he was probably right. 'You don't have the temperament to be that cold-blooded.'

'In other words,' she sighed, 'I have no choice.'

He didn't answer.

They were in bed at nine-thirty that night, and nothing more was said. He kissed her gently on the forehead as he left her in their room. He was taking a taxi to the airport.

'I'll call you every night.' He looked concerned, but also undeniably pleased, and he no longer had that terrifying worry in his eyes, the only sorrow left there was what he felt for Pilar. 'I promise, darling. I'll call every night.' He repeated it, but she looked away.

'Will she let you?' He tried to ignore the remark, but she looked pointedly at him from the bed. 'You heard me, Marc. I assume she's going with you. Am I right?'

'Don't be ridiculous. This is a business trip.'

'And the last time wasn't?'

'You're just upset. Why don't we stop? I don't want to fight with you before I leave.'

'Why not? Afraid I'll lose the baby?' For an insane moment she wanted to tell him that the baby wasn't his, but the worst of it was that if she was two months pregnant, it was.

'Deanna, I want you to rest while I'm gone.' He looked at her with an air of fatherly tenderness, blew her a kiss, and softly closed the door.

She lay there for a while, listening to the sounds of her mother-in-law's house. So far no one knew. It was 'their secret' as Marc called it.

When she awakened the next morning, the house was still. She lay in bed for a long time, thinking, wondering what to do. She could fly to San Francisco while Marc was in Greece, she could have an abortion and be free, but she recognised the truth of what he had said to her. Having an abortion would destroy her as much as it would him. She had suffered too much loss already. And what if he were right? If it were a gift of God? And what if ... what if it were Ben's? A last ray of hope flickered and then died. Two months, he had said, and the young, shy-looking doctor had nodded her agreement. It couldn't have been Ben's.

So she would lie in this beige silk cocoon for a week, waiting for Marc to return, to take her home, so they could begin the same charade again. She felt panic rising in her at the thought, and suddenly all she wanted to do was to run away. She climbed out of bed, steadying herself for a moment against a wave of dizziness, then dressed quietly. She had to get out, to go for a walk, to think.

She turned into streets she barely knew and discovered gardens and squares and parks that delighted her. She sat on benches and smiled at passersby, funny little old ladies in lopsided hats, little old men playing chess, children babbling at their friends, and here and there a girl pushing a pram. A girl – they all looked twenty-one or-two, not thirty-seven. Deanna watched as she rested. The doctor had told her to take it easy, to go for walks, but stop and rest; to go out but come home and nap, not to skip meals, and not to stay up late, and in a few weeks she'd feel better. She already did. And as she walked around Paris, she stopped often, and thought. About Ben. She hadn't called him in days.

It was late afternoon when she finally stopped at a post office. She couldn't stay away any longer. She gave the woman the number and nodded at her, surprised. 'L'Amérique?' It seemed aeons before she heard him, but it was less than a minute before he answered the phone. For him it was eight o'clock in the morning.

'Were you asleep?' Her voice sounded intense even across six thousand miles.

'Almost. I just woke up.' Ben settled back in bed

with a smile. 'When are you coming home?'

She squeezed her eyes shut and fought back tears in answer. 'Soon.' *With Marc – and his baby*. She felt a sob lodge in her throat. 'I miss you terribly.' The tears started to roll, silently, down her face.

'Not as much as I miss you, darling.' He listened, trying to hear. There was something she wasn't saying, something he didn't understand. 'Are you all right?' He knew she would still be distraught over Pilar, but she sounded as though there was something more. 'Are you? Answer me!'

She was saying nothing, only standing in the booth, in silence, in tears.

'Deanna? Darling? ... Hello?' He listened intently. He was sure she was still there.

'I'm here.' It was a sad little croak.

'Oh, darling ...' He frowned and then smiled. 'How about if I come over? Any chance of that?'

'Not really.'

'How about next weekend in Carmel? It's Labor Day weekend. Think you'll be back?'

It was light years away. She was about to say no, then stopped. Next weekend in Carmel. Why not? Marc would be in Greece. If she left tonight, they would have until the end of the weekend, and maybe even one more day before he got back. Together. In Carmel. And then it would be over, as they had foreseen. The end of the summer would have come. Her mind raced. 'I'll be home tomorrow.'

'You will? Oh, baby ... what time?'

She made a rapid calculation in her head. 'About six o'clock tomorrow morning. Your time.' She stood in the booth, suddenly beaming through her tears.

'Are you sure?'

'I certainly am.' She told him the airline. 'I'll call you if I can't make that plane, but otherwise, count on it.' And then as she laughed into the phone, she felt tears sting her eyes again. 'I'm coming home, Ben.' How long it seemed since she'd left. It had only been a week.

That night she left a note for her mother-in-law. She explained only that she had been called back to San Francisco, that she was sorry to leave in such a rush. And, incidentally, she had felt an irresistible need to reclaim her portrait of herself and Pilar. She was sure her mother-in-law would understand. She instructed the maid to tell Marc, when he called, that she was out. That was all. That would buy her a day at least. But there was nothing he could do. He had to finish up in Greece. She thought about it on the plane on the way home. Marc would leave her alone for a week. There was no reason why he should not. He would be annoyed that she had flown home from Paris, but that was all. She was free now. For one more week. It was all she could think of.

An hour before they landed she could hardly sit still in her seat. She felt like a very young girl. Even the occasional waves of nausea didn't dampen her mood. She would just sit very still for a few minutes and close her eyes, and the nausea would pass. She kept her mind on Ben.

She was one of the first off the plane in San Francisco, after it had seemed to drift down through the clouds, racing the sun as everything around it turned pink and gold. It had been a splendid morning, but even that wasn't enough to take her mind off Ben. He was all she could think of as the plane finally ground to a halt at the gate, and she waited impatiently to be released from her seat. She was already wearing a half-smile, as she shrugged on the black velvet jacket over white slacks and a white silk shirt. Her ivory face and ebony hair added to the portrait in black and white. She looked considerably paler than she had when she had left, and her eyes told a multitude of tales, but they danced and sang too as she inched her way towards the door.

Then she saw him, standing there, alone in the terminal at six A.M., waiting for her beyond the customs barrier, with a jacket slung over his arm and a smile on his face. They rushed towards each other as she came through the door, and she was instantly in his arms.

'Oh, Ben!' There were laughter and tears in her eyes, but he said nothing, he only held her close. It seemed an eternity before he pulled away.

'I worried about you terribly, Deanna. I'm so glad you're back.'

'So am I.'

He searched her eyes but wasn't quite sure what he saw. One thing he knew was there – pain, but more than that he couldn't tell. She only reached out to him and held him tightly.

'Shall we go home?'

She nodded, her eyes filled with tears again. Home. For a week.

Chapter Twenty-three

'Are you feeling O.K.?' She was lying back in his bed, with her eyes closed and a small smile on her face. She had been back home for four hours, and in bed with him the whole time. It was only ten o'clock in the morning, but she hadn't slept all night on the flight from Paris. He wasn't quite sure if it was the effect of the long flight that he was seeing, or if the week of Pilar's death had taken an even greater toll than he'd thought. She had shown him the painting when she'd unpacked. 'Deanna? Are you O.K.?' He was watching her when she opened her eyes.

'I've never felt better in my life.' Her smile told him she meant it. 'When do we leave for Carmel?'

'Tomorrow. The day after. Whenever you want.'

'Could we go today?'

There was a tiny thread of desperation woven in there somewhere, but he had not yet discovered where. It troubled him. 'We might. I could see what I can work out with Sally. If she doesn't mind taking on the gallery single-handed while we're gone, then it'll be all right.'

'I hope she can.' It was softly spoken, but earnestly said.

'As bad as that?' he asked. She only nodded, and he understood. He went to make breakfast. 'Tomorrow it's your turn.' He sang it out to her from the kitchen, and she laughed as she walked across the room, naked, and stood in the doorway watching him. It didn't matter now if they made love with Marc-Edouard's child in her belly. They had been doing it all summer, and she didn't care. She wanted to make love to Ben. She would need that to remember. 'Deanna?'

She smiled and cocked her head. 'Yes, sir?'

'What's wrong? I mean other than the obvious ...
Pilar. Is there something else?'

She started to tell him that that was enough, but she
couldn't lie to him.

'Some things came up while I was in France.'

'Anything I should know about?' Like Marc, he was
suspicious of her health, she just looked too frail. He
eyed her carefully from where he stood.

'Slowly, she shook her head. He didn't need to know
about the baby. It would have been different if it had
been his.

'What kind of things came up?' His eyes smiled a
little as he asked, 'Fried or scrambled?'

'Scrambled would be nice.' The thought of fried eggs
turned her green, but she could manage scrambled, as
long as she didn't get too strong a whiff of his coffee.
'No coffee.'

'How come?' He looked shocked.

'I've given it up for Lent.'

'I think you're six or seven months early.'

Seven months ... seven months. She pulled her mind
away from the thought and smiled at his attempt at a
joke.

'Maybe so.'

'So? What's up?'

'Oh, I don't know.' She came into the kitchen and
put her arms around him, leaning into his back. 'I don't
know ... I don't know. I just wish my life were a little
bit simpler.'

'And?' He turned in her grasp and faced her as they
both stood naked in front of his kitchen stove.

'I love you, that's all.' Dammit, why did it have to
be now? Why did she have to tell him so soon? Her
eyes filled with tears, but she forced herself to look at
him. She owed him that. 'And ... things aren't going
to work out as easily as I thought.'

'Did you really think it would be easy?' His eyes
never left hers.

236

She shook her head. 'No. But easier than it is.'

'And how is it?'

'I can't leave him, Ben.' There. She had said it. Oh, God, she had told him. She looked at him for an endless time, tears filling her eyes.

'Why not?'

'I just can't. Not now.' *And not even later, not once I've had his child. Call me in another eighteen years ...*

'Do you love him, Deanna?'

Once again, she shook her head. 'I thought I did. I was sure of it. And I know I did once. I suppose I still love him in a way. He has given me something for eighteen years, in his own way. But it's – it's been over for years. I just didn't understand that until this summer. I understand it even better now, after this week.' She paused for a breath, then went on. 'There were even times, with you, when I wasn't sure if I should leave him or not. I didn't know. It seemed as though I had no right. And I also thought that maybe I still loved him.'

'And you don't?'

'No.' It was a small choking sob. Finally she looked away and wiped her face with her hands. 'I only realised it a few days ago. Something happened ... and I knew.' *Because I don't want his baby, Ben, I want yours!*

'Then why are you staying with him? Because of Pilar?' He was strangely calm as he spoke to her, almost like a father speaking to a child.

'That and other reasons. It doesn't matter why. I just am.' She looked at him in agony again. 'Do you want me to go?' But he only stared at her, then silently left the room. She heard him in the living room for a moment, and then heard him slam the bedroom door as hard as he could. She stood in the kitchen for a time, wondering, stunned. She knew she had to leave now. There would be no Carmel. But all her clothes were locked up with him, in his room. She had no choice except to stay until he came out. At last he did, an hour later. He stood in the doorway, looking red-eyed and distraught. For a moment she wasn't quite sure if he was insanely angry or simply upset.

'What exactly were you telling me, Deanna? That it's over?'

'I ... no ... I ... oh, God!' For a moment she thought again that she might faint, but she couldn't, not now. She took two deep breaths and sat down on the edge of the couch, her long, slim, bare legs hanging gracefully to the floor. 'I have a week.'

'And then what?'

'I disappear.'

'Into that lonely life again? Into a life by yourself? In that mausoleum you lived in, and without even Pilar now? How can you do that to yourself?' He looked tormented.

'Maybe it's just what I have to do, Ben.'

'I don't understand.' He was about to walk back into his bedroom, but he stopped, turning to face her. 'Deanna, I told you ... I said it could just be for the summer and ... I'd understand. That was what I said. I have no right to change that now. Do I?'

'You have every right to be furious, or very, very hurt.'

She saw tears well up in his eyes and felt them well up in her own, but he never wavered as he watched her.

'I'm both. But that's because I love you very much.'

She nodded, but she could no longer speak. She only walked back into the circle of his arms. It seemed hours before either of them let go.

'Shall we go to Carmel today?' He was lying on his stomach, looking into her face. She had just awakened from a three-hour nap, and it was almost five. He had never gone to the gallery – he had explained that he'd be gone all week and Sally would have to hold her own. 'What do you really want to do?'

'Be with you.' She said it solemnly but with a small happy smile in her eyes.

'Anywhere?'

'Anywhere.'

'Then let's go to Tahiti.'

'I'd rather go to Carmel.'

'Seriously?' He ran a finger down her thigh. She smiled.

'Seriously.'

'O.K., then let's go. We can have dinner down there.'

'Sure. It's two o'clock in the morning, Paris time. By the time we have dinner, I'll be ready for breakfast.'

'Jesus. I wasn't thinking about that. Do you feel half dead?' She was looking very tired but she seemed to have more colour now.

'No, I feel fine, and happy, and I love you.'

'Not half as much as I love you.' He took her face in his hands and pulled her closer. He wanted to kiss her, hold her, and touch her, and have all of her that he could for the few days they had left. Then he thought of something. 'What about your work?'

'What about it?'

'Will we still work together at the gallery? Will we still represent you – will I?' He wanted her to be incensed, to answer 'of course', but for a long moment she said nothing. Then he knew.

'I don't know. We'll have to see.' But how could they? How could she go to see him at the gallery in a few months, when she would be swollen with Marc-Edouard's child?

'It's all right,' he said. 'Never mind.'

But the look of pain in his eyes now was too much for her to bear. She burst into tears. She seemed to be doing that a lot.

'What's wrong, love?'

'You're going to think I'm like her – the fake, the girl you were married to.'

He knelt on the floor at her side. 'You're not a fake,

Deanna. Nothing about you has ever been fake. We just undertook something difficult and now we have to live up to the deal. It's not easy, but it's honest. It's always been honest. I love you more than I've ever loved anyone in my life. I want you to remember that always. If you ever want to come back, I will always be here for you. Always. Even when I'm ninety-three years old.' He tried to make her smile, but he failed. 'Shall we make another deal now?'

'What?' She was pouting as she looked up at him. She hated Marc-Edouard, and hated herself more. She should have an abortion. Anything so she could be with Ben. Or maybe he would accept Marc's child, if she told him the truth from the start. But she knew that she could never tell him. He would never understand.

'Come on, I want us to make another deal. I want us both to promise that we won't talk about it being "just one more week". Let's just live each day, love each day, enjoy every moment, and face that time when it comes. If we talk about only that, we'll spoil the time that we have. Is it a deal?' He took her face in his hands and kissed her gently on the mouth as her hair fell softly down around her face from the loose knot she had wound it into on the top of her head. 'Deal?'

'Deal.'

'O.K.' He nodded solemnly, kissed her again, and left the room.

An hour later they left for Carmel, but it was difficult not to feel the pall. Things weren't the same as they had been before. It was almost over, and whether they said it or not, they both knew. It was much too near. The summer was coming to a bittersweet end.

Chapter Twenty-four

'Ready, my darling?' It was midnight, on Monday night. Labor Day. It was over. Time to go home. She looked around the living room for the last time, then silently took his hand. The lights were already out, the woman on the beach in the Wyeth hid her face in the moonlight. For the last time Deanna glanced at her as she left the house. It was chilly, but there was a bright moon and a sky filled with stars.

'I love you.' They were whispered words as she slid quietly into the car. He touched her face, then he kissed her.

'I love you too.' They were both smiling, suddenly it was not a time to be sad. They had shared a bond of joy and peace and love like none other, and it was something no one could ever take away. It was theirs. For a lifetime. 'Are you as happy as I am, Deanna?' he asked. She nodded, smiling. 'I don't know why I feel so goddamn good, except that you make me happy, and you always will. No matter what.'

'You do the same for me.' *And you will.* She would cling to the memories in the long winter's night of her life with Marc. She would think of him when she held the baby, thinking that it could have been his. She wished that it had been; suddenly she wished that more than anything in her life.

'What are you thinking?'

They had started the drive back to San Francisco. They planned to be back by two in the morning. The next day they'd sleep late, and then after breakfast he'd take her home. Marc was due in that afternoon. Tuesday, at three. That was all his telegram had said. Margaret had read it to her on the phone when she called to make sure that all was well at the house. Tuesday, at three.

'I asked you what you were thinking.'

'A minute ago I was thinking that I would have liked to have your son.' She smiled into the night.

'And my daughter? Wouldn't you want her too?' They both smiled.

'How many children do you have in mind?'

'A nice even number. Maybe twelve.' This time she laughed and leaned against his shoulder as he drove. She remembered the first time he had said that, the morning after her show. Would there ever be another morning like that one?

'I would have settled for two.'

He hated the tenses she used. It told him what he didn't want to know. Or remember. Not tonight.

'Since when did you decide that you're not too old?'

'I still think I am, but ... it's easy to dream.'

'You'd look cute pregnant.' This time she said nothing. 'Tired?'

'Just a little.'

She had been tired too often all week long. It was the strain, but still he didn't like the dark circles under her eyes, or the pallor of her face when she got up in the morning. But he was no longer to worry after today. This was his last chance. Miraculously, on the morrow, he was to stop.

'Now what are you thinking?' She looked earnestly up at him.

'Of you.'

'That's all?' She tried to tease, but he wouldn't play.

'That's all.'

'What about?'

'I was thinking how much I wanted our child.'

She felt a sob make a fist in her throat and she turned her head away. 'Ben, don't.'

'I'm sorry.' He pulled her closer, and they drove on.

*

'And what is that supposed to mean?' Chantal glared at Marc from across the room. He closed his suitcase and swung it to the floor.

'It means exactly what it sounds like, Chantal. Come on, don't play games. I've been here for almost three months this summer, now I have to do some work over there.'

'For how long?' She looked livid, and her eyes showed that she had been crying.

'I told you. I don't know. Now be a good girl, and let's go.'

'*Non, tant pis.* I don't give a damn if you miss your plane. You're not going to leave me like that. What do you think I am? Stupid? You're just going back to her. Poor, poor little wife, all heartbroken because she lost her daughter, and now little darling husband is going to console her. *Alors non, merde!* What about me?' She advanced on him menacingly, and a muscle tightened in his jaw.

'I told you. She's sick.'

'With what?'

'A number of things. It doesn't matter with what, Chantal. She just is.'

'So you can't leave her now. Then when can you leave her?'

'Dammit, we've been over and over this for a week. Why do we have to do this when I have to catch a plane?'

'The hell with your plane. I won't let you leave me.' Her voice had risen dangerously and her eyes were darting around the room. 'You can't go! *Non,* Marc-Edouard, *non!*' She was in tears again. He sighed as he sat down.

'Chantal, *chérie*, please. I told you, it won't be for much longer. Please, darling. Try to understand. You've never been like this before. Why do you have to be so unreasonable now?'

'Because I've had it! I've had enough! Whatever

happens, you stay married to her. Year after year after year after year. *Bien merde alors, j'en ai marre.* I'm fed up!'

'Must you be fed up right now?' He looked at his watch with despair. 'I told you last night, if it looks as though it will be a long time, I'll have you come over. All right?'

'For how long?'

'Oh, Chantal!' He had the look of irritation he had previously worn only with Pilar. *'Voyons.* Let's see how it goes. You can stay in the States for a while, if you come over.'

'How long is a while?' But she was beginning to play now, and he saw it, with an exasperated gleam in his eye.

'As long as my foot. Will that do? Now, let's go. I'll call you almost every day. I'll try to be back in a few weeks. And if not, you'll come over. Satisfied?'

'Almost.'

'Almost?' He shouted the word, but she tilted her face up for a kiss, and he couldn't resist.

'Toi, alors!' He kissed her, and they both laughed as they raced back into the bedroom, teasing and touching and hungry again.

'I'll miss my plane, you know.'

'So what? And afterwards let's have dinner at Maxim's.'

One would have easily thought that she was the pregnant one, but they most emphatically knew she was not. They had once thought she was pregnant, and it had produced such an appalling scare because of her diabetes that they had decided never to take chances again. They couldn't afford to. Her life was at stake. And she didn't really mind not getting pregnant, she had never been particularly anxious to have a child. Not even Marc's.

Ben stopped the car halfway down the street. 'Here?'

She nodded, feeling as though the world were going to end. As though someone had announced the Apocalypse to them. They knew it was coming, they even knew when ... but now what? Where to go? What to do? How would she live every day without him? How could she exist without the moments they shared in Carmel? How could she not wake up in that yellow bedroom, figuring out if it was his turn to make breakfast or hers? She wondered, as she sat there, if it could even be done. She looked at him long and hard and then held him tightly in her arms. She didn't even care if anyone saw her. Let them. They would never see her hug him again. They would think it had been a mirage. She wondered for a moment if that was what she would think in years to come. Would it all seem like a dream?

Her words were a whisper in his ear. 'Take good care. I love you ...'

'I love you too.'

They clung to each other then, saying nothing. At last, he snapped open her door. 'I don't want you to go, Deanna. But if you stay any longer, I won't be able to ... to let you go.' She saw that his eyes were too bright, and she felt her own fill with tears. She looked down into her lap, and then quickly up at him. She had to see him, had to know he was still there. Instantly her arms were around him again.

'Ben, I love you.' She held tightly to him, then slowly peeled herself away and looked at him for a long, agonizing moment. 'Can I tell you that these months have made my whole lifetime worthwhile?'

'You can.' He smiled at her and kissed the tip of her nose. 'And can I tell you to get the hell out of my car?' She looked at him in surprise. Then she laughed.

'You cannot.'

'Well, I figure there's not going to be an easy way to do this so we might as well have a good laugh.' And she did, and at the same time started to cry again.

'Jesus, I'm a mess.'

'Yes, you are.' He said it with an appreciative nod and a grin that gave way to a slightly sobered look in his eye. 'And so am I. But frankly, my dear, I think we've got one hell of a lot of style.' And then, with a lopsided grin, he bent to kiss her once more, looked at her very hard, and said, 'Go.'

She nodded, touched his face. With her hands clenched into tight fists she slid out of the car, looked at him for an interminable moment, turned, and walked away. As soon as she had turned her back, while she still fumbled in her bag for her keys, she heard him drive away. But she never turned, never looked, never saw, she simply buried him in her heart and walked back inside the house she would share for the rest of her life. With Marc.

Chapter Twenty-five

'Good morning, darling. You slept well?' He looked down at her in bed.

'Did you miss your plane?' There was no mention of the past week, of the fact that she had literally run away from Paris.

'I did. Stupidly. I couldn't get a cab, there was a traffic jam, ten thousand tiny incidents, and I had to wait six hours for the next flight. How do you feel?'

'Decent.'

'No more than that?'

She shrugged in answer. She felt like hell, and she wished she were dead. All she wanted was Ben. But not like this. Not with Marc-Edouard's baby.

'I want you to see the doctor today,' Marc said. 'Shall I have Dominique make an appointment for you, or do you want to do it yourself?'

'Either way.'

Why so docile? He didn't like what he saw. She looked haggard and pale, nervous and unhappy, and yet indifferent to everything he said. 'I want you to see him today,' he repeated.

'Fine. Can I go by myself, or will you have Dominique take me?' Her eyes spat fire into his.

'Never mind that. You'll go today?'

'Count on it. And where are you going today, Athens or Rome?'

She walked past him into the bathroom and quietly closed the door. It was going to be a delightful eight months, Marc thought grimly. When the baby came a month later than Deanna expected, he was simply going to tell her it was overdue. That happened all the time, babies born three weeks late. He had thought about it all the way over on the plane.

He walked to the bathroom and spoke firmly at the closed door. 'I'll be at my office if you need me. And be sure you see the doctor. Today. Understood?'

'Yes. Perfectly.' She kept her voice steady so he wouldn't know she was crying. She couldn't go on like this. She couldn't live with it. It was too much. She had to leave him, to find her way back to Ben, with or without this damned child. But she had an idea. When she heard the front door slam, she emerged and went directly to the phone. The nurse told her he was busy but when she had the woman explain who was on the phone, he took the call.

'Deanna?' He sounded surprised. She rarely called any more.

'Hi, Dr Jones.' Her voice sagged with relief just to hear him. He would help her. He always had before. 'I have a problem. A very large problem. Can I come see you?' He could hear the urgency in her voice.

'What did you have in mind, Deanna? Today?'

'Will you hate me if I say yes?'

'I won't hate you, but I may tear out the little hair I've got left. Can it wait?'

'No. I'll go crazy.'

'All right. Be here in an hour.'

She was, and he settled back in the huge red-leather chair that she always thought of when she thought of him. 'So?'

'I'm pregnant.' His eyes didn't waver. Nothing moved in his face.

'How do you feel about it?'

'Awful. It's the wrong time ... and everything about it is wrong.'

'Marc feels that way too?'

What did he have to do with it? What did it matter? But she had to be honest. 'No. He's pleased. But there are a thousand reasons why I think it's wrong. For one thing, I'm too old.'

'Technically, you're not. But do you feel too old to cope with a small child?'

'It's not so much that, but ... I'm just too old to go through it again. What if the baby dies, what if something like that happens again?'

'If that's what you're worrying about, you don't have to, and you know it. You know as well as I that the two incidents were totally unrelated, they were just tragic accidents. It won't happen again. But I think what you're telling me, Deanna, is that you just don't want this baby. Never mind the reasons. Or are there reasons you don't want to tell me?'

'I ... yes. I – I don't want Marc's child.'

For a moment the good doctor was stunned. 'Any special reason, or is that a whim of the moment?'

'It's not a whim. I've been thinking of leaving him all summer.'

'I see. Does he know?' he asked. She shook her head. 'That does complicate things, doesn't it? But the baby is his?' He would never have asked her that ten years before, but now things were apparently different, and he asked with such kindness that she didn't mind.

'The baby is his.' She hesitated and then went on. 'Because I'm two months pregnant. If I were less pregnant, it wouldn't be his.'

'How do you know that you are two months pregnant?'

'They told me in France.'

'They could be wrong, but they probably aren't. Why don't you want the baby? Because it's Marc's?'

'Partially. And I don't want to be tied to him any more than I am. If I have the baby, I can't just get up and leave.'

'Not very easily, but you could. But then what would you do?'

'Well, I can hardly go back to the other man with Marc's child.'

'You could.'

'No, doctor. I couldn't do that.'

'No, but you don't have to stay with Marc because you're having his child. You could get out on your own.'

'How?'

'You'd find a way if that was what you wanted.'

'It isn't. I want ... I want something else.'

And then he knew.

'Before you tell me, let me ask you how your daughter fits into all of this. How would she feel, one way or the other, if you had another child?' But Deanna was looking sombrely into her lap.

At last she looked up at him. 'That doesn't matter any more either. She died two weeks ago, in France.'

For a moment everything stopped, and then he leaned forward and took her hand. 'My God, Deanna. I'm so sorry.'

'So are we.'

'And even given that, you don't want another child?'

'Not like this. Not now. I just can't. I want an abortion. That's why I'm here.'

'Do you think you could live with it? Afterwards, you know, there's no getting it back. It's almost always a situation that creates remorse, guilt, regret. You'll feel it for a very long time.'

'In my body?'

'In your heart ... in your mind. You have to want to get rid of it very badly, in order to feel comfortable about what you've done. What if there were a mistake in their diagnosis in France, and there was a chance that this were the other man's child? Would you still want the abortion?'

'I can't take the chance. I have to get rid of it in case it's Marc's. And there's no reason to think they made a mistake.'

'People do. I sometimes do myself.' He smiled benevolently at her, then frowned as he had another thought. 'Given what just happened to Pilar, do you feel able to cope with this now?'

'I have to. Will you do it?'

'If it's what you want. But first I want to examine you and make sure I agree. Hell, maybe you're not even pregnant.'

But she was. And he agreed, it was probably two months though it was always difficult to be precise so early in a pregnancy. It was just as well to do the operation quickly. Deanna seemed so determined on it.

'Tomorrow?' he asked her. 'Come in at seven in the morning, and you can go home by five. Will you tell Marc?'

She shook her head. 'I'll tell him I lost it.'

'And then?'

'I don't know. I'll have to work that out.'

'What if you decide to stay with Marc and have another child, but after this one you find you can no longer conceive? Then what, Deanna? Will you destroy yourself with guilt?'

'No. I can't imagine that happening, but if it does, I'll just have to live with it. And I will.'

'You're quite sure?'

'Totally.' She stood up, and he nodded and jotted down the address of the hospital where he wanted her to go. 'Is it dangerous?' She hadn't even thought to ask until then. She didn't really care. She would just as soon die as be pregnant now with Marc's child.

But Dr Jones shook his head and patted her arm. 'No, it's not.'

'Where are you going at this hour?' Marc picked up his head and glanced at her as she slid out of bed, annoyed at herself for having awakened him.

'To my studio. I can't sleep.'

'You should stay in bed.' But his eyes were already closed.

'I'll spend a lot of time in bed today.' At least that much was the truth.

'All right.' But he was sleeping again by the time she was dressed and he didn't see her go. She left him a note: She had gone out and would be back in the afternoon. He might be annoyed, but he would never know, and when she came home it would be too late. As she got into her car and started the motor, she looked down at her sandals and jeans. She had last worn them in Carmel with Ben. As she waited for the car to warm up, she found herself thinking of him again and looking up at the pale morning sky. The last time she had seen a sky like that, it had been with him. Then for no reason at all she remembered what the doctor had asked her: What if the baby were Ben's? But it couldn't be, how could it? Two months before, she had made love with Marc. But she had also met Ben at the end of June, it could have been his too. Why couldn't she be certain? Why couldn't she be only one month pregnant instead of two? 'Damn.' She said the word aloud as she put her foot on the gas and backed out into the street. But what if it were his child? Would she still want the abortion? She suddenly wanted to talk to him, to tell him, to ask him what he thought, but that was insane. She drove straight to the address, her mind beginning to swim.

She looked pale and drawn when she got there. Dr Jones was already waiting. He was quiet and gentle, as always, and he touched Deanna's arm.

'You're sure?' he asked. She nodded, but there was something he didn't like in her eyes. 'Let's go talk.'

'No. Let's just do it.'

'All right.' He gave instructions to the nurse, and Deanna was led to a small room where she was told to change into a hospital gown.

'Where will they take me?'

'Down the hall. You'll be gone all day. You won't be back here all day.' Suddenly for the first time she felt frightened. What if it hurt? If she died? If she haemorrhaged on the way home? If ... The nurse proceeded to explain the suction technique to Deanna, and she felt herself grow pale.

'Do you understand?'

'Yes.' It was all Deanna could think to say. She suddenly, desperately, wanted Ben.

'Are you afraid?' The nurse tried to look gentle but didn't succeed.

'A little.'

'Don't be. It's nothing. I've had three.' *Jesus*, Deanna thought. *How wonderful. At a discount?*

Deanna sat in her little room, waiting. At last she was led down the hall and then put in a room, where they positioned her on a sterile table, her feet strapped into the stirrups. It was like the delivery rooms she'd been in when she'd had those two baby boys, and then finally Pilar. A delivery room – not an abortion room. She felt herself break into a sweat. They left her alone for almost half an hour. She lay there, with her feet up, fighting the urge to cry and reminding herself that it would be over soon. Over. Gone. They'd pull it out of her with that machine. She looked around her, wondering which piece of ominous-looking machinery was The One, but they all looked equally terrifying. She felt her legs start to shake. It seemed hours before Dr Jones came into the room, and she felt herself jump.

'Deanna, we're going to give you a shot to make you a little woozy, and a little more at ease.'

'I don't want it.' She tried to sit bolt upright, and struggled with her legs in the air.

'The shot? But it will be a great deal easier for you if you take it. Believe me. It's a lot harder like this.' He looked immensely sympathetic, but she shook her head.

'I don't want it. Not the shot. The abortion. I can't. What if the baby is Ben's?' The thought had gnawed at her for the last hour, or was that only an excuse to keep it? She wasn't sure.

'Are you certain, Deanna? Or are you just afraid?'

'Both. Everything ... I don't know.' Tears filled her eyes.

'What if the baby were just yours and no one else's? If there were no man involved. If you could just have the baby to yourself. Would you want it then?'

She raised her eyes to his and silently nodded.

He undid her legs. 'Then go home, love, and work things out. You can have that baby all by yourself, if that's what you want. No one can take it away from you. It'll be all yours.'

She found herself smiling at the thought.

Marc was in the shower when she got home, and she quietly went up to her studio and locked the door. What had she done? She had decided to keep the baby, and what the doctor had said was true. She could have the baby alone and just make it hers. She could, couldn't she? Or would the baby always be Marc's? *Just as Pilar had been.* Suddenly she knew she would never escape. The baby was Marc's. She didn't yet have the courage to have it alone. And what did it matter? She had already lost Ben.

Chapter Twenty-six

'Good morning, Deanna.' Marc glanced at her as he settled himself in his chair. The usual assortment of newspapers was properly displayed, the coffee was hot, and Deanna was eating an egg. 'Hungry this morning?' It had been weeks since he'd seen her eat.

'Not very. Here, you can have my toast.' She pushed the lacy, blue Limoges plate towards him on the table. The tablecloth that morning was also a delicate pale blue. It matched her mood.

Marc looked at her carefully as she played with her egg. 'Are you still feeling ill?' She shrugged, then after a moment looked up.

'No.'

'I think perhaps you ought to call the doctor.'

'I'm seeing him anyway next week.' It had been three weeks since she'd seen him last. Three weeks since she'd run away the morning she could have had the abortion. Three weeks since she'd seen Ben. And there had been no news. She knew there wouldn't be again. She'd run into him some day, somewhere, some place, and they'd chat for a moment like old friends. And that would be all. It was over. No matter how much either of them cared. She felt her whole body sag at the thought. The only thing she wanted to do was go back to bed.

'What are you doing today?' Marc looked vague but concerned.

'Nothing. I'll probably work in the studio for a while.' But she wasn't working. She was just sitting, staring at the mountain of paintings that had been sent back from the gallery, despite Ben's initial protests. But she couldn't do it. She couldn't let him sell her work and not see him at all. And she didn't want him to see her pregnant that winter. She had had no choice. She had insisted to Sally that they be returned. Now they leaned against the walls of her studio, bleakly faced away, their mud-coloured canvas backs staring at her blindly, except for the one portrait of her and Pilar, which she looked at for hours every day.

'Would you like to join me somewhere for lunch?' She heard the words as she walked away and turned to see him in his seat in the dining room, looking like a king. He was her king now, and she was his slave, all because of this unborn child that she was too cowardly to abort.

Again she shook her head. 'No, thank you.' She attempted a smile, but it was barely a ray of sunshine in winter, less than a glimmer on the snow. She didn't want to go to lunch with him. She didn't want to be with him, or be seen with him. What if Ben saw them together? She couldn't bear the thought. She only shook her head once more and walked softly to the little studio, where she hid.

She sat huddled there, clutching her knees, with tears pouring down her face. It seemed hours later when she heard the phone.

'Hi, kiddo, what are you up to?' It was Kim. Deanna sighed to herself and tried to dredge up a smile.

'Not much. I'm sitting here in my studio, thinking I ought to retire.'

'Like hell. Not after the beautiful reviews for that show you had. How's Ben? Has he sold any more of your work?'

'No.' Deanna tried not to let her voice betray what she felt. 'He – he hasn't really had the chances.'

'I guess not. But I'm sure that when he gets back from London, he will. Sally says he'll be there for another week.'

'Oh. I didn't know. Marc got home three weeks ago, and we've been awfully busy.' Kimberly found that hard to believe; with the recent death of Pilar she knew that they weren't going anywhere. At least that was what Deanna had told her the last time they spoke.

'Can I lure you away from your studio for lunch?'

'No, I ... really ... I can't.'

Suddenly Kim didn't like what she heard. She heard a tremor of pain in Deanna's voice that frightened her, it was so raw. 'Deanna?' But there was no answer; she had begun to cry. 'Can I come by now?'

She was going to tell her no, she wanted to stop her, didn't want her to see, but she didn't have the strength.

'Deanna, did you hear me? I'm coming over. I'll be there in two minutes.'

Deanna heard Kim on the studio steps before she could come downstairs. She didn't want her to see the rows of paintings lined up against the walls, but it was already too late. Kim knocked once and stepped inside, looking around in astonishment, not understanding what she saw. There must have been twenty or thirty paintings lined up against the walls.

'What is all this stuff?' She knew it couldn't be new work. As she pulled the paintings free of the others that hid them and saw familiar themes, she turned to Deanna with surprise in her eyes. 'You've withdrawn from the gallery?' she asked. Deanna nodded. 'But why? They did a beautiful show for you, the reviews were good. The last time I talked to Ben, he told me he'd sold almost half your canvases. Why?' And then she understood. 'Because of Marc?'

Deanna sighed and sat down. 'I just had to withdraw.'

Kim sat down across from her, concern furrowing her brow. Deanna looked godawful, wan and pale and drawn, but worse than that there was something tragic stamped in her eyes. 'Deanna, I – I know how you must feel about Pilar. Or really I don't know, but I can imagine. But you can't destroy your whole life. Your career has to be separate from everything else.'

'But it isn't. Because – because of Ben.' The words were muffled by her hands and her tears.

Kim moved closer to Deanna and took her firmly in her arms. 'Just let yourself go.'

Without knowing why, Deanna did. She cried in Kim's arms for what felt like days, for the loss of Pilar, of Ben, and maybe even Marc. She knew she had lost him to his mistress. The only thing she had not lost was the baby that she didn't want. Kim said nothing to her, but let her spend her sorrow in her arms. It seemed hours before the sobs finally stopped, and Deanna looked up into Kim's face.

'Oh, Kim, I'm so sorry. I don't know what happened. I just . . .'

'For chrissake, don't apologise. You can't hold it all inside. You really can't. Do you want a cup of coffee?'

She shook her head but then brightened a little. 'Maybe a cup of tea.' Kim picked up the phone and rang the kitchen.

'And maybe afterward we could go for a walk. How does that sound?'

'What about you? Did you give up your job, or just take the day off to play shrink to me?' Deanna smiled through her red, watering eyes.

'Hell, if you can withdraw from the gallery, maybe I should just quit. It makes about as much sense.'

'No, you're wrong. I was right to do what I did.'

'But why? I just don't understand.'

Deanna was about to tell her something to put her off. Instead, she simply looked at Kim. 'I don't want to see Ben any more.'

'You've ended it with Ben?'

For a long moment everything stopped in the room as the two women looked into each other's eyes. Deanna nodded.

'You're going to stay with Marc?'

'I have to.'

She sighed and brought in the tray Margaret had left

outside the door. She handed Kim her coffee and sat down with her tea, taking a tentative sip before she squeezed her eyes tightly shut and finally spoke again. 'Marc and I are having a child.'

'What? Are you kidding?'

Deanna opened her eyes again. 'I wish I were. I found out when I was in France. I passed out in some country church a few days after the funeral, and Marc insisted on taking me to the local hospital. He thought I had something terminal, but we were both so hysterical at that point, who knew? All they found out was that I was two months pregnant.'

'That makes you how pregnant now?'

'Exactly three.'

'You don't look it.' Still looking shocked, Kim lowered her gaze to Deanna's still totally flat stomach zipped into jeans.

'I know I don't look it. I guess I'm just small this time, and I've been so nervous that I've been losing a lot of weight.'

'Jesus. Does Ben know?'

Deanna shook her head. 'I couldn't bring myself to tell him that. I was thinking of – of having it ... aborted. And I tried. I had it all set up, but when they got me on the table I just couldn't. Not with two dead babies, and now Pilar. No matter how much I don't want this child, I just can't.'

'And Marc?'

'He's ecstatic. He'll finally get his son. Or a replacement for Pilar.'

'And you, Deanna?' Her voice was painfully soft.

'What do I get? Not much. I lose the one man I truly love, I get locked into a marriage that I've discovered has been dead for years, I have another baby who may or may not live – and if it does, it will be Marc's and he'll turn it against me again, make it two thousand per cent French. God knows, Kim, I've been through it. But what are my choices, what can I do?'

259

'You could have it alone, if you want the kid. Ben might even want it, even if it isn't his.'

'Marc would never let me go. He'll do everything in his power to stop me.' It seemed a nebulous threat but she looked terrified by her own words. Kim watched the pain in her friend's eyes.

'But what could he do?'

'I don't know. Something. Anything. I feel as though I could never get away. If I tried to make it on my own, he'd do everything he could to stop me. And somehow he shakes my self-confidence, he convinces me that I can't.'

'Tell me something, Deanna.' Kim looked at her long and hard. 'Are you painting these days?'

Deanna shook her head. 'What's the point? I can't show.' She gave a small useless shrug.

'You didn't show for twenty years and you painted anyway. Why did you stop now?'

'I don't know.'

'Because Marc told you to? Because he thinks it's foolish, because he makes you and your artwork seem very small?' Kim's eyes were blazing now.

'I don't know, maybe ... He just makes everything seem so trivial and pointless.'

'And Ben?'

Deanna's voice was suddenly very soft, and there was that light in her eyes again, the one Kim had so rarely seen. 'It's very different with Ben.'

'Don't you think he could love that baby?'

'I don't know.' Deanna came back to reality and she looked long and hard at Kim. 'I can't ask him. Do you realise that I was pregnant with Marc's child the whole time I was sleeping with him? Do you have any idea how outrageous that is?' Deanna looked for a moment as though she hated herself.

'Don't be so goddamn uptight for chrissake. You didn't know you were pregnant. Did you?'

'No. Of course not.'

'You see? For God's sake, Deanna, it might even be Ben's!'

But Deanna was shaking her head. 'No. There's a discrepancy of a month.'

'Could they have made a mistake? You ought to know.'

'Yes, I should, but it's a little hard to tell. I'm irregular. That makes things very confusing. I have to rely on their theories, not mine. And they say I got pregnant in mid to late June. It could still be Ben's ... but it's not very likely.'

Kim sat silently for a long time, watching her friend, before she asked the one question that seemed to matter to her. The rest really did not. 'Deanna, do you want the baby? I mean, if none of this existed, if they both fell off the face of the earth, and there was just you, would you want this kid? Think about it for a second before you answer.'

But she didn't have to. Dr Jones had asked her the same thing. She looked up at Kim with a small tender light in her eyes. 'The answer is yes. Yes, I'd want it. I'd want it to be my baby. Mine.' She looked away with tears in her eyes. 'And I could always tell myself it was Ben's.'

Kim sighed and put down her cup. 'Then for God's sake, Deanna, have it. Enjoy it. Love it. Be with it. Thrive with it ... but have it alone. Leave Marc, so at least you can enjoy this child.'

'I can't. I'm afraid.'

'Of what?'

She hung her head as though in shame. 'The bitch of it is that I don't know.'

261

Chapter Twenty-seven

'I don't know, Kim. I don't like the layouts, and the whole look just isn't polished enough.' Ben ran a hand through his hair and stared absently at the far wall. He had been impossible to deal with all morning, and Kim knew what was distracting him as she watched him.

'Maybe if you'd gotten some sleep last night after your flight from London you'd like them a little better.' She tried to tease, but it was useless. He actually looked worse than Deanna had, and that wasn't easy.

'Don't be a smartass. You know the look I want.'

'All right. We'll try again. Will you be here long enough to check them out in a couple of weeks, or are you running off again?' He had been doing a lot of that lately.

'I'm leaving for Paris next Tuesday. But I'll be back in a couple of weeks. I have to do something about my house.'

'You're redoing it?'

'I'm moving.'

'How come? I thought you liked it.' Over the months that Kim had been handling the account, they had become friends. And his relationship with Deanna had forged an extra bond between them.

'I can't stand the place any more.' Suddenly she found his eyes boring into hers. 'Have you seen her?' Silently Kim nodded. 'How is she?'

'All right.' *Heartbroken, lousy, like you are.*

'Good. I wish I could say the same. Kim, I – I don't know how to say it. I'm going nuts. I can't stand it. I've never felt like this. Not even when my wife left me. But it just doesn't make any sense. We had everything going for us. And I promised her ... I promised that it would be just for the summer, that I wouldn't pressure her. But, Jesus, Kim, she's burying herself with that man. I don't think he even loves her.'

'If it's any consolation, I've never thought so either.'

'It's not. She still decided to stay with him, no matter what you or I think. Is she happy? Is she painting?'

Kim wanted to lie to him, but she couldn't. 'No. Neither one.'

'Then why? Because of Pilar? It just doesn't make any sense to me. She could have asked me to wait, I would have. She could have stayed with him a while. I wouldn't have pushed her. What hold can he possibly have on her?'

'Relationships are funny that way. It's hard for outsiders to see that. I've known people who hated each other and stayed married for fifty years.'

'Sounds delightful.' But as he spoke to her, his face looked grim. 'I'd call her, but I don't think I should.'

'What about you, Ben? How are you doing?' Her voice was painfully gentle.

'I'm keeping busy. I don't have any choice. She didn't leave me any choice.'

She wanted to tell him that he'd get over it, but it seemed cruel to her to say something like that. 'Can I do anything to help?'

'Yeah. Help me kidnap her.' He looked away again. 'You know, I can't even stand looking at my Wyeth any more, it looks so much like her.' He sighed and stood up, as though to get away from his own thoughts. 'I don't know what to do, Kim. I don't know what the hell to do.'

'There's nothing you can do. I wish I could help.'

'So do I. But you can't. Come on, I'll buy you lunch.'

Kim put the ads for the gallery back in her briefcase and replaced it on the floor. It was agonizing to see him like that.

'You know, I find myself wishing I'd run into her. Every restaurant I go to, every store, even the post office, I find myself searching ... as though if I look hard enough, I'll see her face.'

'She doesn't go out much these days.'

'Is she all right? She's not sick, is she?' Dumbly Kim shook her head, and he went on, 'I suppose the only solution is to keep moving, travelling, running.'

'You can't do that forever.' She stood up and followed him to the door, as his eyes looked at her sadly from behind his private prison walls.

'I can try.'

Chapter Twenty-Eight

'What did the doctor say today?' Deanna was already in bed when Marc got home. 'Everything fine?'

'He said for four months I'm awfully small, but he assumes it's just nerves and the weight I've lost. He wants me back in two weeks this time though, to make sure he can hear the baby's heart. He's still too little to hear, and Jones said he should have heard him today. Maybe in another two weeks.' But Marc didn't look worried at any of the news. 'How was your day?'

'Excessively tiresome. But we got a new case.' He looked pleased.

'Where?'

'In Amsterdam. But I'll share it with Jim Sullivan.' He looked down at her with a smile. 'I told you I wouldn't be going away all the time. Have I been true to my word?'

'Absolutely.' This time she smiled too. He had been home for two months, and he hadn't stirred. Not so much as a weekend trip to Paris. Not that it really mattered now. In some ways she'd have been relieved, but he had told her that it was over with that girl. 'There's no reason for you not to take the case though. When will it go to court?'

'Probably not till June. Well after the baby comes.'

The baby. It still didn't seem real. Not to her. Only to Marc.

'Do you want something to eat? I'm going downstairs for a snack.' He looked back at her from the doorway, again with that tender smile. All he could think of now was their child, and her well-being, as it related to their son. Sometimes it touched her, most of the time it annoyed her. She knew it had nothing to do with her. It had to do with the baby. With his Heir.

'What are you going to eat, pickles and ice cream?'

'What would you prefer, Deanna? Caviar and champagne? That can be arranged too.'

'A few crackers will be fine.'

'Most unexciting. I hope the baby has better taste.'

'I'm sure it will.'

He was back a few minutes later, with crackers for her and a sandwich for himself.

'No strawberries, no pizza, no tacos?'

It was the first time he had seen her sense of humour in months. But she had had a pleasant day. After her visit to the doctor, she had gone to lunch with Kim. Kim was helping her to keep her sanity, in these strange, lonely days. And Deanna could tell her how much she missed Ben. She was still waiting for the hurt of that to stop. So far, though, it had shown no sign of abating.

Marc was about to offer her a bite of his sandwich, when the phone rang next to her. 'Want me to get it? It's probably for you.'

'At this hour?' He looked at his watch, then nodded. It was eight in the morning in Europe. It was very probably for him. He sat down on the bed again, next to his wife. He hadn't seen her this friendly in weeks. He smiled at her once more and picked up the phone. 'Hello?' There was the usual whir of lines from overseas, and he waited to hear which of his clients was in dire need.

'Marc-Edouard?' It was a voice frantic with desperation, and he felt himself grow suddenly pale. Chantal. Deanna saw his back stiffen slightly, and he turned away from her with a frown.

'Yes? What is it?' He had spoken to her only that morning. Why was she calling him at home? He had already promised her that he would be back in Europe within the next few weeks. He was sure he could get away from Deanna just after Thanksgiving. By then, he would have paid his dues. Two-and-a-half months at her side, in the States: 'Is something wrong?'

'Yes.' She let out a long strangled sob, and he felt fear flit through his heart. 'I'm – I'm in the hospital again.'

'Ah, *merde*.' He closed his eyes, and Deanna watched him frown. 'Why this time? The same thing?'

'No. I got my insulin mixed up.'

'You never mix it up.' *Except on purpose*, he thought, remembering the night in the hospital and the panic he'd felt. 'After all these years, surely you must know ...' *Shit*. It was so awkward sitting there, talking to her, with Deanna looking on. 'But you're all right?'

'I don't know.' And then after a pause, 'Oh, Marc-Edouard, I need you. Can't you please come home?' Damn. How could he discuss it with her here?

'I don't have the right papers here to apprise you of that situation. Can we discuss it tomorrow from my office?' He picked up the phone and walked across the room to a chair. Deanna had gone back to reading her book. The conversation sounded dull, and Marc looked annoyed.

But Marc was finding the exchange anything but dull. Chantal had given a small shriek at his suggestion of discussing it from his office the next day.

'No! You can't keep putting me off!'

'I'm not putting you off. I simply don't know when I can.'

'Then let me come to you. You promised before you left that if you couldn't get away, I could come there. Why can't I?'

'I'll have to discuss it with you tomorrow, when I have the files. Can you wait ten hours and I'll call you back?' There was steel in his voice now. 'Where can I reach you?' She gave him the name of a private clinic, and he was grateful that this time at least she was not at the American Hospital, he couldn't have borne having to call her there. 'I'll get back to you as soon as

I reach the office.'

'If you don't, I'll just get on the next plane.'

She was behaving like a spoiled child. And a dangerous one. He didn't want any more trouble with Deanna. Not until after the child. Then they would just have to see. But because of his own nationality the child would be legally French, as well as American. And when in France it was under French jurisdiction. It would be his. If he chose to take his child into France, there would be nothing Deanna could do to get him out. Nothing. The thought of that would keep him afloat for the next seven months. When the baby was a month old, they'd take him to France to see his grandmother for the first time. Deanna would come of course, but then she could make her own choice. She could go or stay. But the baby would not leave the country again. If necessary, he would live with Marc's mother, and Marc would see to it that he spent more of his time there. That baby was his ... as Pilar should have been totally – would have been if it hadn't been for Deanna. The thought of the new baby kept his mind off Pilar. This was going to be entirely his child. In the meantime he needed Deanna. He needed her healthy and happy until she delivered the child. And afterwards, he would be perfectly happy to stay married to her – if she wanted to stay with the baby in France. He had it all worked out -- all of it. And now was not the time for Chantal to rock the boat.

'Marc-Edouard? Did you hear me? I said that if you didn't come over, I'd just get on the next plane.'

'To where?' His tone was icy.

'San Francisco of course. Where do you think?'

'Let me make that decision. And I'll let you know. Tomorrow. Understood?'

'*D'accord*. And Marc-Edouard?'

'Yes?' He softened a little at the sound of her voice.

'I love you so much.'

'I'm absolutely certain that is a reciprocal agreement.' For a moment he almost smiled. 'I'll talk to you in a few hours. Good night.'

Marc put the phone down with a sigh. He didn't notice that Deanna was watching.

'Disgruntled clients?'

'Nothing I can't work out.'

'Is there anything you can't work out?'

He smiled, watching her eyes. 'I hope not, my dear. I sincerely hope not.'

He was in bed half an hour later; Deanna lay awake at his side.

'Marc?'

'Yes?' The room was dark.

'Is something wrong?'

'No, of course not. What would be wrong?'

'I don't know. That call ... should you be travelling more than you are?' But she knew the answer to that question.

'Yes. But I can manage as things are. I don't want to leave you alone.'

'I'd be fine.'

'Probably. But as long as I don't have to go anywhere, I won't.'

'I appreciate it.'

It was the first kind thought she'd had of him in months, and he closed his eyes for a moment as she touched the back of his hand. He wanted to take her hand, to hold it, to kiss her, to call her *Ma Diane*, but he couldn't any more. Not any more. Not now. Already, thoughts of Chantal were crowding his mind.

'Don't worry, Deanna. Everything will be all right.' He patted her hand and turned his back to her on the very far side of the bed.

'What kind of madness is that, calling me at home in the middle of the night?' Marc-Edouard's voice raged at her over a continent and an ocean. 'What if she had answered the phone?'

'So what dammit, she knows!'

No. She *knew*. Past tense, not present. 'I don't give a damn what she knows, you have no right to do that, I've told you not to.'

'I have a right to do whatever I want.' But her voice wavered. Suddenly she was crying in his ear. 'I can't, Marc-Edouard. I can't go on. Please, it's been more than two months.'

'It's been exactly two days more than two months.' But he was stalling. He knew that if he was not to lose her, something had to be done. It was going to be a difficult winter, running between them both.

'Please . . .' She almost hated herself for begging him, but she needed him. She wanted to be with him. She didn't want to lose him again to his wife. Events were always conspiring against her, even to the death of Pilar, things that brought him and Deanna closer, moments when they needed each other. Now she needed him more and she wasn't going to lose. 'Marc-Edouard?' The threat was back in her voice.

'Chantal, darling, can't you please hang on for a little while longer?'

'No. If you don't do something now, it's over. I can't go on like this any more. It's driving me mad.'

Oh, God, what was he going to do with her? 'I'll come over next week.'

'No, you won't. You'll find an excuse.' Suddenly, her tone hardened again. 'I was brought to the hospital by a friend, Marc-Edouard, a man. The one I mentioned to you this summer. If you don't let me come to you once and for all, I'll —'

'Don't threaten me, Chantal!' But something in her words and her tone made his heart turn over. 'What are you telling me, that you'll marry this man?'

'Why not? You're married, why shouldn't I be as well?'

Christ. What if she meant it? If, like the suicide attempts, she actually went ahead and did it? 'If you come over here,' he said, 'you can't just run all over town. You'd have to be extremely discreet. You'd get bored very quickly.'

'Will you let me decide that?' She could tell that he was wavering, and at her end there was a small smile beginning to dawn on her face. 'I'll be good, darling, I promise you.'

And then he smiled too. 'You are always good. Not even good – extraordinary. All right, you determined little blackmailer, you, I'll arrange the ticket today.'

She gave a whoop of victory and joy. 'When can I come?'

'How soon will they let you leave the hospital?'

'Tonight.'

'Then come tomorrow.' They were both smiling openly now. To hell with the complications, he was dying to see her. 'And Chantal ... ?'

'*Oui, mon amour?*' She was all innocence and power, like a nuclear missile wrapped in pink silk.

'*Je t'aime.*'

Chapter Twenty-Nine

Chantal was the first person through customs, and as he watched her wend her way towards him, he felt a smile wipe itself all over his face. My God, she looked beautiful. She was draped in pale-champagne suede, with a huge lynx collar and matching hat. Her auburn hair peeked out at him, and the sapphire eyes seemed to dance as she ran to his side. He saw that, for a moment, she was going to kiss him, and then she remembered. Instead, they walked side by side, whispering, talking, laughing; they might as well have kissed and torn off each other's clothes. It was clear how happy they were to be together again. He had almost forgotten how incredibly appealing she was, how special. Reduced to their exchanges on the phone, he had almost forgotten how heady were her charms. He could barely keep his hands off her as they disappeared into his rented limousine. It was there at last that his hands touched her body, her face, that he pressed her close to him and drank her mouth with his own.

'Oh, God, you feel so good to me.' He was almost breathless as he held her, and she smiled. Now she was in control again, and her power laughed at him from her eyes.

'Idiot, you'd have kept me away for a year.'

'No, but I ... things just got too bogged down.'

She rolled her eyes and sighed. 'It doesn't matter. It's over now. As long as we're together, I don't give a damn.' For a moment he wondered how long she was planning to stay, but he didn't want to ask. He didn't want to speak to her at all, he just wanted to hold her and make love to her for the rest of his life.

The car pulled up outside the Huntington Hotel, and Marc helped her out. He had already checked her in and paid for ten days. They had nothing to do but disappear into her room. He had told his office he would be gone for the day.

'Marc?' She picked her head up sleepily in the dark and smiled. It was well after two in the morning, and she'd been asleep for two hours.

'No, it's the President. Whom did you expect?'

'You. How come you're so late?' He hadn't even called, but she hadn't really been worried.

'Clients in from out of town. We had sequestered meetings all day. We didn't even go out for lunch.' They had ordered room service instead, and he had made special arrangements to have dinner sent up from L'Étoile.

'It sounds very dull.' She smiled in the dark and turned around in the bed.

'How do you feel?' He was getting undressed and he had his back to his wife. It was strange to come home to her now. He had almost stayed out for the night, but he had to prepare the stage for that. He had promised Chantal the weekend, and a few other days.

'I feel sleepy, thank you.'

'Good. So do I.' He slipped into their bed, touched her cheek, and kissed her somewhere on the top of her head. *'Bonne nuit.'* It was what he had said to Chantal when he left, except to her he had added, *'mon amour.'*

'I don't care,' Chantal said, 'I'm not leaving. And if you stop paying for the hotel, I'll pay for it myself or find an apartment. My visa says I can stay for six months.'

'That's absurd.' Marc glared at her from across the room. They had been arguing for an hour, and Chantal's delicate chin jutted towards him in petulant fury. 'I told you. I'll be back in Paris in two weeks.'

'For how long? Five days? A week? And then what? I don't see you for another two months. *Non! Non,*

non et non! Either we stay together now, or it is finished. Forever! And that, Marc-Edouard Duras, is my last word. Make up your mind what you want. Either I stay here now, and we work out something together, or I go home. And we're through. *Finis! C'est compris?'* Her voice was a shriek in the elegant room. 'But this game we have played is over for me. No more! I told you that before I came over. I don't understand why you want to stay married to her. You don't even have Pilar as an excuse now. But I don't give a damn. I'm not going to go on living without you forever. I just can't. No, I'm staying. Or –' she looked at him ominously '– I go for good.'

'What about six months from now when your visa runs out? That is if I let you stay here.' His mind was racing and he was thinking ... six months. It could work. Chantal could go home then, and he'd follow in a few weeks. Then he'd establish Deanna and the baby on the rue François Premier with his mother. It might even make sense for him to spend most of his time there. He'd be commuting back and forth to the States, but Paris would be home base. 'You know, Chantal,' he said, 'things might just work out after all. What if I were to tell you that I am thinking of moving my main residence back to Paris next year? I would still keep the office here, but instead of travelling from here to Paris all the time, I would do it the other way around, and live over there.'

'With your wife?' She eyed him suspiciously. She wasn't sure what he had in mind.

'Not necessarily, Chantal. Not necessarily at all. I am planning a number of changes next year.' He looked at her with the faint hint of a smile, and something in her eyes lit up too.

'You'd move back to Paris? Why?' She wanted to say 'For me?' but she didn't quite dare.

'I have a number of reasons for moving back, and you're not least among them.'

'You're serious?' She stood watching him and she liked what she saw.

'I am.'

'And in the meantime?'

'I might just let you stay here.' He wore a half-smile. Almost before the words were out of his mouth, she flew across the room and into his arms.

'Do you mean it?'

'Yes, my darling, I do.'

Chapter Thirty

Marc-Edouard parked his Jaguar at the corner and pulled the large plainly wrapped box off the seat. He had already sent her flowers, and they would have been awkward to carry down the street. The box was cumbersome, but discreet. He stopped at the narrow house tucked between the palaces on Nob Hill and pushed one of two buzzers. It was a quiet flat up a shallow flight of stairs. The floors were black-and-white marble, the fixtures all well-polished brass, and he waited in amusement as he heard her run to the door. They had rented it furnished from November until June. And they had found it in less than a week. She had been in it for exactly two days, but this would be their first dinner 'at home'.

He listened to her footsteps hastening towards him, and couldn't suppress a smile. It had been the right decision, even if she had forced his hand, but it would be good to have her there all winter. Spring. Deanna didn't keep him company any more; she hid in the studio most of the time, not that she seemed to be working there. She just sat.

'*Alors!*' He pushed the buzzer again. Suddenly the door flew open and there she was, dazzling in a white chiffon caftan with silvery sandals on her feet.

'*Bonsoir*, monsieur.' She curtsied low, then rose with a mischievous grin. The lights in the apartment were dim, and in the back room he saw a small round table set for dinner with flowers and candles.

'How pretty everything is!' He held her in one arm and looked around. It was all silver and candlelight; everything sparkled and shone. It was a pretty little apartment, owned by a decorator who was spending the winter with his lover in France. A perfect arrange-

276

ment. He pulled her closer into his arms. 'You are a beautiful woman, Chantal, *ma chérie*. And you smell heavenly too.' She laughed. He had sent her a huge bottle of Joy the day before. It was delightful having her so nearby. He could run away from the office at lunch, meet her at night before he went home. He could stop by for coffee and a kiss in the morning or for love in the afternoon.

'What's in the box?' She was eyeing the large package with curious amusement. He slipped a hand slowly up her leg. 'Stop that! What's in the box?' She was laughing, and he was running his hand up and down her bare legs.

'What box? I didn't bring anything in a box.' He brought his mouth to the back of her knee, and then slowly upward, on the inside of her thigh. 'I find you much more interesting, my love, than anonymous packages.' And so did she. In minutes the caftan lay crumpled on the floor.

'*Merde!*' She jumped away from his arms, as they lay drowsing on the bed. They had been asleep there for almost half an hour. Marc-Edouard sat up in surprise.

'*Merde?* What do you mean?' He tried to look offended as he stretched his long naked body across the bed. He looked like a very long, very pale cat. But she was already halfway across the room.

'The turkey! I forgot!' She sped into the kitchen, and he lay back on the bed with a grin. But she was back in a minute, looking relieved.

'*Ca va?*'

'*Oui, oui.* I've been cooking him for almost six hours, but he still looks all right.'

'They always do. They just taste like straw. And why, may I ask, after a mere three weeks in the States, have you already started cooking turkey?' He laughed at her as he sat up, and she came to sit next to him on the bed.

'I cooked it because tomorrow is Thanksgiving, and I am very thankful.'

'Are you? For what?' He lay back again, as he tousled her thick auburn hair. It touched her shoulders now and delicately framed her face. 'What are you so thankful for, pretty girl?'

'You. Living here. Coming to the States. *La vie est belle, mon amour.*'

'Is it? Then go open your package.' He tried to conceal a smile.

'Oh, *toi alors*! You!' She ran into the other room and came back with the brown-paper-wrapped box. 'What is it?' She looked like a little girl at Christmas and he smiled. *'Qu'est-ce que c'est?'*

'Open it and see!' He was enjoying it now almost as much as she was as she tore off the brown paper and discovered a very plain-looking brown box. He was delighted at the ruses he had used. She sat staring at the box, afraid to open it, still enjoying the surprise.

'Is it something for the house?' Her eyes were enormous as they held his, but his gaze rapidly slipped down to the perfectly shaped breasts as she knelt, naked, next to him on the bed, clutching the large box.

'Go on, silly ... *vas-y.*' She pulled off the lid and burrowed into the tissue paper to discover what was there. Her hands shot backward as though she had touched flame and instantly flew to her mouth.

'Ah, *non*! Marc-Edouard!'

'Oui, mademoiselle?'

'Oh ...' Her hands burrowed back into the tissue, and her eyes grew even wider as slowly, carefully, with exquisite caution, she pulled it out. This time she gasped as she held it aloft, then ran her hand gently up and down the pelts. It was a very beautiful, bittersweet chocolate, Russian sable coat. 'Oh, my God.'

'Let's try it on.' He took it from her and slipped it carefully over her shoulders. She shrugged herself into it and buttoned it to her chin. It was beautifully cut and it looked magnificent on her as it fell in sleek lines over her tiny waist and narrow hips.

'*Bon Dieu, chérie, que tu es belle.* How incredibly beautiful you are, Chantal. Oh, my dear!' He looked on in mingled awe and ecstasy as she twirled on one foot, the coat opening subtly to reveal a bare leg.

'I've never had anything like this.' She looked stunned as she watched herself in the mirror and then back at him. 'Marc-Edouard, it's such ... such an unbelievable gift!'

'So are you.' Without another word he left the room to get the bottle of champagne. He returned with the bottle and both glasses, set them down, and took her into his arms. 'Shall we celebrate, my darling?'

With a golden smile she nodded and melted again into his arms.

'What's Marc doing tonight?'

'Business meetings, as usual.' Deanna smiled at Kim. 'He has clients here from Europe these days. I never see him.' It was the first time she had actually let Kim drag her out to dinner. Between the death of Pilar and her pregnancy, Deanna had been nowhere for months. They had decided, as usual, on Trader Vic's. 'Jesus, I hate to admit it, but it feels good to get out.' And here she had no qualms about running into Ben. She knew he hated places like this.

'How do you feel?'

'Not bad. It's hard to believe I'm already almost five months.' But it was finally beginning to show, just the merest of bulges in the A-shaped dress of black wool crepe.

'Do you want a shower?' Kim looked at her with a grin over the hors d'oeuvres.

'A baby shower?' Deanna asked. Kim nodded, and Deanna rolled her eyes. 'Of course not. I'm too old for that. My God, Kimberly!'

'You are not. If you're not too old for a baby, you're not too old for a shower.'

'Don't start me on that one!' But Deanna was looking at her with a wry smile. There was no anger or pain in her eyes tonight. Kim hadn't seen her looking this peaceful in weeks, and her sense of humour seemed to have returned. 'What are you doing for Thanksgiving by the way? Anything special?'

'Nothing much. I'm having dinner with some friends. You?'

'The usual. Nothing.' Deanna shrugged. 'Marc will be working.'

'Want to come with me?'

'No. I'll probably manage to drag him out to dinner somewhere. I always did with Pilar. A restaurant or a hotel, it's not what you'd call a real Thanksgiving, but it'll do. And at least we won't be stuck with turkey sandwiches for two weeks.' But suddenly she found herself wondering what Ben was doing. Probably going to Carmel, or maybe he was still back East. She didn't want to ask Kim.

The conversation drifted on to other subjects then. It was ten-thirty when at last they stood up, a little tired, a lot full, and having spent a very pleasant evening without any strain.

'Can I lure you out for a drink?' Kim asked. But she didn't look as though she wanted to drag out the evening any longer. And Deanna was tired.

'Maybe another time. I hate to admit it, but I'm beat. I'm still at the stage when I'm tired all the time.'

'When does that stop, or does it?'

'Usually almost exactly at four months, but this time it seems to have dragged on. I'm four and a half, and still sleepy all the time.'

'So enjoy it and be glad you don't work.' But she wasn't. She wished that she did. It would give her something to think of while she didn't paint. She still hadn't been able to start her work. Something stopped her every time she sat down. Her thoughts would shift instantly to Pilar or Ben, or she would find herself panicking about the baby. Hours would drift by while she did nothing but sit, staring blindly into space.

They brought Kim's little red MG up to the door. With a groan Deanna got in as Kim tipped the valet and slid behind the wheel.

'I'm going to have to give up driving with you in a couple of months.' Her legs were cramped almost up to her chin and she laughed, as did Kim.

'Yeah, I guess you'd have a hell of a time getting into this thing with a belly.' They both laughed again, and Kimberly drove off, turning left out of Cosmo Place and then left again, until she made a sharp right at Jones to avoid some construction blocking the street. 'We might as well drive past Nob Hill.' She glanced over at Deanna with a smile, and they sat together in silence. Deanna was longing for her bed.

They had stopped at a stop sign when she saw them. For a moment she marvelled at how much the man looked like Marc, and then she realised with a start that it was he. She felt herself gasp. Kim looked sharply at her, then in the direction she was staring. It was Marc with an elegant woman draped in a magnificent dark sable coat. They were wrapped in each other's arms. He looked like a much younger man, and she looked especially beautiful with her hair loose and full and a bright red dress peeking through the coat. She threw her head back and laughed, and Marc kissed her full on the mouth. Deanna stared.

As the woman pulled away, Deanna suddenly saw who she was. It was the girl from the airport – the one she had seen him with the night Pilar died. She suddenly felt as though all the air had been squeezed out of her until she had to gasp for breath. They climbed into his car. Deanna clutched Kimberly's arm.

'Drive, please. Let's go. I don't want him to see us ... he'll think ...' She turned her head away from the

281

window, wanting to see no more, and as though by reflex Kim stomped her foot on the gas. The car lurched forward, and they sped towards the bay as Deanna tried to settle her rapidly whirling mind. What did it mean? Why was the girl there? Was it ... did it ... had he ... but she knew all the answers, as did Kim. They had sat there for five minutes, silent and staring, in the little red car. It was Kim who finally spoke first.

'Deanna, I – I'm sorry. Is there ... shit! I don't know what to say.' She glanced at Deanna. Even in the darkness she looked terrifyingly pale. 'Do you want to come home with me for a while until you calm down?'

'You know what's very strange?' She turned to Kim with those huge, luminous green eyes. 'I am calm. I feel as though everything has suddenly stopped. All the whirling and confusion and fear and despair ... it's all over, it's gone.' She stared out the window into the foggy night and she spoke to Kim without turning to see her face. 'I think I know now what I'm going to do.'

'What?' Kim felt worried about her friend. It had been one hell of a shock. She herself was still shaking.

'I'm going to leave him, Kim.' For a moment Kimberly didn't respond, she only looked at Deanna's profile, sharply etched against the night. 'I can't live like this for the rest of my life. And I think it's been like this for years. I saw him with her in Paris ... the night Pilar ... she came in with him from Athens. The joke of it is that when he came home in September, he swore it was over.'

'Do you think it's serious?'

'I don't know. Maybe it doesn't matter. The trouble is' – she finally looked back at her friend – 'there isn't enough in it for me. No matter what. I'm alone all the time. We don't share anything and we won't even share this child. He'll take it away from me, just as he did Pilar. Why should I stay with him? Out of duty, out of cowardice, out of some insane feeling of loyalty that I've dragged with me over the years? For what? Did you see him tonight? He looked happy, Kim. He looked young. He hasn't looked like that with me in almost eighteen years. I'm not even sure any more if he ever did. Maybe she's good for him. Maybe she can give him something I never had. But whatever it is, that's his problem. I'm getting out.'

'Why don't you give it some thought.' Kim spoke quietly and looked at Deanna. 'Maybe this isn't the right time. Maybe you should wait until after the baby comes. Do you want to be alone when you're pregnant?'

'Maybe you haven't noticed – I already am.'

Kim agreed, but she was afraid of the look in Deanna's eyes. She had never seen that burning determination there before. It was frightening. Finally they came to a stop in front of her house.

'Do you want me to come in?' At least they knew that Marc wouldn't be home. But Deanna shook her head.

'No. I want to be alone. I have to think.'

'Will you talk to him tonight?'

She looked at Kimberly for a long time before she answered, and this time Kim saw pain in her eyes. It did hurt. Somewhere inside her she still cared. 'Maybe not. He may not come home.'

Chapter Thirty-one

Alone in her bedroom, Deanna slowly pulled off the black dress and stood staring at herself in the mirror. She was still pretty, and in some ways still young. The skin on her face was supple and taut, her neck had the graceful sweep of a swan, the eyes were large, the eyelids didn't droop and the chin didn't sag, the breasts were still firm, the legs thin, the hips small. There was no real sign of age, and yet she looked at least ten years older than that girl tonight. She had had the glow and the glamour and the excitement of a mistress. There was no fighting that. Was that what he wanted then? Did that make the difference? Or was it something else? Was it that she was French, that she was one of his own ... or maybe only that he loved her. Deanna wondered as she climbed into her robe. She wanted to ask him all those questions, wanted to hear all the answers from him – if he'd tell her, if he'd ever come home. She didn't want to wait all night long to ask him, she wanted to ask him now, but it had been clear that he and the girl were going out on the town. It might be daybreak before he came home, claiming that he had been involved in interminable negotiations and had had a sleepless night. She suddenly wondered how many of his stories had been lies, how long this had gone on. She lay her head back in the chair and closed her eyes against the soft lights. Why did he go on with the marriage, now that Pilar was gone? He'd had the perfect opportunity to leave Deanna in Paris, to tell her they were through. Why didn't he? Why had he stayed? Why did he want to hang on? And then suddenly she knew. The baby. That was what he wanted. A son.

She smiled to herself then. It was funny really. For

the first time in their nearly twenty years together, she had the upper hand. She had the one thing he wanted. His son. Or even a daughter, now that Pilar was gone. But Marc wanted her child. It was mad really. He could have had a baby with that girl, since he appeared to hang on to her too. But for some reason he had not. It amused her. In a way she had him now. By the throat. She could leave him, or stay. She could make him pay. Maybe she could even force him to get rid of the girl. Or pretend to, as he had. He had let her think the affair was over, but it very clearly was not. With a sigh she sat up in the chair and opened her eyes. She had been living with her eyes closed for too many years. Silently she walked out of the room and down the stairs of the darkened house. She found herself in the living room, sitting in the dark and looking out at the lights on the bay. It would be strange not being there any more, leaving this house – leaving him. It would be frightening to be alone, to have no one to take care of her, or the new child. It would all be terrifying and new. But it would be clean. It wouldn't be lonely in the same way ... It wouldn't be a lie. She sat there, alone, until dawn. Waiting for him. She had made up her mind.

It was just after five when she heard his key turn in the lock. She walked softly to the door of the living room and stood there, a vision in white satin.

'*Bonsoir.*' She said it to him in French. 'Or should I say *bonjour*?' The first light of day was streaking pink and orange into the sky over the mirror-flat bay. For once there was no fog. The first thing she saw about him was that he was drunk. Not disgustingly so, but enough.

'You're already up?' He tried to hold himself steady, but he pitched forward slightly and steadied himself on the back of a chair. He looked uncomfortable to have to be talking to her at all. 'It's terribly early, Deanna.'

'Or terribly late. Did you have a good time?'

'Of course not. Don't be absurd. We sat in the board room until four o'clock. And then we had drinks. To celebrate.'

'How wonderful.' Her voice was like ice. He stared at her, as if hoping to find the key. 'What were you celebrating?'

'A new ... deal.' He almost said 'coat', but caught himself just in time. 'A fur trade arrangement with Russia.' He looked pleased with himself and then smiled at his wife. Deanna did not smile back.

She looked like a statue. 'It was a very beautiful coat.' The words fell between them like rocks.

'What do you mean?'

'I think we both know perfectly well what I mean. I said it was a beautiful coat.'

'You're not making sense.' But his eyes seemed to waver from her gaze.

'I believe I am. I saw you tonight with your friend. I gather this is a lasting affair.' She looked wooden as she stood there, and he spoke not at all. After a moment he turned away from Deanna and looked out at the bay.

'I could tell you that she was passing through.' He turned to face her again. 'But I won't. These have been difficult times for me. Pilar ... worries with you ...'

'Does she live here now?' Deanna was relentless with those enormous green eyes. He shook his head. 'No, she's only been here for a few weeks.'

'How nice. Am I to accept this as part of my future, or will you eventually make a choice? I imagine she asks you the same questions. In fact right now I daresay the choice could be mine.'

'It could.' For a moment he seemed to be wavering again, then he stood up very straight. 'But it won't be, Deanna. You and I have too much at stake.'

'Really? What?' But she knew exactly what he meant. They had nothing at stake any more though.

After tonight the baby was hers. Not theirs. Hers.

'You know exactly what. Our child.' He tried to look tender but he only glared. 'That means everything to me. To us.'

'Us? You know what, Marc, I don't even believe there is an "us". There is a you and a me, but there is no "us". Your only "us" is with that girl. I could see that in your face tonight.'

'I was drunk.' For a moment desperation crept into his eyes. Deanna saw it, but she no longer cared.

'You were happy. You and I haven't been happy with each other in years. We cling to each other out of habit, out of fear, out of duty, out of pain. I was going to leave you the weekend after Pilar died. If I hadn't found out I was pregnant, I would have. And now that's exactly what I'm going to do.'

'I won't let you. You'll starve!' He was angry now, and there was a vicious light suddenly in his eyes. She wasn't going to take away the one thing he cared about now – the child.

'I don't need you to survive.' They were words of bravado, and they both knew it.

'What will you do to eat, my darling? Paint? Sell your little sketches to people on the street? Or go back to your own lover?'

'What lover?' Deanna felt as though she had been slapped.

'You think I don't know, you self-righteous, cheating bitch. You make me speeches about my ... activities ...' He swayed slightly as he hurled the words at her head. 'But you are hardly lily-white yourself.'

She was suddenly pale. 'What do you mean?'

'Exactly what you think I mean. I left for Athens and you obviously had a little fling. I don't know with whom and I don't care, because you're my wife and that's my child. I own you, both of you, do you understand?'

Everything inside her raged. 'How dare you say that

to me! How dare you! You may have owned me before, but you don't own me now and you never will, and you'll never own this child. I won't let you do what you did with Pilar.'

He grinned at her evilly from the stairs. 'You have no choice, my dear, the child is mine . . . Mine, because I chose to accept it, to be its father, to keep you in spite of what you did. But don't you ever forget that I know. You're no better than I am, in spite of all your saintly airs. But remember,' his eyes narrowed and he swayed again, 'it is I who will keep your child from being a bastard. I'm giving him my name. Because I want him, and not because he's mine.'

Deanna's voice was like measured ice. She stood immobile, watching Marc. 'The baby isn't yours then, Marc?'

He bowed awkwardly at her and inclined his head. 'Correct.'

'How do you know?'

'Because the woman you resent so greatly never wanted children and to please her I had a vasectomy several years ago.' He stared at Deanna, satisfied with the disclosure, as Deanna steadied herself unthinkingly on the back of a chair.

'I see.' There was a long silence between them. 'Why are you telling me this now?'

'Because I'm tired of lies, and your miserable pathetic face, and your feeling put upon and used and abused by me. I have not abused you, madam. I have done you a favour. I have kept you, and your child, in spite of your appalling behaviour. In spite of the fact that you're an adulteress. And now he's gone, and you have no one to turn to but me. You are mine.'

'To do with as you choose, is that it, Marc?' Her eyes raged at him, but he was too drunk to see it.

'Precisely. And now I suggest that you take yourself and my son to bed, and I will take myself to bed. I will see you in the morning.' He marched solemnly upstairs, totally unaware of the effect of his admission. Deanna had been freed.

Chapter Thirty-two

The door to the back of the house, behind the kitchen, had been locked, and she had the key. She had called Kim and asked her to rent a car – a station wagon. She would explain later. She had had the grocery store deliver a dozen boxes. The equipment in her studio went easily into three. Her photographs and albums fitted in five. The paintings were all neatly stacked next to the back stairs. Six suitcases waited to be packed. She picked up the phone and asked Margaret for her help. She would not do this alone. She had been working in her studio since six, and it was almost nine. She knew that Marc had probably already left the house. He didn't follow her to her studio after she left their room, and the silence in the house had been deafening. The end had come quietly, in silence. Now she could put away the past. In a dozen boxes and a few valises. She was leaving him everything else. It was all his. The furniture from France; the paintings; the rugs; and the silver, which had been his mother's, almost all of it sent from France. All that she had collected over the years was in her studio – art books, brushes, paints, a few trinkets, some bits and pieces that she liked but were worth nothing. She had her clothes. And the jewellery she would take too. She would sell it to eat, until she found a job. She was taking all her paintings, they meant nothing to him, and she could sell those too. All except the one of herself and Pilar. That was not a painting to sell, it was a treasure of a lifetime. The rest he could have. He could have it all.

She unlocked the door at the foot of the studio stairs and hesitantly made her way through the house. What if he was still there? If he was waiting? If he knew what she was going to do and how soon? But it didn't matter now. He couldn't stop her. He had told her what she needed to know last night. The baby wasn't his, it was Ben's. And he had known all along. But it didn't matter any more. None of it did.

'Margaret, is ... ?' She wasn't quite sure what to say.

'He left for the office at half past eight.' Margaret's eyes were brimming with tears. 'Mrs Duras, you're not ... Oh, don't leave us, don't go ...'

It was the speech that should have been made by Marc, except that he already knew he had lost and he was too drunk the night before to follow through on his fears. He must have figured that if he slept it off and let her hide in her studio, he could come home with a handsome piece of jewellery, an apology, and a lie, and all would be well again. Not this time. Deanna put an arm around Margaret.

'I have to. But you'll come and see me.'

'I will?' The old woman looked crushed; Deanna smiled at her through her own tears. She was crying for herself now, not for him.

The doorbell rang as they finished the second suitcase. Deanna jumped, startled, and for a moment Margaret looked like she might panic, but Deanna sped down the stairs and discovered that it was Kim.

'I got the biggest station wagon they had. It looks like a boat.' She tried to smile but saw that Deanna was not in the mood. There were dark circles under her eyes, her hair was dishevelled, and her eyes were rimmed with red. 'Looks like it must have been a great night.'

'The baby's not his.' It was the first thing she could think of to say, and then suddenly she was smiling at Kim. 'It's Ben's, and I'm so glad.'

'Jesus H. Christ.' For a moment, Kim didn't know whether to laugh or cry, but somehow she felt immensely relieved. Deanna was free. 'Are you sure?'

'Absolutely.'

'And you're leaving?'

'Yes. Now.'

'I had a suspicion it was something like that. Because of the baby?' They were still standing at the door. Deanna started slowly towards the stairs.

'That and everything else. The other girl, the baby. It's not a marriage, Kim. And whatever it is or it isn't, it's over. I knew that for certain last night.'

'Will you tell Ben?' But it was a dumb question. She knew that Deanna would. She knew it, until Deanna shook her head. 'Are you kidding? Why not?'

'Why? So I can run from Marc's house to his? So he can take care of me too? I left him, Kim. I walked out. I went back to Marc and never told him I was having a child. What right do I have to call him now?' Her eyes looked too big in her face. Kim stared at her, trying to make sense of what was being said.

'But you're having his baby. What more right do you need?'

'I don't know. I just know I won't call.'

'Then what the hell are you doing?' Kim grabbed her arm as she started up the stairs.

'Leaving here. I'll find an apartment and take care of myself.'

'Oh, for chrissake, will you stop being so noble? How the hell will you eat?'

'Paint, work, sell my jewellery ... You'll see. Come on, I have to finish upstairs.' Kim looked sober as she followed her up the stairs. She thought leaving Marc was the best idea Deanna had had yet but not calling Ben was insane.

Margaret had just finished packing the last bag. There was nothing left in the room except the things that belonged to Marc. The little trinkets and photographs, the tiny mementoes, the jewel box, and the books ... all were packed and gone. She stopped for only a moment on the threshold, then hurried down the stairs.

It took them twenty-five minutes to pack the car, with Margaret crying ceaselessly and Kim carrying all the heavy bags. Deanna carried only her paintings, which were light.

'Don't touch that!' Kim shouted at Deanna once, when she had been about to pick up a valise. 'You're five months pregnant, you jackass.' Deanna smiled.

'No, I'm not. Probably a lot more like four.' Then they both grinned. Deanna had figured that out in the early morning as she cleaned all her paintbrushes, wrapped them in newspaper, and put them away. He had told her that she had conceived at the end of June, which was when he'd left. But it was probably more like late July, when she was with Ben. That explained too why Dr Jones hadn't heard the heartbeat until a month after he thought he should have and why she was so small. Also, why she was still so tired. She was probably almost exactly four months pregnant. 'Oh, my God.' She suddenly looked up at Kim. 'Is today Thanksgiving?'

'It is.'

'Why didn't you tell me?'

'I thought you knew.'

'Aren't you supposed to be somewhere?'

'Not until later. We'll get you settled first. You can have a nap. And then we'll get dressed and have a turkey dinner.'

'You're nuts. You act as though you've been planning for weeks to have me stay.' The two women exchanged a smile as they stowed the last painting in the back of the car. 'I'm going to stay at a hotel, you know.' She said it firmly as she looked at the paintings and packages in the car.

'No, you're not.' Kim was equally firm. 'You're staying with me. Until you're ready to move out.'

'We'll discuss it later. I want to go back inside for a minute and check.'

'Is there any chance Marc might come back? It is a holiday after all.'

But Deanna shook her head. 'Not for him. He works on Thanksgiving.' And then she smiled a half-smile and shook her head. 'It isn't French.' Kim nodded and got into the car as Deanna disappeared back into the house. Margaret was in the kitchen, and for a moment Deanna was alone. For the last time in what had been *her* house – except that it had never been. It had always been his. Maybe the little French girl in the fur coat would like it, maybe it would all mean something to her.

Deanna stood in the hall, looking through the living room, glancing at the portraits of Marc-Edouard's ancestors. It was amazing, after eighteen years she was leaving with almost as little as she'd brought when she had come. Some boxes, some canvases, her clothes. The clothes were more expensive now. The jewellery would keep her alive. The paintings were better, the art supplies finer. But it all still fitted in one car. Eighteen years in as many boxes and bags. She sat down at her desk then and pulled a piece of paper out of a drawer. It was Wedgwood blue, trimmed in white, and the letterhead said MME MARC-EDOUARD DURAS. She pulled out her pen, thought for a moment, and then wrote only a few words:

I loved you, darling.
Goodbye.

She folded the sheet of paper, wiped a tear from her face with the back of one hand, and left the note stuck in the mirror in the hall. When she turned away, she saw Margaret watching her, the tears streaming from her eyes. Deanna said nothing, only went to her, held her tightly for a moment. Then, with tears streaming from her own eyes, she nodded and walked to the door. She said only one word as she left, and she said it so softly that Margaret could barely hear. She said it gently as she closed the door and smiled. 'Adieu.'

Chapter Thirty-three

'Why won't you come?' Kim looked disappointed. 'It's Thanksgiving, and I won't leave you alone.'

'Yes, you will. I'm an uninvited guest, and an exhausted one at that. I can't, love. Honest. I'm just too goddamn tired. Leave me here, and I may even revive by tomorrow.' But Kim wasn't sure of that either. The last twenty-four hours had taken their toll. Deanna looked exhausted and bleak. Kim had even gone so far as to call Dr Jones from the kitchen phone, where Deanna wouldn't hear. She explained to him what had happened. His advice had been to just let Deanna be. Let her go at her own pace and do what she wanted. He felt sure that she'd be all right. On the strength of that Kim decided not to push.

'All right. But you're sure you won't be lonely.'

'No, more likely I'll be asleep.' She smiled tiredly at her friend and suppressed a yawn. 'I don't think I'll miss Thanksgiving at all this year.' The two women exchanged a smile, and Deanna was asleep before Kim left. Kim tiptoed out the door and quietly locked it.

The key turned in the lock around eleven that night, and for a moment he held his breath. It had been insane not to call, but he hadn't known what to say. What could he tell her? How could he take back what he'd said? He had wanted to buy her something pretty, something to buy her back, but all the stores had been closed. Thanksgiving. A day of thanks. He had spent half the day working at his desk, and the other half quietly with Chantal. She had known that something was wrong, but she was not quite sure what. He had clung to her in their lovemaking in a very odd way.

He opened the door and looked up. There was no

light and no sound. She was obviously asleep. Her car had been in the garage. He didn't even see Margaret's light shining under her door down the hall. The entire house was still, and he put on only a small light as he hung up his coat. And then he saw the note paper, stuck into the frame of the mirror near the door. Was she out? Had she gone somewhere with a friend? He reached for the paper and held it, a sudden, odd feeling clutching at his heart. He stood there for a moment, as though waiting to hear her voice or her foot on the stairs. He looked up again and heard only silence, and then slowly he opened the folds of the paper at last. His eyes swam and his head pounded as he read it. 'I loved you, darling. Goodbye.' Why 'loved'? Why in the past tense? But he knew. He had told her the one thing that she could never know. That the baby was not his. She knew now that he had lied to her about the baby, and about Chantal ... She knew about his other life. She had seen him with Chantal in Paris and again the other night. With feet like lead he tried to race up the stairs. He would find Deanna there. She would be asleep in their bed. All day he had ignored what had happened between them, hoping it would go away. Calling her would make it real. He couldn't. He didn't want to do that. Now all he had to do was run to the bed and he'd find her there, asleep.

But when he reached their room, he found it as he dreaded he would – empty. She was gone. Deanna was gone.

Marc-Edouard stood deathly still for a long moment, not knowing what to do. Then fighting back tears, he reached for the phone. He needed her. Desperately. She had to be there for him now. He knew she would be. He dialled, but when Chantal answered, she sounded strange.

'Chantal ... I – I have to see you ... I'll be right there.'

'Is something wrong?' She sounded distracted and in a hurry.

'Yes ... no ... Just be there. I'm on my way over.' She had wanted to tell him to hurry, but she hadn't known quite what to say, and she was still feeling awkward and looking a little bit confused when he arrived only moments later. But he saw nothing. He only took her quickly in his arms the moment she opened the door.

'Darling, what is it? You look ill.'

'I am ... I don't know ... She's gone.'

Poor man. Pilar again. Was he still so excessively haunted by that? But what had happened to trigger it so suddenly? 'I know, my darling, but you have me.' She held him close as they sat together on the couch.

'But the baby ...' And then he realised that he shouldn't have blurted it out.

'What baby?' Had he gone mad? She looked frightened as she pulled away from him.

'Nothing ... I'm upset ... It's Deanna. She's gone.'

'For good? She left you?' He nodded numbly, and Chantal grinned.

'I'd say that's cause for celebration, not despair.' Without thinking further, she rose from the couch and went out to the kitchen to find one of the bottles of champagne Marc had left with her only a few days before. She returned with the bottle and two glasses, and then stopped as she saw the agony on Marc's face. 'Are you that unhappy then?'

'I don't know. I'm stunned. I said some things ... I shouldn't have ... I – I overplayed my hand.'

Chantal stared at him with chilly eyes. 'I didn't realise you were that anxious to keep her. Now what? You fight to get her back?' As he watched her, he slowly shook his head. He couldn't get Deanna back and he knew it. While trying to tie her to him forever, he had told her the one thing that had severed her from him. The baby wasn't his. 'By the way' – Chantal paused only for a moment – 'what was that business you just mentioned about a baby?' He said nothing, he only stared at something she could not see. The death of hope. 'Was she pregnant, Marc?' Her words were like a vice at his throat, and silently he nodded.

'Did she know it wasn't yours?'

'Not until last night.'

'I see. And that was why you stayed with her until now – for a child that wasn't even yours . . .' Her voice drifted away like a kind of distant death knell, disappointment filling her heart as well. 'I didn't realise it meant that much to you.'

'It doesn't.' He lied to her and tried to take her in his arms.

'Yes, it does.' The champagne stood unopened. They looked at each other in despair. 'Yes, in fact, it does.'

'We can adopt a child,' Marc said. Slowly Chantal nodded. She knew that she would have to if it meant that much to him, but she didn't want children. She never had.

'Yes, I suppose we can.' And then with sudden recollection, she glanced at her watch. 'What are you going to do now?'

'Marry you.' He tried to smile as he said it, but the words felt like lead in his mouth. 'If that's what you still want.'

'It is.' She sounded solemn, but there was a filament of worry lurking in her eyes. 'But I didn't mean that, darling. I meant tonight.'

'I don't know. Can I stay here?' The idea of going back to his own home was unbearable to him, and it was too soon to take Chantal there, to sleep in the bed Deanna had vacated only the night before. She had slept in the studio after his disclosure.

'Why don't we go out to dinner?'

'Now?' He looked at her, shocked. 'I'm hardly in the mood. A lot has changed for me in the past few hours, and no matter how much I love you, I need to adjust.'

For a moment he wondered if he had made a mistake coming to Chantal so quickly, before he had absorbed the shock. She seemed to understand nothing of what he was feeling. 'Couldn't we just eat here?'

'No. I want to go out.' She said it nervously now, as though she were in a hurry, and he noticed suddenly that she was wearing a black silk dress, as though she had been planning to go to dinner anyway.

'Were you going somewhere when I called?' He looked as though he didn't understand.

'I just thought I'd go out somewhere for dinner.'

'Alone?' He looked shocked.

'Obviously.' She laughed at him, but it had a tinsel ring, and before she had said more, the doorbell rang. She looked rapidly at Marc-Edouard and then hurried towards the door. 'I'll be right back.'

From where he sat on the couch, his view of the doorway was obscured, but he heard her open the door and step outside, and then suddenly something inside him raged. He strode across the room, following her path, and reached the almost-closed door where he could hear her speaking softly on the other side. He pulled it sharply open and heard her gasp as she jumped slightly aside. She was speaking to his partner, Jim Sullivan, who looked somewhat shocked to be facing Marc.

'Am I interrupting you, or would you care to step inside?' He was looking at his partner, but his words were addressed to both of them. Silently the trio walked into the apartment. Chantal closed the door.

'Darling, it's really ... Jim just thought I'd enjoy Thanksgiving dinner. I thought you would be ... at home ...' Her face was taut with embarrassment, and her borrowed gaiety fooled no one.

'I see. How charming. Odd that neither of you mentioned it to me.'

'I'm sorry, Marc.' Jim looked at him soberly as they stood uncomfortably in the middle of the living room.

'I don't think there's much more I can say.' Marc-Edouard turned his back to him. Jim simply touched his shoulder, and a moment later Marc heard the sound of the front door close. He turned slowly to face Chantal.

'Is that what you've been doing?'

Her eyes were wide as she shook her head. 'I've only had dinner with him a couple of times. I didn't really think you'd mind.' But they both knew it was a lie.

'What do I say to you now?'

'That you forgive me. And I say to you that it will never happen again.' She slipped herself quietly into his arms and held him close as he slowly bowed his head and felt the silk of her hair on his face. Tears hovered in his eyes as he held her, because he knew that it would happen again and again ... and again.

Chapter Thirty-four

Kimberly drove down the narrow streets of Sausalito and then into a small alley leading towards the bay. She glanced at the paper next to her on the seat and confirmed that she was going the right way. Another turn, another alley, a dead end, and then she was there. There was a tiny white-picket fence, a huge bush covered with daisies, and a little house hidden beyond. It was the gem Deanna had described, and Kimberly loved it on sight. Her arms were filled with packages, and she wrestled to reach the bell. A moment later Deanna pulled open the door.

Deanna was wearing jeans and red espadrilles and a full, red sweater over a bright yellow blouse. Her hair was held up in a knot, and there was a gentle smile for her friend in her eyes.

'Merry Christmas, madam. I'm so glad you could come!' She held out her arms to Kim, and they hugged. 'I only left you two weeks ago, and I'm already homesick.'

'Don't be. This is divine.' Kim followed her inside and looked around. Deanna had been working industriously, painting the kitchen, cleaning the floors. In the corner there was a tiny Christmas tree with silvery balls and blinking lights. There were three packages under the tree, and they were all marked KIM.

'Well, do you really like it?' Deanna looked like a little girl as she grinned. For the first time in a long time she looked happy and at peace. In only a few weeks she had found something of herself. There was not a great deal of furniture in the bright little front room, but what she had was comfortable and inviting. There was wicker, freshly painted white, and a wonderful old couch she had reupholstered in a soft blue.

There were plants everywhere, and old bottles filled with flowers. Some of her favourite paintings hung on the walls, and she had bought a wonderful, richly patterned carpet. There were copper pots on the mantelpiece and brass candlesticks on a little wooden dining table just large enough for two, and the room had boasted a small bronze chandelier of its own. She had made the curtains herself out of a starched, lacy fabric she'd found in a trunk. She looked as though she'd lived there for years. There was one tiny bedroom she'd endowed with a wonderful old print wallpaper in a warm, dusty rose, and another tiny bedroom next to it, empty save for a bassinet and a rocking horse, huddled near the door.

Kim looked around appreciatively and settled herself in a chair. 'I'm in love with it, Deanna. Can I stay?'

'For at least a year. But I think you'd find it has a few kinks. The hot water comes and goes, the oven takes about a week to warm up, the windows stick, the chimney smokes ...' She grinned. 'But I love it. Isn't it just like a little dollhouse?'

'Exactly. I like it much better than my place, which has absolutely no charm.'

'Yours has more class. But this will do.' No one would have believed that a month before she'd been living in grandeur. She seemed perfectly happy to be where she was. 'Coffee?' she asked. Kim nodded. Deanna disappeared, then returned with two steaming mugs.

'So what's new?' But the easel in the corner of the kitchen told her what she had been wondering. Deanna was already back at work.

'I'm painting again.' She looked happy and proud.

'So I see. What are you going to do with them?'

'Sell them probably. I've already sold two or three. They paid for the furniture, the dishes, the sheets.' Three paintings and the jade-and-diamond earrings.

But she didn't explain that to Kim. And she didn't give a damn. There was nothing left that she wanted, except her child now. The rest didn't matter any more. Not at all.

'Where are you selling them?' Kim looked at her with a purpose in mind, but Deanna saw her coming.

'Never mind that.' She grinned and took a sip of her tea.

'Why don't you at least let him sell your paintings for chrissake? You don't have to see him.' Kim had seen him only last week, and he looked like hell. She wanted to slip him Deanna's address, but she knew she couldn't. Deanna had to find her way back to him herself. If she ever did. Kim was beginning to doubt it. Deanna seemed happier by herself. 'Why don't you at least call Ben about your work?'

'Don't be silly, Kim. What would that prove? I can't. And he'd probably spit in my eye if I called him and asked him to handle my work.'

'I doubt that.' But maybe she was right. He never asked Kim how she was any more. It was a silent agreement between them. Neither of them spoke of Deanna. Kim understood. 'What about Marc? Have you heard anything from him?'

Deanna shook her head. 'I called him once after I spoke to my lawyer. He understands. There's no argument really.'

'Do you think he'll marry that girl?'

Deanna sighed and then looked up with a smile. 'Maybe. She's living with him at the house. But I think' – the smile slowly faded – 'I think this has all been kind of a shock. A lot has happened to both of us this year.'

For a moment Kim wondered if Deanna missed him; she looked as though she did. Maybe it was merely a question of habit. In any event she had certainly come a long way.

'How do you know he's living with that girl?' It seemed an unusually honest admission for Marc to have made.

'Margaret told me when I called one day to see how she was. Apparently she's quitting next month. It's probably just as well. He doesn't need any more reminders of me around there. We might as well all get a fresh start.'

'Is that what you're doing?' Kim asked. Deanna nodded with another smile.

'It's not always easy, but I am. The house keeps me busy, and my work. I want to fix up the nursery next month. I found some adorable fabric. And I want to do some funny little Mother Goose people for the walls.'

Kimberly smiled at her and they settled back for a nice cosy chat. It was after five o'clock when Deanna finally got up and turned on all the lights.

'Good Lord, we've been sitting here in the dark.'

'And I really ought to get home. I still have to cross the bridge. Are you doing anything for Christmas, by the way?' But she was almost sure she was not.

Deanna shook her head. 'This isn't really the year for that. I think I'll enjoy spending it quietly ... here.' Kim nodded and felt a pang of guilt.

'I'm going up to the mountains for some skiing. Want to come?'

Deanna laughed and pointed at her now swelling stomach. She was at last almost five months, and now the evidence tallied with the dates. She had a nice round little tummy under her blouse. She patted it with a warm smile and looked at Kim.

'I don't think I'll be doing much skiing this year.'

'I know, but you could come up anyway.'

'And freeze? No, I'd much rather be here.'

'All right. But I'll leave you my number. You can call if you need me, you know.'

'I know. I know.' She scooped up Kim's presents, then loaded them into her arms and looked warmly at the things Kim had left under her tree. 'Merry Christmas, love. I hope it's a beautiful year.'

Kim looked smilingly down at her friend's growing waistline and nodded. 'It will be.'

Chapter Thirty-five

Christmas came and went without any of the splendour or ceremony of years gone by. There were no expensive peignoirs from Pilar, selected by her and charged to her father's account. There was no French perfume in crystal bottles, no diamond earrings, no fur. There were four presents from Kim, opened at midnight on the first Christmas Eve she had ever spent alone. She had been afraid of it at first, afraid of what it would be like to be alone, afraid that she wouldn't be able to stand the loneliness or the pain. But it wasn't lonely. And it was only a little bit sad. She found herself missing Marc and Pilar, because Christmas had always been theirs – the celebration, the noise, the ham or the goose or the turkey, Margaret in the kitchen, and mountains of boxes under the tree. It was the activity she missed, more than the riches; it was the faces she missed late at night. Pilar's young shining one, and Marc's in the days of long ago. There was no reaching back to them now though, they were irretrievably gone. It never occurred to her to call Marc, to hear his voice in the middle of the night. She drank hot chocolate and sat near her tree. But it did occur to her to call Ben. She guessed that he was in Carmel. Was he also alone?

In the distance, she could hear carollers wandering past, and she found herself humming 'Silent Night' as she undressed. She was less tired than she had been in months, feeling better in fact than she had in a very long time. But life was much simpler now. Her only worry was financial, but she had even that under control. She had found a tiny gallery on Bridgewater that sold her work – for only a few hundred dollars each canvas – but it was enough money to pay the rent and buy whatever else she might need. She still had some money left from the jade-and-diamond earrings. And she had a safe-deposit box filled with jewellery she could sell in the next months. She would have to sell more when it came time for the baby, and eventually Marc would have to give her something after they went to court.

She smiled to herself as she slid into bed. 'Merry Christmas, Baby.' She patted her stomach and lay on her back and for a moment she fought back the thoughts of Pilar. Maybe it would be another girl. But this time how different it would be.

Chapter Thirty-six

It was nine o'clock on a February morning. Ben sat in his office, looking at his new ads. He pressed a buzzer on his desk and waited for Sally to come into the room. When she did, she had an armful of papers, and he looked at her with a scowl.

'What do you think of this stuff, Sally? Does it work or not?'

'Yes.' She hesitated as she looked. 'But maybe it's a little too showy?'

He nodded emphatically and tossed them back on his desk. 'That's exactly what I think. Get Kim Houghton on the phone. I have to see an artist in Sausalito at eleven. See if she'll meet me at the Sea Urchin around twelve-fifteen.'

'In Sausalito?' Sally asked. He nodded distractedly, and she disappeared. It was almost ten o'clock when she popped her head in the door. 'She'll meet you at the Sea Urchin at twelve-thirty, and she said bring the ads. She's got another bunch of possibilities to show you and she'll bring those too.'

'Good.' He looked up at her with a vague smile and sighed at the work on his desk. Sometimes it seemed endless. He had added four new artists to their roster that winter, but he wasn't really in love with their work. They had been the best of what he had seen, but they weren't wonderful, they weren't Deanna Duras. People still asked him about her, and he tried to explain. She had 'retired'. Another sigh escaped him as he plunged himself back into his work. He had done that since September, and it had almost worked. Almost. Except late at night and early in the morning. Now he understood how she must feel about Pilar. That feeling that you'll never touch someone again, or hold them, or hear them, never laugh with them, or be able to tell them a joke and see them smile. He stopped working for a moment and then chased the thoughts away. He was good at it now. He had had five months of practice.

He left the gallery at exactly ten-fifteen. That gave him time to cross the bridge, drive to Sausalito, and park. This at least was an artist he liked, a young man with a wonderful eye for colour and a kind of magical flair, but his work was far more modern than Deanna's, and not nearly as good. He had never made the young man an offer, but he had decided that he finally would. Until then the young artist had been represented by a gallery near where he lived, a small cosy gallery in Sausalito that handled a mountain of very diverse work. Ben had first noticed the artist's paintings there, buried with some good and some bad, and he knew the young man was getting terrible payment for his work. A hundred and seventy-five was his top price. Ben would up the price to two thousand, right from the start. And he knew he could get it. The artist would be thrilled.

And he was. 'Oh, my God. Wait till I tell Marie!' He grinned broadly and pumped Ben's hand. 'My God. We might even be able to afford to eat something decent for a change.' Ben laughed, amused, and they walked slowly to the door. It was a big airy studio in half of what had once been a barn. It was now surrounded by houses and ersatz Victoriana, but it was still a wonderful studio and a nice place to work. 'By the way, whatever happened to that girl you handled last summer? Duras?'

'Handled.' It was an interesting choice of words. But he didn't know. No one did. 'We don't show her work any more.' Ben said it very calmly. He had said it a hundred times before.

'I know. But do you know who does?'

'No one. She retired.' Ben had the speech down pat.

But this time the young man shook his head.

'I don't think so. Are you sure?'

'Quite. She told me she was retiring when she withdrew her work.' But something in the man's eyes bothered him. 'Why?'

'I could swear I saw one of her pieces at the Seagull the other day. You know, the place that's been showing my work? I wasn't sure, and I didn't have time to ask, but it looked like it. It was a beautiful nude. And they were asking a ridiculous price for it.'

'How much?'

'I heard someone say a hundred and sixty bucks. It's really a crime for a fine piece like that. You ought to take a look and see if it's her.'

'I think I will.' He looked at his watch. It was only eleven-thirty. He had enough time before his lunch with Kim.

The two men shook hands again. There was a profusion of thank you's and smiles. Ben slid into his car and drove a little too quickly down the narrow road. He knew exactly where the gallery was, and he left his car parked on the corner. He wanted to just stroll in and look around, but he didn't have to. Her painting was prominently displayed near the door. He could see it from where he stood, rooted to the spot on the street. It was indeed her canvas. The young man had been right.

He stood there for a moment, wondering what to do, trying to decide if he should go inside. He was about to walk away, but something drew him into the gallery. He had to get closer to the still life. He had seen her paint it. She had done it on their terrace in early July. Suddenly he felt pulled back into the summer.

'Yes, sir? May I help you?' She was a pretty blonde in sandals and jeans. She wore the usual uniform, T-shirt and pierced ears, her hair held up in the back with a wide leather thong.

'I was just looking at the painting over there.' He pointed to Deanna's piece.

'It's a hundred and sixty. Done by a local artist.'

'Local? To San Francisco, I suppose you mean.'

'No. Sausalito.' She was obviously confused, but there was no point arguing.

'Do you have any more of her work?' He was sure that they didn't. Much to his astonishment, the girl nodded.

'Yes, we do. I think we have two more.'

As it turned out, there were three. One more from the summer, and two of her earlier works, none of them priced over two hundred dollars.

'How did you get these?' He found himself wondering if they had been stolen. If there had only been one, he might have suspected that someone who had bought one from him had been desperate to sell it, but that seemed unlikely, and it was obviously not possible since they seemed to have so much of her work.

The little blonde girl looked surprised by his question. 'We have them on consignment from the artist.'

'You do?' Now it was his turn to look stunned. 'Why?'

'I'm sorry?' She didn't understand.

'I mean why here?'

'This is a very reputable gallery!' She looked unhappy at his remark, and he tried to cover his confusion with a smile.

'I'm sorry. I didn't mean that. I just ... it's just that I know the artist, and I was surprised to see her work here. I thought she was away ... abroad.' He really didn't know what to say. On the spur of the moment he looked at the blonde girl with another smile. 'Never mind. I'll take them.'

'Which ones?' He was obviously crazy. Or maybe just stoned.

'All of them.'

'All four?' Crazy, not stoned.

'Yes, that'll be fine.'

'But that'll be almost eight hundred dollars.'

'Fine. I'll write a cheque.' The blonde girl nodded then and walked away. The manager checked with Ben's bank, and the cheque was good. Ten minutes later he walked away, and Deanna and the gallery were each four hundred dollars richer. He still wasn't sure why he'd bought them when he put them in his car. All he knew was that he had wanted to have her work. And the prices were insane. He didn't understand it. He would sell the four pieces in his gallery and turn the far larger profit over to her. As if she cared ... What was he trying to prove?

He was annoyed with himself as he parked in front of the Sea Urchin to meet Kim for their lunch. It had been a grandiose thing to do, buying all four of the paintings. When she found out, she'd probably be mad as hell. But something about the whole episode irked him. What did they mean, a 'local' Sausalito artist?

Kim was waiting for him at a window table, enjoying the view of the city across the bay.

'Mind if I sit down?' She turned towards him, startled, then laughed.

'For a minute I thought you were a masher.' She grinned up at him, and he smiled. He looked as pleasant as ever, as nicely put together, as well dressed in blazer, slacks, and striped shirt, but she thought there was something troubled in his eyes.

'No such luck, Ms. Houghton, mashers are out of style. Or maybe they're all women these days.'

'Now, now.'

'Would you like a drink?' he asked. She nodded, and they both ordered bloody marys. For a moment he looked out at the bay. 'Kim?'

'Yes, I know. You're going to tell me you hate the ads. I don't love them either. But I've got some other ideas.'

He shook his head and dragged his eyes back to hers. 'Never mind that, though as a matter of fact you're right. We can talk about that later. I want to ask you something else.' He paused for a long moment, and Kim waited, suddenly wondering if this was what she had seen in his eyes.

'What is it?' He looked so troubled, she wanted to reach out a hand.

'Deanna.'

Kim's heart almost stopped. 'Have you seen her?'

But he only shook his head again. 'No. Have you?' Kim nodded in answer. 'Is something wrong? I just found four of her paintings in a local gallery, and I don't understand. Why would she sell her work there? You know what they were selling them for? A hundred and sixty, one seventy-five. It's crazy, it doesn't make sense. And they said something about her being a local artist. Local to Sausalito. Now that really doesn't make sense. What the hell is going on?'

Kim sat looking at him for a moment, saying nothing. She wasn't sure what she could say. She had a date to visit Deanna that afternoon, right after lunch. She had been delighted with the excuse of having lunch in Sausalito. This way she could stop and see Deanna before heading back. But what could she say to Ben? How much could she tell him?

'Kim, please tell me. Do you know?' His eyes pleaded with her; they were filled with concern.

'Maybe someone else sold the paintings to the gallery after he bought them from her.' She had to ask Deanna before she said anything to him. She had to. She owed that to Deanna, but she wanted to tell him now.

'No, that's not the case. The girl said they had them on consignment from her. But why? Why a gallery like that, and over here? Is she trying to sell them without her husband knowing? Is she in trouble? Does she need cash?' His eyes pleaded with Kim to speak, and she let out a long, troubled sigh.

313

'Oh, Ben. What can I say? A lot of things in Deanna's life have changed.'

'But apparently not enough for her to call me.'

'Maybe she will. In time. She is still very shaken up about Pilar.' He nodded silently, and they didn't speak for a while. The last thing he wanted to discuss today was business. All he could think of was Deanna. He knew something was terribly wrong.

He looked up at Kim again, and she wanted to die from the look in his eyes. 'Is she in some kind of trouble?' But Kim shook her head no.

'She's all right, Ben. She is. I think in some ways she's happy for the very first time.' She wanted to tear her tongue out for saying it. Deanna had been even happier during the previous summer, but Kim wasn't sure how to alter what she had just said. 'She's painting a lot.'

'And she's happy.' He looked at the bay and then at Kim. 'With him ...' But suddenly Kim couldn't stand it any more. She very slowly shook her head. 'What do you mean?'

'He went back to France.' Deanna had told her that just last month. Marc had finally gone back to his home.

'Permanently?' Ben looked stunned. Kim merely nodded. 'And she stayed?' Kim nodded again, and now there was despair in his eyes. She hadn't called him. Marc was gone, and she hadn't called. But as he looked down into his drink, he felt Kim's hand gently touch his.

'Give her a chance, Ben. A lot of things have happened. I think it may take her a few more months to sort it all out.'

'And she's living here? In Sausalito?' None of it made any sense. Why wasn't she living in their house? Had he just run off and left her? 'Do you mean to tell me they're getting a divorce?'

She took a deep breath. 'Yes. I do.'

'Was it his doing, or hers? Kim, you have to tell me. I have a right to know.'

'I'm the first person to agree with you, Ben.' *But try telling her ...* 'It was her doing, but he agreed. He really had no choice.'

'How is she? Is she adjusting? Is she all right?'

'She's fine. She's living in a funny little house, working on some new paintings, getting ready –' And then she stopped; she had gone too far.

'Getting ready for what?' He was confused again, and Kimberly was driving him crazy. 'For chrissake, Kim, is that lousy gallery giving her a show?' He was incensed. How dare they? Suddenly Kim laughed. She looked at him with a bright light in her eye.

'You know something? This is crazy. We're sitting here playing twenty questions about how Deanna is, when the one thing she needs is you.' She pulled a pen out of her handbag and grabbed a piece of paper from among her ads. She jotted down the address and handed it to him. 'Go. That's the address.'

'Now?' He looked stunned as he took the piece of paper from her hand. 'But what if ... if she doesn't want to see me?'

'She will. But from now on it's up to you.' She laughed. 'And if she gives you any trouble, just punch her in the mouth.' He grinned and looked at her again in confusion.

'What about our lunch?' All he wanted to do was get the hell out of there and go to find Deanna. He really didn't want to sit there a moment longer with Kim, but she knew it, and she smiled.

'Screw our lunch. We can talk about the ads some other time. Go.' He bent to kiss her and squeezed her shoulder very hard.

'One day, Kim Houghton, I'll thank you. But right now' – he finally smiled back – 'I've got to run. Tell me, do I break the door down or just climb down the chimney?'

'Throw a chair through the window. It works every time.'

He was still smiling when he got to his car, and he was at the cul-de-sac five minutes after he left Kim. He glanced at the piece of paper again and quickly saw that it was the house hidden by the large daisy bushes and surrounded by the little picket fence. He wondered if she was at home. Maybe she wasn't in. He was frightened now. What would he say to her? What if she was angry that he'd come? He couldn't bear to have her do that to him now, after all the long months of dreams.

He got out of the car and walked slowly to the door. He could hear someone moving around inside, and there was a radio softly playing jazz. He rang the bell and then knocked. More quickly than he expected, her voice rang out from the back of the house.

'Hi, Kim, it's open. Come on in!' He opened his mouth to tell her it wasn't Kim, but he closed it as quickly. He didn't want her to know the truth until he was inside, until he saw her, just once, even for a moment. Just once more. He pushed the door open with one hand. He was standing in the bright little front room, and there was no one there.

'Are you in?' She called out to him from the back. 'I'm painting the other bedroom. I'll be right out.'

He felt as though his guts were melting as he listened to her voice for the first time in five months. He simply stood in one spot and waited for her to come out. He wanted to say something to her, but he couldn't. He almost felt as though he didn't have the strength. But then she called out again. 'Kim? Is that you?' This time he had to speak; he didn't want her to be frightened.

'No, Deanna. It's not.' There was silence then, and he heard something drop. He stood there, silent, immobile, waiting. But no one came. Nothing happened. No one moved. And slowly he began to walk towards the back of the house. He didn't have far to go. A few steps and he was standing in the tiny bedroom door-way.

'Deanna?' She was standing there, one hand on a bassinet, leaning against the last unpainted wall. His eyes went to hers and he couldn't repress a smile. 'I'm sorry, I ...' And then he saw, as her eyes grew wide and he saw her chin tremble. 'My God, you're ... Deanna ...' He didn't want to ask her, he didn't know what to say. When and how? And whose? And then not caring whose, he closed the gap between them and pulled her into his arms. That was why she was selling the paintings, why she was alone.

'It's ours, isn't it?' He asked. She nodded, tears spilling on to his shoulder. He held her tightly in his arms. 'Why didn't you tell me? Why didn't you call?' He pulled away just enough so that he could see her face. She was smiling.

'I couldn't. I left you. I couldn't go back to you like that. I thought that maybe ... after the baby ...'

'You're nuts, but I love you. Why after the baby? I want to be there with you, I want to ... oh, Deanna, *it's ours*!' He pulled her back into his arms, triumphantly, with laughter and tears.

'How the hell did you find me?' She laughed as she held him close and then sniffed. When he didn't answer, she knew. 'Kim.'

'Maybe so. Or maybe that atrocious little gallery that's selling your work. Deanna, how could you ...' His voice trailed off, and she grinned.

'I had to.'

'Not any more.'

'We'll see.'

'You prefer Seagull to me?' He laughed at the thought, and she vehemently shook her head.

'I've just managed to do it all for myself though. I've gotten independent. I've made it. Do you realise what that means?'

'It means that you're wonderful and I adore you.

Are you getting divorced?' He was holding her in his arms and gently touching her stomach. He jumped as the baby kicked. 'Was that our kid?' The tears glazed his eyes again when she nodded yes.

'And yes, I'm also getting divorced. It will be final in May.'

'And the baby?'

'Will be final in April.'

'And in that case, you crazy, independent, mad woman, we will also be final in May.'

'What does that mean?' But she was laughing now and so was he.

'Just what you think. And' – he looked around the room with a quizzical air – 'pack your stuff, madam, I'm taking you home.'

'Now?' I haven't finished painting the baby's room. And –'

'And nothing, my darling. I'm taking you home.'

'Right now?' She put down her paintbrush and grinned.

'Right now.' He pulled her close to him again then and kissed her with all the longing of the past five months. 'Deanna, I'll never be without you again. Never. Do you understand?' But she only nodded, smiling, and kissed him, as his hand travelled slowly to their child.